The Year of the Red Door

A Fantasy

by

William Timothy Murray

"Whosoever discovers the Name of the King,

so shall he become King."

The Year of the Red Door

Volume 2

The Nature of a Curse

William Timothy Murray

"Whosoever shall discover the Name of the King,

so shall he become King."

pfbisrev1/b

To
Albert and Billie

Table of Contents

Preface

Welcome to *The Year of the Red Door.*   For those of you who are curious, I invite you to visit the accompanying web site:

www.TheYearOfTheRedDoor.com

There you will find maps and other materials pertaining to the story and to the world in which the story takes place.

The road to publishing *The Year of the Red Door* has been an adventure, with the usual ups and downs and rough spots that any author may encounter. The bumps and jostles were considerably smoothed by the patient toil of my editors who were, I'm sure, often frustrated by a cantankerous and difficult client. Nonetheless, I have upon occasion made use of their advice, which was sometimes delivered via bold strokes, underlines, exclamation points, and a few rather cutting remarks handwritten across the pristine pages of my manuscripts. Therefore, any errors that you encounter are due entirely to my own negligence or else a puckish disregard of good advice.

For those of you who might be a bit put off by the scope and epic length of this story, I beg your indulgence and can only offer in my defense a paraphrase of Pascal (or Twain, depending on your preference):

I did not have time to write a short story,
so I wrote a long one instead.

The Author

Maps

A Note from the Cartographers

The geography and place names depicted on the following maps are generally accepted to be accurate as of the year of their preparation (869 Second Age). Distances are approximate, given the scales of the maps. However, these are only intended to give a general sense of the scale and relationship of the various regions and features. They are not intended for travel or navigation. Any mishap as a result from the use of these maps for such purposes of travel are the responsibility of the user, not the mapmakers.

For maps more suitable for travel within particular regions of the world, all interested parties are invited to inquire at our establishment.

Brannon & Gray Cartographers
No. 16, Miller's Pond Lane
Duinnor City

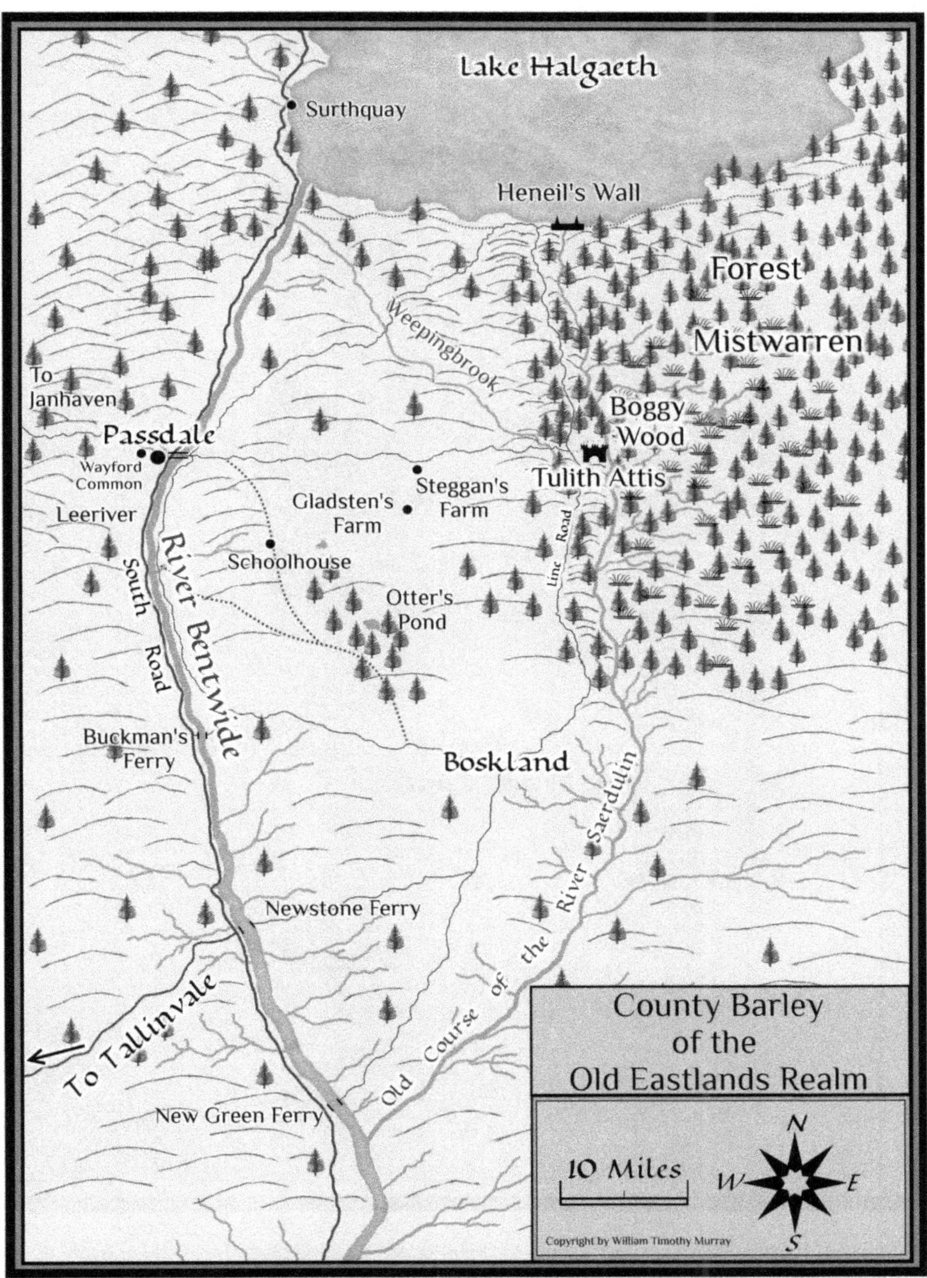

County Barley
Detailed maps can be found at:
www.TheYearOfTheRedDoor.com

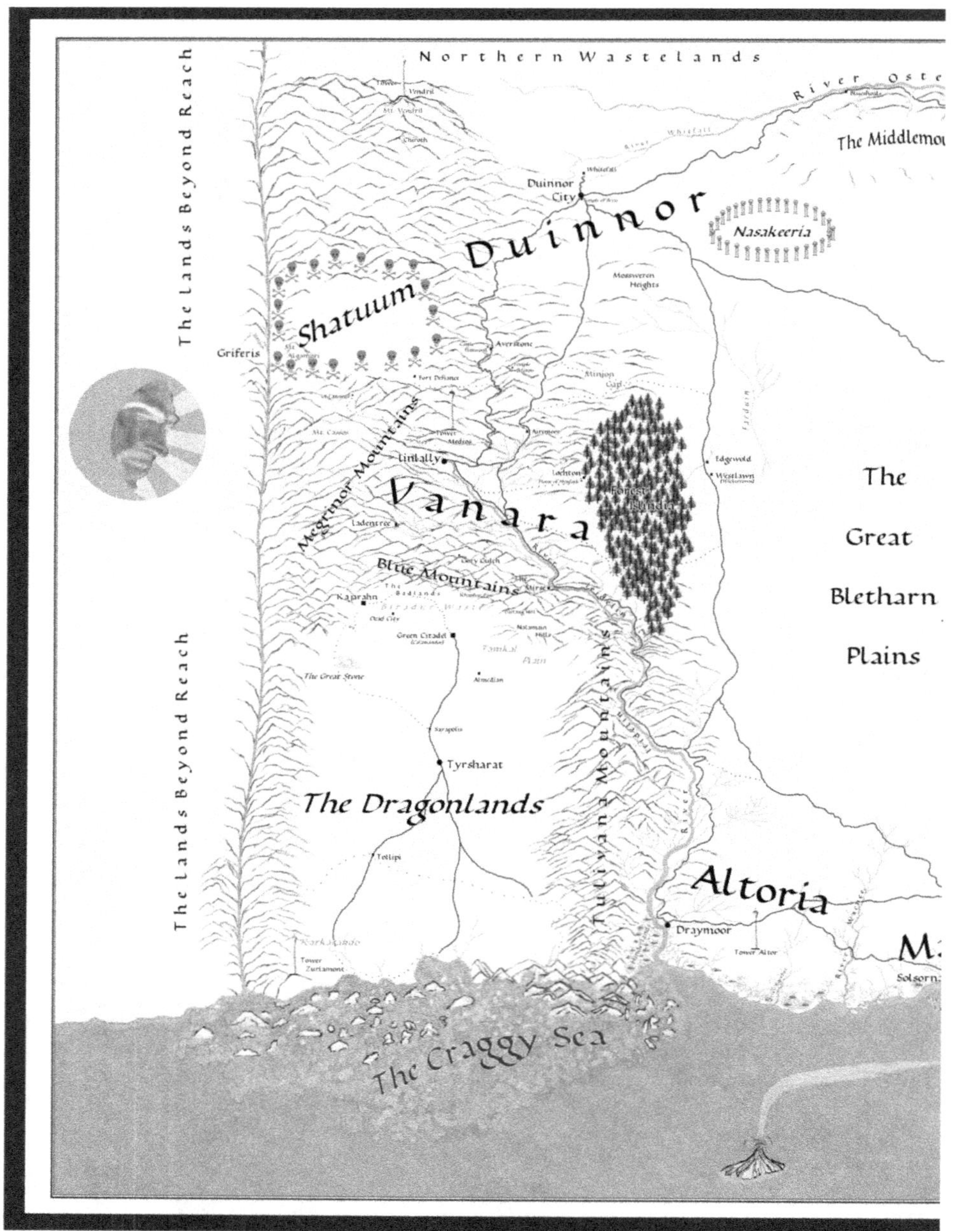

The Western World

Detailed maps can be found at:
www.TheYearOfTheRedDoor.com

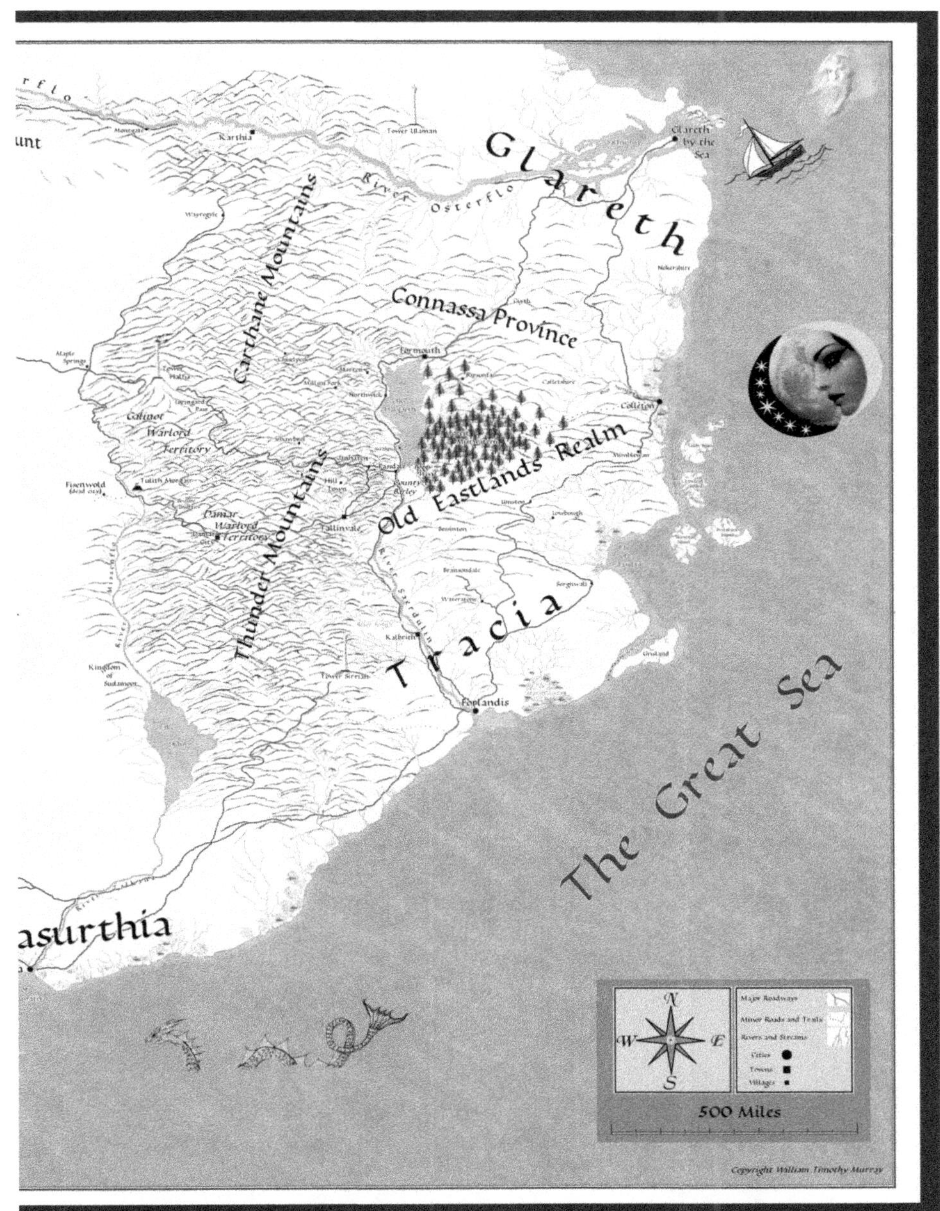

The Eastern World
Detailed maps can be found at:
www.TheYearOfTheRedDoor.com

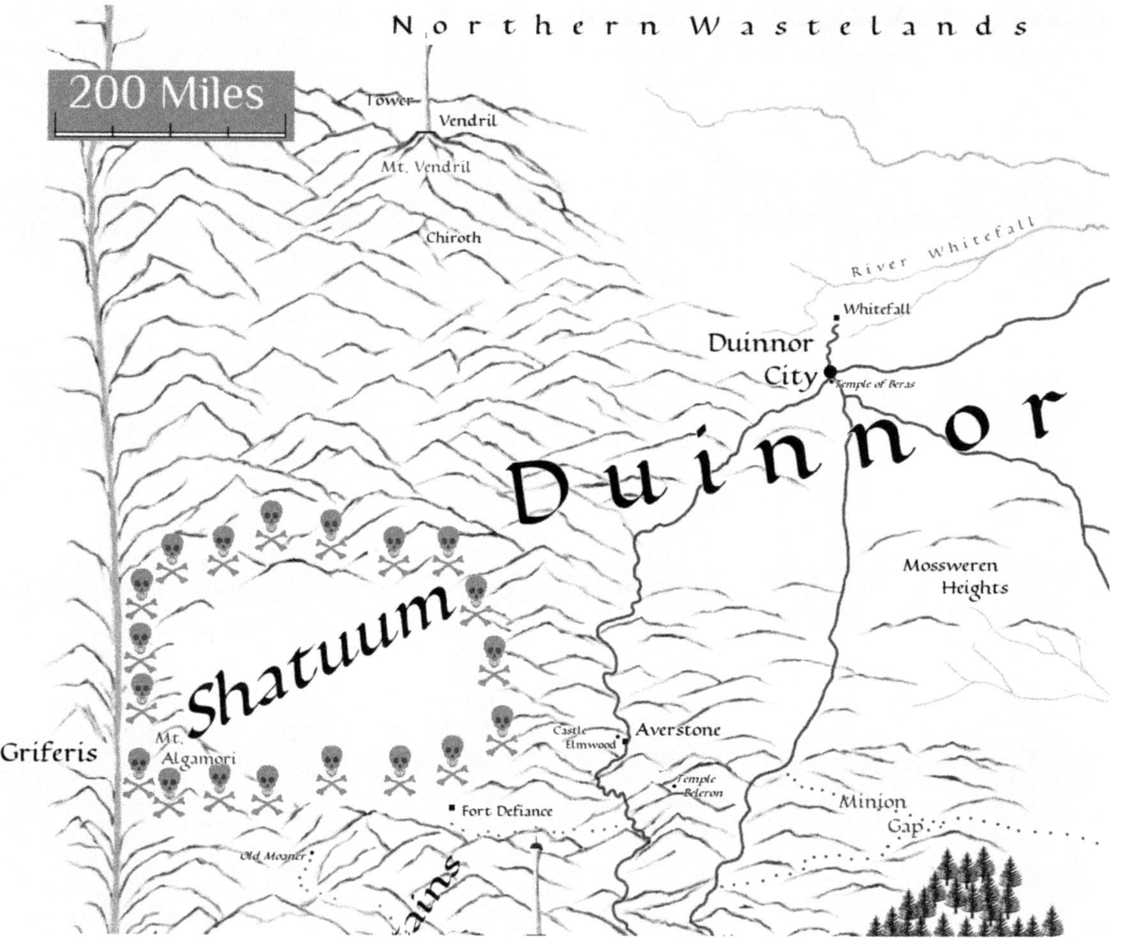

Duinnor & Shatuum
Detailed maps can be found at:
www.TheYearOfTheRedDoor.com

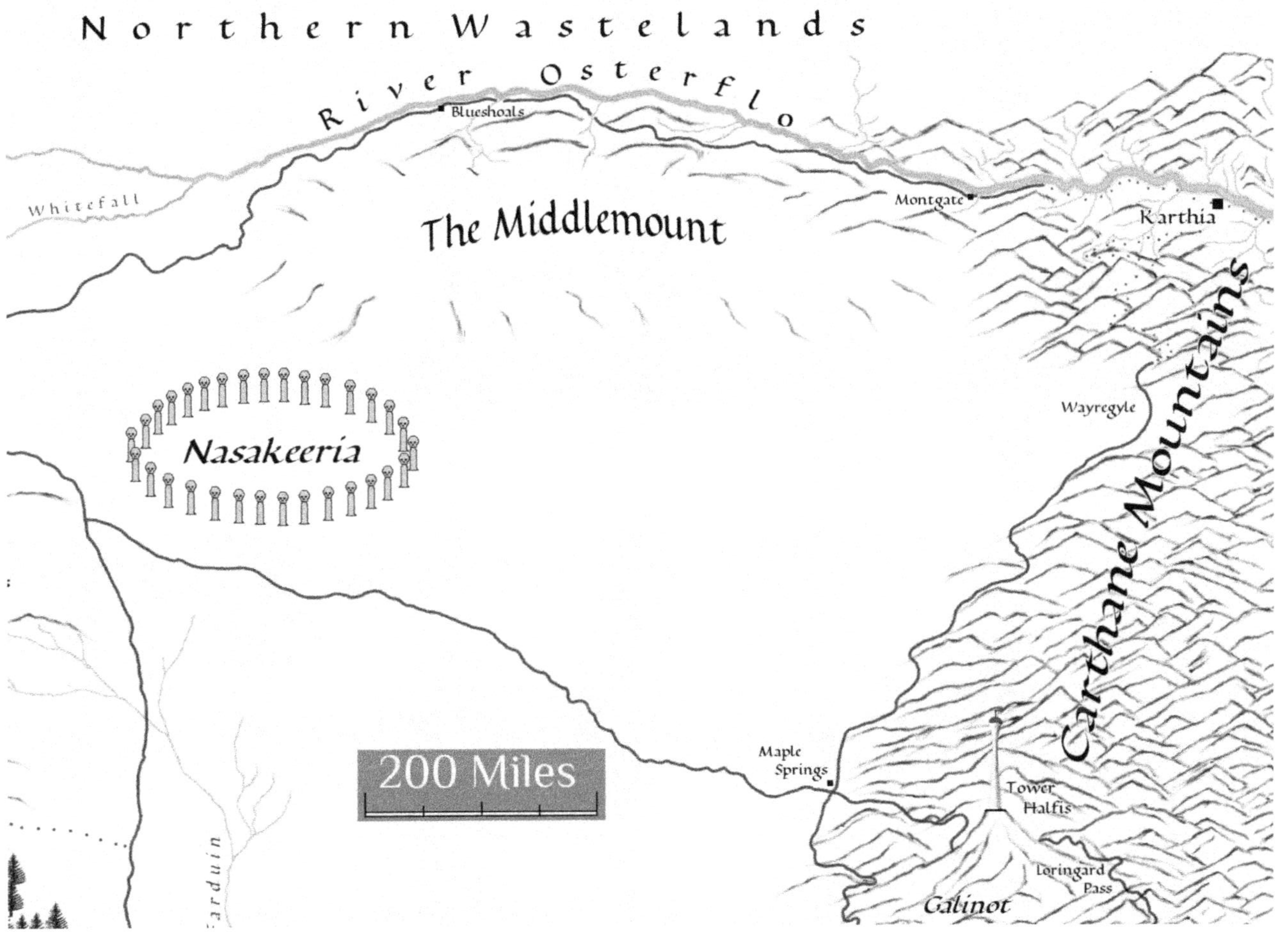

Middlemount & Nasakeeria
Detailed maps can be found at:
www.TheYearOfTheRedDoor.com

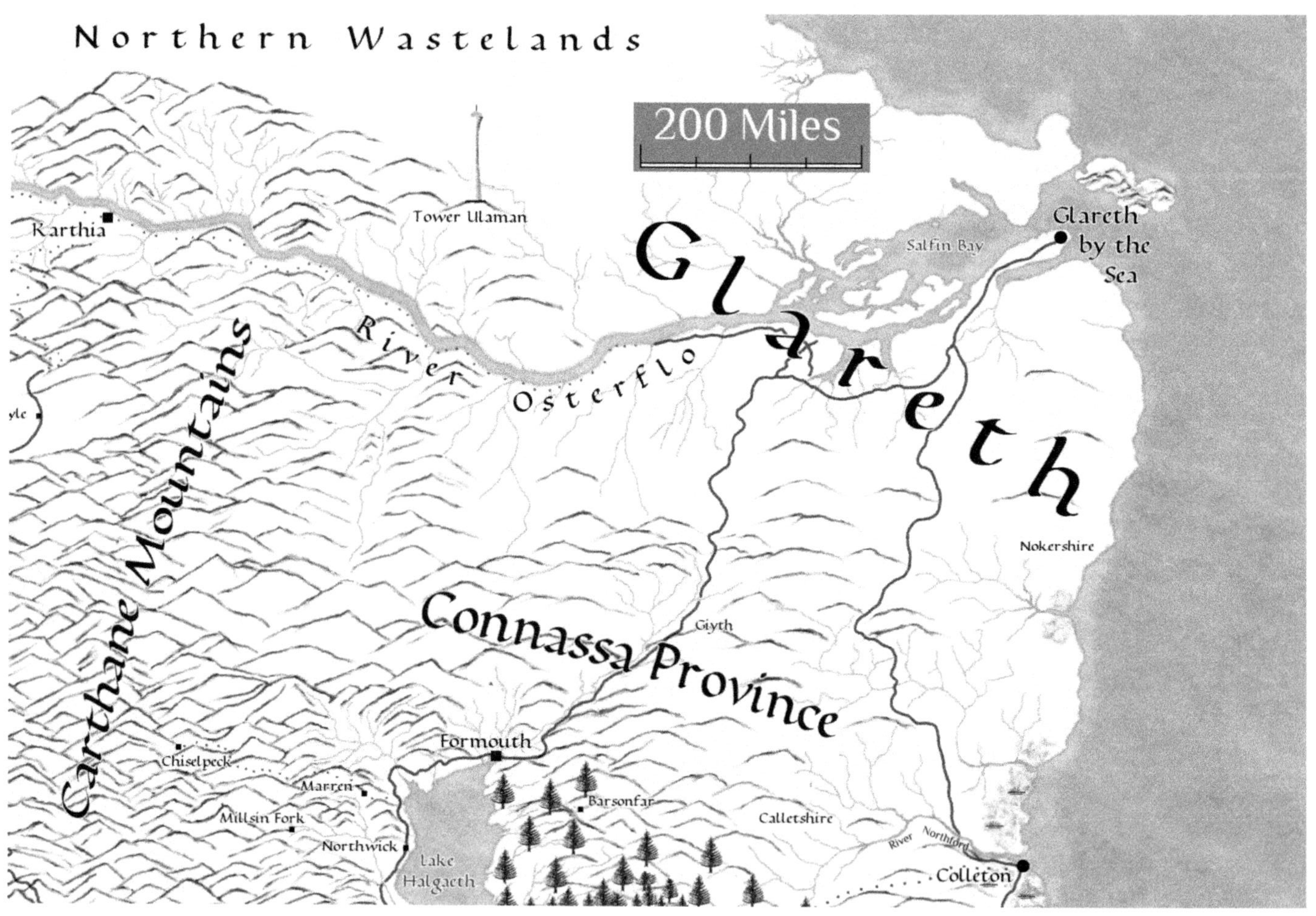

Glareth
Detailed maps can be found at:
www.TheYearOfTheRedDoor.com

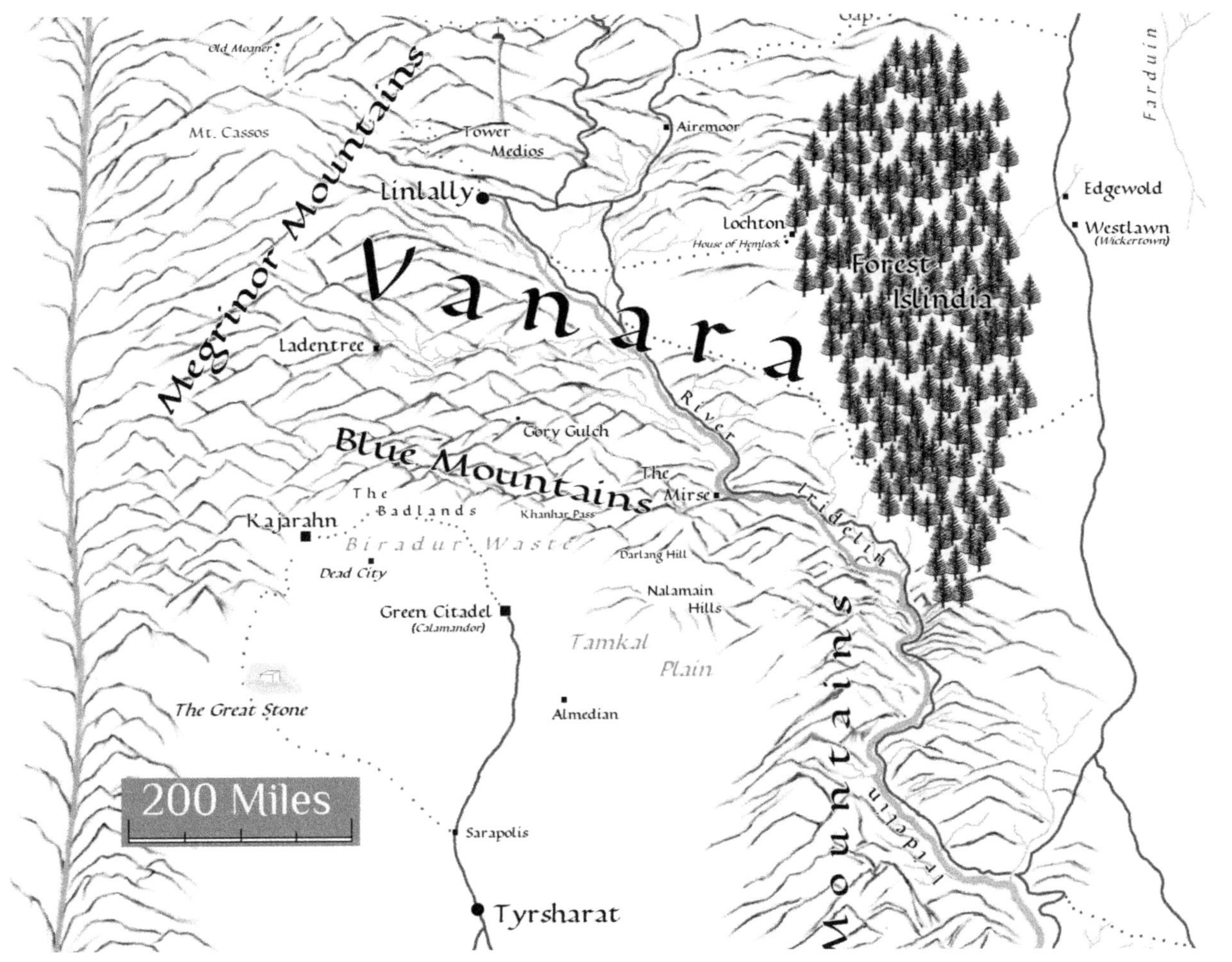

Vanara
Detailed maps can be found at:
www.TheYearOfTheRedDoor.com

The Great Plains of Bletharn
Detailed maps can be found at:
www.TheYearOfTheRedDoor.com

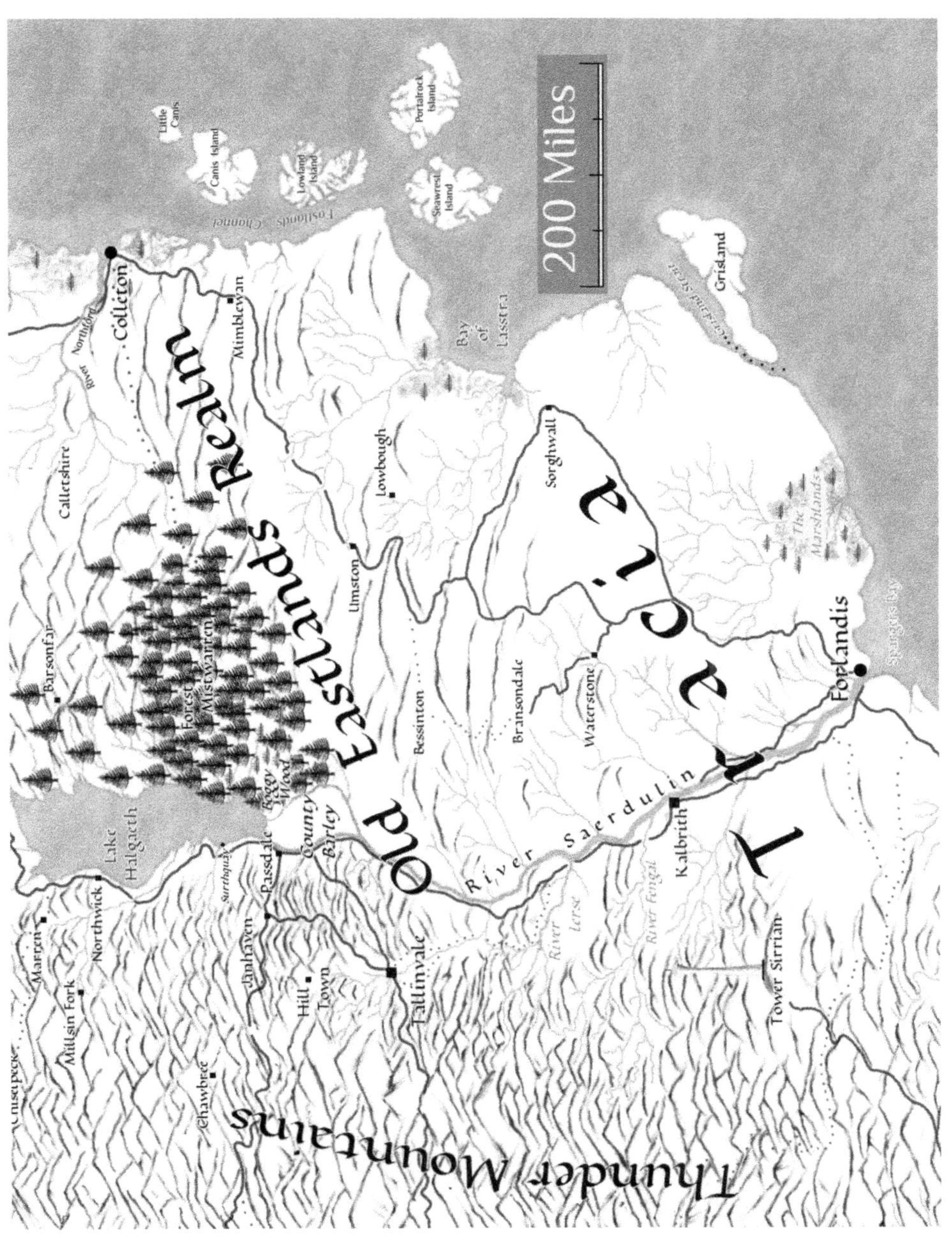

Tracia & the Old Eastlands Realm
Detailed maps can be found at:
www.TheYearOfTheRedDoor.com

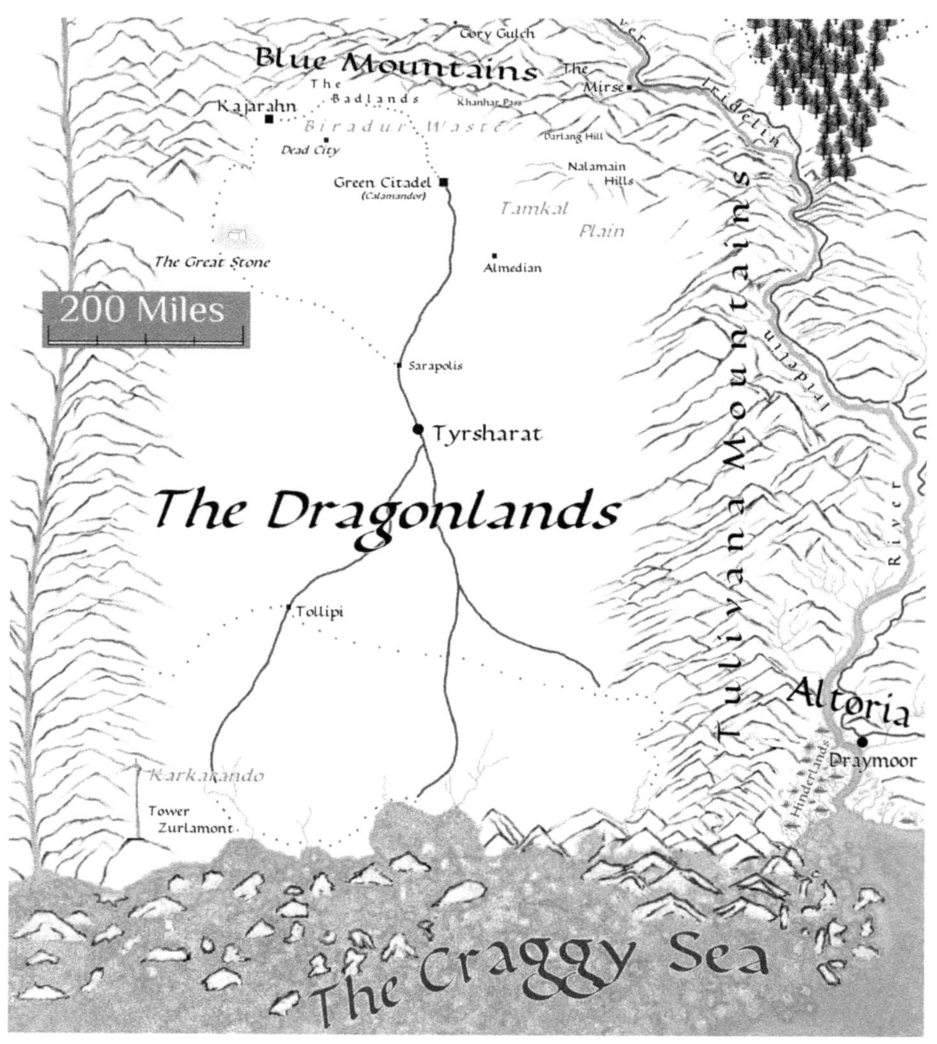

The Dragonlands

Detailed maps can be found at:
www.TheYearOfTheRedDoor.com

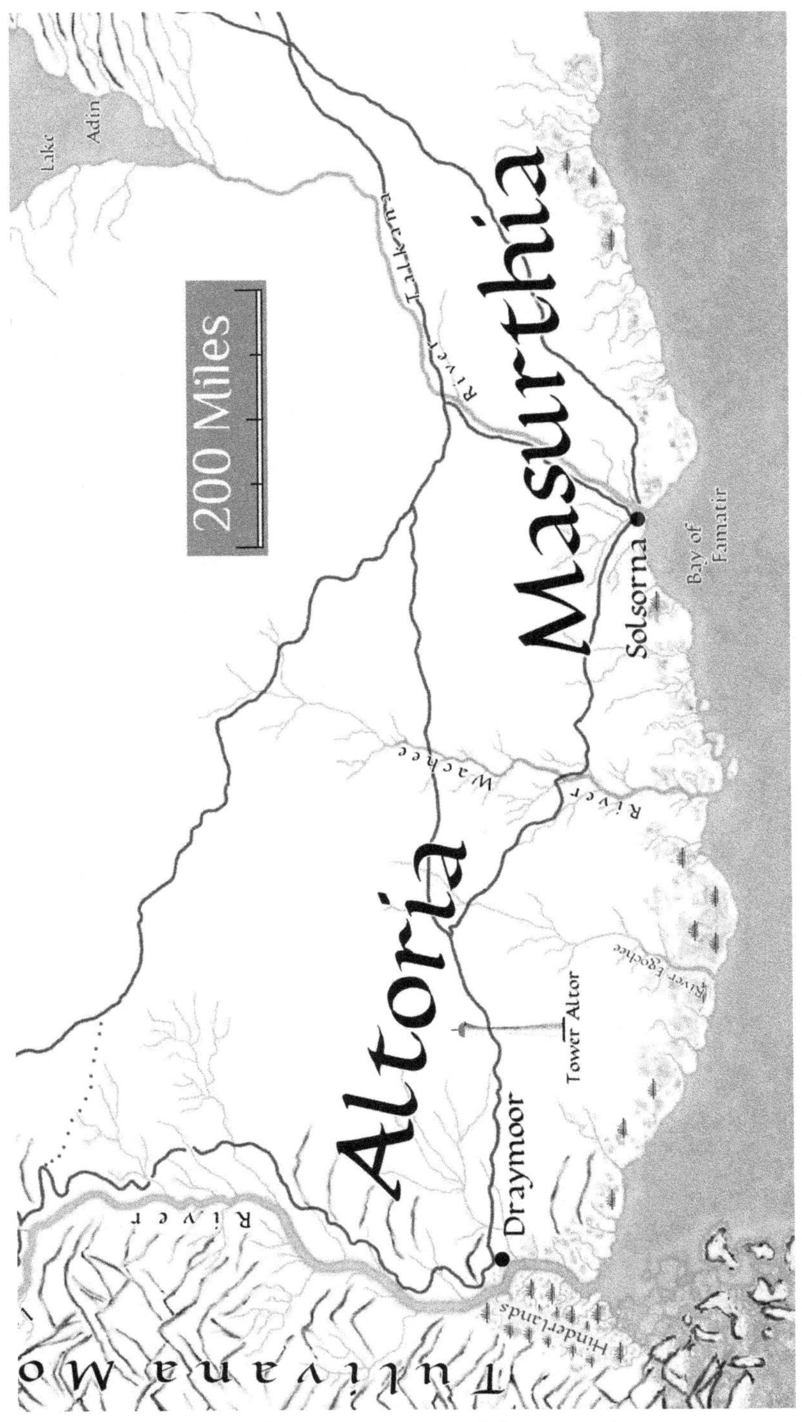

Altoria & Masurthia
Detailed maps can be found at:
www.TheYearOfTheRedDoor.com

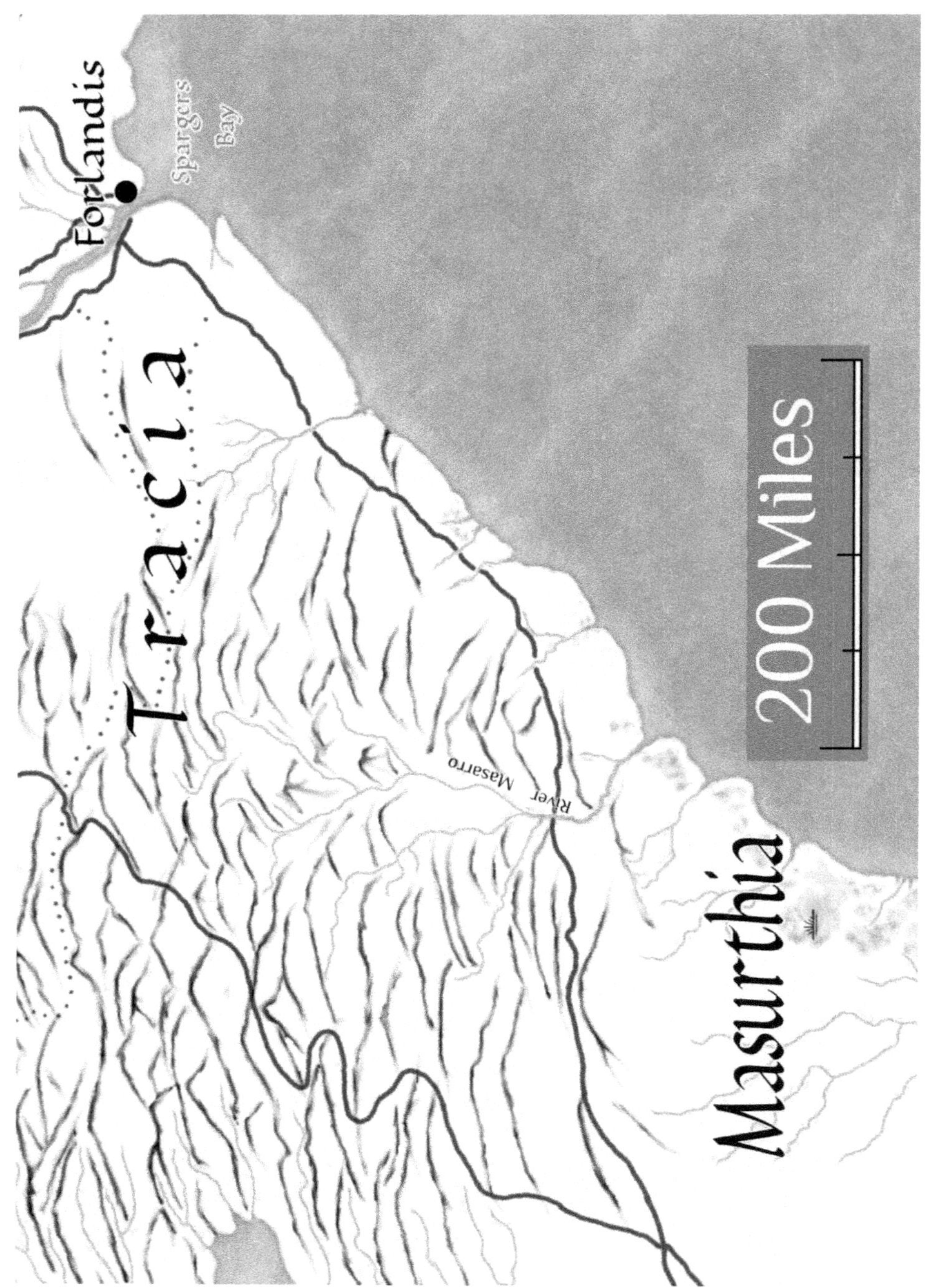

The Frontier between Tracia and Masurthia
Detailed maps can be found at:
www.TheYearOfTheRedDoor.com

The Nature of a Curse

2

Prologue

The White Dragon

Dalvenpar Tallin, Robby and Ullin's uncle, was killed in the Dragonlands years before Ullin was even born. He died during a shoddy retreat from what proved a disastrous invasion of the desert lands. Crying "Remember Tulith Attis!" the attackers managed to sack and pillage the Green Citadel, one of the chief cities of the northern desert provinces. Although the invading forces would be defeated and ultimately repelled, few lessons would be learned from either side, and history would repeat itself in but a few years.

However, six weeks after the useless death of Dalvenpar Tallin and so many others, a group of seven mysterious riders moved along the final stretch of dusty track toward Kajarahn, the Free City in the northwestern desert. They were mysterious because they were dressed in black robes and coverings, such as assassins of the city sometimes wore, and they rode under no banner or standard. The guards of the city saw them while they were still far off, wavering in the heat, and they examined them carefully with their spyglasses. They were not renegades, clearly, since they rode handsome horses and were all dressed alike. No, not renegades, but it was unusual, and risky, not to ride under some banner, for without the protection of a powerful or influential house, few travelers stood much of a chance within the city, unless of course, they had plenty of gold for bribes. Indeed, soon enough, each guard held several coins of Dragonkind gold, and their captain a double amount, and the visiting riders were permitted to enter. They knew their way, and rode on through the bazaar and past the fine palace of the ruling lord of the city. They continued on beyond the gardens and baths and rode into the district of the town where merchants lived. They entered a small courtyard, and as the clatter of horse-hooves bounced from the surrounding walls, the owner of the house, seeing them from a window, hurried his wife and his young son into hiding. He then girded a sword and rushed out with many of his servants to challenge the arrivals. The son broke away from his mother, picked up his own small sword, and ran to join his father. The merchant glowered at the boy, but it was too late to send him back in, and he turned his attention to his unexpected visitors. The lead rider dismounted, approached, and bowed low.

"Peace," said the dusty stranger, loosening the coverings from around his face.

"I hope it is in peace that you come," said the merchant, bowing curtly. "Pray, who are you? And why do you disturb my home's tranquility?"

"Forgive us, good sir," said the stranger, bowing again, "but we come at our master's bidding. You may call me Tareef. Are you not Emal the Merchant?"

"I am. And is your master so low that you dare not ride with his standard?" asked the merchant sharply, eyeing the stranger and the others who came with him. His keen eye did not miss much, not the bearing of the strangers before him, the make of their saddles, the cut of their robes and light armor, nor the workmanship of their sword-hilts or even the stitching on the stranger's gloved hand. He saw clearly that these were no ordinary men since, for Dragonkind soldiers, they were fine of frame and had little sign of the desert sickness. Only a powerful master could provide the darakal elixir in such amounts to make his servants so strong. He also noted that a long bundled object, perhaps seven feet long, was strapped to the side of one of the horses. Tareef sensed the merchant's assessment, and he seemed oddly at ease with it.

"I assure you that we are here on peaceful business," he said to Emal, "but it is such that our master must keep to himself, as much as may be possible, as you may soon understand. He, our master, says that Emal of Kajarahn is a shrewd merchant and a wise trader. Furthermore, he says that Emal is an honest man who lives not in the way of so many of this city, but is proud to have his fortunes rest with his own acumen and skill rather than upon swindles and lying."

Emal's eyes narrowed. His son stepped up.

"The flattery and praise of strangers has no merit but is to soften the cheat which follows!" the boy declared defiantly.

"Radasa!" Emal said harshly, pushing the boy back. "Know your place to speak when spoken to! I beg you forgive my son's outburst. I fear he listens to the sayings of his father too much, but has not yet learned the wisdom of silence."

Tareef only grinned and looked from the boy back to the father.

"I bring a commission for transport," he said as he produced a small folded parchment and offered it to Emal. Emal studied it for a long moment, then squinted back at Tareef.

"What your master asks will be difficult to do without arousing many questions," he said. "And it is a long way to go and will require many bribes. The only roads north are closed to our kind since the great battle of Calamandor, so I must commission trustworthy northmen to carry out this task."

"My master quite understands the difficulties," said Tareef, gesturing to one of his comrades nearby. Immediately two saddlebags were brought. The stranger took one and removed from it a purse and handed it to Emal.

"There is here twenty such purses to defray your costs and to yield some profit to yourself and to those you deem trustworthy to undertake this commission."

Emal nodded as he looked inside the purse. Then Tareef handed him the saddlebag.

"As well, I am instructed to also give you this," he said, holding out the other, much lighter saddlebag to Emal. Emal gave Radasa the first saddlebag, so heavy that the boy had to hastily put away his sword so that he could hold the bag with both arms. Then Emal took the second saddlebag that was offered, undid the flap, and looked within. His expression went from puzzlement to surprise then to astonishment. Inside was enough refined darakal to supply his family with the precious life-saving elixir for two years at least. Emal quickly closed the flap and glanced around to be sure no one else nearby had seen its contents.

"A king's ransom," he said, gesturing at the bag his son held, but meaning the one he himself still clutched. "And the object to be transported and delivered?"

Tareef turned and gestured to his men. They quickly untied the long object from the horse, and two of them brought it forward, handling it with great care. It appeared to be a thin carpet, rolled and tied within a sheet of heavy linen. The two men placed it gently and ceremoniously on the ground before him. Then they bowed and backed away. Emal noted that they bowed to the object and not to him.

"I pray you deliver this on behalf of my master," said Tareef. "And that you see to it that his note is included with it."

Emal took the note and read it.

"I do not understand it," Emal said.

"It is not for you to understand," said Tareef. "Does my master have an accord with you for the transportation of this object to the destination that he stipulates?"

Tareef held out his hand. Emal slowly reached out and took it, holding it for a long moment, making sure of the sincerity in Tareef's eyes.

"It shall be the honor of my House to do so," he said at last, bowing. "Rest assured, it shall not be tampered with in any way, nor shall it be examined by anyone acting on behalf of this House."

At this, Tareef bowed very low, putting his hand to his breast. He looked at the boy, at Emal, then down at the long bundle on the ground before turning and climbing back into his saddle as his men did likewise. Just as he started to rein away, Emal stepped up.

"I hope," he said, not too loudly, "that all is well in Almedian."

For the first time, Tareef frowned.

"I do not know what you mean, sir."

Emal nodded and backed away. Tareef turned his horse around, then paused.

"But," he said to Emal, "should I pass that way, I shall relay your good wishes. Peace!"

And with that, the secretive riders rode away, disappearing from the courtyard and down the street.

"Father," asked Radasa, "who were those men? And what is this thing they wish you to send northward?"

Emal slung the light saddlebag over his shoulder, took the heavy one from his son, and said, "Take the other end of it, son, and we shall carry it in together."

"My lord," said one of the servants, stepping up, "allow us to carry this thing!"

"No. My son and I will see to it. You may dismiss everyone back to their work."

Emal and Radasa lifted the long object and carried it into the house, up the stairs, and into Emal's bedroom. Hearing them enter, Emal's wife emerged tentatively from her closet as the two were putting the object down on the floor. With a finger held up, Emal stopped her questions and turned to Radasa.

"My son, hear me. You are not to ask after this object again, nor may you ask after those men or who their master might be," Emal said.

"But, Father—"

"Listen to me!" Emal said gently. "Only you and your mother are of greater worth than this object. But if any surmise what this thing is, or that you might know who this comes from, or where it is bound for, they will do cruel things to you and to your mother to make you tell all that you know. Even friends of this House would do so, I fear! By taking this commission, I place our House in great danger for the rest of its days, and all its servants likewise, long past the end of my own life. So I must keep it a secret from you and from your mother, insomuch as I can. And I will say this, too: I marked those men correctly, and I would do this for their lord merely for the asking, and I would consider my purse brimming with the pride of doing so. Count yourself blessed if ever you should have such esteem for another!"

"Father," said the son, "I know where Almedian is. And who lives there."

"Ah." Emal, distressed, glanced at his wife. "I see you have been at your maps. Very well, then. Let your lips be sealed!"

• • •

It was three weeks later that Emal completed the arrangements. The long object was carefully rolled into yet another carpet and sent northward in a shipment of goods bound for Vanara. Indeed, only goods from Kajarahn could make it out of the desert and into the north, unless they were goods taken as spoils of war, for Kajarahn was far from the centers of power, and its status as a Free City meant that trade could take place between its merchants and any they chose to deal with, be they

Dragonkind, Man, or Elifaen, as long as payment was had and tribute was given. So it was a large, well-armed party of Men who departed Kajarahn with the long bundle that Emal sent north, Men who were paid well to defend their goods from renegades and Dragonkind soldiers alike, and who would also defend their goods from the Elifaen should they attack the train in the mountains. Their arms were put to use, too, for hardly had the train entered the foothills than they were attacked by renegades. But Emal's men were zealous in their duty and determined in the defense of their goods, and they beat back the robbers easily. An early snow made their way treacherous, so it was another month before the company made it through the mountains to Ladentree, in the western reaches of Vanara. In Ladentree, Emal's representative and long-time trading partner took charge of the goods, disposing of them according to Emal's careful and well-paid-for instructions. Thus the bundle from Emal, seemingly an ordinary carpet, was crated and sent eastward to the icy River Strayborn, and then by boat down to the River Iridelin where the crate was loaded onto a southbound barge destined for Altoria.

It remained in the Altorian port city of Draymoor for two months until it departed within the hold of the Selkie, a Glarethian merchantman. The ship made the passage to Solsorna, in Masurthia Realm, in good time, and was shortly afterwards back at sea, laden with trade goods and manned by a crew that was eager to see their families once again in far away Glareth by the Sea. Winter storms battered the Selkie, forcing it into Forlandis of Tracia Realm for almost two weeks. A few days after departure, the ship was again almost lost when it was nearly driven into the rocks of Grisland Strait by a sudden violent squall and was only saved by its quick-thinking captain, who ordered a bow anchor dropped, which spun the Selkie into the wind and permitted its crew time to reef its sails. The squall passed, the ship safely cleared those treacherous waters, and the crew made good sail with fair winds so that the heavily laden ship lumbered easily northward. Two weeks after departing Forlandis, the Selkie docked at Colleton on the coast of the Old Eastlands Realm. By now it had been over five months since the contents of the crate began its journey.

In Colleton, the crate and much of the cargo in the ship's hold were unloaded and stored in a warehouse along with many other goods to await the passing of winter and early spring rains so that the roads might be better for transport wagons. Eventually, the roads cleared of snow and ice, and spring mud dried away. So it was early summer before the crate was uncovered within the warehouse and then consigned, along with many other goods, to a wagoneer for transport overland. Thus the crate slowly bounced and jogged across the Old Eastlands countryside, passing through one town or village and the next. The wagoneer stopped at virtually each and every hamlet to barter and to trade, and the long crate at the bottom of his wagon was shifted around, shoved over, covered and uncovered by various sacks, boxes, and bundles as he went. The season passed by as he traded and negotiated his way westward, driving through broad croplands and teeming woods and camping under starlight when no inn or barn was near. At last, in early autumn, the wagoneer came to the Saerdulin River. Crossing over by way of a ferry, he made his way up the Old South Road along the river and turned west again before reaching Passdale to carry the battered and travel-bruised crate on the final leg of its journey. He thus arrived in Tallinvale almost a year to the day after its contents were delivered to Emal in Kajarahn.

The housekeeper of Tallin Hall accepted the shipment, and he had it brought into the grand foyer while a footman went to notify his lord of the arrival of the unexpected item. Lord Tallin entered the foyer as workmen waited with their tools.

"What can this be?" asked Lord Tallin.

"Shall we open it and see, my lord?" asked the housekeeper.

"By all means."

Soon enough the crate's lid was removed and from it was taken a long roll of what appeared to be thin, low-quality carpet. But when they unrolled it and found yet another bundled roll of thin carpet, they were further baffled.

"Perhaps these rugs are for the Hall?" Lord Tallin asked.

"Not any that I have ordered," said the housekeeper. "They appear entirely unsuitable, if I may say so. The wagoneer said that it came from Colleton."

Meanwhile, at the housekeeper's gesture, the bindings on the second carpet were untied, and, as it was unraveled, they were all surprised when a long pole rolled out of it and across the floor, its metal caps ringing. In its wake unfurled a long green standard, hemmed in gold, with a white dragon finely embroidered upon it. Tallin stared as the servants backed away.

"Gurasa," he muttered.

For years, tales of this name had filtered north out of the Dragonlands, tales of glory told on the lips of captured Dragonkind, stories breathed with fear by renegades in the badlands of the desert, and exploits related by smugglers and mercenaries. Gurasa. He who smote the rebellious Dragonkind generals that defied their Emperor. Gurasa, who swept across the fabled southern deserts like a sandstorm, scouring the land free of criminals and discontents, annihilating larger armies by dint of his cunning and bravery. It was said that no army that marched under Gurasa's banner would ever know defeat. A green banner emblazoned with a white dragon. The battle standard of Gurasa, who had once been a guest of this very Hall.

Seeing a bit of parchment wrapped around the pole's base and tied with twine, the housekeeper tentatively unfastened it and handed the curled paper to Lord Tallin. Tallin took it absently, his eyes still fixed by those of the white dragon, his mind full of the image of his eldest son, whose death had only recently been reported to him. Dalvenpar died, he had been informed, when a truce between Gurasa and the forces retreating from the Green Citadel was broken. Lord Tallin had too many questions, ones that would never be answered for him. Finally, he broke his gaze and looked at the small note. Upon it were written only five words, brushed in a careful, almost delicate hand with distinctive flourishes.

"In exchange for one ring."

Part I

Chapter 1

Micerea

Not far from Janhaven, in the rustic environs of Mr. Furaman's stockade, within the meeting room of the main building, the small group of Robby's friends, along with his mother, made a decision. By doing so, though it was farthest from their intent, they made themselves traitors of the King, rebels against the ruler of Duinnor, forming a secret pact around a secret purpose. Though they agonized over their deliberations, and remained baffled by the revelations that led them on, afterwards it seemed inevitable that they should make the plan they made. It was as if it had been written somewhere long beforehand, and they were only fulfilling some prior design. And though it was outrageous in its audacity, given the circumstances as well as the facts brought to light by their discussions, there seemed little else to do.

It was resolved, then, that Robby would depart Janhaven along with his companions to seek out the hidden place called Griferis, if it still existed, and there to try himself against the tests of kingship and to be judged of his worthiness to become King of Kings, Lord over all the Realms. If possible, Duinnor would be warned of the treachery of the Tracian Redvests, of their invasions and of the alliance with the Dragonkind. And if the present King chose not to act and refused aid to the east, or if he failed to prepare for the defense of the other realms, a New King might be the remedy.

As the weight and implications of this conspiracy fell upon the group, Sheila and Billy became taciturn. Mirabella retained a pale look of fear, and Ullin was far away in thought. Robby and Ashlord merely looked at each other, sympathetic to the group and the mood that had settled over them, each unwilling to break the silence. For what seemed a long while, they abided quietly, turning over their own thoughts until Frizella Bosk arrived, and she clearly saw the strained faces. But she had her own concerns, and she explained that help was needed to distribute firewood to their people. As Ullin and Robby moved to the door, Billy told her briefly, what they had been discussing, mentioning nothing about kingship, but only that they needed to go to Duinnor for help, and he promised to tell more after they had gotten the wood delivered. Frizella, seeing that Mirabella and Ashlord had no desire to leave just yet, asked Sheila if she would help her with the sick until they could be settled somewhere. And so Ullin and Billy and Robby went to join Ibin, already at work chopping and sawing and splitting. Sheila went with Frizella to tend the sick and wounded, relieving some of the other women so that they could rest, asking everyone along the way if they had seen Raenelle, Frizella's missing daughter. But none had.

Ashlord stirred the fire, his back to the table, letting Mirabella mull through her thoughts. Sooner than he expected, she spoke, and he turned to face her.

"Yesterday," Mirabella started, "when you and Robigor rode out to meet the Redvest general..."

She paused, looking away, as if trying to remember, though Ashlord knew that she had perfect recall and was instead looking for words.

"I was loading the wagons in front of the store," she went on. "There was a moment, when I looked across the river and up at the hills of Barley, where the enemy on the crest stretched across the skyline like jagged red shadows, the sharp glint of their steel in the sunrise, their war-drums like hammers upon my heart. There was a moment, when I saw you and my husband riding back to the bridge, that I knew what was about to happen. It seemed to me—I thought to myself, 'The end has come.'"

Ashlord nodded, seeing her ageless concern and the dark despair of her green eyes.

"So think any who see the closing of one age and the beginning of another," he said gently. "All things come to an end, just as all things must have their beginnings. Some easily and without notice, and others with great turmoil. In that way beginnings and endings are not so different."

Mirabella nodded. "Yes. Perhaps that is so. All my life I have feared the future. Those of my bloodline are naturally cautious, and our dreams are rarely comforting. After you and Robigor returned across the bridge, he looked at me from many yards away, where you and he and the men spoke together, and he nodded and smiled at me as he listened. I knew, then, at that moment, what was to come, and what I must do. As we looked at one another across the distance that separated us, I knew that it might well be the last time I ever looked into his eyes. I could not go to him. He could not come to me. Time was too pressing, and our duties were upon us. He smiled at me, over his shoulder, nodding as someone said something to him," her voice broke as she struggled to go on. "I saw it in his eyes. He was having his last look at me."

Few loves ever touched Ashlord's heart as did that of Mirabella and her husband Robigor, for he had recently made it his business to learn their story, and he understood the transformation it had brought to Mirabella. He felt through her words and saw in the pool of her eyes their love for each other, the strength of it, and the pain of their parting so, in the confusion before battle, without even a kiss, a touch, or even a word for each other. His heart, too, broke for them.

"All I wanted... He is the only man in all the world," she went on, continuing her struggle to speak, swallowing often, her voice cracking. "The only one who gave me peace and taught me joy. Through him, modest man, I learned of the greatness of Men, of their true strength and power. Through him, I found serenity and humble purpose. All I wanted was to spend my days with him, to see him through until the end of his own, then, afterwards, afterwards...I could carry him in my heart until, until..."

She stopped, her eyes a sea of anguish as she looked up at Ashlord. He was leaning on his stick, his shoulders slumped, old and wise and tired, his eyes a deep and dark well, and he smiled painfully. Her own watery eyes could not see the sympathetic mist in his.

"I watched him take his place on the bridge. When I heard that he rode away north, I have since had a kind of peace. Or perhaps it is resignation. In spite of my fear. But now that my son is going away, my fears are greater, and my anxiety cannot be expressed in words. I do not know how I am to go on. But go on, I must."

"Yes," Ashlord replied softly, "you must. You must have hope, and it is up to you, now, to give it to others, just as your husband would want you to do."

"I have little!"

"You may have very little of it, but it is more than many here possess. And, like friendship, hope is not weakened by the sharing of it."

• • •

By torchlight, Robby worked through the night, chopping and loading firewood onto a cart and driving it through the camps and distributing his loads along with blankets. He and the other men who labored with him spoke very little in the misty darkness. And though they were not sullen, they toiled with little enthusiasm. When dawn began to dimly show in the east, Robby found himself on the far side of Janhaven, having returned the cart to its owner, and it was a long walk back to the stockade. Fires burned lowly in the fields along the roadsides, and smoke hung in the motionless predawn air. He could hear the people stirring on the cold ground—a cough here and there, a baby crying in the distance—and he picked his way carefully through the campsites, trying not to trip over slumbering forms or tangling himself in the ropes of improvised tents that caught against his leg. More than once Robby stopped, recognizing a face huddled before a fire, and he asked after the folk there. In this manner, he saw the blacksmith, a bandage covering a gash on his head, lying on his side, smoking his pipe, staring into his small campfire. Later he spoke with Mr. Arbuckle, the former bridge tender, and his wife, and several others as he went along his way. He passed the Greardon nephews, too, who had labored so hard to put the mill back into operation after the terrible storm that killed their uncle. Mrs. Greardon, though, was nowhere to be seen. The heavy mill wagon, which used to haul flour and seed, was now their home, a tarpaulin thrown over the top of it as a roof. Stopping, Robby asked after Mrs. Greardon.

"We don't know where she is," said one of the boys. "She left Jay with us to look after, an' went back to the house for something."

"We think she got taken by them Redvests," said the other.

"Oh. I'm sorry to hear that. I'm sure she'll be fine, or turn up soon," Robby said, trying to be encouraging. They nodded, and he continued on his way.

It was a sad lot, indeed, and Robby grew more depressed as he went. He wondered at the misery that had befallen everyone so suddenly. Over and over he asked himself whether there was something else that he could do, something other than run off on some unpredictable adventure. The idea came to him of leading an attack on Passdale, perhaps winning back their town, driving out the Redvests and returning these people to their warm homes. His mind filled with grandiose visions of a well-organized offensive, with himself at Ullin's side, sweeping down on the unsuspecting invaders. "Let them have Tulith Attis," he muttered, "but surely we can take back Passdale and keep it!"

Out of the smoky mist ahead emerged the shape of a wagon parked near the edge of a field under some trees, and he heard a lonely pipe. It was from one of the minstrel's vans, lately belonging to Thurdun's people and given to the musicians when the boats departed. Robby paused, listening to the plaintive voice of the pipe, wavering through the melancholy air, and in the half-light of predawn he could just make out the player sitting on the back step of the wagon. His hand brushed Swyncraff about his waist, and he remembered Thurdun and the Queen. Her words came back to him.

"When you do what you must, it is as it should be,
and leads to the next and the next."

He knew that if he stayed here to serve his people, to help organize a resistance and to take back their homeland, many things could be possible. After all, they were a resourceful people and, as the recent floods showed, they knew how to work together. But the darkness of his heart told him that even if he did so, and had every success against the invaders, it would be folly in the end. A more formidable opponent was stirring in the world, against which no army could withstand.

• • •

It was a difficult decision for Billy Bosk, who was beginning to feel the burdens of his duties as leader of Boskland. His initial inclination, in spite of the discussion of the evening before, was to take a few men and ride in search of his sister, going around the back ways toward the southern parts of Barley. Frizella dissuaded him, saying it would be a foolhardy quest, and that as the new laird, he had a greater duty to the land.

"Ain't nobody left what can speak for the House of Bosk," she told him. "An' if a great war is upon us, then somebody's got to get word to Duinnor an' bear witness concernin' these things. Yer sister's got a head on her shoulders, an' we must trust that she'll use it. An' though I hate to see ye go, I'd be comforted that ye'd be goin' off with the likes of Ashlord an' Ullin to see to things. I already talked to Mira 'bout all this. Robby's goin', too. At least ye'll be with good friends what'll look after one another."

So Billy was resolved to go with Robby. He consulted with several of his kinsmen who had survived the attack and were at Janhaven, and, with his mother, he explained to them that he was called away to Duinnor, to take warning and to seek aid.

"I'll not say this goes easy on me," he said to them at dawn. They had gathered together in a hut which was given over to them by a farmer who had been a childhood friend of Billy's father. "Yet Bosks have sworn allegiance to Duinnor, an' it's with Duinnor that our hope lay. The fate of Barley'll be shared, an' the Redvests turned back only by might greater than we an' Glareth can muster. If I stayed, me sword an' me voice would only harry the enemy. But if I go west, I'll carry with me the full word of our need. If chance an' fortune favor, I'll return with aid, or, should the way show otherwise, I will do me utmost to wrench the enemy from these lands by other means. But the two of ye, Tonifor Bosk an' Parth Bosk, elder cousins of mine, have all to do with fightin' an' keepin' our people. If ye honor me father an' the House of Bosk, ye'll do honor to the name of Bosk by what means ye have."

Hearing Billy speak thus, with stern determination, was new to them, for they well knew his reputation for sport and jest. And the fire in his eyes was fiercer than his words. The cuts and bruises about his face, his bandaged head, and the reluctance with which he spoke of his ordeal with Bailorg only filled them with a kind of awe of his transformation. Seeing him thus, and hearing his words, softly spoken yet full of authority, they could not but be moved, even though his cousins were older by nearly a generation.

"Aye, Bilaylin," they nodded vehemently, using his given name, and said, "we'll see the House of Bosk restored."

Ibin sat in the corner by the meager fire, a blanket draped over his shoulders, his face unusually void of the smile that he lost somewhere on the road to Janhaven and had not yet recovered. He understood least of any the talk going on about him and repeatedly asked Billy what was the matter. Billy gave an earnest and urgent explanation, lacking only in certain details he thought best kept to himself. Ibin listened carefully, full of effort to comprehend as they made their way to the hut.

"ThenIwillgo, I'llgotoo, Billy," Ibin said.

"Ye'll be needed here, good friend."

"But, but, butIdon't, butIdon'twanttostayhere!" Ibin pleaded. Billy could not say no. Ibin had as much a right to go as anyone. Though Robby had made it clear that he wanted no one to go with him except Ashlord, Billy and Ullin insisted they would be going along, too, regardless of Robby's objections. Billy sighed and put his hand on Ibin's thick shoulder.

"Well, I reckon one more'll do no harm."

Now, as Billy explained to his kinsmen that he would not be back before spring, Ibin sat silent, looking on as still as a statue. He was accustomed to being treated as if he was not present, left out of conversations, remembered as an afterthought, or smiled at with the same tolerant condescension given to children. Though it was impossible for him to articulate, Ibin felt this treatment just the same, and had done so all of his life. It did not bother him as it might have bothered someone else, owing to his good nature, and he rarely felt any sense of offense or cruelty. Though he paid intense attention, as was his way, he rarely gained much understanding about the many deep concerns and interests that those around him discussed. Thus he had come to feel that many things were simply beyond his comprehension. He had little trouble with "whats" and he was a master of "whens," and he never forgot a name or a face or the link between the two. However, "whys" were often a puzzle to him, and "hows" he often failed to grasp. Ordinary things seemed something of a mystery to him, like why folks worked so hard, always making even more work. To them, these activities seemed a-purpose to something else, always something else. But to Ibin all activities were a joy, even if those who worked with him seemed not to find joy in the work. They acted as if chores were a distraction from having a nice time, from dining and singing, drinking and playing. To Ibin all these things were just as natural as leaf and limb, and he hardly saw the difference, though he had to admit he took particular joy from mealtimes. There were things that he recognized as ordinary and self-evident, so much so that he took them for granted, but he was seldom ever able to express those things in words, and his efforts to do so only seemed to mystify others.

These late events had upset all of his routines and all of his expectations of what each day should be like. It was hard for him to grasp the idea that his old room in Bosk Manor was forever gone. And, though he was quicker to adapt than most, due again to his affable and acquiescent personality, he knew the feelings of confusion and anxiety that he suppressed were shared by everyone, and that, at least in some small way, he was now no different than all the rest. So he sat patiently and waited for the Bosks to finish their chat.

Those gathered in the hut concluded their discussion, and Billy's kinsmen departed. Billy looked at Ibin and sighed. Ibin sensed the heaviness on Billy's sagging shoulders, and his own feelings of weariness were nothing compared to the expression on his friend's face. Billy nodded, though, and tried to smile. However, it was Ibin's smile, appearing at last, that gave the most comfort.

"Iwillgo, Iwillgowithyou, BillyBosk," he said.

• • •

"I must stay, Robby," said Mirabella that same hour in the hastily prepared building that would serve as a ward for the sick and wounded. Pulling her son aside to be out of the way of the men bringing in cots, she spoke in low tones. "I would have you stay, or flee after your father to Glareth, except I see that your mind is made up to go. And I would go with you if I could, but the need here is so great. These are my people, too, and I will not abandon them. Not only are there women and children and hurt ones to attend to, but I think my sword will be needed again."

"I understand, Mother." Robby nodded. "I do not want you to go with us. I want you to be here when Daddy returns, and I want you to keep safe, if you can, and be with those that need you. The winter will be hard, I know, and the Redvests stubborn."

"The winter will not be as hard nor the enemy so stubborn as we, I think." She managed to smile. "When do you depart?"

"We meet tonight for more reckoning on that. But I think as soon as we can make ready."

"Come to me as soon as you know."

• • •

"Find a place an' get some sleep, dearie," Frizella ordered Sheila. It had been a long night, making and applying clean bandages, soothing the wounded, and holding the hands of the dying. Sheila cried with the survivors as eyes closed for the final time, and she cooled brows of the delirious with wet rags to somewhat ease their pain. Now, away from the wounded and the sick, her thoughts were as muddled and indistinct as the gray predawn light, and she walked without knowing which way she went. She stumbled into a small throng of lost children being tended by Mr. Broadweed. Seeing her weariness, he invited her to have some blankets and gestured at a place under a wagon where she could lie down and rest. She accepted his offer, in spite of her dislike of the schoolmaster, and curled up on the ground between the wagon wheels. Sooner than she knew, she slipped into a deep and profound sleep. She never noticed when Broadweed came and gently covered her over with several more blankets. It was Broadweed, too, who woke her midmorning to offer her a bowl of steaming-hot oatmeal.

"Wake up, Sheila Pradkin," he said to her, touching her shoulder. She roused herself and saw him crouching under the wagon on his knees to reach her, two small boys peering cautiously at her from behind him. "That's a decent sleep you've had, I hope. And here is a modest breakfast for you."

Sheila sat up on one elbow and took the bowl and spoon he offered.

"Thank you for your kindness, Mr. Broadweed," she said.

"Not at all, my dear!"

She ate a couple of spoonfuls of the honey-sweetened stuff and felt life come back to her. Mr. Broadweed was clumsily backing out from under the wagon when she asked, "Who are these children you have with you?"

"Why, I suppose they are my charges," he said, stopping to kneel next to a wagon wheel so that he could chat. "Younger students at my school who are separated from their parents, or, in the case of Sam and Tom, here, those who have none. I suppose they look to me, now, for things other than letters and numbers. At least for a while, anyway."

Sheila now understood something she had missed all her life. There were adults who would not abandon children, or beat them, or do other worse things. There were a few to be trusted, and there always had been. She should have known this, from her knowledge of Mr. Ribbon and Mr. Bosk. As a brat, she had revolted against Mr. Broadweed and his school. But now she realized that his school had been a shelter for his students, even if only for a few hours each day.

"You have no children of your own, do you?" she asked.

"If I take your meaning, no. Alas, Mrs. Broadweed and I have none." he sighed. "But I try to treat any child who comes to me as my own as far as I can."

"I remember you," she said. "I remember you and your wife coming to see my uncle. I was very little, I think. Maybe only six or seven years old. He abused you most severely, as I recall."

"I came to see your uncle many times," Mr. Broadweed said. "But he would not force you to attend my school, and I had no power to force you, either. Yes. He was a difficult man. I'm afraid I do not think of him with much fondness."

"That's fine. I hated him. And now I hate the memory of him."

"I can understand."

"Oh, can you?" She made no effort to keep the sarcasm from her voice even though she knew he did not deserve it.

"Yes," he said with no sign of noting her tone. "You see, like you, my parents died when I was too young to remember them. My uncle and my aunt kept me as a house servant until I was ten years old. That's when I ran away." A look of pain crossed Mr. Broadweed's face. "I should have, well, I should have made more of an effort for you, my dear. I am so sorry! Yet, as I have heard, you have taught yourself to read and write. That is a great accomplishment! You did not need me at all. Still, I wish I could have offered you something."

Sheila was astonished.

"You did all that you could do," she said. "What more could you have done? I blame only my uncle and myself for my misfortunes. I should have done as you did and run away from him. If only I had." She shrugged. "But I didn't. Not until it was too late. Anyway, I did not teach myself. Robby Ribbon and Ashlord taught me. I'm sorry, too, for all your wasted efforts on my behalf."

"There, there. It is all done and in the past," he said as his pained face turned tender. "I'm afraid we have much else to worry about, now. Well, I need to go and see to the new schoolroom being prepared for us. I hope to see you again soon!"

Sheila watched him get to his feet, noting that he did not look as old as she once thought. There was something in his face, too, a certain droop of his cheeks, perhaps, or turn of his lips, that before she had taken as a kind of timidness. Now she saw him differently; his face, the same as ever it was, seemed to her framed with a quiet but powerful reserve. She suddenly remembered seeing him, the day before yesterday, loading books into the wagon along with as many children as he could muster. She had not been paying a lot of attention to him, though. The fight was beginning as the Redvests poured down the hill to the bridge. She remembered, too, during the flight from Passdale, seeing a man, sword in hand, standing over a crying child as he swung against three Redvests coming at them. She now realized that it had been Mr. Broadweed. She watched him recede, a bloody bandage tied around his left leg, trailing a gaggle of little boys and girls as he limped along, and she felt the bitter irony of coming to know these people only now that all had been lost to them. And she wondered, not for the first time, how her life might have been different if only her parents had lived a little longer. At least long enough for her to remember them.

• • •

Ullin stood at the high outcrop that overlooked the roadway, the place from which the Thunder Mountain Band made their headlong descent the day before. It was a hard climb, and he, along with Winterford and one of Billy's kinsmen, stood together, still panting with the effort. Glancing around, he quickly realized the value of this position.

"Let's get some signal fires up here, ready to light," he said. "And by day, some brightly polished looking-glass to signal warnings down to our points along the road and at the Narrows."

"Aye, but at night it might be better to use a covered lantern," suggested Winterford. "Like the kind we use. Ye can open a shade on one side and point the light. That way ye can wave all ye like and none behind ye can see it. No sense in lettin' onto the Redvests they've been spotted."

Ullin nodded and smiled. He liked the way this fellow thought.

"You Thunder Mountain men have a number of things to teach, I imagine," Ullin said.

"Well, we've gotten along pretty well by being careful, if that's what ye mean."

"And this path, here," Ullin pointed south. "Where does it go?"

"Back along this here ridge. 'Bout six mile er so on, it splits away west across the south road at Fox Gap an' then on up into the mountains," Winterford explained. "An' the other way, along the east side of the ridge for 'bout two miles, crossin' down to the bottom of the ridge goin' on southward that way. We don't use these paths much, except for keepin' out of other folks' way. Anyway, as ye can see, ain't nobody gonna come up the paths without givin' off plenty of notice, either way."

"And a fine command of the West Road below, going both ways," Ullin said turning back around. "Almost within long arrow shot. This is a great place for a watch. It's bound to get icy cold up here, though."

"That it will, for sure. Already pretty chilly with this breeze."

"I'd say it'd be worthwhile to go ahead and start working on some kind of keep. With four men up here standing watch, a small shelter can keep them warm as they take turns."

"Good idea. Maybe build it right up on the side of that rock face right over there," Winterford gestured at a flat, fairly smooth cliff just above and behind them. "Plenty of stone up here to make it with."

Several hundred yards below and to the east, Mr. Furaman was pulling up a wagon to the Narrows along both sides of which his men and others from Passdale were building log walls. Their intention was to make places from where archers could command the road between the two. Here, the road cut deeply through a gap in the ridge, rising steeply to it from the east then, passing through, making a long slow descent westward toward Janhaven. The men already had both walls up and were working on scaffolding behind them for platforms where the watches would stand. A thick rope had been passed between the two walls, some forty feet above the roadbed, and a system of blocks and pulleys allowed the passage of messages and supplies from one side to the other. Mr. Furaman brought with him food, blankets, and more rope, along with casks of oil for torches. He watched with satisfaction the progress that had been made since yesterday and realized that fear increased their efforts.

• • •

Ashlord remained alone the entire night after the others had left. He sat by the fire, smoking his pipe and thinking. Every so often, he would suddenly stand from his stool and pace about the room muttering or shaking his head, only to take his seat by the fire again as it died lower and lower. Hour passed hour, and he cared not when the last flame licked out, leaving only dull coals, and was not concerned at the dense chill that soon after crept into the room. When morning came, the men of the stockade began stirring to their wagons and to their tools, coming and going through the room with their things and talk. Still Ashlord sat, seemingly oblivious to the increasing bustle. But he noticed all those things and more; he simply gave them little attention, putting his mind's ears and eyes instead to stirrings of greater subtlety and moment.

"Excuse me, sir."

Ashlord turned and looked blankly at the man before him, standing with his arms full of wood for the fireplace.

"Excuse me," the man repeated.

Ashlord realized that he was sitting in the way and jumped up.

"Pardon me!"

The man dumped the wood into the box near the hearth and dusted his hands.

"Ye must be Ashlord."

"I am."

"I'm Durlorn, buildin' foreman." He shook hands with Ashlord.

"Oh, yes."

"We'll be usin' this here room for breakfast in a little bit, Mr. Ashlord, sir, if ye don't mind. Our usual place across the way is kind of crowded an' there ain't 'nough room," he explained. "Mr. Furaman always has breakfast with his top foremen. Goes over accounts, gets the men ready for the day, sort of. He's already out, though, takin' stuff to the men buildin' the gate at the Narrows. But he left instructions for his foremen to gather here for breakfast anyways."

"Well, I'll be moving along, then," Ashlord said, pulling on his cloak and lifting his walking stick.

"Won't ye have somethin' to eat with us?" Durlorn asked. "We'd be honored to have ye."

"Thank you very much for the offer. But I have some things I should see to."

Ashlord walked out into the chilly morning air, smoky with the many campfires that now surrounded the stockade, and made his way across the interior grounds to the far buildings. He hardly noticed when Certina landed on his shoulder, only nodding as she clucked in his ear.

"Yes, yes," he mumbled as he pushed open the door to the old warehouse. Inside, folk were busy creating a makeshift hospital, and he saw Robby speaking with his mother across the room. Robby watched her go back into the main room to help make beds, and then he turned to see Ashlord in the doorway. Ashlord noted the wear in Robby's face as he neared.

"How are you this morning?"

"I don't think I slept a wink," Robby said, looking back over his shoulder at his mother. "In fact, I know I didn't."

"That makes two of us," Ashlord said. "Perhaps you should find a place to get some rest. The last few days have been a trial for you, I know. You will need your strength, and it will do no one any good for you to falter."

Robby followed Ashlord back outside where the sun was burning away the morning mists and blue sky was emerging.

"I am tired," Robby said, pulling his coat around him against the chill. "But there's so much to be done."

"Yes, there is much," Ashlord nodded, looking around. "Not only here, but elsewhere."

Robby looked at Ashlord blankly.

"We must make our preparations to depart, Robby."

"I know. It's just that I feel, well, I dunno," Robby shrugged and shook his head.

"It's just that you feel torn," Ashlord said. "You feel responsible, somehow, about all this. You are having doubts about last night, and you think you should stay here and help your mother and the others. I understand your feelings, Robby, believe me, I do. But it would be folly to stay and foolish to delay."

"But, my friends, my home." Robby faltered for a moment thinking of his father, wondering what had become of him, and thinking of his mother doing her best to hold things together.

"I know that you feel pain at the thought of leaving here. It will not go away when you depart. The things you miss are those that you love. But others may have little hope to regain what has been lost, whereas you have a chance to do so. The right thing to do is almost always the hardest thing to start. Get something to eat, then find a quiet place and sleep for a time. Go in yonder and ask for Mr. Durlorn. Tell him that you come to eat breakfast in Ashlord's stead. He'll understand, and I'll wager he'll set a hearty plate before you. Ask him if there is a place where you can sleep undisturbed. Ullin and I will meet with you this evening and work out our plans."

"Have you seen Sheila?" Robby asked as Ashlord turned to go.

"Not since last night," Ashlord said. "I believe she will want to go with us."

"I think she ought to."

"Why? She would be of great service here. And there will be many dangers on our road," Ashlord said. "Do not mistake me. Sheila is capable of taking better care of herself than most full-grown men. I only wonder if it is best."

"I don't know, Ashlord." Robby shoved his hands into his pockets. "I only think I'll, well, I think I need her. I know I want her to come along. Maybe I'm mixing the two up."

"It should be her choice," Ashlord said. "I'll not object, if that is your fear."

Robby watched Ashlord head for the gate and then turned to find his breakfast. After introducing himself to Durlorn and giving him the message from Ashlord, a place was quickly set among the men at the table who had come in from their early morning work. At first, Robby thought them a rough group, but as he chatted with them over eggs and bacon, answering their questions about Passdale and Barley, he came to understand that they were just tired and worried, like everyone else. When they discovered that Robby was the son of Robigor Ribbon, the "great man of business," they warmed to him, saying that since Ribbon opened his store, a flourishing trade had been established with Barley, giving many besides themselves good work to support their families. One foreman, on in years but bright-eyed and friendly, even went so far as to say that if it hadn't been for Mr. Ribbon, "Janhaven might've dried up an' blown away years ago." This was surprising to Robby, for he had never considered what his own hometown might be like without the store.

"Oh, not the store only, no, no!" said the man. "But the bridge, too, an' all his works. Yer father's known far an' wide, er, at least nearby, as a man of acumen. Aye! Ac-u-men!"

"Hear, hear!" nodded a couple of the other men. "Ac-u-men!"

The talk turned to the Redvests and the refugees, and the group speculated on their trade routes south and north. They got around to wondering how long it would be before the Lakemen and their allies, the powerful Glarethians, fell upon the Redvests.

"It'll be summer, earliest," said one brooding man. "They ain't got the men like they used to."

" 'At's right," said another, talking with his mouth full. "Them Redvests ain't stupid. They'd a never come this far north if they had any fear of Glareth by the Sea!"

"Naw," said another. "I'll wager they'll be pourin' through afore the last frost. They's still a mighty people, them Lakemen an' their kin. An' with Passdale taken, the trade route's been blocked. Now I ask ye: how long ye think they'll stand for that?"

"Well, not afore we run short here, is what I say. More an' more folk're comin' in every hour, stragglin' from over the north ridge, mostly, some up from south parts, too."

"What d'ye think, son," one of the men asked Robby. "I seen that Kingsman 'round yesterday. Is thar gonna be an attack on Passdale to roust out them Redvests?"

Robby swallowed his coffee and wiped his mouth.

"I don't think we're in much shape," he said. "We've been licked pretty good, and it's as much as we can do right now just to take care of one another." They had all stopped eating, some with bits of sausage halfway to their mouths, and were all looking at him, listening. "But with arms provided by you folk, and a little preparation, I'll warrant that the Redvests will soon feel the sting of Barley steel," Robby added bravely.

"Thar ye go!" said one man.

"Hear, hear!" cried another, raising his cup of coffee in salute.

"Barley steel!"

"Aye!"

The men nodded and smiled, and Robby was impressed by how much encouragement they seemed to have taken from his words. But one man kept eyeing him without reacting at all, silent as he had been during the whole of breakfast. The others finished eating and hurried out to their duties, bidding Robby a good day as they went, but this man was the last to rise from the table. He was a big swarthy man with short-cropped hair and a matching beard of graying-blond. He stood, finished his coffee, then came around the table to stand next to Robby.

"Ye talk a brave talk, lad," he said without smiling. Robby realized that he knew the man, one of Furaman's wagoneers that often came to Passdale on deliveries.

"Only, is it good to give folk hope where there is little?" the man went on.

Robby did not answer at first, but slowly stood to face him.

"I'll not say there is always much hope," Robby said. "But it is better to have what hope there is, I've been told, and let a candle serve when there is no sun."

The man nodded as a careworn smile crossed his face. He took a step toward the door, then hesitated.

"My sister an' her husband lived in Barley," he said. "They have a little place down river-way, on the south Bosk line. They have two little girls, one's four years old. The other's not yet two."

Robby knew the place and realized that if Boskland had fallen so quickly, this man's relatives were probably captives, or worse.

"Went after 'em soon as word came," the man went on. It was terrible to see the man's face quake with all the restraint he could muster, and Robby's throat suddenly went dry. "Found me little nieces, down in the storm cellar hidin' 'mongst broken barrels an' the like. Took 'em up, one under each of me arms an' ran as fast as I could. On past where they mother lay. On past where they father lay. Holdin' the little one's faces close so they couldn't see."

The man went to the door and opened it, put his hat on, then turned and faced Robby.

"I mean to go back to Barley," he said, and never had Robby heard any simple phrase uttered with such black and certain threat. The man turned away and stood in the doorway a moment longer, looking out at the light of morning, then stepped away. Durlorn shut the door on the cool air and brushed past Robby, picking up plates and cups.

"If he ain't careful," he said to Robby, "he'll get himself done in like was his sister an' her husband. Mr. Furaman's gonna have a time keepin' a hand on the men now that war is on us."

"I guess so," Robby nodded. "Thank you for the breakfast, Mr. Durlorn. I wonder if I might trouble you to show me a place where I can get some sleep. Somewhere out of the way, I mean."

Durlorn straightened up from the washing tub where he had dumped the plates and wiped his hands on his apron.

"Well," he said, "thar's bound to be a good bit of business 'round here, today. Hm-m. I reckon the best place I can think of is Mr. Furaman's upstairs back room. Right this way, Mr. Ribbon. Thar's a cot, an' it's on the back side of the buildin', away from comin's an' goin's. Mr. Furaman catches a nap thar sometimes, but I doubt if it'll be used at all today."

"Just for a few hours," Robby said as he followed Durlorn up some side stairs and down a hall to the back of the building. Durlorn pushed open a door and showed Robby a small room with a desk, some chairs, shelves with account books, and the normal things that one might expect in a clerk's office. And in one corner was the cot, covered with quilts. Durlorn went to a small window and pushed back the shutters to let light in.

"I'll light a far in the little stove, thar," Durlorn said. "An' bring in a wash basin for ye."

"Oh that's not needed. Please don't trouble. I only want to get a bit of sleep."

"No trouble. Ye go ahead an' lay yerself down. Don't mind any stirrin' ye may hear. It'll only be me an' the men."

Robby sat down on the cot and took his boots off, then unbuckled his belt and removed his coat and tunic. Straightening out Swyncraff, he leaned it against the wall beside the cot and sank down into the straw mattress, fiddling with his shirt buttons. That is as far as he got before he closed his eyes. He vaguely heard Durlorn come back and the squeak of the stove door, but after that he heard nothing for a long, peaceful while.

• • •

While Robby slept, the people of Barley and Passdale continued their efforts, much aided by the Janhaven folk, finding accommodations and sizing up their situation. More people had trickled in overnight and into the morning, with some being happily reunited with friends and family. There were impromptu meetings among the people, striving to discover what they were to do. Furaman and others of Janhaven tried to reassure them that they would not be abandoned to fend for themselves, or left to the mercy of the elements, but this was of little solace to people so suddenly uprooted from their lands and shops and homes. Ashlord and Ullin spoke, too, telling them what they knew of the Redvests, and that the enemy would more than likely be gone by spring, perhaps even before. There was the inevitable talk of striking back at the Redvests, and at a large gathering just outside the stockade, many of the displaced people debated, with tempers and passions rising quickly.

"There are at least two or three thousand trained soldiers to face, perhaps many more," Ashlord shouted. The crowd turned toward the commanding voice. "They are armed, they are organized, and by all accounts they are well led," Ashlord went on. "They would be a match for any similar, well-trained and seasoned army, and to go openly against them with less would be folly!"

"What would ye have us do?" shouted back a particularly agitated man of Barley. "Give up our homes without a fight!"

"We ain't done no such thing!" came a shout from Billy who suddenly appeared at the back of the crowd, pushing his way through and climbing onto a wagon so that all could see him. "Good men whar lost in the fightin' at Barley an' Boskland, more in Passdale an' on the road. Would ye dishonor thar blood by uselessly pourin' out more?"

Sheila, coming up from behind the wagon, could hardly believe that it was Billy who addressed them so adamantly.

"This is what I say to all me kinsmen an' all else who'll listen," Billy said. "Look first to survive the winter. Make warm camps for the children, our elderly, an' our sick an' wounded. Take care of what ye still got!"

"Then what? Sit on our arses 'til them Redvests come trampsin' up the road to take us? What'll we do then, eh?"

"We shall fight!" called someone from the other side of the crowd. The crowd parted, and Sheila saw Mirabella, her sword hilt over her shoulder, striding to the wagon where Billy stood. Any who had not seen her take on the Redvests on the road had by now heard of her valor. All were in awe of the fighting skill she had displayed. There was even a rumor going about the camps that Mirabella was a Faerekind warrioress of old, and every imaginable tale was being circulated about how she came to live in Passdale all these years as a lowly storekeeper's wife.

"Fight, I say! But not as the enemy may expect. If you are anxious to fight, then join with me! Let us first make our place here secure. Then, if you will follow my command, I will show you how to make the Redvest fear us! We will reform the militias, and we will not wait for the Redvests to come to us. But here is where our first fight is, here in Janhaven. We must fight sickness and cold. We must fight hunger and disease. If we cannot win against these things, we cannot win against the Redvests!"

Ashlord leaned against his walking stick with an expression of satisfaction. Ullin shook his head with a chuckle.

"I think my aunt will fall upon the old ways of our people if she is not careful," Ullin said.

"And not a moment too soon, if you ask me," Ashlord replied.

Frizella then appeared, adding with her strident voice the ways in which people could help each other and demanding that each send a representative of their family to meet with her and Mirabella at the stockade this very afternoon.

"We get ourselves good an' organized-like," she said. "An' ain't nobody gonna go hungry nor freeze. We all got worries 'bout missin' an' hurt kinfolk an' friends, but we gotta get on with managin' our situation. So, let's do what we must to keep ourselves fit for what's ahead. This day at mid-afternoon! Let everyone know! We'll make articles of law, if needed, bindin' our fates, just like in Barley when we took our oaths. Now, get on with yer chores! Go on! Time's wastin'!"

Effectively breaking up the crowd, Frizella turned to Mirabella.

"Just what on earth d'ye have in mind, missy?" she asked her slyly. "If I didn't know better, I'd say ye've got a bit of soldierin' on ye mind."

Sheila eased over to Ashlord and caught his arm.

"Do you know where Robby is?"

"I last saw him this morning," Ashlord said. "I think Mr. Durlorn, at the stockade, might know where he is."

Ullin approached, and as she turned to go, he spoke to her.

"Sheila," he asked, "do you mean to go with us?"

"Yes."

"It may not be safe for you. That is, less so even than for the rest of us."

"Because I am not a man?"

"There are many rogues, and worse, along the roads we may take," Ashlord put in. "We may not be able to avoid them."

"I am strong," Sheila said, defensively. "And no more can be done to me than what has already been."

Ashlord looked at her and nodded.

"I am also concerned for Robby's sake," he said. "If he had to choose his own safety or yours—"

"Robby would choose anyone's safety over his own, as I think you know," Sheila retorted before Ashlord could finish. "Can you foresee it would be me in the choice and not some other of his friends?"

"No-o, no," Ashlord said. "If you are determined in this, then your bow and your wit will be welcome, and put to good use. Only of that am I certain."

"Then I will come," Sheila said, turning away and walking off, leaving Ashlord and Ullin looking after her.

"I have misgivings about her coming along," said Ullin. "But no more than I have about Billy and Ibin."

Ashlord nodded. "I am concerned, too. But those three have as much at stake as anyone, and they may be a comfort to Robby later on. I doubt if much good would be served by leaving any one of them behind. But if we do not depart soon, others may wish to join us, too."

"You may be right," he said. "Then let us make all our arrangements as soon as we can. Tonight? In the place where we met before?"

"Yes."

• • •

Sheila walked on, perturbed by the brief conversation. Although she readily admitted that Ashlord and Ullin had sincere concerns for her safety, she wondered at the implication about Robby and possibly the others.

"Do they actually think *they'll* have to protec *me*?" she muttered to herself. "As if I haven't been the one protecting them! Where do they think those arrows came from? And where were they looking during all the fighting? Was I invisible? Did they not see me there? Did I not fight as hard and as valiantly as any man? Do they say the same about Mirabella?"

Then she caught herself, and quelled her old temper. Her months with Ashlord, gentle and always sincere, came back to her. His teachings. "You must calm yourself," he had told her on more than one occasion, "and think of what is as it is, not as what you take it for."

So she came full circle, realizing that Ashlord and Ullin worried about much. That she was included in that worry somehow soothed her. Suddenly she felt the weight of their concern and realized for the first time what difficulties must lay ahead. She had stopped walking, and found herself standing in front of a little shop, one of several on a small alley along the edge of Janhaven. Through the dusty window of this shop, past her own grimy reflection, two women were cutting pieces of linen cloth from bolts and fitting the bits together on a table in preparation of a garment. She walked on a few steps, then suddenly turned back and entered.

• • •

"Soon, you must be on your way. Forces are gathering to oppose you and there is much you must accomplish."

Robby stood on top of the dune facing the Dragonkind woman. He could see only her eyes, gold and cat-like, gazing at him from under her shemagh-wrapped face. Her eyes were soft, but the way they narrowed at him told of her forehead, creased with concern. The air blew hard, tugging at her robes, revealing her feminine shape, in spite of her copper-hued light armor, while the low sun bathed the desert in orange hues. She pulled her robes back to her, but not before Robby saw the sword hilt at her side. Though the sand was hot, the gust of wind was cool, as if telling of the coming night.

"Who are you?"

"That is not important. You will know me soon enough."

"Am I dreaming?"

"Yes, after a manner," she said. "But this is the only way I may speak with you."

"You are one of the Dragon People."

"Yes."

"Do all your kind have this power?"

"Yes. And no. That is to say, all creatures have this power. They need only to find it. You are beginning to find it yourself."

He was frightened of her, yet strangely assured that she would do him no harm.

"Do many travel abroad in this manner?"

"No. Very few discover this gift. Fewer still survive its discovery, for it is seductive and may entice an unnatural desire to remain asleep. Many have starved to death, lost in dreams. Many more have died in their tombs or upon the pyre made for them by those lacking wit to see they were merely asleep and had not yet died. Very few of us walk the dream place. I have only ever met with two others, my Kundorlu—my teacher, who instructed me—and another student of his."

"Why should I trust you?"

"There is no need of trust. I do what I must for my people just as you do for yours."

"Our people are at war with one another," Robby insisted. "Why should I heed one of the enemy?"

"Our people are at war, but you and I are not," she said. "And the war at hand is but a skirmish compared to what may come. I fear for my people as you fear for yours. We have much in common, actually. You seek to displace a powerful but unwise ruler of your lands. I strive for the freedom of my people from even harsher tyranny. I think our interests may make us allies."

"You are afraid of me."

"Yes."

"Why?"

"For the same reason you should fear me. Betrayal. If I let it be known who and where you are, word would spread beyond my lands, and you would not live much longer. There are many who would wish to stop you from your quest. However, among those who would wish to stop you may be those who would wish to discover me. The things that we seek are bound up in each other. So it is that I cannot betray you unless I also betray that for which I strive."

"And I cannot betray you, either," Robby said. "For one, you are only a dream. And, for another, I do not know who you are or who it might be that I could betray you to."

"That is why I come to you in this way, directly, rather than through some messenger that may be untrustworthy."

"I have had dreams before, some that recurred."

"You mistrust your senses. That is understandable. I ask nothing of you. That time may come. If you do not wish to meet me in this way, or in any way, you have it within your power to wake from this dream. You only need to will it so."

Robby thought about this. He felt her presence fade and the sensation of a blanket over him, and he felt oddly horizontal.

"You sense what I say is true."

Robby redirected his attention back to her and saw her become solid and clear again, and the sensations of the bed where he slept faded away.

"I think you have the better of me," he said. "For you obviously know the ways of this dream-realm, and I do not. You must know I am full of doubts about all this and whether you be real or some spirit, or worse, come to misguide me."

"Perhaps," she said. "But I will give you a sign so that you may know I am no mere dream."

She lifted her hand and held it out, palm up. In it was a ring of black, banded by interwoven strands of gold, and set with a stone the color of dark wine. Just as Robby beheld it, a black form swooped down from the air, snatching it from her hand. Robby, alarmed, stepped back, and watched the large bird flap away swiftly into the sky. But the woman was unperturbed.

"When you go westward, insist that you go first to a place your people call Tulith Morgair. It is an abandoned keep near Bletharn Plain. There, look to the hand of your great grandfather. I leave there a sign for you. A token of my reality and my earnestness."

"My great grandfather?"

"Yes. I must go, now. You will not see me again until you have found the sign I speak of. Remember, look to your great grandfather. Until then, may care guide your steps!"

She turned to walk away into a cloud of fading scenery, then paused. Turning back to him, she said, "I will tell you my name. It is Micerea."

Chapter 2

Mirabella's Tale

Day 84
161 Days Remaining

Robby woke with a start and was even more startled to see a boyish figure squatting on the floor across the room, back against the wall, head down, with brown shoulder-length hair. Hearing Robby stir, the figure looked up.

"Sheila?"

"Hello, sleepyhead."

"Your hair!"

"Yes, it's nearly all gone."

"It looks awful!" Robby blurted out. "I mean, oh, your hair! It was so long and beautiful! Why did you cut it?"

"Actually, a seamstress cut it for me."

"Why?"

"It was too much to worry with, what with everything else to take care of," she said. "It'll be easier to keep clean this way. And I don't think any of us can count on many niceties for a while."

Robby continued to stare at her until his face lost its sadness and went blank.

"I guess so," he nodded.

"You were dreaming," she smiled.

"Yes, of a desert princess," he said.

"Oh?" She stood and came over to him. "And was this desert princess beautiful?"

"I don't know," Robby replied. "She was covered in robes and a scarf was across her face."

"Oh, mysterious! That's even worse."

"No more mysterious than you!" Robby chided.

"What's so mysterious about me?" she said, slipping onto the cot and pulling the blanket over the two of them. "I think you should not try to understand me so much, and just take me at face value. Or however you wish to."

• • •

Afterwards, they talked, and they gave each other a fuller accounting of their experiences over the last few days. There was much to say and for each to ponder. As Sheila related her story, Robby was impressed by her strength and stalwartness, though her words were far from boastful.

"During the fight at the bridge," she said, "I think I killed six men. Each fell with one of my arrows and did not move afterwards. I had to aim for their necks or their faces, so covered with armor and shields they were. Nine more I managed to stop with an arrow in their legs or hands. It was horrible. I did not know I could do such a thing. It wasn't like the fight we had on the way back from Tulith Attis. This was slower. It was more…intentional. I can't explain."

She talked for a long time about how confusing and useless the fighting had been. About the mad retreat from Passdale, how the night was spent on the road making traps for their pursuers, and about trying to make a defense at the Narrows, and how the mounted Redvests broke through so easily. She described seeing Robby amid the wild horsemen, the Thunder Mountain Band, that poured onto the road ahead of her.

When Robby's turn came to tell his tale, she thought it very interesting. She shook her head when he expressed guilt over breaking his oath to tell the truth.

"You lied because you thought it was the only way to save Billy's life," Sheila said. "Don't worry about it. You may have to lie again before our journeys are done, and do other dreadful things besides. I only wish you had not killed Bailorg."

"Why? I would think you of all people would want him dead, after what he put your uncle up to."

"My uncle put himself up to that," retorted Sheila. "I only mean that it would have been good to see what Ashlord might do with Bailorg, what news or knowledge Bailorg might have given up to him."

"Oh."

Robby went silent. Sheila realized she had hit a nerve.

"I'm sure he deserved to die," she said, trying to recover. "And I'm sorry that you had to fight him. One of Martin Makeig's men said you fought like a lion."

"Oh? They told you about it?"

"Well, of course Billy told his story of it all, about being captured and how you rescued him. When I had a chance, I asked a Hill Town man who was there when you killed Bailorg. Lantin Rose, I think the man's name is. He told me how well you fought."

"Well, Ullin's training certainly helped."

"He said you used a dagger and what he called a living staff. Is that the staff over there?" she nodded at Swyncraff leaning against the wall. "I thought it was only an odd-looking piece of rope. Ashlord says there are few like it, and that Bailorg had one, too, or something of the sort. He said you got yours from Queen Serith Ellyn."

"Yes, from her brother, actually."

"I still find it hard to believe that you really met a queen."

"Me, too. Anyway, yes, that's it. Its name is Swyncraff," Robby said. "What it actually is, I'm still not sure. Only it does what I want it to do, taking shapes that I bend it to, sometimes like rope, sometimes like a rod. And watch this."

Robby rolled over onto his side and stretched out his arm, hand open, toward Swyncraff. Sheila saw him close his eyes for a moment, and his hand and arm trembled as if every muscle was straining against some invisible force. Swyncraff stiffened visibly, and the end leaning against the wall began tapping. Suddenly it bowed into an arc and sprang across the room into Robby's hand so fast that Sheila instinctively ducked behind him. But he held it firm and now relaxed, breathing heavily from the effort.

"It is hard to do," he said, sitting up and laying it across his lap. "But I'm getting better at it. Though—funny thing—it's as if *it* is learning what I want. Like we're getting to know each other."

"You speak as if it is a living thing."

"I know. It's the only way I can explain it. In a way, I have come to think of it as alive. More than that. Like one would think of a horse or a favorite dog. I actually think it wants to please me."

He handed it to her and she examined it closely.

"It is some kind of wood? Oak, maybe? And what are these iron caps on the ends?"

"I don't know." Robby touched it, and when it flopped into a rope-like object across her hands, she jumped in surprise. Robby touched it again, and it stiffened into the dangling shape.

"It is truly magical!" she uttered in amazement. "And it will only do these things for you?"

"Yes, that's right," Robby said. "Magical? I don't know. Maybe that's as good a way as any to put it."

"I daresay it's a useful thing to have along with us, even if only you can use it."

Robby took it from her, straightened it, and leaned it against the bed. When he reclined, Sheila put her head on his shoulder and nuzzled against his cheek.

"So you are coming?"

"Yes."

Robby nodded.

"It isn't a trip for a girl to undertake, even during the best of times," he said mildly.

"I've already had this conversation with Ashlord and Ullin," Sheila answered. "I have been taking care of myself for a long time, now. I haven't always done too well, but I've survived. And I'm as good a fighter as any of us, I think, except maybe Ullin. I'll hide my girlishness as best as I may when we are around others."

"I'm not sure that's possible," he joked.

She turned and raised herself on an elbow, looking down at Robby's face.

"You know I'm not like other girls," she said. "I'll not miss the niceties that I never had, at least never had until I lived with your family. I can hunt and fish and clean what I catch and cook it, too. Without even a pot! I've slept outside more times than most men I've met. I can ride hard and run fast and walk far without tiring. You know all that."

"I dare say I do!" Robby smiled, fingering the edge of her newly shorn hair. "And I doubt if any among the company can do any better. I just wonder if you would not be safer staying here, at Janhaven with my mother and Mrs. Bosk, than wandering off into goodness knows what."

"As long as I know what I know, about you, that is, I'll not be safe anywhere. If I come with you, at least I'll be with others who share the same danger. Are you against me coming?"

"No, my love," Robby said. "I'd worry about you if you came or if you stayed. And, well, I've been thinking about things, and I'm wondering if I should just go alone."

"You're joking!"

"No, I'm not."

"But you don't even know the way."

"That's a problem, I admit. Perhaps Ashlord could instruct me concerning the way to go."

"Don't be silly! Even Ashlord is unsure of the way. You'll need help. And, no matter what you think, you'll probably need protection, too."

"I know, I know. It's just that so many will be at risk."

"At risk either way," Sheila countered. "You should let people decide for themselves how to deal with their own risk. You're not King, yet, you know."

"And unlikely ever to be."

"Don't say that! If it is not your fate to be King, perhaps it is only your fate to try. Then so be it. And if you are determined to try, your friends are determined to help if they can."

"So I guess that's that."

"I think so," Sheila said, kissing him on the lips.

• • •

When the two finally came downstairs into the great room below, Durlorn was clearing away the plates from the mid-afternoon meal. He offered them each a serving of ham and bread along with a bowl of gravy, which they took and thanked him for as they sat down at the long table across from each other.

"I need to go see my mother," Robby told Sheila. "I forgot to ask her if she managed to save any of our maps."

"I think she might have," Sheila told him. "I remember seeing a cart full of books and scrolls, anyway. I don't know how much of it was from your place and how much of it might have been from Broadweed's school or from the Common House."

"I hope the Redvests haven't gotten hold of them."

"Why's that?"

"Because they show Barley and these parts very well. Roads, streams, crossing points, even most of the farms and houses are marked on some. The Redvests would find them very helpful, I'm sure. But if they were saved, I'd like to look them over. Especially the maps of the west country, Thunder Mountains and farther off."

"To get an idea of where we're going, I suppose."

"Yes."

"Well, I think Ashlord will want us to meet again tonight," she said. "I've never seen him so anxious or so grave. I think he's more worried about things than all the rest of us put together, yet..."

"Yet, what?"

"I don't know," Sheila shook her head. "He has a kind of faith, I guess. No matter how grim things are, and no matter how angry he gets, there's always some sort of confidence that he has in things. That things will somehow work out. That, in the end, all will be well."

"Could've fooled me! His talk never ceases to frighten me!"

"You don't know him well enough, yet. But you'll see what I mean. He's good to have around. He's good to *be* around."

Sheila got up and took her plate over to the tub and dumped it in with the rest.

"I think I'll go make myself useful, if I can. My guess is that I'll see you later tonight."

She kissed Robby and he watched her go. A pang of desperation seized him for a moment, wishing everything could just go back to the way it was before.

"I'd ask her again to marry me," he thought. "I'd take her to Glareth with me, to be there while I go to school. Afterwards, we'd find some little place somewhere not too far from Passdale. Close enough to town for me to walk to the shop and close enough to the woods and fields for Sheila."

Then he wondered how anything could ever be as it was before, heaving a sigh and pushing his plate away. After a moment of thought, he left, determined to find Billy.

• • •

"We had a short meetin' this afternoon, just so as to clear the air a bit. But a lotta folk warn't thar. So yer mother's askin' all to gather at the stockade two days from now."

Mrs. Bosk talked to Robby and Billy as she pulled a few potatoes from a sack. She had a kitchen of sorts set up in an abandoned stone hut on the edge of Janhaven, and with other wives and daughters helping, it was cleaned and set up with rough tables for preparing and cooking meals. It was cramped and hot inside, and as she bent over to push the sack back into its bin, her ample bottom nearly toppled a pile of bowls resting on a stool behind her. Billy dodged out of the way of a little girl hauling a bucket of water to pour into the great cauldron, and Robby reached out suddenly to catch an iron pan from striking another woman when it was knocked off the nail from which it hung on an overhead rafter.

"She's gonna ask folks to sign a pact," Frizella went on, pushing Billy out of the way so that she could get to a high table where she began washing and chopping vegetables. "I think she's over at the woodshop down near the mill. Went down thar with me carpenter from Boskland."

Having finally gotten the bit of information they wanted, the boys moved to the door.

"Will ye be back to see me?"

"Yes, ma'am," Billy said. "I'll be back soon to help ye out here." He dashed back to her quickly and kissed her on the cheek. "Don't ye worry."

Robby caught the misty look in her eyes, and he knew it was not from the onions.

"I'm just goin' down to the camp," Billy said to Robby once they were outside. "Me aunt's thar, an' I need to square away some things with the kinfolk. If ye see Ibin, tell him to get on over to the kitchen!"

Robby nodded and waved as they parted at the fork. Billy headed down the east road, while Robby walked along a little track that ran beside a stream behind Janhaven and on down toward the old mill. The mill itself was about a mile away, and Robby had the track to himself. There were bright orange and golden-yellow and burnt-red leaves blowing across the way and still falling from the thick overhanging poplars and sweet gums that were just beginning to prepare for winter. There was still plenty of green, though, and Robby thought it unusually warm for the time of year; he had not yet seen any frost, though each night was colder than the one before. Still, in the shade of this path in the late afternoon, the light breeze bore the slight scent of coming winter on its breath, mixed with the dry mustiness of autumn.

Coming over a rise, Robby looked down and through the trees at a few buildings at the edge of a clearing near a stream. He surmised from the cords of wood and planking piled neatly up against one shed that this must be the woodworker's place, and as he turned to take the path downward, he saw his mother emerge from the shop and stride up the path toward him. She had changed her clothes and was now wearing the same sort of buckskin breeches that Sheila commonly wore and a blouse of equal ruggedness made of thick dark-green linen. Her hair was braided and fell over her left shoulder like a scarlet rope. Behind that shoulder jutted the hilt of her sword, and the fletchings of a quiver full of arrows jutted up behind her right shoulder, over which was strung a bow. Robby imagined her as a stranger, and wondered what impressions might be inspired in any who first saw her like this. Her expression was stern, she had not yet seen Robby, and her stride determined. Robby decided she was a dangerous beauty. He continued on down the path into her view, and when a smile lit up her face, she did not look as dangerous as before.

"Hullo!"

"Hello. I didn't expect to see you here."

"I wanted to talk with you," Robby said as they came together. She took his hand, they kissed, and they began the walk back to Janhaven.

"I'm sure you have a lot on your mind. More, even, than the rest of us," she said.

"Different things, is what I would say, not more. Though I am still bothered by leaving."

"You have to go. That has been decided. You cannot help us here by staying, especially if it brings strife our way from those who look for you."

Robby nodded, feeling a pang at the hardness in her tone. "I know."

"Remember," Mirabella went on, "that you will be taking no fewer risks than the rest of us, and probably more. If you become, well, what it is that you go to become, then you will be able to help us in ways far greater than you ever could if you stayed."

"Yes, I realize that."

"Well, then."

"Mother," Robby put his hand to her arm, and they stopped, facing one another. "Well. It's just that I'm scared, Mother. I don't know if I am capable. I'm afraid something will happen to my friends. I'm afraid I'm not worthy to be a king. And it all seems so pretentious! And I'm afraid I'll not know what to do."

Mirabella searched Robby's face for a long moment.

"You do your best," she said at last. "It sounds so simple, but truly that is the hardest thing in life, to do one's best. Keep your wits and do not forget to use them. Use your knowledge. Use your friendship with others to help you understand new people. Use your strength of body and the fortitude of your own mind. Be determined to do your very best to be patient not only with others, but also with your own self. When the right thing to do is revealed to you, do it in full measure, though all others may oppose you. When the right thing to do is hidden from you, trust in hope."

"Hope," Robby repeated. They continued on, each bearing the burden of their own mind in silence until at last Robby asked.

"Where did you learn to fight, Mother?"

Mirabella looked at Robby and smiled.

"When I saw you the other day," he went on, "you were so terrible! I've never seen anyone so full of wrath!"

"It was an awful thing, Robby," she answered. "And I am as surprised as any to have taken up the sword again after all these long years."

"You see," she continued, "when my brother Aram, Ullin's father, went to Duinnor to become a Kingsman, I ran away from home and followed him. Aram did not know that I followed him until it was too late, and too far, to send me back. From my youngest days, he taught me the use of the sword and the bow, and while Aram studied at the Academy in Duinnor, I studied, too, taking private lessons and furthering my skill at arms. When he graduated and became a full Kingsman, he was sent south to Vanara, and I followed. Once there, Aram and I learned war, and we fought many skirmishes together. We fought together, made merry together, worked and toiled together. His commander ordered Aram to send me away, but I would not go. His comrades called me his red-haired shield maiden. Aram laughed, and warned them not to say that to my face. But I didn't care. I longed to fight the Dragonkind, to have vengeance, as Aram did, for our older brother's death. And the Kingsmen respected that."

A weak smile crossed her face, but it faded quickly.

"After a year of soldiering, we found ourselves taking part in a great conquest. Two hundred thousand men and Elifaen crossed the Biradur Waste to lay siege to the desert city called the Green Citadel. It was the second time we of the north sent an army against that city, the same city that cost the life of our brother and many others. I saw many terrible things in that place. Even before we sacked the city, many were slaughtered. It was senseless. There were atrocities. We freed many slaves, Men and Elifaen, who were in bondage there. There were enslaved Dragonkind, too. But they were slain, or left to the ruin of the great city and to the retribution of their masters."

She paused in her tale, and they kept walking until she stopped abruptly.

"You need to know," she said earnestly, "that people are capable of the vilest acts. Although our enemy was the creature of the deserts, I witnessed honor and dishonor on both sides. When the battle was over, and our armies retreated victorious, there was no satisfaction in our victory. And fewer than one in three of us made it home. Soon, our withdrawal turned into a rout as avenging bands of the enemy marauded and harassed our retreat. And it was in the Blue Mountains of Vanara, at a place called Gory Gulch, that my brother died, pierced through with arrows. I took up his sword, it is here on my back, but I had to leave his body for the carrion. He died in the very same manner as our older brother before him, during a shabby retreat from a shabby victory against the same great city. Perhaps this sword is fated," she added, touching its hilt protruding over her shoulder and turning to resume her walk. "Every member of our family who has ever wielded it in battle has died. It was taken from my older brother Dalvenpar's body by a survivor and sent to our house with news of his death. It was then taken up by Ullin's father, Aram. And now, your mother wields it."

Robby was pale with shock and surprise at these revelations, But many strange and mysterious aspects of his mother's behavior now seemed explained, at least in part.

"Perhaps you ought to get rid of it, Mother."

She smiled and nodded.

"Perhaps I shall. When it is truly no longer needed. Let me tell you more. After my brother's death, when I made it back to Vanara, I just kept walking. Sick with grief and sadness, I abandoned the army and slowly wandered, desiring no company, relying on no one to help me along my way. A year later, I came home to Tallinvale. The wretched news I brought with me was the death of my mother, so grieved was she at the loss of her last son. My father became hardened in his sternness, and I became a recluse, existing only in the gardens of our estate or in the high chambers of my father's manor. Years passed. More than I counted. My father invited many suitors to our home. Elifaen and high-born Men. They came, and they went, but I rejected them all. Eventually my father tired of trying to marry me off.

"That's the way it was until, one day, a young man came to sell grain. While he waited to receive his silver, he wandered into the gardens of Tallin Hall, and it was there we met. Thinking I was a maidservant of the house, perhaps because of my plain way of dressing, he was rather fresh with me, though kind and witty, telling me about his home and the plans he had for his future. His way of silence was in his prattling on, ever watchful of my reactions. My way of screaming in pain was my silence, yet he pierced my soul with his bright smile and his laughing brown eyes. He was simple without being a simpleton, and sincere while at the same time of irrepressible spirit. His talk made me laugh, and I could see that my laughter pleased him. I did not tell him who I was, not even my name. When my father's purser came to pay him, I shrank away into the hedge as coins were counted out to him. The young man looked around for me, and then he departed. My sadness immediately returned to take his place, and my melancholy thoughts returned, too. Even so, all that afternoon, my thoughts wandered back to the bright-eyed country fellow. I made it a point to find out where he was from, and when he might come back, but none could say for sure. That night, my heart was troubled by the memory of his company, and I was sadder than ever. I remember crying myself to sleep, so lonely I felt.

"But, guess what? He came back the very next morning, asking for the cheery maidservant with red hair. When he was told there was no maidservant with red hair, he was thoroughly abashed. They told him, 'There is only one woman with red hair in this hall, but she is hardly a maidservant and, anyway, she is anything but cheery, being none other than the Lady Tallin who has shunned the merry company of all for many years, and is as dour and gloomy as a dark wood on a rainy day.' He was not convinced at first, thinking they made jest with him. Eventually they prevailed, so he reluctantly departed. When I learned of all this later that afternoon, I was mortified that I had missed him and immediately rode out to catch up to him. I found him on the road, letting his mules pull his cart without even bothering to hold the reins while he slouched back on the bench lost in thought with his eyes closed. So engrossed in his own cares was he that he did not notice me riding alongside gazing at him. Nor did he seem to notice when I slipped from my saddle and onto the bench beside him. I spent a long while looking at his face. He was not the most handsome young man I had ever seen, nor the best dressed, and certainly not the most graceful as he slouched there with his head tilted back to the sky, his eyes closed and his brow furrowed with some problem he was trying to work out, and the long curly locks of his hair wild in the breeze. But I thought his was the most beautiful face I had ever seen, though I could not say why. When he opened his eyes, he was not startled to see me sitting there right beside him. He sat up slowly, and smiled.

" 'Are ye some kinda sprite? Er, spirit-like creature?' he asked easily. 'For I was just thinkin' on ye, an' wonderin' what kind of charm was laid on me. I suppose yer a garden sprite, inhabitin' the gardens of the Tallin place an' capturin' what hearts might happen along?'

" 'No, I'm flesh and blood,' I assured him. 'You came back to look for me.'

" 'Yes, I did. I had somethin' to ask ye. But I was told ye don't exist.'

" 'And you believe that?'

" 'No, I don't. I don't pretend to understand the ways of folk what live in fine castles an' great estates. But ye exist for me regardless of what they say,' he said, 'if even in a dream.'

" 'Why did you come back to find me?'

" 'Well, that's easy to answer: I wanted to ask if ye was spoken for.'

" 'Oh! Well, the answer to that is, no, I am not.'

" 'Well, in that case, I'd like to ask if ye'd have me for a husband an' if ye'd consent to bein' me wife?'

"Well, I nearly fell off the cart! Your father—for naturally that is who I am talking about—he saw that I was greatly perplexed and began telling me, all in the most gentle of ways and perfectly at ease, all about his plans for a store and how he promised a comfortable life, though full of hard work, and that he'd be the best father to my children that a man could be, and on like that."

" 'I'm afraid I cannot speak yes or no this moment,' I told him. I told him I had to think about it. But, in truth, I had already made up my mind. I had already fallen in love with him, just as, I suppose, he had fallen in love with me. 'Though I am not a maidservant to Fairoak, I owe my fidelity to that household unless I am released from it. If you can gain the consent of Lord Tallin to release me, I will be your wife.'

" 'I will present meself afore Lord Tallin this very night,' he said to me.

" 'Then I wish you well, good sir,' I told him. 'And I leave you my name. It is Mirabella.'

"So I joyfully leapt back onto my horse and galloped home. I remember I had no care of my father refusing him. I thought that he would be so relieved to be rid of me that he would readily assent. But things didn't quite work out in the way I hoped they would.

"That evening, your father appeared again at our gates and bid his way into the manor house, saying he had business with none other than the Lord and Master himself. While I watched from the far shadows, he was led into the great hall of our home and before my father who was seated on his chair.

" 'What business have you with me?' my father demanded.

" 'I bid ye release the one called Mirabella from yer service and from yer fidelity so that she may become me wife,' is what I heard your father boldly state. You should have seen the stir it caused! My father sat bolt upright. His chief lieutenant of the guard stepped forward as if to strike Robigor, but my father's gesture stayed him. Others, hearing the commotion, pushed into the room and watched.

" 'You are most impertinent!' my father said. 'Do you know what it is that you ask?'

" 'A man may have no peace if long separated from his love, nor may any woman, good lord,' said Robigor Ribbon, unmoved by the glares given him. 'I will provide for Mirabella's welfare an' well-being as well as any, an' better as years go by. What work an' toil she may do will be of her own pleasure an' desire, an' not at the pleasure an' whim of others. I ask only that ye release her to her own decision, that she might say yea or nay her own self.'

" 'Do you know who it is that you ask to marry?' asked my father indignantly.

" 'I care not, sir, what family, high or low, she might have. Nor do I care for any dowry or boon from her family, however great er small. I care not if she be useful to ye or a burden, whether she be clumsy an' witless, or whether she be careful an' diligent in service to ye. Neither do I care whether she be a joy to ye or a shame upon yer house.'

"Oh, I was truly in love then! Never had I seen anyone speak so to my father. And never had I heard words so ardently spoken.

"My father thought about it for a moment and even conferred, over his shoulder, with his counselor. Then he looked at Robigor for a long while.

" 'How will I be assured of you?' he asked at last. 'What means have you to support her and what honor can you bring in union with her?'

" 'What means I have will, like me honor, only increase as the years pass.'

" 'I will consent, then, only if you succeed in carrying out one task,' my father said.

" 'Name the task, an' I will abide by yer word if I succeed or if I fail,' your father said.

"Well, the task he was given was this: My father bade Robigor wait while he and his counselor departed the room. After a short while they returned. My father gave to your father a little chest, no bigger than two hands wide and one tall. The box was not sealed, nor was it locked, but my father instructed Robigor not to open it for one year. He was to return with the box so that it could be examined. My father gave his word that if the contents of the box were still within it after one year, he would give his consent to marry me, if I also then consented."

"What was in the box?" Robby asked.

"That is getting ahead of the story somewhat," Mirabella answered. "But in fact it was full of precious jewels. Anyway, I did not know at the time what the box contained, and I did not understand what my father was about, either. Soon after Robigor took the box and departed, my father came to me.

" 'Mirabella,' he said, 'I have turned away a suitor this day whom you would have surely scoffed at, just as you have scoffed at all those who have come before.'

" 'Why do you tell me this, Father? Do you think I care?' All the while, I was trying with terrible determination not to let him see my worry!

" 'No, I do not think you care,' he said. 'But he may be back. And if he does return, it may be that I will give my consent to his marriage to you, should you then have him.'

" 'Why should it be different when he returns than when he left?' I asked. 'Will he be handsomer? Will he be a king? Will he be more worthy of me than now in any way?'

" 'I cannot say. I only tell you this because I think I saw in him something I have rarely seen in my fellow mortals. I set for him a simple task, knowing it is in the simple things that men most often fail. If he succeeds, he will have proven his honor and will set himself somewhat apart from other men. At least in my estimation.'

" 'What task did you set?' I asked him.

" 'To abide one year and to remain an honest man.' "

"What did he mean by that?" Robby asked.

"He meant that your father was not to take any jewel from the box, not one, much less run off with the entire treasure. He was not even to look within the box. My father was testing him, you see. As I learned later on, my father and his counselor laid obstacle after obstacle before Robigor. They sent their agents to buy at a higher price the trade goods that your father had deals for. They took notes of exchange from all the farmers and made them to sell not grain nor product to any but them. So Robigor struggled to live, you see, and yet, with each obstacle before him, he found some other way to profit. When the farmers sold all their goods to my father's agents, rather than to Robigor, they had no way to transport the material. Robigor had in the meantime made a deal with Mr. Furaman for contract on all the wagons and carts as agent, and so any transport costs were paid to Robigor. When my father realized that Robigor could not be outwitted that way, he turned against Robigor's neighbors, or so one tale of it goes. It is said that three witches from the north were hired to brew hail and storm against all of Barley. I doubt if that is so, but it is true that there were awful storms. Houses were destroyed, crops were ruined, and Passdale starved. My father then sent his agents, pretending to be emissaries from Tracia offering the sale of badly needed goods. But they would only take jewels or precious metal in exchange. The people came from all over with their meager rings and bracelets and their gold combs. Each was made to sign a deed naming themselves as rightful owners of the item exchanged. But no diamonds, no sapphires or emeralds appeared, none of the jewels from the chest. However, it came to pass that Robigor approached the men and offered to buy all their grain and all their blankets, in fact all of their goods, on the spot, wagons included, for one hundred pieces of gold. Well, my father's agents agreed, thinking he had sold the jewels, and they took Robigor's gold. But it wasn't Robigor's gold at all. Robigor had bargained with the Passdale masters to allow him to use the town treasury for the relief of the townspeople. Passdale was so grateful to him that they talked to him about becoming mayor, but he declined."

"He did become mayor, didn't he?"

"Yes, he did, but that was later."

"So a year passed."

"Yes, and all kinds of tribulations, though Robigor never knew they were aimed at him. During that year, I met a person who lived in Barley and who knew Robigor, and through her I was able to find out what had been happening. I'm talking about Frizella, who at the time was a young house servant for hire. I hired her and paid her to be my housemaid, but instead of working at my father's estate, I arranged for her to take employment in Barley, too."

"So she was your spy!"

"Well, more like a hired busybody. And we became fast friends. Though very different, we both had certain romantic interests that we shared with each other. Her eye was on a certain Boskman, and you know how that turned out. Anyway, Robigor returned the little chest after a year and repeated his bid for my hand. My father counted out every jewel, twice. And even he was amazed, I think, at your father's integrity and honesty. But I'm afraid my father was quite shocked when I actually consented."

The two had by now made it to the main road leading through Janhaven and they walked along between the cottages at a good pace.

"On the day of our wedding, held in the gardens where your father and I met, my father bid me farewell. He told me that my world was now the world of Barley. My father never told Robigor who I truly was. No one did. Robigor was obviously taken aback by the pomp of the ceremony, though it was a small, private affair. And, though he was a happy man that day, he was perplexed by the way I was treated, with such fine elegance for a mere servant. And Robigor may have even thought it impertinent that I kissed the Lord of Tallinvale when we parted. I did not tell him until that night that I was the daughter of the Lord Tallin. Your father was shocked, at first. Then we laughed until we cried."

Robby and his mother smiled at each other.

"Why did you never tell me before now? It is a wonderful story!"

Mirabella shrugged and nodded.

"We kept too much from you, Robigor and I," she said. "We thought it was better that way. We were wrong. I'm sorry."

"Well, I don't resent it. I might have done the same. Tell me, have you heard from your father recently? Do you think the Redvests have attacked him, too?"

"I have not seen him in years. As for the Redvests attacking Tallinvale, perhaps they have. His is a powerful land, and it would take a powerful army to threaten it. At any event, he should be informed of these events. When things settle down around here, I'll send word even though he has likely already heard what has happened."

They drew to a halt in front of Mrs. Bosk's kitchen.

"I suppose you will be meeting with Ashlord and Ullin soon?" she asked as she pushed a strand of curly hair from his brow.

"Yes. I expect we'll be leaving any day. As soon as we can pull ourselves together."

"Do you know who will be in your party?"

"I have a good idea. Ashlord, Ullin, and Billy. Ibin, I expect. And Sheila."

"Sheila?"

"Yes, she insists on going with us."

"Is that wise?"

"Maybe not, but she's determined, and I think I want her to come along. In fact, I know I do."

Mirabella shook her head, shrugging. "We'll miss Sheila's abilities. It's bad enough to lose five good men."

"I know, Mother. I'm sorry."

"Don't be. There's no getting around it. You need Ashlord and Ullin. Billy's determined, and Ibin cannot be without his friend. And Sheila has apparently made up her mind. Alas! I wish I could come!"

"I wish you could, too. Truly, I do."

• • •

That night, they all met again at the same place and made their plans. Ullin said they would need horses for each and two pack animals, since their journey would be long and the ways rough, and winter was coming.

"If I understand right," he told them, "Ashlord means to take us west, to Vanara, and then northward from there to Duinnor. Under the most favorable summer conditions, it would take us at least a month and a fortnight to reach Vanara. If we only had to contend with the road and the weather. This time of year, who knows? From Vanara to Duinnor won't be so long or hard. Once we leave here, there are few places to lodge or to reprovision until we reach Vanara. So we will have to travel light, carrying only clothing, blankets, weapons, and food. Fodder should not be a problem, but we should take some, just in case. Our mounts and two pack animals, at most."

"That is so, Ullin," Ashlord said. "I think we should stay off the roads as much as possible, especially the well-known ones, and travel cross-country as much as we can. Yes, yes. I know that will slow us even more, but we should risk the fewest encounters as possible. We will have a hard enough time explaining ourselves. The curious or the well-informed may see through any yarn we may spin. Our story should be like this: We travel from the Eastlands to Duinnor to plea for aid against the Tracian Redvests. If asked why we travel the way we do, we say that we take a circuitous route in order to baffle those of the enemy who may try to stop us from reaching Duinnor. Let us not try to explain too much, nor spin too much yarn to tangle ourselves in. We have our own business, and it is ours alone."

"What about the people here?" Sheila asked. "They are bound to ask why we're leaving."

"We tell 'em the same," said Billy. "We go to Duinnor. That's what I've told me kinfolk already."

"Others may want to join us," Robby put forward. "There are many here in Janhaven who have seen too much bloodshed. Some have already lost everything, their homes destroyed and farms, too, from what they say. Some are talking of putting more distance between themselves and the Redvests. They may want to come away with us."

"We cannot permit that," Ullin spoke up immediately. "We will have to move quickly, with few comforts. As it is, we cannot make the pass of Loringard for the snows, and must go the long way around the Carthanes, through the Thunder Mountains and territories held by warlords and bandits. We will have enough to manage looking after ourselves. Others, if they go, must find their own way west."

"That is something that only haste on our part may take care of," Ashlord said. "Let us try to be ready by noon tomorrow. Each of you must see to warm clothes and gear this very night. Furaman knows that we plan to depart and will provide packs and mounts for us. He is willing to provide more if there is anything we think of that he has. Ullin and I will select horses and have them here by first light."

"Bring only what you can wear or carry on your back," Ullin continued. "We'll have horses each, and two more for our supplies and food. But anything may happen and we may lose our horses."

Ashlord looked around the room. Ibin sat at the end of the table, closest to the fireplace, with a blank look on his face. Billy and Sheila stood beside him and nodded.

"Then we are agreed," Ullin said. "We gather our horses and supplies at daybreak. With luck, we can depart even before noon."

They all nodded.

"One last thing," Ashlord said, seriously. "Arm yourselves. Light, strong, quick weapons."

• • •

Later, in the upstairs room that Robby was permitted to use, Mirabella held out a vest.

"I want you to wear this," she said.

Robby had been stuffing the other pieces of his clothing into a pack, along with a few other small things, when his mother came back into the room. She had earlier dropped off a bundle of clothes for him to pick through and had just returned, closing the door behind her.

"It is a good, sturdy vest made of heavy cloth. Let me show you."

She turned the vest inside out and revealed a flannel lining and showed him several slyly-sewn patches around the bottom of the vest. "Feel," she said, handing it to Robby. He took it with a quizzical look and felt along the patches. Through the cloth he could feel the shape of large round discs.

"Coins?"

Mirabella nodded. "*The* coins. When you have a chance, show them to Ashlord. I meant to do so, but never did. Show them to Ashlord privately, with no one else around. Let no one else know that you have them, not even your other companions. Not unless there is special and urgent need."

"I understand," Robby said. "I'm sure they are of great value."

"Yes, Robby. I think they are. I think they..." Mirabella paused, then changed her mind about what she was about to say. "I fear to think how valuable they may be, and that you will be carrying them. But I know they are too valuable to stay here with us. Remember, show them to no one except Ashlord, and mind what he says about them."

"Yes, Mother."

Robby slipped the vest on for size, and buttoned it up.

"Here is some silver and gold, about twenty-weight of silver and ten of gold, in various coin."

She handed him a small leather purse, such as the kind he had often carried on his routes to collect or pay bills of the store.

"For more ordinary needs," she added. "Do you have all of the other things that you'll need?"

"I think so. It will be getting cold, so I'm leaving behind all the light stuff," he told her. "Just heavy shirts, sweaters, and a coat. And lots of socks. And Mr. Furaman gave me a travel cloak with a good hood for bad weather."

"Did you get the sewing kit from Mrs. Bosk?"

"Yes. Sheila dropped it by a while ago."

"It's good that you each should have one. I hope you will only need it for clothes."

"Me, too, but I'm carrying along some grayhort root salve and a little bit of brandy to clean any wounds that may need stitching."

"Have you ever done that, Robby?"

"No, but I watched Sheila do it once, to a little baby rabbit that we rescued from a cat. It was only a small wound, though I imagine the method would be pretty much the same."

"Oh, I see. Probably so."

Mirabella watched Robby finish packing and said nothing else for a long while. Robby, too, was silent. There was so much to say, so much more to ask about, but Robby could not think of anything in particular that was most important. Finally, after cinching up the straps on the pack and checking the bedroll tied to it, he turned back to his mother, who had by now taken a seat on the plain wooden chair near the dark window. The candle burned steady and the unwavering light silhouetted the soft contours of her face. Though she smiled, Robby saw immense sadness in her face, and she uncharacteristically clutched her hands pensively in her lap. Robby sat down on the edge of the bed, his knees touching hers, and he took her hands in his.

"I love you, Mother."

"Oh, Robby!" she cried. "How I pray for strength! To be parted from the two I hold most dear in all the world!"

Robby's eyes burned with all his effort to hold back the water forming there.

"I'll come back and rejoin you and Daddy," he said. "I think you will see him sooner than you believe. He is proud of you, and will be prouder, still, when he returns. As for myself, I carry with me the good fortune to have two such parents. I will always strive to honor you both and to carry in my heart the gentle goodness that you have taught me. I will miss you and long for your counsel, just as I miss and long for Daddy. Although I know it will be otherwise, I ask that we try not to worry too much about each other and keep a mind to the business we have at hand, for that may be worry enough."

Mirabella tossed her hair and smiled, nodding.

"You are starting to sound like Collandoth," she said. "And you are right. Oh, I love you so much! In spite of what you say, I shall worry for you each day and every night!"

• • •

The night was an active one for all the company, each busily putting together their travel gear and attire. That did not take very long, so the rest of the night was spent sharpening blades, sorting through arrows and spare bowstrings, resewing straps, buckles, and buttons, remembering the odd little thing or two, and wondering what they would forget to bring. Although they were making their preparations in different places around and about Janhaven, they all felt a sense of urgency, and each was determined to be ready by dawn.

Billy and Ibin spent the night in the hut taken by the Bosk kinsmen. Ibin peppered Billy with questions about Duinnor: the distance, whether they would meet other Kingsmen like Ullin, how they might trudge through winter snow, and what kind of food they would eat along the way. Billy answered in short but not unkind statements. Ibin saw that Billy was busy and preoccupied, but he could not help himself and kept thinking up more questions that seemed important. Would they see any lions? Was Billy sure there were no more trolls? Would they have bacon or sausage for breakfast? And why, again, were they going?

Ashlord and Ullin had the most to do. Besides getting their own things together, Ashlord put himself in charge of food, and Ullin moved about Janhaven selecting the best mounts and saddles he could find at that late time of night. Anerath, he decided, would stay and serve Mirabella. There would be little reason, he felt, to outpace the others, and Mirabella may have more need of his speed and intelligence. He delivered Anerath to her as she returned to the infirmary, whispering in Anerath's ear. He stroked his mane and scratched under Anerath's chin as the two nodded at each other.

"He'll obey you," he told Mirabella. "Trust him. He has a knack for picking a way through rough terrain, and a good sense for danger."

Mirabella took the reins and hugged Ullin.

• • •

By the fifth hour after dark, all of their tasks were accomplished. Sheila, Billy, and Ibin turned in for a few hours of sleep, each to their own borrowed cots or bedrolls. Ashlord, bringing packs into Furaman's great room, found Robby poring over all of the maps his mother had taken from their home and the Common House before fleeing Passdale. She had done so to keep them from the Redvests, and Robby was grateful that she could not bring herself to burn them.

Robby nodded at Ashlord when he came in and continued studying while Ashlord checked over the pile of saddlebags and packs he had assembled on the floor near the door. When he was satisfied that he had brought in everything, he lit his pipe and turned to Robby.

"What do your maps tell you?" he asked.

"Well, not much, really." Robby sighed and shrugged as he straightened up from hunching over the table. He waved his hand over the dozens of charts and maps strewn before him. "Most of these maps are old, and few have much detail about what is between here and Vanara, and nothing as to what lies beyond. Any way we look at it, we have a long way to go!"

"Indeed, we do."

"What can you say of the way to Griferis? Have you ever been there?"

"No-o," Ashlord smiled. "I have not. But I can tell you this concerning the travels before us. Keeping off the main paths, we must first pass through the Thunder Mountains, a place of warlords, mercenaries, and other threats. Beyond the mountains, we will move swiftly across the broad grassy plains, bearing ever westward. Then we will likely come before a vast and deep forest, which we will strive to go around, if we can, for we may not be welcome there. On the other side, we will be in the Vanaran frontier. Then our way will be more arduous, for we must go up, up into the high western mountains. We shall certainly take every care to avoid the shadowed lands of Shatuum, and continue on and up through snowy passes and across icy peaks until, at last, we shall come to the very edge of the world. Thus will end the easy part of your journey."

"The easy part?" Robby blurted out. "Then what's the hard part?"

The door opened, and Ullin strode in.

"There you are!" Ashlord said.

"And there you are!" Ullin replied. "Our horses are stabled across the yard. I think they will be good mounts. Ah! I see you have the packs ready. What are you looking at?"

"Maps."

"Maps?" Ullin bent over the table, looking over the charts as he took off his cloak.

"All paths look easy when drawn in ink," he commented. "This chart isn't so bad," he touched one, "if only we were going north!"

"We were just discussing our route," Ashlord said. "I think we should make our first stop at Hill Town, where Makeig's people are. We may be able to gain some knowledge from them as to the safest way to avoid trouble with the warlords. I'll count us lucky if we can make it through the Thunder Mountains without being waylaid. Once on the other side of the mountains, we should be able to make fair distance each day, especially across the plains."

"What of a place called Tulith Morgair?" Robby suddenly asked.

"It is an old watchtower, long in ruin," said Ullin.

"Where is it?"

"I have only seen it once," Ullin said. "It is along here, overlooking the River Missenflo."

"It is at the highest point of a line of hills bordering the foothills," Ashlord said, who had eased up behind Ullin and Robby. He reached between them and put the stem of his pipe on a map indicating a place west of the Thunder Mountains. "It overlooks a ford of the River Missenflo and the plains beyond. Built during the early years of this age. It is the largest of a line of such places that once crossed the Thunder Mountains. From its heights it could give fair warning by beacon fires of armies approaching from the west or southwest across the plain toward the gap."

"Will we be going that way?" Robby asked the two.

"It is somewhat off of what I expect to be our course," Ashlord said, tentatively. "The Damar have made the area dangerous, though they do not control the place, it being north of their strength and there is little of value to them there."

Robby nodded and turned back to the map while Ashlord and Ullin exchanged questioning looks.

"Is there something special about that place?" Ullin asked.

"I'm not sure," Robby told them. He did not want to talk about his dream, not before he had something more tangible. He tried not to show his nervousness as he went on. "I think I need to go there, but," he hesitated, "I cannot tell you why. Not yet."

"Is it important?" Ashlord asked. "It may be difficult."

"I wish I could be certain," Robby answered. "It could be very important, or it may turn out not to be important at all. Finding out is one reason I need to go there. Perhaps as we get closer I will know more."

"Very well." Ashlord shrugged. He was clearly troubled by this addition to their plans. "We shall see."

"Thank you."

"I suggest we try to get some rest," Ullin said, stretching out on the floor next to the hearth. "We will need more than we will get as it is, I'm afraid."

Robby bade them good night as he climbed the stairs to his room. Entering, he was surprised to see Sheila's pack and travel gear leaning against the wall. Sweeping his candle around, he saw her form under the covers of the cot.

"It's about time," she muttered as he undressed and slipped in beside her. "Oo! You are cold! Here, let me warm you."

Robby gladly spooned her and put his arms around her.

"This probably won't work out very well on the road," Robby whispered.

"I know," she said. "But I want you to know that I love you. Even if things have not worked out for us, and even if they never do. When we are on the road, I will do what I can to look out for you. I will do my part to protect you and to get you to your destiny. I will strive to be your lover, if you want one, and your guardian, should you need one. I will try not to make the others feel awkward or embarrass you by clinging to you. When it is time for you to let me go, I'll not protest, and I'll try not to cry."

"I'll never let go of you!"

"I hope not," she pulled his arm around her tighter. "But, if ever you must, I'll not question it."

• • •

When Robby awoke, Sheila and her things were gone. He hurriedly got up, dressed, and rinsed his face in the wash basin. When he came downstairs, he found a gathering about the table, breakfasting. Mirabella was there as was Frizella and two of her nephews, and there was Sheila and Ibin and Ashlord. Mr. Furaman was there and also Captain Makeig. They greeted Robby and as he sat down to a plate put before him, Billy and Ullin entered from outside. Together they were all served a large breakfast of eggs, honeycakes, ham, fried potato slices, and coffee. As they ate, they talked of plans for harassing the invaders, of the journey west, of the camp conditions of the Barley and Passdale folk, and of the coming winter and all the work that needed doing. Ashlord and Makeig discussed the first leg of the journey, to Hill Town, in rather guarded tones, for Ashlord did not want Furaman or Billy's cousins to know too much of their direction of travel. Meanwhile, Robby and Mr. Furaman talked of business and the Ribbons' shop and what may have become of the stock there.

"I am more concerned with the building itself," said Robby. "That was our home, too, you know. I just hope they don't do too much damage."

Frizella shook her head and laughed with Mirabella about some of the more inexperienced Passdale women who were trying to cope and to be helpful in their present situation, but they were doing poorly at both in spite of their good efforts.

Ullin listened quietly while he ate, saying very little. Billy talked with one of his cousins while the other cousin chatted with Sheila, the one conversation about the use of bows and the other about the making of arrows. Ibin hardly said anything unless it had "pleasepassmethe" in it, and he paid little attention to the conversations around him, preferring instead to concentrate his efforts on cleaning plate after plate after plate. As the meal progressed, and by the time most (but not Ibin) had pushed their plates away, the mood was less jovial, though still of good spirit, and at last the two cousins pushed their chairs back and stood. They bade the company safe journey, and Billy shook their hands and hugged them before they departed to go to their guard duties.

"Billy, let's bring around the horses," Ullin said. The two thanked Mr. Furaman for the breakfast and departed for the stables.

"Did you and Billy bring the things you'll be taking along?" Robby asked Ibin.

"Yes," Ibin swallowed a half-chewed sausage, "yeswe, yeswe, yeswebroughtourstuffits, yeswebroughtourstuffits, ourstuffitsoutside."

"And you?" Robby asked Sheila.

"My packs are by the door, there."

"Well! I guess I'd better start packing!" he said, turning to go up the stairs.

"Ye ain't packed yet?" Frizella said incredulously.

"Ha ha! Gotcha!" Robby laughed. "I just need to fetch my things from upstairs."

"I knew Billy'd be a bad influence on Robby!" Frizella said to Mirabella, shaking her head.

Sheila admonished Ibin to stop eating and to help her clear away the table while Captain Makeig and Mr. Furaman and the two ladies conferred about the situation among the new arrivals in Janhaven. It was not long before the horses were saddled and brought around and the two packhorses were loaded. Ullin assigned each to a horse and each traveler got their saddles and stirrups adjusted, tied on their packs and saddlebags and, lastly, buckled, belted, and slipped on their weapons, their swords over their shoulders, quivers hanging nearby, and knives sheathed in their belts and boots. Captain Makeig, who would guide them to Hill Town, assured Mirabella and Frizella that he would be back in two or three days, and was the first to mount up. He then waited while the others made their farewells.

They did so quietly, with tight hugs and tender kisses and strained smiles, and each got astride their mounts until only Robby stood before his mother, his reins in his hand.

"I will be back," he said to her bravely. His voice was steady and determined, and Mirabella looked deep into his dark eyes.

"I will be waiting for you," she said.

"If I can, I will send word as we go along."

She nodded and gave Robby another hug and kiss.

"Your father and I are very proud of you and love you very much," she said into his ear.

She watched Robby get into his saddle as Frizella's arm slipped around her. Together they waved as the company passed through from the gate and out of sight. Mrs. Bosk watched Mirabella turn away toward the infirmary, taking only a couple of steps, then falling to her knees like a little girl, weeping most bitterly, clenching the dirt in her hands. Frizella hurried over and knelt beside her, pulling Mirabella's hair from the dust and hugging her, their tears mixing on the ground.

"I will never see either of my Robbys again!" Mirabella sobbed, clutching handfuls of dirt against her breast, the soil running out between her fingers as she rocked back and forth.

"No, no, no, sweet dear. Don't ye say such a thing!" said Frizella through her own tears. "Whether ye think ye will or ye won't ain't important, but how ye stand up to it is. Ye must live to see them again, for if ye do, they will need ye strong. An' if never ye do again, ye need to honor thar strength with ye own. An' others are needin' ye now, too, me heart!"

• • •

Outside the gate, people stood along the way, having heard that a party was leaving for the west to seek help, and they wished them well as they went. Many familiar faces impressed themselves upon Billy, Sheila, and Robby, people they had grown up with and had known all their lives. It made Robby proud to be doing what he was doing, yet he had a pang of guilt, too, for leaving them.

As they came to the intersection of roads, several voices called Sheila's name. Pulling on their reins, they turned and saw Mr. Broadweed hurrying along toward them with a few small children running before him, calling and waving for her to wait.

"Miss Pradkin," Mr. Broadweed said when at last he came up to her. "I was afraid I had missed you. Oh, my! Your beautiful hair is all but gone!"

Before Sheila could react, he shook his head at her to tell her no response was needed.

"I heard," he continued, "that you were going west with the others, and I thought…well, I thought you might like to have this to take along."

He reached up and handed Sheila a small leather-bound book.

"It is just a little collection of poems and songs," he told her. "Something to help you keep up with your reading, if you have the time."

"I don't know how to thank you," Sheila said awkwardly. "You shouldn't have."

"Perhaps when you return, you can tell me which poem might be your favorite," he smiled.

"Thank you."

"Be safe!" he said, taking her hand. She leaned down and kissed him on the cheek.

"I will try."

The people of Passdale and Barley, and many of those from Janhaven, watched the riders recede down the road and out of sight. They lingered, quietly chatting with each other for a few moments about the travelers' prospects. Then they slowly returned to their work.

Chapter 3

Hill Town

Day 85
160 Days Remaining

They headed west, into the crisp air of autumn, bearing along the road for a few miles until they turned south and followed Makeig along a narrow track that wound up and down, but mostly up. By noon, they had traveled nearly twenty miles, and before them stood the Thunder Mountains, dark and thick-shouldered. They pressed upward into the cooler air of the heights as the afternoon wore on, going deeper and deeper into the rugged forest, through shady oaks, maples, and gum that were showing their first weariness of green, and through mighty pines and thick firs that never tired of their sage and loden coats. Makeig led them across many streams and underneath waterfalls, the rough terrain sometimes forcing them to dismount and led their horses along narrow passes or up steep inclines. Sometimes the path opened onto a ridge or hill that was sparse of trees wherefrom the expanse of the mountain range revealed itself stretching south, west, and north as far as the eye could see, with many of the nearest mountains looming high over their heads. It was mid-afternoon before they made their first stop, in a grove of oaks that surrounded a small waterfall. Makeig told them to water themselves and their horses for a few minutes.

"We're 'bout halfway to Hill Town," he told them. "Though this way we go is the shortest, it ain't without risk. There's a warlord what thinks this bit of forest belongs to him, an' ever' now an' then sends some of his ruffians along to remind folks of his claim. They ain't usually much to worry over, unless they number a dozen or more. Right poor fighters. Anyways, from this place up an' 'til the next ridge over yonder, we move fast. This stretch is easy, thank goodness, but that's why they like this pass so much, I reckon. I don't 'spect any trouble, but keep ye wits close by, if ye take me meanin'. From here on, let me do all the talkin' if there's anyone met along the way. Most likely it'll be some of me own people, but ye never know."

After a short pause, they continued on, the air now decidedly cooler and gusting over the hills, shaking loose the brownest leaves from the branches. They descended into a wide steep-sided ravine so thick with trees that they could not see any hint of the surrounding mountains. Saying little, they crossed back and forth over several small streams, negotiating shoals and pools and banks. Other trails led away to the right or left, but Makeig kept them to their own path, twisting and turning until at last they were moving upward again against the other side of the vale.

"By now, me watchmen have spotted us," Makeig said to Ashlord. "Though we won't see 'em at all. They'll have signaled our approach, an' a party'll be dispatched to make sure of us. We'll meet 'em in a couple hours."

"Do they expect us?"

"No, no. It's the ordinary way of things with us, very organized ye might say," Makeig explained. "We may not hold the pass, but we keep sharp eyes on it, day an' night. This is one of four approaches to Hill Town, an' the least used since our business seldom takes us this way. No good for wagons, as ye see, an' too close to them warlords for reg'lar supplies. Anyhow, me people don't 'spect to see me 'til on the morrow, an' though they'll recognize me hat an' coat, they'll set about markin' who's wearin' 'em. An' I guess seein' several horsemen what with pack animals, too, strangers all, they'll be double careful. But don't ye worry none! We well mark friend from foe afore lettin' fly with arrows!"

"I'm glad to hear that," muttered Ullin before Billy could say the same.

It was a steep climb, and they led the horses by the reins for the better part of the ascent. They reached the top and took a breather, looking at the vast wilderness of forest and mountains behind and before them. The sun was already slipping nearer the highest of the far mountains to the southwest, and long shadows were reaching across the view. Robby thought the scene one of bitter beauty, and a terrible loneliness surprised him as he gazed northeast where he imagined his home was.

"Gar!" said Billy coming up next to him. "I'd never find me way back out of this!"

Robby nodded in agreement. "Let's hope we don't have to."

"How far have we come from Janhaven?" Sheila asked Makeig.

"Oh, I reckon we're 'bout ten or twelve leagues, as the arrow flies. 'Bout twice that as the road winds, I reckon," he answered as he mounted his horse, "an' another five to go. But the next several should be a bit easier."

Indeed, the way was not so steep up or down, and they rode at their best speed, being careful of the footing of their animals. Following a broad ridgeline, they continued upward, and the character of the forest changed so that many of the trees, gnarled scarlet oaks, yellow birch, and red maple, were shedding their autumn colors, with leaves of red and yellow scattering in the gusts.

"Doyouever, doyouever, doyoueverseeanytrolls?" Ibin asked. He had somehow worked his way to the front of the group just behind Makeig. Though he longed to hear the answer, Robby took the reins of the pack animals from him and fell back to take Ibin's place at the end of the line.

"No, never, not in all the years I've been here," Makeig said. "Some of me people swear they've seen 'em, way back, long afore I came along. These mountains are filled with troll houses, though, an' caves, an' all manner of leavin's. Look right up yonder, for instance."

He pointed at another ridge a few miles away, toward a line that angled across the face of the distant slopes.

"What is that?" asked Ullin.

"Why it's an old troll road," answered Makeig. "I've been over there. It's devil hard to get at. The funny thing, it just starts up, out of nowheres, like, an' after maybe a mile stretch, it just stops. Yet, it be paved with flat stones with not a crack between, smooth as ye please, an' all along it are old stone houses an' caves. I even peeked into a couple. Not much to find, 'cept some pots an' pans too big to carry, an' stone chairs an' benches an' like furnishin'. We'll pass along a piece of road like that up near Hill Town, too."

"What happened to them? To the trolls?" asked Sheila.

"Well, there's few what know, if any. But there's a feller what lives among us at Hill Town, one of them prospector-types that's older than even he knows. Well, he's got a notion or two that he don't mind jabberin' 'bout. Says they were all called away, sudden-like, on a moonless night laid with winter snow. Says they marched off southward, settin' off such a mighty thunder by their tramp that the ground shook all the way to Barley, an' made folks remember why these mountains are named as they are. An' they never came back. So says Warley Rinspoon, the ol' geezer I got the tale from. I'm sure he'd be more than happy to relate it to ye, if ye have a day or two. Kind of a slow, roundabout talker, in a way."

"I hope we won't be lingering quite so long," Ashlord said. "We need to be on our way as soon as we can. I'm counting on some advice to get past the warlords, too, or we'll have an even longer trip of it."

"Well, as I told ye back at Janhaven," Makeig shrugged, "if we can round up them Blaney brothers, what know them western parts best of any, ye'll be well supplied with directions. If it were up to me, though, I'd move way south afore crossin' through. That Damar lord, Lord Cartu, they calls him, he runs a mighty mean outfit, an' it's his territory, so he claims, just west an' south. Wants to run things all the way up to the west road near Janhaven, if he can put down the Galinots up that way. Anyhow, if any knows a way, the Blaneys can figure it out for ye."

"How many people live at Hill Town?" Robby asked.

"We reckoned one thousand nine hunnerd fifty-three, last spring," Makeig stated. "Of them, 'bout a quarter are children with less than ten years. Most of them born at Hill Town. Many more families live out an' around the town. The last time we had a real fight on our hands, 'bout three years ago—that was with some Damar—we raised nearly six hundred fighters."

"Do you have much trouble with the Damar?" asked Ullin.

"Naw, not too much any more. They send out raidin' parties, mostly after cattle an' women, just testin' us, I think. Anyways, though we ain't very many, we control the territory all 'round, an' ain't none got away alive in six years. Ever' now an' then, them Galinots from up north foray through the pass, an' we let 'em go on through, so long as they ain't too many. We treat the Damar just the same. Our rule of thumb is if there's less than two-score men an' horses, we let 'em through. Any more than that, an' we take 'em on their way back. They've learned to move in small parties an' sometimes they try an' meet up with each other. Only we keep good count an' that don't pay for 'em any more. We got lots of rules 'bout them warlord men. Another one is that we don't parley. Sometimes they send somebody up to badger us to trade with 'em, standin' on a hilltop or down in the pass callin' at us. But we never show our faces unless we mean that to be the last thing they see. That way, they can't ever reckon our strength."

"Somewhat brutal, isn't it?" Ashlord asked.

Makeig gave him a sidelong glance and snorted.

"Not as bloody unkind as what I found when I first got here!" he said. "Bloody Galinots an' Damar all over the place, rapin', lootin', killin'. I didn't lose seventy fine seamen runnin' out of Tracia only to get the others killed when we got here. So I kinda took over, like. War's war, I say. Whether it's against a highfalutin tyrant, or a lowdown bully. Pretty soon them Damar an' Galinots figured this part of the mountains was cursed an' haunted, an' we encouraged 'em. In the early days, we always spared one or two as prisoners an' staged it so as they saw or heard the wildest, vilest, most terriblest, an' spookiest things. All a big put-on. Afterwards, we let 'em escape, like, takin' the tales back. I think it worked purty well. Too well, in fact, since it got us a bad name with other folk what could've been friendly with us, traders an' such, an' folk in nearby towns an' so forth. Aye, we overdid it maybe, even if them tales we spread have helped to keep the warlords off our backs."

They traveled on along the path, moving gently up and down the ridge, which eventually flattened onto a broad rolling forest, thick with ancient trunks. Makeig's pace slowed perceptibly, and though he led them on comfortably and with no word of care, Robby sensed that he was watchful. They heard running water, and soon after they were following alongside a tumbling stream, spraying over rocks and mossy boulders, and jumping around nooks and gurgling crannies. Ahead was an arched stone bridge, and as they approached it, two men stepped out from the trees, blocking the path with notched arrows at the ready. A third man stepped between those two, holding up his hand as a signal for them to halt.

"Say the word, or stand an' deliver!" the man shouted.

"Swordplay's the word!" cried Makeig back at him.

"Right, then. So what business have ye on this road?" the challenger demanded.

"Mad Martin's business, that's what!" bellowed Makeig.

"Doff ye hat, then, an' come ahead slowly on foot."

"Best do as they say," said Makeig, dismounting. "I told ye they'd make sure of me."

The three men, dressed in similar tan and green leggings and tunics, with patchwork cloaks of likewise tan and green, stood motionless while Robby and his company dismounted and continued their approach. At last Makeig took off his hat with a grand swoop, and the men relaxed. Their leader turned to the other side of the bridge briefly and made a hand sign that produced thirty other men, all dressed and armed alike, emerging from the trees all around them and from the far side of the bridge.

"Capt'n," said the leader of the band, "we didn't expect ye back so soon, an' suspected foul play with yer clothes."

"Just so, an' right in bein' cautious, too."

"An' yer companions?"

"Trusted men of Barley, the ones I sent word about, on their way westward," Makeig replied as he gave his plumes a few strokes and crammed his hat back onto his head.

"Might one of 'em be Robby Ribbon?"

Makeig was surprised at the question, but no more than the rest.

"I am Robby Ribbon," Robby said, stepping forward.

"Well, there's a messenger for ye, just arrived at Hill Town," the man said. "He waits there as we wouldn't let him pass on. He says he's come from yer grandfather's house."

"My grandfather's house?" Robby asked, glancing at Ullin who shrugged and shook his head.

Turning to Makeig, the man went on, "He arrived just when our scouts brought news of yer approach through the pass. Not knowin' what was afoot, I thought it best he stay there. He would not say his business, but I suspect it ain't much to do with us."

"Why do ye say that?" Makeig asked.

The man looked around at the newcomers and then said softly to his captain, "He is an elfkind. Wears the livery of one of the ancient houses that is no more. Nornus, the old woman who does medicine an' knows the lore of the past, says so."

"Aye, she's one to know," Makeig said, scratching his chin and glancing over at Robby. "What say ye to this, Mr. Ribbon?"

"It is unexpected," Robby replied, shrugging and shaking his head. "I can't imagine what he might want."

"Maybe, he's onto us," Billy whispered to Ashlord, who glanced sharply at him to hold his tongue.

"I hope ye treated the feller well," Makeig said. "I don't want no trouble with Tallin or any of his people."

"He ain't one of Tallin's folk. He only came from there. He gave no trouble, Capt'n, an' we put him up at my place to wait."

"Well, then," Makeig said, mounting his horse, "let's get on. It'll be past dark as it is, an' we don't want to keep Mr. Ribbon from his meetin' any longer than need be."

The man whistled and horses were brought out. He and several others took the lead as the rest of the Hill Town soldiers faded away into the forest. Robby noted the ease with which they moved and how suddenly he lost sight of them.

"I think these people can help our own, if ever they may join together," Robby said to Billy.

"Aye. Did ye see how they moved nearly without a sound?"

"What do you think of the news?" Ullin asked, coming up on the other side. "About the messenger waiting for you?"

"I don't know what to make of it," Robby said. "He is your grandfather, too. What do you think?"

"He has always been a secretive one," Ullin said. "And I hardly know him, though I grew up under his roof. He probably doesn't even know I am anywhere near. I haven't seen him in years."

"Do you miss him?" Robby impulsively asked and immediately regretted.

Ullin thought for a moment, then said, "He is a hard one, and is hard to miss, I must say. He keeps too much bitterness within him, having lost his wife and two sons. He is never anxious to see me, but he has always treated me fairly, even if he is cool and distant. I do miss him, though, for in my grandfather's face I see the likeness of my father."

"What became of our grandmother?"

"Ah, well, that is a sorry tale that no one fully knows," Ullin said. "I was told by my mother that her name has not been spoken in that house since she died of a broken heart."

"Can someone actually die of a broken heart?" Robby asked.

"Surely," Sheila said under her breath.

"Surely," Ullin said to Robby. "Her father and mother had no sons to send to Duinnor to serve the King, and had to pay heavy tribute instead. The Fairoak lands were later laid waste by war, and when our grandfather met Lady Kahryna of Fairoak, that House was all but ruined and bankrupt. The two married, but things went badly for Tallin lands in Vanara, too, as a result of the wars with the Dragonkind. So Fairoak and Tallin signed the last of their Vanaran lands over to the King, and my grandfather brought his family back to the Eastlands, to Tallinvale. So bitter was our grandfather that he cut all ties to Vanara and Duinnor alike, and he swore he would have no more to do with the troubles of the west. But my uncle, his eldest son, Dalvenpar, was soon of age and was called to serve the King of Duinnor, as had our grandfather, as Kingsman. He went willingly, though our grandfather was against his going, and

Dalvenpar served with distinction for many years. But then news came that he was slain. Such was our grandmother's misery, I was told, that all of the spring blooms on all the lands of our estate withered and fell away at her mourning. A shade, they say, covered the night so that no stars could be seen, and the summer air of our lands was cold and foggy while all those lands around enjoyed the light and warmth that is expected of the season. Anyway, that was the tale.

"Then a messenger came with summons for my father to take his brother's place in the service of the King. One year and one day, he was given, before he was to report to Duinnor. I was very small, but I remember, all during that year, my father prepared himself gladly, and my mother supported him as cheerfully as she could. Lord Tallin, our grandfather, opposed his going, too, just as he had opposed his first born son's service. Lord Tallin was wealthy enough to pay the heavy fines, and he demanded that my father stay in Tallinvale and refuse the call of duty. But my father wanted not only the honor of service, but also vengeance for his brother's death. Our grandmother, though, succumbed to her grief and went mad, tearing at her clothes and mourning for my father as if he was dead. Grandfather locked her away in the east tower of the hall and set a watch to keep her from harming herself, and to provide for her needs. She became a kind of prisoner and was allowed to see no one else, save grandfather, alone, who went to her each day and each night to see to her needs and to comfort her. Months passed and the day came for my father to depart. My grandfather took my father and me to see her, and she received us calmly and kindly, kissing my father many times, weeping all the while. She hugged me and told me to be strong for my father. It was all very quiet and very sad. As I said, I was very young, but I remember."

Ullin paused as they negotiated under low tree limbs.

"My father departed later that morning," he went on. "Then, on the next day, Mirabella disappeared, leaving a note that she, too, sought service as her brothers. Years later, I learned that she followed my father, remaining hidden from him and at a distance. She eluded the parties sent by Lord Tallin to bring her back, and she made it all the way to Duinnor, and took up training there, privately learning all she could about warcraft while her brother attended the King's Academy. Later, she somehow managed to join the Kingsmen armies going south, where she and my father fought side by side. She was with him when he died. It was she, Mirabella, who brought news of his death back to Tallinvale. Grandmother's hair, the color of polished copper, turned white at the news. She uttered a few words to our grandfather so that he turned pale even as his cheeks reddened with shame. I don't know what she said, but she never spoke again to anyone, as far as I know. She took to her bed, and our grandfather stayed at her bedside as she slept. She never again opened her eyes. By nightfall her spirit had left her body.

"For the next three weeks, our grandfather kept to himself, and I later heard that during that time it was feared that he had gone mad, for the servants reported that he raved, going from laughter to crying in an instant. It was said also that he would sometimes act as if he was in another place, speaking with people who were not there, or dressing in full battle gear, swinging his sword at imaginary enemies. But, at last, he emerged from his mourning, or his madness, and took up his duties as Lord of Tallinvale once again, and with an even greater zeal than ever before."

Although Ullin told his tale matter-of-factly, his companions felt its heaviness. For Robby, who had only the day before heard a version of the tale from his mother, it explained part of the reluctance of his parents to talk about his mother's side of the family.

"A sad tale," commented Makeig.

"And what of your mother?" Robby asked. "Does she still live in Tallinvale?"

"No. My father's death broke her heart, too. She remained in Tallin Hall for a time, then departed to rejoin her kin in Glareth. I went with her, but I came back later. I stayed at Tallinvale until I left for Duinnor to become a Kingsman."

"Do you ever get to see your mother?"

"Yes. I saw her just a few months ago, when I was in Glareth on the business of Queen Serith Ellyn. She is very frail. But we were very happy to see each other."

Ullin's tale left the group in a somber mood, and they went for a long while afterwards without saying anything. They made their way easily, led onward by Makeig's men who, Robby noticed, sometimes gave signals with their hands to unseen recipients. Makeig acted as if he barely noticed these gestures, but Robby realized that he was keenly aware of them, and he thought perhaps the Captain was pleased that their approach was being treated with such care.

"Captain Makeig, are your people always so cautious?" Robby asked him.

"Aye! Indeed we must be," Makeig stated. "With warlords all around, an' with rebel agents from Tracia comin' an' goin'. We know that if our harvest is too bountiful, or if we bring too much ore out from our mines, there's bound to be raids an' such. An' many of our folk're like me, wanted by the realm they fled from, though none of us are justly accused, I warrant. I meself have a bounty of one hundred pieces of gold on me, an' twenty-five on each of me crew what came with me. Treason, we're accused of. Treason! We who defended the rightful Rulin' Prince! So, aye, we're a careful lot!"

By this time Sir Sun had strolled below the western mountains, the sky above was a darkening blue with faint wisps of pink high and away, but the shadows were deep along the forest trail. Over a rise they came to a small gorge spanned by a long stone bridge barely wide enough for two men to walk abreast, yet Makeig and his man guided their horses straight onto it while Robby's mount hesitated and balked at the edge.

"Lead 'em over if ye have to," Makeig called back without turning. "It takes 'em a time or two to get used to it."

Robby dismounted and led his horse across. While the others followed Robby, Ullin told Ibin to wait.

"Billy and I will come back over and each take one of the packhorses," he explained.

It was a deep ravine with sharp rocks jutting up dimly far below, and though the bridge was solid enough, Robby felt a little off balance when a stiff wind suddenly picked up and blew crossways.

"There are many of these stone walk-bridges in the forest," Makeig explained as Robby finally stepped off the bridge and remounted to wait for the others. "Some fancier an' wider than this one, but many too crumbly to trust. Don't worry, this one's sturdy, an' a good place to set a watch." He nodded back up the rise, and Robby saw a small, squat hut of stone about fifty yards off on top of which were several men keeping an eye on them. "Wind seems always blowin' through here," Makeig observed to Ashlord coming up, "so we call this Windy Crossin'."

"A troll bridge?" Ashlord asked getting into his saddle.

"Aye, we believe so. More like a footbridge to a troll, I imagine. See here?" Makeig pointed down. "This here's another troll road, pickin' up on this side of the bridge. It'll go our way about two miles an' quit. See how neat the stones are laid? Hardly a crack between them."

Soon Ullin and Billy were across, along with Ibin, and after they retied the harnesses, the group set off again. By now there was a definite chill in the air, and even the character of the forest seemed changed. The trees were old and thick and sparse of leaves, and only a few pines were seen at all. The stone roadway was well used and ran like a pale stream through the carpet of fallen leaves. They passed by many a troll house, low stone structures overgrown with ivy and brush, and in the tangle beside each was a massive stone just the shape and size to fit into each doorway, laying as if cast lightly aside. Even the roofs were made of stone slabs, roughly cut and laid out across the walls. There were no windows, and it was apparent that the ruins, as gloomy as they were, had never been cheerful. Billy shuddered at the thought of going inside one, yet he was curious, and Ibin once turned his horse aside to explore one, but Billy stopped him.

"No time for peekin' 'round," he said.

"Ain't nuthin' there anyways," said Makeig. "Like I said, just a few pieces of junk too heavy to lift."

The paved road ended, and the way became a path as before, and it took them winding along the side of the ridge, then it led them across an open field and straight to the base of a low cliff. There, the path proceeded into the gate of a keep set with stone in the wall of the cliff. Torches were already lit along the top of the wall where men stood watch. The gate was opened for them and as they passed into the keep they entered the mouth of a well-lit tunnel that was cut into the mountain. It was high enough to ride through and reminded Robby of the troll house where Billy had been taken. Except this one was better lit and not as smelly. The passage inclined upward, and the cobblestone floor rang loudly as they went, making it difficult to talk.

"Was this made by trolls?" Robby asked.

"Aye, for the most part," answered Makeig. "But we laid the cobblestones an' worked the braziers an' cut channels along the sides to let the water run out an' keep the road dry. We built the keep outside, too."

"It seems a long tunnel," commented Ullin.

"It is fair long, about a half-furlong. It gets pretty steep, so mind yerselves!"

Indeed it got steeper, and at one point Robby worried his horse might slip. But all their mounts were sure-footed, and they moved slowly along without incident. Still climbing and rounding a bend, they could see a purple sky through the opening above and ahead of them. When they emerged, they were on the top of a broad ridge. Above them on their right, lights from many buildings and houses glowed from a town that crowned a hill about a mile off. Between here and there, they passed through fields and farms, and several folk came from their houses to greet Makeig as he passed. The path took them gently along, crossing wooden bridges over swift-running streams, and soon they were riding through the main street of the small town, dogs barking at them, music coming from a tavern, and folks going about their evening chores before bedtime. Makeig took them on until they came to a large building of stone and logs, and there they stopped.

"This is our Great House," Makeig said. "It is where I stay when I ain't at me cottage, an' where we meet an' make our government, too."

"You have some kind of government?" Ullin asked.

"Aye, an' I'm the mayor. We got a sheriff, some judges, councilmen, clerks, an' even a jailor. There's the Council for Defense, the Council for Crops, Livestock, an' Commerce, an' the Roads an' Works Council, too. Purty much everone's on some kind of council or other."

"Impressive," said Ashlord.

"Well, we've been tryin' to get away from the thievin' line, if ye take me meanin', an' more into the real way of livin'," Makeig said as he dismounted. "But it ain't easy, what with warlords on two sides, an' enemy agents forever out to arrest any who try to trade with the south parts. Janhaven is about our only real partner in these parts. When the mountains are good to us, they yield good rubies an' other stones, so we've done trade with Glareth an' Duinnor, even, through roundabout ways. But we have to be independent-like, least-ways until there's some change in Tracia, which don't seem likely to happen all too soon. Here, let me men take yer horses. They'll get stabled right. We got some rooms inside where ye can stay the night. Meanwhiles, we'll have a pint or two over at the tavern whilst we round up this messenger feller."

"I'd rather we not make too much of a show of ourselves," Ashlord said.

"Ah, ye mean to keep yer business private-like. I understand," Makeig nodded, slapping Ashlord on the back. Ashlord winced as Makeig continued. "No problem. Ye ain't got that much to give away, do ye? Just wantin' a way west, is all. I'll send word for them Blaney brothers, too. Ye can ask them questions 'stead of the other way 'round."

As the horses were led away, they took their gear inside to a room that looked something like a barracks, with cots lined through it. Then Makeig led them back outside and down the way to the tavern, called the Green Sail. Soon they were settled at a table, and pitchers of beer were being put before them. It was a surprisingly well kept place, and there was a sense of pride in its decidedly nautical theme. Everywhere were ship's fittings, brass lanterns, blocks, netting, and swinging rudders served as doors. It soon came out that the barkeep, and master brewer, was a shipmate of Makeig's on many voyages and fell by the same fate as many of the others when the Royal Family was ousted. Most of the accoutrements were locally made or carefully collected over time from the gleanings of passersby or from Furaman's connections. At any rate, the beer was fine and the wear of the road was soon forgotten. The barkeep, under Makeig's orders, kept the travelers' table stocked with fresh pitchers, as well as fried potatoes and cheese, and he stoked up the fireplace. There were few locals and none asked any questions, though they were friendly enough and smiled and raised their own tankards to the strangers. But they kept an eye on Robby's group. Sheila, not exactly trusting, kept her face away from them and pulled her collar up. Billy prattled on about what adventures these folks must have, with Ibin nodding in agreement between gulps. Ullin and Ashlord were more restrained, saying little as they puffed their pipes and kept an eye on the door.

Soon enough, Makeig came in with another man, and at the sight of him, Ullin stood. The man was thin, but tall, and very pale in the face, with light almost yellow hair, and dressed in fine light armor. Seeing Ullin, he approached quickly and bowed.

"This here's the feller what come from Tallinvale to speak with ye," Makeig said.

"I am Tyrillick, of the House of Sycamore," said the man. His blond hair draped down across his shoulders, glistening in the light, and his blue eyes glittered with a repressed spirit. Though his build was slight, and he had the spryness of youth, his age was a mystery, his face at once young and ancient, as if it had known no change for a thousand years. "Are you

Ullin Saheed Tallin?"

"I am." Ullin bowed.

"I am honored." Tyrillick returned the bow. "I am to escort one of your party to Tallin Hall. Your cousin, Robby. Is he here?"

"That is him," Ullin motioned at Robby who was by now standing across the table looking on.

"What business does my grandfather have with me?" Robby asked.

"I do not know what, if any, business he has with you. I am not in service to him, nor am I privy to his business. I serve and am sent by one who wishes to meet you at his estate. I am to say this to you..."

The words he then spoke were in the First Tongue, and everyone in Robby's party understood them instantly. Sheila slowly stood as an odd chill ran down her spine. Tyrillick's voice resounded in the same manner that Robby's words had done when he declared his love for her those many weeks ago. There was the same chiming sound, the same melancholy rhythm and intonations. But the message delivered by Tyrillick also carried a powerful counterpoint, like the distant clap of iron thunder resonating across the sky and through the earth.

The Bell of Attis loudly rings.
It raises stones and casts down kings.

The noise of the tavern slowly replaced the fading sound of Tyrillick's words. Ashlord and Robby glanced at each other. Whoever sent this messenger knew Robby to be the Bellringer. Makeig stood silent, baffled that he understood the haunting words, though they were in a tongue he had never before heard.

"Tallinvale is out of our way," Ullin finally said, sharing the apprehension that suddenly gripped the group.

"We know your way lies west and that you must go with all speed," Tyrillick nodded. "It is not our intention to delay you unnecessarily."

"Can you but tell us who your master is?" Ashlord asked.

"I am not permitted to say, Collandoth," replied the messenger sharply with a mischievous glint in his eye. "But I offer this as a token of who sends me."

He took from his pouch a small box and drew forth a tiny crystal vial that glittered like a yellow jewel. He uncorked it, and a strange golden mist wafted out from the vial. With it floated an aroma like springtime along a mountain meadow full of blossoms and clean air and youth. They all felt refreshed and invigorated by the scent though it was so light and airy that it was barely a scent at all. Ashlord smiled and looked at Robby.

"No one knows the brewing of that perfume except one House of all those of the world," he said to Robby. "And it is wise that Tyrillick does not speak his master's name. I would encourage us to go there if at all possible, even if it is out of our way. But the decision is yours."

Robby looked at Ashlord, then at Ullin.

"We still need to meet with the Blaney brothers," said Robby. "So we cannot come right away."

"They'll be here soon," spoke up Makeig, who only now roused himself from a faraway daze brought on by the perfume. "Ye can't leave afore mornin', anyways. Ye need to rest."

"Rightly so," said Tyrillick. "Nor need all of you come. If you say you will come, and if Ullin Saheed will show you the way, then I will carry word ahead of you to make all ready."

Robby gave the group a questioning glance, but they were all silent, waiting for him to decide.

"I'll not commit any but myself and Ullin, if he will guide me," said Robby. "But I will come as soon as I can. How far is it from here?"

"One day, giving a swift horse no rest. Two, with ease."

Robby shook his head. He already had in mind one detour, to Tulith Morgair, that would cost them time.

"Then I will leave early tomorrow," he said.

"Very well, I will depart now and carry the word," Tyrillick turned to go. "Until then, safe journeys!"

"That's awful strange," said Billy after Tyrillick had departed. "Very abrupt-like, if ye ask me. An' what about that perfume? Mighty strange sensations it gave off! Who's the maker of it?"

"Billy," Ashlord advised him, "it is best not to ask too many questions just now. All will be revealed when we return."

"Huh?"

"You and Sheila and Ibin will stay here while Robby, Ullin, and I go to the Tallin lands."

"What?" cried Sheila. "Why can't we all go?"

"Someone needs to stay and see to our route west," Ashlord coolly explained. "And I think we may save time if we travel with fewer in our company."

Before Billy or Sheila could protest, Ibin spoke up.

"Ithink, Ithink, weshould, weshouldallstaytogether, Mr.Ashlord," Ibin said flatly.

Surprised by Ibin's statement, Billy stared at him and nodded.

"Well, I suppose we all have a stake in this journey," said Robby. "If this is business that has to do with us, then maybe it's best we share in the knowledge of it."

Ashlord leaned on his walking stick, intent upon Robby. Perhaps Robby was beginning to assert himself, at least in small ways. Ashlord perceived, too, that the others were in no mood to be left behind.

"Very well," he sighed at last. "Captain Makeig, is there any chance that we might meet with the Blaney brothers this night?"

"They've been sent for," he said, "an' should be here in a couple of hours. They'll be tired an' wantin' food an' sleep, though. Been out on the south patrol for a week."

"Can you tell us if our westward route may be taken up from the Tallin lands?" Robby asked. "Or should we come back through here?"

Makeig rubbed his nose in thought.

"Well, it's a bit south of what I reckon the Blaney brothers might commend to ye," he said, as if thinking aloud. "O' course, it's only a day or so out. But, then again, them warlords, hmm. Ain't no easy way west. Well, I reckon them Blaneys'll be best to tell ye," he said at last. "Meanwhiles, drink ye fill. An' supper's on the way! All on the house, ye might say, even though there's a jar up on the bar for loose coins, if ye take me meanin'."

"So what about that perfume?" Billy pressed as soon as Robby and Ullin sat back down.

"Its making is a secret," Ashlord said. "And that's all you need to know for now."

Billy rolled his eyes, took a long drink, and shook his head. The door opened, and a few women came in with baskets of food, and one of them, seeing Robby, hurried over to greet him.

"Master Ribbon! We meet again!"

"Sally Bodwin!" Robby stood and bowed. "Here I am."

"An' lookin' something better than the last time we met, too."

"I should hope so."

"An' these are yer friends? I hear yer bound for Duinnor."

"That's right. Here, let me introduce you to them."

Ashlord she had met, and he greeted her kindly. Ullin and Billy bowed, and Billy would hardly take his eyes from her for the rest of the night. Ibin also made an effort to bow, but immediately went back to his fried potatoes.

When they came to the last person, who remained seated and somewhat hunched, Sally asked, "An' this is?"

"Pradkin," Sheila interrupted, making her voice strangely low and gravelly. She kept her head down and had pulled up her hood as soon as the women entered. "Mr. Ribbon's particular bodyguard." She took Sally's hand into her gloved one and gave it a hard shake, still keeping her head down.

"Oh!" Sally said as Robby gave his bodyguard an odd look. "I had no idea ye needed a bodyguard."

"I don't actually need one," Robby said as he guided Sally away, shooting a puzzled look at Sheila. "But he's an old friend and a might strange in his ways. Somewhat attached to me, in an odd kind of way."

Sheila kept an eye on Robby and Sally as they moved across the room, Sally rubbing her arm and glancing back with a frown. Billy, too, looked after them as they pulled up stools at the bar.

"What was that all about?" he asked Sheila. But he was not inclined to hear her answer, so intent on Sally was he, and Sheila was not inclined to answer, anyway. Ibin, meanwhile, had absorbed himself in the food that was being laid out, and between "Thankyouthankyouthankyou," was snatching up bits of cheese, roast beef, and applecakes.

Ashlord and Ullin sat back down and neither ate enthusiastically, each in their own thoughts while Makeig excused himself again to look after more of his affairs. The tavern's business picked up and soon it was fairly crowded, in spite of Makeig's prediction, though most of the folk merely came in and after chatting with the barkeep, left soon after. Not before they had given the strangers a good once or twice over. Some greeted them by nodding their heads or tipping their wide colorful hats. Indeed, though the local people seemed well off—for none were ill-dressed—the travelers overheard snatches of ordinary talk about cows, crops, and weather. They were well-spoken, and the thick accent of the Tracian coast was pronounced by most of them. Ashlord's attention landed on one gentleman who was dressed in a dark coat of blue velvet and knee-high boots, a cocked matching blue hat with a white plume reaching from it, and a white blouse with frilly ruffles. He stood, one foot on the bar, one hand lifting a tankard while the other rested on the pommel of a sword hanging at his waist. It happened that their eyes met just as the man finished his draught, and, without taking his eyes from Ashlord, he put his tankard down and approached.

"I take it you are the one called Ashlord?" he asked.

"I am."

"I am Ramund Drayworth, late of Tracia, too long of Hill Town," he bowed. "I welcome you to our little community. I am the sheriff of this place and make it my business to look to any strangers that happen through."

Ashlord smiled neutrally while Ullin coolly studied the man's outfit.

"Mayhaps you are only passing through?" Drayworth asked.

"Yes, on our way west."

"West? Surely Hill Town is out of your way from Barley?"

"We come from Janhaven," said Ullin. "Perhaps you have not heard that Barley has fallen?"

"And you might be?"

"Ullin Saheed Tallin. And these are my companions."

"Ah, one of the Fairoak amongst us!" Drayworth grinned and bowed again. "An elf-blood, a wise man, a few Barleymen, and," he looked askance at Ibin, "a man of modest intellect, though prodigious appetite, I must observe. We are most honored by your visit, indeed. As for Barley, yes, we have all heard. And we know you come from Janhaven. Yet, out of the way it still seems for a westward trek. Yes, we have heard about the battle at Passdale and the refugees at Janhaven. But do the Redvests press you so that you cannot take the west road from there?"

"The west road be blocked by warlords," Billy stated, having taken an instant dislike to the fellow. "An' the north passes'll be covered by ice before we could reach 'em."

"You have not traveled westward very much, I think," Ullin added.

"No. No, I have not," Drayworth said as he drew up a stool. With a sweep of his coat and his scabbard, he sat at the end of the table, picking over the applecakes until he found a little one to his liking, daintily holding it to his mouth with two fingers. "I have had no need, and I lack the desire to go west," he said, nibbling. "My heart lies to the south and east."

"Are ye one of Makeig's crewmen?" Billy asked.

"That ragtag ruffmuffian rabble? I sincerely hope you are not serious."

Billy shrugged.

"I am the nephew of the Duke of Sharlofiorn, Prince Lantos, and how I came to be mere sheriff of this place is a sorry tale I'll not bore you with. But we have done well for ourselves here, don't you think? It is not easy to be out of one's place, as you are learning. Do you think your people will do as well, eh?"

"We don't mean to wait long enough to find out," Billy shot back. "Yer countrymen will learn a thing or two 'bout messin' with Barleyfolk!"

"Oh?" said Drayworth in an amused tone. "Do you mean to find help? Is that why you go west?"

"That is our intention," Ullin said bluntly.

Drayworth shook his head and took a tiny bite of the cake he had been waving about.

"Tsk, tsk," he said, producing a handkerchief with a flourish and daubing the corners of his mouth. "Duinnor will not help you. Why would they bother? Did they come to our aid? Did they send a single sword? Not even Glareth came, except to rescue some of my kin, and rather late in the game, at that."

As he spoke, he attempted to lower his head enough to see under Sheila's hood by letting his feet slide away under the table and slouching down on his stool with as much nonchalance as he could muster, but with an obvious and uncomfortable attention to balance as the seat of the stool ran into the small of his back.

"And now look what has happened," he went on. "The Red Tyrants spread their villainous empire. Allow me to share a thing or two about losing your country: First, you learn that you cannot count on all your countrymen."

He reached for another piece of applecake, but he did not lift it. Instead, he bent his head sideways very close to the table as if to examine it carefully, trying very hard to see under Sheila's hood as he continued to speak.

"Many are taken in by the glory of the new order, drunk with new-found power and position that they could never otherwise deserve or hope for. Second, if you oppose your conqueror, you do so at the loss of land, love, and friends, for he will have them all in his purse or else in their grave. And last, your enemy is as much those who have broken their promises to help as it is those who attack you. No, no. Go west if you must. Find out for yourselves."

At this point, he nearly slipped off the stool, but he deftly straightened back up, giving up his attempt to view the hooded one.

"The sooner you get accustomed to the idea that you are on your own, the sooner you will form new alliances, and the sooner you will begin to rebuild your strength. Do you think this town is a permanent place for us? No, there is not one amongst us who was not born here who does not breathe for the day he stands on his own lands again."

Drayworth suddenly stopped himself.

"Ah! I said I would not bore you, and there! I have! I only mean to say that if it is fighting the Redvests you mean to do, there are many here who would likely join you. If for no other reason than to strike back at those who have wronged us."

"Captain Makeig has already given us assurances of that," Ashlord said smoothly. "But it is good to hear it from another."

Drayworth rose and bowed.

"So there," he said. "I bid you a good stay and a safe journey."

"We thank you," Ashlord said. "Good night."

Drayworth strode out of the tavern with Billy glaring after him.

"What a fop!" Billy snorted. "I think he gave me a headache!"

"That fop was the greatest swordsman in all of Tracia," Ullin said quietly, pulling apart a piece of bread. "And he has killed as many men in single combat with his blade as he has in battle, it is said."

"Aye," whispered one of the women who had leaned past Ullin to pour more ale into his tankard. "An' seventeen assassins have died in pursuit of him. So far as we're countin', that is. Four of 'em this year alone."

Billy huffed disbelievingly as he rubbed the side of his head near his recent wound.

• • •

While Drayworth held forth with his friends, Robby and Sally sat at the bar having their own conversation.

"Captain Makeig told me once that the Prince sent to Duinnor for help many years ago," Sally said, "tellin' the King through his envoys that his rule over Tracia would fail if Duinnor did not send help. Two years later, his prediction came true. Later, not long after Martin took over here, he, too, sent an envoy to Duinnor. In fact, the Blaney brothers went, along with three others."

"When was that?"

"Oh, let's see. About ten years ago, I think. But nuthin' came of it."

Sally looked sympathetically at Robby.

"I don't mean to put ye off yer hope," she added, touching his arm. "There's always a chance they'll listen to ye, an' that ye may convince them to act. Especially since Tracia seems set on movin' against its neighbors."

"Well, we must try," stated Robby, looking blankly into his near-empty tankard. More people had arrived, many in jovial moods. And with all the loud talk and laughter and clanking tankards, the noise of the place was such that Robby and Sally had to lean their heads close together to keep from shouting. A few of the patrons had taken up instruments, fiddle, pipes, and mandolin, and their jaunty tunes also filled the smoke-laden air.

"Come along, Sal," a nearby man called over. "Give us a song!"

This was followed by a chorus of encouragement and entreaties, until at last she rolled her eyes and nodded.

"Duty calls!" she said to Robby as she stood off her stool. "Perhaps I'll see ye again?"

"I hope so," answered Robby. She joined the musicians, and Robby moved back to the table with his comrades.

"She's very pretty," Sheila said as he sat on the bench between her and Billy.

"Not to worry," grinned Robby. "I know where my heart is!"

"I think I know where Billy's might be, too!" she commented, nudging Robby to look around. Billy's gaze was fixed upon Sally. "Poor thing. She hardly knows he exists. And, anyway, we'll be leaving soon."

The plucking of a dulcimer joined the other instruments, and soon a melancholy aire somewhat quieted the crowd as expectant heads turned to face Sally.

'He rode through the night on a pale gray horse,
Through the moonlit shadows of the forest-land,
Back to the house where his true love was,
Galloping swift with sword in hand,
To take her away,
To get her away,
To flee and away from the Redvest band.'

'The Redvest band marched through the hills
Sweepin' the villages with anger and hate,
An' made for the glen by the standin' stones,
To the house on the shore of the River Slate,
To take the rebel's love
To bind the rebel's love,
To use the rebel's love as their bait.'

The ballad went on, clearly a familiar one to most of the listeners, and it ended with a rousing climax describing how the two lovers escaped into the night before they could be captured. Near the end of the song, Ullin saw Makeig re-enter the tavern with two other men. They hung about near the door, respectfully allowing the song to end before Makeig gestured for Ullin.

"I believe our guides have arrived," Ullin said to Ashlord and nodded toward the door. The group rose and followed Ullin. Robby and Billy glanced over their shoulders at Sally who watched them leave amid the applause.

Outside the tavern, Makeig made introductions.

"This here're the Blaney brothers, Gargeoff an' Markum," Makeig said as they all shook hands.

The two brothers were tall, swarthy men, with an unusual combination of black hair and green eyes. They appeared almost as twins, though separated by two years, in their early forties, and were similarly dressed in the oddly stained riding cloaks common among the men hereabouts, cloaks meant to make them blend more readily with the forest. Though obviously tired and weary, with several days of beard, they were patient and good-natured.

"I apologize for keeping you from rest," Ashlord said to them. "I hope we may make it up to you someday."

"Martin tells us ye mean to go west by a southerly route," Markum Blaney said. "If ye manage to get Duinnor to send aid, where others have failed, that will be payment aplenty!"

"Your captain tells us that you two know the westward passes and byways best," Ullin said as they walked briskly to the Great House.

"We know them as well as any," Gargeoff Blaney replied. "In the Great House we have maps, an' we can better show ye an' tell ye what we know. But I must say it is a dangerous route. The passes are narrow, an' it is easy to get caught by the Damar what swarm the western side. I would not want to go west that way."

"How else would you go?"

Gargeoff shrugged.

"As for meself," Markum said as he pulled open the big oaken door of the Great House, "I'd rather go farther south, crossin' at the frontier between the Damar's southernmost territory an' closer to Masurthia."

"That is too close to the way the Tracian Redvests would take if they were to invade Masurthia," Ashlord said. "And I fear troop movements may already be taking place. And it is too far and too dangerous for friends of Duinnor."

"Friends of Duinnor!" Makeig huffed. "Duinnor should learn to be a friend!"

The brothers led the way into a large hall. Various pennants and tapestries hung, some depicting coastal scenes and others showing signs of battle-wear. The wooden beams were carved with seafaring motifs and various Tracian scripts, and at the far end of the room was a dais upon which an ornate chair sat.

"This is our meetin' hall," said Gargeoff, "where we hold court of justice, an' where our councils meet an' plan. Over here is our map room."

They were led through a side door into a smaller room in the center of which was a wide table. The room was walled in by several scroll shelves, and brightly burning lamps hung down over the table to illuminate its surface. Markum pulled out a chart and spread it across the table and pointed out where they were, southwest of Janhaven and nearly due north of Tallinvale.

"If ye left from here, ye could travel almost due west," he said. "With caution ye might make it through the passes an' safely out onto the plain beyond."

"But if ye plan on goin' from Tallinvale," Gargeoff took up, "ye'll be two days, at least, out of the way. We just returned from the western limits of Tallin territory, an' those parts are teemin' with Damar scouts an' patrols. "

"We think they make ready for some action," said Markum. "They're raidin' their own villages with press gangs, an' besides gettin' men for their army, they're takin' slaves an' provisions. A western path from Tallinvale would almost certainly take ye right into them, since Damar City, the warlord's stronghold, is that way."

Robby and his group were gathered closely around the table, paying close attention. But after discussing several possibilities, it was apparent that the brothers did not have confidence in any of the routes they studied. Ashlord frowned, and Ullin crossed his arms in thought. Robby, who was growing sleepy, was also becoming impatient.

"Look," he said at last, "we mean to go west. We must first go to Tallin Hall. Why should we not go straight to the Damar City?"

Everyone looked at Robby in astonishment.

"That is the chief city of the Damar, where the warlord Cartu rules from," said Ullin.

"But they do not expect us, and they should not suspect our business," Robby said. "Surely many travelers go there on business. This road here," Robby traced a line on the chart, "runs west into this road here. From there to Damar City, but look, here, just before it turns toward the city, there is a fork that goes around, passing south of their city. And then it turns back to the northwest."

"Ye'll need writs of passage to travel them roads," said Markum. "All are examined carefully by their posts and patrols."

"Well, how does one obtain one?"

"They're letters," Makeig said, moving over to a drawer and rummaging through it as he spoke, "marked with the current seal of the Damar Watch, an' signed by at least four—ah, here we go!"

He handed Robby a parchment. It was written in the common speech but with many symbols at the top, with several signatures in different places, and there was a large embossed seal was pressed into the document in green ink.

"That one's pretty old, 'bout four years, I'd say," Makeig said, leaning against a bookcase. "I lifted it off a passerby what got caught up in the middle of one of our skirmishes. Don't know how he came by it. Warn't much in the talkin' way by the time I found him, if ye take me meanin'."

"If ye mean to go to Tallinvale," said Markum, "why not take a letter of transit from Lord Tallin?"

"What?"

"He does business with them Damar, I do believe," Gargeoff said.

"What kind of business?" Robby asked, his face reddened somewhat.

"Don't know," said Makeig. "There's a feller from Tallinvale what goes back an' forth to Damar City. But we figure we're better off lettin' Lord Tallin's people pass on through. We don't care to get on the wrong side of Tallinfolk."

"Why spare them of any others?" Ullin asked pointedly.

"Well, because," Makeig shrugged, "in the first place they ain't never done us no harm. An' in the second place, I ain't heard of nobody crossin' Lord Tallin an' havin' long to brag on it. Ye seen that feller what brought up the summons. He's in with them western Faerefolk, as ye of all should know. Them Elifaen are a stern lot with arrows an' steel, an' I ain't never seen one of 'em that warn't the match of any five of us. Why, one time, back when I was capt'n of the Golden Swallow (that was the name of me ship), I seen a single ship-load of 'em come into Spargers Bay, right up in the midst of a ragin' battle. They took to the docks, fought their way up the hill to the villa of the Prince Lewtrah, took his family entire, fought their way back through town to the ship, the whole city burnin' to the ground around 'em. An' then they made off with their rescue, neat as a pin, not a lost man amongst 'em nor a hair touched on Prince Lewtrah, nor his wife. Them was a Glareth lot of Elifaen, an' I hear them Tallinfolk take more after those ways than the ways of Men, which they mostly are."

All remained silent, and Makeig and the Blaney brothers felt uneasy at their statements.

"I was forgettin' meself, Master Ribbon, no offense was meant," Makeig said at last as Robby handed the pass back to him. "If any was taken, I sincerely regret it to ye an' yer cousin, here."

"No offense taken, on my part," said Robby.

"Nor on mine," added Ullin.

"But you present a mystery to me," Robby went on. "What doings my grandfather has with the Damar warlord would be an interesting one to unravel, if the chance presented itself."

"Well, be that as it may," Makeig replied. "I still think the best thing for ye would be to come back here to town, an' then go west. Movin' up through Damar country's bound to stir trouble. An' I gather ye don't want attention, neither. If them Damar was to get wind of where it is yer bound for, they ain't likely to let it go. I don't imagine they want the eye of Duinnor cast this way."

"Whether we pass this way or not can only be decided after we learn what there is to learn at Tallinvale," said Ashlord. "But the hour is late, and we are all tired."

"Course ye are! We got plenty of bunks right here. Room for all!" Makeig said.

They thanked the Blaney brothers who, like themselves, needed sleep, and soon the company was shown to washrooms and a barracks room with a dozen cots lining two walls. Sheila chose a cot near the far side of the room, while Ibin flung himself down on the nearest one, creaking and groaning under his great weight. The others settled quietly, and Makeig said his good-nights. Ashlord sat down on a cot near the door and propped himself up against the wall to light his pipe. Robby, the last in bed, blew out the candle and settled down next to Sheila. For a while, he watched Ashlord's face glow at each puff of the pipe, the strange man's black eyes glittering from the dark shadow of his face. Soon Robby's own eyes were closed, and he wondered no longer about Ashlord's habits.

Chapter 4

Ullin's Tale and Robby's Dream

Day 86
159 Days Remaining

They rose very early, and after a good breakfast at the tavern they set off with Makeig riding along as far as the east gate of the town. There he stopped and wished them well, bidding them to come back through Hill Town if at all possible, and promising his aid to those in Janhaven. Soon after, they were winding their way into the sunrise and between the hills, making south and east by a narrow path through the forest. They spoke little and rode as fast as they could, taking no breaks for water or to rest the horses. The day turned bright, but the still air never lost its midmorning cool and, on this second day since leaving Janhaven, they were for the first time truly on their own. Ullin led the way, with Ashlord behind him and then Ibin and the pack animals, followed by Billy and Sheila, with Robby at the rear. He wondered about those they had left behind in Janhaven and how they would fare, and he hoped that his father, wherever he was, was safe. And he pondered what he had gotten his friends into, thinking about the dangers ahead, and the warnings given by the Blaney brothers. After most of the morning riding in silence, and at a place where the path widened for a stretch, Sheila dropped back alongside of him.

"How are you?" she asked.

"Good. And you?"

"Well enough," she answered.

"Do you truly think that you fooled anyone back there?" Robby asked. "About being my bodyguard."

"All they had to do was to try me," Sheila retorted with a smirk. "I'm thinking it's better not to be too much in the trusting way."

"I don't guess you've had the best experiences with men," Robby nodded.

"It's not that," she replied. "I do not judge all men by the cut of a few. You and the rest of our friends are who I hold to be the real examples of men."

"Oh? Then why all the pretending at Hill Town if you are not afraid?"

"I did not say I wasn't afraid. I fear men and women alike. I pretend because any weakness perceived in us is a strike against you."

"Hm. Well, I don't see how pretending to be what you are not would show strength. And you are as strong and able as any of us here."

"Maybe so in some ways," she said. "But men and women think differently, as you well know. Among men, many things are left alone or just accepted, things that would provoke comment, or at least attention, when found in a woman. Well do I know, my whole life being the testament, that to gain a man's respect as an equal is a hard thing for a woman to do, and, once had, it is ever in the earning, it seems to me."

"You are probably right," Robby said. He and Sheila had often talked about such things, and they knew their opinions were closely akin. "I dare not gainsay you on that. But it seems to me that it is sometimes better to be underestimated by the proud and haughty, than to make a show on their terms."

"Sour the vinegar or sweet the pie," Sheila nodded, "as the apple falleth into the pot. Or so Frizella would say. It just depends on the situation, that's all. And anyway, I think that Drayworth fellow nearly made me. No telling what he might have done!"

"Yes, quite the rake. I saw him talking to you at the table while I was at the bar with Sally."

At the mention of Robby's acquaintance, Sheila fell silent and looked ahead at the others with a blank face.

"I hope we will not become like Sally and her people," Sheila said. "Making some home away from our homeland. Or like the Elifaen of Vanara who are cheated from theirs."

Robby nodded, and Sheila fell back behind him as the path narrowed. Their way was one of steady descent, and when they came onto a roadway, Ullin led them to the right. At last they were able to ride alongside each other with greater ease, and soon Billy and Ibin were engaged in a rather one-sided chat, as were so many of their conversations, with Billy holding forth on the merits and drawbacks of riding as opposed to those of walking.

"An' it seems to me, ol' boy," he was saying, "whilst horses may indeed be faster overall than walkin', a man can ever trust his legs to carry him whar he aims 'em, if ever thar be strength in 'em. Howsoever, a horse's apt to canter off this way an' that, an' even spring to full gallopin' all of a lark, like, bouncin' the hapless rider wherever he may be borne."

Ibin nodded, fascinated.

"Now as for me, I hold with usin' horses, mules, donkeys, asses, an' even oxen to bear a burden far an' wide so long as the road be sure an' familiar-like. It's these here unknown ways what's liable to get a man thrown." Here Billy waved his arm around in a knowing way with a look of serious caution on his face. "An' if it warn't for such a long way to go, an' much to carry, we'd be better off, surely, at the pace of our own legs."

"You wouldn't think so if we met up with bandits, Redvests, Dragon People, mad elves, capering lions, or cold water up to your chest," said Ashlord, barely turning his head around toward Billy.

"Yeah, Billy, whatif, whatif, whatifwehadtorunfromalion,Billy? Whatif, whatifwecameontosome, ontosomemadelves?"

"Well, in them cases, a horse may be just the thing, I do admit," Billy conceded. "But, they ain't no mad elves for miles, I'll warrant, an' they ain't probably been no lions in these parts ever."

"Ihopenot, Billy, Isure, Isure, Isurehopenot. I'm, I'm, I'mscaredoflions. I'mscaredofbears,too,andsnakesandwolvesandhornets. Igotstungbyahornetonce. Ithurt!"

"I got stung by a wolf, once," Robby said softly aside to Sheila. "It hurt, too!"

"AndBilly, Billy, Billy, listen, BillylistenI'mscared, I'mscaredofgalafronks,too. Ihategalafronks!"

"What? You hate what?" Sheila asked.

Robby and Billy both rolled their eyes.

"Galafronks," Robby told her.

"Galafronks? What on earth are those?"

He and Billy knew well enough all about Ibin's fear of galafronks, but before either could explain, Ibin twisted around in his saddle to call back to Sheila.

> *Galafronks, galafronks!*
> *Big as a house, small as a mouse,*
> *Brown and black and gray.*
> *Squeezing between the door-cracks*
> *Up between the floor-cracks*
> *As thin and flat as smoke are they!*
> *With iron-strong arms,*
> *And saucer-plate eyes*
> *They mumble their charms*
> *Through teeth like scythes*
> *To get you they come, rum duma-dums!*
> *Stomping their trollfeet like thunder, like drums.*
> *Galafronks, galafronks, shadows and dust!*
> *Galafronks, galafronks, gristle and rust!*
> *Rude little girls they love to boil*
> *With beetles and spiders and bugs.*
> *And bad little boys they like to broil*
> *With maggots and leeches and slugs!*

Billy and Robby added their voices to the last four lines and the two of them laughed heartily while Ibin looked blankly from one to the other. Sheila smiled, shaking her head at them. At last, when their mirth had subsided, Ibin turned straight in his saddle and looked sternly ahead, his bottom lip jutting out.

"It's not funny," he stated.

The roadway widened and steadied downward out of the foothills with only a few sharp turns, and the more they went along, the more Robby wondered if this was the same road his father used years earlier to cart grain to the Tallin place.

"This is the north road from our lands," Ullin said, as if reading Robby's thoughts. "It joins by forks and turns behind us eventually to the Great South Road that leads to Passdale, a ride of three days along that route. These roads have never seen much coming or going, but Tallinvale maintains them, nonetheless. These columns we come upon mark the beginning of Tallinvale lands."

Robby looked at the round columns as they passed, set on either side of the road almost like gateposts. They had no writing carved into them, but each was capped with a verdigris cone of aged copper and at the point of each cone sat a small unlit brazier. Now that the way was easier, their pace naturally quickened, and they covered many miles through the forest without break until noontime had long passed and mid-afternoon was yielding to cooler air. The forest thinned, and after a few climbing turns of the road, fields appeared, newly shorn of crops, the cornstalks neatly stacked and tied into standing bundles, and only a few distant fieldworkers were seen. Rounding a bend, they suddenly found themselves entering a small village of neatly rowed cottages and workshops.

"This place is called Bluepine. There is a tavern up ahead, if you care to stop," Ullin told Ashlord. "Nothing fancy, but the ale used to be passing fair, and the horses could use some water."

"Yes," Ashlord nodded. "If it were not for the horses I would have us push on. But rider and ridden both need refreshment, I think. And my backside could use a stretch."

There was a fair amount of curiosity on the faces of the people they passed, not unfriendly, but rightly cautious of six armed horsemen. Deference was paid to Ullin, sometimes with bows and touching of heads as he passed, and Robby realized this behavior was directed not at Ullin himself, but at his uniform and bearing. Indeed, as Robby watched from just behind him, Ullin seemed a lordly figure compared to his companions. Such a man—dressed in cloth cut for a Kingsmen of Duinnor, and in company with such a striking figure as Ashlord at his side—certainly must be a rare appearance, Robby thought. He thought, too, that he had taken much for granted, and though they were only Ullin and Ashlord to him, kinsman and friend, he saw now an aspect of nobility about them that he had never really noticed before.

Ullin turned them aside at the far end of the village, past a staring blacksmith, hammer raised in mid-stroke, and a woman who was quickly herding several young children out of the yard and into the doorway of a cottage, closing it hard behind them. The tavern would have been unrecognizable as such if it had not been for a hitching rail and water trough and a sign swinging over the door that professed it to be the Blue Tree. Otherwise, it was like most any other cottage, except it had wooden shingles instead of fernleaf thatch. No sooner than they dismounted and were hitching their horses than a middle-aged man, round and bald, came running across the road past them and on through the door of the tavern without so much as a nod. As Ullin approached the door, it swung open again and there the man stood, a bit out of breath, struggling to don an apron.

"Greetings! Greetings, noble travelers!" he said proudly as he ushered them inside. His face was red with enthusiasm, and, as he spoke, he kicked chairs into place and swept clouds of dust from tables with a rag, trying to manage straightening, cleaning, greeting, bowing, and talking all at the same time.

"Welcome to the Blue Tree! Finest ale an' coolest beer this side of Tallinvale. Forgive that chair, I'll move it. Yes, we're open, open are we. Watch that tub thar, I got it. Yes, just the thing for weary travelers, for not a penny more than worth!"

It was a modest establishment, obviously not expecting them, or anyone else, and the proprietor and the six travelers quickly filled the small space.

"Marly!" the man called loudly out through an open back door, and a small child immediately appeared beside him.

"Yes, Papa?"

"Food or drink for ye gentlemen? Marly! Just have a seat anywhars."

"Yes, Papa?"

"Make yerself comfortable. Marly! No don't sit thar, sir. Bad leg that chair has, been meanin' to fix it. Marly!"

"Yes, Papa!" the child at last got hold of the apron and tugged hard.

"Marly, whar've ye been, girl? Run over to Mrs. Chulwinkie's an' fetch ye mother. Tell her we've got company an' to get the stove fire goin'."

"Yes, Papa!"

"Wait! We only want a drink before moving on," Ullin tried to say.

"Nonsense! Ye look famished, if ye pardon me sayin', good sir. Run along, Marly."

"No, no. Just beer," Robby confirmed.

"No food," Ullin stated. "We must move on as soon as the horses have had a rest."

"Nofood?" asked Ibin.

"No food?" repeated the proprietor. "Well, surely, ye ain't come all the way from Duinnor just for a beer? Though many's the one who've traveled just to put a pint of me own brew in him! Good enough for any Kingsman, too. Made of the finest Barley barley, an' me brother's own hops, it is, as always has been! Kept cool in the spring house out back right up 'til the sippin'. No taps in here, no siree. So! What'll it be? We got brown ale, golden ale, an' a good stout."

"None of that," Ullin said. "We'll all have a pint of your spring house beer."

"Ah, I see yer no stranger, after all. Or ye've heard far an' wide, I suppose, of me beer."

"I've told of it far and wide," Ullin grinned. "But in fact, I am a personal friend to your beer and have been since I was no higher than the back of that chair."

"Ye don't say!"

"I do. And many's the time ye've thrown me out, along with my friends."

By now the man was squinting hard into Ullin's face, and even took out a pair of spectacles to have a closer look. Suddenly an expression of shock overcame him, and he went red-faced as he gasped.

"Oh, Master Ullin! Er, Lord Ullin, I mean. Forgive me for not knowin' ye," he bowed low. "I've gotten to be such a fool in me old age."

"No, no. None of that," Ullin raised the man up by the shoulders. "I am just a Kingsman, now, Mr. Deedle. Was that one of your granddaughters?"

"Oh no, that's me great-granddaughter, that was. But let me fetch out the pitchers an' haul up some beer!"

The pitchers came soon enough, foamy and full, and Mr. Deedle's grandchild helped put out tankards as the elder poured.

"Don't get a lot of travelers. Never have. Mostly just local folk an' folk from down Tallintown-way," he said to them. "An', ever once in a while, folk from Hill Town."

"What news of the Hall?" Ashlord asked.

"Things go on as they always have, I reckon," Mr. Deedle said as he wiped his hands on his apron. "I've seen more riders an' Talliners soldierin' about this past year or so, though they seldom stop by. Most of the menfolk been called into the ranks, to report after they've got the harvests in, an' some say thar's war to the east an' west an' south."

"And to the north," Ullin said. "Passdale and Barley were taken by invaders out of Tracia five days ago."

"Lo! Ye don't say! Oh, dear! I've a cousin over in Barley, a Bosklander, name of Mumpas. Garv Mumpas."

"Then we're kin," said Billy. "I'm Bilaylin Bosk. I know Garv, but I ain't seen him since the attack. I warn't thar at Boskland when the Redvests came, so I can't say what might've happened to him."

"Oh dear, oh dear! An' he's got a family, too!"

"I'm sorry we bring you bad news," Ullin said. "Many made it away, most to Janhaven. Perhaps you will hear from your cousin soon."

"So yer makin' for Tallin Hall?"

"Yes."

84

"To ask for help?"

They looked at each other, but Ullin shook his head.

"No. I doubt if much help will be offered, and we do not go to ask."

Mr. Deedle looked around the group, some standing, some sitting, and he nodded, picking up an empty pitcher.

"Ah, well, yer business, not mine. Redvests in Barley! That's purty close by, too," he said turning to fetch another pitcher, then, turning back, he said, "The day's gettin' on. Ye'll not make Tallin Hall before well after dark."

"We don't mean to," said Ullin. "We'll sleep out tonight, on along the way."

Mr. Deedle departed but returned just in time to refill the tankards.

"I don't think we'll be having another pot of beer," said Robby. "Will this cover us?"

He handed over several coins, and Mr. Deedle handed one back to Robby.

"Is it not to yer likin'?"

"Oh it is the finest beer ever," said Ashlord.

"Indeed!" agreed Robby.

"But we mean to move on."

"Yer welcome to stay as long as ye like," Mr. Deedle said. "We can find ye lodgin' for the night easy enough, if ye don't mind being put up in various places."

"No, thank you kindly. We'll be off in just a bit. I especially wanted my friends to taste your sweet beer."

Sweet and refreshing it was, too, golden-yellow and cold, and soon their second pints were gone, and they were riding away, with Mr. Deedle, and now his wife, as round and jolly as he, waving them off and bidding them good journeys.

Indeed, the day was nearly spent and after an hour or so, the sun was well behind the trees and the coolness of the evening was already descending. The road took them past many fields, dotted with cottages, and then upward into a deep wood.

"We can safely camp anywhere in these woods," Ullin told them. "Though I think we can go for another hour before it gets too dark to see our way, and I know a good place to stop."

The shady wood seemed gloomy compared to the open fields and sun, but their spirits were still high from the beer and also from being together. Troubles might be before them, and certainly they left many behind, but for now they all seemed content to do just what they were doing, so long as they could be doing it together. So they rode along at a good easy pace, enjoying the day and the peace of the surrounding forest.

• • •

"I still don't understand 'bout the Faere Folk," said Billy to Ullin. "I mean, why are they sometimes called elf, sometimes called Elifaen, an' other times Faere, an' so forth? Ain't they all the same?"

"Yes, mostly. It is simple," Ullin explained. "The Faerekind are first. They inhabited the world when it was still being formed. And they were made by the gods to be the embodied spirits of all good things, of sunlight and cool water, of stone and branch, root and vine. When the Dragon People appeared—no one knows whence—some of the Faerekind decided to take up arms and to fight them. The gods watched with dismay, but they did nothing as the Faerekind forged iron into steel and made their swords and arrows and bows and shields. When they formed themselves into armies, some of the Faerekind pleaded with the others, saying that war was not their way. And the gods listened to them and were aroused, and they offered the Faerekind a way to depart the woes and conflicts of the world. Many accepted the offer and departed from the world. Those of the Faerekind who refused to go out of the world, or who still had war in their hearts, were stripped of their wings and were cursed and called Elifaen, meaning the Fallen Ones. Still, cursed though they might have been, the Elifaen clung as much as they could to their ways, to the Faere spirit still within them that connected them all to one another and to the world and all the things that happen in the world, for good or ill. That spirit has faded out of them, for the most part. And they are still called the Faere People, though some hold that is not proper respect to those who departed. Later, when Men came to these shores, they began to call the Elifaen by a shorter name: Elf. And so it came about to be as it is today."

"But are you not Elifaen, yourself?" asked Sheila.

"No, I am not, though my father and my grandmother were. Man and Elf may conceive, but of the mixed unions, only those where the mother is Elifaen may bear Elifaen children, children who inherit the immortal qualities of the mother, including the curse laid upon all their kind. My mother was mortal and so, though my father was Elifaen from his mother, I am not."

"The curse?" asked Billy.

"So the children of mortal women and Elifaen males are mortal?" Sheila asked before Billy could pursue his question.

"That is so. Very few are born to such unions, but, even though the children are of the race of Men, they sometimes do inherit long life by the union."

"The curse?" asked Billy again.

"The mortal offspring are not cursed, and so do not bear the mark of the Fallen Ones on their backs."

"Oh."

"Needless to say," added Ashlord, "much tension and discord arises from both such unions. On the one hand, an Elifaen husband of a mortal cannot see his lineage carry on, except as mortals who may perish long before their sire. On the other hand, the Elifaen wife of a mortal supplants Men with her kind, sometimes to the ending of the man's surname and his lineage. Yet, mortals who marry Elifaen may be but one of many spouses, over the course of their mate's long and immortal life. They tend to be very jealous, these mortals, of their position and that of their children, if they have any. So the House of Fairoak, joined to the Tallins, is a very unusual family. Only a very powerful love could hope to overcome the inevitable strife and prejudice that would ensue."

"Ye mean between Robby an' Ullin's grandparents?"

"Yes. It was a passionate courtship that brought about their marriage. Lord Tallin was a brilliant and dashing soldier. A great general. It is said he won Lady Kahryna's heart by deed and gallantry on the battlefield, and by wit and charm in court. Is that not so, Ullin?"

"Yes. That is the gist of the story. And my grandmother had many Elifaen suitors, I have been told," Ullin said. "So I suppose her selection of my grandfather over all others was quite scandalous."

"So Robby's immortal? His mother is Elifaen, ain't she?" asked Billy, forgetting his earlier question.

Ullin glanced back at Robby, at the rear near Ibin.

"There are so few from such unions that no one may be sure," said Ullin. "Many males of such unions have died in battle, and there are very few females born. Mirabella is indeed of the Faere blood. She is this very month seventy-seven years of Men."

"Naw! Ye don't say! An' she don't even look half that!"

"But wait," interrupted Sheila. "I thought your grandfather was or is mortal. Yet, he still lives."

"Yes, he is one hundred and twenty years old. It is a strange thing, a blessing some say, but a man who has children by union with the Elifaen ceases to age as other men do. Some say not at all, but that is not true. I have seen the changes brought by age in my grandfather, Lord Tallin, that others might not perceive. And Robby's father is just beginning to gray, though he is fifty-two years, and he looks very much the same as he did when Robby was born. A bit heavier, perhaps. Mortal women are not always touched with long life as is given to men. Yet another cause of some resentment."

"So a mortal woman does not often conceive a child by union with an Elifaen male?" asked Sheila thoughtfully, falling back as she pondered.

"Oh, she may conceive," Ashlord replied softly, slowing his mount alongside hers. "She will not likely give birth, though. At least, very few have. Some say the gods are against such unions, yet that they, at rare times, do grant children who survive and are healthy. Ullin, here, is an example of such an exception, for his mother was mortal. Such children are hard for a woman to carry unto birth."

"Few have," she repeated. She turned her head to look back at Robby with an expression of confusion and concern on her face.

"I know what you are thinking, my dear," Ashlord said to her. "It is not your fault, and the gods are not against you. It is not the fault of Robby or any curse laid upon him, nor is it the fault of the child that would have been."

"But—"

"It was a vile man who took your child, one made the worse by drink and the influence of someone even more despicable than he," Ashlord told her firmly. Then he smiled. "And when I say that few have given birth in such a union, I speak of the past. Robby's hope, and yours, is in the future. You can only be guided by the past, not led by it."

"What are you saying?"

"Only that there are many mysteries to be solved. Curses, wives tales, and prophecies all have their day. Some come into light by reason, others remain concealed from our understanding, while still others are overturned, cast off, and forgotten. Whether they are fulfilled or thwarted is often a matter of the will and determination of people rather than the will of the gods."

"Then what good are the gods?" Sheila said in frustration.

Ashlord nodded and chuckled, "Sometimes even I wonder."

"So how do ye tell the difference," Billy was asking Ullin, " 'tween a mortal an' an Elifaen who ain't gone through the change yet?"

"You can't. Even the Elifaen can't tell them apart. The only difference in appearance between Elifaen and mortals are the scars upon the Elifaen's back. Otherwise, they look like everyone else. So, until a person goes through the Scathing, when the scars of the Elifaen form, they are not truly Elifaen."

"Hmm. That's very interestin'," Billy nodded deeply. He glanced at Ibin and shrugged, shaking his head. "I reckon."

Ullin turned his horse and led his party off the road and onto a path into the woods and uphill. It was a narrow track and wound past great oaks, forcing them to dismount to walk under the low branches. When they reached the heights, he showed them to a hilltop clearing ringed around its crest by the ancient stones of some long decayed structure. It was flat and grassy, and a good place to camp, and as the sun set behind the west mountains, they could see Tallinvale for the first time, stretching out in the distance to the south, a broad valley of forests and fields, and of lakes and streams.

"It's so beautiful!" Sheila said. "Like a dream."

"What is that glint, way off there to the southeast?" Robby asked pointing.

"The spires of Tallin Hall, a few leagues away," Ullin said.

"I'mhungry!" said Ibin.

"Then I suggest we make a fire and see what is in those packs," laughed Ashlord.

Soon enough a fire was going, blankets were spread, and a pot was hanging by a tripod with potatoes, carrots, and onions, along with some coined sausage, boiling away in a brown broth. Ashlord and Billy studiously watched after it while Ullin and Ibin took care of the horses and saddles. Robby and Sheila had already laid by a large stack of wood for the fire and were bringing a last load as Ibin and Ullin returned to the campfire as well.

"Doyou, doyou, doyouhavemagicalpowers?" Ibin asked Ullin.

"Ibin!" Billy hissed, shaking his head. The others were a little embarrassed, but said nothing since they were as intensely interested in the answer as Ibin. Ullin chuckled.

"None that I know of," he said, squatting nearby to smell the pot. "Though some say my ability to sense danger is uncanny."

"What? Yer hair stands on end, like?" Billy asked.

"Indeed. Yes, that happens," Ullin said thoughtfully. "It is more like a mood that comes with no reason, sometimes very suddenly, getting stronger. Over the years, I have been taught—and I have learned from my days of fighting in the west—ways of reading the signs of danger. Sounds, tracks, and so forth. But this mood, this feeling, is something other than that, something that can't be read, as a track on the ground might be or the nervousness of birds or horses. The first time I remember it happening was when I was a small lad."

Sensing they were in the mood for a story, he continued.

• • •

"After my father died, my mother and I moved away from Tallinvale and went to Glareth by the Sea. I was seven or eight, and I was very unhappy. I'm afraid I got into a lot of trouble, was disrespectful of my elders, my mother especially, and cared little for my school work. I suppose I missed my friends back in Tallinvale, and I missed my father, too, even though I was so little when I last saw him that I barely remembered him."

Ullin situated his saddle on the ground near the fire and stretched out to recline on it, pulling a twig out from under him and tossing it into the fire. The others sat around, listening, while Ashlord continued to stir the pot of stew.

"There was a tidal pool close to where I lived, and one day a few other boys and I snuck off from school to go swimming there. After a long afternoon of playing and swimming about in the water, the mood came upon me for the first time. I suddenly wanted to get away, though I couldn't say why. I threw a terrible fit when my friends would not leave with me. I began to panic, such was the fear that gripped me. I begged and pleaded with the other boys for us to go back home, but they only laughed at me. Although I did not want to walk home alone, I became so worked up with desperation that I abandoned them. Oh, they jeered, calling me a crybaby and so forth. As soon as I got on the path home, my fear only grew worse, and I ran all the way, a league or more, crying and screaming as I ran. When my mother saw me coming, she instantly knew something was terribly amiss, though I was in such a state that I could not say what it was, even if there were words for the dread that had overcome me. She quickly got enough out of me to immediately take a party of neighbors on horseback to look for the other boys. They found only one of the three lads, cowering in the rushes at the edge of the water. He was in such fear that he could say very little, except that the other lads had been taken away. Soon a larger party of men arrived and began searching. They searched for weeks, but no sign or hint of what had taken the boys was ever found. They questioned and questioned me, but, as I told them, I saw nothing at all to cause me to have such panic, and I couldn't explain why I acted as I did."

"A bar, mebbe! Er else, a wild boar!" exclaimed Billy. "Or mebbe some great serpent comin' up on 'em."

"Maybe. Afterwards, I became even more unruly than ever, and I begged my mother to let me go back home to Tallinvale. She eventually did so. And, for the most part, once I was back in Tallinvale with my old friends, I was happy. Meanwhile, the boy that I told you about, the one found hiding in the rushes, he never regained his wits. He was eventually shut away by his family because of his ravings, and he became unwilling or unable to tend to his most basic needs. I went to see him, once, some years ago. Somehow, he recognized me immediately and was overjoyed at the sight of me, hugging me and holding my hand the whole while. He asked me—the first words, I was told, that he had spoken clearly for twenty years—he asked about the other lads and how they were doing."

Ullin shook his head and shrugged.

"I lied. Told him they were fine, living far away. That made him very happy. Three weeks later, he died."

"Lo!" Billy said softly.

The fire crackled and night settled suddenly around the camp, and no one said a word for a few moments.

"Tell me, how is your mood these days?" Robby asked, trying to smile.

"The same as it has been these many years," Ullin replied. "Though some days are better than others. I was worried the day the Redvests came into Barley through the Boggy Wood, but I paid little heed to it, thinking that I was nervous about other things. When Billy was kidnapped, I thought that was it, the reason for the mood. Who knows? Just because I have a mood does not mean I know why it comes."

There was another long silence as the group considered his tale. Ashlord looked at Ullin blankly, who shrugged back a silent apology for his depressing story.

"How many wars have there been with the Dragonkind?" Sheila asked.

"Many," Ashlord said. "Some short, some long. Ibin, break up some bread and pass it around. I'll ladle this out. The first war was when the Faere fell, sometimes called the War of Kalzar and Cupeldain. That was during the Time Before Time. In the First Age, there were many wars. The same has been true of this age. The Dragonkind invaded twice, the last time when Tulith Attis fell, over five hundred years ago. And twice in this age there have been large invasions by Men and Elifaen into the deserts. In between, there have been brief periods of peace and truce. There have always been skirmishes and clashes. Some say the first war, the War of Kalzar and Cupeldain, which started it all, still goes on."

"What do you say?" asked Ullin, accepting a bowl from Ashlord who shrugged.

"I say it does continue, from the time of the Fall of the Faere. People seldom resolve their differences until they see that it is in their interest to do so. And even then it is difficult. Peace requires a greater valor than war, the valor to lay aside pride, to resist retribution, and it requires the courage to forgive. I think we are coming once more into a time of great strife. But also," he smiled at Robby, "perhaps a time of great hope."

"The Dragonfolk, Redvests, warlords, an unwillin' Duinnor, an' some unknown place we mean to go to, right through the middle of all that," stated Billy. "Very hopeful, indeed!"

Ullin smiled. "You're as glum as an elf!"

"I thought elves were a merry folk," said Sheila.

"You have not known many of the Elifaen," put in Ashlord, handing her a steaming bowl.

"Well, then, you're one to say so," she said back to Ullin. "After your gloomy story!"

Ullin nodded, but said nothing.

"I'm sorry," she immediately said. "That was thoughtless of me."

Ullin shrugged.

"Ullin is a fair judge of gloom," Ashlord said so that only Sheila could hear. "As are you, somewhat."

Sheila did not look at Ashlord, or at anyone else, and took another small sip of the broth. Pondering Ashlord's mild rebuke, she placed it down carefully and stood.

"Please excuse me," she said, and she went to her bedroll and made it ready. Then, still in thought, she went to the horses, to give them a little petting. Robby watched her, knowing that she still mourned, that she still suffered from rebuke and rejection, from years of having no friends and little help. In Robby's mind, it was as if the beatings of Steggan continued. He was somewhat amazed that the goodness of her heart still endured, in spite of her years of torment, and even though that torment continued. Robby turned back and caught Ashlord looking across the fire at him. Ashlord turned his attention back to the pot, a mild smile crossing his lips, as Robby wondered about the mystic's influence on Sheila, about the profound change in her, her speech, her bearing, her patience. In so many ways, and in spite of what Sheila often said, Robby felt as if it was she, and not he, who was the worthier person.

• • •

Soon their supper was finished, and, satisfied with their meal and feeling the wear of the day upon them, they bundled into their bedrolls for the night. It was agreed that Ullin would take the first watch and each would be awakened for their turn as it came. Billy was soon settled, and Ibin was snoring gently nearby. Sheila made her bed against Robby, some distance from the fire, while Ashlord sat and smoked his pipe and stared at the flames, eyes squinting, but with a flickering gleam showing. Ullin moved away to the promontory and sat on a stone, gazing at a faint glimmer from distant Tallin Hall before the evening mist settled into the valley and obscured the light. Still, the stars shown brightly overhead, and Ullin watched their movements, hearing nothing more threatening than a night bird's song and the chirp of crickets. Only once was he startled at the nearby flutter of wings, but, turning quickly, he saw a little shape land on Ashlord's shoulder.

So Ullin's watch passed easily and peacefully, as would each of the other's in turn. Ibin and Billy would share the next, followed by Sheila, and the last watch was to be Robby's. Each spent their time in quiet and watchful contemplation under the starry sky, and the troubles of the world, before and behind them, seemed just as distant and detached. As Ibin and Billy chatted in low indiscernible tones, Robby and Sheila snuggled together, he more uncomfortable than she on the hard ground. But after only a little tossing and pulling the blankets back and forth against the chilly air, they both fell asleep, she to dark dreams oft-repeated, and he with mixed images of his father passing through a misty wood and his mother sitting in their parlor back in Passdale. After those visions passed, both fell into the deepest slumber, without disturbance of mind or heart. It was after a long while that Robby mentally stirred, a strange feeling overcoming him, and he found himself standing up, staring across the low burning embers of the fire at Ashlord, who puffed gently on his pipe without taking notice of him. Blinking, Robby rubbed his eyes, trying to get at the sand that strangely blurred his vision. As his vision seem to clear, an odd light illuminated all, yet the moon was too low behind the western hill to be the source, and the low fire gave only a sparse reddish glow. A shape moved on the ground to the left of the fire, in the corner of his vision, and he turned and saw Ullin stirring under a blanket. Between Robby and the fire slept Billy and Ibin, and beyond Ashlord was the distinct shape of Sheila sitting some distance away on the ground at the promontory. He felt lightheaded and almost airy. He had no sense of fear or danger, but things did not seem quite right, and he was filled with a bewildered concern. Taking a step toward Sheila, a falling, lunging sensation overwhelmed him. He threw his arms out to catch himself, but no sooner than he reacted than he found himself standing right beside her, two dozen yards away just a heartbeat ago. Blinking away a dizzy spell, his heart began to thump.

"Am I drunk?" he asked himself out loud. His voice surprised him as it shattered the stillness. Sheila did not stir. She sat easily, staring at the distant horizon where bright Therepolon, the yellow wanderer, was hanging low over the dim valley.

"Sheila," he said. Still she did not stir. As he so often was, he was struck by her beauty, and he reached out to touch her and to brush away the hair that fell across her brow. He stopped, aghast at the appearance of his own hand, for it was glowing with a pale blue light, rippling like water across his skin. Raising his palm to his face and turning his hand back and forth, he was nearly spellbound by the light. Suddenly, his perception cleared even more, the glow disappeared, and his own flesh and all else gained their natural colors.

Sensing a movement, Robby turned abruptly and saw Ashlord, who was now staring toward him, but as if he was looking through him, not at him. Ashlord shifted his gaze back to the fire. Robby began to realize what was happening. His heart thumped nervously, and he looked across the fire toward where he had first stood. There he saw a shape on the ground, bundled in blankets. Quickly he counted his mates and missed none. Wondering who the stranger was, yet fearful of knowing, he made to approach. After another brief sensation of falling—this time akin to sliding rapidly forward—he stood over the sleeper. Cautiously, he reached down to pull the blankets from around the face, but as he did so, he felt a queer sensation of fabric rub across his cheeks and that of butterfly-wings fluttering across his eyes and nose. His heart skipped as he saw his own face. At that very moment he sensed another form standing a few feet away. As he turned to this new figure, he seemed to lose consciousness and a profound dizziness overcame him.

"Wake up!"

Robby struggled to throw off the hands that pulled at his blanket. Sitting up with a jerk, he stared into the astonished face of Sheila, recoiling from him, on her knees beside him and holding the edge of his blanket.

"It is time for your watch, Robby," she said in a low voice. "Are you alright?"

Robby rubbed his eyes, saying, "Yes, yes. Just dreaming."

"Well, it's my turn to dream for awhile," she said. "And I'll have your warm blankets, if you don't mind."

They kissed, and Robby put his arms around her to draw her down to him, but she resisted.

"You must stand watch, and I must sleep!" she scolded him tenderly.

"Yes, yes," he answered, struggling to his feet. "Yes, alright. I know."

He stood and stretched as Sheila took his place. Ashlord was still sitting before the fire, his eyes still open, and Certina was perched on his shoulder, preening. Ashlord absentmindedly sucked on a long-cold pipe, but never moved his gaze from the dwindling fire. Robby added a little more fuel, being careful not to disturb the mystic. So, taking up his duties, he walked around the camp, listening and watchful, quickly growing accustomed to the peace and quiet, still wondering about his strange dream. The dream that seemed something other than a dream. He remembered what the Dragonkind woman, Micerea, had told him, *"All creatures have this power. They need only to find it."*

During the first hour or so of his watch, he tried to shake the strange dream from his thoughts, its odd sensations lingering in his heart. But then a peaceful mood came to him just as it had with the others who had their watch before him. He slowly walked back to the promontory to gaze across the dark and misty valley, feeling apart from all happenings upon the earth. Yet, as he sat on the same stone that Ullin had earlier occupied, the place where Sheila had been just a little while ago, he felt also the weight of so much change happening so quickly. He wondered again whether those changes were only in the world, or within himself, too. He was still thinking on this a couple of hours later when Ullin rose from his sleep and approached.

"Good morning," Robby said to him.

"Morning."

"Is it time we were up?"

"I think so. It looks like a foggy dawn."

"Indeed, it was misty when I came on watch and now the land below is blanketed."

Robby had wrapped a cloak around himself to keep warm during his stint and now it was wet with dew.

"These mists are common to the valley," said Ullin. "You have never been here?"

"Once, but I do not remember it. I was only a baby, and my parents brought me to see Lord Tallin. To show off the new baby, I suppose. I don't guess it went very well."

"I imagine it went well enough," Ullin said, gazing at the shrouded valley. "Our grandfather is a hard one. Difficult to fathom. As you know, your mother was fairly banished when she and Robigor wed."

"Yes. I don't suppose my reception will be a warm one, then."

"Nor mine, I don't think, so you won't be alone in that, at least."

"Why is that?"

"I'm not sure," Ullin shook his head and sighed. "Too much heartbreak, perhaps. Too many harsh words, ill-considered and unkind. His. Mine."

"He did not want you to go to Duinnor?"

"No. He wanted me to go to Glareth and to enlist into the service of Ruling Prince Carbane. You see, by an act of Duinnor it was agreed that no one serving the Royal House of Glareth would be required to enter into service of Duinnor. But I refused. I was foolish, perhaps, but I wanted to take my father's place among the Kingsmen of Duinnor.

Perhaps to find vengeance against the Dragonkind for his death. Maybe I just wanted to be like him."

"And you said yesterday that your father's death was a mortal blow to your grandmother," Robby said.

"Yes, it was."

"Surely it was out of his fear for you that our grandfather wanted you to go to Glareth."

"Certainly. I admit that, now. But that was long ago, and things are the way they are, not as they might have been. We must make the best of what we cannot change. Besides, had I never gone to Duinnor, I may never have met Ashlord, and would probably not be with you now."

"Is that a good thing?"

Ullin laughed, "Of course! Now I have a chance to serve kith, kin, and King, too. Maybe even to help right old wrongs, if you turn out to be a good ruler."

Now Robby laughed, "Let's not get ahead of ourselves!"

Ullin laughed again and pulled Robby close by the shoulder.

"Why don't you rekindle the fire for a breakfast while I rouse the others and prepare the horses."

• • •

Soon, their hot breakfast of coffee, fried sausage, and potato hash, and an apple each was eaten, and their cookwares were cleaned and packed. All were anxious to be on their way, rested and in good spirits. After their first night on the ground, none of them were without aches, but, though there was much stretching and a little groaning, none of them complained. They knew this was only the first of many such nights to come. Ullin saw their stiffness and smiled.

"In the future, it may be better if you spent some time piling pine straw, fern thatch, or leaves into a mound to put your blankets on," he suggested. "It will make the ground somewhat softer and a great deal warmer."

Billy looked at Ullin, then at Robby.

"Now he tells us."

Chapter 5

An Uncomfortable Interview

Day 87
158 Days Remaining

They started out before sunrise and found their way back to the road for the final short leg. It remained misty, and the forest birds were waking from slumber even after the sun had risen, and the clop of hooves seemed a loud intrusion on the sleepy morning. The road carried them up and down gently, but they could see little in the gray air, and Robby could not tell if they climbed more than they descended. Even though the sky grew brighter, the cool air barely moved at all. They could sense occupation around them, smoke from kindled hearths, the clank of a harness being hitched away to the left, the closing of a door from somewhere ahead, and the cry of a distant cock. They passed a few cottages, attended by their owners, chopping wood outside, or drawing water, or taking out the chamber pots. All eyed the travelers suspiciously, but without greeting or challenge other than the occasional civil wave. The mists evaporated somewhat, and they could see a gentle rise before them, leading between two fields, and then more steeply upward through a sparse wood. Suddenly the way was open, and the road turned, curving downhill. There lay Tallinvale, a patchwork valley widening into the distance between bordering hills, plaid with lines and squares and other shapes. The fields directly below were crisscrossed with stone-laid canals feeding the neatly ordered fields and orchards as well as the moats bounding the city walls, less than a half-mile from the bluff where the company paused to look.

Tallin Hall with its graceful spires predated the walled city that surrounded it. They could see that the city was about a half mile or less from its center to each of the four walls that enclosed the town. The ramparts were of gray polished stone and on this, the north side, they loomed three stories high, topped with tall battlements. Where each wall joined one to another, a watchtower jutted up. Yet the graceful domes and spires of Tallin Hall, away on the far side of the city, stood in contrast to the stern city walls; it was a banner-bedecked structure of a light tan complexion, roofed in green copper, with ample windows of gleaming glass. Iron and stone balconies flew gracefully from its five spires and its highest stories. Four of the spires were at corners of the structure, slim turrets, topped with tapered roofs of green copper. The fifth, standing three times the diameter of the others and somewhat higher, was otherwise of the same design but located midway on the western side of the Hall.

It was a striking view, indeed, looking as they did from the wooded heights while the morning mists rose up over the fields. Here and there, the early golden sun broke the vapors apart, and a gentle breeze pushed them away so that the glint of glass and the fluttering of pennants on the battlements and spire-tops gave the place something of the inviting aspect that it must have once known in happier days when the Hall was full of children and laughter and song. Sir Sun, as if turning over in his bed after a sleepy look about, pulled the skyward sheets back up around his crown and disappeared once more into the pillowy mists. Thus, the scene returned to its somber if not sullen appearance, as if a great sigh was heaved after a brief happy thought.

"Home," Ullin said.

He dismounted.

"I think it would be better if Ashlord took lead of our company while we are here," he said. "I am a King's soldier, and here, though I be kin and kith, I should expect no rank or station other than that of my Duinnor commission. In truth, I do not know what to expect in the way of greeting or hospitality."

Ashlord nodded as Ullin led his horse aside and, with long practice, rechecked his cinches and straps as he did every time he dismounted.

"Even though we do not come here to meet Lord Tallin, we must present ourselves before him, as is customary and courteous," Ashlord said to the group. "You may as well know that Lord Tallin is a brooding and somewhat resentful man these last many years. It has been a long time—well before your father's time, Robby—since visitors to Tallin Hall received much welcome. Though the hospitality shown to us will be correct, it will likely be somewhat cool. I beg you, do not speak to Lord Tallin or any of his counselors or courtiers unless they bid you do so. And then, keep your answers short. He is a shrewd man. If he desires, he will have more out of you than would be wise to reveal. I will speak for us when I may. Those we are to meet here may be his guests, but we cannot know on what terms they may be here. And we should not presume that Lord Tallin knows any of their business with Robby. Let us hope we meet with Lord Tallin first, while we ourselves are innocent of that business, rather than afterwards when we may be indiscreet."

"Do you know who it is that asked us here?" Sheila queried.

"I have guessed, but I have no certainty," Ashlord told her. "And, remember, it was Robby who was bid come. The rest of us were not asked and may not be expected. Whoever it is that invited Robby may not wish us to be there. We will just have to see what unfolds."

Ashlord nudged his horse onward, Ullin remounted, and they followed after, descending onto the valley floor and through a high vine-covered iron archway. The road led them through fields, orchards and vineyards, bearing straight through the center of the valley, toward the north gate of the city. They crossed over narrow stone bridges that spanned the network of canals. Looking down into one as he crossed, Robby was surprised at how deep it appeared, the water dark and slow-moving, the stone sides of the same gray polished granite, laid without mortar, as the city walls. It would be nigh impossible to climb out, he thought, if one were unlucky enough to fall in. The short bridges were also made of the same stone, each laid across an arched span. Jutting out of each span was an iron bar that extended into the side of the canal.

"What are those iron bars for?" he asked, pointing to a bridge not far away that was parallel to the one they were crossing. "Do they help support the bridges?"

"No," Ullin answered. "Quite the contrary. These canals bring water to the surrounding fields, but they also defend the town. The keystone of each bridge is attached to the end of one such bar as you see there. It is laid underground through a small tunnel. By a series of bars laid end to end through the small tunnels, they run back to the interior of the city walls. There, over the end of each run of bars, is poised a huge hanging hammer that will, when released, drive the bar and knock out the keystone, thereby collapsing the bridge. The other bridges, like the one over there, see it? They are made of wood. They are built so that the farmers may easily cross at various places to tend the orchards and fields, but they can be easily taken up if need be."

"Oh."

"Yes, an ingenious design copied from Heneil himself," Ullin went on. "He was one of the greatest builders, especially concerning fortifications. No stronghold built by his hand and manned by willing defenders has ever fallen."

" 'Cept Tulith Attis," Billy said.

"He did not build that place," Ashlord corrected him. "Only the inner chambers and workings. And it was by treachery, not by skill at arms, that Tulith Attis fell."

"Oh. But these canals ain't very wide. Wouldn't ye just have to fill up the canals with rocks an' stones an' stuff?" Billy asked. "Make yer own bridge across, so to speak?"

"That is ever pointed out to Lord Tallin," nodded Ullin. "But he always replies the same, 'Let them try.' "

"Sounds like famous last words, Ullin. Has Tallinvale ever been attacked?" Sheila asked.

"Never yet."

At the next bridge Billy and Sheila fell back behind Ibin and Ullin, allowing Ashlord and Robby to have the lead. Billy nudged his horse nearer to Sheila.

"They say the walls of this place rose overnight," he said to her softly, mindful of Ullin ahead of them.

Sheila nodded. "I have heard it said so."

"Aye, an' it's said that the master of this place made a dark pact to get it done," Billy added.

"I never heard that," Sheila said skeptically.

"Aye, it's said. Me mum told me so. She said it was done before the Lord Tallin brung his family eastward, an' that it was all done secret-like, to host an legion of warriors durin' a time of war, if need be. An' that the villages an' farmlands sprang up only afterwards, with folks feelin' safer under Lord Tallin's watch."

Sheila admitted the walls looked beyond the skill of any she had ever imagined. They seemed to be made of a continuous polished rock, without seam or crack or any line where any stone was laid upon another. The sun broke through the hazy lifting mists and now the walls positively gleamed, so polished they were. "Hm," was all she said, but it was enough to embolden Billy, who nudged his horse up closer behind Ullin.

"Ullin," Billy asked, "who built this place?"

"Our ancestor, who was among the first Men to come to these shores, built the original Tallin Hall," he said, "near the beginning of this age."

"But what about these walls?"

Ullin looked right and left, as if examining the walls for the first time. He shrugged.

"Lord Tallin will never say. But workers of Endeweir is what I have been told, master craftsmen employed by my grandfather in the years while our family lived in Vanara."

"Endeweir? The ice people of the far north?"

"Yes, that is what I was told. There are many other rumors and much speculation."

"But they live far away, far beyond the lands of Glareth, do they not?" Sheila said.

"They do. And they are not known for their stone craft."

Though early, they could see activity on the parapets. At the open gate ahead stood a line of guards dressed in light green trimmed in gold with swords at their sides. A line of heavy lances stood against the inner wall of the arched entrance, and beside each was hung a shield for quick retrieval. Before the riders passed over the last canal, the guards neatly donned their shields, took up their lances, and lined across the drawbridge in two staggered ranks, each six men across. In front of them stood two figures, one tall and blond-bearded dressed like the other soldiers, but without shield or lance. He held his helmet under one arm while his other hand clutched the sword hilt at his side, impassively watching the company approach. The other man they easily recognized as Tyrillick. He stood with this arms crossed but with not so stern a look as his companions on the drawbridge.

"Who goes!" the captain of the guard challenged.

"Kingsman and company for the Hall!" answered Ullin from the rear of the group, dismounting and leading his horse forward.

The rest dismounted also, and Ashlord said, "We are invited."

But the captain's eyes were on the Kingsman.

"For the Hall, Kingsman," he said loudly. "Let pass!"

The captain stepped forward to Ullin with outstretched hand and a look of happy recognition while the ranks behind him parted to either side in well-practiced coordination.

"Welcome, Lord Ullin Saheed!"

"Weylan!" Ullin took the hand, and they clapped each other on the shoulders warmly. "So you are made captain?"

"Aye, these six years ago, winter. Of the North Gatesmen. We were not expecting you, or else I would have made a proper welcome to Tallin the Younger!"

"None of that! You know how things are. I am Kingsman, now. Seeing you is welcome aplenty."

"Indeed," said Tyrillick, "only one was bid come."

Ullin smiled at the blank-faced elf and said, "I came as guide to companions not easily parted from each other."

"I see. Well. Lord Tallin has requested that you be shown to him as soon as you arrive. I informed him of a visitor, and he received word yesterday that your party was approaching."

"Very well, then," Ashlord said, a bit impatiently. "Please lead us on."

Captain Weylan nodded and turned sharply around, marching ahead of them.

"Hono-o-or, STANCE!" Weylan ordered.

The guardsmen snapped to attention, drawing their feet together and smartly bringing their lances at an angle against their shields with a saluting bang. The company passed under the portcullis and into the thick wall, going between the stern ranks, and each soldier in turn snapped his lance upright as Ullin passed. Ashlord noting this, smiled. Ullin remained expressionless, his eyes down.

"I'll have your mounts and baggage seen to," said Weylan as they cleared the inner portcullis. He motioned over several men. "And perhaps I will see you later."

"I hope so," replied Ullin, handing over his reins. "But, remember, here I am but a Kingsman."

"Aye, sir. But a much honored one, long missed."

• • •

Within was the small city of Tallinvale. Brick and stone houses stood in orderly rows, and there were buildings of all shapes and sizes in the broad space bounded by the walls. Paved streets fanned away left and right between the buildings, and were full of activity all around, the sort that one might expect to find in any town—children playing, carpenters working, market stalls, craftsmen's shops, comings and goings, carts and wagons moving here and there. There was military activity, too, with men drilling upon the many large yards and tourney fields within sight. Scaffolding was erected in several places around the walls and great hoists were lifting nets and buckets of materials upwards to be unloaded onto the parapets. Robby eyed one gang of workers nearby who were attaching a heavy ballista, like a large bow, to the ropes of a nearby crane. On into the town, they passed out from between a row of buildings and into an open area where dozens of archers were drilling, releasing their arrows in volleys that whistled through the air, and the passersby could hear the drumming thump of them into their targets. On the other side of this field, there was a large foundry with anvils ringing away and smoke belching from bellowed furnaces. Tyrillick led on briskly, and they passed a cluster of glass-fronted shops and taverns. Through the windows of one, Billy saw workers pouring molten glass into molds. They kept for some distance along the straight way, seeing Tallin Hall rising ahead of them as they approached, its graceful towers watching over all.

The old original walls still surrounded the estate, but were nearly invisible under the ivy that encased them. Robby's company passed through another gateway and onto the estate grounds, entering a very different kind of space than the town they had just passed through. Here, the hedge-bordered street was paved with small white gravel, and at regular intervals topiary archways on either side led out to the open grassy lawns of the estate. Looking through the archways as they went, they saw fruit trees on neatly trimmed lawns, banks of rose bushes, and islands of ornamental gardens. There were a few massive oaks with low, drooping limbs that spread out and nearly touched the ground, some of them dripping with long beards of swaying moss. Like an island, of sorts, of beauty out of place, it seemed to Robby, imbued with a restful feeling. The grace and calm seemed to emphasize a sense of isolation from the town. Yet here, too, was activity, though of a more domestic kind, with gardeners and groundskeepers busy at their trades.

"My master is not yet arrived," Tyrillick said to Robby.

"Surely you may tell us now who your master is? Now that we are here."

"That will be revealed to you this evening, I imagine."

Ullin, now at the rear of the group, kept his head down in contrast to the others who craned their necks this way and that to gape at the magnificence of the manor house, Tallin Hall. It was imposing, but without the sullen look that Robby imagined. Rather, with its tan stones and its graceful balconies and many windows, it seemed light and airy. And, though he saw arrow slits and other defensive aspects, the place appeared to have been built for comfort and pleasure. There was a side path that led away around to the back of the Hall, but Tyrillick kept them straight on to the front where a series of broad stairs took them up to a covered portico where tall doors were being opened as they neared. There emerged an older man of medium build, with long gray hair tied back in a ponytail and dressed in dark blue tunic and pants. Behind him stood another soldier, dressed very much like Weylan except with a black cape buckled to the shoulder straps of his breastplate. His beard was iron-gray, and his hair was shorn very close to his balding scalp. A third man appeared, thin and tall, wearing a fine black waistcoat, jacket, and breeches, and wearing polished black shoes with silver buckles underneath white silken stockings. He was clean shaven, his hair was white, and he looked to be in his seventies at least. His face, like the others, was blank, but it was not unpleasant, and his blue eyes sparkled like a distant lake in sunlight as he looked them over. The man in the blue tunic took a step forward.

"Welcome to Tallin Hall," he said. "I am Dargul, counsel to Lord Tallin. This is Captain Bekund, of the House Guard, and this is Windard, Keeper of Tallin Hall. Windard will see you to your rooms later and will look after your needs during your stay."

The soldier snapped a bow in military fashion. The elderly housekeeper made his bow, which was less distinct but somehow much more elegant.

"I am Collandoth, called Ashlord by many," Ashlord motioned at Robby, "and this is Robby Ribbon, son of Robigor, of Passdale and Barley. And these others are our travel companions. Tyrillick, here, bid us come."

"I am honored to meet you. Yes, you are expected," Dargul said, studying first Robby, then Ullin. "Will you please come this way?"

"I will come to you later," Tyrillick said to Robby. "When it is time."

Tyrillick turned and departed back the way they had come.

Robby and his group followed Dargul on into the Hall and through a grand foyer with high arching ceilings, lit by glass skylights. Polished rose-colored marble clicked under their footsteps and the sound echoed from the wide walls. A curving staircase wound upward on either side to a high balcony overhead, but they were led straight on to a square gilded door, outside of which there was a table and four guards.

"Visitors may not bear arms beyond this point," said Captain Bekund. "Save only the Kingsman who, by the King's Law, must be exempted."

They deposited their weapons onto the table, and the visitors were each in turn inspected by Bekund. Robby was tempted to undo Swyncraff from around his waist and lay it on the table, too, but a light touch and a subtle shake of the head from Ashlord stopped him. Bekund hesitated when looking at Swyncraff, but quickly moved on.

"Lord Tallin will see you now," said Dargul, nodding at the guards who pushed open the doors, revealing an even larger hall within. It was also lit by skylights, and its floor was tiled with the same rose marble, but checkered between tiles of white. The style of the arches very much reminded Robby of the bell room at Tulith Attis, but hanging from their apexes were many-candled crystal lamps suspended by long silvered chains. As well, the columns below the arches supported additional lamps, dangling from gold hangers, and many small elegant fireplaces lined the walls. Here and there were pennants and battle standards carved of wood on staffs tilting out from rings of iron set into the columns and walls. More pennants and cloth flags draped down from the balconies above, along with shields and bucklers of various designs and heraldry.

Dargul led the way, walking ahead of Ashlord and Robby. Sheila, Billy, and Ibin followed, staring and gaping at the room and its contents, while Ullin came lastly. Ashlord and Robby kept their eyes ahead where, at the far end of the room, there was a low dais spanning the width of the hall and flanked by banners and hung with intricate tapestries behind. Unlike the main floor, the dais was carpeted with rich heavy greens and blues. Two fireplaces, the grandest in the hall, burned to either side, and two low-hanging chandeliers glowed brightly. There were two great and ornate chairs pushed to the side, apparently to permit room for the large long table that was there. Beside the table stood two men with their backs to the approaching group. They were discussing a large map and other charts unrolled between them on the table. One of them was dressed in military fashion. The other man was robed in splendid silks, green and yellow and silver with ruby studs along the cuffs. He had long red hair spread across his shoulders, and, when he turned to glance at the visitors, Robby saw a gray-streaked red beard that came down to his chest. In the moment that he briefly looked his way, Robby thought he saw an angry flash in his eyes that made his stomach flutter. Robby did not want to appear weak before Lord Tallin, and he did not want to seem too proud or arrogant, either. But Robby had no doubt that he would be verbally cut to shreds by this man if he made one slip.

Dargul stopped a few feet before the dais and gestured for the visitors to wait while Lord Tallin finished his discussion. Robby could hear their voices, and he gathered that the military man was sharing something of vital importance. This soldier had white hair that flowed over his hard leather cuirass, made in heavy bands, and fastened about his shoulders was a long purple cloak, unbuttoned and flung back as a cape. He stood with his feet apart, and when he turned to face the group, Robby saw one of the sternest faces he had ever beheld. Two long braids of gray-white hair hung over his shoulders and his hand rested on a heavy brass-hilted sword at his side. He crossed his arms, but did not take his eyes from the group as he listened and nodded, piercing each visitor in turn with his brooding eyes until they settled long and hard upon Robby. His thin lips, his clean-shaven dark face, his high brow—his entire face, in fact—frowned.

"Very well," he said, still not taking his eyes from Robby. "Please do me the honor of remaining for a few moments."

"Certainly, my lord." The red-bearded one bowed low and stepped aside, rolling up the map and taking a position to the left before the group.

Dargul cleared his throat and, in a voice that was louder than was necessary, said, "Lord Tallin, the expected visitor has arrived, with company. I present to you Robby Ribbon, late of Passdale and Barley."

Robby hardly knew who to bow to, so surprised by his own mistake. Yet it was clear that the white-haired warrior, not much older in appearance and vitality than Ullin, was in fact his grandfather, the Lord Tallin. Somewhat flustered, Robby managed to bow not too awkwardly.

Tallin lowered his arms and took a step toward the group.

"You have the appearance of your father," he said, "but the bearing of your mother. They are well, I trust?"

"My lord," Robby said, "have you not heard? Passdale and Barley have fallen to Tracian Redvests, and my people are scattered. Your daughter, my mother, is near Janhaven, and she is gathering all the forces she may muster to counter the invaders and to protect those who escaped. Her husband, my father, is making his way to Glareth, there to plea for aid. Perhaps some of our people have made it away safely, perhaps some have come here. But many are missing and may be dead or captured by the enemy."

"I have heard. No one has come out of Barley as far as we know. I thought your mother would have brought her family here," Tallin said, "and I wonder that your father did not travel here to seek assistance."

"My father took the only way that the attackers left open for him. And my mother will not leave her people in the time of their need, my lord."

"She left her people long ago," Tallin retorted coldly. He flung himself down into the left-hand chair and slumped. "I understand your aim is to go to Duinnor. To seek assistance there."

"Yes. If none can be found closer at hand," Robby said.

"If you mean to imply Tallinvale should go to the rescue of Passdale," Tallin said, suddenly rising from his seat and stepping down from the dais toward Robby. "Let me put that from your head immediately. The strength of this valley is in the south where a Redvest army of two hundred thousand is gathered, we think, to move westward. Two hundred thousand so far. Should they choose to turn north, all of Tallinvale would be open to them. Meanwhile, to our west is the Damar warlord who looks with envy upon our lands, hoping that the Tracian Redvests will strike so that he may send his forces through the mountains against us. An uneasy treaty is all that stands between Tallinvale and those two powers. And while trade and commerce continues between us, I have only seventy thousand to put against them should either attack. Dare I provoke such a disaster by interfering with their doings in Passdale? I, too, have sent couriers to Duinnor. For years, I have seen the gathering clouds of war, and I have forewarned the West of the days that have now come upon us. Duinnor has done nothing! No supporting army has it raised for the relief and security of the eastern realms. No treasure has been sent for the purchase or production of arms. No emissaries have gone with threats or reasoning to Tracia. Duinnor! You should go back to your mother. Your journey is a waste of time." He shot a glance at Ullin before turning away. "Even if you do have a Kingsman to vouch for you."

"But we are determined to go, my lord," Ashlord said. "We hope only to pass the night and then be on our way."

"Your way is as confused as ever, Collandoth, Watcher," said the red-bearded one, stepping up with a smirk. "What do you watch for that none else may see? Do the stars not shine upon us all? Be there messages upon the wind and water that none but you may read? You skulk from realm to realm, from court to court, seeking new signs in ancient scribbles. Yet, ever is your effort futile. I am surprised at the gullibility of your comrades. At least the Kingsman should know what folly it is to heed one such as you. A mystic! A dreamer of days long past, and of kingdoms fallen into dust. Tell me," he said, now addressing the group, "has he told you of his lost empire? Has Collandoth the Mighty promised you riches and glory, wealth and honor beyond imagining, as soon as he is returned to his imaginary magic throne?"

While he spoke, the red-bearded one stepped down from the dais and walked among the group, nearly snickering at his own words.

"Lord Tallin," Ashlord said. "Hear my words." At this, Ashlord snapped his fingers in the red-bearded one's face who then stumbled back, blinking and rubbing his eyes. "Poison has ever been the specialty of Toolant the Red! Beware who you keep in company during these days of doom, and those entrusted with your secrets! There are greater powers at work in the world than even Duinnor may imagine. In times such as these, you deserve the workings of a more subtle mind than this one will ever possess, though his words be sweet and welcome, like honey. Do you know the last House he served and what became of them? What of those he served before that?"

Tallin managed a wry smile, but said nothing as he glanced at Toolant, whose face was now nearly as red as his hair.

"Do you call me traitor before my own lord?"

"Now, now!" Tallin said, holding up his hands before Ashlord could answer. Turning to Ashlord, he said softly, "My advisors are of my own choosing. Do not impugn them before me! I know the unfortunate circumstances that befell the Ruling Prince of Tracia before Toolant came here. And I hold him blameless. I also know," he said to Toolant, "that your words to Collandoth are unjust, ill-chosen, and grossly misinformed. He and his company are guests in my Hall, and I will not have them challenged or insulted while they are here."

"Yes, Lord," Toolant said, bowing. "I beg your forgiveness. Perhaps I should now attend to our other matters?"

"Yes. Indeed, do so. And I will see you in a fortnight."

He watched Toolant leave. When they heard the side door slam angrily, Tallin heaved a sigh that seemed uncharacteristic to his stiff demeanor. Dargul faced the group and put his finger to his lips, as if listening. For a few moments, they stood silent. Bekund, the Captain of the Hall, entered.

"Toolant has departed, my lord," he reported smartly.

Dargul nodded, then, as Bekund retired, he turned to Ashlord.

"Well do we know that Toolant is a spy. He weaseled his way into our court some years ago, and, in order to use him to spread false news to our enemies, we play along."

"We allow the appearance that he has displaced Dargul, here, as my chief counselor," said Lord Tallin. "As I alone hold rein over the armed forces of Tallinvale, and as I still privately confide all with Dargul, Toolant does little damage and we do much. He has been useful, for he moves between our lines and the Redvest lines without challenge. He has unwittingly carried word to my agents in the southeast and to those amongst the Damar in the mountains, and he has unknowingly brought word back from them. As well, we have used him on several occasions to mask our true weakness at arms, for we can field far fewer armed men than the enemy thinks."

"A risky course, Lord Tallin," Robby said. "If they decide to come, they will do so with overwhelming force, thinking their adversary mightier than it is." He realized immediately that he had spoken out of turn, that Ashlord was to be their spokesman. But the words were out of his mouth before he could stop them. And Robby did not notice Ashlord's subtle smile.

"True," said Tallin, squinting in appreciation of Robby's quick assessment of the problem. "Then our walls will be our only defense, if we can gather into them quickly enough. But we seek, as we have done so far, to avoid bloodshed."

"Let us just hope our ruse holds," Dargul said. "Perhaps they will not turn their armies this way."

"Why are you telling us this?" Ashlord said. "How do you know you can trust us any more than Toolant?"

"Because I know the reason you have come here. That is, I know who it is that you shall meet," said Tallin. "Toolant must never find out lest all of the enemy is poured out against you."

"It was a surprise and shock to us when Tyrillick came before us, in secret, and told us of his master's desire to meet young Robby," Dargul said.

"We still do not know who that is," Robby said.

"You know enough to keep you until this evening," Tallin said. "And by then Toolant will be far away to the west, carrying our latest wishes of goodwill to the Damar. I do not know what business you have with our coming guest, but I could not refuse the liaison, and I would not even if I could. And I am deeply disturbed by this turn. I believe you, Collandoth, when you say that these are days of doom. I do not trust in hope, and I have not these many long years. But if you have any word that may bring encouragement, I beseech it of you."

"I have none, Lord. Yet there is ever hope. If you haven't any, perhaps you may look to that of others, for none may weaken it by the sharing."

"I see. Then I wish to speak privately with the Kingsman and with my other grandson, Robby Ribbon. Windard, will you see to the others?"

"Yes, my lord."

None of the group had noticed Windard's entrance, but there he stood behind them, and he motioned for them to follow. He ushered the others out, with Ullin and Robby remaining, and Robby caught a look of warning from Ashlord as he turned away.

"This way, if you please," Dargul said, motioning Robby and Ullin to follow Lord Tallin. They were led through a side doorway, followed by Dargul, along a narrow hall, and then up a winding staircase to a broad landing. Tallin opened a door and motioned them into a small room, no larger than a closet, lit by small elegant oil lamps overhead. It was a snug fit for the four of them, then Dargul closed the door and pulled on a gold braided cord that dropped through a hole in the ceiling. The floor shook slightly, and to Robby's amazement the walls, including the door they had just stepped through, began to slide away downward. Somewhere below was the sound of gurgling of water. The platform on which they stood, more like a cage, literally floated upwards inside a shaft within one of the great spires of Tallin Hall. Tallin stood beside Dargul, arms crossed, and said not a word. Ullin, seeing Robby's surprise, could not help smiling, and chuckled silently to himself. The noise stopped, as did the cage, and Dargul opened a door for them. They stepped out into a short hallway and then through another door into a spacious room very much like a large parlor. It was lined with shelves of books, tables with charts and instruments of mapping, stands with swords, and from its ceilings hung marvelous tapestries. Here and there on the walls, in spaces between the shelves, were framed canvas paintings. Some of these were of landscapes, one depicted ships of the sea, sails billowing, and several were portraits. Robby saw one of a little girl that very much resembled his mother. There was a fireplace and several nearby chairs, and, on the adjoining wall were glass-paned doors, outside of which was a balcony. The doors were open wide, and Robby saw the blue ridges of the Thunder Mountains.

"Please sit," Tallin said, gesturing at two wing-back chairs upholstered in dark blue paisley linen. "Dargul will you pour for us?"

When all had glasses of pale wine in their hands, Tallin sat, too.

"Ullin, do you still ride the King's Post? It appears you are now involved with the Barleyfolk and their troubles."

"I am commissioned to carry special dispatches from Duinnor and Vanara to Glareth and back. Collandoth is my liaison in the Eastlands. However, I was asked by the mayor of Passdale to help train a militia there. I had completed my deliveries, so I agreed to assist them."

"Yes. I see. We heard there was a new militia in County Barley. How did they fare against the invaders?"

"Barleyfolk, for all their quiet ways, are natural fighters when they are put to it, Lord. They fought for their homes with honor and spirit, though hopelessly outnumbered and outclassed by the disciplined Redvests. The fight was brief but decisive, and Tracia holds all of Barley, including the fortress of Tulith Attis and the remains of the bridge in Passdale, which we set afire to hinder them. Many escaped to Janhaven. Our forces hold the roads and passes to Janhaven, and the Redvests have been denied that place. So far."

"That agrees with what has been reported to me. Furaman's stockade would be a plum worth picking, if the Redvests could manage it. But I have had other reports, too, of strange goings on at the fortress, where Collandoth had taken up. And then there's the Bell."

"Did you hear it, sir?" Robby asked cautiously.

"As I sat in this chair, it shook this tower and every wall and every stone of this hall," Tallin said. "Three times it tolled, each toll mightier than the last. See that portrait over there, on the floor, leaning against the wall?"

It was a large portrait of a robed Elifaen standing behind a table spread with scrolls and drawings. In one hand he held a divider and the other rested upon the table, holding down a large sheet that was spread out among inkwells, straight edges, other compasses and dividers. The other curled end of the sheet was held down by a sword.

"It is a portrait of Heneil. It still rests where it fell from its hook on the wall above, brought down by the third mighty toll. Do you know the story of Tulith Attis?"

"Somewhat."

Tallin eyed Robby closely, but Robby said no more, unwilling to let the wine loosen his tongue.

"I see you wear the ring of the Queen and Lady of Vanara," Tallin abruptly turned to Ullin. "Is she now in Glareth?"

"Yes, Lord. It was my honor to prepare the way for her," Ullin stated simply.

Tallin nodded.

"And you now act as guide for this journey westward?"

"Yes."

"How do you mean to go from here?"

"We have not decided on a path as yet. Either back through Hill Town or else straight on west through the territories of the Damar."

Tallin rose and walked onto the balcony. Ullin and Robby immediately stood, too. They watched Tallin gaze out from the balcony for a moment, the wind tossing his light hair and tugging his caped cloak.

"My words were true," he said. "You cannot obtain help from the west."

"Yet we are determined to try," Robby said. Tallin turned and looked at Robby.

"I know something of the determination of Barleymen," he said, and Robby saw the painful turn of a smile on his lips. "And if you take after your father, beware the man who tries to stop you! He may lose more than he bargained for."

"Sir. I do take after my father, but equally after my mother, in what ways a man might. I mean to do what I can for my people, even if the obstacles are many and great. If there is help to be brought back from the west, I shall do so. If there is none ready, I shall try to build some. If I come back, I will not be alone."

"Hm. And do you stand by your cousin?" Tallin asked Ullin.

"In all that he says, with my heart and with my sword," returned Ullin.

"Yet your sword and your allegiance belong to another."

"I believe they serve one and the same. And, anyway, the hand that wields the sword and the heart that holds faith are both my own."

"I see."

Tallin's expression softened as a deep weariness passed over his demeanor. Some of the haughtiness left his stance.

"I believe what you say, young Robby. When your father came to me for Mirabella's hand, I tested him severely. And I was made the fool! I will not be the fool again and test you likewise, yet I perceive that if you fail, much more may be lost than one man's daughter. Look yonder! Thereby is your path westward, between yon two mountains. The way takes you through Damar lands, but it is not so often patrolled. Dargul here will give you a pass to travel in case you are stopped. We cannot vouch for the safety it might bring. Lang Cartu is the current warlord holding sway over the Damar, but he is capricious and prone to bribery. So you must be wary. Some of the Damar are undisciplined, no more than mercenaries, and they often disobey their masters. Others are professional and well-trained, zealous in their loyalty to Cartu. Avoid crossing them if you encounter them. But if you must, show no mercy and hide the bodies. Once you make it through the passes, and cross the bridge at Redwater Gorge, you can turn northwest through the last of the mountains and then be out of Damar territories once you cross the Missenflo River."

"We have not decided a route," Robby said. "But we will consider that one. We may go back the way of Hill Town, if the west road from there seems better to us."

"So be it. Whichever way you deem best. I would like to ask that you carry a letter to the King. It is already prepared," Tallin said as Dargul got up and retrieved a packet from the desk. The letter was not yet folded and

Dargul held it out for Robby to see. "This is asking much of you, and so you should know its contents."

"I would be happy to carry it," Robby said.

Tallin looked hard at Robby. Dargul glanced at Tallin as Robby read the letter, but Robby's expression did not change when he handed it to Ullin to read. The letter put forth the situation in the Eastlands most frankly, giving estimates of the Redvest forces, the areas it had invaded and captured, and assessments of the movements of its armies. Tallin pleaded with Duinnor for assistance and promised dire consequences if an army was not raised and put into position by springtime to face the enemy.

"I'm not sure you realize, young sir," said Dargul, "that if you are caught with this letter, by the Damar or others, it would be your death warrant."

"I do understand," Robby replied. "If we are captured or if capture is threatened, it will be destroyed. I will carry your news with me and will impart your message myself if no better courier can be found."

"Pardon me for saying so," Tallin said with a slight smile, "but I do not think you have the credentials to beg an audience with the King himself."

"I assure you, sir," Robby stated, "that, if I enter Duinnor, the King will not only hear your cry, but will heed your words. You may presume that, should I reach Duinnor, the King has received your message."

"You speak as if you held the authority to…"

He stopped, his amused smile completely vanished, and his eyes narrowed. Then he looked at Ullin who gave a slow silent nod.

"I sense that you go west with another burden, or secret, that is of far greater urgency than my letter could ever have," Tallin said slowly, speaking carefully. "And I believe I now am gaining an inkling of what is truly afoot."

Tallin turned away and went slowly back to the balcony doorway and gazed to the northwest. When he spoke, he did not turn around.

"You hide your true reasons for going west, Robby Ribbon. You have spoken little of other events, and you have not offered your version of the night the Great Bell of Tulith Attis rang. Your companion, the Kingsman, wears upon his finger the ring of the Lady of Vanara. And you yourself have a token of the most ancient days wrapped about your waist. You were born in secret of me and raised apart from this house, one long watched by Duinnor. And by others, I am sure. And tonight you are to meet with one whose name I dare not even breathe, for fear of upsetting the world."

Now he turned around to face them. A breeze puffed in behind him, pushing his long cape around him, and his face was dark against the bright blue sky behind him. In the contrast, Robby could see no expression, but he felt his grandfather's eyes upon him.

"These things are not without meaning to me. Indeed, my fear only grows with the realizing of them. Do not think because I am an old man, removed from what little family he has left, and do not travel from this valley, that I do not have it in my power to know the happenings of the world. Long have I puzzled over them, just as I have gathered ancient books and writings to chew upon, compelled by the sense that the fate of my House is tangled deep within the strands of too many powers, like so many strands of a net. Dreams, strange and without interpretation, have come to me these last years. Signs, I am told, are being seen in the world, in the heavens, and upon the waters of the sea."

Tallin spoke slowly, deliberately, almost as if speaking to himself.

"Yet only now, only at this very moment, as I stand here, do I put together the puzzle of the years," he said. "Of unspoken words, unfulfilled promise, and unseen actions. Of unnamed children."

Robby's heart thudded at this last statement.

"Yes," Tallin went on, "the evidence is all around for those with eyes, if we only look. Even though many pieces may be hidden from me, there is enough for me to see what form the days to come will take. The Hidden One will soon come to power. This age will end, and soon the world will be broken and remade. If these times are upon us, and the prophecies of our forebears are come into life at last, then dark days indeed are upon us. Yes. I see," he nodded, bowing his head. "I see what my children knew, and what my sons carried with them to the next world. My house of Men is thrown down, and there is arisen from it, as the fabled bird from ashes, a new House, to be blessed among both Men and Elifaen. For the blood of your mother and your mother's mother is true within you. Yes," he sighed, still nodding his head. "I know my way, now, and the way of my people. No help will come. And these walls will not stand if weakened by my continued doubt and indecision. Too long have I renounced any action in the world beyond this valley. But if I cannot put off the ending of this age, I may at least shape the making of the next. If only I may bring myself to do it, and lead my people into doom."

He came and knelt before Robby who stiffened in surprise at this gesture.

"I swear this oath to you: I will purchase time for you," Lord Tallin stated with fire in his eyes. "I can give you three months that you did not have, and perhaps more if we are favored."

"Sir, I don't understand. What do you mean?"

Ullin touched Robby's elbow, interrupting him, and he said to Lord Tallin.

"No one can know, Grandfather. Even Robby does not fully comprehend what has come upon him."

"Indeed," Tallin said, rising. "What greater shock can there be? I have reason enough to do what I must," he held out his hand for the letter, and

Ullin gave it back to him. Tallin took it, smiling, and threw it into the fireplace. Dargul stepped forward in surprise, and Tallin laughed at him.

"Consider it delivered, Dargul! Hard questions are now before me, and they must be answered. Tallinvale must go one way or the other. Balance is no longer possible. No, old friend, do not at this moment ask my meaning. I speak more to myself than to you."

He turned back to Robby and Ullin.

"Pray tell Ashlord that I wish to see him, once he has rested, and that I desire that he call upon me as soon as he may. Please excuse me for now, my lord."

With that, Tallin bowed low to Robby, and strode from the room. Dargul remained, staring at the door through which Tallin had departed.

"I beg your pardon," he said to Ullin and Robby, "but what has just happened here?"

"I cannot…," Robby began, then faltered.

"It is not for us to say," Ullin said. "Let Lord Tallin say to you what he will and in his own time and way. And, I beg of you, do not press him too much on these matters."

"Well," Dargul stepped to the door and glanced down the hall, "can you tell me why he knelt? Why he addressed you so?"

"By his gesture, he does me a great honor," said Robby. "One of greater affection than could ever be expected, under the circumstances."

"I see. Well, then," Dargul said, unsatisfied. He looked at the two, from one to the other, with a slight frown.

"I believe I should accompany you to your rooms," he said at last. "This way if you please."

"I know the way to my own," Ullin said, "but perhaps you may ask one of the household to lead Robby to his. I'm sure you wish to wait upon Lord Tallin."

Dargul nodded and tugged a bell rope.

"How does he mean to buy us time?" Robby asked. "What does he mean by that?"

"I am not sure," Ullin said.

"He is a close one, your grandfather," said Dargul to Robby. "And though I have been with him for many years, I hardly know his thoughts." As they passed out into the hallway, Dargul said to Ullin, "I was very sorry about your rather cool reception earlier. But now, well, perhaps his heart thaws somewhat. My hopes have always been that time would heal some of the pain between you two."

"It has, kind sir. Somewhat." Ullin took Dargul's hand. "I am most happy to know you are still at his side. He will need your counsel now more than ever before. And if I know my grandfather, a plan is already forming in his mind."

"I will do my utmost to help him in all he asks of me," Dargul said, "even though he does not confide in me as much as I would wish. He is a stern man, and cool, but I knew him from an early age and know some part of his past. For all his hardness and distance, there is no man better with compassion and care for his own people when it comes to it. That may be difficult for members of his family to believe, since all are estranged from him. Perhaps he makes up for the love he has lost from his family by giving it to his duty, to his people and their lands. Still, it's a great shame such misunderstandings of passion have come between you and him, and between him and his daughter. But this conversation just now…it is a riddle to me."

Ullin sighed, taking Dargul by the elbow, saying, "I am sworn to say nothing. That we mean to go to Duinnor is no secret. However, we mean to take an unusual route, and by going the long way, to accomplish sooner what might not otherwise be accomplished by taking the short way."

"More riddles!"

Ullin shook his head.

"I am sorry if it sounds so. But if ever my grandfather asks for your advice, give it as you always have, with honesty and wisdom. And if ever he utters a strange command, I beg that you carry it out without question. He may indeed be stern and cool, even secretive, but he is the most cunning man I have ever known, and wise in his own close way."

Ullin looked down the hall where Lord Tallin had disappeared around a corner.

"Yet I fear for him. Now he faces a grave decision, upon which all our fates may rest. I do not fear the wisdom of the choice he will make, only its price. You should be with him. And this I will tell you: He may seem to have lost his love of family, what is left of it, and their love in return, but I know better. And I, for one, will forever love my grandfather."

"I am glad to hear it," said Dargul as a young girl appeared and curtseyed. "Ah, will you please see our guest to his room? I hope to see you later, Lord Robby."

"Thank you, sir. Ullin?"

"Oh, I'm sure Windard has your rooms already prepared for you," Dargul said to Ullin.

"I'm sure. Thank you," Ullin replied as Dargul walked on down the hall. "And I'll see you after a while, Robby."

They all parted their own ways, with Robby following the girl to a narrow winding staircase that descended steeply. Ullin watched him disappear downward, and then he walked away, smiling at the thought of sleeping in his old bed. And he was surprised that he already felt so at home in a place he had not even seen for many, many years.

Chapter 6

A Grand Place, But Somewhat Dour

Soon after parting company with Robby and Ullin, Dargul looked for his master in the meeting chambers, where the two were to review the inventories of the harvests, the disposition of the armed forces, and various other matters at hand. But Lord Tallin was not there. He looked, too, in the Lord's chambers and did not find him there, either. At last, hearing a sound from the library, Dargul entered and saw Tallin pulling old manuscripts from their shelves and unrolling them. Tallin had been spending more and more time here, often taking his meals at the table where he read and studied, but usually only in the evenings, after the day's work had been accomplished. He had for the past several months been studying all of the manuscripts, books, scrolls, and even a few stone tablets pertaining to the ancient days, the lineage of the various houses of Men and those of the Elifaen. Also, of particular interest to him, were the works of two or three of the so-called Fate-Seers of old, legendary, and some said nonexistent foretellers of future events. Some of the things they foretold, such as the coming of Men to the shores of the Faere and the rise of the Dragon Peoples, had come to pass.

Dargul thought Tallin's interest in such things was mild and was not much alarmed at first. After all, Tallin was a hard-nosed, practical man at heart, not much given to spiritual things or superstitions. And Dargul had never heard the Lord of Tallinvale speak of the well-known lore that surrounded his wife's family. According to that lore, if the Elifaen House of Fairoak was ever to join with Newcomers, as the Elifaen sometimes called Men, a new and subtle power on earth would emerge from the union, one which would overtake all realms and all empires. Although some of the serving staff bandied the tale about from time to time, it had never been a topic of interest to the Tallin family as far as Dargul knew. But then, Dargul did not know Lord Tallin from the "old lands," as Vanara was called, and only came into his service some years after Lord Tallin had brought his family back east to Tallinvale. Dargul was at first employed only as a sort of general manager of various construction projects. After a few years, however, he became Tallin's chief and most valued advisor on all matters, including those involving their delicate political relationships with the powerful neighbors directly to the west and to the southeast, meaning the Damar and the Redvests. As the years passed, the old man became more concerned, if not alarmed, as Tallin occupied himself more and more with the old tales and legends.

But Dargul had to admit that Tallin remained as busy as he ever was, mindful of his responsibilities at all times, in spite of the long hours at night spent with his books and scrolls. Tallin sometimes consulted Dargul concerning some point of history or other, and several times even arranged through Dargul's contacts the purchase of more manuscripts from the south or from Glareth or even from faraway Duinnor. What worried Dargul was that his master never explained what it was that he was looking for. It was as if part of Lord Tallin's mind was always working on a secret problem, or some nagging concern. Now, seeing Tallin standing at the table, with one hand holding open a book and in the other a letter recently received, he knew that something specific was definitely on Tallin's mind—something that pertained to real events, real choices, and real decisions, not mere superstitions or old wives' tales. Something that had to do with the visitors that had just arrived and those who were coming. But these mysterious matters would have to wait until Tallin revealed his thoughts, if he ever did. Though he was protective of his employer, Dargul would not presume to intrude unless the utmost need required it. He cleared his throat. When that did not arouse Tallin's attention, he ventured to speak.

"My lord?"

"Dargul. Yes, what is it?"

"Sir, do you wish to go over the tallies and the accounts? Also, I know Brennig returned late last night from his tour of the south, and he awaits to give you his report."

"Yes," Tallin said absently. He put the letter within the book and closed it thoughtfully. Turning to Dargul, he snapped out of his thoughts. "Yes, of course. Have Brennig come into the meeting chambers as soon as is convenient for him."

"He has been waiting this past hour."

"Then by all means let us go to him."

The two quickly made their way to the meeting chambers, just off from the great hall, and Brennig was shown in. Tallin's chief military aide, Brennig held the highest military rank in Tallin's service, a tall man, clean shaven with the tan face of one who spent a great deal of time out of doors, and smartly dressed in his best light armor. He was in his early forties and with gray around the temples of his black close-cut hair. These three were completely comfortable with each other, but Tallin and Dargul could see that Brennig was anxious the moment he was shown in.

"My apologies for keeping you waiting," Tallin shook Brennig's hand. "I had company that needed attending, and, frankly, I became distracted. Though I was aware that you had arrived, I did not wish to hear you until Toolant had departed from us. He would have insisted on hearing your report, too. And, knowing him, he would have thrown a fit to know why he wasn't told of your mission. I hope you have had some rest?"

"Yes, my lord. I understand. Yes, I am quite rested. I hope the situation with Toolant is quite in hand?"

"You may rest your mind at that," Dargul put in, offering Brennig a seat. "Toolant is today traveling to Damar. He carries with him a fairly accurate assessment of the strength of our forces. Officially, he is to tell the Damar that we are far stronger than we are. If he betrays our true strength, which I fear he will, it will be his death warrant. We have a man in the Damar court who will hear Toolant's report. This man is aware of our suspicions concerning Toolant. It is all very complicated, but it boils down to this: We think Toolant will use his information to seal a pact between Tracia and the Damar. The Damar are too weak to threaten us outright, unless they are supported by an overt Redvest threat from the south. They have been reluctant to join with Tracia, yet they, too, fear Tracia's strength to their south. Since the Damar and Tallinvale currently have a treaty, permitting trade and travel between our lands, the first sign of a new alliance on their part with the Triumvirate who rule Tracia will be the closing of trade with us. Our man will carefully watch the movements at court and will report to us any actions. If he suspects a treaty has been reached between the two, he is under orders to immediately deliver a trade order from us for arms from Damar. Their refusal of the order will be confirmation enough. Our man also carries papers with him that, when they are found on the person of Toolant, will see him to the block."

"Papers?"

"Yes, papers in code, easily broken, addressed to Duinnor, confirming that the assassination attempt on the Damar warlord will take place as planned."

"What assassination attempt?" asked the soldier.

"One that will be carried out shortly after those papers are found and the cipher broken," said Tallin.

"All this seems a bit far to go to implicate one spy!" said Brennig. "Why not just cut his throat here, when you had him at hand."

"Because," said Dargul, "we know that Tracia and the Damar will soon reach an understanding. But we do not know when. If we can force that inevitable pact, and have it confirmed, we will at least know where we stand even though they will try to make it a secret from us. Until they form an alliance, we are forced to diplomacy alone. But should the Damar attempt any more incursions, we will know it for what it is, and not some playing with us."

"I'm not sure I see," said Brennig. "Nor do I think it matters. All that I have seen in the south points to conflict. Word is that the Damar are now even waylaying riders of the King's Post, and sending all dispatches they capture to Tracia."

"That explains why no word has been heard from our contacts in Duinnor. What else did you learn?" Tallin said.

The southern portion of the valley that made up most of Tallinvale lands opened broadly from around Tallin City through gentle hills between the Thunder Mountain range to the west and the lower but still rugged Greensward Hills to the east. It was just outside Tallinvale territory that the Redvests were massing their armies, south of the convergence of the Fengal and Saerdulin Rivers, near the town of Kalbrith. It was a land long in dispute, being the southwesternmost reaches of the old Eastlands Realm. Both realms claimed the territory, but the Redvests had occupied it many years ago, even though most of its inhabitants felt more kinship to Tallinvale than to Tracia. From that region, it would be an easy march northward to River Lerse that was at the southern boundary of Tallinvale lands. In those parts, Tallin had established checkpoints and keeps, in a line along the north banks of the Lerse, manned with enough soldiers to challenge any crossings the Redvests might attempt. Along the western side of Tallinvale, in the foothills of the Thunder Mountains, a similar line of encampments had been established for patrolling against incursions by the Damar. During the past three weeks, Brennig had toured all these encampments, moving quickly on horseback southward along the Thunder Mountain line, then going eastward along the River Lerse. The last leg of his journey brought him up along the Old South Road that ran along the River Saerdulin before reaching the confluence of the Bentwide.

"I found our men all in good spirits all along the way, but spread thin, it seems, given the areas they patrol. The local people support them well, and, as you know, many are serving as regulars and have therefore more knowledge of the nooks and crannies, as it were. However," Brennig took a deep breath, "all reports are that the enemy means to move west come spring. They are building storehouses all around Kalbrith, and each day more rafts and boats come down the Saerdulin with provisions. Wagons are beginning to move along the road, too, laden with grain and supplies. Our scouts, who cross the Fengal with ease, tell me that new roads are built and more troops and supplies are being brought across the Saerdulin every day. At present, we estimate the Redvest strength at somewhere around one hundred and eighty to one hundred and ninety thousand men, in sixty or so encampments. And their numbers are growing rapidly. By month's end, they will number over three hundred thousand. Virtually all of the towns and villages south of the Lerse are taken over by them, and the folk there are pressed into the army or made to work as slaves. Small groups of Redvests move across the Lerse, sometimes at night, to test our guard, but all have been turned back without much bloodshed so far. I don't know how long that will stand, though, for our people grow weary of their arrogance. I made my way back by the Old South Road, passing more troops and many people pressed into their service, moving stores and provisions. The lower Eastlands are being emptied of food, fodder, and livestock and taken southwards to feed the army. I was challenged all along the way, but was allowed to pass without too much in the way of argument. Apparently, there have been some attacks made on the Redvest wagon trains. They claim that a few hundred of their soldiers have been killed. Ambushes, traps. Night raids."

"Attacks? Who is behind them?" Dargul asked.

"Dunno. The Redvests don't seem to know, either, but they're very suspicious that Tallinvale is behind them. Seems to be the work of bandits, or some such loose-knit groups. I saw no sign of them, though, and I'm not sure the Redvests aren't making up tales. It might be the work of the Thunder Mountain folk, from around Hill Town, though that's quite far from their territory."

Brennig went on to describe in more detail the disposition of the troops, and Dargul, with one eye on Tallin, asked many questions. At first, Tallin was very interested, but then he slouched in his chair and said little, seeming more remote as the meeting progressed. He nodded as Brennig touched upon some important point, and Dargul saw Tallin's face grow stern, his eyes narrow distantly, his brow furrowed in thought.

"Pardon me?" Lord Tallin asked suddenly, looking from Brennig to Dargul.

"I was just wondering if we should continue rotating the units as we have been, my lord," said Brennig.

Tallin stood up and the other two did, too. "Until further notice, all is to remain exactly the same. A change in our ways may come soon enough, but let the relief companies be on their way today as planned. I'm sure it will be appreciated by those who have not had sight of home for this month past."

"Yes, my lord. Yes, it will."

"You have done well, Brennig," Tallin said as he walked out. "I would like for you to be nearby these next few days. Keep yourself in readiness, please."

"Certainly, my lord."

Dargul and Brennig exchanged looks of bewilderment, but Dargul soon mastered himself and went on to tell Brennig of the local happenings during the past two weeks, about the visitors that had arrived that morning, and that other visitors were coming. Walking Brennig down the hall, Dargul said, "I know little of the west ways, but I feel something important is going on that we are just on the edge of. Lord Tallin is very close with his thoughts these days. I feel a crisis may be taking shape. Yet, I cannot say what it may be."

"I may be able to say for you," Brennig said at the front doors. "Tracia is hungry. Damar is opportunistic. Their pact will soon be open. If Tracia aims west, she can hardly afford to leave Tallinvale as a threat to her flank. If we do nothing, they will eventually attack us."

"But what can we do?" asked Dargul.

"That is for you wise men to think out!"

"The situation may be beyond anyone's thinking. I'm afraid what will come will come!"

"Then sharpen your dagger, good counselor, and sleep lightly!"

• • •

Ullin was pleased to find his old rooms opened for him. The suite of two smallish chambers had served as his bedroom and study from his earliest years in Tallinvale. Located on the third floor of the west wing of the Hall, its balcony was some distance below and north of the West Tower that he had just left. Still, it afforded a good view over the little town, encompassed by the great walls, and a picturesque view of the mountains in the distance. The windows had been left open to air the room, and a cool breeze sent a wave of chill bumps along his arms. He absently rubbed them away as he looked westward. Many a sunset had he seen from this window, watching Sir Sun walk slowly over the mountains toward the faraway homeland of his ancestors.

"I hope you will find everything in order, sir."

Windard was standing in the doorway.

"I thank you, Winny. As if I never left."

"A little tidier, I think," Windard said with twinkle in his eye. "The staff change the sheets and clean and air the room every fortnight, at least, so you should find it fairly fresh. I have also taken the liberty to lay out a change of clothes, should you like."

"That's very good of you, but you shouldn't have gone to all the trouble," Ullin said, fingering a fine selection of robes and tunics draped over the bed.

"Not at all, sir. Your guests are in the lower east wing, and we are making them as comfortable as possible. We have offered the young lady some clothing that is perhaps more suitable for the Hall than her own attire. But she is reluctant to accept."

"She is not one to accept loans or charity very easily, Winny. She will likely remain in her own clothes."

"I see. I hope I did not offend her."

"I am sure you did not."

"I thought perhaps after they were settled in, they might enjoy being shown about the Hall and the town. Captain Bekund was kind enough to offer his services for that purpose."

"I believe they would like that very much. But I don't know if they will be able to do so."

"Very well. You have but to pull the bellrope, and I or one of the household will attend," Windard said, turning to depart. He stopped and turned back to Ullin. "If I may be so bold, my lord?"

"Yes?"

"Is it true that your cousin, Mirabella's child, had something to do with the ringing of the Bell at Tulith Attis?"

"What makes you think that?"

"It was rumored to us by a troupe of musicians who passed through some while back. They said it was well known among a group in the company of the Queen as she passed Lake Halgaeth. They called him Harbinger, but said the elves called him Bellringer."

"I was not at Tulith Attis when the Great Bell rang," said Ullin casually, as he tried to hide the sudden concern that gripped him. "And all I can say is that Robby was there. Yet, in truth, I do not think he knows precisely how the Bell came to ring."

"I see. And if I might inquire after your aunt, Mirabella? Is she safe? We have heard all manner of news, some of it hardly credible."

"I saw my aunt two mornings ago, when we set off from Janhaven. She is as beautiful as ever she was, well, and as safe as any can be in those parts."

Windard nodded. "Like you, she is still missed in this house. It is good to have you home."

"It is good to be here."

"I will leave you, then. Please do not hesitate to summon, my lord, should you desire anything at all."

"Thank you, Winny."

• • •

In other parts of the great house, Robby was led along sundry passages and hallways to his room. The servant who showed him the way said little, but she glanced at him suspiciously several times. As he followed along, Robby was continually awed by the finery he saw, the elegant tapestries that adorned various rooms they passed through, the magnificently carved columns and archways, and the lofty windows that poured light into passageways. The people of the house smiled and bowed or curtseyed as he passed, but he was too intent on the sights to pay much attention to them or to speak more than a good morning or how-do-you-do. On they went, crossing tiled floors and carpeted rugs, and everywhere Robby saw the evidence of a rich and glorious heritage, the result of a union of one of the greatest ancient lines of Men to that of Fairoak of Vanara. Statues of his forebears, some stern, others rather benevolent-looking, appeared here and there. He passed one adorned in the same accoutrements worn in life, banded breast armor of gold, shoulder-cape of green, and pointed helmet of gold-trimmed steel. He and his guide suddenly turned a corner and there opened a long hall of light-colored wood. At the end of the hall was another great window, but before they came to it, his guide turned and opened a door.

"Here we are, my lord. We thought you should have your own room," she said as she entered and stepped aside. "Your companions share rooms next to you, the two boys together, and the older man and the lady with separate rooms, she at the end of the hall."

She waited and watched as Robby inspected the large bedroom. It was light and airy with windowed doors leading out into the east gardens. The bed was turned down for him and there were clothes laid out for his choosing. There was a writing desk, a cold fireplace with a bucket of wood beside it, and through a little door, a washroom complete with pumps for water and an iron bathtub.

"I hope this suits, my lord?" the girl asked when he looked back to her. For a brief moment, he thought she had spoken to someone out of sight in the hall, then he realized from her questioning expression that he being addressed.

"In the first place, this is far grander than any bedroom I have ever seen, much less stayed in. And, in the second," he was so overwhelmed by the extravagance of the place that he laughed as he spoke, "it will suit me far more than I deserve since I'm no lord but just a store clerk from Passdale."

"Pardon me? Are you not Robby, grandson to Lord Tallin and heir of Fairoak through Lady Kahryna, his wife, your grandmother and your mother, who is also one of the Elifaen?"

Robby was glad she wielded no feather, for she surely could have knocked him over with it after such a surprise question so lightly asked. But he locked his knees and stood rigid while his expression served only to confuse the young girl who was now just as red-faced with embarrassment as Robby.

"I am Robby Ribbon, son of Robigor and Mirabella. Lord Tallin is my grandfather," Robby said stiffly, but stopped, unsure of what else to say. "I thank you for your kindness and all who have gone to so much trouble for me and my friends."

The girl managed an uneasy smile and curtseyed.

"Tell me," Robby asked. "Whose rooms are these? I hope no one had to move on our account."

"Oh, no, Lord, er, Master Ribbon."

"Most just call me Robby."

"Yes, your honor, er, I mean, no, Lord Robby, sir. No one was turned out. These are guest rooms always held in the ready for company, though we have had very few since I came here to work."

"And how long has that been?"

"Oh, sir, I first came here to serve Lord Tallin and his family, oh, it must be fifty-one, no, fifty-two years ago, by the reckoning of these parts."

"You astonish me! You look no more than a little girl, no more than ten or eleven years old! So you are of the Faere folk? From the west?"

"Oh, yes, sir! Of the House of Persimmon, sir. My family has served Fairoak for generations, and we serve still, though the Lady has passed away and all the children have gone."

"I see."

"Please give the bell rope a tug if you need anything," she bowed and curtseyed.

"Just one more thing?" Robby stopped her.

"Yes, my lord?"

"May I wander in Tallin Hall? I have never seen such things as I have seen here."

"There are no rules forbidding guests from any parts of the Hall or grounds," she answered. "And especially not you. But I would suggest you stay clear of the topmost floor. Lord Tallin has his rooms there, and he is rather stern about his privacy."

"I will do as you say. How many floors are there?"

"Not counting the towers, the Tallin Hall has five floors above ground, and two more below."

When she had departed, he again looked over the room. It was about five times bigger than his old small bedroom at home. It had an iron-lined fireplace, simple framed landscapes on the pale blue walls, and a large bed, which he tested and found to be very comfortable. Nearby to the garden doors, the writing desk was stocked with quills, ink, writing paper, and a sealing candle. He went to the washroom and looked again, testing the pump and, picking up a cup there, drank his fill of cool water. Next, he opened the glass doors and stood for several minutes gazing at the profusion of flowers and shrubs still in blossom in spite of the lateness of the year. After washing, he made his way down the hall to greet his friends. The door of the adjacent room was ajar and, peeking in, he saw Ibin sprawled across a tremendously large bed, and Billy likewise on another across the room, and they were snoring in competition to one another as if they were sleeping off a night of revelry. Passing Ashlord's room, he went on down the hallway and knocked on Sheila's door. After a moment, she opened it and smiled.

"I was wondering how long you would be," she said, inviting him in. "Aren't these rooms wonderful?"

"Quite nice, indeed!" he answered as he looked about. It was obviously a room for a lady, with fine silken curtains and dainty paintings, flowery sheets on the bed, edged in lace, and an elegant dressing table with an assortment of fine combs and brushes. There was a large floor mirror in an ornate stand, another vanity at the dressing table, and several looking-glasses with silver handles and frames. She, too, had thrown open the garden doors and the sweet aroma of the blooms mixed with her own as she took his arm and showed him about. "And how did your chat with Lord Tallin go? Did he pry much out of you? Or did you get much out of him? Will he send help to Janhaven?"

"I don't know if he will send help or not, but, and this is a strange thing, I suspect he is not overly fond of Duinnor. And," Robby hesitated, "he knows why we go west. My part, anyway. I think he had guessed as much before we arrived, but something, maybe something I let slip, seemed to confirm it for him. There was a point in the conversation when he changed his tone. He became—I don't know how to say it—very respectful? I think he knows as much about things as Ashlord. Maybe more. I don't know. It was a strange meeting."

"Does he know you are destined to be King?"

"Does anyone know that? I hardly know it myself, except by what I've been told." Robby shook his head. "It hasn't sunk in. I'm not sure it ever will. Whenever I think on it, my head swims. As for Lord Tallin, I believe he is convinced. Not so much by meeting me, I don't think. More from other knowledge, though I haven't the foggiest what. Lore, legend, old books, maybe."

Sheila looked at him and furrowed her brow.

"Is something else bothering you?"

"Yes. Perhaps we should see Ashlord, if he is in, and I'll share it with you both at the same time."

• • •

"Come in!"

They entered Ashlord's room to find that, he, too, had flung his doors open to the gardens, but was sitting at a small desk, much like the one in Robby's room, writing furiously with a quill, his back to them.

"Ah," he said, without turning around, "Robby and Sheila. Good of you to pop in. I was just writing a few notes to be sent as dispatches to various points east, west, north, and even south. I have just this one left to finish. Windard assured me that they would be carried by the regular riders who go forth from Tallinvale each week. They ride tomorrow. One of the riders will go to Janhaven, and so a note to your mother is here, as well as another to Furaman. You might consider writing a little note, too, since you may not get another chance for some time to come."

He then fell silent, and the scratch of the pen sounded strangely loud until a wren just outside began to sing emphatically. Certina sat on Ashlord's shoulder, peering down at the notes, following his hand as if reading what he wrote. Robby noticed thin streaks of silver running through Ashlord's long black hair, and, as he and Sheila took chairs nearby to the open doors, it occurred to him how much he had trusted Ashlord since Tulith Attis. Even now, as Ashlord sat with his back to them folding his notes and sealing them carefully, Robby felt confident that Ashlord was doing something wise and thoughtful. He remembered, too, that day on the road to Janhaven when in the company of Captain Makeig and his men, how Ashlord had fought. True, after the melee began in earnest, Robby did not seen much of him, but now frozen flashes came to him, and he saw again glimpses of the fury of Ashlord's sword, held high to strike a Redvest, his hair flying about his head, his arm outstretched in warning to a fellow even as he plied his strokes. That was Ashlord, ever mindful of more than one thing at a time, so that during the panic of any moment, he was watchful of those other things of great importance, too. The Watcher, he had been called, by more than one person. Before now, Robby had taken it to mean something more sedate or meditative, studious and distant. But now he realized a truer aspect of Ashlord the Watcher, and remembered the walk back from Tulith Attis and how he cast his attention to every movement and bent his ear to every sound, even as they conversed.

Aspects of Ashlord's mysterious nature revolved in Robby's mind. Ashlord never seemed to sleep, was possessed of uncanny awareness, and somehow communicated with animals and transmitted his words, and warnings, through Certina. To Robby, all those things, and more, made Ashlord something other than a Man. Yet, surely Ashlord was no Faerekind. A Melnari, Thurdun had said. Robby wondered deeply what Ashlord's story was, where he came from, and who, if anyone, he served.

Ashlord turned around in his chair, smiling warmly at them with his eyebrows up in anticipation of the gist of Robby's visit. But there was also something in his expression that seemed to say, "Yes. I am here. Who it is that I am, I have always been becoming. You have some inkling of me. I am here."

"How do you find the Hall of your forebears?" Ashlord asked. Robby shook himself from his thoughts and glanced at Sheila.

"Well," he replied, somewhat hesitantly, "I am a bit overwhelmed at what I have seen so far."

"The wealth and power of Tallinvale is renown throughout the Seven Realms, though it is but a small region. And the heritage of the Joined House of Tallin and Fairoak is one rich in history and legend."

"I am beginning to get some sense of that. And I would like to ask you something about what happened during my talk with Lord Tallin. Oh, I must tell you first that he wants to see you at your convenience and says he desires you to wait upon him whenever you might."

"Very well," Ashlord said. "I confess I have a desire to see him, too. I sense change in the air. You might think our reception cool and without much in the way of welcome, especially as you are his kin. But I find it somehow less cool than in the past. The last time I was here was three years ago, on business. But what is it that you wish to tell me?"

"Well, I know I've been sheltered, knowledge withheld from me about my mother's side of my family," Robby began. "And, since I don't have much kin on my dad's side, I am a stranger to the inner workings of most families or clans, except when it comes to Bosklanders. But the servant girl who brought me to my room acted rather, well, rather too respectful of me, saying 'my lord' and so forth, calling me 'heir' to Fairoak, too. And we went all around the house, it seems, before we got to my room. This is truly a wonderful and grand place! Like I've never imagined. Along the way, I saw all sorts of marvelous things—statues, paintings, battle gear, flags and pennants, just to name some of them.

But, the thing of it is, it was as if the servant girl was not only showing me the house, but showing me *to* the household staff as we came through. They would stop what they were doing and bow and curtsey and say 'my lord' and such as I passed."

Ashlord nodded with a somewhat bemused expression as Robby spoke.

"I don't mean to make something of nothing," Robby wrapped up, "but suddenly it is as if something is expected of me. Some way of acting, or some action. It may just be some misunderstanding. I just wanted to ask you about it, before I have any more dealings with these people."

"You are not making something of nothing," Ashlord said. "As for family matters, one can never tell in the great houses what conflicts or happenings may sway the line of inheritance one way or another. Yet, this is a sign to you, Robby Ribbon, that indeed something is expected of you. Some people expect this, others expect that, but few know what it is that gives them the sense of expecting anything of you. They latch upon this and that. You are heir to Fairoak and Tallin. These people expect you to act as such. You are a messenger from Passdale to Duinnor. Those people expect that of you. Such are the times we live in, that few comprehend the reason behind their feelings, and they give to those feelings reasons they may reasonably accept. You are to be King. *King.* It is in your face and in your blood. It is in the earth and stars, and no age falls or arises except that those who live in the changing of ages come of themselves into what they are to be. You are to be King. This, too, is what people sense, yet cannot form in their minds, so fearful a thing that it is. So, instead, they may rightly call you by other names, Lord and Heir, Messenger, Hidden One, and Bellringer."

"What do you call me, Collandoth?" Robby asked.

Ashlord's brow went up quizzically, just as a glint of sunlight struck a silver thread of his hair. His eyes grew sad, somehow, yet earnest.

"I hope to call you King," he said. "But my greater hope is, regardless of what I call you, that you may call me friend."

Robby returned the smile.

"My hope is that you will not regret that I do," he replied.

"Never in life," stated Ashlord. "Nor in what may come afterwards."

At that moment, Billy and Ibin burst in, yawning and jabbering about their room, pummeling Robby with questions about Lord Tallin, about the grandeur of the Hall, about what o'clock it might be, and, naturally enough, about how those who stayed in this great house might take their meals, and, more importantly, when? Just as they turned to that subject, a tall and finely dressed figure appeared in the doorway, and it was a moment before they realized it was Ullin. His beard was gone, showing now his youthful face, his hair was combed and glistening, and to both sides two long locks were braided after the fashion of his grandfather. His loose-fitting robes were of a pattern of small green diamonds on a field of dark blue, hemmed in embroidered gold. He wore comfortable deerskin slippers with long curled-up toes. About his waist was a dark leather belt with silver tassels at the knotted end. And, incongruous with what they knew of him—but entirely suiting the look of this person who now stood before them—he held a mandolin.

"Ullin!" cried Robby.

"Yer beard!" said Billy.

"Your clothes!" admired Sheila.

"Yourman, yourman, yourmandolin!" uttered Ibin.

"You're late," said Ashlord flatly. "We were just discussing food."

"I beg your pardon," Ullin bowed. "I did not mean to cause a stir or a delay. But it is fitting that I should change into something clean within my own home, and I had to rummage somewhat for this."

He held up the mandolin, stroked across the strings, then proceeded to pick a light melody. It was a brief phrase, a lively passage from an old ballad, and the group was fairly astounded at his talent. He stopped, mid-phrase, looked at the mandolin as if sizing it up, and nodded. "It is for you, Ibin," he said, holding it out.

Ibin was stunned with joy overflowing, his mouth wide in astonishment, and his wide eyes flitting to Billy, then to Ullin, and then back to the mandolin nearly a dozen times before his arms slowly came up to accept it.

"My father taught me somewhat how to play on this when I was only a toddler and it was bigger than me," Ullin said, handing it to the thrilled and still speechless Ibin. "And my mother taught me somewhat more. I thought you would enjoy it. Though it is old and worn, the strings are fairly fresh, thanks to Windard's care of my things, and it still sings warm and true."

"I ... do ... not ... know ... how ... to ... thank ... you ... dear Ullin!" Ibin said, slowly and deliberately with great concentration, his eyes shimmering. None of the others had ever heard Ibin speak this way, and it was evident to them that Ibin was deeply touched as he took the mandolin and admired it. "But, Ullin ... I ... do ... not ... know ... how ... to ... play—"

"I will teach you what I know," Ullin said. "And you will probably wind up teaching me more, if I have you right. You are welcome. Now. In this household, with such honored company—and you are honored company, even if your reception was somewhat off—you will be well dined this evening, I'm sure, should you desire it. In the meanwhile, it is the tradition of the house whenever guests are present to keep the kitchen fires hot at every hour of the day, and to always have in waiting some buffet in the great room of the guest wing. If you follow me, I will lead the way."

Ullin showed Ibin how to sling the mandolin over his shoulder with the strap and then he led them down the hall and around the corner, Billy and Ibin almost tripping over each other with eagerness. Ashlord gathered up his letters and came along, too.

"I have rarely seen any so enthusiastic for food or sleep at every opportunity," he muttered. Then, to Robby, "If you write a note to your mother, I will include it with these. But the riders leave early."

"Thank you. I will do just that."

"Keep it short and vague, if you can. Who knows what may become of the rider who carries these? And, if misfortune should befall, into what hands our letters may land."

"Indeed. I will try."

Ullin was waiting for them at a doorway, Billy and Ibin having already entered, and he ushered them into a large room. It was also brightly lit with glass doors all along one wall. On the opposite side was a massive fireplace of white marble with two rampant horses carved into the pillars supporting its high mantel. There were tables and chairs of various styles and sizes, in no particular arrangement, it seemed, as well as a settee here and there, placed near the sitting chairs for comfort and for ease of conversation. There was, in fact, one longer table where members of the staff had put out pitchers, platters, plates, and bowls all filled with soups, meats, fruit, breads, ale, wine, coffee, tea, and sweet cakes. Ibin and Billy were there, each with plates already piled high. Though the staff eyed the two with a mixture of amazement and dismay, Robby had little doubt that those stationed at the serving table would remain strangers to his friends for very long.

Not as hungry as his friends, Robby continued to look around the room. On one wall were murals and paintings, most depicting pastoral scenes of Tallinvale, as well as several old but still colorful banners and pennants, trophies from past conflicts. On the opposite wall were more of the same, but also several plaques supporting ancient helmets, swords, and other small arms. In a corner leaned a tall pole, and Robby's eye was drawn to the white dragon embroidered on a green banner that hung from it. Ranged around the dragon figure were other, smaller symbols, done in gold; Robby could not make them out but thought they must be some kind of writing.

"That is the battle flag of the House of Saltani Gurasa, which was carried before the armies that he led," Ullin said, coming up beside Robby.

"Saltani Gurasa?"

"Saltani means 'great leader,' and Gurasa was one of the greatest generals the Dragonlands have ever known."

"Was it taken in battle?"

"It is a strange thing," Ullin said. "It arrived here not long after news of the death of our uncle, Dalvenpar, brother of my father and your mother. That was ten years or so before I was born. Your mother thinks perhaps Dalvenpar took it in battle or traded for it. She told me there was a note with it saying it was in exchange for a ring, but that was all."

"Why is it not with the other banners and trophies in the great hall upstairs?"

"Because its price was too dear," Ullin replied. "You see, Dalvenpar and Gurasa were friends, each despising war, yet each loyal to their duty. Ashlord may tell you more, for he knew them both, well before I was born."

"Their friendship began during a brief time of peace," Ashlord joined in. "Or it seems brief now, as all things do when their time has departed. At the time, I was member of a mission of representatives sent from Duinnor to the Golden City, Tyrsharat, and there I met a boy filled with curiosity about the inhabitants of Vanara. He was curious about all things. He loved to cultivate exotic flowers, he collected interesting insects, and he studied the movements of the stars and heavens. He read all the histories he could find, even learning the languages of Men and Elifaen to do so. He wished for trees that would grow needing little water, for his desire was to learn if such could provide shade and shelter to crops grown beneath them, protected from the harsh desert sun. Since he was a distant member of the imperial family, I saw him often, and he constantly pestered me with questions. He convinced me to bring him back to Vanara when I returned, and so I did, with the Dragonkind boy disguised as a malformed and sickly vagabond to hide the fact of his race. From there we went to Duinnor, where he met Dalvenpar. Someday perhaps I will tell you the whole of it. Suffice it to say that Dalvenpar was of like nature and temperament as Gurasa, and they struck up a close and deep friendship, Dalvenpar knowing Gurasa's true identity. When Dalvenpar returned to Tallinvale, Gurasa accompanied him and stayed in this very house for a time. Eventually, Gurasa returned to his homeland and the two friends lost touch with each other, though Gurasa sent a ring to Dalvenpar from the Dragonlands as a token of their friendship. Tragically, they may have met upon the field of battle many years later, when Gurasa's name was as great as it was feared amongst the forces of Vanara. At any rate, I knew them both well, and their friendship was true and fast. Dalvenpar was proud of the ring Gurasa sent to him, and, in spite of the note that came with this, I do not think he would have ever traded it for anything in the world. Not even this banner."

Ashlord gazed at the banner, heaving a great sigh, and leaned heavily on his stick.

"Yet, it is said that no standard of Gurasa has ever been taken in battle," Ullin continued the story. "Perhaps Dalvenpar acquired it by some devious means and sent it here so that it would not be given to Duinnor. But surely he would have written home about it. And, our grandfather placed it here rather than upstairs in the great hall because it was in this room that Dalvenpar and Gurasa last saw each other in peacetime. If it was Dalvenpar who sent it, perhaps he desired that the banner would remain within the Tallin family, to honor his friendship with Gurasa. So it was leaned into the corner, simply and without embellishment. Alas, Dalvenpar never lived to see it there. So it represents many things to us. Mystery. Sorrow. Regret. Maybe hope."

"It is a sad family history you have," said Sheila, listening from behind.

Ullin nodded and shrugged, "It was not always that way. And I have faith that it will not be so forever."

"Sheila, look at this!" Billy called over from the table where he was balancing a plate in one hand while at the same time holding out his other hand for a tankard being filled for him by one of the serving staff. "Barley ale! Clean made, High Bend Special, too!"

Sheila and Ullin wandered over to the food table so that they could be served.

"I think I'll go look for Lord Tallin," said Ashlord to Robby. "Don't forget to jot a few words to your mother!"

Robby nodded as Ashlord departed, then he walked about the room looking over the displays. In this one room, there was a fair representation of the history of both the Tallin family and that of Fairoak. The Tallins seemed to have been among the so-called First Families, those who came off the original ships of Men that landed on the shores of the world, and Robby recognized among the various portraits of family ancestors the same pale-blue star he had seen in the murals within Tulith Attis. Only in what he took to be later paintings did he see the addition of the ivy entwining it, and he realized that it represented the union between the races of Men and Elifaen which took place. He had no notion who the people portrayed were, nor the significance of the weapons that he assumed had belonged to some of them, or had played some role in their history—in his own history as it turned out. Lost for a moment in thought, he found himself staring through the doorway at another small painting that was in the hall. He couldn't quite make it out from where he stood so he left the room to take a closer look. It was not a painting at all, but a scrap of cloth artfully mounted under clear glass, framed and hung for display. It looked to be a remnant of clothing as it had the same blue star dyed upon it, almost faded beyond recognition. It was not long before his curiosity overcame his reluctance to leave his friends, and he wandered along the hallways, up and down flights of stairs, studying the artwork, statues, and paintings that he came upon.

Along one upstairs passage, he stopped at a window to gaze out at the bustling town. He wondered again, sighing at the thought, why it was that he was never encouraged to come to Tallinvale. It was in keeping with all of the other secrets his mother and father kept from him.

"Still," he said, "had I known it was such an interesting place, I might have made an effort to come on my own, just to see the sights."

Turning away, he saw a large chart on the wall nearby and, going to it, he saw that it was a family tree. It outlined the Tallin family ancestors, going all the way back to the last generation to live aboard the wondrous ships that had brought them here. It also, to one side, outlined the Fairoak lineage, with far fewer names listed, presumably owing to the long lives of the Elifaen, going back over two thousand years to the Time Before Time. He studied the chart for a long while, and was surprised to see that unions between Tallins and Elifaen had occurred twice before his own mother and father had married. The first such union was between the nephew of Heneil and a Tallin woman. Their son, his grandfather's father, took the Tallin name and passed it on. Robby realized that he had Elifaen blood not only through his grandmother's lineage, but from his grandfather's, too. As he looked over the names, his eyes tracing up and down and back and forth across the genealogy, he wondered at the people listed and their stories. He wondered, too, whether his own name might someday be listed on a similar chart.

"Oh, I forgot," he muttered, walking away. "I don't have a name, do I? And, if I do, and if I become King, then only the person who will ever know it will be whoever it is that replaces me."

This only served to remind him of the recondite tasks before him, not the least of which was to learn the Name of the King. Ashlord said that he would be able to solve the problem. But Ashlord always seemed to think the best of people, Robby thought.

He paused at another window that overlooked the estate, and he watched some of the groundskeepers tend the gardens for a few moments before wandering on. Household staff came and went, but did not disturb him, though a few stopped to ask if he desired assistance, bowing low and addressing him with what he felt was too much deference. He thanked them, returning their bows, but refused any offers, content to be lost for the time being as he explored Tallin Hall. Somehow or other, he found himself down in the deep workings of the structure, in what he at first thought to be the ground floor, but now he perceived that many of the corridors were carved out of living rock. It was lit with lamps of amazing quality that gave off splendid white light. At last he rounded a bend in the corridor and came to a huge double iron door, outside of which were several guards who immediately snapped to attention.

"Lord Robby!" one of them said. "I did not expect so quick an inspection!"

Robby recognized him as Ullin's friend, Weylan.

"Captain Weylan, I believe?"

"Aye."

"I thought you said you were of the Gatesmen."

"North Gatesmen, my lord. But we of the Fortress Guard also serve the Hall. I am here to bring routine orders."

"I see. And what is this room?"

"This is one of the Hall's armoury vaults, sir. Just a storage place for spares and various fighting gear."

"May I see?"

"Certainly! Open up, there! And light the way!"

Two of the soldiers pushed hard on the great doors, swinging them inwards as a third lit a small torch. He entered and quickly marched through the room touching off torch after torch that jutted from walls and columns. Robby followed Weylan into a very long wide room, nearly as wide and as long as the great hall above. But this room had low ceilings and thick stone arches crisscrossing throughout. Everywhere in neat orderly lines were racks upon racks of swords, shields, helmets, lances, breastplates, chain mail, bows, and baskets of arrows. He looked at Weylan in wonder.

"It looks as though you have enough to arm thousands!" he said.

"Three hundred archers with fifty arrows each," Weylan said. "Two thousand footmen with shields and pikes and shortswords. Seven hundred and forty light skirmishers, and three hundred lighthorse. Plus several light ballistas, some to launch fire, some for bolts, others for spikefists."

"Spikefists?"

"Yes, these little pretties, my lord," Weylan went over to a box and lifted the lid. Reaching in, he gingerly picked up a small ball about the size of a fist, bristling with dozens of long sharp steel spikes each about four inches long.

"It looks like the center is made of some kind of glass," Robby said. "And the whole looks very nasty."

"Nasty they are! Our spikefist ballistas fling thirty of these at once in a tight grouping and can reach up to fifty yards away with accuracy, much farther if we don't care. The spikes penetrate anything they hit while the glass center shatters, sending the other spikes hurling at nearby targets."

Weylan gently returned the weapon to its bin.

"It is best used against lightly armored mass assaults of closely packed attackers," he said dryly. "This is only the house armoury. Lord Tallin has kept our forges ringing day and night these past few months, and the products fill three other much larger warehouses and many smaller stores around the city."

"So you are preparing for war."

"Well, we prepare the implements, anyway. Our treaties with Damar and Tracia still hold. We are certain their spies watch our movements and report the activity of our forges. We may be fewer in number than they, but we are well-armed, at least. And Lord Tallin has seen to it that we are trained as well as any. Perhaps better. If our enemies come against us, they will find Tallin Town a hard nut to crack."

"If only my people could have had time to prepare," Robby said wistfully, picking up a lance and looking at its tip. "We could have used some fine weapons such as these, if only we had the men and training, too."

Weylan nodded.

"Riders came through three days ago with news of the Redvests in Passdale," Weylan said as they left the room and the doors were closed behind them. "Do you now go back upstairs? Or are there other things you wish to see?"

"Oh, no. I am just wandering around. I don't exactly know how I made my way down here. Indeed, I think I'm rather lost. But I would like to see whatever I am allowed to see, and I'm in no particular hurry to rejoin my friends."

"In that case, might I show you around?"

"I would like that more than anything, if you have time for me. I'm sorry that I am woefully ignorant of so many things. Perhaps you would tell me about the walls, too. But first, tell me, what was the reaction here concerning the events in Barley?"

"We were all of us shocked," Weylan said, pointing to a side hallway and gesturing for Robby to go that way. "Dismayed, concerned. Surprised that the Redvests managed to cut through the long way 'round, north through the Boggy Wood."

"I don't mean to sound ungrateful for your hospitality, but was there no talk of sending aid?"

"Certainly there was talk! Some mighty loud talk, indeed! And none too sparse of language, either. But Lord Tallin forbade any action, saying we were not prepared to break our treaty with Tracia, and that if we sent men to oppose Tracia in Barley, we could only do so by weakening our southern and western flanks."

"But now Tracia has your eastern flank as well. Surely they mean to move from Barley southwards along the Old Road."

"Certainly. Well, that is my opinion, anyway. And rumors have it that much activity of horsemen, messengers and the like, move from the Redvests in Barley to their main forces in the south. Let us turn here and go along these steps."

Weylan led on through the brick-lined corridor, still well lit and not as damp or close as one might imagine.

"Where are we going?"

"You'll see. And be surprised, I think."

"What do you think Lord Tallin will do?"

Weylan shrugged.

"I do not know. Many of his most loyal grumble that he does nothing. Many are unhappy that Lord Tallin refuses to engage the Tracian Redvests, or even the Damar unless pressed by their forays. There are many here who once lived in Tracia, and we have commerce with those of Hill Town, too. It is well known here that honor means nothing to those who now rule Tracia, though their army is professional and for the most part are a credit to the sense of the word most of us know. But their leaders are not military men, and they are ruthless. Their orders are most despicable, even against their own people. They give their word on paper and then toss it aside when it suits them. They have mismanaged their commerce. Their farms, which were failing even before the great summer storm, have collapsed. Those who have escaped or been driven away say that most common folk go hungry while the army and those in power eat well enough, indeed. It is rumored that some sickness of mind has gripped the new Tracian leaders and that, after having murdered most of those loyal to the Prince, they now are filled with fear and mistrust lest their own ways are used against them. Meanwhile, Lord Tallin tolerates the fact that the Redvests to the south encroach, forcing tribute from those nearby to our lands. Many of those people have left their homes and farms to escape such abuse, and they add to the resentment that grows. And to the discontent with Lord Tallin's treaties and such. It is a balancing act, some say, that must fall one way or the other."

"So now they go to war, attacking the Eastlands," commented Robby as they came to a long upward slope.

"It seems so, though we have heard of no fighting yet, outside Barley, that is. And they probably move first in the Eastlands to gather food and such for their armies."

"Hm. This is an extraordinarily long tunnel!"

"Yes, the city is crisscrossed with them. It makes for easy movement by our soldiers. We take the straight-ahead fork this way."

"And Lord Tallin built all this? Years and years ago?"

"Aye," Weylan nodded. "Or, rather, those he hired to do so. From what I've heard, it was some Masurthia folk that did the work."

"Masurthia? From the south?" Robby looked at Weylan as the Captain nodded. "I heard Endeweir folk made the city."

"Endeweir? Look at these joints. Not a speck of mortar, and dry as a bone, too. Smooth. Some say it is some kind of glass. The Endeweir are fisher-folk, I heard tell. And that's a far place, indeed, up where the snows don't even melt, they say."

"Oh."

They marched on, sometimes turning aside so that soldiers could pass, until Robby could hear noise of activity coming from ahead, and as they neared a bright exit, several soldiers appeared.

"Who goes?"

"Weylan of the Guard! With Lord Ribbon! Open!"

"Why do you call me lord?"

"Why? Er, well, I reckon there's no other term. I mean we all know you're not *the* Lord. But in these parts, any descendant of Tallin is called lord or lady."

The pair neared a gate of iron bars that groaned as two men pushed it open for them to pass. The way continued upward, curved sharply to the left, and bright daylight poured through an open arched portal. Before they reached it, Weylan turned and led Robby through a side opening and up a steep staircase, dimly lit at first but growing brighter as they climbed. When they walked out blinking into brilliant daylight, Robby was surprised to find himself at the very top of one of the outer walls of the city. He could clearly see the road he had traveled along earlier that morning and well beyond it to the forest. The air was cool and refreshing, and the handsome pennants snapped in the breeze.

"Captain on the Gate!" cried a soldier nearby, and, as quick as you like, several soldiers lined themselves up as their leader approached.

"All correct, sir. Little traffic today. A fine morning."

"Thank you, Eglan. Very good. Yes, fine."

Then, as the soldier stepped aside, Weylan turned to Robby, grinning.

"Welcome to the North Gate of Tallin City! Are you not amazed?"

"Indeed I am! Never would I have guessed! A most impressive passage, and one that no doubt may serve an important military purpose, should the need arise."

"It is so. The passage, but one of five like it, each from the outer walls to the Hall. They permit the movement of arms whichever way is needed. Should the walls ever be breached, which is not likely, the underground corridors are made to collapse, if need be, blocking the enemy's use of them. Along the way, there are many upward-leading egresses to sally ports and such, to let us come up behind any force in the streets above. Should any enemy make it through our walls, that is."

"Ullin said your defenses are based on a design of Heneil, and that none of his defenses ever fell by arms."

"That is so, but there are secrets to these walls that only Lord Tallin himself knows, for only he among us was here at their construction."

Robby started to ask more questions about that when Weylan's face lit up. Turning around, Robby saw Ullin coming up the stairs.

"You are something of a wanderer!" Ullin said to Robby.

"Just a little tour of the place," put in Weylan. "Perhaps you would like to accompany us?"

"I'd be delighted! I must confess I was looking for Robby with the same thought in mind. That is, to show him around."

"Weren't you going to teach Ibin how to play the mandolin?" Robby asked.

"Oh, yes. And I did, sort of," Ullin laughed. "But after a couple of lessons, I realized he would be the teacher and I the pupil. He seems to have an uncanny gift and is already plucking out tunes far beyond my meager ability. I left him still playing, Billy nodding away, and Sheila being given a tour by Windard, who has taken a keen liking to her. Very uncharacteristic of him to take such a liking to anyone. He is formal of a nature, and no less so with her to a point, but I found them chatting away about keeping house, of all things. Windard, who rarely has more than a word or two for anyone, was telling her all about the workings of Tallin Hall with an enthusiasm I have never seen in him."

"She has a way of bringing that out, sometimes."

Chapter 7

Puzzles

"I wanted to speak to you about several matters," Tallin told Ashlord as the two entered the library. It was a large room, Ashlord's favorite in all of Tallin Hall, with rows of shelves for bound manuscripts in abundance as well as racks for scrolls and rolled maps. It was well lit, day or night, by south windows and doors, and by ingenious lamps at the tables that burned highly refined oil beneath polished hoods. Ashlord had been here several times before, the last time some years ago, and as a figure of some status with both Men and Elifaen, he was allowed the use of the place. It held not only copies of all of the greatest works of literature and lore, but also many materials devoted to the early ages, some even in the hand of the original chroniclers of the First Age before Men came. Upon locating Tallin, Ashlord immediately asked if he could spend the afternoon reading and studying, especially the accounts of the early Kings of Duinnor. Tallin was proud of his library and glad to have it used by such a scholar as Ashlord, and he escorted him there personally, saying they could talk there as well as any other place.

"But," he went on, waving Ashlord to a chair, "much of what I wanted to confer with you on is now moot, I find."

"Oh?"

"Yes. I must say that my interview with my grandsons has affected me in a peculiar way. I find, through no slip on the part of Robby or Ullin, that Duinnor may soon have a new king."

Ashlord stiffened in his chair.

"Oh? And how did you come to that conclusion?"

"Come, Collandoth! I am not as old or as wise as you, but it only takes a fair observer who has studied the chronicles and lore to see the signs. My House has long been foretold to play some role in the changing of the world and the coming of the new age. That is certainly why we were banished, in a manner of speaking, from the West. It is also why Duinnor has ignored our messages of warning and has sent our sons to almost certain death in battle time and again. Ullin survives only due to your intervention, I am convinced, having him reassigned to the King's Post. Evidently, your contacts in Duinnor are still loyal to you."

"It is not to me they are loyal, but to the doing of right things," Ashlord said. "I am not opposed to Duinnor. Indeed, I am united with many loyal servants of the Realms in wanting the wrongs suffered by many to be righted, and for an end to the continued abuse of power. Ullin was guided to me by a friend not to protect him from battle, which he has seen plenty of, but from those who would read the signs as we have, and think he might be the One."

"I opposed Ullin when he left for Duinnor."

"I know. But that was unwise. Your opposition was apparent to all close to this House, and word of your dislike of the King was widely spread. As a result, while you may have the sympathy of many, you have little open support. Few will respond to any petitions you may send, even when your interests and those of Duinnor's are the same."

"Ah, you speak of the present situation," said Tallin.

"Yes."

"But why was Ullin thought a threat? Why was he deemed to be the One?"

"Many made the same mistake. Even I very nearly came to that conclusion. But, in fact, it is here in this room that the key piece of knowledge came to me a few years ago. The last time I was here, in fact. You have the original manuscripts of Uden of Selacia, who was among the First Men on these shores. Those writings have not been widely translated or copied, and Duinnor knows nothing about their contents. But Uden referred to Heneil's wife, Lyrium, who had the gift of Sight. She foresaw the fall of Tulith Attis in a dream, and she warned her husband, Uden tells, and so Heneil constructed the bell room to catch the traitor. Everyone knows the stories of that battle and how Heneil constructed the Bell so that only one of the Elifaen who could speak the First Tongue could open the Iron Door and set the Bell ringing out its warning. But Uden was writing before the battle at Tulith Attis and did not know the outcome."

Ashlord had gotten up from his chair and was searching among the manuscripts as he spoke. He tucked one under his arm and kept searching for another.

"How is that a clue about Ullin?"

"Aha!" Ashlord cried. "Here it is! The Aldergiest Toll, an account of the battle by one of the survivors."

"But that was not written by Uden."

"I know. I have Uden's manuscript here, too. The Aldergiest Toll was written by a Dragonkind soldier who was at Tulith Attis and who managed to return to his homeland. I am still amazed that you have a copy of it."

"It was a present of Gurasa," Tallin stated as Ashlord put the books on a nearby table. "Apparently he is somehow related to the author."

Ashlord opened one of the books, located a passage, and, keeping his hand on the open page, opened the second one with his other hand and rapidly flipped through it. It took some looking to find the passage he desired, but at last he stood straight and looked at Lord Tallin.

"One of the peculiar things about the battle of Tulith Attis was the wolves."

"Wolves? What do you mean?"

"I mean, according to this account of the battle, let me read: 'Our legions swept easily up the south bank of the Saerdulin, crossing to both sides to cut off any escape. We came as a shadow over the land, driving wolves and all manner of beasts before us and into the ranks of our enemy as a prelude to battle. The wolves upon the ground before us, and the carrion birds following in the wake of our destruction.' "

"Yes, I remember that passage. But I still do not see—"

"That is one piece of the puzzle. Here is another: From Uden's accounts of Lyrium's vision I now read, please forgive my coarse translation: 'And so Lyrium, much disturbed by her dream went unto her husband, and, finding him, said unto him, 'Dear one, listen to me. I have had a dream that foretells of the fall of this place in days to come. In my dream I saw a young Elifaen. A great battle raged and the very clouds strove to overturn one another, amidst fire and thunder, and from this came a devastation of water upon the land. I saw the young Elifaen coming up through the river passage of our fortress, bearing a fiery brand. I saw this Elifaen enter our stronghold, coming into the very midst of our fortress, and behind him came an army of wolves. And wolves came from all sides. There was a great struggle, and my vision failed me. But I saw him again, in another age to come, bearing in one hand the crown of Duinnor, and in his other hand he held seven golden rods. I saw a Prince of the Dragon people bow down before him, and great ladies of ancient Elifaen Houses do the same. I saw a nobleman lying dead upon the street, and others taken away in chains. Tell me, oh husband, what can this mean?' And, considering, Heneil said unto Lyrium his wife, 'A warning, no more, though a powerful one. Your dream foretells of a traitor who may conquer the Seven Realms and unite them under his servants, the Dragon People. But I will thwart this traitor by my skills. I will construct within the passage from the river a chamber to hold a great bell. An iron door, too, I will make. And I will have a charm laid upon it so that it will open only to one of the Firstborn who can still speak the First Tongue. Beside the door, I will set great sentinels watching, and about the chamber, too. Moreover, I will raise a wall to block the River Saerdulin so that it may shrivel and no boats may bring enemies against us. And if any but I open the Iron Door, the great bell will toll and the sentinels will awake. The traitor will pass unharmed, so that we may capture him, but his army of wolves will be slaughtered behind him. And the great wall that I shall make will then tumble so that, returning violently to its course, the Saerdulin may sweep away any enemies upon the riverbed. And if any reach within our castle, I will set upon them my personal guard as well, who, by incantation, shall wait patiently howsoever long as is required, protected by stone such as the kind that Alonair might fashion. They, too, the great bell will arouse, to repel any intruders within.' "

Ashlord closed the books slowly and looked at Tallin.

"Although I suspect it did not happen precisely as it is recorded here, the rendition of Lyrium's dream is, I think, fairly accurate. For me, this was my proof that Ullin was not the One, and that Robby is, though I was too long in seeing it."

"Then you have guessed who it is that comes tonight?"

"Yes."

"But how is that passage proof that Ullin is not the One?"

"Because young Robby, seeking to escape a storm and beset by packs of ravenous wolves, entered the bell room, and his only escape was by means of the Iron Door, which he opened, being Faere Blessed and able to do so, thereby setting off the Great Bell, destroying the dam that blocked the flow of the ancient Saerdulin, and awakening the stone sentinels."

Tallin crossed his arms, looking away in thought as Ashlord put the manuscripts away.

"I remember hearing," he said to Ashlord, "that he was sick once. As a very young child. Almost unto death. Strange folk from far away came to him, was what I was told. Those that are Faere Blessed, so they say, can only become so during a great trial of their life, or else be born to the blessing. If his visitors were..." His voice trailed off, but he resumed with another thought, "But he is not one of the Firstborn. And, besides, the Elifaen do not become sick, except perhaps of heart."

"That is true," Ashlord nodded. "But Robby has not yet been Scathed, so is not yet Elifaen. To be Faere Blessed is another matter. It is still a mystery to me, and we may never know the answer. It happened some years before I took up in the region, so I knew nothing of it. But I was led to take up a place of watching at Tulith Attis by my reading of events and signs, some so vague that I cannot explain them in words."

"It seems you are not the only one who has been watching," Tallin said. "For this evening there comes one, so I am told, that particularly wants to meet my grandson. A messenger, Tyrillick, came to me this last spring. You saw him. Like you have probably guessed, I, too, knew from his livery who sent him. And he confirmed it to me when I asked who it was that wished to use Tallinvale as a place of rendezvous, and with whom they wished to meet. He told me that I should take from him a twig about two feet long and a finger thick, but it was heavy, as if made of lead. I was to cast the twig from my window and watch the place where it fell. I was told that if ever I did not wish to have Tallin Hall as the meeting place of these parties, I only need cut down anything that might grow up from where the twig fell, and the appointment would take place elsewhere. So I took the twig and, standing at my tower balcony, I threw it as far out as I could."

Tallin rose from his seat and walked to the outside doors, and flung them open.

"It landed there."

Ashlord stood, and his eyes widened as he went to the door and saw the breadth of the massive tree that grew some forty yards away. Its great roots curled over a bench of newly cut stone, its dark gray trunk was over two yards thick, straight and tall, it was crowned by strangely symmetrical limbs bearing silvery-green leaves, and it stretched up higher than any other tree in the gardens.

"It is an Iron Oak!" said the astonished Ashlord. "I have not seen one since, since..." This time his words trailed away. "But they grow very slowly, and this tree looks to be several hundred years of Men."

"Yet the twig I threw landed just behind that new bench not even six months ago," Tallin nodded. "So you see, I asked no more questions, nor did I cut it down while I could have, as a young sprout only a hand-thickness wide at the trunk. Now it would take my best smithies toiling away night and day for the better part of a year to take it down. Not that I have the least intention of trying," he added, turning back into the library.

"You have had your signs, Collandoth, and I have had mine. And though I am a stubborn man, quite often not willing to see the hand before my face, I am not a fool. This morning, as I talked with Robby, the puzzle for me was solved. I cannot now say precisely what it was that enlightened me, but I knew it was he. Not at first. It only came to me in the middle of our interview. Something he said. Or, perhaps rather how he said it."

Ashlord gazed at Tallin, nodding in understanding. "So what will you do? Now that you know what may come."

Tallin looked away and shook his head.

"Do? I wonder, can anything be done? What might we do other than what we are already doing? It seems little, in the face of it all. Yet, Tallinvale must do its part, whatever it may be, with whatever hope may be had. What more may we do? Only things too terrible to contemplate."

"Yet contemplate such things you must," Ashlord stated. "And there are those who would come to your aid. Though few in numbers, and scattered into many places, they may be of assistance. The people of Hill Town, Tracians mostly, who yearn to free their country but have no means to make a difference. They know the hills and mountains as well as any, and they can act as raiders. I beg you, send a trusted envoy to Martin Makeig, their leader, putting your plan before him. Janhaven, too, holds many from Barley and Passdale who would join with the Thunder Mountain folk. They may keep your northern flank protected if they have some support. They need food and arms and only the most basic of supplies. And they, like the Hill Town folk, long to take back what is theirs. But you must be openly bold. Else they will see no purpose in joining with you."

"Yes. Bold," Tallin said softly, a painful expression on his face. He suddenly seemed preoccupied and distant as he went to the door.

"I leave you to your studies, then," he said quietly and without turning as he left the room. Ashlord saw Dargul hovering about the door with an anxious expression. He made as if to say something to Ashlord, then, thinking better of it, turned to follow Tallin.

• • •

Two hours later, Ashlord was still studying the precious manuscripts of the library, the staff having delivered to him some light wine and refreshment. Before him were maps and books strewn about, scrolls unfurled and hanging from tables, and various loose papers and folios.

"Tulith Morgair, Tulith Morgair," he mumbled, sliding papers and maps back and forth. He looked once again in the book nearest him, read over a passage. "Year 322 of the Second Age ... many stations along the western slopes of the Mountains of Thunder ... gave notice by its beacons of the coming of the desert armies ... hmm."

He shook his head, "No, not here," and dashed back over to the bookshelves, running his finger along the spines.

"No, no. Where might it be? I definitely sense some connection." His finger passed over a thin leather volume and hesitated. He pulled it down and looked to its title page.

"Poems of Starlerf of Everis," he read aloud, and he turned a few pages. It was written in the poet's own hand with a dedication to Lady Kahryna, Lord Tallin's deceased wife, Robby's grandmother.

"Ah!" he cried, putting the book back and turning swiftly to the scroll rack. He pulled down one, then another, and yet another, each time unfurling them somewhat and putting them back until at last he found what he was looking for tucked beside a portfolio. It was a small one, covered with dust, and he unrolled it carefully onto the table.

From Danthis of Duinnor
To Kahryna of Vanara, House of Fairoak.

Written this day, the Fourth Day of Tenthmonth
In the Year 243 of this our Second Age.

It is my greatest hope that this letter finds you well and that your family is enjoying a safe and prosperous autumn. With great pleasure I report to you the completion of Tulith Morgair, and it is my honor to say that the structure has been adorned with images of various great figures of our people, arranged in a circle to serve as the columns to support the beacon platform above. Among these is one which is carved in the likeness of your late father. As do the other figures, this one of your father stands about fifteen cubits tall. He is represented holding the staff I so often saw him carry, with his arm outstretched, his hand palm up, as he frequently did when explaining some point of custom or law. It is my hope that you will soon receive drawings of the structure that will in some way impart to you how we hold proud the memory of your father now as we did during his life, with honor and esteem. Should you ever come into the East, and should you desire to look upon the work, it would be my pleasure to escort you there. You would then see that, just as the wisdom and guidance of your father continues to serve his people long after his departure, this place, too, will also be of lasting service.

Ashlord leaned back in his chair, putting the letter down. Looking back at the shelf, he reached over and pulled down the portfolio. It contained several drawings of the structure described in the letter.

"That's it. But how did Robby know about Tulith Morgair?" He absently picked up and sucked on his cold pipe. Somewhere inside his head he noticed no smoke was drawing, but he was so deep in contemplation, his brows furrowed and his eyes narrow, that he paid little attention. "How did he know?"

Twice, a light tap came upon the door, but Ashlord did not react. Only when Sheila cautiously entered into his view did he stir from his thoughts and look at her.

"I hope I'm not disturbing you," she said tentatively.

"Oh, no, no. You should have just come on in. I was taking this chance to catch up on some reading, to confirm my memory a little, and so forth."

"I was thinking of doing the same. Windard told me about the library here and asked one of the girls to show me the way. But when I saw you, I hesitated to enter. You looked rather deep in thought."

"Oh, if I was, it shouldn't keep you from anything here!" Ashlord waved his arm about, gesturing at the riches that surrounded them. "For one, you've been with me often enough to know better than to be so formal. For another, it is a wonder to me that this room isn't crowded with people. Such a glorious collection of histories, tales, letters, maps—many done in the authors' own hand, I might add—enough to keep one's noggin busy for years!"

Sheila looked around the room for a few moments.

"One hardly knows where to begin. Is there any order to any of this? It looks so confusing."

"Oh, much of the mess is my doing, I'm afraid. But, yes, there is somewhat of an order. Over there are collections of tales and legends, and next are chronicles of various kinds. Those are letters and old household documents. Over here are poems, songs, and music. There are excellent drawings in many of these works. Across from us are sundry official documents, land title records, deed exchanges, census counts of Tallinvale of the various years and so forth."

Sheila hesitated.

"One place to start might be where your present interest may be," suggested Ashlord.

"Well, we don't have much time here, and I feel I need to practice my reading of the Ancient Tongue since we go west into lands where it is more often spoken."

"Oh, yes, very well. If that is what you wish."

"But I am not sure where my interests are, exactly."

"Well, why don't you try this." Ashlord picked up two volumes. One was slightly smaller than the other, and looked older. "This is called *'Esin dur to Lumenii'* and it is a collection of poems and tales from the First Age. This other volume is called "Hope of the Stars," and it is a translation of the first into the Common Speech of our present day. Over there, on that table, is an ingenious book, within which is a list of words and letters in the Ancient Tongue and gives beside them a list of the same or similar words as they are written in the Common Speech, and in various other languages of the Realms. Start with the original and if you have trouble, turn to the other two for help. Or, you may ask me if you wish. I find that one thing often leads to another, and that connections are sometimes made in the most surprising ways between interests that may seem far different and separate. But start with these and see where they may lead you."

. . .

Meanwhile, from the great room of the guest wing came the continual plucking of light tunes produced by a mandolin and accompanied by a smooth tenor voice. Windard came gliding down the hall and, hearing it, stopped to make sure of the sound. Yes, it was coming from the great room. Though he recognized the tune, a harvest song he had not heard since he was a youngster, he could not place the voice. Just as he neared the door, Billy shot out with an exasperated expression, and the two nearly collided.

"Oh! Pardon me, sir!" Billy cried out, red-faced.

Nonplussed, Windard straightened his jacket. "I beg your pardon, Master Bosk. Is there something amiss?"

"No, no. Yes," Billy said, throwing up his hands and moving around Windard. "How's a person to nap? If I hear another bloody ballad I may as well go stark ravin' amuck! What a fierce headache! By yer leave, sir. I must retire!"

Billy managed an awkward bow and stomped off down the hall to his room. Windard returned the bow, ever-so-slightly, and turned to look into the great room. The staff were all seated around Ibin, who was giving air to aires, so to speak, and holding them in a kind of rapture. His touch on the mandolin was clean and clear, and the slight quavering of his voice gave an understated passion to the words of the melancholy song. His listeners wore expressions of deep sympathy to the haunting and lonesome lyrics. Even Windard, dismayed by the familiar conduct of his staff, was momentarily captivated, and only when Ibin drew the last note on the mandolin and it had faded, did he shake himself back from the distance of his thoughts. As the staff around the singer gave their praise, Windard floated into the room, stiff and expressionless. Seeing him, one of the boys leapt up, and instantly the others of the staff did, too, turning his way. Realizing they had been caught out, they faced Windard expectantly.

"You have an exceptional voice, Master Brinnin," he said, glancing at the dirty dishes left by Billy. The staff sprang forward to clean things away, but having so few things that the five of them struggled for a moment to determine which one of them was to take the bowl and which the saucer and which the platter, so that all could appear busy. Windard seemed to ignore them. "I have not heard that tune for many years. Pray, where did you learn it? I do not think it is of this realm."

"OhIlearnedit, Ilearnedit, Ilearneditfrom, fromlistening, fromlisten-ingtotheminstrelsonenight."

"I see."

"Wouldyouliketohear, Iknowanother, Iknowothersongs,too."

"I am sure that you do, and I thank you. But, alas, I must attend to my duties." This Windard said pointedly toward the embarrassed staff who had by now retaken their stations at the buffet tables, each and every one solemnly adjusting the placement of some carafe, fruit bowl, napkin, or fork.

· · ·

Robby had been shown many aspects of the outer walls, the various positions of defense where men might set up the ballistas like those he had seen earlier in the armoury, stages from which archers could rain their lethal arrows upon attackers, and even the great bridge-hammers, as they were called. These were located at special casemates at the base of each wall. They were massive iron weights, each carefully designed so that its swinging fall would strike an iron pin protruding through the wall. The blow would drive the pin which would transmit its push to the connected iron rods and bars that Ullin had spoken of. They would move but just a few inches, yet so precise was their working that those few inches would make the difference between a standing bridge and a tumbling pile of rubble. Asked if they were ever tested, Weylan explained that each year, a different bridge was selected to be tested so that over the course of years, every bridge was knocked down and rebuilt. If there was a problem, it was corrected, and the test was made again.

"We have not had a bridge fail in more than fifteen years," Weylan told Robby, patting a nearby pin.

"And what are those?" Robby pointed at tall brick tanks nearby to the hammers.

"Those are our oil stores," Ullin said. "In each of them are nearly a three hundred barrels of light oil. See those small stone troughs below them? Those caps at the end of the troughs are removed so that when the tap is turned, the oil flows into those troughs and on through holes cut into them and then into the same little tunnels in which the iron rods for the bridges are laid."

"Oh. To make the iron bars slip more easily."

"No, there is no need for that. The iron bars are well-laid by themselves," explained Weylan. "No, the oil runs out from around the bars near the bridges and so into the moat and the canals. Our archers may then send flaming arrows into the canals, setting the oil ablaze."

Robby looked at Ullin blankly at first, then blinked, thinking of what it might be like to be caught in such an inferno. "Oh, my. Is that ever tested, too?"

"Aye, every late winter," Weylan nodded. "And it's a fine way to keep back the brush that may make handholds on the canal sides."

Robby looked at Ullin, who nodded a confirmation of the seriousness of the defenses.

"I think Robby and I had best be getting back to the Hall," he said to Weylan. "I regret we'll not be here long. My guess is that we'll be leaving tomorrow early. It was good to see you."

"Likewise, Ullin. Perhaps we'll see each other again before you depart."

Robby thanked Weylan for his attentions, and they wished each other well before Ullin led him back through the town and so toward Tallin Hall.

"So you and Captain Weylan are old friends?" Robby asked.

"Yes. We grew up together. Had our letters together," Ullin said. "And a fair amount of mischief, too."

It was well past mid-afternoon, and more people were out and about than when they had first arrived. Robby sensed a change in them, too, as they passed by. It was not merely that there were more soldiers, but also that they seemed extraordinarily well attired, with every piece of metal polished, every leather strap blackened, and wonderfully colored plumes affixed to their helmets. The horsemen were busy, their grooms brushing down the clean coats of the mounts while saddles were being prepared by others. There was a long line of helmets, he saw, each having its long horsehair plume brushed and combed, and everywhere along the way, outside of shops and houses, sat men with towels over their shoulders having their hair trimmed and their beards shaved. People seemed in a hurry, though they smiled, and some, taking closer notice of Robby and Ullin, bowed as they passed. Some did this modestly and others in a very showy fashion with even a flourish or two. Three ladies, who came giggling out of a house and who were wearing lavender, pale rose, and turquoise gowns with broad skirts and billowing sleeves, and bodices laced low and tight under their high bosoms, stopped short of the two men, bumbled into one another and then stood aside silently. As Robby and Ullin passed, the ladies smiled and nodded, and they curtseyed so elegantly and so precariously low, with their heads bowed, that Robby feared they might all tumble in a heap on the ground.

More people came along, and Robby had to watch where he was going, but he threw a look over his shoulder at the ladies and saw them moving off as before, one giving him a brief flirtatious glance. Tyrillick then appeared in the crowd before them, and when he saw them, he quickly turned to walk with them.

"I hope you are having a good day," he said in a friendly tone. "I was just going back to the Hall, so I'll join you if that is where you are going, too. And if you don't mind."

"Yes, it is," said Ullin.

"We'd be happy for you to join us!" said Robby.

Several gaily-ribboned carts rolled by, filled with children with garlands of flowers in their hair and singing happily as they went.

"What is happening, Ullin?" Robby asked. "Why all the activity? Is this usual, or is there some celebration taking place?"

"No celebration that I know of," he said. "Well, maybe. In a manner of speaking."

"Word has gotten out, late this morning," said Tyrillick. "All great things come in threes, they say. First, rumor has it that the Redvests and the Damar will at last be faced, though I don't know how that rumor started or what there is to it."

"Do you mean war? And these people are excited about it?" Robby asked incredulously.

"For a long time Tallinvale has tolerated the ill treatment and raids of the Damar," Ullin said. "And long have we simpered to the threats of Tracia, it is spoken. It is said that our grandfather, Lord Tallin, has allowed insult upon his people, doing nothing while their trade is cut off and while the houses and farms to the south are taxed and made to pay Tracian tribute. They do not long for war, but they have been fed up these past many years, and they yearn to do something about it."

"Hrumph!" said Robby, much as his father might. He noted that Ullin said "we," but he knew enough of the state of things to know Tallinvale was a sideshow, at best, to the strength of Tracia.

"What about the other two things you mentioned? Coming in threes, as you said?" he asked Tyrillick just as another crowd parted before them. The plain folk bowed, and the soldiers saluted as they passed through.

"Do you not see?" the elf replied, amused at Robby. Tyrillick and Ullin exchanged a glance. Robby saw this. Ullin smiled, lowering his head in a slightly embarrassed way, but he said nothing. Robby looked back at Tyrillick and shook his head with a questioning shrug.

"They say the Lords of Tallinvale are returned," Tyrillick said to Robby. "And that it is a sign, no less, that the great Joined House of Fairoak and Tallin will stand and may be restored to the glory of the ancient days."

"They do?"

"They do. I have with my own ears heard it said not an hour ago, a butcher telling a carpenter on the street with a certainty. And then again, just before we met up, from a governess to her charge. It is a small place, after all, and word has spread like the wind. And now, as the pair of you stroll, they see for themselves."

"So you are to take the place of our grandfather?" Robby asked Ullin innocently. "And become Lord Tallin?"

"They do not speak of me, Robby," Ullin said gently, yielding to a passerby. "I am not Elifaen, and so I cannot be heir of Fairoak."

"So who..., oh!" Robby stopped himself, embarrassed at his own ignorance. "I didn't realize."

Ullin nodded, and Tyrillick chuckled and shook his head, then went on.

"And of the third thing, it is rumored that a great visitor will arrive this night from the West. A party of the First Ones, they tell each other, the likes of which has not visited Tallinvale since before anyone can remember. They have, suddenly, many reasons to turn out in their finery. In one day, no less, all these things come to them. It is much to deal with, and their scurrying about—the fine clothes, the preparations—is, I would say, a kind of release of hope for many restrained hearts. Would you not agree, Ullin Saheed?"

"Yes. You put it well."

"First Ones?"

"That is what they say, Robby Ribbon."

"But not you."

"Not I, for I have said nothing."

"That would be enough to feel honored, if it were true. As to us lords," Robby nearly laughed out loud at the word—not so much as how it applied to Ullin, for he was lordly enough. "Do these people know we'll not be staying?" Robby asked Ullin.

"Evidently not. But I doubt if that would matter."

"And what about the visitors?" Robby turned back to Tyrillick. "Who are they?"

"You try me, Robby Ribbon of Passdale! I promised not to say," Tyrillick said kindly. "But the rumors are, well, not without some accuracy. As far as rumors go."

Robby could see that Tyrillick would tell him no more. By now they had passed through the town and were climbing the gentle slope to the gates of the estate. Looking up at the Hall, Robby saw new banners had been hung. And along the broad path that led from the gate to the Hall, men were cleaning the oil lamps on their posts by standing on long narrow ladders.

"I leave you for now," Tyrillick said. "I bid you rest before this evening. You will be summoned when the time comes."

Tyrillick bowed and took his leave of them. Ullin continued on into Tallin Hall, and Ullin showed Robby back to the guest wing.

"I have a few people to look in on," he explained, waving goodbye. "But I will be back later."

Robby, suddenly hungry, went to the great room in his hall and was served a plate of fruit and nuts and a tankard of ale. Ibin was reclining on a sofa plucking softly at his mandolin, and Robby thought he detected a familiar melody. He listened for a moment then took his meal to his room. There, he sat at the little desk, pulled over a sheet of paper and dipped a quill.

> Mother,
> I find myself writing to you from your old home, Tallin Hall. I don't know whose room they have given me, but it is very nice and opens eastward into a garden. How I came to be here, and off our course, I am not at liberty to say. Though you recently told me something of this place, you never mentioned how beautiful or grand it is. I have only imagined such places, and only as the abode of kings or queens, and I find my past imaginings have fallen short of the mark by far. Certainly you must have been very much in love to have left this place for the simple ways of Passdale!
> I have seen many of the paintings, statues, and murals depicting and portraying various aspects of what I now realize is my own family's history. It has been very interesting, and I feel somewhat enlightened. I do not blame you and father for keeping so much to yourself, but I think it will make you feel better to hear that I have been treated very well, too well, in fact, for my comfort.

At this point there was a gentle knock on the open door, and Robby turned to see Windard standing there.

"I am sorry to disturb you, my lord," Windard said.

"Not at all. Please come in."

"I just wanted to know if you are satisfied with your room, as I missed you earlier when I came by."

"Oh yes, thank you," Robby said, rising from the desk. "It is very nice."

"We would normally have you in the family wing," Windard went on. "But our thinking was that you would prefer to be closer to your friends. Especially since Tallin Hall is a strange place to you."

"Yes, it is good of you to be so considerate. To tell you the truth, I do feel out of place here. But I am fascinated by Tallin Hall and the town, too. And, like anyone accustomed to more modest surroundings would be, I am more impressed by all I have seen than I have words to tell. I wish I could have visited before now. When I had more time to explore and to learn, that is. But I suppose my grandfather would not have been too pleased at that."

"Yes, it is a shame upon us that we have not been more inviting."

"Oh, no! I did not mean it that way at all! I'm sorry if I did not express myself very well. It's just that I knew so little about my family until very recently, and the opportunity on my part never came about. I only meant that I don't wish for anyone to feel obliged to me in any way because of my connections with Lord Tallin. I had rather be treated like anyone else. I regret any awkwardness my presence may be causing."

At this, Windard smiled.

"A little awkwardness, as you say, is not always so bad a thing, if I may be so bold," he said. "Your presence here is very exciting to many of the household, and to others. And, if I may, I would like to ask after your mother. For myself, and for others of the staff, we hope she is safe and well. We have all heard about the events in Barley and Passdale. We have also heard that your father has not been heard from since departing for Glareth by the Sea."

"Thank you for asking. That is so, and we all hope he is safe. I was just writing a note to my mother. I left her safe in Janhaven. She was organizing the people there, seeing to those who, like herself, have lost their homes. She is surrounded by many who honor and respect her, and I don't doubt she will soon be in charge of things there."

"That is good to hear. I will share it with others who have asked after her. There are some here who remember the day she left us. She is missed, of course, and all of us wish her well."

"Thank you."

> Windard asked after you and I told him a little about your situation in Janhaven. I believe some of the nice treatment I have received here is due in part from the love and respect the servants still have for you. But, beyond that, I do not understand why they treat me so well. You probably know more about that than I.
>
> I met Grandfather earlier today. He is a stern man, indeed. Much younger-looking and stronger-looking than I expected, in spite of his white hair. I think he has guessed everything, and I think he struggles with some hard decision. Ullin and I met with him privately, and by the end of our meeting he seemed more sympathetic to our cause. I cannot say what he will do, but I do not think he counts

on Duinnor for help any longer, if he ever did.

There is no word here about anyone who made it from Barley, I'm sorry to say. But if any can make it here, I think they will find good welcome.

You may not hear from me again for a long, long while. It is only by chance that I have this opportunity to write. From here we resume our way, having hardly started on our journey when we took this turn. I can only say that I have been brought here to meet someone, but no one will tell me who it is, and they have not yet arrived. I do not know why it is so important. Afterwards, perhaps as early as tomorrow morning, we hope to be on our way again.

I should also say that our overnight stay in Hill Town was very enlightening. They are something of a rough people, but not artless by any stretch. We met many unusual characters, too, some helpful to us and others just curious. But this I have to say: I think they would make good allies if that can be brought about. I believe, as you have seen, that they can be useful as a fighting force, but they have much to share along other lines, too. Perhaps you might speak with Captain Makeig about forming stronger ties with them. And should you meet one called Sally Bodwin, know that I believe her to be an upright and forthcoming lass, and her singing voice is as pretty as she is. She would be a good person to tell you about the Hill Town folk.

With all my love,

> Your devoted son,
> Robby

Yawning, Robby folded the note and sealed it, addressing the outside to Mirabella Ribbon, Janhaven, in care of Furaman's Stockade. He went to wash his face, hoping it would refresh him. It did not, and, yawning again, he decided a nap would not go amiss. He took off his shoes and his shirt, hung Swyncraff over the bedside table, and stretched out onto the bed. No sooner than he had noticed how comfortable it was than he was asleep.

It was a delicious sleep, and the only dreams he had were of fair days and pleasant company, no anxiety, no dark fears, and no strife. He slept soundly until an insubstantial rustling sound filtered into his notice, and he opened his eyes and sat up. It was dark, Lady Moon was still finding her pace across the sky and peeked faintly through the glass garden doors. The hall door was still ajar, and the bright light from the hall cracked across the room. Then, hearing the sound again and looking toward it, Robby saw, sitting at the writing table beside the garden doors, a figure bent over pen and paper. He heard the scratching of the quill and saw the quick movements of the writer's hand as he dipped the quill into the well and wrote more. But, most curious of all, even though Robby could only barely make out the mysterious person, and then only in a sort of dim silhouette, he could tell, somehow, that it was not one of his companions. Robby felt no sense of fear or alarm until he said, "Hello?"

The figure turned to face him, and every hair on Robby's body stood on end. It was clearly the face of a Dragonkind man that gazed at him curiously. Robby's heart pounded, and he instinctively thrust out his hand. Immediately, Swyncraff flew into his grip. A breeze ruffled the drapes, and Robby saw that what he had taken for a person was only a bit of gauzy curtain that had caught over the chair, and the scratching sound must have only been a twig or vine rubbing against the glass.

He jumped at the gentle knock at the door and the shadow that suddenly appeared there.

"Robby?" Sheila put her head in.

"Yes!"

"It's almost time," she said, slipping in with a lamp in her hand.

"Yes, yes. I'm coming," Robby replied, quickly scrambling out of bed and rushing to the washroom to throw water in his face.

Chapter 8

Lyrium

No one knew from whence they came. As Lady Moon at her most bold began her trek from the eastern rim of the world, the mysterious travelers appeared from the west on the roads leading into Damar territory. They traveled with eerie ease, and they passed swiftly by, with drummers drumming and pipers piping, escorted by troops with lances and bright, holly-emblazoned shields. With every step they seemed to glide ten paces, their progress a contradiction to the eyes of those they passed by. So suddenly did they come that the Damar could only stand aside in amazement and awe as the train passed right by their city. From the battlements of his town stood Lord Cartu, the Damar warlord himself. He watched with many of his generals and officials, all summoned by the sudden signal fires lit on the far hills, a sign of great alarm. But there were no orders he could give that could be carried out in time. He quickly realized that no command could stop the uncanny apparitions, and he stood agape as did all those around him. His generals waited in nervous anticipation of what their leader would demand.

"Let them pass," Lord Cartu said at last, weakly, nervously, more as a prayer of hope than of a command to his forces.

And pass they did, without care of the confusion in their wake, slipping over the eastern hills and into the forest. Soon couriers were pouring in from east and west alike, from checkpoints and armed keeps along the way, all a-babble with news of the passing. Some, who had been very close to the train, said the travelers looked neither right nor left, and they acknowledged no challenge nor even the presence of the Damar soldiers. Others reported how the tollgates burst asunder at their approach, and still others said that the feet of the strangers seemed not even to touch the ground, leaving no sign or track of their passing, not even hoof prints or wheel marks of the peculiar carriage.

The sound of their drums and pipes faded with them, but the firefly glow of their lamps lingered in sight as they went over hills and along the mountain road leading east until even that disappeared beyond the ridge and completely out of view from the city.

"That road is to be secured at all costs!" bellowed the warlord, as shaken as those around him. "From this moment, not even a flea may pass along it without orders from this castle!"

• • •

The last hues of dusk in the distant west were replaced by the evening shadows, now less deep in the east as Lady Moon climbed the stairs of night. And although the mysterious company moved quickly, more quickly by far than seemed possible, it was still some long while before the light of their lamps could be seen by those who lined the walls of Tallin City. Since sunset, the occupants of this town had gathered, not knowing from which direction the visitors might come. By now all manner of rumors had spread throughout the city, and had gained credibility only by the repeating of them, as rumors often do. Even the ranks of soldiers were infected by it, having freshly blackened their boots and polished their belts and shined their buttons and helmets and swords and shields with such vigor that much metal was removed in their enthusiasm. Each and every squad was now at its proper post, at the gates of the town and the outer bridges, and along the ramparts of the city. Not a man was absent, and, in fact, more were present than the evening orders called for. The city councilors sent delegation after delegation to the Hall asking for guidance, inquiring what sort of visitor was coming, from where, and of what rank? What would be expected of the town fathers? Would they be desired to address the visitors or give any accounting? Should they prepare a reception, a banquet, perhaps? What protocols should be followed?

Each delegation and each question was met by Dargul, kindly at first, but with growing exasperation after the fourth or fifth time he was interrupted to meet with yet another urgent request.

"Only a private visitor to Tallin Hall," he told them. "Not an official visit," he said. And, "no reception is needed," "no delegation required," "no observation of rank would be asked for, only free passage to the Hall," and "I am not at liberty to say."

He never indicated that he himself was as concerned as they, or that he, in fact, knew not much more than they. Indeed, the only thing he did know was that it was not Lord Tallin that the expected guests were coming to see, but Dargul never indicated that to the bothersome townsmen. What business was it of theirs? So the town leaders joined the rest of the crowds, in ignorance and anticipation. Since nearly every family had at least one member serving in the ranks, many people managed to find admittance to the walls, and so crowded it was in places, though the walls were wide, that movement was difficult. Others thronged onto balconies and rooftops, and many more lined the streets. Dargul, in an effort to find some peace from the constant entreaties, begged his master's leave. Tallin, who seemed not to care a whit for the visit but remained cool, distant, and distracted by other things, nodded his permission. So Dargul slipped away home only to find that his wife and all his family, except the cat, had gone out to watch with the throngs. He poured himself a glass of wine, then he and the cat mounted the stairs of his apartment to the roof where he, too, looked over the city toward the west as he sipped and pondered.

So when the mysterious glow was spotted, moving against the night-darkened far-off western hills, word spread quickly, for it was apparent by its movement and color that it was an unnatural sight, and those who crowded the other walls raced to the western side. So tightly packed the parapets became that soldiers had to prevent any more from climbing up. The western entrance became lined with hopeful and curious onlookers, and from the walls in various places people called down to those below to give word of the progress of the approaching lights. By now the city was lit with all its lamps and braziers. And the many-colored costumes of the rich and poor, the soldiers and the shopkeepers, and all the people in their finery, gave the city an aspect of a great festival or celebration.

"It is a visit from Duinnor," some said.

"Aye, I heard the King himself is come," said others.

"No, it is a Faere Princess who comes, to visit the husband of her sister, Lord Tallin," others held.

"Not a bit of it!"

Thus the crowds chatted and speculated loudly, and refreshment vendors moved about taking advantage of the nervous excitement that drew the people out and together. Yet there was very little laughter or mirth, for it was a most uncanny light that moved so swiftly down the far hills of their valley, disappearing, now and again, and reappearing later as the approaching party passed below or behind rises in the land. After only a few minutes, the coming van had cleared the hills and could be seen on the western road, a fairly straight route of over a league, lined in places with trees and passing over many stone-bridged streams and, closer by, the stone-bridged canals that surrounded the walled city. It was at this point that the sound of their approach was first heard, faintly wafting across the cool air, distorted by the distance and by the following echo. Droning pipes, low, harp-like strings, and the beating of two-tone drums, all of a march-paced cadence, accompanied a heavy melancholy aire played in a ghostly fashion. This sound silenced the crowds when it reached their ears, and as it grew closer, it filled them with an awe somewhat of reverence, somewhat of foreboding. It was now reported by those on the wall to those below, that they numbered about two hundred. Fifty horsemen, every horse white as snow, at the front and at the rear, in line five abreast with every other outside rider carrying a tall staff mounted with a bright lamp and each rider between with equally tall lances with green and red pennants. Silver breastplates and holly-wrapped helmets they wore, and green capes and livery. Following behind the first group of riders were twenty drummers, ten men blowing pipes, and ten blowing horns, and twenty players plucking lyres. Fifty soldiers came next. They were afoot, dressed and armed in a manner like the horsemen, but these footmen also carried shields upon which was painted the likeness of a stag's head, its antlers entwined with holly and ivy. Then came fifty ladies in strange robes, some that shimmered like the wings of a dragonfly, others that were feathered like the wings of a hummingbird. These mysterious robes wrapped the ladies completely, yet revealed their feminine forms, and draped over their heads as hoods so that only their arms, crossed over their breasts, could be seen. At last came the carriage itself, drawn by twelve creatures as large as horses, but more akin to deer. They were mighty buckmarls, each with a regal rack of antlers and each haltered and harnessed with silver ribbons so light and delicate that no one could reckon how they drew on the carriage. No one led these beasts, and no driver sat behind them, and no rein was there, but they drew on the glorious carriage of their own accord. The carriage itself was enameled black as night, its sides the shape of the wing of a bird, with silver wheels and spokes, and red and green ivy adorning the silver stars that encrusted the coach. It was as if a mysterious night sky, as glimpsed through a break in a green thicket, was passing by those who looked on. And as it did so, whether by the flickering light of the lamps or by the movement of the coach, all who saw it thought those stars twinkled and glittered just as the real heavens above.

As they neared to within a furlong of the western gate, they seemed to slow; that is, they took on the aspect of speed in keeping with the natural way of things. The rhythm of their cadence did not slacken, and the passing of them through the gates was a mighty affair and no less eerie. The crowds parted to let them by, and the Tallinvale soldiers saluted while the other spectators bowed. Thus the mysterious company made its way easily to the intersection at the center of the town, passing from there onto the way that led up to Tallin Hall.

● ● ●

Tyrillick had by now led Robby and his companions to the West Garden, just outside the family wing of Tallin Hall, the same garden where Mirabella first met the Barleyman who would become her husband. A nervousness infected Robby's company as the sound of the approaching visitors grew closer. Lady Moon enthusiastically looked straight down on the bright and glorious profusion of white and pale blue flowers amongst the shrubs and on the vines that grew all around in the garden that Lady Kahryna had dedicated to her and had so carefully planned and tended during her life here. Though long passed away, Kahryna would have been pleased that her husband had meticulously continued its maintenance, and pleased that it would be the reception-place for such a renown visitor. For every blossom was at its peak, every leaf and vine seemed perfectly attuned to the evening light. Even the pink and red blooms that grew about the many arbors and statues mysteriously showed their color with a strange vibrancy in the silver light. Indeed, the lamps along the portico, and those hung here and there throughout the garden, seemed superfluous to Robby. For everything seemed radiant of its own accord, strange and alluring, as if it was not night-time at all, nor daytime, and neither dusk nor dawn, but some other time of day joined of all the others.

Lord Tallin was nowhere to be seen, nor Dargul, though surely they knew the visitors had arrived. Ashlord seemed pensive, and Sheila was likewise restless. Billy and Ibin wore blank looks and remained uncharacteristically quiet, while Ullin leaned against a column of the portico with arms crossed and his head down as he often did, but Robby could not tell if he was relaxed or deep in thought.

There was a sudden crescendo of sound. Outside the garden gate not far from where they stood, the entourage came to a halt, the strange and wonderful carriage turned around widely so that it was just outside the gate entrance facing the way it had come. Soldiers dismounted and formed lines all around the carriage, and the female attendants entered the garden some little distance within, forming a line to either side of the path. The door of the carriage opened briefly, and brilliant golden light spilled out. Squinting, Robby could see vague shapes moving in silhouette toward them between the ranks of attendants. He also sensed Ashlord's presence very close to him.

"I warn you, Robby Ribbon," Ashlord said quietly in the sudden silence of the garden, "these folk are not to be taken lightly. There is one here who will offer you gifts, and it is your right to accept what you will, but such gifts often come with unexpected consequences."

"What do you mean?" Robby asked, thinking of Swyncraff about his waist.

"Merely this: If it is not within your power to control or to wisely use what things may be offered to you, it would be better to refuse them."

Before Robby could press Ashlord, several figures appeared at the gateway, all on foot. Except for the two women who led the group, Robby saw that they were all sternly dressed warriors, in banded armor the color of brass, and upon their heads they wore the same helmets that the soldiers on Tulith Attis had worn. On their black cloaks, these soldiers wore the same insignia, too, the ivy-entwined star, that he had seen there. They approached quickly and without noise, and the two women cast back their hoods, smiling as Robby stepped down from the portico. One, with red hair flowing, wore a cloak and gown of black, trimmed in red with blood-red rubies in the ring on her hand. The other, blond hair flowing, was similarly attired as the first, but in a silver-white fabric with green trim and with emeralds rather than rubies. Robby and his group bowed as they came before them, remaining silent and respectful. The two ladies gazed at Robby, smiling benevolently, as if sizing him up, and he stepped forward from the group and bowed again.

"I am Robby Ribbon," he said.

"My name is Elmira," said the one in silver.

"And I am Belmira," said the one in black.

"I think you remember..."

"...from some years past..."

"...our visit to you..."

"...when you saw us last."

"Yes. Yes, I do," said Robby. Butterflies fluttered in his stomach, and his breath quickened. "You came to me when I was sick. When I was a child."

"Your banshee sang…"

"…and your fever was hot..."

"…but you were strong…"

"…and she took you not."

"T'was a night filled with fear,"

"…that ended in joy."

"And now you are grown…"

"…and no longer a boy."

"And now as a man,"

"…with your burden to bear,"

"…surely you wonder…"

"…why we are now here."

"I do wonder," Robby answered, his voice still shaking, looking back and forth from one lady to the other. "I hope it is not to claim payment for my recovery all those years ago," Robby answered, "for we have very little these days."

"No debt do you owe,"

"…it has already been paid…"

"…though we did not see…"

"…how it would be made."

"The Great Bell was rung…"

"…and tolled the end of these days…"

"…and these days must end…"

"…before the new age may come."

Robby glanced at Ashlord behind him, wondering how they knew.

"I rang the bell accidentally," Robby began.

"What one does accidentally…"

"…another calls fate."

"And what some call fate…"

"…others call destiny."

"So I have heard it said. But of such things I know very little," Robby put in while he could, "except what I have been told. I only desire peace for my people and their well-being. I do not desire destiny, or fate, or any more accidents."

"Well spoken!" said a small voice from behind the two ladies. "It is as was foretold to me, 'The Hidden One shall not know his own way for many years. And when he learns it, he shall yearn to refuse it.' "

Elmira and Belmira parted one to either side, bowing to a third woman who emerged from behind them, an old bent crone, dressed in a simple gown of plain cloth. Her sparse hair was white, and with one thin and arthritic hand she leaned on a wisp of a cane that looked as frail as she, and with the other she held her shawl together at her neck. Her voice was thin, as a child's voice in the distance, but clear and without cracks or wavers. She approached Robby, and he saw in her silver-gray eyes a whisper of blue and green, bright with enthusiasm as she turned her head sideways to look up at him.

"I am called Lyrium, of the House of Fairfir."

Upon hearing the name, Ashlord bowed his head. Ullin gaped, then he, too, bowed and put his hand on his breast. But Robby did not remember the stories just yet, and simply nodded a courteous bow as he would to any new acquaintance.

"I am Robby Ribbon, of Passdale," he said to her. A smile crossed her face as she saw that he did not know who she was, and she came even closer to Robby so that he was looking down into her searching eyes.

Then he recognized her face from the likeness he had gazed upon in the bell room, carved in stone and painted in life-like illusion.

"Oh!" he said. "It was your statue that I saw in the fortress."

"No. That was my twin sister, Myrium."

"Oh. Pardon me."

"Come," Lyrium said, holding out her hand. Robby took it, and she became tall and erect. Her plain dress changed to elaborate robes and gown. Her face lost its wrinkles, her lips became full and red, her cheeks filled with a mild blush, and her hair became thick and black and long to her waist. Her figure became pleasing, and her flimsy cane grew and strengthened into a tall ornate staff of silver-laced fir. Robby held her hand, and, as he did so, he bowed to one knee before the striking young lady.

"I am no queen," she said, her voice now deeper and with no hint of frailty, "though I am honored by your gesture. Please rise and accompany me along this walk. It is such a beautiful garden that your grandmother planted, in moonlight and in sun. You know, we are distantly related."

Robby rose, glanced at Ashlord, who nodded, and then escorted Lyrium along the garden walk.

"No, I didn't know."

"Very distantly. My sister, whose likeness you saw at Tulith Attis, was your great-great-great-grandmother."

"Oh, yes. I saw a chart of the Tallin family tree earlier today. I remember, now. Myrium was Dalcadian's mother, and he was my grandfather's grandfather."

"Yes, that is so."

"Did your sister make it away from Tulith Attis as you did?"

"No. She was unable to escape," she said.

"Oh. I am sorry."

"Thank you for saying so," Lyrium paused to gaze at Robby. "But you must be wondering why it is that I have come to see you. Why I sent Tyrillick to ask you here."

"Yes, my lady, and I wonder at many other things, besides."

"These last months have been trying ones for you. You wonder what it is that you must do and how things have come to pass that so much should be placed upon your shoulders. You think you are too young and too inexperienced. Though perhaps you have yearned to know more of the wide world, you never dreamed in your darkest moments that this is how it would come about."

"True. That is all true."

"Tell me," she asked, "what do your friends think of you, now? They know, do they not, who it is that you may become?"

"Yes, they know," Robby told her. "But I cannot say for sure what they think of it all. I hardly know my own mind on all of this."

"Are you determined, then, to go through with your quest? To find Griferis and to enter therein and to strive for kingship? It will be dangerous. And not only for you, but also for any who accompany you."

"Yes. I see no safer way. I do not relish the idea of hiding forever, essentially useless, spending my life in fear for my safety and for the lives of those dear to me."

"That is what I thought," she said, stopping to look at his face. "I know what it is to live in hiding and fear. We were given refuge by one who wishes to remain unnamed, and who loaned to us our transport and escorts. Within that refuge, that hiding place, my daughters and I have enjoyed well-tended secrets and have been shielded from the disturbances of the world. We see the world from there, and know the passing of its careworn years. We have waited and watched. I have come now to offer to you our allegiance, for we will not serve the one who now sits in Duinnor."

"I am honored," Robby said, bowing.

"Do not bow to me," she said kindly. "It is I who should bow to you, and kneel, but I do not. I do not trust what other eyes may be watching."

Robby caught a note of warning in her voice.

"Many years ago," she went on, "my daughters, Elmira and Belmira, visited a young boy. He was sick with a strange fever, and his parents feared for his life. And in the delirium of his fevered dreams, the little boy muttered in a tongue that filled them with wonder, and a strange light covered his face. My daughters told me how they came to his bedside and how they strove with each other to see whether the boy should live or die, with Belmira representing the Halls of the Dead and Elmira the following days of his life. Yet, they told me that they could not utter his name, for he was nameless, and therefore he could not be bid to follow one or the other. So they soothed his fever and sang to him to calm his pains. They stayed with him into the night, giving him their blessings. When he had come through his struggle with death, all on his own, and took again the aspect of the living, and when his banshee ceased her song and had departed without him, my daughters then departed, too. And they came immediately to me and told me the tale.

"I was anxious to learn about this boy, for it came to my knowledge that a strange star had appeared on the night he fell ill. The eye of the Behemoth opened and burned brightly for seven days, closing again on the night my daughters departed the little boy's side. I later learned that when the prisoners and thralls in the faraway lands of the Dragon People saw the star, they rejoiced and endured their hardship and slavery with gladness, saying to one another that the star was a sign that their deliverer was coming, he who would redeem their freedom. Many other strange things happened in that week, terrible and wondrous, omens of the coming end of days and the beginnings of a new age. I learned, also, that old enemies were stirring and saw these signs, as well. Ever yearning to bend the world to their dark will, they sent their agents far and wide, in among the great Houses of old they sent them, and amongst courts, and into the villages of seldom-noticed peoples, seeking everywhere the new coming king. Seeking to slay him and preserve their own power. But they failed to find him, and found none who knew of him. The years passed. The boy grew into a young man, strong and with a good heart, hidden amongst the ordinary and the humble. A store clerk. But fate has found him at last."

"You speak of me."

"I do."

"But I have never heard these things," Robby said. "Until lately, no one has hinted of any such fate."

"These things were hidden from you," Lyrium explained. "And, I hope, from all others, perhaps even your mother and your father. Your Melnari, there, perceives much, though he is still struggling to put meaning to the things he sees. It is a great burden to have your secrets. Your friends are beginning to feel the weight of it. One slip of the tongue, one errant letter or revealing gesture, and all would be lost. Until your enemies are defeated and utterly smitten, no one is safe from them. Not you, Robby Ribbon, nor your friends or family."

"That is why I have come to you now," she stated. "Now that it has been revealed to you and to others, and now that you have chosen your path, you will have doubts, naturally, and will be tempted to turn away from your goal. I offer my encouragement, such that it is. And I have it in my power to give you a choice of gifts. You may choose one or the other, but not both. Either gift may serve you equally well, but in different ways. And either gift may become a thing of loathing to you, if not used wisely."

She nodded at her daughters, who still stood near the others on the far side of the portico. They turned, and in a moment, one of their escorts, a proud soldier in armor and flowing robes, strode up to Robby and Lyrium. He bore in his hands a bundle, held before him, and kneeled, offering it to Lyrium.

"You may choose knowledge, such that I can give, or this," Lyrium said, throwing back the covering on the outstretched bundle, revealing a brilliant sword. "Ethliad, it is called. It once belonged to Silmain, first King of the Elifaen. He lost it in battle, and I later found it and kept it hidden. It was foretold that this would be held by he who would bring liberation to the lands. For many years, I thought it would be my husband, Heneil, who would wield it. But it was never my husband's destiny to do so. I offer it to you, if you wish to have it."

She handed it to Robby, who had never seen anything like it. It was long and straight, its blade gleaming with such brilliance that it seemed to be made of something other than steel. Its hilt was black metal, polished and inlaid with silver and gold, and its handle wrapped in fine leather, and he felt a welcoming grip when he took it. Upon the pommel was an emerald the size of Robby's thumb, surrounded by a circle of diamonds. Robby lifted it, surprised at how light it was. As he held it up easily with one hand, he felt a stirring in his spirit, and he stepped away from Lyrium, unable to take his eyes from the upheld blade before him. In the reflections there, he seemed to see vast battles unfolding before him as if looking through a narrow window. He would swear later that he even heard the cries of war and the thunder of drums and the ring of steel in his ears. He impulsively swung the sword through the air, as light as a reed, whistling as it went like a finger rubbing the edge of a crystal goblet. He felt power in his grip, his heart skipped a beat, and his stomach fluttered. He felt what he could do against the Redvests with such a weapon as this. He had the certain knowledge that no power in the world would resist its bite, nor turn its blow. Again, his stomach fluttered, his heart pounded a throb, and sweat broke across his brow. He noticed these sensations, and he took their warning. With cheeks reddened with embarrassment, he reluctantly offered the sword back to Lyrium.

"I do not think I am destined to be a warrior," he said.

Lyrium smiled enigmatically.

"I will not question your decision," she said. "But I have one other thing of power that I may offer to you."

She gave the sword back to the bearer, who retreated with some confusion on his face as a second soldier approached and bowed, holding out to Lyrium a small box, which she took from him. Showing it to Robby, she opened the lid, revealing a plain iron ring cradled by a small pillow. Robby looked at Lyrium, who was watching him carefully. He looked more closely at the ring. But he could see nothing special about it as it was without adornment or decoration of any kind.

"It is the Ring of Hearing," Lyrium told him, "and there is only one of its kind in all the world. It was forged by a sorcerer of old. With it the wearer may know the thoughts of all those within sight. No thought of any such person may remain hidden. To the Faerekind it is useless, and its power can only be tapped by a child of Men."

Robby looked at the ring, dully gleaming in the moonlight.

"With this ring, I may know the thoughts of others, be they friend or enemy?"

"That is so."

"And they would not know their thoughts were seen? My own thoughts would remain hidden from them?"

"Truly."

"And thus I may know whether truth or falsehood is in the words they speak aloud?"

"Yes, and many other things besides."

Robby looked at the ring again, touching the box that held it.

"Such a ring has untold power. What leader would not wish to have this? Surely it is beyond price!"

Robby's hand reached closer to it, his eyes wide with anticipation and his mind reeling with possibilities. He ran his finger across the cool metal of its form, imagining the ways he could use it. He put his fingers on it to lift it from the box, then hesitated, pulling his fingers back.

"Why is this ring not now worn?" he asked.

Lyrium tilted her head, saying nothing, but her smile increased just a little.

"What madness must come to he who puts it on his finger?" Robby went on. "For what person in the world does not have vile thoughts, at times, and speak cruel things in his mind that no other may hear? What must it be like to hear them in others? Who would dare remove such a ring, once it is put on? For any thought missed may be the one that explains all the others. Yet, is it thoughts that matter? Or the actions those thoughts put into the world? How often have I changed my mind about things! How often have I regretted decisions made, wishing them unmade! Could I be the fair judge of such things, those most private and intimate musings?"

Robby spoke almost as if to himself rather than to Lyrium. His heart pounded with desire for the ring, but his knees quivered and his stomach twisted. He knew that such a ring was not lightly offered, no more than the sword. He shook his head, "I don't think so. Though I may regret the passing of these great and powerful things that you offer, this ring I must also refuse. Moreover, I wish it could be destroyed, somehow, and banished from the world forever, for I see too much danger and little hope of anyone putting it to good use!"

Robby closed the lid upon the ring and looked at Lyrium.

"Destroy this ring, I beg you!" he said earnestly. "For I fear that any who use it will be corrupted by it. And I fear the madness it could bring would do more harm in the world than any good its wearer might ever accomplish."

Robby was overcome with the greatest sense of relief as he said this, and he was filled with a firm opinion of what he said, even though he was confused by Lyrium's offering of the ring.

"It does not take a magic ring for me to see that you are baffled by my offered gifts," she said. "I test you. Just as you will be tested again and again. The sword, the ring, these temptations are unworthy of the king who must lead the world into a new age. But I offered them honestly, for though I loathe the use of them, I dare not part with them foolishly, nor do I throw them into the sea, for even the sea may give up its treasures. You are wiser than your years, Robby Ribbon. Or else blessed with plain common sense, as I have often heard it said of the people of Barley. Then are you firm in your choice and of your wish that this ring be taken from the world?" she asked with a benevolent smile.

"Most certainly, I am."

"Then, look once more upon it," she said, reaching to open the box. When the lid was swung open, a flash of yellow light appeared, and the ring glowed brightly, then fell into ash that blew away softly on the breeze.

"It is done!" she said. "This ring, a great evil in the world, was bound by its creator to grant one wish to any who could refuse the gift of it."

As the last dust blew away, Robby felt a sharp pang of regret. The realization gripped him that he had just become responsible for the loss of a thing of power greater than he may ever know again. Gone to all and lost forever. Then he felt a sense of relief, for he knew no one wise enough for such things, except perhaps Ashlord.

"Your wish is granted. You have destroyed a thing of great power. And, perhaps by doing so, you have rid the world of a great evil. Little else do I have to offer you, Robby Ribbon," she said, "except my friendship."

"That's more than I deserve, I'm sure. But I am sorry that you traveled all this way for nothing."

"The decision to come was longer and harder than the way itself. And the way back will be easy. Is there nothing I can do for you before I depart?"

"You do not stay?"

"No. I have placed too many at risk by coming here, and I would not have them remain at risk by overstaying my purpose. And I must travel on."

Robby glanced at his friends waiting patiently nearby, looking on with some anxiety and seriousness. Robby wondered how much Ashlord perceived of what had just happened. And he wished that he was standing among them and someone else was in his place.

"Like you, they think I am to become King. They think that I know the Name of the King. But I don't even know my own name!"

Lyrium smiled sympathetically. "You are caught in a paradox. It is not the one that you think you are caught in, but another altogether."

162

"What do you mean?"

"The prophecies are difficult to interpret. They spell out with fine detail certain things, but leave other matters open to anyone's guess. They say that he who shall become King shall be the one who knows the name of the King. But what name? We are given many. Which name is the right one? Is it truly a name that is secret from all? Or did the prophets mean only that the King will be replaced by one who knows the King?"

"I can only go by what I am told," Robby shrugged. "That he has a name, and that I am to know it. And, they tell me, knowing it will bring down the present King and deliver the throne to me. I know. My friend Billy, there, says that it is preposterous, and he's right. And, anyway, what hope have I, if all is so uncertain? How am I to know what to do?"

"You can only go by the calling of your heart and the answering of your mind, Robby Ribbon of Passdale, and find for yourself the meaning of these things. It is not for me, one who has Sight, to reveal all that I see, and there is much that remains hidden and mysterious, even to me."

Robby shook his head, thinking how useless such words seemed, and his disappointment showed in the slump of his shoulders and his sigh of irritation.

"Do not be vexed, I beg you," Lyrium said, touching his arm. When he turned to her he saw through her eyes that she truly felt his plight, and that she chafed at some limitation on her that prevented her the clarity that he so desired and that she longed to give. He was touched that a stranger would feel such concern for him, and he gave her a wry smile.

"Sometimes," she said, "it is better for things to take their own course, and people likewise, than to push them along this path or that one. You have chosen yours. Yet, there are many forks and many turns along every way. You think that the crux of your challenge is a name that cannot be known yet must become known. To you, that seems a paradox. But this I tell you, Bellringer: The name itself has no power and merely knowing it will avail you but little. The true paradox that surrounds your quest is not a matter of names, as you will come to see in your own time. It is a deeper one you face, an enigma that cuts through our existence, whether Mortal or Elifaen. You think I speak in riddles. But I do not. I ask only that you have some trust in what I say; if you stay true to your purpose, let your heart guide you, and ponder all these things, then the answers will come to you. You will remember this conversation when the answer becomes clear to you, and, remembering, you will find confirmation of it. Then you will know what it is that you must do."

• • •

As the two talked, the others of the group waited patiently and without speaking. Elmira and Belmira smiled enigmatically whereas the others had blank expressions, each wondering what was passing between Robby and Lyrium. Ullin had moved to stand very close to Ashlord, and he bent his head to speak. But Ashlord, still gazing at Lyrium and Robby, held up his finger. Ullin nodded and remained silent. Billy, glancing at Sheila and Ibin, then to Ullin and Ashlord, could no longer bear being silent, and finally cleared his throat softly. The two sisters looked at him.

"So. Did ye come a long way, then?"

The sisters' smiles broadened, and Belmira said, "Yes, a very long way, that is so…"

"…but not as far as you have to go."

"Our journey nears to its end…"

"…while yours will soon but begin."

Billy nodded, half-entranced at their sing-song voices. He suddenly felt little desire to talk further, but it was a lack of boldness that for once gripped him, not a lack of curiosity.

• • •

"I cannot repay the kindness of your visit," Robby went on. "And I am reluctant to impose upon you. But perhaps there is something else you might do, if it is in your heart."

"Pray tell me."

"I have heard it said that the First Ones have the power of prophecy, and you say that you have the power of Seeing. Could you look ahead and give us some notion of the path before us?"

"I do have it in my power to See, after a certain manner. But I cannot always see upon those things I wish to divine. It is a practice I avoid sharing because of the trouble it can cause among others. And it is a gift that commands me more than I command it. My visions come to me unbidden in dream or in trance. If I am to force them to come, I must prepare for many hours or even days. And the more I force them to come, the less likely I will have the words for sharing what I See. I cannot do this thing that you ask, not for lack of desire, but merely because the hour is late and I have not prepared myself for it."

"Oh," Robby said, unable to hide his disappointment. Lyrium looked at him, then at his companions nearby.

"Perhaps there is some comfort I may give," she said. "But in ordinary words. That is, to tell you why I have come. It is in the hope of seeing with my own eyes the King who will bring this age of waiting and watching to a close. Who will bring through the building strife a time of peace when the world, though broken, may begin afresh. Long have I waited and watched. Since from the days when our wings were taken from us, days when the forest knew no axe, and before the air was cut by steel or pierced by arrow. Here, sit next to me."

By now they had wandered to the end of the garden, and she led him to a small stone bench, and they sat.

"Long has been the decline of my people, and we would surely have dwindled to nothing had it not been for the coming of Men. But the curse laid upon us is not broken; even the alliance of Men and Elifaen has not been strong enough to endure it. From the earliest days it was foretold that there would be a time of healing, when once more our kind will take joy in the earth and once again soar through the forests and valleys, over the mountains and seas as we once did. A time when melancholia will know no place in our hearts, when memory is not a torment, and when the bounty of the world will be open to all. It is said that the power of Aperion's curse cannot endure He whom Aperion serves, the Creator of all the world, the earth, the seas, and the heavens. It is said that a wearing away of the strength of our curse would take place, and that our curse will pass away as all things do, even so-called immortal things. It has been prophesied that only the One True King of all the Earth may remove this curse upon us and heal the world. Only the One True King of Men and Elifaen may heal the wounds made by Aperion, King of the Faere. I do not say that it is you, Robby Ribbon. But that is my hope, for who else can it be? I have never had such hope or signs of hope in any king of earth until I learned of you. Even then, and for a long while, I did not believe the signs as they were given. They may yet prove fallible. But how much can be ignored, how many portents of change does one need?"

Lyrium looked for a moment at Robby's companions, standing with her daughters across the garden. Robby followed her gaze, and he had the odd sense that this meeting with Lyrium was years in the making, perhaps eons in the making.

"I struggled with the decision to come here," Lyrium went on, "not because I do not place my hope in you, but because I long so much for hope. But I fear to have it! My history is long, unto the beginning of things. Men, they come, they live, and they die. They do good or evil that lasts beyond their days, and even that passes away. Yet, my people remain, seeing generation after generation of Men grow stronger and greater in number, while we dwindle and retreat, weak, forlorn, distracted by reminiscence and melancholia, persecuted, cheated of our lands by the axe, by the law, and by the numbers of Men. And though we fight the Dragon King with glory and many victories, against Men we are nigh upon helpless. Still, we do not hate Men. Indeed, our salvation from annihilation came from Men. Ironic, is it not, that we look to Men still, even though they are now the source of much of our pain? Who else is there? You, Robby Ribbon, store clerk of Passdale, Bellringer. You are both Man and Elifaen! Though your time has not yet come, you, too, will enter Faerum, and feel its loss. No wonder the signs and portents have been confused and misunderstood! For here they point to the Faere Folk as those that may lead the way from ruin, and there they point to the children of Men who may give the earth its healing. But now all is clear to me, and to others who see."

Robby leaned on his elbows, his hands clasped together between his knees as she spoke to him.

"You know much more than I do about signs and portents, surely," he said. "And Ashlord is like you in that way. But I have seen no signs that I understand, and have only stumbled from trouble to trouble. The road of my life seems already paved, yet I cannot see where it goes."

"It is not already paved, nor is even your path blazed, for none have gone before you," she said. "No one has a ready-made path in life. Even when choices are few, the choosing of this over that makes a world of difference. Choice by choice, stone by stepping stone, your road is paved with choice. The hope placed in you is the hope that you, above all others, will make the right choices. Is it not so in every person's life that touches another? Is not that the hope mothers and fathers have for their children, friends have for each other, and the low have for the mighty amongst them and the lords that rule over them? To make right choices is not always easy, but neither is it always hard for those who have goodness in their hearts. I do not place my faith in you alone, Robby Ribbon, but in that which moves within you and moves all things in heaven and upon earth."

"Beras."

"If you call it by that name. Many do."

"I know little about such things," Robby replied. "But is there not some word you might give my company, some encouragement or sign, no less to me, that this quest is a worthy one? That it is not a hopeless waste, when we might instead be giving aid to our kin and countrymen?"

She looked at him sympathetically, and then turned her gaze to his companions. As her eyes moved from face to face, she saw indeed the care in each. She also saw fear and fatigue, and she was moved by Robby's request.

"In the days of old, when Men were new to these shores, they would often come among my people seeking advice and guidance, thinking our way somehow blessed, rather than cursed, by the gods. It is true, Robby Ribbon, that we hold to the world differently than Men, and touch the things of the world differently, the air, the water, for those things once conversed with us and told us their secrets. But no more; their voices have faded from us, year by year. It is also true that our immortality permits us to grow in wisdom and insight beyond the years of Men. But our hearts are just as full of passion, our jealousies just as strong, and our love as dear to us as to any child of Man. We are not without blame or mistake. I myself mistook the dreams sent to me as a sign of threat, once, when I now know they were merely a foreseeing of far away days of change. My kind are fallible. And, owing to our long time in life, we have more chances to make mistakes. But I will greet your friends, if you will introduce me."

"It will be my pleasure!"

He offered his arm and led her back to the waiting group. As they watched the pair approach, each for the first time saw her aspect change from the disguise of an old woman to the haunting young beauty that she was. Except, perhaps, for Ashlord, Robby's companions were stunned and surprised. Billy, especially, seemed affected by her transformation, and when Robby approached him first, he felt his stomach flutter and his cheeks redden. For the first time in his life, and in a rush of emotion, he felt a humility he had never known, and he felt all his carefree past was but a shameful waste of time when he should have been learning his responsibilities to become Master of Boskland. Her presence, to him, was a tangible reminder of his own mortality, for she was in the world when it was created, and would likely still be here when Billy was dust. He felt brief, as if his place in the world was rushing past. And all his friends felt exactly the same way as he did in her presence. Yet, even though Lyrium's aspect was penetrating, there was nothing but kindness in her eyes.

"I first introduce Bilaylin Bosk, late of Bosk Manor in County Barley," Robby said.

"I am Lyrium, and I am happy to meet you."

"The pleasure is all me own, Lady Faere," Billy bowed low, with surprising elegance.

"Unless I mistake it, are you not named for a mighty captain of Men? The one my people called Bilaylin the Hammer?"

"Yes, ma'am. That was me ancestor from long ago, indeed, who served it is said in the faraway lands of Vanara. It was he who came back east an' 'stablished our lands. He died, it is told, fightin' at Tulith Attis, an' his bones are what lay this day in a tomb nearby to our hall."

"I remember him well," she said, her smile diminished for a brief moment. "I see that you are lately wounded. Do you suffer much pain?"

"Oh, no ma'am. That is to say, just a bit of headache now an' again. Nuthin' to speak of. Yet, I thank ye for askin'."

"And you have a stalwart companion. What is your name, good sir?"

"Myname, mynameis, mynameisIbinBrinnin!"

"I am Lyrium. Do you play the mandolin?"

"OhyesIplayit. Ullin, Ullingaveittome, tometodayandhe, heshowed, Ullingaveittometodayandheshowedmehow."

"Perhaps someday, when you return from your journey, you will play it for me?"

"Ohyes!"

They bowed to each other, smiling, and Robby led her next to Ullin.

"Lady Lyrium," Ullin said, bowing low with his hand to his chest. "I am honored to greet you."

"Ullin Saheed of the House of Fairoak and the House of Tallin, son of Aram. I knew your grandmother's family, as well as others of your grandfather's lineage, long ago, of course. And I have heard of you, of your service both to Duinnor and your aid to Vanara and to Queen Serith Ellyn. I'm sure it was a comfort to the Queen to have one so capable as you to serve her passage to Glareth."

"My part in things is exaggerated, I am sure," he bowed again. "I am afraid the Queen's travels have not been without hardship, as it is with all

Vanarans who travel eastward. But what little I have done to ease her way has been an honor for me."

"For you, yes, and an honor to others," she said to him. She paused, casting a long glance up at the hall. "Do you perceive, as I do, that a great cloud has been over this house for many years?"

"Yes, Lady. Though these lands prosper in the peace it has known, the House of Tallin and Fairoak has been troubled for many years by sadness and grief at the loss of its sons and its mistress."

"That is so, indeed. The burden of regret is heavy, and its weight of grief long borne. Yet, tonight, a storm breaks quietly upon your grandfather, I think, just as a greater storm will soon break upon this land. He is a perplexing man."

Ullin followed her gaze upward to a window high in the tower above, where the silhouette of a single figure stood, then turned away.

"So it has been said before," he said. "I fear for my House and what these days may bring upon it."

"You are not alone, Ullin Saheed," she nodded and took his hand. "It is in the power of this House to shape the world, and he who has long been withdrawn from the workings of the world may, if he has the will to choose, play a part at last."

"Perhaps, Lady," Ullin bowed.

"But that is beyond your influence, I see. Your path is elsewhere, with this company?"

"Yes. I have bound myself to Robby and to this company, for what help I may give."

Lyrium looked long into Ullin's eyes and saw much, and he, in turn, felt her seeing. Then, in the language of the west that none but Ashlord and Ullin understood, she said, squeezing his hand, "I see that the malaise of indecision that afflicts your grandfather does not exist in you, for you have ever been decisive and determined in your duty and in your quandaries. But ever have your choices been for yourself alone. Soon you may taste of the cup of worry that your grandfather has long lived upon. When decisions are made for others, the weight of them may be as mountains to the caring and concerned. Your strength of body and the prowess at arms you possess will be tested, yes, but so too will be the resolve of your heart. Men have disappointed you, and so have the Elifaen, for why else would you remain alone and not a powerful leader of armed companies, entrusted by Duinnor?"

"I have seen my share of fighting in the west, Lady, as have all my family. My way has taken me far from those fields of honor, and I have for these past years served my duty to Duinnor, and continue to do so, in my way, by aiding those who wish to preserve the Seven Realms. I have given up the ambitions I once had. It is now my desire, my hope, to be a steadfast helper in the task before us, no more."

"Yes. Yet you are still drawn back to those desert lands. Drawn by what, I wonder?"

Ullin did not reply, and held her gaze with difficulty. Ashlord, nearby, was attentive to what passed between the two, and his eyes darted back and forth between them.

Lyrium nodded and smiled, saying nothing more to Ullin, who appeared somewhat shaken by the question. Robby drew Lyrium's attention to Ashlord.

"Ashlord, called Collandoth in other tongues," Robby said.

"One of the Melnari," Lyrium said as she and Ashlord bowed to each other.

"Yes, Lady Lyrium," Ashlord replied.

"I have heard of you. A learned one, a servant of the powerful and a friend of the meek. A Watcher, but also a Doer. Yours has been a long tread upon the earth, with many twists and turns, many roles to play, and much to see."

"I have had many paths to follow, my lady. And many mysteries and wonders to delve."

"Then you must wonder at me, too."

"I do, my lady. I am happy to know that you escaped Tulith Attis. Might I ask after the other members of your household?"

"Of my family, I, alone, escaped. My husband, sister, and her husband were all lost. Only my daughters, who were not there, now remain of my family."

"I am deeply sorry," Ashlord said, bowing again. "My condolences. And I assume these items that you offered to Robby are amongst those things you brought away from Tulith Attis."

"Only the sword. I came by the ring much later," Lyrium said. "I sense that you wonder about other things that were in my keeping."

"I do, since the House of Fairfir was one of the Seven High Houses, and the only one, besides Fairlinden, that still remains."

"Only the sword, Collandoth, was I able to bring away. I do not know the fate of the other things that you may wonder about. They are lost to the world, likely smashed for their jewels and melted down for their gold by the Dragonkind. I have long since learned to live without them, and I do not pursue or search for such things anymore. They are gone."

"I see. I am sorry. Please forgive me."

"It is I and my House who should beg forgiveness," Lyrium said. "So much and so many were entrusted to Fairfir, and we failed to protect them. I sense, too, that you have many questions concerning Tulith Attis. I have traveled far, coming from the west. And the nearer I came, the more I felt the power of those lost objects grow, like a weight upon my heart. Since arriving here, my anxiety is almost unbearable, as if the Seven that I lost were present here within this garden, crying out to me. I do not understand the sensation, and I did not expect such feelings when I set out to come here. It must be that I am near to Tulith Attis, where I last saw them, and where so much else was lost, too. Husbands, sisters, friends."

Lyrium hesitated, her eyes momentarily misty and distant, her forehead wrinkled in thought. Then her expression changed and hardened somewhat as she looked again at Ashlord.

"However, my purpose in coming here lies not with the past, nor the things of the past, but with the present and with the future."

"Of course, Lady Lyrium," Ashlord nodded. "But the water penned up long ago waits to break upon us, so that the past will flow violently into the present, I fear, and threaten to sweep away our future. The betrayal of Tulith Attis still infects the world, and it clouds the minds of Men and Elifaen with suspicion and mistrust. If that, at least, could be put to rest, one way or the other—"

"I fled the fortress when it was betrayed," interrupted Lyrium. "I saw the creature who caused our gate to be opened to the enemy. He was attired in unfamiliar armor from head to toe. I will not speak further of it."

"Ah. Once more, I beg your pardon, Lady Lyrium," Ashlord said with a sympathetic bow. "As you say, I have been a Watcher, and such things that reach out from the past and cast a shadow over the present are amongst the things I watch and study."

"I quite understand. It is your way. And mine, too. But it seems that your watching may be nearing its end, for few signs remain to be divined, and the ending and beginning of things is at hand. Do you now play both mortician and midwife to those things, to the passing away and coming of things?"

"If that is my place, then that is my duty."

"Then your time is nigh at hand," Lyrium said, smiling sadly, turning back to Robby.

Ashlord bowed once more as Robby gestured to Sheila.

"And this is my particular friend, Sheila Pradkin, late of Barley."

"Lady Lyrium." Sheila bowed rather than curtseyed since she was wearing her usual breeches and blouse instead of a gown.

"Sheila Pradkin," Lyrium repeated, offering Sheila her hand. Sheila took it, and Lyrium held it, looking deep into her eyes, and Sheila's face reddened with an odd sensation of being exposed. Suddenly, the awkward sensation was quenched by a stilling peace and an inexplicable sense of pride filled her heart. As Sheila drew herself up to stand proudly, Lyrium's smile vanished, her grip upon Sheila's hand tightened as an expression of recognition and shock briefly crossed her face. It was only a moment, but such a moment as only the Elifaen may know, when all coming moments pause and all receding moments hesitate.

"Do I know you?" Lyrium asked, more to herself than to Sheila.

Sheila, bewildered as much by Lyrium's expression as her question, shook her head and was about to answer.

170

"Pardon me," Lyrium said, her smile reappearing. "I sense that you have been through much. More than any of your companions may ever know. Yet your healing is not yet done."

"I am mending as well as can be," Sheila said. "I thank you for your concern, though I am baffled by how you might know."

"I See," Lyrium said.

Lyrium tilted her head sideways, and with curiosity's brow she studied Sheila again, and once more seemed on the verge of recognition. Suddenly, she grinned and said, "Will you come sit with me for a time?" Sheila, surprised, looked to Robby as if asking for permission. He smiled and gave Sheila a little bow.

"Mother," said Belmira, "the hour is late...

"...and our carriage will not wait."

Lyrium nodded at her daughters and led Sheila quickly across the garden and back to the bench.

"Perhaps I know some member of your family, from years past," said Lyrium, "and that is why you seem familiar to me."

"My mother and father both died of fever when I was very young," said Sheila. "And I do not even know their names. So I can tell you little about my ancestry."

"You are not Elifaen, then. Yet there is a special quality about you, rare in Mortals."

"I am flattered that you say so. No, I am not Elifaen," Sheila replied.

The anxiety that Lyrium had only moments before expressed to Ashlord seemed to ease. Glancing quickly across the garden at Sheila's waiting friends, she realized that the tense and fearful feelings in her heart had reached a climax when speaking with Robby. Now, sitting some distance away with Sheila, Lyrium's heart felt inexplicably lighter. It was baffling. As baffling as the face of the young girl she now sat with. A face so much like a dear friend that Lyrium had lost during the battle for Tulith Attis. Her anxiety was replaced by curiosity, and by a tenderness so powerful that it was all she could do not to take Sheila's face in her hands and kiss her in loving memory of her lost friend.

"Tell me, then," said Lyrium, "are you and Robby very much in love?"

"Does it show?" asked Sheila.

"One need not have the gift of Sight to see it."

Sheila's companions watched as the two sat and chatted in low tones, unable to hear what they said to each other. From time to time they laughed and giggled, just as small girls might, and every now and then Sheila, or Lyrium, or both would glance in Robby's direction as they spoke. They talked in such a manner for a long while, still holding hands and looking earnestly at each other the whole time, as the rest of the group waited, silent and somewhat awkwardly. Robby was curious that they continued to speak for so long, but the happy glow on Sheila's face was one that he had not seen for a long time, and he hoped that

Lyrium was speaking words of encouragement. In time, Lyrium and Sheila stood and walked back together to rejoin the others, smiling as they came.

"Where do you go from here?" Sheila asked as her friends gathered around them.

"I was to return to my place of hiding," Lyrium said. "But now I feel the need to visit Glareth by the Sea."

Strangely, as Robby and the others gathered to listen, Lyrium felt her anxieties return.

"Oh. To take word of the Redvests," Sheila said.

"No. To look into other matters. I will take word nonetheless. However, the hour is late, and I must depart," Lyrium told them. "I would offer to you our conveyance into the west, but my borrowed carriage will not serve any but those of my race. And, besides, the carriage and escorts are only mine for this night. They must all return to their owner and master before moonrise tomorrow evening. So I have little, it turns out, to offer you, except my blessings and the friendship of myself and my people. Wherever your road may take you, our prayers and hopes are with you." She looked at Robby as she continued speaking. "For many generations of Men, I and others like me have watched the great Houses of our people and those of Men, looking for the One, the Hidden One, who will bring justice and unity to all our peoples. It is significant, perhaps, that Tallin Hall be the place of our meeting, Elifaen and Men, for not only is this place the result of one of the greatest unions between those two races, but it is rich in the history of reaching out to others. Even a Dragon Man was once welcomed here, did you know? Now, in this place of goodwill, beclouded though it is, you truly begin your quest. I bid you all look for signs, in your hearts and in the earth and sky, to encourage you. Trust and rely upon each other. Remain true, and you will find the courage that you need. Farewell!"

Her voice faded into almost a squeak. Her frame shrank and her clothes deteriorated into the simple dress she wore before. Her back hunched, and her thick black hair became thin and gray. Elmira and Belmira took her by the arms and led her to the carriage waiting at the garden gate. Tyrillick appeared, standing beside the carriage, and as he opened the door, brilliant gold light flowed out, as when one opens curtains to the bright morning sun, causing the company to blink. Through the opened door Robby caught a glimpse of a garden-like wood, with trees and blooming flowers, and he heard the sound of tittering birds and gurgling brooks. The ladies entered, the door closed, making sudden darkness, and the caravan was away. The soldiers, mounted alike on their steeds, followed quickly behind. Their departure was eerie and silent, with not a hoof nor a wagon wheel heard. No drum tapped, no horn blew, and no string was plucked. Robby and his company of friends blinked and peered after it, but could see nothing and hear nothing of its travel away from Tallin Hall. They felt the distinct sensation one has when waking from a mysterious dream. Lyrium's words and something of her presence remained with them as they turned to go into the Hall. As they made their way to their rooms, each said very little, but gave each other long searching looks as if none knew quite what to make of the visit.

Walking close to Ashlord, and speaking quietly, Ullin struggled to put his sense of wonder into words, and gave up, shaking his head.

"I know," said Ashlord. "That she survived the massacre is a great wonder. And to emerge from hiding only now, after all these centuries."

He was fully aware of the melancholy mood that had settled on the group, and he spoke to Ullin softly, not wishing for his words to intrude upon the thoughts of the rest of their companions.

"Still," he went on, "she has much to hide, I suppose. If her whereabouts became known to our enemies, no doubt she would be in great danger. Why she chose this time and this place to meet Robby I cannot say. And I think she said much less than she knows."

Ullin nodded and paused outside the door to Ashlord's room as the others passed by.

"Get a good night's sleep," he told them. "We'll be on our way tomorrow."

Sheila hovered at her door, as if to say something, but then went inside. After the doors were closed, Ullin turned back to Ashlord.

"But surely," he said, "Lyrium's visit is a great sign that we are right about Robby, is it not?"

"It is, indeed," Ashlord nodded. "To come out of hiding and to give us her encouragement, in spite of the danger of doing so, was a brave and kind gesture. But she tested Robby, too, and measured him. And, I think, she was pleased by his response. Lyrium is surrounded by mystery, though, and she keeps to herself much that she knows and Sees."

"I heard you question her about the objects kept at Tulith Attis, the Seven Bloodcoins entrusted to her House. So they are truly lost."

"Yes. You saw her distress. If she does not have them, they are gone. As for the traitor, I think she knows, as a certainty, who he is. But why she would not say, I cannot guess."

"Could he have taken them?"

"It is possible."

"Hm. Much to think on," Ullin said. "What will you do tonight, Collandoth?"

"I will look in on your grandfather, I think. Afterwards, I hope to spend the night reading," Ashlord replied. "I have borrowed some books from the library and intend to finish them before dawn. And you?"

"I walk the walls with my friend Weylan. Then I turn in."

"Let us strive to be away from here by noon, if we possibly can," Ashlord suggested to him. "I fear the red-bearded one may have alerted the Damar about our presence. Our way west will thus take longer with the greater caution we will need."

"Aye," Ullin nodded. "Those are my thoughts, too. Word of tonight's honored visitor will surely spread, too. And that may not be without risk to Robby."

Chapter 9

Perfect Memory

The uncanny carriage and its escort passed through Tallin City and out through the eastern gate. The people, many of whom had lingered outside of Tallin Hall's grounds for some sign of the mysterious visitors' business, marveled as much at their silent departure as they had at their sensational arrival. When the carriage and its escort passed out of sight into the eastern hills, the watchers were just as full of speculation as ever. Many insisted that whoever had the means to come and go in such a manner was very important indeed. Others argued that the visit was a sign of great change to come, and that it might not be the kind of change one might wish for. Gloomy or otherwise, the speculation did not do much to diminish the celebratory mood within Tallin City. And since the people had no desire to waste an opportunity for merriment, they were soon enjoying a late night of dining, drink, and laughter.

Within the carriage, the mood was less merry. Inside its spacious interior, no sensation of movement or sign of its passage through the countryside could be felt. Indeed, it was as if they were not inside anything at all. Rather, they were free to stroll a springtime forest, with bright sunlight beaming through thick canopies of green. But the carriage did move, though not as quickly as before owing to the hesitancy of its primary occupant. As it rolled toward the coming dawn, Lyrium's thoughts guided it, while her daughters and Tyrillick tried to dissuade her of the decision she had just announced to them.

"But why, my lady?" asked Tyrillick. "The very thought of returning to Tulith Attis fills me with dread."

"You can have no more dread of that place than I do," said Lyrium. "I cannot say what it is that I wish to See. So much was lost there. My husband, my sister, your wife and children, and all our dear friends. Their memory has ever since weighed upon me, as it does you. For though we escaped, there is no end to our mourning. But a different memory now pounds upon my heart with hammers. I speak of those Seven objects that were entrusted to me. I sought to protect them, Tyrillick, by sending you and the others away before the end came."

"We searched before," Tyrillick said, "far and wide, high and low, for the one burdened with their safekeeping. She and the Seven Bloodcoins she carried are long passed away. They are lost, my lady. Lost forever. I am sorry that we failed you in that task."

"Tyrillick, good friend!" Lyrium reached out and took Tyrillick's hand. "I do not blame you or those that were in your company. As I have said many times before. I blame myself, only. For not taking them away much sooner. Failing in that, for not going with you to lend my aid, though I doubt that I could have saved the Seven from their fate. And had I known that I would be able to escape from Tulith Attis, and evade those who have sought after me, I would have kept them with me. So it is I who failed, not you."

"Nevertheless," replied Tyrillick, "it would mean a great delay, if we are then to go on to Glareth. For it would be necessary to go on foot from Tulith Attis to the coast, a journey of some weeks through forest and field."

"Before very long, our escorts must forsake us," said Elmira.

"And without protection, the Redvests might take us," said Belmira.

"I carefully scouted the lands before your arrival," said Tyrillick. "There is no safe way to go through Barley. If we are to go on without our escort and carriage, rather than return to our refuge in the west, then we must by needs pass by Tulith Attis. It is the only way. By all accounts the invaders have blocked the north road around the lake. And the Saerdulin is now too swift and broad to make a crossing farther south. So, to even begin our journey to the coast, we would have to first pass over the bridge at Tulith Attis, going directly below the fortress summit. But I alone cannot protect you against the company that is garrisoned there."

"Yes, yes. I well know the risk. Yet I still have Ethliad, which Robby refused to accept," said Lyrium, gesturing to the sword leaning against a nearby tree. "If it comes to that. If we move only by night, perhaps we shall not be seen."

Tyrillick shook his head.

"To abide nearby the fortress, in enemy-held lands, while you strive to See, will add to the risk. Will you not tell us, to ease our fears, or to bolster our courage, what it is that you wish to See?"

Lyrium turned away and walked to the edge of the garden then stopped and ran her hand along the smooth trunk of a myrtle. Her daughters, coming to stand with Tyrillick, waited. She looked up through the fuchsia blooms and into the blue sky above. Then she bowed her head, still clutching the myrtle, and watched the water of a nearby brook glisten and shimmer as it jumped around one mossy stone and the next. She listened to its soft patter, and tried to hear its words. But she could not make them out.

"I can no more explain my heart, my feelings, than to explain the color of the sky," she said, turning back to face Tyrillick and her daughters. "Yet I cannot deny them. As we recede from Tallinvale, the sensation fades. I am beginning to suspect more of Robby Ribbon than I did before. Perhaps the enchantment of the Bell permeates his aura. I do not know. In his presence, especially when I was nearest to him, my heart was filled

176

with an anxiety such as I have not known since departing Tulith Attis. It was as if some portion of that place and the events of that terrible time was present. It was all I could do to push those feelings aside and attend to the purpose of our visit. I cannot explain it. But, as I said, the farther we go from them, the calmer I feel, and other mysteries now perplex me. Robby's friend, Sheila Pradkin, is as mysterious as Robby. Those two are powerful individuals. Did you not observe her face? Her bearing? None of you have said anything, but I know what must have passed through your minds."

Belmira and Elmira glanced at each other while Tyrillick gazed intently at Lyrium.

"I do not deny that the resemblance to Faeanna was uncanny," he said at last.

"Yet she is from Barley, so how can it be?" said Elmira.

"And, too, she is Mortal, as was plain to see," said Belmira

"I cannot say! I cannot say!" said Lyrium, exasperated at her own confusion. "I can only say that meeting her had the most profound effect upon me. It is something I must delve. Something I must strive to See. First to Tulith Attis, where there may be some power that will bring Sight to me, and then to Glareth by the Sea."

"My dear Lady Lyrium," said Tyrillick, "if going to Tulith Attis will help you See, if it will resolve the quandaries of your heart, then by all means let us go and look upon that place. I will not forsake you. And I will escort you as best as I am able as far as you wish to go. Not only to Glareth, but unto the ends of the earth, should that be your desire."

Lyrium's daughters nodded, and Lyrium smiled weakly.

"We turn north, now," she said as the carriage gained the road that ran along the Saerdulin and toward the confluence of the Bentwide. "We shall make the old Bentwide soon. And then we must say goodbye to Islindia's escort and to the comforts of her father's carriage. We will ford the shallow Bentwide on foot, find some place to bide the day in hiding. Then, going slowly and carefully, moving only at night, we will cross through Boskland and go to the fortress. I will first look upon the place from afar. If it is possible, I'll strive to See from a distance. Afterwards, in darkness, we will approach close to the fortress and pass it by. If we are fortunate, we will avoid the invaders and cross the bridge into the old forest and be away. As you say, Tyrillick, it will be an arduous journey to the coast, but with caution and luck we shall safely arrive. Let us hope that the Redvests have not taken the coastal towns and that we may hire a boat to take us on to Glareth."

• • •

It was not to be a restful night for any of the visitors at Tallin Hall. In the wake of Lyrium's visit, Robby and each of his friends privately pondered the meaning of her visit, and the meaning of other things, too. Others of Tallin Hall were also contemplative, even though they were not present at all within the moonlit gardens. And especially one who had looked down upon the gathering from a high window, but had turned away to pace his home's passages and hallways like a restless shade, brooding and silent.

• • •

Robby sat at the desk in his room, looking eastward through the open doors and out at the dark gardens on that side of the Hall. Lady Moon had wearied of Tallinvale, and she was now descending into the west so that the trees and shrubs that Robby stared at were in the shadow of tall Tallin Hall, lit only by starlight and the glow from windows nearby and on floors above his room. He recognized the constellation of Tameron, the Seven Princesses with their bluish sapphire-bejeweled tiaras twinkling as they played. He remembered a time, just about a year ago, when he and Ibin and Billy had watched them rise just as he did now, but from a hilltop in Barley. They spent the night out, making a camp under the stars and together drank a keg of Barley beer until they were all three stupid drunk and silly with laughter, freezing with cold because they hadn't the sense to keep the fire up. And he recalled another time, just a few months or so after that, on another hilltop nearer to Passdale, bundled together under several blankets with Sheila when his parents thought he was camping with Billy and Ibin some two miles away. That night he felt as if he was holding one of those princesses in his arms, wishing that he had a jeweled tiara to give her. That was a cold night, but little notice did they take of the chill, for the fire within their hearts needed no kindling. Now Robby wondered what it was about Sheila that fascinated Lyrium so.

• • •

While Robby mused, so did Billy, nearly in the same position in his room next door. Ibin was already snoring away in the broad expanse of the massive bed, but the desire to sleep had not yet come to Billy. He saw the same constellation that Robby watched, but his thoughts were on the future rather than the past. He wondered what would become of Boskland now that his father was dead and the land occupied. His head hurt constantly with worry, though he rarely showed any concern, and he wondered if coming along with Robby was a mistake, if his place was back in Janhaven with what was left of his people. What was being said about Duinnor was not encouraging, and the idea of Robby becoming King was unsettling and complicated. It made his head hurt even worse when he thought about it. What was Barley to a great power such as Duinnor? And if Robby did by some miracle become King, of what importance would a little farming land be when compared to the problems faced by the new ruler? Billy thought of the paintings in Bosk Manor, now lost in its destruction, those showing his ancestors and their achievements in battle and in commerce. He worried for his sister, hoping that she had by now found safety. He thought of his mother and nearly wept with grief for her loss, strong though she was, but he was thankful at least that she was with Mirabella. Mirabella. Robby's mother was always a fascinating point of interest to Barleyfolk, and Billy was no exception to the common curiosity. Beautiful, tall, thin and strong, well-spoken and kind. But both aloof of and held aloof by most others. Now that he was in her ancestral home, Billy understood much more of the nature of her grace and history, and he briefly wondered what Robby thought of it all. Tallin Hall made Bosk Manor look shabby, and yet never did he hear of Mirabella speaking a word about her home. Only a few times did his mother mention Tallinvale to Billy, but always as if it was some faraway village, and he doubted if even his mother had any notion of the grandeur that surrounded Mirabella before she came to Passdale. And so nearby! He didn't understand why Lord Tallin could not spare a few soldiers to Janhaven. Was it to spite his own daughter? Or was he being honest when he said that Tallinvale was in a precarious position, with massive armies poised to strike? If that was the way of it, how long would Robby have to find this Griferis place and to do what was needed? How soon would be too late to save Barley or the refugees now scattered in Janhaven and elsewhere, and those captured by the enemy?

• • •

Ashlord made his way back to the library, wondering, as he had already done six hundred and twenty-seven times that day, how the pieces would come together. All was a jumble of possibilities, probabilities, and certainties, but how would the pieces connect? He knew that some pieces would be discarded as others came to light and were tossed into the mix. Tonight's meeting with Lyrium did that. Other events, he was sure, would, too. Still, as he entered the library and adjusted the flame of a lamp, he reflected and theorized, shuffling the bits and pieces, the signs and messages, the clues and questions.

Robby, he was certain, was destined for kingship. But how could he become *the* King? How would they find Griferis in time? And could Griferis truly provide Robby the knowledge and skill to lead?

Then there was Tallinvale, seemingly paralyzed, its situation precarious, yet unable to act decisively. Lord Tallin seemed fully aware of the consequences of continued inaction, though Ashlord sensed that the crisis within the stern lord was reaching its most intense pitch. A decision was imminent, and would soon be forced by the enemy's inevitable advance. Tallinvale would play a vital role, but what role would it be? Ashlord knew how much Lord Tallin cared for his people. Would he continue to barter and bargain in order to avoid bloodshed? If so, at what cost?

And there was Bailorg. Surely other agents would be dispatched soon, suspicious of Bailorg's silence. Perhaps he was merely a mercenary, favoring the highest bidder for Robby's head. No, that would be too much to hope for. Ashlord regretted that Robby had killed Bailorg before he had a chance to question him, but they were hardly in a position to hold the vile one prisoner. Worrisome, too, was the red-bearded Toolant, obviously working as liaison between the Redvests of Tracia and the Damar warlord, spying for both against Tallinvale.

"I must remember to ask Dargul if Bailorg was met here by Toolant," he muttered as he paced back and forth before the shelves of books and scrolls. "Or anyone else."

He abruptly halted, his shoulders hunched, his forehead creased with concern.

"Lyrium," he said softly, shaking his head. "Poor, brave Lyrium. All that she has witnessed. All that she has lost. But she still lives!"

Ashlord remained motionless for many long moments. Suddenly, as if flinching from a surprising crack of sound, his posture straightened. Then he hurried from the room.

• • •

In her room down the hall from her companions, Sheila lay in bed looking up at her dark ceiling. She was still dressed, but had not lit the candle. After the meeting with Lyrium, she tossed herself down on the bed to contemplate the encounter. Thought turned to thought, often of Robby, sometimes with longing, sometimes with awe, sometimes mindful of the words of Lyrium, and sometimes even with some anger that she should feel so strongly about one who was in many ways beyond her. It was not sadness she felt, but more akin to curiosity and bewilderment. Robby was suddenly important, not just to her, but to *everyone*, and in no ordinary way. She found herself thinking of him abstractly, like one would think of an object rather than a person, and about the division between them that she had always felt but had never truly understood. It was not that he might someday be Elifaen—she didn't care at all about that one way or the other. And it wasn't that he might become King—she was sure that he would. Now she felt torn between her desire for Robby, the flesh and blood, and her fear for Robby, the King to be. As her thoughts drifted and she edged toward sleep, visions of woodland frolics and pasture rollicks, mixed with incongruous imaginings about ceremonial crownings.

She suddenly thought of the night she clawed her way to Boskland, dripping blood and sobbing with pain and terror. There was a point when, in her misery, she lost all sense of struggle, gave in to the pain, and, when darkness poured over her, still a mile or more from Boskland, she stopped crying, stopped crawling, rain pouring down on her, and she slid into a black swoon. She remembered only complete helplessness. Then, vaguely, she recalled a lightness surrounding her that further muddled her vision, like a dizziness, like spinning upward, floating through the air toward Bosk Manor. As she lay on this soft bed in Tallin Hall, she turned over onto her stomach, her head in her arms. She remembered slumping heavily down onto the doorstep of Bosk Manor, and it opening to her.

There were the memories of her delirium, wild and strong, pleading with Mrs. Bosk, begging her, screaming with agony and fever and despair until a draught came to her lips and was forced down her. Then faintness and sickness like she had never known, a sickness that could only mean one thing. Later, in her delirium, she felt as if she was pulled apart and that, somehow, Robby was being pulled and beaten out of her.

Now, far away from those places, she fell toward slumber, crying into the softest pillow she had ever known at the persistent memory, clutching it with both fists against her face, until the blackness of sleep approached. Then, dimly, a vision of Lyrium's face appeared. It grew clearer, yet retained an aspect of immense distance, and Lyrium's words gently hummed in her head like harp strings.

"I will be with you, Sheila Pradkin, whose right name is Shevalia, I know. I will keep you in my heart and in my thoughts and in my prayers. And now that we have spoken, I know that it was no king, but you that I was destined to meet."

• • •

Ullin leaned against the battlement and tapped out his pipe, watching the coals tumble and glitter downward into the darkness and suddenly disappear altogether in the moat below. He and Weylan had already walked nearly the whole way around the city wall, the crowds having long since dispersed in something of a disappointed muddle after the strange visitors' silent departure. At first the two chatted, somewhat merrily even, for they were old chums and there was much to catch up with. At Weylan's mention of the tensions with the Tracians, the conversation turned serious, and their tones, which had been noisy, even boisterous, became low and solemn. They strolled west along the south wall, speaking very little, and then turned northward along the west wall, saying nothing at all until at last they stopped some distance along it. Ullin put away his pipe and sighed.

"The Hall is restless tonight," Weylan observed, nodding toward the residence on the hill some distance away. They were nearly level with the middle floors, and yet from this distance they saw that a light moved along the windows of the fifth floor corridor, Lord Tallin's floor. Someone moved there with a lamp, walking behind the glass, and lighting the hallway lamps as he went so that soon the entire length of windows was lit. Ullin knew that hallway to be lined with tapestries and paintings, a record of the family's history, or rather the families' histories since the two great Houses, that of Fairoak and that of Tallin, were joined in this House. He knew, too, that his grandfather was pacing the hall in his brooding way, as he was known to do. His grandfather would study each painting, lost in thought, sometimes standing close to the artwork and at other times viewing it from a distance, his arms crossed, or his chin cradled in one hand as he slowly moved from depiction to depiction.

"He has much to decide," Ullin said. "Much to consider, I fear."

"Aye," agreed Weylan, "and the sooner the better, I say. Meaning no disrespect, mind you, but too much scratching of the head makes for a cold head and no hat."

"And I guess you ought to know!" Ullin chuckled, affectionately rubbing the shiny spot on Weylan's crown.

"I reckon so! And I only have the North Gate to keep, and not all of Tallinvale and more."

Ullin and Weylan continued on, each smiling once again. But they were grim smiles.

"Things don't seem to be turning out quite how we dreamed when we were lads, do they?"

"No, Ullin, not exactly. Though we ain't done too bad. You a Kingsman, and still alive, and me a right proud soldier, complete with a sweet wife and two fat little brats. I hope you'll have a chance to meet them before you're off."

"That isn't likely, though I would like nothing more in the world than to congratulate the lass who managed to tame you! No, we'll be off early, I'm sure, with many miles to make up for."

Weylan nodded. "So it's on to Duinnor, is it? And right through Damar lands, if I understand you right."

"Yes, there's no other way, it seems, this late in the year."

"I'm wishing I could talk you into staying here. We could use someone with your experience in the fight that's sure to come."

"If there's to be a fight."

"Oh, there'll be one," Weylan insisted. "Whether it comes to us or we go to it, there'll be one. And a right mean one it is sure to be, too."

"I wish I could stay and help out, but I'm committed. My companions will need me more. Ashlord and I are the only real fighters among us, should it come to that, though the others are all scrappy enough."

They stopped again, this time to let a squad of sentries go past, but they paused for a while, each gazing again toward the Hall.

"Many's the night I've seen those lights, often wondering 'bout the thoughts going on in there."

"Wish I could tell you," Ullin said. "But he's as much of a mystery to me as to you. Perhaps even more so, since I have so seldom been here these past many years. Yet, I am impressed, frankly, by what I have seen today."

"What's that?"

"I've been all over the Seven Realms. Even to Tracia, and rarely have I seen or met people as loyal to their lords as these folk are to my grandfather and my family. I'm not really sure why, except that he is fair and looks to his people's welfare as any decent lord should do. Only in Glareth and in some parts of Vanara have I seen the like. Yet, Tallinvale is far away from any court and any Regent or King."

"That may be why," Weylan said. "Your grandfather keeps us. He is a tough man, true. And words of rebuke from him land like boulders. But never was a man more loyal to his people. I know, it sounds odd that a man might be so good to his people and so hard on his family. But it is true. He spills out his treasury during drought or pestilence, he directs our defenses and parleys with our enemies for our safety, at his own risk. He sees to the direction of the law and the appointment of fair judges. He asks no tribute but relies solely on the earnings of his own holdings and lands, no more, and takes no property as is his right as liege. He orders and directs our education, and hardly a person in Tallinvale cannot read and write. And he himself leads patrols along our most dangerous borders. I myself have had the honor on more than one occasion to draw swords with him against the Damar intrusions. No man in Tallinvale can match the swiftness of his arm or the power of his blows, not even I who am a less than half his age and twice his weight in muscle. Oh, we would be lost without him, I fear!" Weylan looked at Ullin curiously. "And who will be his heir? Will it be a fighter, like him? Or a store clerk?"

Ullin looked up from his feet with a blank expression, but his eyes glinted with sharp response.

"Do not underestimate clerks of stores," he replied. "Or the sons of Passdale. I need not remind you that they have spilled more of their own blood and more of the blood of the enemy in this past week than Tallinvale has done in your lifetime. Moreover, the one that goes to Duinnor a clerk may not return as one."

Weylan bowed, stunned at the cutting tone of Ullin's words and embarrassed at his own.

"I deeply regret what I said, and I meant no disrespect to your cousin or his fellows," he said. "Yet, I only try to express my sentiment to have you here with us. Not only mine, but many, many others of your people here in the valley."

Ullin took Weylan by the shoulder and turned with him to continue their walk.

"Come, come, good friend. I am sorry for my rash response. I am honored by your sentiment. But I cannot stay, as I told you earlier. I am committed to my cousin, and the mission of my company. And I will see it through."

Weylan nodded, though the turn of his lips and the bow of his head showed that he was disheartened by Ullin's reply.

"I fear for Tallinvale," Weylan said simply.

"These walls are strong, and the people stronger still," replied Ullin as they walked slowly on. "If the enemy in Barley and Passdale are any sign of the rest, they put appearances over fighting prowess, and any man here is more than a match for three of them. My sense is that many Tracians serve unwillingly."

• • •

Tallin Hall was indeed very large, but it was not so vast that a man—one who knew its passages and chambers, its stairs and back corridors—could not walk every hall and every back passageway from top to bottom in little more than an hour. And this the Lord of Tallin Hall often did, sometimes during the daytime, sometimes in the evening, but more often late into the darkest hours of the night when all was quiet and all but a few servants and guards had retired. Those that knew the Hall best knew their lord might at any moment appear, at any hour and during any task in any part of the place. They were accustomed to this behavior, if any could be, their master appearing as an apparition, his almost silent footfalls giving little warning of his approach, often wrapped in a cloak against the evening chill, his head bowed in thought, sometimes with a small lamp in his hand, but just as often in complete darkness he wandered. He would sometimes stop, especially when a maid or footman would rise from their seats, pausing long enough to acknowledge each person by name, to ask after their family, or to make a small inquiry or comment concerning this or that business of the household. Though no room was barred to him, he respected the servants' chambers and rarely ventured into those parts of the house except only to pass through the kitchens or workrooms on his way elsewhere. And when he did so, it was never with the air of lord and master, but rather as a visitor, a passer-by, humble, and not wishing to intrude or disturb their privacy or their work.

Likewise, he could often be found during these hours between the middle of the night and well before dawn along the battlements at any part of the outer wall, or in the armouries, or at any given turret or gate. So, like the staff of Tallin Hall, the soldiers of Tallinvale stood their watches and minded their stations with meticulous attention and readiness, knowing that at any moment the Lord Tallin himself might ask a report of even the lowest rank.

Where he got his stamina no one could say with any certainty, though many rumors abounded, some having to do with Faere spells of his late wife, others pertaining to peculiar and mysterious herbs he put in his pipe to smoke. Some tales even had it that the Lord Tallin was not one man but many, each alike in aspect and character and each taking his turn in the place of the others. But so accustomed were its inhabitants to this fact of Tallinvale life—this awesome and mysterious presence that ruled them so effectively—that most inhabitants of the valley wondered very little about it anymore. And, like their lord, Dargul, too, was often seen during these nocturnal walks. Sometimes he was at Lord Tallin's side as a friend, the two strolling like old chums. But just as often, Dargul kept some paces behind, entering a room just after Tallin had left it, or standing some distance away, but within easy calling distance, as Lord Tallin paused to study a trophy, some pennant or shield, or contemplated the town through a window, or the scenes painted within one of the many alcoves throughout the Hall. The two had long since given up telling each other to get rest, of kindly scolding each other for keeping such late hours when important duties lay in the morrow. Dargul usually retired first, and then he often found Tallin was already up and about before him the next morning, if indeed Lord Tallin had slept at all.

It was with habitual concern that Dargul thus followed and looked after his master. And for more than sixty years this went on, since Dargul came into his present position of Counselor to Tallinvale. But Dargul no longer had the stamina of those earlier years, though Tallin had aged hardly a day. During the early years of their association, Dargul worried over his master like a faithful and loyal dog, ever at his master's side awaiting his lord's word. Then came a time when Dargul was more confident in the well-being of Tallin, and this lasted for several decades. Now, Dargul was aware of some further tension within his lord. It was as if those earlier years of worry and fret had come again; and once again he strove to be nearby as much as he could. Dargul could not ride out with Lord Tallin as he once had, being now too frail of bone to endure the rough horseback travel to all parts of the valley. Nor could he even keep apace on foot, marching hither and yon across the city or out into the countryside, his breath now too shallow and his stride now shorter than it once was when youth's strength made up for difficult paths. So he most often confined himself to the Hall and to his business there, enlisting several young helpers to accompany Lord Tallin whenever possible, ready to send for Dargul should he ever be needed.

It was one of these, a reliable young man, who knocked this night on the door of the apartment where Dargul lived with his wife. Here, they were just next door to his son's home, and on Dargul's rare days away from the Hall, he spent every moment he could spoiling his grandchildren in whatever way was possible for him to do. His butler gently woke him, trying not to stir Mrs. Dargul, but he failed, as he always failed at such attempts, and she, too, arose as the two men hurried to the foyer where the young messenger awaited.

"Sir, he's up as usual," said the messenger. "But he lights the lamps of the West Hall and is muttering and speaking to himself most vehemently. I left Sprately with him and came directly. Don't know if it signifies, but I ain't seen him act as such."

"You did right, Johons, quite right," Dargul assured him as he turned to his man who was now holding out proper clothes to replace Dargul's nightshirt and slippers. As he quickly dressed, he could hear his wife in the nearby kitchen putting together a bit of food to shove into his pocket. So often had he been called away in the night that Dargul and his wife acted as one, and, as Lord Tallin might well know, the service of his most trusted counselor was due in great part to the counselor's devoted wife.

• • •

Dargul was met when he arrived at Tallin Hall by another young man who told him that Lord Tallin was still on the fifth floor. When he and his assistants had at last climbed all the stairs, Dargul a bit breathless at the effort, they found the hall lamps of the family wing lit. Halfway down the passage stood Lord Tallin gazing at a wide mural. Ashlord was there, too, standing a few feet behind Tallin, leaning on his stick. Dargul quietly dismissed his helpers and contented himself by watching cautiously from this distance.

"Was it so long ago that these ships came?" Tallin was saying. The painting was similar to the one Robby had seen deep in the bell room of Tulith Attis, and was in fact done by the same artist. The subject was a seascape of many large ships coming over the bright rim of the horizon and bearing for shore, heeling from the wind, their sails taut and their bow waves white and determined. The nearest ship in the depiction had a golden hull, and its billowing sails displayed the emblem of the House of Tallin. "This one brought my own namesake, though he was but a youngster. He was born at sea, as were all who landed on these shores. In these lands, he established himself as a man and later built this hall. Did you know he used timbers from that very ship to frame the doorway of the original hall built here on these grounds? Those timbers still stand four floors below us."

Ashlord stood silently by, letting Tallin talk.

"His line was nearly wiped out. By plague and disease, famine, war. His descendants hung on. One of them, called Leander, moved our family to Vanara, fearing the war that he saw coming. He and two of his brothers lost their lives at Tulith Attis. His son, safe with his family in Vanara, was rewarded for his father's service, and with the trust of the Queen, Serith Ellyn. Many came back east with me when we were forced from there, and here in Tallinvale, our ancient holdings, we have once again grown and prospered, indeed even beyond the accomplishments of our fathers." He threw Ashlord a fiery look, saying, "But what will my people say of me, now? Will they say that age has robbed my mind at last? That time has left a dotard in a young man's frame? Do they know, I wonder, how precarious these last years have been? Can they imagine the utter destruction I could invite by one false decision or another?"

Dargul stepped a little closer.

"These people have never known real war. Not like we have, Collandoth. They are young, and few have faced more than a skirmish. They are happy, I think, and healthy, and their zest for life and its bounty is matched, I dare say, in few other lands of Men. Yet, even they have grown more stern these last years. Do they suspect the doom that creeps upon us? I cannot say. In later years, will this Hall still stand? Will the children of these good people spit at my name? Are these last years of peace to be purchased with a final payment of blood?"

Still Ashlord said nothing, and Tallin turned away, stepping toward the next painting.

"Would not slavery be better than that? Who am I to say for these people that slavery and death are little different? I, who have enjoyed long life beyond the time of natural men? I, who am prosperous and safe behind my walls! Who am I to make such judgments for these people?"

Tallin paused before a small delicate depiction of a baby boy, barely able yet to stand, playfully reaching out for a butterfly with one hand as he steadied himself by clutching the gown of his mother with the other hand. Ashlord recognized the pair as Ullin and his mother, and the fanciful field where mother sat and child played was sunlit and golden-green. So charming and cunning was the depiction that Ashlord could see the grass move under a gentle breeze.

"I have tasted the bitterness of battle, Collandoth, as you have," Tallin took up after a moment. "I know the terrible joy of survival when all my comrades lay dead around me, the sick happiness of remaining alive among the lifeless gore and slaughter of friends. I remember it still, aye. This long life that I have been granted is cursed by a memory that does not fade, and every experience of happiness, every memory of fear, each recollection of fury or despair or sadness has for me the same power of emotion as ever it had. The joy and delight of the birth of my children and the satisfaction of seeing them grow to be fine and strong. What can match those feelings but the overwhelming grief at the death of my two sons and my wife! Yet, one is not more powerful than the other, nor is one memory softened any more by time than another, and all combine into a confusion of despair that ever draws me closer to madness, day by passing day. Perfect memory is a perfect curse that no man should endure for long. And I know where it drives me; I fear that someday I shall give up the present altogether, and live my life as long as it lasts in memory alone.

"No color of sunset seen may fade from me. No thunder of battle drum may soften, but ever again and again, even with its first beat crack ever again in my ears. No rebuke has lost its sting, nor any mistake its shame. Yet my children's tiny fingers forever caress my hand. And the taste of love's kiss never leaves my lips. But, alas, all are gone away, yet will not depart. Oh dear Forgetfulness, thou minister of relief, will you not come to me? Come take from my heart some slight feather of this weightless world that crushes without sweet harm. With your elixir rust away some nail of this ever towering house so that some moment's room may cave away and so be barred from my roaming thoughts never to enter there again. To be absent of mind but once! To have one moment, one only! Some unfilled place in my heart to exist, some space not to be piled upon with memory upon memory, some brief nothing to be mindful of! Some sleep from this cacophony of experience, some repose, if only for a passing eye-blink, so that one moment might be recalled with perfect peace. Oh, peace, peace! Perfect memory is but a perfect hell! Hated Time, that coach ever in the arrival, it delivers to my door its never-ending passengers, an unending family of uninvited recollection, each one a despised guest who will not depart, but ever demands my hospitality and welcome, though I would cast them all out, if I could. Oh, that I could!"

During this quiet but coldly passionate speech, Dargul drew even closer and stood just behind Ashlord, his eyes now glistening in pain for his lord and friend.

"This condition that is upon you is matched by your great will to sustain, to continue," said Ashlord softly to Lord Tallin. "Surely it keeps your madness in check."

"Aye, but it is the will of necessity, not the will of the willing," came the reply as Tallin slowly moved down the hall, with Ashlord and Dargul following. Ashlord's knowledge of Tallin was not so exact as Dargul's, but these two knew Lord Tallin better in certain ways than any other living soul. In spite of the harsh and tough exterior, one enforced, these two knew, by the cruel nature of perfect memory, they knew Lord Tallin was not a man without a heart. Indeed it was his heart, so shattered and broken by the loss of his children and his wife, that made him into a stern man these many, many years. Those pieces of his heart, which had once been strong enough to be broken and to heal, he had guarded too long, allowing nothing to touch them. Little comfort had he desired, nor did he need. His was the business of everyday musings that led to anger and short patience. Those closest to him, who had known him the longest and whose own demeanors were much a result of living within the influence of so brooding a man, knew that his outbursts were passionless and cold. An astute man of business, with a keen eye to the welfare of his domain, Lord Tallin was ever on horseback checking the fields, purchasing the best seed for his lands, and negotiating with Furaman or other traders for the best prices on behalf of those who farmed and toiled in the valley. A warrior by upbringing and, for many years of his life, by trade, he still rode out with his men at arms to push back the creepings of the Damar with many skirmishes fought and won. And, though his days of great and mighty battles seemed over, he still dressed daily in the raiment and armor of a soldier. But his losses were too many. Battles had he lost with great slaughter of friends and fellows. He had lost his lands, the ancient realm of Fairoak, upon the western slopes of Vanara. He had lost his western titles and no longer had the honored standing he once held in Duinnor. As misery follows strife, one after another, he lost his sons, his wife, and his daughter. But none hurt so much, nor cost him so dear, as the loss of his wife. Lady Kahryna was the only person who had ever been able to truly love him without hesitation, who could provoke him so easily to laughter, and whose memory would now provoke him to tears if only he had not locked away the crumbs of his heart so fast and so far, and sealed over the deep well of his eyes.

This night, as so many nights before, Lord Tallin wandered the empty and immensely lonesome passages of the Hall, hearing in spite of himself the echo of children's laughter from the still rooms, or the sweet singing of his little red-haired girl as she wove a delicate tapestry beside her mother. Again he felt the shadow of his own stern face against the memory of harsh words that haunted him again and again. He relived, now as in memory.

"Tallinvale is not strong enough to resist Duinnor," his wife said to him. She turned away from the mirror and stood, her body lithe and firm beneath her sheer gown, and she glided across the room to the bed where he lay watching and waiting for her. "Unless Dalvenpar goes west, your obligation to Duinnor will be seen as broken. Would you risk the honor of our House, and the liens upon Fairoak? Dalvenpar is strong and little harm may come to him if he is sent south to the desert."

"I fear not Duinnor," he said to her as she slipped from her gown and then under the covers beside him. Lying on his side, he ran his hand along the curve of her side to the waist, then around the small of her back and along the scar that ran along her left side up to her shoulder as she snuggled close to him. "I fear useless waste of youth and treasure. Look what it has cost us. Do we send our first-born to pay an even heavier tribute?"

"It is the way of our people," she answered. "And yet we are now far from that strife, in peace here in the Eastlands, safe from the Sun King, maybe, but not from the frown of Duinnor. Our place here is not yet firm, and we have no resources to support any resistance. And, I need not remind you, that Duinnor fears this House above all others, for the prophesies made upon it."

"Yes, yes," Tallin said aloud.

Ashlord's eyes narrowed.

"Yes, yes," Tallin said impatiently, "we have all too often heard the poems of old, foretelling the great throne to be remade of 'oak, fair and strong,' and of the sovereign new-come from the east who will plant anew the healing trees of Vanara. How many times have I heard it, from you and from those of your proud family? But we are Tallin, too, and my fathers and forefathers, too, swore their allegiance to the Unknown Name. Have I not fought for the crown? Have not my lands and yours been laid waste by the wars? And what has Duinnor done? It continues to raise army after army, leading them into the desert. Where are the builders of old? Where are the craftsmen and the yeomen needed to retake and keep our old lands? Do not think that since we are among the first to be shorn of our properties that we will be the last."

"It is not hopeless, my love," Kahryna replied. "Not so long as those of our blood fight alongside Duinnor. Where would the Seven Realms be without the

valor of our people? Wherefrom may the lands be restored, except by force of arms? Yet, you are master of Tallin Hall, and Lord Tallin of the House of Fairoak. I do not easily give up any son for vainglory or for hollow honor. Let Dalvenpar go, as his fellows must, and he will do us the honor by his service to the King."

"It will seem a hollow honor, indeed, if he never returns," Tallin said bitterly.

He had immediately regretted those words. He regretted them now as bitterly as he ever had. And now, as on so many previous dark nights of his soul, he wished them back. But they could be no more dismissed from his memory's possession than the endless halls of recollection that he was doomed to wander. Those words! Indeed, his fears came about soon enough, and never was his son's body recovered from the faraway field of war. But Duinnor had called, Fairoak had answered, and Kahryna was crushed by grief and remorse. Then Duinnor called again. He commanded his second son, Aram, to remain in Tallinvale or flee to Glareth, and Duinnor be damned. But the son did not obey his father, and so Aram went west to join with Duinnor and to seek vengeance for his brother's death. Lord Tallin had no words that could comfort his wife, and any he gave she threw back into his face. From that day onward, she rarely ever spoke, mourning her first-born and in perpetual fear for her second son. Then it was discovered that Mirabella, too, had run away after Aram. Tallin led men and horses after her, but she eluded them most cunningly. When he returned without her, never another word did his wife speak to him until the day Mirabella returned, years later, with the bitter news of Aram's death. Even now he shuddered at his wife's words, her last words uttered, as she wasted into dust before his eyes.

"I give you now all your memories," she said as she faded, her eyes ablaze with what he could only interpret as hatred. "May you never forget!"

Now, as always, he remembered these things without reference to time. Indeed, the laughter of their courtship among the waterfalls of Vanara was just as clear to him this night as the cries of her anguish. And it was just as this memory reached him that he arrived at the end of the long hallway, Ashlord trailing respectfully along and Dargul now only a few feet behind them. Here was where Tallin most often paused the longest, to muse upon a fair portrait done of Lady Kahryna shortly before their eldest boy was killed. Tallin put aside the little lamp with which he had been lighting all others and let the soft light from down the hall render upon this portrait as he contemplated it. As he looked upon the lovely countenance, Dargul wondered what new brooding his lord took before the painting. For a long time Lord Tallin stood, as silent and as still as his wife, tall and beautiful, her dark green eyes looking down at him from where she stood in her garden on a bright moonlit night.

Dargul edged closer, not trying to hide, yet reluctant to make his presence known or to disturb his master.

"Oh, Kahryna! It is not fitting for a mortal man to live so long as I!" Tallin said, speaking her name aloud for the first time in Dargul's long memory. "A curse of itself, perhaps. For we Men are weaker than your people, and we cannot bear this heavy weight of time! To the elderly, forgetfulness may be a kinder madness than anguish, and poor memory a blessing. For who can bear to witness the passing of those one loves, and the beauties of the world, yet keep company with them at every waking moment? What dire fortune is it to have memory of the world when it was young as we once were? That I remember trees and forests that have long perished before fire and plow, even at my own hand! That I still see my father's face. My mother and all my sisters and brothers, as clearly as if they were standing with me here. Yet, they are distant. Not even in spirit do I feel them anymore. But, alas, I see them. And I remember the laughter of my children in faraway Vanara and in this very house, and I see their toys and their play, and I hear their little cries of bruised knee and pouting anger, and even the whisper of their breath, now, just as clear as I once did looking upon them late at night peaceful in their slumbers. And now where are they? Gone. Into the dust of the great desert. Into the green grass of the hills of Vanara, they are. Not even their graves are known to me. And now, so full of loathing and fear am I become that I turned away our own daughter and know not one grandson while hardening my heart all these years against the other. I know. They will go the way of their fathers. Like all mortals do. And I must bear witness to whatever may come. I have turned my fear into steel and into chain to bind me against hurt! My anxiety I have forged into distance and time to shield me from caring. And not only have I done this with those of my family, those who are left to me, but in doing I have ill-guided my people. Why should they pay for my folly? What a fool am I! What a fool! Oh, what have I done? What have I become? Oh, how I wish that life would flee my bones! I am a wretch and cannot bear this weight of memory!"

He put his hands over his face and clutched his hair, crying out these last words, as he looked between his fingers at the image before him, not noticing that Ashlord had closed his eyes and was muttering soft words, low and indiscernible. Tallin groaned, swaying right and left as he pulled his hair. Then there came a breeze, gentle and sweet from an unseen place. And with it came a note of music, light and airy. Tallin opened his eyes and saw the folds of Kahryna's gown flutter, and her head bend a little toward him. She held in her hand a simple white flower and, as if for the first time in his life, he saw her there as he never had before, and it seemed to him that, for the first time, a look of gentle sympathy and forgiveness came into her face. So powerful was the sense of her expression that he cried out and fell to his knees before the portrait, weeping for the first time since his wife had died, weeping into his hands most bitterly as only a man could who had lost everything he had ever loved. Little was he aware of the kind hands that rushed to him from behind, or the faithful man who kneeled beside him to hold him as one might a child. Dargul, long waiting for this moment, wept, too, but his were the tears of relief.

"There, there, my lord," he said, cradling the much more powerful frame. "All will be made right in time."

Ashlord turned away, leaving them together, and walked slowly out, muttering some thanks to the air for Tallin's final catharsis. Though deeply moved by Tallin's torment, the mystic was now confident that one crisis had passed. Another crisis, of quite a different sort, could now be faced by Tallinvale. Sad but satisfied, Ashlord returned to the library to study while his companions slept and while Dargul helped Tallin recover himself.

Chapter 10

Lord Tallin's Plan

Day 88
157 Days Remaining

Hours later, as dawn quickly approached, but sooner than Ashlord might have expected, Lord Tallin found him.

"I wish to thank you for your patience, Collandoth," Tallin said as he took a seat across the table from Ashlord. "I'm afraid I acted out rather shamefully. Dargul, faithful man! I am afraid I gave him a fright. I'm sure he believes I have lost my wits at last. But perhaps I begin to find them. I thank you for abiding with me as you did."

"I think you needed only someone to hear you," Ashlord replied. "The crisis and doubts you feel within may be a mirror upon those that cloud these days, surely. But I trust you have now come to a greater resolve regarding all?"

"I have. Though I have resisted the last measures I should put in place, I will no longer put off what must be done. I cannot put off."

"Then you have a plan?"

"I do. It is a hard one, and I shall tell you about it in a moment. But first, I must ask you if you truly intend to go to Duinnor? To take Robby there?"

"It is our intention to go to Duinnor, yes, but I hope to see Robby to Griferis, first."

"Ah. Griferis. Then you answer my concern. I have read the old books, in Vanara and elsewhere. Books we do not have here. Yes, he must go first to Griferis. It seems the only way to prepare him. But how do you propose to pass through Shatuum?"

Ashlord shook his head and shrugged. "It is my hope that a way will be made for us, or else we may find our own way."

"I see. I wish there was some aid I could offer along those lines. But if you find your way to Duinnor before spring, would you be willing to carry a message for me?"

"Certainly."

"I will not trust it to ink, so I must tell you. There is a person who resides in the Temple of Beras. His presence there is a secret, guarded by myself and the monks there. Many years ago, this person performed a service to me at great risk to himself. He helped me lay the stones for our defensive works. All was done according to my wishes, with nothing done amiss. But I was told by him that in order to make use of our defenses, I would need a secret word. I will not explain how it is to be used. However, the word was never revealed to me, as a safeguard for this person's secret. He trusts no one, and especially not mortal Men."

"A stone worker, you imply."

"Yes, of the highest caliber. Renown throughout the world."

"How were you to obtain the secret word, when needed?" Ashlord asked. "And I assume you now need it."

"Yes, I fear that I shall need it to secure our defenses against the enemy horde that I shall entice to battle. More of that momentarily. I have sent trusted couriers to the Temple, begging for the secret word. For years they have been rebuffed, the monks not permitting my couriers an audience with their guest. I, myself, aimed to go there in the spring. But time has run out. I am needed here. Would you go to him as my ambassador of sorts? And obtain the word?"

"I would be most happy to do so. Though it will be months before I may reach Duinnor, and months longer before I could return with the word."

"You need not return with the word. He has the means to send it swiftly. All I wish for you to do is to go to him and ask him to do so. I believe you can lay out the situation for him faithfully. And, being Melnari, I believe he may listen to you. If he refuses, then we shall do without his help, as well as we may do."

"Then I shall do it. I know who it is that you mean for me to see. For who else can you mean but he who has the greatest skill in stoneworking? I shall do it, and we shall hope for the best."

"Good. That is all I can ask of you. Now, it is best that you know my intentions. I tell you first, then must I hurry off to inform others."

• • •

Morning came early, and earlier, still, for many who were called to duty by Lord Tallin's orders much sooner than they were accustomed. Dargul, who had taken Tallin back to his chambers, and who was assured by Lord Tallin that the morning would see certain great changes begin, had hardly gotten back to his apartment and his bed when another courier came to wake him. Alarmed, he and his wife were told by the courier that Tallin merely wanted to get an early start on the day's activities and wished that Dargul would join him as soon as was convenient—Tallin's way of saying, "Right away."

Still disturbed by the previous night, Dargul took the sandwich his wife made in haste and hurried to Tallin Hall. There, he went immediately to Tallin, noting the unusual number of aides and footmen reporting to their stations even though it was well before dawn. When he reached the door of Tallin's small office behind the great hall, he saw Tallin at his desk. He knocked politely and entered, and Tallin looked up, grinned uncharacteristically, and waved him to a chair.

"Please be seated," Tallin said, turning back to the papers and books on his desk. "I will be with you shortly."

Dargul quietly sat, eyeing his lord with concern, for it was strange to see this new animation in Lord Tallin's eyes. A happy resolve, incongruous and somewhat disturbing to Dargul, creased Tallin's forehead over a genuine and rather bittersweet smile. Dargul wondered if the previous night's breakdown, which was surely embarrassing for the lord, forced Tallin to take on a lighter attitude in order to alleviate worry in others.

He patiently watched Tallin pore over documents of land holdings, scattered on top of a few maps on the cluttered table. Though he did his best not to squirm or fidget, Dargul's old bones, never comfortable for long, were least comfortable when waiting. The silence was bad enough, but as Dargul abided, absently fingering his wedding band as he thought, an out-of-place sound entered his awareness. It was nearby, soft and low. At first, Dargul could not believe the source, but he realized that his Lord Tallin was actually humming to himself. Thus, it was a bewildered Dargul that Tallin now looked up and saw. After so many years of serving a demanding master, of seeing the cold evidence of a brooding intellect, to see Lord Tallin now, smiling warmly upon him, topped the cup of anxiety that filled Dargul with a froth of nervousness unlike any he had ever known. It was simply too much. Dargul, for the first time in his life, actually squirmed.

Tallin was a powerful man, rich and influential, but one who had always resisted using any power or influence for the sake of their increase alone. Instead, as Dargul well knew, the Lord of Tallinvale gained and lost his fortunes by his own wits rather than by coercion or favor as such men often did. True, Tallin severely tested all who knew him, his family, his servants, and all his friends, if he had any. But the rewards he gave for loyalty and good work had always been beyond the expectations of most. In all his doings, in his dealings with folk high and low alike, his actions had always been for the good of the valley, respecting the bonds of tradition to blood and earth, and the virtues of justice and honesty. Never had he deceived any but his enemies, and even then never for his own gain alone. Yet, now Dargul wondered what he was about to hear, for something unusual was surely afoot. Just a few minutes before, when he had first arrived in the room for the usual morning meeting, Dargul had to shuffle about to stay out of the way of the accounting clerks who were departing, having left stacks of ledger books on the floor and on the far table. After last night's scene, Dargul felt positive that Tallin was so exhausted that he would sleep late for once in his life. The evidence all around the room, the ledger books, the crumb-filled plates, and the morning dispatches already written and ready, convinced Dargul that his master had not slept a wink. But Lord Tallin appeared rested, and, another peculiarity, he looked less strained, even younger than ever. As

Dargul scratched his chin, resisting the temptation to interrupt his master's thoughts, Tallin suddenly picked up a set of dividers, measured out a length against a map, tossed it aside, picked up a document and ran his finger down it, looking for a bit of information.

"Ah!" he said. He tossed the document aside and, tapping the dividers lightly on the map, looked at Dargul serenely. Here it comes, thought Dargul, and he stiffened.

"I am probably the richest living man in the entire world," Tallin said easily, and with a little laugh. Lord Tallin leaned back in his chair, actually putting his feet up on the desk. Dargul only nodded. Lord Tallin stirred his hot morning drink with another chuckle. "Indeed, my vaults are so overflowing with gold and silver that these past years I have contrived for the estate to accept no more, and have taken trade and service as payments for our crops and our goods. You know all this better than any. However, to have such wealth is a waste if it is not used. And, now, I do mean to use it. To accomplish my aim, I will use every grain of gold and every ounce of silver that I have in my possession. Every diamond, every ruby, and every sapphire. Every copper coin, if need be!"

Dargul shifted in his chair, "Do you propose to undertake some grand construction? For years you have talked about rebuilding the bridges along the South Road."

"Hardly! It is more along the lines of destruction that I aim. But as the ground is plowed before the seed is laid, and as old stones are cast aside to make room for a new foundation, sometimes destruction is merely the first part of something greater to come. I hope so. But we haven't much time, and there is not a moment to be lost. I know this is beyond your normal duties, but I trust you above all others to see things done properly. This is it: I want you to prepare such a store of food within the walls of the city that may sustain the entire population of Tallinvale for a year, until early summer, at the very least. Not only sustain those of us already here within the city, but also every man, woman, and child in this valley. I want you to undertake to buy all crops and all animals within our valley. At the same time, you will need to see to the construction of ample storage buildings, granaries, and stables. You undoubtedly have associates that you can call upon to oversee some of these tasks. Regardless, all must be done quickly."

Tallin suddenly stood up and began pacing back and forth as he spoke.

"I wish to purchase a lease on all lands and houses in the valley with an assurance that an equal portion to the lease paid will be given the owners should any damage befall their property. All those who accept our lease are to do so within the fortnight, and, as a condition of the lease, they are to remove themselves here. A fortnight only, and no more, is allowed, so you must send heralds out with the news to prepare them. I have here a written list of what will be paid as lease according to acres, buildings, cropland, and rents as listed in this past census, just completed last month. You must understand that this lease is my way to encourage our people to leave their farms and their outlying shops and lands for a time. All men and boys above twelve years of age and less than eighty who are strong enough to bear arms will be called to duty, lease or no lease, and all farming and husbandry are to be put aside. The women and children are to be employed wherever possible or necessary with the granaries or mills in Tallin Town or any other suitable occupation that is productive and may be protected within the walls. Schools will be established, and those masters engaged in the village schools will be moved here. All within a fortnight, do you hear?"

"Yes, Lord. A massive undertaking in so little time. But why? Do you mean to increase our armies? Why do you seek to lease the lands?"

"We are going to war. If we act swiftly, we can prepare in time. After a fortnight from today, we must all be gathered within the walls. We will then have but another fortnight, after all are gathered, to prepare. But in time or not, prepared or not, I intend to provoke the Redvests and the Damar to enter into war against us and to lay siege to this city."

"My lord! Why? Our treaties, though precarious, still stand. Surely every day without bloodshed has value?"

"Indeed, it does. Value to the enemy! But bloodshed is coming. Already the enemy has tested our lines to the south. They are prepared to turn north. I am convinced that they believe Tallinvale will be an easy capture, rich in plunder, though costly in time and men. They would rather wait until the war in the southwest and west is fully within their control. By that time, according to what I believe to be their reckoning, we will be isolated. This is our chance. We do not have the means to stop their attack on the west. But we may tax their strength, force them to expend their precious resources, and weaken their ranks. If we are fortunate, we may even upset their plans. By turning north against us, they will have fewer men to commit to the western battles to come."

"What reason will you give them for turning against us?"

"I will close the South Road near the Lerse. It is the plan of the Redvests to use the South Road to send supplies and food to their southern armies now gathering. The message will be clear. To secure the road, and their captured harvests, they will have to traverse the whole of Tallinvale, land we know well, and they hardly at all. We will draw them northward to us, burning as we retreat, leaving not so much as an ear of corn or a sack of potatoes for them to scavenge. They will be forced to lay siege upon us. The Damar will strike against our western flanks while the Redvest forces will build from the south. When they realize our power, they will move quickly, but not quickly enough. It will soon be winter. Their long march and their siege will be more costly still. They will be harried from the north by the Janhaven and Hill Town forces, and they will have nothing to eat but what they bring. They will be cold and sick and far from home. To relieve them, Tracia will pour northward with more troops and supplies, and then still more and more. Yet, we will hold on. Thus, we will bleed them like an open wound in salty water. Their final assault upon us, if all goes along my expectations, will be in the late winter or early spring. Their victory over us will permit the resumption of their original plans. Once we are annihilated, nothing will stand between them and the lands to the southwest. But if the Tracian Redvests are to be allied to the Dragon Peoples, we will see to it that they are a weakened and bruised partner. The alliance with Tracia permits the Dragon armies to be secure on their eastern flanks, and they may at last throw their whole strength at Vanara, or march past Vanara and straight north to Duinnor. Either way, one by one, the Realms will be cut off from one another. And, one by one, all of the Seven Realms will be overrun and conquered."

"Lord Tallin, I hear in your voice and see in your eyes that you are serious in this matter and that your mind is set upon this course of action," Dargul said. "But what assurance do you have that we may defeat them without Duinnor's help?"

"I have no hope of defeating the Redvests, only to delay them. To hurt them, reduce their numbers, and strain their treasury. To wear them down."

Dargul blinked.

"Then why? Why bring this destruction upon Tallinvale? If Duinnor does not come to our aid, then what?"

"We must first go to the aid of Duinnor, and to our King!" Tallin looked at Dargul and smiled again. "I know what you are thinking, but will not say and have never said in all the long years of our friendship. You, like most of us, have no faith in our King. You, like most of us, feel the sting of Duinnor's neglect and even wonder why we should remain loyal. But it is for hope that we fight! For hope of our survival. Maybe, even, for hope that tomorrow's Duinnor will not be the same as today's."

"Not the same? I don't understand. What do you mean?"

A rap came at the doorway, and Weylan stood there, along with a dozen other soldiers.

"Remember, Glareth will not be idle for too long," Tallin said to Dargul, then stood and turned to Weylan and the other soldiers. "Ah! Captains, come in!" Tallin grinned, waving the men into the room. "I have many orders for you and much to discuss. The first of which cannot wait, so have your aides make ready to dispatch fast-riding messengers to Hill Town, Janhaven, and to Glareth by the Sea. Dargul, good friend, perhaps I will be able to tell you more at a later time, but for now, please begin preparing those leases."

• • •

"Windard told me I'd find you here."

Ashlord looked up from the parchment he was studying.

"Ah, Robby! You are up early."

"I thought we'd be getting an early start."

Ashlord took another paper and looked over it as they talked. Robby entered and roamed, looking at the books, sometimes taking one down and reading a little.

"Early enough, though a bit later," Ashlord said. "It has already been a busy morning for some."

"Yes, I noticed a great deal of hubbub out in the front yard and down in the great hall. Looked like lots of messengers and soldiers coming and going and many of the townfolk, too. What is it all about?"

"War, Robby," Ashlord said plainly, without looking up from the page he was running his finger down. "Lord Tallin is taking his people to war against the Tracian Redvests and the Damar."

"What? Why? When did this all come about? Just yesterday my grandfather spoke of delicate treaties! What has changed his mind? Lyrium's visit?"

Ashlord looked up and smiled.

"No. He came to a change of heart on his own. These events we are living through have been in the making for many generations, each development along the road to the present shaped by countless choices, decisions, and actions great and small. Now, choices are being forced, and indecision may be the worst sort of answer. In other words, it all came together for Lord Tallin last night."

The two gazed at each other for a long moment.

"If you are wondering at your role in this," Ashlord put forward, "you should know that Lord Tallin seeks to buy you time. He hopes to disrupt the westward movement of the enemy armies, to delay them, and to interfere with the Damar's efforts to build their forces. He aims to weaken the accord between Tracia and Damar and to undermine their effort to join with the Dragonkind. And, perhaps, if we hope beyond luck, to even prevent the coming together of that alliance. I have no doubt that he sends out his provocateurs as we speak."

"But what of Duinnor? What role does Duinnor play?"

"Duinnor sleeps, Robby. And until some other king comes to rule, I fear it will remain in a slumber. There is little hope of otherwise rousing it as Tallinvale has been, until it is too late and the enemy is at the gate."

"But isn't it the most powerful of the Seven Realms?"

"Perhaps. But how can Duinnor know of Lord Tallin's decision? I am doubtful even that they know of Tracia's movements and plans, its efforts to ally with Damar and the Dragonfolk. This morning before dawn, I sent Certina to deliver the news, but though she is swift and will not rest, Duinnor is over four hundred leagues from here, as the owl flies. It will be many days, at least, before she arrives and then many more after that for her to return."

"When will the fighting start? I mean, around here."

"Not for at least two weeks, perhaps a month. We must be far away by then, well beyond the Damar lands. We cannot risk your capture, and I'm afraid those who may wish to stop us will soon learn of our plans and may guess our way. Besides that, there are many who will not know of us but would find it profitable for their own ends to have captives. To sell, or worse."

"Or worse?"

"Or worse. Do not forget Bailorg and his abuse of Billy. Nor his casual disposing of Sheila's uncle. Surely there are others like him."

Robby nodded. "Yes, of course."

"We will be on our way soon enough," Ashlord concluded. "Ullin and his friend Weylan are preparing our things now, and by noon all will be ready. I just want to quickly look over a few more of these manuscripts. Why don't you browse around? It is a fine library, one of the best between Vanara and Glareth. There are some particularly good histories over there, some with quite artfully done illustrations of remarkable accuracy."

"That is what Sheila told me."

Robby did as Ashlord suggested, quickly finding many interesting volumes. Some of them told of histories that he had learned from Broadweed's school, but in much more detail. Others told of completely new places and people he had never heard of but who did mighty and wondrous things. There were many, indeed, with fine illustrations, one in particular with paintings on every few pages that seem so realistic he could almost feel the breeze that tugged the banners on the castles illustrated, or hear the cry of battle from those scenes, terrible and shocking to view. Soon he was no longer mindful of the passing of time, so absorbed he was in this treasure of knowledge. There were several books on the Dragonkind, and he was amazed when he perused them that their cities were so fine and beautiful, for he had always been of the impression that they were a crude and artless people. He saw a small book, written in the western script that he struggled to understand, and he noticed right away on the binding an embossed inscription, in gold leaf, that resembled a familiar name.

"Did you write this?" Robby asked, holding up the book.

"What? Oh, that. Well, no," Ashlord said smiling. "It says there 'An Interview with a Late Traveler from the Dragon Lands, one Collandoth of Duinnor.' It is an account of a portion of my time in those lands, very long ago."

"It's about you!"

"Yes, it tells of my work and my observations," he sighed, "but few ever read it, and fewer still minded what they read or else many troubles might have been avoided."

"All these writings," Robby said, fingering the spines of some of the bound volumes. "These histories full of great people and mighty feats, thinkers and kings, you and others, warriors and poets and builders. I feel so small before them, though they are only page and ink. What can I do compared to these? How is my own single life to be measured against these long histories, Ashlord?"

"It is not the books you write, nor the buildings you build that matter when life is done," Ashlord replied, putting one book aside and reaching for another. Then he looked up at the boy. "It isn't the battles you fight, or the tragedies you suffer, or the successes or failures. When life is over and done and you are gone away, it will be the connections you made that count most. If during your life you do not make those connections, then surely the afterworld will be cold and dark, for there, just as here, our way is lit only by those things to which we attach our hearts and minds. Whether friend, family, or stranger, the hand that we take or the one we offer is the touch that lasts and lasts. It is the power of that touch, so vast that the mind cannot encompass it, nor the eye see its bound, that goes on long after the breath has left the body and the world has forgotten the name."

"So all these things don't matter? These great works?"

"Oh they matter a great deal, Robby. They are the offspring of little things, of the efforts and loves, the struggles and trials, and the character and spirit of all who take a part in bringing things to be as they are. History is not written. It is lived. It is not carved, cut, cast, or charted. It is formed by the works, great and small, of every living being, of even the plants and animals of the world, the seas that beat upon its edge, and the stars that shine down upon it. You are history, Robby, and so am I. We shape it by what we do with what we have, when we have the time and strength to do those things. Certainly there are ways that can be foretold, even events predicted. Any man may say that a leaf will fall in autumn. But who may say where it will land and what will be its consequence?

"In fact, a story is sometimes told of a leaf that fell one summer, long before any others, and landed upon the still waters of a forest pond. The leaf made a slight ripple and upset a mayfly from its buzzing and caused it to fly near to the surface of the water. A fish snatched the mayfly and ate it, giving the fish strength to last another day. The next day a bear caught this fish, and so the bear lived another day, too. The day after, the bear discovered a honeycomb and upset the bees therein, which flew away and stung the horse of a passing messenger. The horse's rider was thrown and killed, and the message never delivered to the prince of the army. That army, then lacking the message, marched into folly and was destroyed, and so the kingdom fell to its enemies. Did the enemy cast down the kingdom? Or the horse, or the bee, or the bear, or the fish, or the mayfly? Or was the mighty kingdom toppled by the silent fall of a single leaf?"

"Hm. It seems to me that it was a long chain of things," Robby replied, "of many weak links that could have been broken, if things had but gone another way here or there."

Ashlord smiled. "You see clearly, then. Blame has little purpose. You may as well blame the mayfly as the army. Nothing is without consequence. Not even small things."

"Small things, indeed," Robby chuckled wryly. "I am overwhelmed by all the big things to notice the small things, it seems. I am so behind, so backward! How can all this be so? How can I be here, with the purpose I have? Hope? Now *that* seems a small thing!"

Robby shook his head, but Ashlord remained smiling.

"Much is demanded of you, Robby. I do not have all the answers, nor do I know how so much may be accomplished in so very little time. You must chase the wind, it seems, and I have no wings to give you. Those you must find on your own. I hope and believe that you will. A small thing? Hope? Yes. Maybe it is. And maybe sometimes it is even skittish, like the little finch, never still for very long. But it contains within it all the true treasures of the world. Those that our hands may touch and hold, and those treasures we may only feel with our hearts. Within hope's little breast, the greatest trove may be found."

• • •

Not very long afterwards, Sheila sat with her arms around her knees and watched from the top of the old wall that surrounded the Hall. She saw the comings and goings, anxious riders speeding to and fro, some in the livery of the Hall, some soldiers with light arms, and some ordinary looking boys. As more came, more went, bearing away from the Hall saddlebags of scrolled parchments. All left at a gallop, some turning south and others northward, the dust of their passing barely settled before the next rider thundered by.

"It'stime, it'stimetogo,Sheila."

She turned and saw Ibin, his mandolin slung over his shoulder, looking up from below. She smiled at him and jumped down from the wall, and soon they rejoined the rest of their company at the stables. Ullin and Billy were lashing the last of the supplies onto the pack animals while Robby led out their riding horses, already saddled. Her things, her bow and sword, and her saddlebags were neatly stacked where she had left them, and as she checked her saddle and tied on her gear she looked around.

"Where's Ashlord?"

"Went off to see that Dargul feller," Billy said, jerking his chin at the Hall. "Said somethin' 'bout last minute somethin' er other."

"He wanted to know a few things about Toolant," Robby told her.

• • •

"Why yes, of course he was watched," Dargul was telling Ashlord. Ashlord trailed Dargul as the elderly counselor went quickly hither and yon about the Hall making necessary and urgent arrangements. There was lease-writing he had to supervise, done by a group of scribes. There were messages to be written and messengers to summon for their dispatch. And there were accounting books to review, deeds to locate, census rolls to check, all with quickly summoned clerks and foremen helping (and new ones arriving every few minutes), and a myriad of other things needing haste but also care. With Ashlord in tow, Dargul did all this, passing from room to room, dodging aides and assistants who trotted back and forth across the halls from one doorway to the next with stacks of papers and books, and avoiding collision with soldiers who were reporting for duty here or there, or being sent out to all parts of the valley. It was as busy a place as any place could be, and busier than Tallin Hall had ever been before. Yet, amid the seeming confusion, Dargul went competently about, resolving arguments, putting the final touches on various letters and decrees, going over routes, and authorizing the purchase of building materials for various storehouses, barracks, workshops, and kitchens that were to be assembled. Alarmed city fathers and leading citizens came, were told what they needed to be told, and left to hurry to their assignments and to make ready their businesses. Sheriffs and their deputies came to receive arrest warrants for known Tracian spies staying nearby. The lawmen were also given various decrees and proclamations to carry out, especially in the line of closing certain establishments known for providing haven and illegal trade for Damar agents and conspirators, and for the establishment of guards at every well and every spring within the walls.

"And as counselor he had a fair number of visitors from foreign parts, just as I do."

"He may have come alone or in the company of a few others," Ashlord told him, stepping out of the way of a clerk who charged around the corner. "His name was Bailorg. And he was one of the Elifaen, from Vanara, I think."

"Bailorg, Bailorg. I can't say that the name strikes me in any particular way."

"He was tall, blond,"

"Yes, yes, yes!" Dargul exclaimed. "I remember him, now. Yes, he came here several times. I am sorry I am so thick! I only actually met him once and did not care for the looks of him, too shifty-eyed by far. He had men with him that always lurked nearby but never spoke, remaining in arms the whole while, helmets, even. I took them to be his bodyguards."

"Several times, do you say?"

"Yes, I met him when he came the first time, about three years ago, applying for use of the library. In fact, Toolant brought him to me. I took him to be from Duinnor, though. It is not unusual for our libraries to be visited, and Lord Tallin is generous in his permission. He returned last winter and then again in the spring. I only know because I signed the house pass for him each time. It was one of the few duties left to me when Toolant displaced me, so to speak. I did not pay much notice to Bailorg, my attention by then wholly concerned with Toolant's intrigues."

"But they could have conspired together?"

"I suppose. Though I know of no connection. His visit, like all who visit, was reported to Lord Tallin. It did not arouse concern. Excuse me! No, those are not needed in there," he stopped a servant bringing more pots of ink and quills. "Down the hall, to the left, where all the scribbling is going on. Oh how I wish we had one of those new writing presses! You would not believe the imbecilic way some of these 'learned scribes' shape their letters! And I've already dismissed four who were intent on decorating each and every copy with flowery illuminations before each paragraph, each taking two hours on a single copy. At a time like this! School children would be better by far!"

"Do you know what it was that he was looking for in the library?"

"What? No, I cannot guess. I can't remember which of our footmen attended him. I could find out and ask."

"Well. No, that is not necessary, I don't think. You have more pressing matters, and I will not take up more of your time," said Ashlord, reaching for Dargul's hand, "and my companions await me. Please express our gratitude to Lord Tallin, if you will. And also share our thanks with the servants of the house, Windard, especially."

• • •

The others were waiting for Ashlord in front of the Hall as he emerged, but he said little as he slung his bag over the saddle and climbed after it. The yard was noisy still, with comings and goings, and as they made their way through the estate grounds and then out into the city beyond, everywhere seemed all a-bustle and a-jostle, and every few minutes another galloping rider would fly past them. This traffic increased as they made the western gate and passed through it.

"We make our way to the village of Undertree, some few miles from here, at the rim of the valley," Ullin told Billy as they passed through the cultivated fields and over the stone canal bridges that surrounded Tallin City. They followed the same road that Lyrium and her party had traveled the night before, straight westward until it curved to take the first of many turns that would carry them up and into the west hills overlooking Tallinvale. At last, gaining the crest of the first line of hills, they stopped and gathered together to look back over the valley below. The afternoon sun was bright and the day was warm, and all along the roads that crisscrossed below were riders and wagons and carts and people moving. Several times as they watched, one of these riders would overtake them and gallop past, disappearing into the forest northward or southward or straight on along the western road.

"All this commotion," said Billy. "Will thar truly be fightin', like I heard outside me room this mornin'?"

"Looks like it," said Robby. "They mean to buy time by provoking the Redvests and delaying them from their westward attacks, if they can."

"But just since yesterday?" Sheila asked. "Yesterday, when we arrived, your grandfather didn't seem too interested in helping."

"Yeah, but that was afore Robby had a chat with his granddad," Billy said to her. She looked at Robby, who shook his head.

"It is a fearful thing he embarks upon," Ullin put in. "However he came by the decision."

"Yes," added Ashlord, reining his horse around to lead them on. "I'm afraid he has thrown away the sheath."

"Thrown away the sheath?" asked Billy, nudging his horse alongside Ullin who was still gazing across his valley. "What's 'at mean?"

"It means there's no turning back," Ullin replied, pulling his horse around to follow Ashlord.

● ● ●

They passed many crossroads and on through places where the pasture-quilted hills and patchwork woods held small cottages, and on through more intersections where cattle paths and foot paths came and went, and everywhere people were out and about. Riders continued to go by, some coming and others going, but the farther along they went, the fewer they saw, and the hills became more rugged and forested as the day fell toward late afternoon. Several times, Billy tried to strike up some note of conversation, but he found that his friends had little enthusiasm for talking, and they remained silent, for the most part, moving as quickly as their pack animals would allow. So it was a somber group that entered the village of Undertree, a small town of shops and cottages. They found the inn, stabled their horses as the sun set, and, since there were no other travelers staying there this night, they had the keeper and the cook to themselves and the whole of the great room, too, and the bright fire in the hearth. After some beer, they sat at a long table and ate a hearty stew and talked of the days to come.

"Do the Seven Realms rule all of the lands between here and Duinnor?" Sheila asked Ullin.

"No, there are many places amongst and between that have never been part of any realm or kingdom. Wild places, some. Others forbidden and closed to outsiders. Some are forests, others are swamps, and still other places are in the mountains or even the open plain. And there are other places, not forbidden at all, inhabited by Men or Elifaen, that swear no oath to Duinnor and rule themselves apart from all the happenings in the world outside of their lands. Sudamoor is one such kingdom, where men farm and fish and abide together in many towns and villages, led by a line of kings that they have supported for many generations. Gardask is another land, not so hospitable, where the folk live meager but free lives, choosing their chiefs and leaders and making their own laws as they see fit. They are a scrappy folk, easily incited to violence, and not against raiding other lands for cattle or booty."

"What about them forbidden places?" Billy piped up. "Why are they forbidden?"

"Only because few who go into those places ever come away," Ashlord put forward. "Or if they ever do, they wish they never had, living the rest of their days in terror or in some madness of mind."

"Like whar, for instance?"

"Like Nasakeeria," said Ullin, "a high country on the northern plains between here and Duinnor. All travelers avoid that place, even though passing around it takes days. Its boundaries are marked by the discarded bones of those who attempted to penetrate its secrets."

"Discarded?" Billy asked. "By what?"

"By those who live there, it is said, who conjure a mysterious fire to consume any who attempt to cross their border. There have been many witnesses to the fire."

"Get on!"

"It is true," Ashlord said. "During the time of the Dragonkind invasion that destroyed Tulith Attis, Duinnor dispatched an army to the east, and in their haste they attempted to pass through Nasakeeria. Fifteen thousand swordsmen, three thousand archers, and a thousand horsemen, along with their train of supplies entered Nasakeeria. When they did so, they dispatched a messenger to Duinnor with word of their progress. Only he survived. Two weeks later, when no other messengers came, riders were sent. They found only clean white bones laid out in vast arrays. Skulls here, ribs there, leg-bones yonder, and so forth, bleaching in the sun beneath the fluttering battle flags of each company and division. Likewise, the bones of their horses and cattle were found. But no equipment was found, other than the pennants and the lances upon which they flew. No swords, saddles, shields, arrows, or clothing of any kind. And none of the bones bore any mark whatsoever, as would be expected if they had died in battle."

Billy's mouth was opening and closing, as if he was trying to form some word of comment. Ibin's mouth just hung open at the tale.

"Had Duinnor's army gone around, it is likely they would have reached Tulith Attis in time to render aid, if not break the siege entirely. As it was, they sent another army, but it did not reach the east in time, and it caused Queen Serith Ellyn's army to be delayed. That is why, even to this day, Duinnor is often blamed for the slaughter that took place in the Eastlands."

The company fell silent for a few moments as they all wondered at the tale.

"But that's not all," Robby said. "Did not that same fate await another army some time later?"

"Indeed it did, another small army, marching swiftly from the south, nearly three hundred years ago," Ullin said. "Now their bones, too, mingle with the others. You have done some reading?"

"A little."

"But what Duinnor fool would send another army into Nasakeeria after what happened to the first?" Sheila cried incredulously.

"The second army knew nothing of the first," Ashlord said. "It was from the Dragonlands."

"Oh," Sheila was taken aback. She had forgotten lessons that Ashlord had taught her during her stay with him at Tulith Attis. Three hundred years ago, a Dragonkind army moved swiftly out of the deserts, broke through the mountains south of Vanara and, surprising everyone, made a daring and devastating dash straight out and around Vanara, swinging northward toward Duinnor. She now remembered that when she asked what had stopped them, Ashlord only said "Their own bad luck." The lesson had been interrupted by Certina, and then by Ashlord's request that she go to Passdale to meet Ullin. That was the day Robby set out for Tulith Attis with Ullin's delivery, the day he rang the Bell. Suddenly she was lost in a different line of thinking, about then and now, about knowledge and ignorance, and about the smallness of her old life in Barley. In an odd way, she thought, this situation, arising from the misfortune that befell Barley and the hopeless quest pressed upon Robby, was a relief from the oppression of her life before. Then she remembered the kindness of Frizella and Mirabella, the gentleness of Robby's father, and the happiness—yes, she could say that, now—of her stay with the Ribbons. The loss of all that settled somberly upon her heart.

"The Dragonkind?" asked Billy.

"Yes," nodded Ullin. "And had it not been for Nasakeeria, the army would have reached Duinnor with little resistance, the Realm's armies being scattered to the east and southwest. Since that time, Duinnor has grown more reluctant to send its best forces very far, sending instead armies made up of poorly trained and ill-led men. So the burden of defense fell more and more upon Vanara. The Dragonkind army may have failed in its attempt, but it succeeded in weakening the Seven Realms in ways only now coming to light."

"Nasakeeria may have many secrets," said Robby. "But at least we know that it plays no favors with intruders."

"An' none of them folk, er them creatures, whatever they may be, none of them have ever come out of Nasakeeria?" Billy asked.

"Who knows?" said Ullin.

"The place is inscrutable," stated Ashlord.

"But we do not go that way, do we?" Robby asked.

"Not at all. I intend to lead us west and a bit south along these foothills before entering the mountains," Ashlord told them as they ate. "We will abandon the roads, so as not to risk capture by the Damar who are surely on alert after last night. So we must try to make our way cross-country as best as we can for as far as we may."

"That's liable to be rough," commented Billy.

"I know, but unless you can think of a better way to pass through without getting our throats parted, I think we must try."

"How long will it take us to move through Damar country?" asked Sheila.

"Once we enter the mountains, it would be about a hundred leagues, from east to west, as the bird flies," Ashlord replied, passing another bowl to Ibin. "If we make forty miles each day, about a week to cross through."

"That may be optimistic," Ullin said. "The days are growing shorter and night comes early in the mountains, anyway."

"Yes, it will be difficult," Ashlord agreed. "Which is why we should all turn in after we eat and strive to depart before dawn. We have the loft room, upstairs, not so fancy as Tallin Hall, but better than you'll find for many nights to come. So I suggest you go to them soon and enjoy them while you can."

"Did you learn anything about Bailorg?" Robby asked as he tore off a lump of bread for his stew.

"Dargul knew little, except that he came to use the library," Ashlord replied. "I suspect some connection with Toolant."

"And you have some history with the red-bearded one, is that not so?" Ullin asked.

"Yes, I'm afraid I do. Years ago, we were at the same time in the service of Duinnor. He left service and disappeared for many years, turning up first in Vanara and then, later, in Tracia. I have always thought him capable of the most foul deeds, but he surpassed even my imaginations in Tracia."

"Why? What did he do?"

"He was instrumental in bringing down the Prince, I believe. He came into a position of counselor to the Tracian Royal House, and escaped capture even when many were taken and executed. A slippery one, surely. He showed up in Glareth not many years ago, with some plan to rid the Thunder Mountains of the bandits that lurk there, or so he said. It was suspected that he was an agent of the new Tracian overlords who feared the refugees in Glareth would foment resistance. Prince Carbane, I'm happy to say, considered Toolant's proposals to send forces into the Thunder Mountains quite outrageous, and Toolant soon left Glareth with nothing accomplished except the further tarnishing of his reputation. Then, as I gather, he showed up in Tallinvale and established himself there, seeking to accomplish the same that he strove to do in Glareth. Lord Tallin would hear none of it, thankfully, but led Toolant on so as to use him as a means to pry other Redvest spies and agents from the woodwork. I dare say many are being rounded up this day and will soon find their path southward, or worse."

"So you don't think Bailorg and Toolant were partners, do you?"

"No, I do not. But they may have shared sympathies, so to speak. And Toolant, an Elifaen but much younger of the two, was very likely all too happy to assist Bailorg. Remember Bailorg's letters? A more involved plot than Toolant was privy to, I'm sure. If Toolant had known about the plot to kidnap you, and the bounty Bailorg thought to receive by doing it, he would surely have attempted to carry it out himself. He had ample warning of our approach, but did nothing. I only hope we make it through the mountains and beyond his reach, or the reach of the Damar, before they realize their missed opportunity." Ashlord nodded at Robby's bowl. "You should pay more attention to your food. You need to eat and rest well tonight. It gets hard from here on. We'll have plenty of time to talk on the road."

"I think I'm about full. What will you do this night?"

"I will keep vigil."

• • •

That night, restless though they were, they slept soundly enough in the loft upstairs. Sheila, never shy, and anyway accustomed to Robby and the boys, slept with them, cuddled against Robby at the end of the great bed that very nearly stretched across the entire room. Ullin, as usual, was the last to retire, staying up to smoke his pipe with Ashlord well into the night, softly chatting with his elder friend about all things that came to mind. After a long while, they grew silent as the fire grew low. At last, Ullin stood and tapped out his pipe, nodded good-night to Ashlord, and made his way up the stairs.

When he entered the room, he smiled at the peacefulness of the sleepers. Ibin's normal lion's snore was subdued, Billy's competitive bray was altogether missing as he lay with his arm over his head, and the lovers were curled under their blankets. A candle burned low on a nearby table, casting its light upward into the rough-hewn beams overhead. The town was quiet and the breeze rustled softly in the tree tops. A distant dog barked, none too enthusiastically, and from below could be heard the innkeeper giving the great room the last sweep of the night.

Ullin took off his cloak and undid his straps and harness, and laid aside his sword. He put his daggers on the table, and, unbuttoning his leather tunic, sat in a chair beside the candle to take off his boots. A pendant fell from around his neck and dangled in the light as he bent over. When he straightened up, he held it near the candle. It was a small silver locket, and he looked at it thoughtfully for a moment, then he clicked it open with his thumbnail. Within was a tiny likeness of his mother and father, done years and years ago, brought back from the west by Mirabella. He gazed at it, remembering the day she returned, when she handed to him this very locket, the one she had pried from his dead father's grip. Ullin was only a youngster, and had been out playing with his little friend, Weylan. On his return, he knew instantly something was very wrong at the Hall. As he strode up the steps to the doors, Mirabella emerged. Now looking at the locket, he remembered still the flush of joy and relief at seeing his beautiful aunt coming toward him, and then the grim look on her face that instantly shattered his relief. She held out her hand and gave him this locket, saying nothing. When he looked questioningly into her tearful face, she turned away. He knew what it meant. The days that followed were black. His grandmother died of grief and his mother nearly did, too, inconsolable over the loss of her husband. When she departed Tallin Hall for her own kin in Glareth, Ullin begged to stay, claiming Tallin Hall as his home. He went with her to Glareth by the Sea, but was so miserable there that she permitted him to return. But Tallinvale never seemed the same without his father. Nowadays, his mother was feeble and infirm and, unlike his grandfather, her connections to the Elifaen had little lasting effect on her body. Still, he thought, smiling at her image in the low light of the candle, she was once beautiful and strong.

He put his nail under another tiny hidden flange under the image and gave it a gentle push. Beneath the portrait of his mother, snapped open another small chamber. In it was a long strand of jet-black hair, carefully twisted into a tiny braided ring that encircled another tiny portrait. It was of someone he had met in the west while on assignment, someone he had never mentioned to anyone. He fingered the braid, giving an almost imperceptible sigh, and his lips turned up slightly at a pleasant thought that came to mind, a gentle feeling in his heart. It was a long deep moment, full of memory and the visceral sense of vast melancholy distance. Just as his feelings edged toward unendurable longing, he felt an inexplicable presence, as if she was somehow still with him. He gently closed the locket, then, he tenderly kissed the back of it. Ullin blew out the candle, picked up one of his daggers, and slipped onto the nearest cot. Soon enough, in spite of his anxieties, he drifted off, and his sleep was peaceful and deep.

Likewise, the others were less fitful than on many previous nights, and when Ashlord looked in on them some few hours before dawn, he, too, noticed their peace and decided to give them another hour before rousing them. So, instead, he went to the window and peered into the night, wondering about Certina and her travels, among many other things. He stood motionless, as comfortable as sitting, neither blinking nor yawning, hardly breathing, it might seem. In the dim light he could have been taken for a dark statue but for the occasional slight creasing of his brow over his black bottomless eyes. This was his way, his fate one might say, to struggle in his mind, to grapple with problems near at hand and far into the future and long since passed, to relive in acute memory all his long days upon the earth, just as the Elifaen are said to do, and to turn over all things as a puzzle. To him, the beginnings of his habit stemmed from his first memory, unblurred by time, the memory of his first breath, taken on the dawn of his first day upon the earth. It was a deep breath, the firm inhalation of rich, cool, clean air, bathed in golden light that rang with the purity of boundless love, a breath that filled his being with life and ignited his heart. Just as the sunrise over a distant horizon struck a ray into the high, sapphire-blue walls of the icy cave, he opened his eyes, knowing they would never close again until the time of his leaving. Ashlord then exhaled, and he rose up from the granite bed where he had been placed.

"Who?" he asked.

"Collandoth, you shall be called. One of the Melnari, you are, and my agent in this world. You shall learn, and with your learning you shall guide the happenings of the world in the way I shall set before you. You will gain and lose fortunes and friendships, kingdoms and loyalties, but never shall you want of faith. For I am your Father and unto me you shall return when your way is ended. Neither mortal nor immortal are you, neither Man, nor Faere, nor Dragon, nor any other worldly race that may be or may ever come to be. Go! Take up your path and tread with care. It is for you, my agent, to learn and construe the right way of things. This I say: Long may it be before the coming of your time and the consummation of your power in this world. Abide with patience and care, watching all things, fearing not to look in unthought-of places and obscure lands. When the time to act comes, you shall know what to do."

Ashlord nodded.

"And where shall I begin?"

"Begin in youth, and make this day your beginning."

So Ashlord stepped from the cave, his white hair blowing about his head, and he walked out onto the path that led downward into the valley below. It was a long walk and took all day, his limbs learning, his heart becoming strong, his eyes and ears keen, and the grip of his hands firm. By afternoon's end, his hair was black as coal, and, since that day, his form changed very little. But even just a little changing, steady and continuous, amounts to much over long centuries. It was only a few years ago that he absently noticed the white strands returning at last to his hair and the lines on the back of his hands, and he knew the time of his departure was closer at hand than was the day of his arrival.

Chapter 11

Kings and Queens and Frying Pans

Day 89
156 Days Remaining

They breakfasted on hot coffee and cold meats and bread, and were in good spirits and well rested as they set out from the inn at Undertree. Although their thoughts turned to stern matters again and again, the breaking dawn of a fair day, and the good pace they made kept their moods lighter than might be expected. The westward track they took led them higher into the hills then south through farmland. Here, Ashlord led them away from the path and through the fields directly west. Behind them the sun slipped into the rising fog and in front of them steep dark-forested slopes rose up, shedding thin mists like tufts of cotton rising through the pine-greens, maple-golds, and yellow-leafed gums.

This part of the Thunder Mountains was not so pretty as that around Hill Town. They crossed through many barren dales and bald hillsides, scraped clean of timber by the Damar, and there were fewer and fewer homes that, if not abandoned, were more squalid than anything Robby had ever seen. Billy's frown indicated his own opinion of the farms they saw. It was, on the whole, a depressing entrance into the mountains, and the deeper they went into Damar territory the more unwholesome it seemed. Whenever the terrain allowed, they picked their way across the fields and through the woods, avoiding roads and paths. There were few places where they could ride and the need to pick out ways for their mounts and pack animals slowed them even more. On several occasions during the afternoon, they found their way blocked by slopes too steep for the animals, or by brush too thick, or by streams too rapid and rocky, and each time they had to backtrack to find a way around. Billy's opinions as to the advantages of walking over riding often came to mind. But he did not bring it up again, and they said nothing about it, trudging onward, pushing briars away as they went, ducking under rocky outcrops, or splashing midstream along the relatively clear way provided by small brooks. Several times they saw Damar patrols, ahead of them or on the hillsides above or on the slopes below them, always traveling along a path above or below them and making such good time that the group envied their easy progress. Still, each sighting filled them with greater and greater caution. Robby and his fellows knew the risk of being caught, the awkwardness, if not outright danger, of any story they might proffer, and all were agreed to struggle on as they had for as long as they could before risking any open roadway.

At the end of the first day, they were very tired, aching, and dirty. Hardly a member of their company was without scratch or bruise from all the brush they pushed through and the rocks they had stumbled over. Their arms hurt with the exertions of pulling and pushing the horses this way and that, picking out places they could pass through. Now, at the end of the day, even the horses seemed to lack spirit as they had their saddles and packs removed and were watered, fed, and rubbed down. Their masters were not much better off.

"How far d'ye reckon we got?" Billy asked at one point, trying to pull a rock out from the place he hoped to spread his bedroll.

Ullin shook his head, not having the heart to tell them the paltry distance he thought they had made. In truth they had only managed just under six leagues as the crow may fly.

Ibin seemed more interested in food than rest, but was satisfied with a thick bit of bread and some cheese that Billy passed over to him. One after another, they undid their bedrolls and dropped upon them. By the time Ashlord had cleared a ring for a fire, they were all sleeping. Even Ullin, normally the last to take rest, sitting on the ground with his back against his saddle, packed his pipe, but he, too, was asleep before Ashlord could spark a flame to light it with. The ground was hard and cold and at a slant, yet it was a welcome place to them all, at first. But Robby, who had unrolled his blanket across some roots, tossed and turned until at last he, still mostly asleep, dragged his blanket a few feet aside and collapsed again upon it.

Now sleep quickly came to him, but it was burdened by visions of Passdale, confused scenes of Redvests buying pickles and nails at the store, with his father packing goods away through the back door, and Mirabella laughing with Sheila about the folly of men. The visions blew away in a blue-white mist, and he sat up. Looking down between his feet, he saw himself below, stretched on the ground amid the others of his company. He realized he was sitting on a branch several feet above, clinging with one hand on the trunk and with the other the limb on which he sat. Letting go he slid and fell slowly through the air and landed noiselessly on his feet beside his sleeping body. Ashlord was blowing on an ember at the end of a stick, preparing to bring it to his pipe, but all others were asleep.

Robby turned his attention to the west, and he rose upward again, through the limbs and branches, until his feet were just above the highest leaves of the trees. From here, he could see far, but the view was muddled by reddish-brown shadows that closed in. Turning to the east, or what he thought must be east, he watched the rising sun waver through shadows like a fluttering yellow butterfly through autumn leaves. With great effort he tried to discern the land around him, and while he could barely make out the nearby mountains, the lands more distant seemed clearer. Somehow, he saw all the way back to Tallinvale and the city there, bustling with crowds pouring into it. Then, slightly northward, he perceived a line of carts moving slowly out of Passdale, laden with harvest goods and booty, driven by familiar men and guarded by red-cloaked Tracians. They moved south along the old road. Turning his gaze farther north, he thought he saw Lake Halgaeth and a lone sailboat, heading northeast across the tossing waters. In Janhaven, he could only perceive the stockade and could not see anyone he knew. Naturally, he thought about his mother and his father and wondered intensely what had become of them. Yet, his state of mind was that of an observer, and though part of him cared greatly, most of his being seemed only to be watching.

Turning west again, he thought he saw a movement in the treetops. For a moment, he could have sworn someone was standing there, just two or three branches away, looking at him. No sooner had he noticed the apparition than it disappeared into the windblown foliage and the ruddy shadows closed in.

"If only I could somehow get to Micerea," he said to himself. "Perhaps she could instruct me about this strange dream-place."

"It is not time yet for your instruction."

Micerea appeared out of the mists beside him, no more than an arm's length away, standing on the same dune where they last met, and now Robby was standing there, too. There was something different about her, Robby thought.

"When will that be?" he asked.

"I cannot say," she replied, "but certainly not before you make Tulith Morgair. I cannot stay. And you must rest!"

Robby realized that, this time, Micerea wore only an outer garment and none of the weaponry or light banded armor as before. He also noted that, though she still had her head and face covered with only her eyes showing, a thick strand of black shiny hair had worked its way to the edge of her right eye.

"May we not talk for just a few moments?" Robby asked as she made to turn away. She stopped and turned back to him.

"Talk?"

"Why, yes. It doesn't have to be about anything in particular."

"You no longer fear me, then?"

"I wouldn't say that. It's just that sometimes it's nice to talk to someone you don't know. Who doesn't know you very well. Sometimes it's easier to be at ease with a stranger than it is with any others."

Micerea looked down at the slumbering company below and then back at Robby.

"You are fortunate to have such good friends, Robby Ribbon of Passdale," she said. "But I understand that sometimes those closest to you may not accept what is in your heart, and so you dare not speak those things to them."

"That is so. And other times, it's just nice to chat about things that don't even matter."

"Everything matters."

"Yes, I know. I just mean things that aren't so important to your friends. New things, maybe. Little things."

"Like what?"

"Like, well, like trees and rivers."

"There are few trees and fewer rivers in my country."

"Things like that is what I mean. Won't you tell me about your land? Perhaps your family?"

"Perhaps, but now is not the time. I must go, for I need to awaken and do my work. And you must rest."

"Oh," Robby nodded. "If you must."

"I will tell you this: I love the land I am from as much as you love your home. To me, my homeland is beautiful. But there is a sickness in my country. I do not think it has always been there, but there is no cure, and this sickness makes my people the way they are, infirm with short lives. It is part of the reason they drive themselves to attack the green hills to the north and east. Now I must go!"

"Wait! Please. Won't you at least tell me about this…this dream."

Again, she turned back to him.

"It is a bit scary," he went on. "And it seems, well, naughty."

"Naughty is as naughty does," she said. "You can walk amongst the wakeful, but it is like being a ghost. They cannot see or hear you and cannot feel your presence. You can see them and hear them, though."

"The perfect spy."

"Not quite. You cannot move a feather or change any object. You cannot burgle anything of value but what you may see or hear. You cannot turn a page or make a candle flame flicker. Or, at least a way has not been found to do so."

"The idea that someone could be watching you at any time. That's not very comforting."

"No. And those few who have this ability, like us, must be careful not to let others suspect that we have it. Many who have done so have come to terrible ends at the hands of their own neighbors. To be discovered is the greatest danger. When you are in someone's dream you can easily hide by simply taking part in their dream. But when you are outside, when you are dreamwalking, you stand out to anyone else who is likewise as you are. This is how we find each other, by looking for the distant light of those others in this realm."

"Dreamwalking. But didn't you say before that anyone can do this?"

"That was what I was taught. But few waken to it. It is rare among my people and uncommon among Men. There are some Faerekind, it is said, with this ability. They are clever and bold, though seldom will you encounter them directly. I warn you: they have other powers as well that they may use. They can bend the world to appear as it is not. They can cast a piece of their soul into the body of another, and do mysterious things that way. Their trickery is well known to my people. Beware! I must go! It is too dangerous for me to stay."

"What do you mean?"

"I must go! We will not see each other again until after you reach Tulith Morgair."

• • •

By the end of the next day, the company had only managed four leagues farther up and into the mountains. And as they prepared a sheltered campsite, where they hoped their fire would not be seen or the smoke smelled by the Damar, they were too tired for words and almost too tired to cook and eat. Ashlord realized they could not keep going this way and chatted quietly with Ullin about the situation as the two cooked a small meal for the group. After the horses had been seen to, the others spread out on the ground, and all, even the normally energetic Sheila, immediately fell asleep.

"I don't think we can take many days like this one," Ullin said quietly as he crouched next to Ashlord and tossed some diced onions and carrots into the pot that Ashlord was stirring.

"I believe you are right," Ashlord replied, glancing around at the prostrated group. "But I doubt if the way will be any easier until we reach the other side of the mountains."

"Except for one or two, the Damar we have seen today are lightly armed and are in small groups," Ullin put forward. "I doubt if they move at night."

"If you are suggesting we take to the roads by night, there are bound to be checkpoints. Especially as we near their strongholds."

"Unless we give up our mounts and pack animals, I fear we may be weeks in these hills. I'm afraid we must risk the roads. And we must eventually cross Redwater Gorge."

"That is so, and the bridge there is sure to be guarded. There is no way around that."

"But I take it that you do not trust the pass given us by Lord Tallin?"

"I do not," Ashlord stated bluntly. "Merely because it rests upon a very tenuous relationship that may be broken off at any moment without our knowing. The Damar, if they get wind of our destination, would surely sell us to the Redvests. What is worse, if they knew our actual purpose, they may sell us to Duinnor!"

Ashlord stirred the pot for a moment.

"I am grateful for your grandfather's advice and for the papers of passage he gave us," he went on. "But Toolant has been in Tallin Hall a long while, and he is not to be underestimated. By his cunning he has squirmed out of many traps before now, and we must assume that he suspects his position is compromised. If Lord Tallin's agents fail to spring their trap on him, or if the Damar do not believe whatever ruse Lord Tallin has devised, Toolant's position with the Damar will be strengthened and, hence, his position with the Tracian leadership, too. Surely he knows by now of our company's movements, and I don't doubt that soon they will be looking for us. One, or maybe two days at most."

They went on mulling over their options and various choices that came to mind as the evening lost all of its light. When the stew was ready, Ullin woke the others, and Ashlord passed out bowls. They were glad for the meal, and they ate it in silence, circled around the glow of the fire. When Ashlord was satisfied that all would have plenty to eat, he cleared his throat.

"Ullin and I believe the terrain before us is too rough to continue as we have unless we take to the roads and paths."

The group looked up from their bowls and thought about this.

"What about them Damar?" Billy spoke up.

"We think we should try traveling at night," Ullin said. "Moving cautiously."

After another pause, Robby said, "Even with a full moon, which we'll not have again for weeks, I doubt if we can see well enough to avoid Damar who may be guarding the way."

"I do not think they lay in wait as if to spring a trap for us," Ashlord said. "Not yet, anyway, for I doubt if the outposts yet know of our coming. Likely their posts and waypoints will be lit by cooking fires and lamps for us to see well before they see us. And it is unlikely that they have reason to move around at night."

"It is this way," Ullin took up. "We must move with as little sound as possible, you know how noise carries at night. But we must move quickly, too. With luck, we may pass through the Damar as they sleep. Surely they won't expect night travelers. We need to put these mountains behind us as soon as possible and get out onto the open plain, beyond the reach of Damar and Tracia."

"When do we leave?" Sheila asked.

"I think we should stay here tonight and all of tomorrow, resting as we may. Then set out in earnest tomorrow night, well rested."

It was quickly agreed upon, and gladly, too, for they were tired and sore enough for as much rest as they could get. Soon all were asleep again and Ullin, too, stretched out. Ashlord, as ever, did not sleep, but propped himself against a tree and stared open-eyed into his enigmatic thoughts the whole night long. Only once did he stir and that was when the silence of the still air reached his attention. Ullin stirred, too, up on an elbow, to listen. The wind had died and with it the forest closed in, still and peaceful, and the few twigs still burning seemed to crackle ever the louder. Ashlord got to his feet and poured water on the embers to quench them and stirred the hissing remains.

"It will not do for our smoke to be seen in this still air," he said to Ullin, "and dawn is but a half-hour away."

Ullin nodded and went back to sleep, pulling his blanket up around his chin.

Some four hours later, Robby woke stiff and full of aches in places he did not know could ache. Ashlord was still leaning against the tree, his eyes open but with a distant gaze. Sunlight angled down through the tree limbs. Ullin was gone.

"To scout the best way for us," Ashlord told him. "There is some cold sausage and cheese there. Alas, no coffee. We do not chance the smoke. But there is a flask of Fetch beside my saddlebag."

Robby ate his sausage and cheese and chased it with a few swallows of the strong sweet liquor that was a specialty of Barley, one used for everything from wounds and sore teeth to nose-colds and wedding toasts. He coughed inadvertently at the last swallow, but nodded and said his thank you to Ashlord, feeling the warmth of the drink going through him.

"You should move around some, stretch your legs," Ashlord told him. "But do not wander far. You should take as much rest as you can. Our nights will be long ones from here on, and the days are getting shorter."

Robby did as he was told, and so did everyone else in turns as they rose and eventually went back to their bedrolls, except for Ibin who was less inclined to stretch and more inclined to eat. But Ashlord kindly told him that he must do with a bit less so that they might all eat again from their rations in the evening before starting out.

"Inthe, intheevening?" asked Ibin, holding up a sausage hesitantly, near his mouth, looking at it as if he had never seen one before.

"Yes, and until then you must rest quietly so as to need very little."

"I, I, Isee. RestsoIdon'tgethungry," he said, the sausage still poised tantalizingly close to his mouth. He slowly and carefully placed it back into the victuals bag and licked his fingers. Then he slapped his knees and stood up from his crouched position and exerted himself through several exaggerated stretches.

Sheila came to eat when Ibin went to pet the horses, and she took only one piece of sausage and a bit of cheese.

"Surely that is not enough to sustain you," Ashlord said, though he knew that in truth she was more accustomed to privation and hardship than any of them and bore it better, too, with never a complaint. Since leaving childhood, she never had that skin and bone look that many other poor youths displayed, but kept herself trimmed out nicely with never a look of lankiness for one of her height. When she came to live with Ashlord, he nearly spoiled her with food, sensing that he could at least provide regular meals that she never had before. But her constitution, and her discipline, needed little and never was she one to gorge herself. She ate when she was hungry and did not eat for the mere pleasure of it. No wonder she was so strong.

"This will do," she said, simply.

"Very well. Will you give Billy a nudge, for the sake of peace?"

Billy, who had been snoring and sawing logs most emphatically, gave a growling snort, sniffed long and loudly and opened his eyes at the not so gentle nudging of Sheila's foot as she passed by.

"What?" he said, sitting up and rubbing his eyes.

"Food," she said. He instantly got to his feet to take his meager meal and then a hearty swallow from Ashlord's flask, chasing that with many gulps from the water flask. While he was doing so, Robby finished his walk around the area and settled back onto his bedroll with Sheila sitting beside him on hers.

"What do you think about traveling at night?" she asked him.

"Well, I think it's best," he said. "With Ullin scouting out a good start, and with his knowledge and experience, and that of Ashlord, I think we'll be fine. I wish Certina would return, though how she'll ever find us is beyond me. She might help us find a good way onward. I think she acts as his little spy, sometimes."

"Yes, and more, maybe. He once told me, or rather implied, that they've been together for a very long time. Still, she cannot be everywhere, can she? If she was here, how might she help? Even with all of Ashlord's wit and caution, and with Certina looking out, the Redvest army coming through the Boggy Wood took Ashlord completely unawares, and I know he does not forgive himself for missing that. I heard him say as much to your father on the day they took Passdale, apologizing deeply and saying that with earlier warning we could have held them off at the bridge at Tulith Attis."

"Hmm. I never thought of that. I bet Ashlord does feel badly about it. Goodness! But even he can't be looking everywhere at once, I suppose, even with Certina's help. I feel for him and understand how anguished he must be. Still, I have no doubt he will guide us by night better than we would do otherwise. I just wish Certina was back and that Lady Moon was bolder."

• • •

The company spent the day dozing and eating lightly between naps. Sheila took time during one of her waking periods to peruse the little book that Mr. Broadweed had given her as they departed Janhaven. She sat in a beam of sunlight with her back against a tree, and surprised herself that she had little difficulty with the writing in the book. Some of the words were familiar to her, lyrics to common songs sung at Firefeast Time, or at Winter Solstice, and some weaving songs sung by Frizella at her loom. Others were entirely new to her, from far places like Glareth, Altoria, and Vanara. She marveled at the beauty of the words and how clearly they spoke of love and adventure, of springtime and playtime, and of wistful loneliness. It occurred to her that Mr. Broadweed was a keen teacher indeed, to have known that she, a girl he hardly knew, had the ability to read and comprehend the contents of this book. But she owed so much of that to Robby and much, too, to Ashlord who had continued and intensified her lessons. She was still reading late that afternoon when Ullin rejoined them and reported finding a suitable way for them, not too far off.

"I suggest we move before it is entirely dark. You know how fast it comes in wooded mountains. We need to go uphill for about an hour before making the roadway."

In fact, it took them nearly two hours, uphill, indeed, carefully guiding and encouraging the horses and each other, zigzagging upward through dense trees and through a particularly nasty stretch of blackberry bushes. After an hour and a half, the sky over the mountaintops still glowed a royal blue, but below the way was already in night-time shadow and the final furlong was a great struggle to them, as it grew steeper and darker. At last they broke onto a narrow road, more like a path, and fell about panting as the waterskin was passed around.

Ullin gave them a few minutes, then said, "Let us make the most of the night," and they climbed to their saddles without complaint.

The forest road was narrow but well marked, and they had no difficulty seeing their way as it alternately climbed and descended around the mountainsides. Ashlord, Ullin, and Robby went first, with Ibin and the pack animals behind, followed by Billy and Sheila. Though the pair at the rear kept as close in line as they could, such were the turns and twists that often Sheila could not see the leaders of the train. Sometimes, at a rising switchback, Robby could look down and see Sheila and Billy below, and on the descending turns, Sheila could catch sight of the leaders, going in the opposite direction below. Though there was hardly a straight way for more than a few feet, and the road traversed steep mountainsides, they managed easily enough for several hours, going quickly but with caution through the murky shadows and pale starlight. When Lady Moon at last cleared the heights behind them, her light helped immensely, and they found greater confidence in their footings. Hour passed hour and the night grew cool and misty until Ashlord called them to a halt, and Ullin pointed to a likely place where they could move away from the road and seek a camping spot to await the dawn and pass the day.

• • •

As Robby and his companions began their night of travel, Certina had just ended her days of flight and delivered the message that Ashlord charged her with. But it sorely tried her patience. She had a natural tendency to be ill-tempered as far as dispositions go, with a fair dose of haughtiness in her attitude. Though her long association with Ashlord did serve to mellow these aspects of her character, it did not take much to make her irritable, and any separation from Ashlord, in time or distance, was usually enough. Indeed, if it had not been for her anxiety to carry out Ashlord's wishes, to deliver his message and wait for one to return to him, she may well have given up. But the only thing she could abide less than frivolity was the prospect of disappointing Ashlord. Still, she had much to put up with, and with growing exasperation she tried the window, the door, even the chimney, fluttering in a very un-owl-like manner about the gardens and the branches looking for her chance. Raynor did not seem to be aware of her at all. She could clearly see him there, on the other side of the latched window, hunched over his desk, reading, reading, reading, shuffling papers, scratching out notes, and reading and reading. Once, she even tried flying straight into the window with as much force as such a little creature as she could bring. But all of her five inches from head to tail barely rattled the glass, and Raynor did no more than turn his head slightly. Finally, he lit his pipe and stood by the window. At last, he swung it open to let out the smoke and to gaze across the rooftops of the sleeping city. Hardly had his hand dropped from the window latch than Certina shot past his head so close that his thin gray hair trailed after her.

That was over an hour ago.

After the old man realized who she was, and after he understood her message, all he did was pace and mutter, mutter and pace, leaving her to sit on the astrolabe on his table. She blinked and turned her head, following him all around the room, without turning her body. A brown rabbit hopped after him, sometimes tangling him up in his robes, sometimes circling him with various thumps. At least the rabbit knows, Certina thought, that there is some urgency here. Still the man paced and muttered. If it had not been for the bits of meat that he offered her (and that she took greedily), she would have left long before now. But she was hungry and tired, and even if Ashlord and this Raynor never needed sleep, she certainly did, and had not had any to speak of for many days and nights. What was worse, she had hardly a nibble since that barely edible vole, tough as saddle and dry as dirt, three days ago. And her feathers were a mess—of all things, to look like this in the Great City! Between snacks, and while she kept at least one eye on Raynor, she preened until she felt somewhat presentable. Once, the rabbit hopped up onto Raynor's chair and stared curiously at Certina, its nose wiggling and its ears twitching this way and that. Certina stopped preening and gave him a sidelong look.

"If I were just an inch taller," Certina said silently with her chin up and her head turned slightly away, "I would eat you." As Raynor paused and scratched his chin, she added, "And your silly master." The rabbit thumped and hopped off the chair and over to Raynor who approached quickly.

It was then she felt it, and though she always had some fear, the kind that comes with incomprehension, she was relieved. His blue eyes reached into her, his voice, not like Ashlord's, but refined in its way. It was a short message. Too short, she thought, for all the trouble and waiting. In spite of her desire to return to Ashlord, when Raynor waved at the window, she was reluctant to go. After all, she had only just eaten and cleaned up. Not allowed to rest? To get just a wee bit of peaceful digestion? Surely Raynor did not know about Certina's delicate constitution, and she blinked at him with as little expression as she could muster. She continued sitting, purposely blinking even more slowly, as Raynor pointed and motioned at the window. She continued to remain still as his voice grew shrill, and she gained some pleasure from the frenzied waving of his arms, his swooshing gestures, and the redness of his exasperated face. Just when Raynor gave up and let his arms drop to his sides, she flew from her perch and darted between the ears of the rabbit, sending the creature galloping across the floor, and she swooped up so close to Raynor's nose with such suddenness that he knocked off his pointy hat with his wild reaction, stumbling backwards as she shot through the window.

"The impertinence!" she heard him say as she flew upward out of his sight and into the highest limbs of a nearby oak.

"Let him think I am on my way," she thought with deep satisfaction as she alit. "But I need an hour or two!"

She ruffled herself into a ball and slowly closed her eyes.

Who can say where creatures go when they sleep? But if it is a country suited to them as our dreamscape is to us, then Certina certainly reached that place. This time, however, there was something there that shook her into sudden and total wakefulness. Not many hours had passed, and the coming sunrise tinged the east rim of the sky. She longed for Ashlord, to see him and to hear his gentle cooing, to feel the stroke of his kind fingers on her back, and, most of all, to let him have this message. Without further hesitation, she flung herself into the air and darted away, just above the highest branches, following alongside the streets below, rising over rooftops and swerving upward and back down to cross the battlements and walls that circled the city, until at last she was over the surrounding farmlands.

As she flew off into the rising sun, behind her and so high overhead that they could barely be seen, two black forms slowly circled. They tilted gracefully on long thin wings, soaring without effort, patient and exact, as their heads bent downward to gaze between the thin clouds at the city far below. As Certina crossed the first open field, being no more than a speck of dust blowing low across the land, the great black birds banked ever-so-slightly and turned eastward as well. They made four or five smooth strokes with their powerful wings, and settled on a course that would be sure to overtake the tiny owl in a day or two.

• • •

It did not take Ullin long to find a good campsite, and, since none were expecting the night's travels to pass so easily, they were in lighter spirits as they tended the horses and spread their bedrolls. Soon, Ashlord had something ready for them to eat, and by the time the sun came over the hills they were ready to sleep. So they did, peacefully, throughout the day.

All except Ashlord, that is to say, who, as always, seemed not to sleep so much as stare. Ullin, after a long nap, woke himself in the afternoon and went off to scout the way ahead. He picked his way through the forest with the long practiced stealth of experience. He circled the camp, making sure from all sides its best positions of defense and escape, and any likely ways of discovery or attack. Growing more satisfied, he widened his circles until at last he found himself crouching near enough to the roadway to smell the dust of it, but so completely hidden that a man could come within knife's reach and never know he was there. After a long while of waiting and listening, he moved onto the roadway and began following it westward.

• • •

Back at the camp, small creatures occasionally wandered nearby and passed on, skirting around them either warily or curiously, according to their nature. Once a hedgehog waddled by and paused for a long time to stare at the group. A little while later, a skunk, with a trail of four or five little kittens following along, ambled into their clearing and paused only briefly before leading her troop quickly away. Once, Billy awoke thirsty and roused himself to take a drink from the brook. Returning, he stood beside Ashlord who was sitting with his back against a rock with his usual blank stare and his cold pipe in his hand. Billy stretched and yawned and listened to the soft gurgle of the brook and the gentle shush of the breeze through the leaves overhead. Robby, Sheila, and Ibin still slept nearby and, seeing Ullin's blankets neatly rolled up beside his saddle, he understood without asking where the Kingsman had gone. As he tried to figure out what Ashlord was staring at, he heard a sudden sound some distance away in the other direction, and he stiffened, straining to see through the brush. He heard it again, then again, and realized that it was moving.

"What's 'at?" he whispered.

Ashlord's eyes moved to the side, toward the sound, his face as motionless and as expressionless as before.

"Only a bear," he said. "She will not trouble us."

Ashlord's eyes returned to their previous position. Billy stood, looking back and forth from Ashlord to the noise.

"A bar? How can ye be sure?"

Ashlord did not reply, and Billy was uncertain whether or not to believe the mystic until the noise receded. Going back to his bedroll, he stretched out, but pulled his sword closer and closed his eyes with his hand on the hilt of his dagger.

• • •

Very late in the afternoon, Ullin returned to the camp, and reported what he had scouted to Ashlord as he accepted the food he was offered.

"The way seems much like before," Ullin said. "Pretty easy on the road, but fewer places to offer cover should we need to hide quickly. Steep on both sides ahead. The road takes a bend southward, and continues on before turning west again some five or six leagues."

Ashlord was once again amazed at Ullin's ability to travel far and fast. To make twelve leagues, round trip, stealthily, was no mean feat.

"I saw four parties of Damar on foot in groups of twelve or so each, and three riders, each alone and riding hard. I think this way must take us near to the Damar city, perhaps to its south side. But I am unfamiliar with this region, and so I cannot say for sure."

"Hm. If you are right, Ullin, then we may encounter some farmland in a day or two, in the numerous gaps south of the city. It has been many years since I have been that way, and it could be good or bad. Good since the Damar are most secure in their south and west lands and probably have fewer soldiers patrolling. Bad because it may be more populated, and our passing may not go unnoticed."

The aroma of soup roused Ibin, and he quickly joined the two with an eager expression.

"Did you rest well?" Ashlord asked as he ladled out some soup for him.

"Yes, yesIslept, Isleptprettywell."

"Here you go. Some bread there. Only one helping, though."

"HelloUllin!" Ibin said as he sat nearby with his bowl and bread. Ullin nodded and smiled, his own mouth full, but by the time he had swallowed, he saw that Ibin was intent on his own meal and oblivious to any talk for a time.

Ullin finished his bowl, wiped it clean with his last bit of bread, and ate that, too. He stood and went to check the horses before unrolling his blankets and stretching out. Ullin was soon asleep, and Ashlord advised Ibin to try for more sleep himself, "for the nights are longer than the days, and we may be up most of it tonight."

Ibin's sleep was indifferent at best, and he tossed and turned with too much vigor for a satisfying rest until at last he sat up in the late afternoon and fetched his mandolin. Moving away from the others some small distance, he plucked softly as the sun sank behind the mountaintops and the blue sky deepened slowly to purple.

While there was still dusky light in the sky, Robby stirred and got up. After going to the brook and splashing his face, he stretched and yawned and came back as Ashlord was rekindling the fire.

"I hope you had a good sleep, Robby."

"I suppose I slept soundly enough," Robby shrugged. "After that nice bed at Tallinvale, the ground seems especially hard and cold. But I guess the hard ground is a welcome place to rest when that's all one has."

Robby watched Ashlord prepare the fire, noticing how with twig and soft breath he coaxed a tiny flame, as gently as one might stroke a feather, until it crackled and grew.

"How is it, if you pardon my asking, that you don't seem to need sleep or rest?"

"Oh I rest," Ashlord said, raising the tripod for the water pot. "Just not in the way that you do. I must rest, as all living things must, but I do so with my eyes open to the world."

"Do you dream?"

"No. I do not dream. Or, that is to say, I am always dreaming, even now as we speak, I am dreaming. Just as you are, if you think about it. But the dreams that you have are of a different sort than mine."

"Pardon me? That is, how do you know what kind of dreams I have?"

Ashlord detected the note of sudden concern, almost defensiveness, in Robby's voice, but refrained from looking at him and only chuckled.

"I only mean that my dreams do not begin or end, as yours do, when you sleep and then awaken. That is, what I call 'my dreams.' "

"Oh," Robby nodded. He was relieved, though a little embarrassed at his rash reaction. He realized that he would probably need to tell Ashlord about Micerea and his reasons for wanting to go to Tulith Morgair. He almost did so, then and there, but he remembered Micerea's warning.

"Why don't you see to the horses," Ashlord suggested. "Then we'll be off just after we have a bit to eat."

• • •

They dowsed the fire, broke camp, and did their best to hide all evidence of their stay. Then they set off through the woods and made the road with little difficulty, thanks to Ullin's expert way of picking out the best path even in the dark. They traveled for many miles, stopping only twice where small streams cut down and across the road so that the horses could take a sip. Even though Lady Moon's shyness increased, now, with each passing night, spreading her fan wider before her face and beginning her skyward walk later than the night before. When she did at last make her appearance, she showed them the roadway so clearly that they could see the tracks left by daytime travelers. But they did not see or encounter anyone the whole night long, and by the time a hint of dawn tinged the sky, they had reached a bluff overlooking a small misty valley. In the dim light, they could see fields and a few farm houses below, and it appeared that the road they were on passed down and straight through the dale.

"It is as I thought," Ashlord told them as they gathered. "We are south of the Damar city and entering farmlands."

"Would it be better for us to travel through here during daylight? Making the appearance that we have business in these parts?" Robby asked.

"Perhaps," Ashlord said, "though it is likely that they see few travelers, and word of passing strangers is apt to reach Damar patrols fairly quickly.

Unless I am mistaken, there must be, on the other side of this dale, a road leading north to the city, and there is likely to be traffic along it of the military kind. Especially if Damar and Tracia are coming together."

"Now might be the best time to move on through," suggested Billy. "Sun's comin' up, an' the farmers must tend to thar cattle an' livestock, milkin', gatherin' eggs, feedin' an' so forth. They'll likely have little time to bother us, er spare someone to send with word 'bout us."

Ullin nodded.

"I agree," he said, "and if we can get to the other roadway while it is still morning, we might pass on before much traffic comes."

"How far do you think it is from here to there?" asked Sheila.

"No more than a league would be my guess," said Ashlord. "Probably just to the other side of those hills yonder. But we'll soon know."

With that, he nudged his horse on, and they followed, going downward in single file. At the bottom of the mild descent, they came out of the woods, and the road took them across a small wooden bridge spanning a fast gurgling stream and then on between pastures. Ullin, riding second behind Ashlord, threw back the tail of his travel cloak, exposing the hilt of his sword. Seeing this, the others behind him prepared likewise. They passed the first farmhouse, a dim yellow light showing from a window and a thin line of smoke rising reluctantly from its chimney. A cock crowed from the coop nearby. From the next farmhouse just ahead, they heard the thumping of someone chopping wood. As they passed, they saw a woman pulling a bucket of water from a well while a man in the yard split firewood. A dog loped out at them, barking as it came. Ashlord glared at it, and the dog suddenly stopped to scratch itself. The man, worn and haggard, stopped his work and eyed them, axe in hand, as the woman came to stand beside him. The dog retreated between the two and whimpered at the passing strangers. Ashlord nodded, Ullin did the same, and each of the company in turn as they passed, but the couple said nothing and hardly moved, their faces blank. The company was well past and nearly to the next field before they heard the chopping resume. They came to another pasture just as the sun edged over the mountains behind them, and the morning mists began to lift when they encountered a farmer driving a small herd of cows towards them along the way, apparently taking them from one pasture to another. The travelers moved aside to let the herd pass.

"Good morning," Ashlord said to the farmer as he came up.

"G'morn," he said in a friendly enough way.

"Can you tell us how far it is to the city?" Ullin asked.

"Oh, it ain't more than eight leagues as the way winds," he said, stopping and leaning on his staff before Ullin. His cows ambled on without him. "I can see ye fellers're strangers, an' I reckon yer off to join in with all them others. They took me oldest boy last week, an' he ain't no more than fourteen years. Ye might be seein' him, by the name of Darce

Frakorn. An' if ye do his mum'd be grateful if ye tell him he's needed at home if he be done with solderin'."

"Darce Frakorn. We'll tell him if we chance to meet. So it's a great gathering?"

"Oh, me yes! A musterin' an' a makin' of more soldiers, like on account of them Tallinvale folk comin' agin us, they say, though I ain't seen none yet."

"Are many coming to Damar out of the west to join up against Tallinvale?" Ashlord asked.

"I wouldn't know. The west road cuts in a ways south of here, so as they all looks like they come up from the south to me. Farm boys, mostly, like me Darce, ganged by soldiers. I seen a crowd of them red-caped horsemen of Tracia day 'fore yesterday. An a few right professional lookin' riders, too, like ye fellers, all plain dressed, but armed. Right mean lookin'. Yep, looks like a great gatherin' it is, all right. Don't know what's to come of it all. Don't know how they think folks can run thar business right if they take away the hands. An' that after layin' such tax on a land, too! Ain't for an old man to say, I reckon. I reckon if it warn't for wars an' fights an' such other, folks like yerselves, maybe, might done be out of business, eh? Aw, now, look! Me cattle's done gone up the wrong field!"

The old man hobbled away quickly, flinging his staff around to head off the few cows that had not yet made the wrong turn.

"Let's move along," Ullin said to Ashlord. "Before the sun gets higher and the road becomes unwelcome!"

They spoke to no other inhabitants of the broad dale though they saw many coming and going about their morning chores. There were few children to be seen, mostly those too young to bear arms, and all others they saw were old or lame or infirm, all tired-looking and with resigned, careworn faces. The farms and the dwellings had the look of having once been well-tended, but were now somewhat gone to seed, with many of the houses in need of ordinary repair, fences in need of mending, and the only other horses they saw were wizened and bony.

"This land is hungry," Billy commented.

Robby hoped they were too hungry to care about his group. Looking over his companions, he imagined they must look like mercenaries going to join the other fighters gathering against the Eastlands. But if the wary farmers and few silent watchful children thought otherwise or suspected anything else, they gave no indication. At least there was no sense of alarm at the company's passing. Indeed, the inhabitants did not look like they had even the vigor to make a report concerning them if a Damar patrol happened along later.

It was not long before they began the upward climb into the hills west of the dale, and as the sun broke full over the mountains, it lit those before them with a sudden glare. These seemed much higher and more rugged than those through which they had already passed, their green sides already spotted here and there with the red and orange and yellow patches of turning leaves. Once over the first hill, the road intersected another one that was wider and obviously more used, and they turned south.

"We should turn west as soon as we can," Ashlord said, "and get off the road, if possible."

"It looks like we're stuck on this'un for awhile," observed Billy as the road quickly climbed and wound around and into the mountains with a steep rise to their right and an equally steep drop to the left.

"Then let us make haste!" cried Ullin. "And if we encounter any small force, let us push right through them!"

He loosened his saddle sword in its scabbard as he spoke, and they urged their mounts to a canter. Often they had to back to a trot as the road climbed sharply and rounded upward. At one place, it broadened through a flat area, and they saw the clear signs of a recent camp, trampled grass and brush and many cold fire-rings. It was apparent to all that a fairly large party had been there not very long ago. They did not stop for a closer look, and it served only to make them move more quickly, with Ibin often calling words of encouragement to the two pack animals in tow behind him. Steeper and higher the mountains around them became, and the roadway with them, the slopes looming above. After more than an hour of this nervous hurry, they suddenly rounded a bend and came out at a small dale where there was an abandoned farmplace, the small plots grown up and weedy.

"I believe we might turn westward here," Ashlord said, slowing to a halt. "We can get off this road and cut through that gap yonder and to the westward running path beyond. If we stay on this road it may be several hours before we come to the place where they meet."

He hesitated.

"Very well," Ullin said. "What is it?"

"I'm not actually sure if this is the right place. Without Certina, I cannot tell."

"Can we not consult Robby's map?" Sheila called out.

"Actually, I brought two," Robby said. He quickly dismounted and pulled a folded packet from his saddlebag. By now the sun was high and the day was growing warm in spite of the breeze. Billy and Ibin, without hesitation, dismounted and moved off a little way to sit under an oak tree that had not yet lost all of its leaves.

Robby spread out his maps against his horse's flank and studied them, with Ashlord and Ullin and Sheila all crowded close and craning their necks to have a look, too.

"Here," Ashlord said, putting a finger on the map. "I think we are here."

"Is that line there this road?"

"I think so."

"Must be."

• • •

While the others discussed their route, Billy and Ibin waited patiently, Billy looking out over the fields across the road. His attention was drawn to a leftover pumpkin, one that the harvesters had apparently neglected to gather.

"Ye know," said he after long consideration, "I'm not so sure Beras managed things too well when he created the world an' all."

"What, whatdoyoumean, Billy?" Ibin asked with sudden concern.

"Well, ye see that pum'kin over yonder, 'cross the road?"

"Yeah."

"Well, look at how scrawny an' thin them vines are, an' the great big ol' pum'kin pullin' 'em down an' all."

"Uh-huh."

"Well, mostly the Creator did a fine job," Billy went on. "For instance, them cornstalks over thar. They's thick enough to hold all them ears of corn. That seems fittin'."

"Uh-huh."

"An' see that apple tree puttin' out. Why thar must be a ton of apples held up thar. An' the branches all saggin', but doin' a fine job holdin' up them apples."

"Uh-huh."

"Yet look at this here great big oak we're sittin' under. Why, Beras must've got distracted an' mixed up, er somethin'. This great big ol' oak tree, strong enough to hold a hunnerd men up in them limbs. But all it does is put out these itty-bitty acorns, whilst them poor vines over yonder flop all over the place under the mighty weight of that dang pum'kin." Billy shook his head, "I mean, it just don't seem right, does it?"

"I never, I never, IneverthoughtaboutitBilly," Ibin said, looking up into the tree above and them back over at the pumpkin.

"Well," Billy sighed, shaking his head slowly, "sometimes I ponder such things."

Ullin was mounting up and waving at them to come along.

"No time for naps, today!" Billy said. Getting to his feet, he reached out to give Ibin a hand up. Just as Ibin stood, an acorn fell from the highest limb and bounced off of Billy's head.

"Owie!" Billy cried, rubbing his head and looking up. Ibin looked up, too. With a serious and almost reverent tone, he looked at Billy.

"Billythat, Billythatcouldhave, couldhave, thatcouldhavebeenadangpumpkin!" he said. Then he turned and hurried to his horse, leaving Billy flabbergasted and speechless by the casual observation. It was Ullin's call that shook him out of his frozen muddle, and he hurried to take his reins as Ashlord began leading them through the pumpkin patch and westward again.

• • •

Ashlord was right. After only an hour of rough terrain, coaxing the horses along by the reins up steep slopes and through thick brush, they at last came upon a path, little used by the narrow looks of it, that threaded away westward and north. By now, they were far within the Thunder Mountains, and the path carried them onward, upward and downward, winding through the forested shoulders so that each turn of the way seemed very much like the last. At one point, after a long twisting climb, the path passed over the top of a high rocky gap, and they could see away westward, perceiving a break in the mountains far away and, just beyond, what seemed a flat land, blue and hazy in the distance.

"Do you think it is safe to continue during daylight?" Robby asked Ashlord and Ullin.

"Not particularly," said Ashlord. "But my own senses agree with Ullin."

"This way has been little used, at least of late," Ullin told Robby. "I've seen no track of man or horse, no sign of recent movement, and since leaving the main road, we've seen no campsites, new or old, and the brush encroaches on every side. My guess is that if any folk live this way, they travel very little, perhaps keeping to themselves to avoid recruitment by the Damar."

"And the Damar have little reason to guard this region, being their southwest flank," added Ashlord. "So I imagine most of their forces in these parts have been recalled from this area. My guess is that only important crossroads and bridges may be watched."

"Still, we should be cautious," Ullin stated. "Especially as we near the gorge. I imagine they want few people leaving Damar lands, especially any of fighting age, and that the bridge there will be garrisoned. And there is always the possibility of patrols or messengers."

At last the going became easy, the path widened, and they rode along, sometimes two abreast, and none saw anything to increase the caution that filled them. For a long while, Ashlord and Ullin led the way, with Billy and Robby just behind. Sheila and Ibin brought up the rear with the pack animals.

"Y'know," said Billy after a long and uncharacteristic silence, "I don't get it. What's so special 'bout a feller's name? It's only a word people use to call someone by. I mean, how on earth can knowin' a feller's proper-given name make any difference in anythin'? An' it seems mighty peculilar, anyways, for folks to have a king, an' go to all that trouble over one, an' not even know his name! Even though, as I heard, when the present King came to take the place of the Old King, that thar was this big fight between 'em, an' that's how he took over. By winnin' the fight."

Ullin looked at Ashlord, who smiled but did not respond.

"It is a mystery of the ages," said Ullin, more to Ashlord than to Billy.

"An' another thing," Billy went on. "If he's holed up in his palace, like ever'one says, an' he don't come out, how does he get people to do what he wants 'em to?"

"He speaks with his mind to people. To his court and his counselors. And he enforces his will through an agent, a kind of oracle, called the Avatar," said Ullin. "It is the Avatar who metes out the King's will. If a person displeases the King, or if the King wishes to see someone, the Avatar goes and sees to it. Likewise, the Avatar delivers gifts and rewards if a person pleases the King."

"So the Avatar is a man, then?" asked Sheila.

"Well, perhaps I misspoke. I said 'oracle,' but I don't mean like those in temples. I mean that the Avatar represents the King. Each spring, when the King goes to the Temple of Beras to renew his reign for the New Year, his Avatar goes forth before him as the shape of the passing year's symbol. When they return to the King's Palace, the Avatar is in a new shape, the symbol for the new year. The Avatar remains in that shape until the following year."

"Oh? What is the meaning of that? The symbol, I mean?"

"It is a mystery," Ashlord said. "But the Unknown King must go to the Oracle of Beras at the end of each Royal Year, emerging the next morning to begin the next Royal Year. In Duinnor, the Royal Year always begins on the first day of spring. The Avatar casts off the shape of the old year and becomes the likeness of the new year to symbolize it."

"So the Avatar is a person dressed up in the shape of something?" Sheila asked.

"No. It is not a person," Ullin said.

"It is the thing, itself," Ashlord stated.

"What? What kind of thing?" Billy asked.

"All kinds. This year, for example, is the Year of the Red Door."

"The Red Door? What's 'at supposed to mean?" Billy laughed.

Ashlord shrugged.

"I was born in the Year of the Snowflake," Ullin commented.

"Snowflake?" Sheila asked.

"Yes."

"All manner of things have symbolized the years," Ashlord picked up. "There was the Year of the Elk, the Year of the Loom—that was when Certina came to be with me—the Year of the Harp, the Year of the Plow, the Year of the Frying Pan, the Year of the Rabbit, the Year—"

"Hold on, just a dang minnit!" interrupted Billy, most incredulously. "The Year of the *Fryin' Pan*? Are ye makin' fun of us?"

"Never in life!"

"But...a *fryin' pan*? The King of Duinnor, Master of the Seven Realms, goes forth an' afore him goes a *fryin' pan*? Did someone carry it, some cook, maybe? Er did it sprout iron legs an' walk?"

"It floated," Ullin said gently. "Through the air. Just as the Avatar always does."

"It floated," Billy nodded seriously. He shook his head. "The King goes forth an' he speaks to his people through a floatin' fryin' pan. Right. It all makes perfick sense, now."

"Few may ever know the significance of the Avatar's shape, or why Beras, through the Oracle, ordains the year to be symbolized by the given object. The Year of the Snowflake, for instance, was one with only a mild winter by all accounts. Not as people feared it would be. The Year of the Shovel, however, was full of disease and plague. Many graves were dug that year."

"Have you never seen or heard of the Book of Years?" Ullin asked Robby, who shook his head. "I'm a bit surprised that Mr. Broadweed didn't have a set. It is a list of each year, in the reckoning of Duinnor, and is a summary of each year taken from the Chronicles of Duinnor. It tells of each year's namesake and the big events of the year. Every hundred years or so it is revised and a new volume is added and the whole is recopied. We have two copies in the library of Tallin Hall."

"Oh. I did not notice them."

"The Year of the Fryin' Pan," Billy repeated. "But what about the King's Name? How does a name make any difference?"

"It is not the Name itself, Billy," Ashlord told him. "It is the finding out of the Name."

"I thought ye said Robby already knew the Name."

"But I don't know it," said Robby.

"I said that Robby may have the ability to learn the Name. Or that he may already know what the Name is but does not yet realize it."

"But ye think that goin' to Griferis will somehow shake it out?"

"I have no idea if it will or if it won't. To obtain the Name of the King is not why we go to Griferis, but rather to let Robby receive instruction there. To be tested and tried for kingship."

"I thought you said that if he went there and passed their judgment, he'd become King," Sheila asked before Billy could.

"You two must listen more carefully! I did not say that. I repeated only to you what is said about the place, that *it is said* that none who passes through ever fails to take their place as a king or a queen. The last one to do so, *it is said*, was Queen Serith Ellyn. As for Robby, his quest is in four parts: To know the Name. To find Griferis. To emerge from that place. To become King."

"And, then," said Robby with a cynical chuckle, "my challenge truly begins."

> *"The babe is welcomed by the dead*
> *And he who dies, dies not alone,*
> *But alone bestows the Given Name,*
> *And makes a way unto the throne.*
>
> *A verse of comfort and of pain*
> *The banshee will then loudly sing*

> *To ease the way of the passing one*
> *Burdened with the Name of the King."*

"Where did you hear that one?" Ashlord asked Ibin in amazement.

"Mr., Mr., Mr.Arbucklesungthatone," Ibin replied. "Buthesaid, he, buthesaid, hesaidheheardinGlarethbytheSeawhenhewasaboy."

"What's all that about banshees?" Sheila asked.

"There are different kinds," explained Ashlord. "But all are harbingers from the spirit-world. Some say they come to make the passage of the dead easier on them. Others hold that they forewarn the coming of death."

"They are frightful in aspect, I hear, and their song is terrifying," Robby added.

"Yes. They may appear so. But some, though certainly frightful, are said to be beautiful, too. It is said that the living are not permitted to hear the beauty of their lyrics, nor to see the comeliness of the banshee's countenance, lest the witness become filled with a longing to make the passage with her through death's door before they are bidden."

"Oh," said Robby, remembering something Billy's mother once said, on a cold rainy night during a stay at Boskland. "It must've been a night like this when yer granddaddy saw the banshee," Frizella said, picking up some plates and carrying them past a water-glazed window. "I mean, pardon me, the night he died, may he rest peacefully." But, just when Robby was about to ask what she meant, Billy and his father burst through the door with their talk and chatter, and Robby never got around to asking at all. It was like so many other things, things that he now wished he had made the time to ask about.

"Fryin' pan! Me arse!" muttered Billy, in a thoroughly disgusted manner.

• • •

The way turned rough for a while, with low branches and short steep rises and falls. In some places, they had to dismount to traverse difficult stretches, and twice they had to work their way off the path and around uprooted trees that had fallen down from the slopes and blocked the way. That night, fairly exhausted and yet feeling they had made good progress, they made camp on a flat shoulder of the mountain that Ullin spotted above them, and the climb up to it cost them the last of their strength. There was no water there for the horses, but it was well above the path, and covered with soft pine needles which they gathered to put under their bedrolls.

Chapter 12

The Eagle and the Owl

Day 92
153 Days Remaining

Though Certina was no ordinary bird, if any owl can be called such, she still possessed within her all of the skills of those winged creatures, and all of her instincts of flight and direction. Those instincts told her many things, and her unique nature told her other things, too. As the sun rose over the horizon, she knew Ashlord was farther south than her course, and she altered in that direction. But altering it, she knew also that the things that stalked her, high above, would sooner overtake her. She never turned to look, but she could feel the shadow of their presence coming steadily closer, hour by hour. Though she was not easily frightened, panic began to slowly tighten its grip upon her. She beat her small wings with greater deliberation, gleaning every bit of thrust and speed from each stroke as she cruised several hundred feet above the plain. Below, no trees offered cover, no craggy rocks to hide beneath, only green grass and gentle swells veined by the silver lines of streams here and there, and no villages with eaves to dart beneath or barns to rest within. Her breathing, long synchronized to her wings, became more labored as she bore southward. This course, she well knew, would take her across the borders of the Forbidden Land and into a territory that she did not know. But it was the straightest way back to Ashlord.

"Why, oh, why is he so far away!" she, in her own language, despaired.

Far above, one of the dark specks began its descent, pulling its wings inward to speed faster and faster into its final dive.

Below Certina were now the stone pillars, each capped with the likeness of a large human skull, that surrounded Nasakeeria every few hundred yards and which were intended to act as warnings to hapless travelers. A few yards past those dire pillars, and partially covered by grass, were mounds of petrified sun-bleached bones, thousands and thousands of bones. They were all that remained of those who had entered there, having been cast out by the inscrutable occupants of that land. Beyond, not very far away, were trees, green, thick, and low. Her wings beat all the harder, and she threw herself into a long shallow descent. The border of bones now behind her, she made with all her strength toward the trees. For a moment, she thought she might make it, but the chasing shadow grew larger and came faster. Her wings missed a beat. To her, the world below was made entirely of that line of dark inviting leaves, nothing else existed down there, her entire being bent upon reaching those nearest limbs. Still she did not look up toward her pursuer. She knew the world above her was no longer sky blue, but was now filled with black shadow and sharp death, spreading quickly from horizon to horizon as it descended. She could hear herself squeaking now, wheezing her breath as she lost a wingbeat, then another and another. Fighting the urge to fold her wings and fall, she beat on, stroke after painful clumsy stroke, losing height and speed, in terror of the thing falling upon her. Suddenly, a swift, thin shape shot up from below, streaking only a few inches past her with a shrill whistle, and then came a terrifying scream. She squealed and rolled over onto her back as she fell, her talons extended to fend off her attacker, and she saw a great black bird, like an eagle, enveloped in a cloud of blood and feathers, writhing downward past her, transfixed by an arrow. The smell of the thing filled her with disgust as she rolled back over. She only managed a few more beats, uncoordinated and without effect. Exhausted, she folded her wings and fell, still far short of the trees that she hoped for. She opened her wings just in time to break her fall, then tumbled and bounced into a clump of grass. There she panted, her beak open, her eyes wide and blank, her feathers ruffled, her heart pounding, pounding. She heard footsteps crunching through the grass but had not even the strength to look. She felt a touch and smelled the scent of a two-legged one. After a moment of defensive reflex, she resigned herself as she was lifted up, letting out a low sad whistle.

"There you are, little one," a man's voice said in a language she had not heard for many, many years. "Rest. You need not fret."

Certina bent her head and saw, some few yards away, the crumpled remains of the bird of prey that had stalked her from Duinnor. From the gloved hand she sat in, she could see several people gathering around the dead bird, all dressed in black-banded lightweight armor, with green and black cloaks covering all their heads and faces with only their eyes showing. Looking up at her captor, she immediately saw a man bending over her, his dark complexion revealed as he pulled his scarf away from his face, his lake-blue eyes gleaming.

As she was carefully lifted, the remaining eagle circled, too high for any arrow to reach, but with eyes as keen as spyglasses fixed upon the scene far below. The creature banked away northward and flew swiftly back toward Duinnor.

• • •

"Cover it!" said a female voice behind the man that held Certina. "Here, give me that!"

Certina did not have the strength to react to the language that sounded very much like that spoken in the desert lands. The words seemed the same as that of the Dragonkind, but they had an unusual cadence and accent that was new to her. But she could only listen, having not the will to even wonder at what she heard, too distracted by her own fatigue. And she also lacked the strength to resist as a robe was spread over her. She felt herself bundled away, still carried by the man who had picked her up.

"This cannot be an ordinary owl," she heard the woman explain as they moved. "She is a Familiar, I am sure."

"Someone's pet? How can you say so?"

"The black eagles of Shatuum do not fly for pleasure," she said. "Nor do they hunt for food. They serve their lord in all they do, and this little one was its prey, as we all saw before your arrow struck the predator."

"A minion of Shatuum?"

"Yes, and look there! High up and bearing away."

"Another?"

"Yes, no doubt soaring home to report the fate of its brother."

"But what would they have to do with this little creature?"

"This little creature would not have been prey unless it serves the enemies of Shatuum."

"How can that be? It is but a wee thing! What threat may a pet be?"

"Don't be foolish, Aremon! Familiars are not pets! They serve their masters willingly, just as those black eagles serve theirs. This one, I suspect, is a messenger. It was flying south. Hm. My guess is that it comes from Duinnor and heads for the south plains or perhaps the Thunder Mountains. Anyway, either to its master, or on its master's business."

"But it carries no pouch, no ring, and no beads or markings. How else may it carry messages?"

"In ways that would surprise you, Aremon."

By now Certina had her breath back, and was trying to preen out her feathers between efforts to pry her way from under the robe. She had no strength to fly as yet, but the air beneath the robe was stifling, and she preferred to see her surroundings.

"Let us take the creature to my cottage," the woman said.

Certina felt the man halt abruptly.

"And what will you do?"

"I will examine her more closely."

"But you have a cat."

"I will safeguard the bird from Ruse."

"This is a free creature," the man said. "There is no evidence it serves anyone. It has rights to enter our country as do the deer and the geese and the rabbit."

"It cannot be counted as a free creature. It is not like other birds, or like the deer or rabbits that come through our lands. Have you not been listening to me?"

"Yes, but I see no reason to keep this bird with you."

"You may be a great hunter, Aremon, but you are none too wise in these matters!"

"Yes, I am a great hunter, Seleesa, and as hunter I claim this bird as my prize, the spoils of my hunt to do with what I wish. You have no claim upon it."

"Don't be foolish, you tenderhearted oaf! This bird may threaten us, our hopes, our very survival. I promise not to harm it! I only want to—"

"To what? Pick at it with a sharp stick? Pluck its feathers for one of your potions? There, there, little one. Do not struggle so! No harm will come to you. I promise!"

His words did little to calm Certina as she continued to pick at her coverings.

"If you were anyone else, I'd use one of my potions on you! Perhaps then you wouldn't be so dense-headed! Uh-oh. Too bad for you. Here comes Prince Nightar."

Certina heard the sound of approaching horses and soon another voice.

"Hail, Prince," said the man and woman.

"Hail, Aremon, Seleesa. A black bird is reported felled this way."

"Yes, Prince," said the man who held Certina. "A black eagle of Shatuum, most likely. It was my arrow that brought it down after crossing our border."

"Shatuum? Its servants do not travel without purpose. Where is it?"

"It fell yonder, over that hill."

"I will look upon it. What do you have there?"

"A capture from my hunt, sire. A little owl."

"Oh?"

"Lord," spoke Seleesa, "it was this that the black eagle was after."

"Then it is no ordinary bird. And if it crossed our border seeking safety, it must have been desperate indeed. And foolish. A Familiar, most likely."

"That is what I think. And I wish to examine the little owl in my cottage."

"I would hope you would, if for no other reason than to determine its innocence or guilt."

"What is this, my lord? This is but a little owl," said Aremon. "It is the prize of my own hunt. I take it to my dwelling as my rightful capture. I will not have it harmed."

"Your prize, eh? Are not all the creatures of these lands, those that dwell here and those that pass through, subject to my rule? Including those who walk on two legs?"

"Of course, Prince. Forgive me." Certina felt the man bow.

"And are not the rights of prize, whether of hunt or of battle, first claimed by my throne before all other claims?"

"Why, yes, my lord. Only—"

"Then I will have it examined by Seleesa as is her duty."

"Ha!" cried Seleesa. "I told you!"

"But sire, she has a cat!"

"A cat?"

"Yes, Prince. A long, mean cat."

"Yes, I do recall a certain cat."

"Sire," Seleesa said with an air of exasperation. "I will put the cat out."

"My dwelling is nearer, my lord."

"Oh? Yes, I suppose it is. It is settled. Take the creature to your dwelling, Aremon. Seleesa will accompany you. Await me there. I will view the black eagle and then attend with you while she looks over your bird."

"Certainly, my lord!" Aremon said with satisfaction.

"Yes, lord," said Seleesa sullenly.

Certina heard the horses trot away as she felt the man begin walking quickly.

"You are sometimes a little too eager, Seleesa."

"You are sometimes a little too stubborn, Aremon."

"Perhaps if you would take my ring, as I have asked you these many times, you would come to value my stubbornness."

"That is one thing that I am decidedly not too eager about!"

"Too bad. I would make you a good husband."

"I do not long to lose my powers by joining with any man."

"Are your powers so great that their loss would hurt you so?"

"I pray that you do not declare your love for me again," Certina heard Seleesa say in a whispered tone of distress. "Do not torment me so, I beg. For I dare not let such utterances pass my lips. Of my kind, only three remain in this land, as you well know. It is not that my powers are so great, but that only two others and I have them. It is true I have not been called upon, and perhaps I never shall be. But Nightar is needed here, and Traveshia, though she is still powerful, is old and frail of body. If something should happen to them before the Time of Leaving, what would become of us?"

There was silence for many moments until Aremon spoke again.

"Forgive my selfishness, Seleesa," he said. "I sometimes think the time will never come, and I often look to happiness here, if such a thing can be. I hope you will not hold that against me, at least. I will speak no more of it. Here, let us go into my dwelling, see to this little one, and await the Prince."

• • •

But it was to Duinnor, and not Shatuum, that the surviving black eagle flew. Arriving late in the day, it circled the city, hesitating. The creature was tempted to fly instead to the southwest, to the place of its hatching, the place of its true master. As in the early days of its flight from Shatuum, it shared all it saw with its master, and was generously rewarded with special meats, still living. But it had been commanded to render its services to another, and to share those things it witnessed first with that other person. Only then would it be released to return to its true master. Once before, it disobeyed these commands, and was punished with painful treatment. That was enough. It wheeled over and descended to the high slender tower of the King's Palace. Why here, of all places, must it meet the one appointed? Here, in the presence of the enemy, and of that accursed Avatar, to share its vision with an Elifaen. Cruel this was, the creature felt, to give itself over to one of those wingless two-legs. But to please its master, it would do so.

It flapped heavily and landed on the highest ledge and peered into the open window. Another of its kind sat nearby, careless of the new arrival, awaiting its own orders. The newcomer squawked viciously, making the other bird hop farther aside, then it peered deeper into the large room. The Avatar stood there, silent and unmoving, but no one else could be seen. The newly arrived black eagle would have to wait. First would come the King, eventually, or the King's little helper. Then the other one would be summoned. The Elifaen who served the King. And, presumably, who served its master, too. Only afterwards, and only if the Elifaen was inclined, could it fly away and report to Shatuum. The eagle had no words that humans might comprehend, and no thoughts that we might understand. But it felt its master's attention, and his pull. Not strong enough to draw it away, but strong enough so that it was distracted, restless, anxious to be done with this task and return to him.

• • •

Indeed, Secundur waited. Although far from Duinnor, he was aware that one of his minions had some news. He was not as patient as he once was, and felt that, perhaps soon, he would break his pact with Lord Banis. It was during moments such as these when Secundur's form was most restless, upsetting his servants and the legions within his realm with his dark aura. He sensed that news was coming, but until his black eagle related it to Lord Banis and then flew away to come to Shatuum, Secundur would not know what the black eagle saw. Until the black eagle's arrival, he could not guess the import, if any, of the black eagle's tidings, for the growing disturbance that Secundur felt seemed to come from every direction, from the south as well as the east. Distinguishing those subtle, and not so subtle, manifestations of his own long plot from the plots of those who opposed him was no longer an easy task, for his own efforts were ages in the forming, years in the planting, and even those things he himself fomented in the world sometimes had unpredictable outcomes. Secundur was, therefore, ever revising and refining, shifting his game pieces, countermanding orders for new ones, and reversing himself. Since the Queen had left Vanara, many of his plots had to be abandoned. The secret accord with Lord Banis, by which Secundur allowed the use of his eagles, had only produced mixed results, and Secundur, though patient, often considered withdrawing them from Banis. The eagles were necessary, for now, and allowing some to serve Banis could only further Shatuum's plots, regardless of how inconvenient it sometimes was. So Secundur, at last unable to bear uncertainty and inaction, sent forth more of the flying spies, some south toward Vanara, and others east to faraway Glareth. Those eagles, among all of Secundur's vile creations, seemed the least restless, happy to fly hither and yon as his spies and messengers. And only these creatures were permitted to leave Shatuum until all was prepared, until Secundur would lead his legions forth all at once.

It was useful, Secundur had learned, to have such creatures as the black eagles, ones that could bear the full bright light of day to do his bidding. They could go where it was now too painful, or impossible, for Secundur himself to venture. Too long wrapped in the cloak of shadow was he, until the cloak and the shadow and Secundur were one and the same. Darkness was his abode, his security, and his intent. Yet, with their eyes, his eagles could see for him into those places where he could no longer bear to look, and they could touch for him those things he no longer had the ability to grasp. But they had to be handled carefully, these creatures who flew in the light of day. He could enslave them, but he could not envelop them with his nature completely, or else they would be useless to him. He still needed such servants to build his legions, to spawn his followers, to gather and corral those witches and demons that still survived, and to convert those who were brought to Shatuum. The eagles, however, could come and go, watch and report, and even be his bargaining pieces.

The black eagles that roosted in Duinnor were just that, tools loaned to seal a treaty. And Secundur made sure they were useful to Duinnor, indispensable. That was how he kept Duinnor from harassing his borders, from attempting to delve his secrets as did Serith Ellyn and her Gray Guard. Duinnor, not Vanara, was now Secundur's worry. The black eagles he gave over to Duinnor were just part of his bargain. The King, of course, would not use them directly; he was immune to his whisperings. It was a mystery, perhaps having to do with the Golden Mantle that the King wore, and Secundur had long given up the effort to subvert the Unknown Kings. But the Elifaen lord who served the present King was different, was like all the rest of the Elifaen. It was this Lord Banis who arranged the trade of eagles for Shatuum's security, and Lord Banis made good use of Secundur's feathered minions to assure his own rise to power. And now Banis was second only to the King. But could Duinnor be trusted? Certainly not the Elifaen lord; none of that blood could ever be trusted, not even those he had turned into his slaves, not even the highest general of Shatuum. And the eagles? Would they continue to come to Shatuum, reporting to him what they shared with the Elifaen lord? Giving them the choice was dangerous, but necessary. His power over them was greater than the Elifaen lord in Duinnor. Just enough freedom was required, and no more. But he could not give the eagles free reign, either, or else they, like all others, would turn away. It was in their nature, in the nature of all creatures to resist Secundur.

Esildre had taught him that.

Esildre, who was given over to Secundur by her own father in trade for his eagles. Was it a trick? Secundur knew that fathers only reluctantly gave away their daughters. It must have been a trick. But what did the Elifaen lord hope to achieve? Did it matter? The Unknown King, in his paranoia, could no longer do without the eagles, controlled by his Elifaen lord. And the Elifaen lord's place of power was thus assured. Was that not enough?

Yes, the Elifaen who served the King, Lord Banis, gave his own daughter to Secundur, and he convinced her to come as a willing hostage, ignorant of the extent of her father's bargain. Her charms were considerable, coming closest to Secundur's heart, she, who nearly ruined him with her beauty and her pleasures. Too many secrets he shared, mingling with her in her bed. Yet, often they argued for days and days at a stretch. Gently he coaxed her, and tenderly he courted her, using skills he had long practiced on others. He nearly succeeded, for she was not like Islindia, with whom he had once been obsessed. Esildre was not pure of heart nor so attached to the good earth as Islindia. Over a thousand years had passed, and more, since his failed attempt to seduce the forest queen. That should have been a lesson to Secundur. But he spited her and her lands and all her people for her rejection of him. Fie upon Islindia! Later, when Secundur had received Shatuum to be his own land, he had no thought to form any new female liaisons.

But then came Banis with his proposal. And Esildre was easy, almost compliant. She was not so good, nor so imbued with earth's goodness. And she had not given her troth to another as Islindia had done, so had no reason to resist. So Secundur agreed to the Elifaen lord's scheme, and, eventually Esildre came to Shatuum.

For centuries, the Elifaen lord's daughter was Secundur's courtesan, and his paramour. More and more time did Secundur spend with her, and closer they became entwined. Yet she remained a mystery to him, a challenge. She would not give herself over to him completely, always held back something essential, something inscrutable to Secundur. Yes, a challenge, an indulgent challenge. And much of his dark business was put aside for the pleasure of her, delaying his plans. In the dimmest light possible, she vexed him with the temptation of her body, and thus held him back from his final transformation.

For Esildre nearly became his queen. She delved so close to his workings that he gave himself over to her. But then she saw. What was it that made her see? She saw, and she recoiled from him. He could have enslaved her. Why didn't he? He chafed whenever his thoughts turned to her, whenever he remembered her, dimly, now, as through a great distance of time, a speck of painful light, like a single star, alone in the darkness. Yes, he remembered stars, he remembered their stinging pricks of light. He remembered her. Yes, he let her go, though he smote her with a vindictive curse.

She was a mistake he would never repeat. No one was worthy of him. When she left him, she left with his mark upon her, his curse. But he did not realize until after she had gone that, when he had released her, when he shot his curse into her, some last bit of his most ancient being went from him. But that kind of power no longer mattered to him. It was not the sort of power that was really useful, not what he called power at all. Futile creatures of light! Almost immediately upon her departure, Secundur shed the last remnant of fleshly nature. Fie upon light! He was become Darkness. Shadow was now his body.

Now, the memory of her gave him pain and filled him with anger. He should have destroyed her. He should have crushed her body and chewed out her soul. Why didn't he? After an age of contemplation, he realized that the one thing she longed for the most, the thing that he had turned against her, to spite her and to doom her, was that which she conjured from the remains of his own heart. He knew the words well, and had used them countless times in the ears of others. Desire. Affection. Love. And, after she left him, he felt a loss as he had never known. He filled the void with his ancient anger and with resolve. Never would he make that mistake again, and, in her absence, he now had no reason to resist his darkest ambitions. Perhaps he owed her that much, for he had now gathered into his realm all that he needed.

No, not quite all.

Patience. Let Throgallus, his general, his protégé, do his work. He, at least, could never betray him. Throgallus came to Shatuum of his own will, too, having failed the King at Tulith Attis, having failed to bring away the Bloodcoins, having betrayed and abandoned his own family, his own people, and having nowhere else to turn. First, Esildre came. Then, just when she left him, came this traitorous general, pliable and softened by his own gnawing soul, after centuries of hiding, of being on the run from discovery. Secundur knew he would come. But Throgallus was strong, and he resisted the enchantments laid upon the armor he wore, spells that infected his heart and urged him to seek refuge in Shatuum. When Throgallus came at last, he was gladly received, for Secundur had prepared the way for him. Secundur gave the general a new purpose, a new calling, and even a new name. And now, like the black eagles, Throgallus belonged to Secundur. And now, too, Secundur was wiser, darker, and incapable of the weakness that he showed Esildre.

No, he never would make those mistakes again. Morgasir, his old tutor, long vanquished in the Time Before Time, would be proud, for the student had grown mightier than his master. She had done that for him, erased the last vestige of his origins, the last vulnerabilities of his heart. Secundur was no longer Faere, no longer Elifaen. The feelings they had were weakness, to be used and exploited, as he always had done. And now he was stronger, having gained a more subtle understanding of his own power. Shadow, never interrupted, was now his entire being.

Esildre was gone. But patience remained. Angry, smoldering patience. She had given him that, though he had no gratitude for it. For, though parted from him, the memory of her chafed him, though he no longer understood why or how. Doubt and paranoia she planted in him. But, in return, he cursed her with a curse that would bring death and madness to any who succumbed to her eyes. And he gave to her eyes an urging that could not be resisted. It was a fair trade.

And her father? Duinnor? When she left, Secundur was filled with fury and a powerful temptation to unleash his wrath upon that realm, forsaking all other plans. But he needed Duinnor. Only through Duinnor could he achieve his ultimate goal. And Throgallus was not yet ready. So Secundur allowed the pact to stand, and the eagles continued to fly from the King's tower. The pact benefited Secundur's land of Shatuum more than Duinnor.

No. He would not make those mistakes again, not with any creature with eyes to see with light. Though they could be useful, if crushed and reshaped, and he turned many to his service, through a different kind of madness, to serve him. Some, from the most ancient days, still lurked, awaiting his release from their lairs, scattered deep within the lightless bowels of the earth, or moving secretly across the lands. True, some had escaped his leashes, so powerful was their will to gnaw and bite and wound the world. It vexed him, and he punished those who were charged with holding them back. But Secundur made little effort to retrieve them; they could only do his will.

And so he let Esildre go, and seldom considered her. Other matters required his attention, for the fruition of his ancient plan was nearly at hand. Throgallus was almost ready with his baneful army.

She was irrelevant. And the black eagles served Secundur better than Esildre ever could.

So he waited for his eagle. He had no eyes to close, but from his black tower Secundur felt his teeming legions swelling their numbers within Shatuum. Throgallus and his captains ordered and trained them, rank upon rank. Soon the way would be prepared, the world in chaos, and it would be time to march.

Chapter 13

Dashing Through Memories

Day 94
151 Days Remaining

At dawn, eight Redvest horsemen tore along the path from Passdale, crossed the Weepingbrook in great splashes to the far stone-lined bank, and sped up the steep hill of the ridge. As they passed over the top and then down and out across the Line Road, they shot through the stone markers of Oldgate, and continued on. Behind them, four cloaked figures emerged from the mist-shrouded trees atop the ridge and onto the hoof-churned path and watched the riders recede toward Tulith Attis in the far distance.

"Eight," said Tyrillick to Belmira, "just as you sensed."

"Your ears saved us from capture thrice in as many days, daughter," said Lyrium.

"They are so very noisy, it is easy to do," Belmira said.

"Yet I dread to think, had it not been for you!" said Elmira, taking her sister's hand.

• • •

Indeed, it was at dawn seven days ago that they parted from their carriage and their escort, sending them back into the west. On foot, they then crossed the shallow Bentwide and quickly found an abandoned and burned-out house in which to hide for the day. The countryside, they found, teemed with Redvests, riding and marching all along the roads and byways, often herding prisoners before them, and at all hours of the day and night. Cautiously, often spending hours hiding mere yards from the enemy, Lyrium and her escorts inched through the lands at an agonizingly slow pace. For five nights they carefully worked their way north and east, moved through Boskland toward Tulith Attis, and narrowly avoided detection by the restless soldiers that occupied the land. They barely managed more than a few excruciating miles each day. For most of one night and the entire following day, they hid under a small stone bridge, stooping in waist-high water while troops of Redvests and trains of wagons full of Boskland spoils and harvest passed over their heads. Having taken a week to travel the same distance that, in peacetime, would have been a single day's hike, they had at last made it to the wooded ridge that overlooked Weepingbrook on one side and the plains before Tulith Attis on the other.

"My lady, are these woods along this ridge safe enough to abide in?" Tyrillick asked. "Or should we press on to find a place for you to See?"

"With you and my daughters standing guard, I think a more secluded spot along this ridge will do. I would prefer to have the fortress within view, if possible," Lyrium said. She threw a long gaze down the other side of the ridge, toward the large stones that leaned over the stream below. "But I must say that, now that I am once again here, so close to the terrors of my memory, I find that I feel very little. I hear their whisperings," she indicated with a nod the stones. "But they do not hear mine."

Turning around, she faced Tulith Attis, barely visible in the early morning air.

"And, truth be told, I no longer sense any greater dread of that place than if it was merely rock and rubble, but that I know it is occupied by the Redvests. Otherwise, of the past I feel...nothing. And I do not hold out much hope of Seeing anything."

"Since departing Tallinvale, your fears have but eased," said Elmira.

"Yet, you do not seem happy, you do not seem pleased," said Belmira.

"It is a strange thing, yes," Lyrium nodded. "But my anxiety was almost more than I could stand while at Tallinvale. Now, I am calm, but uncertain why that is."

"Then, my lady, let us find a suitable place for you, where you can throw your stones and bones and try to See," suggested Tyrillick.

"Yes, let's do. Lead the way, Tyrillick."

Honoring his lady's wishes, Tyrillick kept them at the top of the ridge, leading them carefully along. Soon, between its height and the warming day that dissipated the morning mist, he found a relatively flat place where the fortress summit could be seen, yet where they were still somewhat sheltered by trees.

"Yes, this will do," Lyrium said as Tyrillick raked aside leaves and loose brush with his boots. Her daughters spread a blanket over the place Tyrillick had prepared, and Lyrium removed her shoulder bag and from it took a smaller bag that was filled with her amulets and placed it on the blanket. Then she knelt, scraped up soil from around the blanket, and sprinkled it in a circle around her amulet bag.

As she worked, she often glanced toward the fortress, where a thin trail of smoke was now rising, presumably from the Redvests garrisoned there. Tyrillick, too, saw the smoke. Frowning, he crossed his arms and moved a few yards away as did her daughters, to keep watch upon their surroundings and to wait for Lyrium.

Lyrium emptied her amulet bag of small bones and stones, softly saying her prayers and the incantations she hoped would bring Sight to her. Repeating her words, she gathered up the objects and tossed them upon the blanket, watching how they fell, and examining the patterns they made. The cool autumn day drew on, passing through morning to noon, and thence from noon toward evening. A light breeze whispered through the multicolored leaves above them, and a few detached to scatter around Lyrium's blanket, but none landed on it. As insects began tuning up their instruments for the evening, Lyrium's companions waited patiently, knowing this was not a thing that could be rushed.

Sir Sun, ending his daily walk far behind them, threw a last gaze at Tulith Attis. Lyrium shook her head and stared through the trees at the fortress bathed in yellow light. She kept her gaze upon the far-off walls until the light of day was all but gone.

"Ugh! Nothing," she pronounced. "It is pointless. I See nothing."

She gathered up her stones and bones, and she put them away. Tyrillick and Belmira shook out her blanket as Elmira gave a hand to help Lyrium to her feet.

"I am sorry for bringing you this way," Lyrium said to them. "But Sight will not come to me today. And I am no closer to understanding things than before."

Elmira and Belmira nodded and began pulling off their cloaks and stuffing them into their bags. Then they rolled up the skirts of their gowns and secured them around their waists to free their legs. Lyrium did this, too, as Tyrillick cinched his shoulder bag out of the way. He put his hand up over his shoulder to grip the hilt of his sword and shifted it somewhat. Lyrium, too, slung Ethliad over her shoulder and pulled its straps tight across her chest. They did all this silently, and when they were thus prepared for the next dangerous leg of their journey, they nodded to each other.

"So," said Tyrillick to the ladies, "we know what we must do, and where we must go from here."

He looked up through the trees and saw the first stars making their appearance.

"Yes," said Lyrium. "We shall move with haste and make the bridge before Lady Moon arrives."

"Let us be as swift as an arrow," said Elmira.

"Let us be as quiet as a barrow," said Belmira.

"Let us go," said Lyrium, nodding for Tyrillick to lead them on.

• • •

Making their way down from the ridge, they came to the old Line Road, setting off at a run. They followed the road for several hundred yards, then, where it turned west to pass through the woods of Farbarley, the foursome turned east, racing along the northern edge of the plain that stretched out before Tulith Attis. As they ran, they skirted blocks of stone and leapt over ancient tumbled columns grown over with grass and vines, weaving around others and around the few saplings that struggled to grow on the battle-blighted ground. They were all alert and wary, but their sight was keen, even under the moonless sky, and none of them tripped or stumbled.

As they sped along, Lyrium and Tyrillick remembered how this plain once appeared, covered by the small city of Attis with its workshops, its houses and mansions. To them, each half-sunken block and every tumbled and shattered column was reconstructed, appearing in their minds as it once had been. They ran through parlors and courtyards, through gardens and playrooms, shops and kitchens, and their nostrils remembered even the aroma of those places. They heard again the sounds of lively families, music and laughter, and the noise of busy trade and commerce. Tyrillick's heart suddenly pounded all the harder, and he felt in his legs a desire to slow, for now they passed through a small bit of ground that had once been his own home. He did not slow. It was all gone. All destroyed by the Dragonkind that assaulted this place over five centuries ago. He and the ladies fast on his heels also noticed, jutting from the ground here and there, thick bars of iron, rusted and corroded by time, the remains of some abandoned engines of war.

• • •

At Tulith Attis, Redvest Captain Pargolis had arrived that morning with several of his lieutenants. He was to see to the condition of the twenty men stationed there, and return the following morning with his report to General Vidican in Passdale, leaving six men behind and taking six back with him. Away from the watchful eye of his general, Pargolis had spent most of the day sleeping. Late that afternoon, he roused himself to an early supper. Afterwards, having also imbibed a quantity of Barley beer, he and the sergeant in charge of the garrison took a turn around the walls of the fortress.

"We do all as ordered, sir," said the sergeant, "and in the proper fashion."

They stood at the northwestern corner of the fortress, overlooking the place where the old road passed by toward the bridge. As they watched, men went about lighting bright lamps and braziers along the roadway, working their way toward the bridge, and continuing to light more lamps across it, too.

"As you can see, sir, they're spaced so that their ain't no shadows between one and the next," continued the sergeant, "though it is a prodigious amount of oil and good fuel used up every night. I worry at our supply."

"It will be worth it to catch any more loose Barley folk who might try to get away along here," answered Pargolis. "The Saerdulin is too swift to swim, and the north road around the lake is blocked, so this bridge is the only way for them to go. I imagine we'll have them all rounded up in another day or so, anyway."

"Are there all that many still loose, sir?"

"Vidican does not believe that so many could have made it away to Janhaven. We have a good tally from our man in Glareth who looked at the census from past years. So, if Vidican is right, there should be several hundred still about. There is urgent need of labor to the south, and we still need to keep enough of them as our own workers. We rounded up thirty yesterday, down at the south end of the county. Including a very feisty Boskland girl. Had to give her a private lesson, if you take my meaning."

Pargolis absently put his hand to a few scratches on his chin. The sergeant glanced at Pargolis, knowing what kind of man he was, and nodded but did not smile.

"She'll need some further instruction, I imagine," Pargolis chuckled. By now the men along the road had completed their task and were returning to their post at the bridge.

• • •

Tyrillick suddenly stopped and crouched. The ladies did likewise next to him. They were two hundred yards from the fortress, and they could see the road at its base being illuminated. Torches were also being lit along the northern top of the battlements, and they could clearly see two men standing at the northwest corner.

"Let's go," said Lyrium.

• • •

Just as Pargolis was turning away, the sergeant shot out his hand to clutch his arm.

"There! Moving quickly!"

There was a shout from another man along the wall, who was also pointing.

"Four," said Pargolis. He hurried down the stair. "Mount up!" he cried. "There are four along the road trying to escape!"

By the time he and his riders were out of the southern gate and galloping around the base of the fortress, Lyrium and those with her had reached the portion of the road directly beneath the looming northern wall. They did not slow, ignoring the shouts from above as they made the paved approach to the bridge. Ahead at the bridge, soldiers scrambled from around their log barricade to face them.

"Halt!" cried one of the soldiers. "Halt and surrender yourselves!"

In the torchlight, the soldiers saw the flash of steel.

"They are armed!" cried the soldier as his comrades brought up their bows and leveled their lances. "Shoot them!"

Tyrillick twisted as an arrow shot past, and another arrow whistled between Belmira and her sister.

"Do not stop!" cried Lyrium as she whirled into the lances, swinging Ethliad. It hummed cleanly through the shafts and dismembered the arm of one soldier. Tyrillick parried another lance and dispatched its wielder as the sisters ran past and around the barricade. Lyrium and Tyrillick were right behind them running across the bridge, the remaining soldiers giving chase as the pounding of horse hooves mixed with the sound of the pouring river. The foursome reached the far side and continued on into the Boggy Wood. But the riders were closing fast. Tyrillick halted and turned to face them.

"Go!" he cried out to the ladies.

But Lyrium stopped also, and she saw the Redvests coming off the bridge a mere sixty yards away, bearing down upon Tyrillick. Quickly looking up and around at the trees, she ran to a tall poplar nearby and with one blow sent Ethliad clean through its trunk at a sharp angle. The tree slid from its stump, teetered, and fell.

"Tyrillick!" she cried. He saw the falling tree and ran to her. The horsemen did not see it in time. Pargolis pulled his reins and his horse reared as the crown of the old tree crashed upon him. Cracking branches and the screams of men and horses filled the night for a long moment, then all was quiet but the gush of the River Saerdulin. Lyrium and her companions fled through the Boggy Wood, turning from the path the Redvests had made from the south to strike off on a northeast course. They did not slow their pace, plunging through wicked briars and miry bogs until, hours later, they entered the higher ground of Forest Mistwarren.

• • •

It took two hours with axes and ropes for the Redvests to hack their way to the stricken men. When they finally extricated Pargolis, they found him bruised and dazed but otherwise miraculously unhurt. The other riders along with all of the horses were killed by the falling tree. Pargolis stumbled away from the wreckage some distance before he regained his balance. The sergeant handed him a flask of liquor which Pargolis drank greedily.

"Well, damn!" he said. "Damn and blast if I know how that happened."

He took another long drink, shoved the flask at the sergeant and lumbered away and back across the bridge with the sergeant trailing.

"How many men did we lose?" Pargolis asked.

"With your riders, ten. Six wounded."

Pargolis fumed, knowing this would be difficult to explain to his general. He did not care about the loss of the men, nor the escapees. The loss of face would set him back. And Pargolis suspected that General Vidican already harbored a dislike for him. He was determined not to let this incident hamper his advancement.

Abruptly, Pargolis turned around and faced the bridge, gazing across it at the woods beyond.

"Three women and a man!" he muttered, saying aloud what he knew Vidican would say.

"It was clearly three dozen who fought their way through," he stated to the sergeant.

"Sir?"

"And they had help from some of their people already in the woods."

"But, Captain—"

"You heard me, Sergeant. Let the men know. At least three dozen well-armed men. Several of them were killed on the bridge and fell over the side. Your men fought bravely, but were clearly taken by surprise by a greater force in a well-planned escape."

"Yes, Captain Pargolis. I'll let the men know."

"Clear the bridge of the dead. And put your men to work on a new barricade. One that does not have a pass-through."

"Yes, sir. Right away, sir."

Frowning, the sergeant watched Pargolis walk off, then turned to join his men who were still chopping away at the fallen tree.

Entr'acte

Entr'acte

Bailorg's Mistake

They made their last stand in and around the Treasury Room. In this small space was stored the wealth of Tulith Attis, the tiaras, jewelry, fine silverwares, and gem-speckled heirlooms of not only Heneil's household, but also belonging to people from the surrounding settlements who had come to this place for refuge against the invading Dragonkind. In later years, some might think it odd that two of the defenders within this vault were Men, fierce and short-lived Newcomers, as the immortal Elifaen called them, who had little connection to the treasure they now defended. They fought well and hard, but they and their comrades were driven back when the enemy poured through the opened gate. They knew their fate was sealed. The thousands of defenders within the fortress, the last holdouts, fought on. Every woman had a sword, and every child a knife, every Man and Elifaen who still drew breath stood bravely. But they were like autumn leaves before the wind, their bodies trampled where they fell. Finally, a few managed to retreat within the chambers of the interior, exacting as many lives of the attackers as they could, with tears of anger and sorrow. And a few made their way into the Treasury Room, shut the heavy door, threw the slide bolts, dropped the cross bar and backed away.

One was tall and of fair complexion with long sandy-brown hair, caked with blood and slick with sweat. He pulled a locket from beneath his mail, kissed it tenderly, and let it dangle by its chain from his neck. He calmly notched an arrow and aimed at the door. A short, barrel-chested man with close-cropped red hair stood beside him, wielding a battleaxe in one hand and a short thrusting-sword in the other. Behind that pair, and standing as well with their backs to the shimmering glory of rubies and emeralds and gold, were six more soldiers. Each was wounded and weak from the loss of blood, but all were ready with sword and bow and axe.

The ring of steel against steel and the thump of edge against flesh just outside the door suddenly ceased amid the muffled cries of the dying and the stamp of many feet. The door shuddered at the impact of a ram. Again the battering ram struck, and the iron-shod oak shifted in its frame. First one hinge gave, then another, carrying away bits of cracked stone.

"So, Captain Tallin," the axe-wielding one said to the other over the din, "this shall be it for us."

"It has been an honor, Bilaylin, to fight alongside—"

The door crashed in.

The end was brief and merciless, and when it was over the bodies were piled high, choking the doorway. It took only a few more moments for the wounded to be dispatched and the dead dragged out of the way. Impatiently, Bailorg strode in across the blood-slicked floor with a party of his wary escorts. He looked around the gleaming wealth then saw what he came for and hurried to it. But the ornate case that he opened was empty. Seeing this, Bailorg realized his mistake.

As he should have expected, the objects he sought were missing. Only a fool would risk keeping them during a siege. He stood in front of the ornate case, staring at the seven empty spaces where the objects he sought had been kept, and his mind chased after every plausible notion of their whereabouts. While his escorts took care to keep out looters, a tall figure entered, wearing black armor with a red hourglass on the breastplate. He stood behind Bailorg, his face obscured by helmet and hood.

"They are not here!" Bailorg cried, pounding the case with his fists. He spun around and, seeing the dark figure, immediately cowered.

"Then Lyrium took them," the warrior said.

"Then we must find her, my lord!"

"If she escaped the slaughter she will not be found. And she would no longer have them. She is far too cunning. I am undone."

"My lord! Perhaps—"

"No!" the figure turned away to leave. "We are both undone. Take what you will of this place and let us go from here quickly. We shall not accompany the army, but instead go west."

Bailorg followed into the corridor and saw his master staring down the passage at the huge iron door at the far end. It barred egress that way, and there were scores of bodies piled against it, those who died defending the outside of the Treasury Room.

"You should open it, my lord," Bailorg said, "so that it will be thought that this place was taken in that manner."

"No. Doing so now would wake powers best delayed. Letting it remain as it is will deepen the mystery of this place. And, too, it will cast doubt upon the Newcomers. That discord, at least, will be my spiteful reward."

Bailorg, never trusting, was quick to grasp the situation, and he made up his mind, right there. Without the objects they came for, this armored warrior would be too dangerous; they would have to part ways at the soonest opportunity. He glanced back at the empty case. He had time to bide, and could turn this problem over and over. Perhaps, eventually, he would find the answer. Or perhaps it would never matter. The things he came for were gone, probably forever.

Bailorg called to the Dragonkind who were assigned to his service and ordered them to have his wagons loaded with all the treasure they could hold. They, in turn, lashed out with their whips to urge on the slaves brought for that purpose.

The loot, though valuable, was paltry compensation for failure to capture the priceless objects they came for, but Bailorg was determined to have it as a consolation. His mysterious companion, preoccupied with his own bruising failure, was impatient to get away, else Bailorg would have tried to obtain more carts. So he cut short his looting, as the Dragonkind began theirs, and they departed, the dark warrior riding silently behind their train. Ahead, and alongside the wagons and carts, Bailorg with his Dragonkind soldiers rode guard, lashing the slaves to pull the carts more quickly. They retraced their path through the litter-strewn battlefield and on through the nearby ruined woods and fields. Before the night was done, Tulith Attis was far behind them, and Bailorg was making plans for his future.

Things did not go as Bailorg wished. In less than a fortnight, events turned against him. In danger of capture by an approaching army, the mysterious warrior rode away. Bailorg's mercenaries, the Dragonkind soldiers, deserted into the forest, and his slaves rebelled, refusing to budge the wagons another inch. Bailorg cursed them harshly, took what he could carry in his saddle bags, and abandoned the wagons of loot and his slaves. Fortunately for him, he eluded the forces closing in, and by stealth and conjured fog, he slipped from their reach.

It was a devastating and embittering blow, and he barely escaped with his life. But he made good his escape, and he remained in hiding for years and years. He knew he had time to make up for his losses, nearly all the time in the world. And while he waited and sulked, the world changed. The Fifth Unknown King of Duinnor was replaced by the Sixth, and a new order was imposed. Bailorg got busy again, and soon found new patrons.

• • •

Generations of Men passed into oblivion, and new histories were written as the old ones were forgotten. Men prospered, and their settlements grew into great and powerful cities while the Elifaen gradually declined, bearing fewer offspring and burying more casualties of their incessant wars with the Dragonkind. Men slowly established new traditions, and they tenaciously hung on and multiplied, in spite of their short lives. Meanwhile, the ways of the Elifaen faltered, their population declined, and their hearts grew weary.

Five hundred and forty-eight years passed, full of glory, full of tears. In that time, Bailorg courted and obtained a new patron, and as this lord rose in power, so too, did Bailorg. Darker powers, too, did he court. Until, at last, with the cruelest of ironies, he understood that his new quarry, just as the old one had been, was in the region of Tulith Attis.

• • •

"Will marvels never cease?" he commented as he leaned back in his saddle and gazed across the misty plain at the ruined ramparts of Tulith Attis. "Never did I wish nor have the least desire to see this place again. Yet, here I am."

Fate has twists and turns. After many years of thought, he came to understand who his former employer, the traitor of Tulith Attis, had become. And, in another twist, he found himself in the odd position of protecting that identity. Someday, he might make use of the knowledge, if only he could keep it from others, reserving that power to himself. Meanwhile, the orders that brought him here officially came from Lord Banis. Lord Banis's orders came from the King. And the King's orders? Bailorg smiled. The mist shifted somewhat, and he could better see the distant walls, now crumbling and brush-covered, long cleansed of the gory streaks that he remembered.

Too bad the place was already occupied by a Watcher. Otherwise, the old fortress would be a good place to establish his own base. He would have to find out who that Watcher was. Ashlord, the locals called him, but he did not recognize the name. A mystic, they said, who came some years ago from the west. Bailorg would have to be careful to hide his presence until the time was right, and use the meantime to learn all that he could about those in this region. The One he was sent to identify was sure to be somewhere nearby. The mist shifted again, and the old fortress was completely obscured. Bailorg shivered as the last gust of winter puffed spitefully through the air.

Coming this close to the old fortress was risky enough, but, in spite of what he just said, he could not resist having a look at the place, even if from a distance. This was where his life's greatest failure culminated. He would not fail again, he resolved. Yes, this is too close, he thought. The caves on the far side of this shire would have to do. It was out of the way, and people feared to venture there. He would have to obtain his own watcher, he knew, someone nearby. So many threads to weave!

One of the four horsemen who accompanied him nudged his mount next to Bailorg and said, "Go we to fortress? Tales my kind say of the place...I desires to see its stones and the brokened gates of it."

The other riders, who eschewed the company of this one, were surprised not only at the way the person spoke, but also by the fact of his speech; it was the most they had heard him say since he came into the group over two months ago. Bailorg shook his head.

"No. But the time may come—soon, I hope—when you will see it up close. Meanwhile, let us go away from here before we are seen or challenged!"

He led them back to the wooded ridge and then downward and across the stream, its banks lined with strangely leaning stones that gave Bailorg chills. They pressed on toward Passdale at a gallop, desiring to cross the bridge and back to their hideout in the hills before the day was full. Only once did he call his men to a stop, when they came on a path that led away to a dilapidated farmhouse.

"Is this the place?" Bailorg asked. "The one you met in the tavern, who told you of this way to the fortress?"

"Aye. Steggan's the name, sir. A drunkard farmer," one of the men said. "This path leads off to his place."

"Does he live alone, or has he family or servants?"

"Servants?" the man chuckled. "He can hardly keep himself! In debt, so I'm told, to nearly everyone in these parts. No servants. The man's wife ran off years ago. But he has a ward, so to speak. A young lass, his niece. But she's never there, I'm told. The Wild Girl of the Woods, the local folk calls her, a tomboyish sort. I believe she prefers the comforts of the field and forest to the beatings of her uncle."

"In debt, you say?"

"Aye, so I'm told."

Bailorg stretched around in his saddle looking back the way they had come. He reckoned it was about ten miles to the fortress. Easy enough walking distance. And only about fifteen or so the other way to Passdale.

"Well-known in these parts, then?"

"Aye, sir. Everyone knows him, and avoids him. But he's a jolly drinker, as I can vouch, though with a mean streak."

"Good. Go on ahead. I shall see if he is at home. I may be able to convince him to be our eyes and our errand boy. If people despise him so, he can carry our letters to Janhaven without molestation."

"Sir," said one of the other men, "we can leave our messages at the general store in Passdale. The Post Rider from Janhaven makes a stop there every week."

"No. It's the Post Station at Janhaven we must deal with. I do not trust storekeepers. Besides, our man, Steggan, may not be welcome in town. And we should not make ourselves familiar. Ride on, keep to yourselves! I will join you before nightfall."

Part II

Chapter 14

The Fall of the Faere

Day 94
151 Days Remaining

Robby's company decided to press on until such a time when Ullin might find a suitable place for them to camp. They spoke little, yawned much, and made a very good pace deeper into the mountains, going higher and higher until, by late afternoon, they had passed over the highest ridges. At last, Ullin took them off into the woods and they made camp as the sun set. They slept the night, grateful for sleep and rest. More confident now of their way, having seen no sign of Damar or any other dangers, it was decided they should resume traveling at daybreak. Ullin departed before dawn to scout ahead for caution's sake, but he was back not long after sunup just as the horses were being prepared. The path ahead, just as he reported, was easy, with no signs of traffic, and soon they had gone many, many miles, gradually descending, it seemed to them, more than climbing.

Conversation between riders varied as they swapped places, sometimes Billy riding up ahead with Ashlord, and sometimes falling back to let Sheila ride with him, but always Ashlord in the front, with Ullin riding well ahead scouting the way for safety and sense. But they were not so strung out that they could not hear each other's comments, for the forest was quiet and the clopping of their mounts muffled in the pine straw and humus of the trail.

Most of their talk pertained to their adventure and the ancient things that touched upon their quest. Beras was mentioned, and Sheila asked about the entity, as she had done many times before when she was staying with Ashlord. And the others listened carefully to what Ashlord had to say. The mystic answered, describing how Beras was considered the personification of the Creator, the Great Spirit that ruled over the wide Universe. Beras was merely an expression of the Creator, he told them, as all things were. Beras represented the Intent, the Tendency, and the Will of the Creator. Ashlord was very learned in these matters and struggled patiently to put things in plain words that his companions could grasp.

"And all things that happen are guided by His Hand, though not forced."

"Even what we do?" asked Sheila.

"Of course," Ashlord replied. "If we listen to the truthful voice within that Beras spoke to all creations at their birth and making, we are guided."

Ashlord smiled and went on with his explanation, "We are seeds, in a manner of saying. We do not stay as we are born, do we? And as we grow, we change. And, yet, we are ever as the seed. The passing of each day, and all the events up until the present, are the circumstances, the soil and sun and water of our planting. But we may choose, if we have the strength, to seek a different soil to grow in, a different sun, and fresher water. Is that not why you came to me, Sheila? Because your choice was for something new, something different, better? Likewise, each day, to start again or continue on is our choice. Is that not a kind of Intent? And a kind of Tendency? And by giving expression to it, are we not acting in the way of Beras? Even when our plight seems so dire, as it may seem now, we are ever faced with choices. It may not be easy, but it is right that it should be so. And things often do go amiss, most times out of misunderstanding, sometimes of clumsiness. We should always be careful not to credit to malice those things that are done of ignorance and stupidity."

They all considered Ashlord's words as they progressed through the mountains. Talk turned back again to the ancient things, and recent events that surrounded their present circumstance. Conversation turned to the subject of Tulith Attis and the people who fought at that place, to the lands their own quest might take them, and what the world must have been like before Men came to its shores. They speculated about how the Elifaen may have lived during those ages before Men came, and what they did to fill their days. Ashlord told them once again that the Faerekind were the last to be born into creation, and how they came out of the spirit of other things.

Then it came Robby's turn to ride with Ashlord, in a wider portion of the way that permitted them to ride side-by-side, sometimes bending in their saddles to duck under boughs. After a few words about the trail, and how pleasant the day was, Robby asked about the Elifaen.

"My mother told me a little about what to expect when I go through the change," Robby said. "I don't look forward to it. I take heart from knowing that so many others have done so. But there is so much I don't understand. Like, why? And, how did it all come to be this way? I mean, I've heard tales, we all have, but it's like when I do the books at the shop and the sums don't tally up. Sometimes my mistake is at the beginning, and sometimes in the middle. And sometimes the reason is that I haven't added in or taken away something that my dad knows about but I do not. All this is like that. Except this is no tally-book! Which parts go back to the beginning? And where, in the line of figuring things, are we right now? I have trouble even explaining my confusion!"

"Hm," Ashlord said. "And no wonder! All this is a great deal to ponder, surely, and, as you say, we do not yet know which parts are missing, and which are yet to be filled into the reckoning of things. Our own adventure stems from a line of happenings that goes all the way back to the beginning of all things."

"As you have said before," Robby nodded. "But, for instance, Queen Serith Ellyn. She is Queen of Vanara, the land of the Faerekind. She is not the first ruler of that land, is she? Some say that she murdered her father to become Queen."

"She did not murder her father, Robby, though he died by her hand," Ashlord corrected.

"Was that Aperion?"

"Oh, no," Ashlord chuckled. "Her father's name was Parthais, and his father's name was Cupeldain. They are not related to Aperion. Sometimes, the ruler of Vanara is called 'King of the Faere' or 'Queen of the Faere' by Men, but that is not correct. Only Aperion may hold that title. The correct way is to say that the rulers of Vanara are 'Kings and Queens of the Fallen Ones,' since the true Faere departed the world long ago."

"Yes, as we have been taught and you have said," Robby nodded, "that 'Elifaen' means 'Fallen Ones.' But that confuses me. The Scathing is bound up in all that, as I have heard and been told by you and by the tales I've heard from others. It is even in some of the lesson books I have seen, and that one of the Faerekind may always be identified by the scars of Scathing and so not mistaken for Men. But why did all that come to pass to be as it is today? And what has it to do with Beras, or Aperion, or Queen Serith Ellyn, or any of us?"

"Aperion," Ashlord said, "was appointed by Beras to be King of the Firstborn, the Faerekind. When the world was made, such was the power of Beras that each thing that came into being answered first to Beras and took form in the First Tongue. Through Beras, the Creator gave to these forms the power to witness and to have joy in the emerging creations of the world. So, as the forests grew, there came into the world the Firstborn of the Forest. As the mountains rose up, there also arose the Firstborn of Hill and of Dale. As rivers flowed, so came the singing of the Firstborn of the Rivers. Thus came into the world all the Firstborn of the Faere. Aperion came last, as the spirit of the Faere was strong, and out of their spirit he was created. It was he, Aperion King, whom Beras gave to the Faerekind as their leader, the one to give guidance to the others when need be."

"Then what went wrong?" Robby asked.

"Much."

"Will you tell us?"

So Ashlord told them the tale, oft repeated in the West, but seldom in the eastern lands, except in and around Glareth where the Elifaen still abided in numbers. And Ashlord was a good storyteller, his voice deep and clear, and his way not too hurried, nor too slow. The first part of the tale he told went like this:

• • •

No one knows how it came to be, but there sprang a jealousy of Aperion from the Faerekind of the mountains. Not all of the Faere were jealous, but some of those among the elders of the Firstborn. They, who had been upon the earth the longest, felt one of their own should be leader of all the Faere, and they chafed against the authority of Aperion, their younger sibling. Into the deep recesses of their mountain caverns they withdrew. They ceased to take fellowship with the others of the Faere family, in sunlight or in moonlight, in forest or field or river, and so the Mountain Faerekind grew apart from the intent of Beras. They rejected Aperion's guidance and heard not his urgings to rejoin the others of their folk. It was one of those who came to power at last and who first brought sadness into the world by creating poison and death. This one, who was later called by the name of Morgasir, sought to have power over Aperion, and it was he who first spread death into the world, and deceit and treachery. Some say that it was through trickery that he gained from Beras the power to beget other creatures, and that it was he who brought dragons into the world. But I have heard none of the Elifaen bards say so, and they take offense that Beras could be tricked. In any case, Morgasir's creatures were made in the most foul and unspeakable way. The shadow of that power, a corruption of Beras, reaches into every age. It was Beras, not Aperion, who destroyed Morgasir, and his domains and the places where Morgasir and his followers once dwelt sank into the sea by the hand of Beras. That place remains unto this day, in the far reaches of the world to the south and west, and it is called the Craggy Sea, a vast sea choked with great rocks, full of treacherous currents and shallows, beset with fog and storms so that no ship can pass through it.

Evil though Morgasir was, some of his followers and some of his creatures were permitted by Beras to escape his wrath, for no creature made by the hand of the Creator is purely evil. Eons passed. Peace and tranquility returned to the world, and the passing of time upon the earth was not counted or noticed. Then there appeared dragons in the lands of the far south, rising up from the depths of the sea, from that place of Morgasir that was destroyed, and they brought with them fire and destruction to the lush forests and fields. Like Morgasir, they, too, beget new creatures to toil and to labor for them and to be as slaves. Great alarm swept the Faerekind. They witnessed the death and disappearance of many trees and animals, and saw for the first time ever death come to some of their own Faere brethren. Thus the world was filled with fear. But it was at this time also that Beras made a way for offspring to come of all living creatures so that they might have some hope of continuing their own kind. And so, for the first time, the love of family came to the Faerekind, as children were born unto them.

Many of the Faere retreated from the devastated lands, but some grumbled against Aperion and against Beras, too.

"We do not know these dragon creatures, nor their slaves," Aperion argued, "and Beras is silent concerning them."

"Let us fashion the land over," said some. "Let us make the rivers run dry from those lands, and let us coax Sir Sun with his heat to parch these unwanted ones."

Those that spoke thus to Aperion then departed from him, and they strove in the earth and sky and changed the path of the rivers and made the land of the Dragonkind harsh and barren. This angered Aperion who said only Beras may have such power. Such was Aperion's ire that he grew fearsome in aspect to his own kind. Indeed, even those that reshaped the lands regretted what they had done, but they were powerless to undo their work. Yet, as a result of their labors, the dragons died away or receded back into the seas or burrowed into deep places into the earth where they yet grumble, sometimes sending forth their flames and their molten bile high into the sky and flowing across the lands, burning the plains with lava and covering vast areas with soot and ash. Even to this day, they sometimes do this.

The Dragonkind, who were the offspring of the monsters and had been made to be their slaves, dwindled in numbers when their former masters were destroyed, and once again peace came into the world.

But there was one among the Faerekind who sought to undo Aperion. He was called Secundur and had been a pupil of Morgasir. Secundur was fond of shadowy places and longed to take up the work of his former master. He nurtured resentment among the Faerekind who had lost their forests to the desert, and by his soft urges they were made to feel discontented. He gathered around him all those who, like himself, had escaped the destruction of Morgasir. Though they were few, they made much mischief among the other Faerekind by whispering against Aperion, and they even hissed against Beras when they dared. It is said that Secundur courted even the Dragonkind of the parched places, seeking to provoke them, but those people for the most part shunned and mistrusted him. The desert people eked out a miserable existence, but they considered themselves free of their former masters, the dragons who were now destroyed or in hiding.

In spite of all these things, the world was still favored by Beras, and the Faere lived happily and without need but for sunlight and moonlight. Dew filled the ever-blooming flowers with nectar to delight the lips of the Faerekind, and the birds sang joyously to delight the ear. With their broad and airy wings, the Faere skipped along the waters and danced among the green forest treetops, and with the First Tongue, they took pleasure in conversation with every creature, every tree and blade of grass, and every stone. And their communion with each other brought forth for the first time children of their own kind, without pain or travail, and new joys were brought into the world.

One day, some of the Dragonkind appeared among the green hills of the north saying they were invited to feast with the Faerekind. As it turned out, it was Secundur who had invited them and welcomed them. Yet many of the Faere were mistrustful of these crude creatures who walked with their feet and were covered with the dust of their travels. Many of the Faere who had been driven out from their lands by the dragons remained aloof and resentful of the guests. But Aperion welcomed them, saying, "Are you not also the children of Beras, though your coming into the world was sad and harsh? Why should we not enjoy together the taste of these fruits and share with one another our songs and our laughter?"

Indeed, it was perceived by many that the Dragonkind and the Faerekind had much in common, and each found beauty where they lived. And it was shown by Secundur that, though the Dragonkind had no wings, they were little different from the Faere. The women of the Dragonkind were especially beautiful, and they aroused admiration for their poise and their grace. These women brought with them gifts made by their own hands of gold and ruby and lapis. Secundur was pleased, for it was he who showed them the art of making such things, and he well knew what the outcome would be.

"What is this?" one of the Faere cried out upon seeing the ruby-encrusted staff being presented to Aperion. "This staff is the arm of my old friend, a great and mighty cedar who once lived in the southlands!"

And another cried, seeing the emeralds that lined a headpiece being offered, "And these are the eyes of my dear friend the hare who danced and played in the meadows of the southlands!"

And so great discord came among them, prodded by the smiling whispers of Secundur.

"Aperion," Secundur breathed from the shadow of an elm tree, "it does not seem fitting that such gifts should be accepted. Our people grow angry, and their hearts turn against our guests. Give back these things and send the Dragonkind away."

This Aperion reluctantly did, apologizing for the temperament of his own kind and begging the guests to take with them what food they wished.

"I fear for you," he told them, "for I have never seen my people act in this manner. But I will see you safely home. Let us wish for a time when such things may be forgotten and when we may be friends."

And so Aperion accompanied them away, back into the desert lands, and he walked upon the ground as they did to keep their company and to converse with them all along the way for many many leagues. At last, when they reached their homes, he bade them farewell and took to the air with his wings and returned to his own kind in the north.

Some stories say that when Aperion returned, he spoke to his own people with anger in his face and in his voice, saying, "Who are we to deny communion with those others of this world who live and breathe? What fault of theirs is it that they may live in lands made barren by evil doers and misguided mischief-makers? What fault of theirs is it that they do not know how to speak with the things of the world? But are these not also children of Beras, who come from the same Font of Creation that brought forth us all? And look you at their plight, for they live but for a very short while, toiling against the ground without wings. Their lives are full of struggles, and then they quickly pass away. Yet we remain. I say unto you: Know now time, its measure and the weight of its passage! Let the day end, and let darkness come to the lands to cause you to think on the end of life for creatures such as these. And, after a while, let day come back anew to remind you that life has its beginnings out of darkness. Give thanks that you enjoy the creations of Beras as you do and are joined with him. Let your heart ponder what otherwise may be!"

And as he spoke, Sir Sun shrank away and sank low into the ground for the first time ever since the world was made, and the sky was filled with the red fire of his trailing robes. Lady Moon followed soon afterwards, alone and without her bright husband, hiding her face behind her hands in shame. All of the Faerekind shuddered at the coming dark of the First Night upon the earth. Yet, by this act, the Dragonkind were given relief from Sir Sun's pitiless gaze, and for the first time the cool of the night air was known in their lands, and they praised and thanked Beras for the respite.

Other stories say that the day and the night were made by Secundur's trickery, and was not Aperion's doing. Regardless, Secundur reveled in the hiding dark of night. He went about with ease and spoke to the others, whispering, "Why does Aperion put the creatures of the desert lands before us? Why does he give greater regard to those who live on lands that were taken from us?" And to others he said, "Aperion has turned away from Beras and has taken favor with those that Beras has punished." Thus he went, stirring dark thoughts among many.

He went also to the far-off Dragonkind and floated amongst them while they rested in the cool of the evenings. There he went about from one to another.

"Why should it be," he spoke, leaning over their shoulders with his lips near their ears, "that those of the northern lands may live easily and without struggle when you must scrape and toil?" And to others he declared, "Aperion sets himself up as a god, and he cares not if he offends you by refusing your gifts and your company. Yet you are the proud offspring of dragons!"

Thus for many passings of the days and nights without count, Secundur patiently aroused some of the Faerekind to doubts and to subtle anger. And he did not neglect the Dragonkind, either, going amongst them to spread worry, resentment, and discord.

There was one among the Firstborn who began to think as Secundur suggested, and yet he also sought to resist Secundur's words. These days, his name is remembered as Cupeldain, and he was one of those who had once favored the coastal forests far to the south and was driven out by the dragons who came from the sea. It was Cupeldain, too, some say, who had striven with rock and river to drive out the dragons and who, with some others lost to memory, angered Aperion by that work. Cupeldain had not forgotten Aperion's anger, nor the shame of his rebuke, but his spirit had arisen in those places now lost to the world, and Secundur's words filled him with melancholy longings for what was no more. Yet Cupeldain had not the power to restore the forests of the south, even though the dragons were gone. It was he who took to heart Aperion's admonishments, and he, more than the others, grieved not only at his loss but also at his failure to restore life to those lands and make them as they once were. Never could he forget the shame of attempting what only Beras might do.

"Aperion's words were true," Cupeldain said to Secundur. "Look at our failure. It was we, not Aperion, who strove to be gods and to do what Beras has not seen fit to do. The dragons are gone, but our seeds grow not in the southlands. Sand and rock are parched, and the rivers we took away cannot be put back in their old courses. Surely it is as Aperion has spoken, that it is not our place to create but only to rejoice in that which is, and, if it must be so, to mourn and remember that which is no more."

This angered Secundur, for he knew Cupeldain to be powerful and that Cupeldain enjoyed the conversation of rock and river and would be a mighty ally if only he could be convinced.

"If Beras is in all things the intent of Creation," Secundur countered, "then how may it be that those things have come to pass and that the spawn of the dragons now roam the dry lands once lush with leaf, root, and twig? Is it not given to us by Beras to decide and to judge? Is that not why Aperion claims to speak for Beras?"

In this manner Secundur slowly urged Cupeldain, coming to him in the shadows of the forest or in the darkness of night. But Cupeldain listened not, it seemed, and Secundur grew impatient and went then to the Dragonkind.

"Why should you struggle so?" he asked them, "when just over yon mountains is cool-flowing water, vines heavy with sweet grape and berry, trees laden with hearty nuts and with peaches gold and juicy?"

"We are not welcome there," was the reply from one.

"This is our place," said another, "given to us by our dragon-fathers."

So Secundur set about causing strife among the Dragonkind, and with his whisperings and shadowy words he created turmoil among them so that they fought among themselves and increased their struggles. This was difficult for Secundur to do, for there are few shadows in the Dragonlands, and Lady Moon watches brightly at night. And the Dragonkind people were mysterious to him. Though he knew that they were the products of dragons and that those dragons somehow were the creatures of his former tutor, Morgasir, Secundur did not understand their resistance to him nor the mystery of their existence. For how could the rude dragon sire such a fair likeness, though crude, of the form of the Faere folk?

Still, for generation after generation of Dragonkind, Secundur patiently plied them with doubts and with longings until there rose up among them one who heeded Secundur's words. His name was Kalzar, a chief of one of the great tribes of the barren lands. To this tribe Secundur showed the secrets of smelting iron and forging weapons and tools. He suggested to Kalzar that he, among all his peoples, was the true descendant of the dragons, and that, with the secret of fire and steel, he held the power of the sun itself.

As Kalzar came to have greater power over his kind, Secundur went also to Cupeldain and said, "Do you not see the stirrings of the south? Yet Aperion does nothing and claims to have kinship with them through Beras. Yet they do not rejoice in life as we do. They do not follow the intent of creation. See how they fight and slay one another? This they do without remorse. And now there is one, named Kalzar, who rises to great power in those lands. He builds cities and commands legions who worship him as a god. Yet Aperion cares not that they do these things."

"What is it to us?" Cupeldain replied. "We have our lands and they have theirs. If Beras is offended, let him make a change. Why do you whisper to me these thoughts and try to put fear in my heart?"

"Is it fear to be aware? Is it fear to be prepared to protect our lands? Or is it folly to be idle as Aperion is and to invite the followers of Kalzar into these untouched valleys."

"What may we do, anyway? Look at our last efforts! In our effort to destroy the dragon, we only made a place for these Dragonkind."

"You must learn what they have learned," said Secundur. "Make steel as they have. Forge and mill. Cut stone and raise up walls."

To this Cupeldain eventually agreed, and so he and those also convinced by Secundur delved into rock and fire, forged weapons and built airy cities of glass and stone. They ceased in their conversations with oak and granite, refrained from singing with river and reed.

Aperion, when he saw this, went to Cupeldain and said, "Why have you forsaken our ways and taken up the works of your own hands over that which Beras has provided?"

"We seek not to offend Beras," Cupeldain replied, "but only to learn and take joy in the abilities that Beras gave us. We wish to fashion with our own hands pleasing things for ourselves and, in doing so, to discover and rejoice in new things."

"For what purpose do you build these temples? Are not the halls of the forest and the columns of the mountains seemly enough places to rejoice?"

"We build them in fond imitation of the earth."

"Why do you then strike iron from the stones and make fire to forge metals?"

"The stone and the trees are willing to our hands, or else they would not give up their metal or their heat."

"For what use do you make, then, these sharp implements of bright steel? And what do you make when you stretch sinew across the cut and carved branch?"

"These swords we make because they are beautiful to hold, and they have within them mysterious powers of life and death. These instruments we make with wood and string to invent music like the brook does or the gurgling stream. Also, we may use these to send short branches far into the air as birds in swift flight."

And though the things they wrought were beautiful to behold and the music of their lyres and bows comely and sweet, Aperion trusted not Cupeldain's words, for he had seen the use of such things in the hands of the Dragonkind. So he went away from Cupeldain full of misgivings. Secundur, watching and listening from the shadows, followed Aperion as a murky cloud and whispered to him.

"O, King of the Faere! Why trouble over the toys and pastimes of your fellows? Their hands were made by Beras, were they not? And so all works spring from him."

Then to Cupeldain Secundur went and suggested, "You answered wisely, Cupeldain, and yet perhaps you should assert yourself more than you do, for Aperion grows weak and you grow strong."

This troubled Cupeldain, and he flew to the sunlit plains where he knew Secundur seldom went. There he pondered all that had come to pass while he drank from the flower-cups of nectar and gave himself over to sing with the larks and to ride gaily on the backs of antelope as they danced across the plain.

Secundur did not follow, for on the plain the face of Sir Sun, ever the servant of Beras, shined unbearably. But he was satisfied with what he had said to Cupeldain. That night, Secundur went unto Kalzar, the new king over the Dragonlands.

"You have done well, Kalzar, and your sires, the dragon-gods, are proud and pleased with your rule. What say you to those Faere who north of here in the green mountains make sharp weapons and build great castles? It is not for each other they do these things, but to come and take back these places that have been given from them to the Dragonkind by Beras."

"Why do you come to me? Are you not one of them? Like them, your spirit is dark to me and arouses me from my peaceful sleep to pace the night in troubled thoughts. Go from me! You are not welcome, and your words do not bring comfort to me!"

Full of anger at the rebuff, Secundur left Kalzar, and he brooded in the deep caverns of the mountains. He prodded, for spite's sake, the ancient beasts of Morgasir who still survived in the deepest recesses. With skills taught to him by Morgasir, Secundur conjured the old dragons to breed demons, and these he set loose to bring pestilence and torture to the Dragonlands and to any place they might roam.

"It is not meet for I, who am Firstborn, to be shunned. It is Beras himself who strikes my heart, and I shall strike his! It will be my place to remake the world. To gain from all the Faere and all the Dragonkind their prideful spirit and their knowledge and turn it against the plan of Beras!"

And for a long time, Secundur was not seen or heard, but his followers, those Faere who bent to his will, gathered themselves unto him and did his bidding. And though seldom seen or heard, his hand has ever since been felt in all the world and no doubt it was he who somehow provoked the first war, and sundered the Faerekind one from another, and caused the Fallen Ones, the Elifaen, to be in the world as they now are.

• • •

When Ashlord finished this part of his tale, he paused. His companions, all except Ullin who still rode some distance ahead, had drawn as close as they could to hear his voice. But they sensed there was more to tell, and had no questions, not even Billy, who listened all the while with squinting eyes and a cocked brow, his lips pursed in consideration. So Ashlord continued with the second part of the tale, which went like this:

• • •

This is how some legends tell of these things:

In the grand White Palace that Cupeldain built, there stayed a Faerekind by the name of Alonair who was skilled in the making of stone likenesses of animals, trees, and even of his own kind. These he would place around the Faere city that Cupeldain had built, and Alonair made them upon the porches and in the gardens. These sculptures were a marvel to all who saw them, so lifelike that, especially in the moonlight, they seemed to move and breathe, sometimes even turning their heads. Alonair's fame spread throughout Faerum and even far away to the Dragonlands. Even Aperion was amazed at the skill of Alonair. Those of the Faerekind who never before went to the city now did so to see the works of Alonair. The visitors, from the plains and from the forests, were amazed at all the doings of Cupeldain and his people, at the grand structures and temples, the fantastic gardens and fountains, and the boisterousness of those who lived in the city. And especially were they filled with wonder when they laid their hands on the statues of Alonair and felt them to be warm to the touch. But the statues spoke no word, the stone of their making was silent, and the visiting Faere understood this not at all, for never had any material of nature been silent to them before.

When Kalzar heard of these statues, he marveled at the tales and sent emissaries to Aperion asking if Alonair might carve some statue for Kalzar in exchange for some similar boon.

"Alonair may decide for himself if he is to do this," Aperion said, "and the measure of his reward, too."

And Aperion summoned Alonair, but when he arrived, Alonair's heart was darkened against the Dragonkind, and he thought to himself, "I will agree to Kalzar's wish and ask a boon of great price of him, for his people walk the land where once I played with deer and where I once danced with the ram. Kalzar's land of sand once was full of green fields and forests that gave to me the juice of their berries. There, the chorus of leaves once spoke back to the beat of my wings as I passed through, and thus the trees sang as Sir Wind moved his fingers through their branches. Yes, it will be a great price."

So Alonair agreed to come to Tyrsharat, the city of Kalzar in the desert plains, and to make for him a statue like no other, and to ask in return a favor of his own choosing.

"But first make ready the stone that I will carve. Cut it twenty times the height of Kalzar and the same in its width and breadth. Quarry this stone in a single block and make a place for it in the center of your city. When it is there and all is ready, send for me and I will begin the work of carving this thing for you."

"In what likeness may we tell Kalzar that you will carve this statue?" the chief emissary asked.

"You may say that it will be in the likeness of what once was but is no more, of what will be but has not yet come to pass."

When Kalzar received the emissaries back at Tyrsharat and they told of their meeting with Alonair, Kalzar asked, "Did he say no more? Did he not say what likeness he would carve?"

"No, Mighty One, only: 'It will be in the likeness of what once was but is no more, of what will be but has not yet come to pass."

"And did he not say what boon he would ask?"

"No, Son of Dragon, he never did."

Kalzar pondered this for a day and a night, then he ordered the preparations to begin. The Dragonkind labored long, and an entire generation was born into the task, for once the massive block was cut from a mountain, it had to be moved over a hundred leagues to the city Tyrsharat. Many of his people grumbled, saying it was impossible to move such a stone, as big as a hill, as heavy as a mountain. But Kalzar would have the thing done, and so he raised armies to conquer all of the Dragonkind and to make of them slaves. And he raised a great host of workers to pry away the stone, to forge tools for sliding it across the sands and gravel of the desert. When they faltered, Kalzar's taskmasters whipped the workers. When his counselors said the task was too great and cost the empire too much, Kalzar had them put to death. When at last the Dragonkind Empire grew weak from the task, Secundur emerged from his place of sulking and went to Kalzar and stood beside him on the high balcony of the palace. There, Kalzar cast his gray eyes over the city, beyond the place prepared for the stone, and outward across the moonlit desert toward where, far beyond sight, the stone still moved, inch by agonizing inch.

"Surely Alonair's gift has become a curse upon you, Kalzar," Secundur said in his ear. "The Faerekind delight in the sufferings of your people and rejoice in your vanity. You do not have the power, as do the Faerekind, to converse with stone and sand, and they resist your will stubbornly. Only the Faere may move this thing here, and this they know. While your empire falters into ruin, the cities of Cupeldain flourish and grow in beauty. Your numbers were once vast, but the ocean of your people recedes, while the Faere grow in number."

Kalzar thought about this and passed the night through with Secundur at his ear until morning when Kalzar walked out into the sun and Secundur departed.

"What power have I to do this thing?" Kalzar cried out at the blazing sun. "Have we indeed been tricked by the immortal ones who may wait with patient ease for our self-destruction? No! I shall not be treated so contemptuously!"

Then he gathered his generals and ordered them to make an army and to go north into the greenlands, fearing not the Faere. There, this army was ordered to capture as many of those who lived there and could be brought back to be chained to the Great Stone and to pull against it. To take the fruit of the lands, too, and all the animals they could find, and to destroy what they could not sack, forest, field, and city alike.

Of course, the Faere saw these preparations. Many still flew the skies that once covered their homes of leaf and twig, looking down at the now-parched lands. They saw the many fearsome creatures below, scorpions and basilisks, which the devastated lands had spawned. And these Faere watched the building up of the Dragonkind and the rise of their cities. They saw how the desert dwellers made fields along the few rivers still flowing there, and how they slaved and toiled and fought and were beaten down by the sun and by the whips of their masters. They saw, often enough, Kalzar himself and his retinues, going forth in glory upon elaborate sedans to survey the movement of the Great Stone or to review the gathering of his armies with his many sons and wives and all the high members of his court. But those Faerekind that flew high overhead and watched did not speak to those creatures below, or those people or those rivers, or to the rows of wheat that they grew in some faint semblance of the grass that had once sprouted there. Rarely did they allow themselves to be seen, except in the distance, perhaps, safe from the bite of the high-flung arrow. To Cupeldain they returned to tell of what they had seen. As the marching armies came toward them, all of the Faerekind in Cupeldain's city watched in horror and disbelief. Some went to Aperion and cried, "What shall we do? For they are grim and vast in numbers, and they have murder upon their faces."

"They cannot fly into the air as we," said Aperion, "nor do they abide upon the earth but for a short while. They are weak creatures and are cursed with all manner of pain and longing, springing from their lowly bodies. What is there to fear of them? Let them be as they are and have what they wish, for all will return to Beras after a time, as is His intent, and we will see their passing away."

"What of our cities? What of our gardens that we made with our hands and that give us pleasure?"

"It is not from such made things that we sprang, but from that which made the stone of your cities, and from that which made the flowers that grow in your gardens, and we sprang also from the water that runs across your terraces, and from the air that blows the scent of your blossoms. The Dragonkind cannot unmake Beras, nor can they stay his Intent."

"But it is cruel, what they do. If we are but the hand of Beras, then surely it is an offense to him that the works of his children are cast down and trodden to dust."

Aperion then understood that many of his own kind had become attached to the things of the earth and to the objects made by their hands, and he saw that they no longer felt as strongly the Force behind those things.

"Beware that you do not act as those you fear," he said to them, "lest you take up their ways and become as they are."

But Cupeldain and the others with him understood little and heeded less of Aperion's words. From their high places in the cities, they watched the armies hack through the forests and swarm through the mountain passes between the Dragonlands and Faerum. Deer and elk, docile and tame, they slaughtered to eat, and birds for their feathers, and the bear for his skin. In horror, Cupeldain watched from the tower of his castle, his eyes stinging with tears. And when the armies came to his city, the Dragonkind were at first baffled, for there was no road into the city and no gate. But what use are these to Faere who are lifted up by their wings over the walls of their cities and who need not tread the ground or crush a leaf with their feet? Here, the Dragonkind camped and made engines of wood and stone and iron, the smoke of their fires and forges choking the air along with the sound of anvils, mallets, and drums. Strange and cumbersome devices they made, dark of purpose, and with them they came again unto the walls of the city. They pounded the walls with the great battering hammers they had made, slung by ropes from carriages and scaffolds. Day and night, they smote the walls, and day after day and night after night, until at last they made cracks in the statue-covered ramparts until they crumbled away into rubble and ruin.

It was then that many of the Faere, still innocent and without understanding, were taken by the intruders. And when Cupeldain saw them murdered, he cried out and fetched his sword and flew into the midst of the enemy and cut down all the Dragonkind that he reached. Others joined him and in their fury they put to death all they found, soaking the ground with the blood of the Dragonkind, those that fought against them and those that tried to flee. But few Dragonkind escaped, and the fey defenders of the forest lands flew across the desert and, coming upon Tyrsharat, wreaked such blood that Kalzar himself was in fear and joined the battle.

Then, as the height of the battle was reached, and Cupeldain plied with Kalzar, sword against ringing sword, darkness fell upon the earth. Torch fires gave no light, nor did Lady Moon or any of her retinue of stars look down from the heavens. And a great fear came over all, Faere and Dragonkind alike, so that they paused in their killing.

Aperion's voice, full of the might and spirit of Beras, parted the black silence.

"Come!" he commanded. And the wings of all Faerekind moved and flew of their own accord, obeying some higher master than the bodies to which they were attached. Away they flew from Tyrsharat, and from all other parts of the earth, over the blackened desert and through the blinded sky and beyond the lightless forests and onto the wide plains where Aperion waited. All the Faere of all the lands of the earth were called, those in battle and those who knew nothing of it. Those of the forests, and those of the rivers, and those of the sea. All were gathered on the plain in a vast host, and they saw each other in the red light of Aperion's golden anger.

"A new place is prepared, and now we must depart this world to await the will of Beras!" he said to them sternly. "Follow now along the way I go."

But there was hesitation among many of the Faere, who muttered, "Why must we go? We have done no harm to any creature, and our conversation with the earth is not broken."

"We cannot depart and leave our work unfinished!" cried Cupeldain, still breathing with the heat of battle and soaked with the blood of Dragonkind. A rejoin of like sentiment went up from his people, still gripping their swords and anxious to complete their vengeance.

"You have parted yourselves from the intent of Beras and love too much that which Beras gives rather than He who gives it."

"We will not go!"

"We cannot go!"

"Look there!" Aperion pointed at Sir Sun, who was red with anger, and who was retreating with haste to that place beyond the western rim of the world. And very close at his side was his Lady Moon, who covered her face for shame.

"All those who stay beyond the passing of Sir Sun's purple hem shall bear the punishment of their desire. Verily, the weight of their hearts shall be their reward. All those who still rejoice are welcome into our new home."

And so Aperion departed quickly upward into the sky, followed by a host of the Faerekind. But many hesitated, not wishing to leave their lovers or their fathers or mothers or children. Some did not wish to leave their fields or forests, and many spoke to one another, muttering words of wonder that Aperion would leave so, and with him such a host of Faerekind. Those of the deep forest or gentle sea who knew nothing of Cupeldain made to depart back to their homes. And those who wished to resume their battle against the Dragonkind moved to return with Cupeldain to those lands. But as the sun disappeared, their wings grew weak, and they fell to the ground or into the treetops or upon the waves of the sea.

"Why does my body fail me!" cried Cupeldain as he alit on a high hill. "What sensation is this to be pulled to the earth? This pain that burns my back and this emptiness that grows in my belly? How is it that this sword grows heavy in my hand when it was but a feather moments ago?"

As he pondered these new and curious sensations, his dripping sword became too heavy to hold. The burning of his back grew more painful, the hunger of his stomach spoke loudly. He cried aloud, gathering his wings about him for warmth against the cold night air. But his wings did not obey him, and he pulled them with his hands, feeling the life go from them. And, as everywhere around him the sounds of agony and shock of all the Fallen Ones rose up from the lands, their wings crumbled and fell away as dust.

• • •

"That was how it was that the Elifaen lost their wings," Ashlord said. "They bear the scars of what they lost even to this day, and all their offspring, too. From that day to this one, those of the Faere race who remained in the world have felt hunger and cold. The stone bruises their feet, and the thorn cuts their flesh. For all the days of their lives, they endure the memory of what they lost, yet they are unable to succumb to sickness, or to hunger, or to pain, or even to age. The peace of death comes to them only through violence or, sometimes, through deep inconsolable sadness."

Chapter 15

Highway Robbery

The day stretched on as Ashlord told his tales, and, early in the afternoon, the company descended into a deep wood where autumn had hardly yet touched the leaves. They listened to the end of his telling and rode along in silent consideration. Robby, who continued alongside Ashlord, still had many, many questions. And he longed to tell Ashlord why he needed to go to Tulith Morgair. Tugging at his vest, he also wanted to do as Mirabella had instructed, and show Ashlord the coins she had sewn into the lining of the vest. But he never seemed to find the right moment with Ashlord, away from the others so that he could speak privately with him. And, besides, until he got to Tulith Morgair and saw the place for himself, and saw what proof, if any, there was to the Dragonkind woman's existence outside of his dreams, Robby thought it best to keep all that to himself. Perhaps his worries were making free with his imagination, and his dreams were merely the reflections of a confused mind. So Robby carried on his internal conversations, circling and circling, pondering Lyrium's visit, the situation at home, the plight of Tallinvale, and, now, the tale Ashlord had just related. As Robby was of late often seen to do by his companions, and noticed no less by Ashlord, he shrugged and shook his head. But he said nothing.

Along this portion of their way, the forest was thick and the path narrowed, though it was well-marked, easy, and unusually flat by comparison to the surrounding lands. It was a quiet place, too, as if the shade had a sleepy quality to it, deep and cool. Robby and the others, tired though they were, felt their spirits lighten somewhat in the pleasant wood. Coming around a bend, they arrived at a fork in the path where there was a guidepost with two signs. There, Ullin waited for the others to catch up and gather around. They did so, remaining in their saddles, and they examined the signs, posted in the middle of the fork, one pointing one way, and the other pointing the other way. On the one pointing left was carved:

Free Way
To
Redwater Gorge Crossing
45 miles

And on the other sign, pointing to the right-hand way, was written:

Toll Way
To
Redwater Gorge Crossing
15 miles

Ashlord looked from one sign to the other in consideration.

"What do you think?" asked Ullin. "Might it be a Damar road?"

"Very strange," Ashlord replied. "Why would the Damar have a toll on such an out-of-the-way path when they have none on the crowded and well-used roads?"

"Maybe it's a private way," Sheila suggested.

"An' how much could they be askin' for it?" Billy put in. "I brung a few coin."

"Me, too," said Ibin.

"Me, too," said Robby, fingering his purse with one hand and running his other along the lower hem of his vest where the seven special coins were sewn in. "But why isn't there a gate?"

"Strange, indeed," Ashlord repeated. "I'm not sure I trust these signs."

"But if they are true, it could save us a couple of days," said Ullin.

"Look yonder!" Billy motioned at the right-hand path.

Coming down the path was a figure, thin and frail-looking, moving slowly toward them with small careful steps and leaning on a staff as he approached. Even with it, the man seemed to have trouble keeping his balance. He was dressed in a long brown cloak that reached to his ankles and was buttoned up to his neck where a hood flopped down about his barely visible ruddy face. He had unusually short arms, and the belt around the cloak was strapped about where a normal person's elbows would hang. He waved to them with a tiny hand on the end of a stubby arm.

"Ho, there, fellow travelers!"

"Greetings to you," replied Ullin, getting down from his horse. "Do you come from the direction of Redwater Gorge?"

"Aye, indeed, young feller," said the stranger as he entered the fork. He stopped in front of Ullin and caught his breath. "A long walk for me! Do ye go that way?"

"Yes. And we are considering whether we can afford the Damar toll."

"Oh it is not a Damar way," said the figure. "It belongs to Herbert."

"Who?"

"Herbert?"

"Herbert the Blue. It is his lands and the lands of his people through which this way goes."

"Oh." Ullin glanced at Ashlord.

"Never heard of him," said Ashlord to Ullin.

"And what of the toll?" Robby asked. "Is it much?"

"Aye, for one such as I it is a ransom! But as ye can see, I must move too carefully to take the long way, for it is hilly and is crossed by rocky streams. At least this way is smooth and has good stone or wooden bridges."

"But what of the toll?"

"A ransom to me, as I said, being but a poor creature. I had to borrow the amount to make the trip. Herbert takes a copper mite for every shoe!"

"A mite? How much is 'at?" Billy asked.

"A mite? Why it's one-twelfth a Damar shilling, or one-fiftieth a silver ounce of Duinnor."

"About a half-penny," Robby said. "That'd be about two—"

Robby almost said "two Eastlands bits" but caught himself, not wanting to give away their home. "We can afford that."

"Well, if ye have it, it may be worth the spending for the ease of the way," replied the stranger.

"But where is the gate? Where is the toll collected?" asked Sheila.

"Oh, it is at a bridge about halfway," said the stranger, resuming his way past them. "If ye don't like the way and don't want to pay, ye can turn around and take the rougher ground."

He ambled on with his odd way of shuffling along, and was soon gone from sight.

"Well?" Billy asked the group.

"Something, I don't know, shifty about that man," Sheila said.

"I agree," nodded Ashlord.

"We have ample the toll," put in Robby. "And what if it may save us a day or two?"

"So, what d'we stand to lose, then, but a couple of bits?" asked Billy.

Ullin nodded to Ashlord.

"Very well," he sighed. "But let us be sharp! I sense some foolery hereabouts."

The rest hardly paid attention as they steered onto the right fork. Just as was told, the way was easy with only gentle rises and falls, and with well-made bridges of stone and wood that crossed the many streams they encountered. It seemed no time at all before they came upon a post with a sign on which was written:

Ten Miles
To
Redwater Gorge Crossing
Toll Gate Ahead

And it was not long after that they did indeed come to a small wooden bridge, made of posts and planks, with a simple toll gate before it. Nearby was a sign in the shape of an arrow pointed down at an iron box chained to the signpost.

One Mite per Shoe
Or Go Back the Way Ye Came
Cheaters Will Be Fined!

"Allow me!" Billy jumped down from his horse and loosened his purse. "Will two silver bits cover us all?"

"For the six of us," replied Robby. Billy nodded and tossed two coins into the box. He then hoisted up the toll bar so that everyone could pass through.

"A trusting sort, this Herbert the Blue," commented Ullin.

"Too trusting, if you ask me," returned Ashlord.

Soon Billy led his horse through and lowered the bar back into place and rode up behind the pack animals.

"When we get to the gorge, do you think there will be Damar guarding the bridge there?" Robby asked Ashlord.

"Most likely. We may need those papers your grandfather provided, though I would prefer not to use them."

"An' how far from thar 'til we get on into the plains?"

"Two days. Three, maybe."

By now, the afternoon sun was long and low and the forest shadows deeper and cooler. Perhaps it was the calming quiet of the woodlands, or maybe it was the ease of the way which gave their fatigue some chance to catch up with them, but all grew sleepy and even the horses slowed, their heads low. Ashlord, too, felt an unusual weariness settle upon him, forming a great desire to stop and ponder over a lit pipe. Still, they moved on. When Ullin yawned, all those behind him did, too, each in turn one after the other, except Ashlord.

Sheila considered asking if they should make camp, but held herself back, not wanting the only girl in the company to make the suggestion. She heard Billy yawn once again behind her.

"Oh, me!" he said. "Kinda drowsy, I reckon."

"Perhaps we should stop and make camp," Robby suggested to Ullin. Ashlord heard this and allowed his horse to come to a halt.

"The day is nearly done," he said. "Perhaps it is time to rest. A cold supper, no fire, somewhere away from the path."

He dismounted, and the others did likewise and followed into the trees where they soon came into a small clearing. As they unburdened the pack animals and stacked the packs and saddles and undid their bedrolls, they could hardly speak a word that was not interrupted by a yawn or even two. Ashlord chose a tree to sit against and was drawing the first puff from his pipe when the last of his companions slipped into slumber.

"A peaceful place," Ashlord muttered. "Strangely calming."

So peaceful, he noticed, that there was hardly a snore to be heard among his companions. And so easy and deep into his thoughts did Ashlord float that he hardly heard the little *Poof!* that sounded nearby, nor did he at first notice the odd glow behind him that quickly dissipated. But when it sounded again, then again, it finally reached his attention, and, alarmed, he immediately sprang to his feet.

"Ye have cheated!" cried a voice behind him. This voice, so shrill and strange, immediately woke the others, and, blinking and rubbing their eyes, they looked with disbelief and wonder at the crowd that surrounded them. Little men, not much more than four feet tall, stood all about the clearing. They were dressed in brightly colored breeches and vests, some with little jackets of scarlet, others in green or gold or yellow or purple, with buckled shoes below and shiny black hats above, some with gay feathers and others with brass buckles above the brim. Robby counted twenty-five of them before being distracted by one dressed in sky-blue who stepped out from the rest. He stood with his lower lip jutting out from his freckled face and his arms crossed. The others stood likewise, or with their thumbs in their belts.

"I say: Ye have cheated! Ye must pay the full amount of the toll to pass this way!"

"We paid at the toll gate," Robby said, hardly believing the spunk of the little fellow.

"I tossed the coins into the iron box meself!" said Billy, affronted by the accusation.

"There must be some misunderstanding," Ullin offered, smiling at the little folk.

The blue-dressed one stepped forward and stood on a log to give himself some greater height.

"Misunderstanding, eh? Are these the coin of yer payment?" he held up two coins.

"Yes, they are," stated Billy, now crossing his own arms.

"Did ye think we would not count? Ye must pay the toll!"

"My apologies, sir," Robby said, stepping in front of Billy. "It was I who did the figuring. Perhaps I did not know the right amount to give in our coin for the amount you ask in yours. What is the worth of a mite in Realm silver?"

"One-sixth Realm silver, it is!"

"Is that not two silvers you hold there?"

"Of course, it is."

"Are there not six of us, then?" Robby asked with some confusion. "Twelve feet in all? And so, there you have twelve mites."

"Twelve feet? Twelve feet!" the little man nearly whistled, he screeched so high and nearly fell off of the log, so agitated he became, while all the others of his kind set to muttering and mumbling, and some even stamped their feet with impatience.

"Twelve *feet!*" he shrieked again while Robby, taken aback, looked to his companions in embarrassment and with some little anger beginning to boil within him.

"I don't understand."

"We do not count feet, ye silly creature! If we counted feet we would have to count every bug and flea, every slug and snail and ant, every chigger and fly that came along. Why, we would be picking yer hair and combing yer mane for lice and counting from here to doomsday! Forever it would take us to count all the mites!"

At this some of the little ones began to snigger and giggle, elbowing each other and winking. "Count all the mites! Get it? All the mites? Hee-hee-har-har-har!"

A glare from their leader stifled their mirth, and they bit their lips to halt their glee, trying to screw serious expressions back onto their faces.

"We count shoes!" he stated to Robby. "Shoes! Did ye not read the sign?"

"Yes, but we're wearing only two shoes each, including boots!" Robby countered.

"Do ye take me, Herbert the Blue, for a fool? For a nincompoop! For an ignoramus who does not know numbers!"

"Well, if you must know," whispered someone behind him, followed by some giggles and elbowing.

"Millithorpe! Millithorpe!"

"Oh, oh!" A wee man with spectacles, a green waistcoat, and an arm full of scrolls and parchments stepped up from the others. "Yes? Yes, Herbert?"

"Millithorpe! Did ye not give me a proper count?"

"Why, yes. Yes, of course. I did, indeed. Yes. I counted with care, sir. No one can count so as I can count! A mark for every one, added up, checked again, counted over. You know how thorough I am in these matters. Why, I even—"

"Yes, yes! Show me yer counting."

"Oh! Of course. Right here it is! Oh, my!" Millithorpe in his nervousness fumbled his bundles, dropped nearly every one, and more as he tried to pick them up.

"The count!"

"Yes. Here it is!"

"Show me!"

Millithorpe unfurled a long scroll.

"See? One with two, here. And two, likewise, making six. And six with six, here, with the rest making a score and a dozen, and two with four, making eight, with the previous, making two-score and four. And here is the second counting, making the same as the first," Millithorpe concluded as he got to the bottom of the length of scroll.

"Oh, oh be careful!" he cried as Herbert snatched it from his hands and held it up for Robby to see. Robby noted the many hen-scratches, the places where tick-marks were inked out and rewritten again, the stick-horse drawings along the margins, and the number, written with an exaggerated flourish, at the very bottom.

"Forty-four? Forty-four!" Robby exclaimed.

"Why, that includes the horses!" Ullin protested.

"Just so!" retorted Herbert. "Of course. Do they not wear shoes?"

Ashlord rolled his eyes, and Ullin shook his head reaching for his purse, saying, "Very well, then. How much remains to be paid in Realm silver?"

"Er, well, it'll be, er, Millithorpe! Tell them how much it is!"

"Yes, Herbert. Well. Let's see. Two mites as to one sixth Realm shilling, given forty-four less twelve, as one-score, one dozen shoes, no, wait. Take away…hmm."

"Will three more shillings pay the toll fee?" Robby asked.

"Why, yes, I would say. That is, yes, but—"

"Well, for the love of peace, take these!" Ullin held out three coins. Millithorpe took them, and examined them with care, then nodded to Herbert.

"Good. Now, then," Herbert said. "Before we leave ye to yer rest, there is just the matter of the fine."

"Fine?"

"What fine?"

Herbert rolled up his eyes in a mocking way.

"The rules were clearly stated: Cheaters Will Be Fined."

"But we paid!" Billy said, angrily.

"Oh, good grief!" Sheila uttered, throwing up her hands.

"How much is the fine?" Robby asked sternly.

"Millithorpe! The amount of the fine!"

Millithorpe, who had almost managed to get his scrolls rolled up again, now dropped them once more and hurried back over to Herbert.

"Oh, that's already figured, just here. No, wait, not that one, either," he patted his vest pocket, then his coat pockets, drawing out bits of parchment and scraps of paper until he at last found the right one. "Aha! Here it is. A complete list."

"Well? Read it out and let's be on with it!" Herbert ordered, giving a nod to the others, who gathered in closer.

"One pack and contents…"

"Ooh, here's one!" said a little yellow-vested one, darting over to the company's pile of packs. He put one hand on a strap, then snapped his fingers and POP!, he and the pack disappeared in a spray of glowing bubbles that quickly dissipated.

"What the…!" Billy cried.

Millithorpe read on.

"…and another pack and contents for measure…"

Pushing through, another little man grabbed another pack as big as he. "Got it!" he cried, and then vanished into a fountain of fading sparkles.

"Hold on there!" cried Ullin.

"This is thievery!" cried Robby.

"How dare ye!" said Herbert, crossing his arms.

"...two fine saddles," Millithorpe read, and before Ibin could block them, two more little ones popped away with a saddle each.

"Pixies!" cried Ashlord, lunging forward. "Grab them! Get hold of one!"

But they were too quick for Ashlord, and in a crackle of snapping fingers and blue bubbly glows, the crowd disappeared, leaving the company stumbling over each other as they tried to take hold of the last one, but only getting armfuls of fading twinkling light.

POP!

Herbert reappeared, standing on a nearby tree limb.

"Ye haven't fully paid. Read on, Millithorpe!" He snapped his fingers as Ullin hurried at him and, with a POP!, he was gone before Ullin could grab him.

POP! Millithorpe reappeared, at some distance and called out, "One good blanket!"

POP!

"...four sharp swords..."

POP! POP! POP! POP!

"...two strong horses..."

POP! POP!

Each time, Robby and the others tried to lay a hold onto the impish fellows, but with no luck as their belongings quickly dwindled away.

"...one brass buckle..."

POP! POP! Ibin's belt fell away, and, with out its support, his drawers dropped to his ankles.

"...and one sturdy walking stick!"

POP! Robby quickly undid Swyncraff and straightened it stiff. "Take this one, then!" he shouted at the orange-jacketed pixie who was reaching for Ashlord's walking stick. He hesitated, eyeing Robby suspiciously, then he looked at Swyncraff.

"Go on, if you must have one," Robby encouraged. "It's stronger than that one there."

"Yes, hmm. It appears so. I'll take it, then!"

As soon as he put his hand on it, Swyncraff snaked around the pixie's arm and held fast with Robby clutching the other end.

"Let go! Let go!" the pixie screamed.

Robby jerked on Swyncraff, pulling the fellow to him, and grabbed him hard by the ear.

"Ow! Ow! Owie!Owie!Owie!"

"Shut up!" Robby yelled. None of his party had ever seen Robby so angry or assertive. Sheila was shocked at the roughness with which

Robby handled the little one, especially now that he was also dodging kicks and bites from the pixie.

"Stop it!" Robby cried, letting go of the ear and drawing his sword. "Do as I say or I'll part your head from your shoulders!"

At this the little one dropped to his knees.

"Yes, yes! Oh, please! I beg, spare me! I'll do as ye say. Anything. Anything ye say!"

"Promise that you will speak truthfully and fully to me at all times!"

"Yes. I promise! An easy one, for we cannot tell a lie, oh that we could!"

"You will answer all of my questions."

"Yes. I promise. If it is in me knowledge, I will tell ye anything. Little though I know."

"You will not try to run away, and you will abide with me until I release you from my service."

"Oh! Yes. I am yer slave," he sniffed. "Please do not harm me, I beg!"

"Do not give me reason to and I will not. I promise," Robby said, releasing the pixie from Swyncraff's grip. The little one rubbed his wrist.

"It is a magic stick, ye have," the pixie protested. "A sorcerer ye are! We've trusted before in one such as ye, to our shame an' grief! He, too, offered life over death in return for service, an' we are cursed for takin' his offer."

"I am no sorcerer," said Robby. "Only an ordinary person, trying to find his way in the world. And, for my part," he went on, sheathing his sword, "I will not hurt you. I will treat you fairly. And, if it is in my means, I will reward you for faithful service."

At these last words, the little one looked up with a mixture of mistrust and hope in his face.

"Men lie," the little one said sheepishly. "Sometimes."

"Yes," Robby nodded. "And to be honest, I lied once, breaking an oath not to do so. I have also, at times, held back the full truth. But this I promise to you: that I will not lie to you, and I will treat you with all honesty and courtesy, as well as I may."

Robby held out his hand, "Are we agreed?"

The little one got to his feet and took Robby's hand.

"Little choice do I have," he said to Robby. "But I have given me promises, an' I'll keep them. I can only trust an' hope that ye'll keep yers."

"Good! What is your name?"

"I am called Eldwin."

"I am Robby, son of Robigor Ribbon. You may call me Robby. These are my friends, Sheila, Billy, and Ibin, of County Barley in the Eastlands. I am from Passdale, a town in that region, too. This is Ullin Saheed Tallin, a lord of Tallinvale, and Kingsman of Duinnor. And this is Ashlord, called Collandoth by the Elifaen. You need not fear any of them as long as you remain in my service. Is it in your power to return our belongings to us?"

"It is not. Yer things are held by others who will not relinquish them."

"Why do you need our things? Do you mean to sell them or keep them for your own use?"

"Oh, no! Nothing like that! It is long to explain."

Robby stood with his hands on his hips looking down at Eldwin, and he realized they had stumbled upon an unusual group of robbers. Thoughts of Makeig and his people ran through his head, making him wonder how they must have acted as highwaymen and how, even among them, there seemed a high sense of honor and loyalty. Perhaps there was more here, too. Robby nodded, sizing up the situation, and he forced himself to calm down. He realized that he would need patience to get to the bottom of all this.

The others of Robby's party looked on, anger and frustration still in their faces, and the impatient Billy was twice halted by Ashlord's gesture from speaking. They quickly came to understand that Ashlord wanted Robby to take charge of this situation. As they listened to Robby and Eldwin, their anger subsided somewhat, though Ullin was already considering how they might manage with only the remaining horses and supplies.

"Sit there, if you wish, and let's talk," Robby indicated a low tree limb. Eldwin held up his hand to snap his fingers and eyed Robby questioningly. Robby nodded, and, with a snap and a pop, the little one disappeared and instantly reappeared sitting on the limb. Robby seated himself on a nearby log so that the two were at eye level, and he motioned to Sheila.

"Could you see what food we may have?"

"There is little left but hard bread and some cheese."

"Then please bring my ration of it, if there is enough, and a cup of water, please." To the others, he said, "Perhaps you will leave Eldwin and me to speak for a bit?"

Ashlord nodded. "Come," he motioned to Billy and the others, "let us make a reckoning of what we have left to us."

They reluctantly moved away, and Robby turned back to Eldwin.

"Is there a name for your people? What do you call yourselves?" Robby asked.

"Some call us pixies," Eldwin said, glancing at Ashlord. "But we are not. We used to call ourselves Picathians, after the small valley we once called our home, Picathia, a place very far away in the southwest, north of Altoria. But we often think of ourselves as the Forgotten Ones."

"Why? Why are you forgotten? And who forgot about you?"

"Oh, sir! That is a long and sad tale, an' the reason for our sorry way of livin' today."

"Perhaps you will tell me the gist of it? And explain, too, why you treat travelers so meanly with tolls and fines?"

"We make our means by the means we have," replied Eldwin. "It is not how we always lived, an' it is no pleasure to us to live at the expense of others. We were once happy farmers an' herders, accomplished craftsmen an' artisans. As happy as any peaceful people who lived fairly in a fair land. It is cruel, sir, cruel! We stood in stature an' in accomplishment as proudly as any Men, an' traced our lines to the first ships of Men who landed on the eastern shores. Yet, look at us now! We are reduced to a wee an' shabby folk!"

Sheila came and handed Robby a cut of cheese and a hard biscuit along with a tin cup of water.

"That is all that can be spared you," she said. "And the same portion for each of the rest of us before all is gone."

"Thank you," he said to her, accepting the food and drink. She glanced at Eldwin and managed a weak smile as she turned to go. Eldwin watched as she sat nearby and pushed her hood from her head, revealing her entire face to him. At this, Eldwin drew in a sudden intake of air and held it, staring at her for a long moment before blinking at Robby.

Robby glanced over his shoulder at Sheila, then back at Eldwin.

"What is it?"

"Oh, forgive me, sir. But she is lovely," said Eldwin. "If ye pardon me, sayin'. In spite of her unusual manner of dress. Might she be someone special?"

"Yes. She is. This is all I have to offer you. It is not much, and you must soak the biscuit first. But the cheese is good."

Eldwin looked at Robby's offering, held out to him. He looked at Robby's face and blinked again.

"We may have nothing more for some time to come," Robby encouraged. Eldwin continued to blink, somewhat agitated, and Robby saw clearly that Eldwin still feared him, but there was some other emotion in the little one's face.

"I, I cannot eat before ye do so, since yer now me master," he said to Robby. "Though I thank ye."

"As long as you are in my service, you are my responsibility," Robby said. "And you look as hungry as any of us. This is only a trifle."

"A trifle is a treasure when that is all ye have!" blurted out Eldwin. "I should know!"

Robby shrugged and put the food aside. "Then tell me about it."

"Very well. Once, me people were as tall as any of ye. We were, indeed. We lived in a valley, as I said, to the south an' west of here, many, many leagues away. Not a rich people, but prosperous, nonetheless, by reason of our happiness an' the bounty of our work. We managed our affairs an' paid no tribute to any lord or king, yet neither did we take part in any of the wars that raged between the Elifaen an' the Dragon Peoples. Our only protection was that we were insignificant in numbers an' our valley difficult to find. Yet, one day, found we were.

"A stranger appeared among us one winter day, a sorcerer or conjurer or some other unnatural bein' he was, callin' himself Bailorg."

At this, Robby's company perked up, and Robby tried to remain expressionless as Eldwin went on.

"He foretold to us the comin' of an army of Dragonkind to do battle in the northeast. He told us that if we placed ourselves under his service, he would see to it that we would be spared, though our lands may be ravaged, an' we would have to leave them for a time. He said that he was a lord among the Elifaen an' yet an ally to Men, too, an' that he had forged a pact with the Dragon King so that he had some influence among the Dragon King's generals. Though his words were soft an' his tongue full of hope, we did not believe him, an' we doubted what he said.

" 'One day,' he said to us, 'one day only shall I give ye to decide.' An' he left us in a cloud made of foul smoke an' disappeared from our eyes. That night, word came to our chief men that, indeed, an army approached our valley. We were told that a village not distant from ours was taken, an' all its people were slain or were marched off to the far southern wastelands to be slaves of the Sun King. We were in a panic an' did not know what to do. Some of us tried to flee, but our valley was surrounded by the Dragonkind soldiers. Others wanted to fight, but we had no weapons, no knowledge of how to use them, an', anyway, our numbers were too few. So when the sorcerer reappeared the next day, we had little choice but to give our oath of service to him.

"There was an old crone there, a witch some said, who lived on the far side of our valley. She came among us as we were about to swear our promise to the sorcerer.

" 'Give not yer oath to this traitor of Vanara!' she cried out. 'Enemy of earth an' sky, servant of Secundur! Never shall ye see yer home again! Fie upon his promises!'

" 'Be still old woman!" cried the sorcerer. "Do not speak to me, Bailorg, in such a manner! What choice do these people have but to live in me service, with some hope, or to die by the Dragonkind?'

" 'Hope! Ye speak of hope, yet offer only the choice of slavery an' death! Fight, I say! Fight as others do! Defy this one an' his scaly allies!'

" 'Silence!' roared Bailorg, an' there was a great rumblin' behind his voice, as the thunder rumbles on the hills. There was a mighty strivin' between the two. Bailorg took something from a little sack that he carried, an' when he threw it on the ground dark clouds boiled down from the sky an' lightnin' split the air all around us. So afraid were we that we could not even run away. The old crone, who now appeared as a young woman in flowin' gauze, cried out in a foreign tongue, an' the lightnin' blinded us. But when the thunder rolled away an' the fog lifted, there stood in her place a gnarled, leafless willow tree, its branches bent an' stark.

" 'See the fate of those who oppose me!' cried Bailorg. Of course we were terrified an' gave our oath immediately, just as the Dragonkind army swarmed down over the rim of our valley. But Bailorg kept his word an' stood before the fearsome horde an' spoke with their generals. They spared us, but only so long as we remained in Bailorg's service an' did his biddin'."

Robby listened carefully as he lit his pipe. Eldwin produced one of his own and, with the same burning faggot from the fire that Ashlord had built, Robby lit Eldwin's pipe. They puffed for a moment until the briars were well kindled.

"Please continue," Robby said.

"Of the next months there is not much to tell, except to say that they were cruel an' hard. We were made to wear plain gray sackcloth, so that the Dragonkind would know us to be the servants of Bailorg an' would not slay us. We were made to carry the supplies for the army, an' so followed it eastward across the plain an' then unto these mountains. Many times along the way we crossed over gory fields of battle. Gruesome sights we saw! Our women an' children, too. All of us were beasts of burden, bearin' their foods, pullin' their wagons of arms, an' buildin' fires for them when camps were made.

"Once, on a battlefield within sight of these mountains, I came across a dyin' Eastlander soldier, somehow missed by the slaughterin' lizardmen who surrounded an' guarded us. I stopped to offer him a sip of water from me flask. Me friends stood around so as to shield the two of us from view as I held his head an' gave him to drink."

Eldwin paused, staring into his pipe's bowl.

"I have not spoken of him for a long time," he said. "Some life came into his eyes, an' I believe he perceived the risk we took for him. He managed a weak smile, an' with his last breath he said to me, 'May the blessin' of Beras be upon thee.' An' he pressed into me hand this locket."

Eldwin tugged at a chain and drew from under his shirt a round locket made of gold, enameled with green and blue, and studded with a white gem encircled by seven tiny rubies. Robby recognized it immediately as the same sort his father had shown him on the day he set out for Tulith Attis. On such a little fellow as Eldwin, it seemed quite large and weighty as he dangled it before him.

"Ye've seen one of these before?" Eldwin asked, seeing Robby's expression.

"Yes. Once. It contained within a small braid of hair."

"This, too, though I will not open it unless ye insist."

Robby shook his head, and Eldwin carefully placed it back under his shirt.

"He died. An' we left him as our guards approached to hurry us along. I came to learn that lockets such as this were given to young soldiers in those days by their mothers or their betrothed, as a token an' reminder of the love they hoped would sustain their men an' bring them safely through battle an' back home again. We gathered many such lockets. Not as treasure or booty, mind ye. Oh, no! As a way of defyin' our keepers.

Some of us hoped to someday return them to those who gave them, for many have inscriptions namin' the giver. But, alas! That was not to be.

"Our masters, set upon us by Bailorg, drove us into the mountains, many miles north of here. That was long before the Galinots were in those lands, an' few lived in these parts other than the trolls, who were friend to no one, Dragon, Man, or Faerekind. The deeper into the mountains we came, the more often we were raided by the trolls at night. But they were clumsy an' unorganized an' seldom posed much of a threat to the Dragon soldiers. Meanwhile, the armies of the Elifaen, with Men among their ranks, constantly harassed us, layin' the most cunnin' ambushes an' traps, but rarely meetin' the Dragonkind in open battle. An' so we pressed eastward.

"It snowed, an' all the rest of that winter we moved through the mountains. Some of our people froze to death for lack of shelter. Some slipped an' fell to their death, for there were few roads back then, an' we made the paths we took. We were fed the vilest gruel, askin' not what it was made of. But it sustained us, an' as we neared the edge of the mountains, our burdens were lighter because the food an' supplies ran low. Up until then, more slaves joined us as more were captured. But as we cleared the mountains, the Dragonkind took no more prisoners, an' those of us under the protection of Bailorg fared better than the others who were taken, for only we who wore the gray sackcloth were given anything to eat.

"By late winter we came to a place called Dalefath where there was a bridge over a river, which Bailorg called the Peninflo. We crossed over the bridge into a wood where we were put to work cuttin' down trees an' haulin' logs. This was cruel work, an' whips were used to prod us into haste, even though we were weak. Many of me people died from exhaustion, or broken bodies, or sometimes broken hearts.

"They made us take the wood to the edge of a plain where I saw that other armies had joined ours, an' where there a great industry of buildin'. There were smithies an' armorers everywhere an' carpenters at work in many places. The smoke from the forges an' camp fires was as thick as the ringin' of anvils an' the thuddin' of mallets. Some of our logs were used to feed their furnaces an' others to build engines of war. Rams were made, shod with iron, towers, an' ballistas, too, an' many other things, all in preparation for some awful battle.

"One day, I was made to carry some of these implements far forward, an' I saw, at the far side of the plain, a great fortress on a steep hill, an' before it a mighty battle ragin'. At the base of the hill on which the fortress stood an' all around its walls were the devices that we by our labor had built. I saw tall towers out of which streamed flamin' arrows thick as rain upon the fortress. There were hordes of Dragonkind, thousands an' thousands, advancin' with long pikes, the shafts of which we had cut from saplings in the forest. Ballistas an' catapults launched deadly missiles through the air, red with trailing fire. Missiles that our own hands an' sweat had provided.

"With one eye, I watched me task, an' with the other the strivin' of the Dragon armies against those who defended the walls. I saw a tumult of armored horsemen pour into the Dragonkind ranks, an' with great slaughter they drove deep through line after line of attackers. Behind them came red-cloaked footmen, wieldin' swords an' lances and battleaxes, hewin' through the Dragonkind as wheat before the sickle. Great confusion fell upon the battlefield, an' the vile engines of siege were torched an' the towers overturned into ruins. I was hurried away with me keepers an' the other men of me people who also assisted. Though I was terrified, me heart sang in delight at every Dragonkind that fell. It seemed we were in a general retreat, an' in the confusion I an' the others with me were blocked by convergin' lines of Dragonkind at the edge of the plain. It was there that a great moan was heard risin' from the battlefield behind us. Turnin', we saw Dragonkind upon the walls of the fortress. They were fightin' the defenders an' throwin' many over the walls to be dashed on the rocks below. By some vile device, they had anticipated the moves of the defenders an' counterattacked, an' by some devious means must have breached the gates of the fortress. All was lost. Me an' me friends wept as the most horrible massacre began.

"I was made to retell what I saw when I reached the camp of me people that evening. Hardly had I ended my story when Bailorg appeared an' took away half our number, while the rest of us were set to buildin' wagons an' repairin' packs to hold the booty that was to be brought away. That night we worked, amid the sounds of revelry most vile, for many prisoners were taken for sport. I'll never forget that night, an' I still have nightmares about it.

"Nigh upon dawn, the rest of our party returned to us, with Bailorg an' his private company of Dragonkind. An' two others were with them, one was the general of the army, an' the other a cloaked figure. His hood was pulled over his awful black helmet. I could see by his build that he was not one of the Dragon people. But whether he was a Man or Elifaen, I cannot say. His armor was different, too. Black iron, with a red sandglass painted on his breastplate. He an' the general exchanged a few brief words, an' then the general departed, an' Bailorg commenced directin' us at the loadin' of the wagons an' carts. The shadowy figure remained on his horse, an' though he said nothing an' did nothing, we felt his baleful eyes upon us, an' we feared him above the whips of our drivers."

"Who was he?" Robby asked.

"I never learned," Eldwin answered, looking at the others, seated at a respectful distance and listening carefully. At this last mentioning of the mysterious figure, they glanced at each other and sat more rigidly. "I see ye've some interest in me tale. Could it be ye know something of these things? Perhaps the battle at Tulith Attis has not been forgotten?"

"You are perceptive," Robby said. "The reasons for our interest would be too long in the telling, except to say that the battle is still remembered, and the troubles of the world today go back to those times and has to do with why we travel this way. Tell me, did you notice anything else about this person who came with Bailorg? Any clue as to who he was? Do you know if he was part of the Dragonkind army's company, or was he already at Tulith Attis when the battle began?"

"I cannot say, an' do not know. He was certainly not a prisoner or any such. Bailorg was extremely anxious about him an' kept reportin' our progress to him. But he never spoke to Bailorg or answered his reports so far as I ever saw or heard. He remained completely silent behind his black helmet. We felt he was Bailorg's master, or someone even more fearful. None of me own people had anything to do with him, not even to cook or bring him food or water over the next days. He led us, with Bailorg, back into these mountains, an' we traveled with great haste, pullin' the wagons as fast as we could, havin' been spared no oxen or horses, ye see, except the mounts that these two rode. A few days after we left there, a messenger came to Bailorg, an' afterwards he made his Dragonkind servants whip us into even greater haste. A week later, we were movin' along a road through the mountains when a Dragonkind came runnin' to Bailorg in a mighty agitation. Bailorg ordered us along a side path, an' after a mile or so, made us gather in a forest clearing. There was only about seventy of us left, men, women, an' children, an' we crowded together with the carts an' packs, relieved to be able to rest whatever the reason for it was. We could see Bailorg pleadin' with the strange one, but could not tell what was the trouble. The dark figure seemed unperturbed, an' Bailorg kept gesturin' at us an' at the wagons of booty. Something was afoot, of course, but we could not make out Bailorg's speech. The dark one then turned an' slowly rode away into the forest. Bailorg watched him disappear into the trees, an' then he turned to us full of anger.

" 'If ye value yer lives, ye'll remain silent!' He made a thick fog come about us, though it was a clear day. 'Soldiers will shortly pass nearby,' he told us. 'They will kill all they find without mercy, an' I cannot protect ye from them.'

" 'Ye ain't done much protectin' so far!' muttered Finniar, a sturdy blacksmith of me village. We noticed the Dragonkind had disappeared, too, slinkin' away into the fog, an' we began to talk among ourselves about what to do.

" 'Silence, I say!' cried Bailorg.

" 'Why should we be quiet?' shot back Berralasa, who is now Herbert the Blue's wife.

" 'Fools! Do ye not hear the drums?'

"Indeed, a throbbin' echoed through the hills an' grew louder as it approached.

" 'It is the armies of the west, comin' to do battle with the Dragonkind!'

" 'Good!,' cried one of the youngsters. 'Let them come!'

" 'Let them smite all of the lizard folk!' called another.

" 'Aye!'

" 'Idiots! Imbeciles! Do ye think they will spare even one of ye when they see what it is ye carry? Spoils of Tulith Attis, bearin' the mark of Lord Heneil's House? They will kill ye outright or hunt ye down, each an' every one, without mercy, sparin' not women nor children.'

" 'At least there will be an end to it! For ye'll never grant our freedom, an' have never intended to do so!'

"All the while, as the sounds of the armies grew louder an' nearer, we grew bolder an' more desperate.

" 'Let us give them Bailorg!' someone shouted, an' at once many of us made at him. But he was strong an' we were weak from hunger an' tired from our labors. He smote us with his magic stick, an' curled it about our raised arms an' flung us away like twigs. I think we went mad at last as we screamed at him, tryin' to claw or scratch him, an' we even threw rocks at him in our fury. All the while an' all around us could be heard the drummin' of war drums an' the stampin' of feet an' the clinkin' of armor as armies passed to our left an' to our right. But no soldier appeared among us either to save or to slay us. Bailorg, retreatin' a few steps, pulled something from a pouch at his belt an' he threw it upon the ground, an' he stirred a mighty storm out of the clouds. Rain fell hard an' cold, an' lightnin' grazed all around, an' hailstones pelted us an' beat us back.

"Then Bailorg drew a bolt of lightnin' to his staff an' held it, an' with the other hand pointed at us sayin', 'Obey me, or ye will never leave this wood!'

"But we were still defiant, an' one cried out, 'We will never again do yer biddin'!'

" 'Until pigs grow in trees!' cried another.

" 'As ye wish, then! Curses be upon ye! To bind ye to spoken fates! Curses three! One by me, two by the next who pass this way. Mine is thus: Ye shall never leave this wood or pass beyond these mountains until all memory of ye has been forgotten an' me body withers upon a pyre of me own makin'! Never, I say, until pigs grow in trees! Let the other curses, two, come from the mouths of passersby. So be it!'

"He released the lightnin' with a mighty clap of thunder. When our sight came back to us, Bailorg was gone. We were still in a terror, an' the sound of the passin' armies was all around us. We knew not whether to run to them or hide ourselves, an' so we did neither, but huddled together, some cryin', some shushin' those that made noise.

"It took hours an' hours for the armies to pass, but when their sound faded away, the fog lifted an' with it our hearts lifted also. For the first time in what seemed forever, we were free of Bailorg. We set on our way, but the curse he laid upon us was no idle threat. When we had walked a long way, the fog came back, an' we lost our way until we came again upon the carts an' wagons we had left behind. So we set out again, thinkin' we had turned ourselves around in the unknown forest. But again we only found our way back to where we started. No matter which way we turned or which path we took, we came into a fog just as each time before, an' each time came back to where we began.

"The next day we tried again. Three times we tried, an' three times again we came back to where we had started from. At last, we found a place near a stream where there were fish that we could catch an' eat. For weeks, we camped, an' each day we would try again to leave. Each time with the same result as before. Months went by, an' we were a poor, starvin', an' sad lot. But we did not give up tryin'. Each day, we tried. Spring passed to summer, an' summer bore on into fall. Gradually, we began tryin' to leave these lands less often, once a week, maybe, or twice a month. In the place near the stream, we fashioned crude shelters, we fished an' ate nuts an' roots. But we never stopped tryin' to leave, all of us goin' together, holdin' hands so as not to be separated from one another. An' each time, regardless of which direction we traveled, we always came into a fog, then wound up back where those wagons were.

"Then, on a fall day, when we tried again an' failed again, there was a tall man, standin' at the wagons, lookin' at the things therein with a ghastly expression on his face. He was dressed as a soldier, in armor an' helmet, an' when he saw us, he drew his sword an' made at us.

" 'Did ye bring this booty here?' he demanded. His aspect was fierce an' his blue eyes, I remember, were fired with anger, an' his voice was so full of rage that we shook in our worn-out boots an' fell to our knees.

" 'Answer me! This goblet, bearin' the mark of me comrade Heneil, did ye take this from Tulith Attis?'

" 'Yes, lord. But we were forced by Bailorg an' the Dragonkind as their slaves.'

" 'Looters! Traitors!'

" 'No, lord!' we cried to him. 'We were made to do so. We were forced to haul these things an' are cursed because we refused to carry them further!'

"In a gush of babble we all tried to explain, but he made to strike the nearest to him.

" 'Stop!' Suddenly there was a woman on a buckmarl at the edge of the clearing. 'Stop, I say!' she cried again. He did stop, but did not lower his sword.

" 'A pack of thieves!' he said harshly to her. 'Looters of our slain brothers an' their families. They are not worthy of sparin', even as prisoners.'

" 'Look at them, Navis! Do they have the look of an enemy?'

"It was true, we were a pitiful sight, I'm sure. Our clothes were tatters an' rags, an' we were lean an' sick from our long toil, with the wounds of our mistreatment, an' with hunger.

" 'How did ye come to be here?' she asked, an' we all spoke at once until she raised her hand an' pointed to me, nearest to her. When her golden eyes rested on mine, I thought I would burst with desperation, an' me heart caught in me throat. Never have I seen so beautiful a woman, nor so terrible in her beauty. 'You,' she said to me, 'You tell the tale.'

" 'Oh ma'am, I have but a poor manner of speech, an' our tale is too sorrowful for me words, an' the things we have seen too terrible for me to tell.' But she looked at me with compassion, an' then the tale flowed out of me in truthful words, fair to our ordeal.

"But the one she called Navis only spat.

" 'Fie! Fie an' lies!'

" 'No. I do not think so,' she told him.

" 'Then cursed they are! A little people, unwillin' to stand up to evil. Without courage to fight or flee! Petty an' small!'

"As he screamed at us we indeed grew smaller an' smaller until the rags that were our clothing fell away from us, an' we tripped in our shoes, an' we cowered, tryin' to hide our nakedness.

" 'An' 'til these things are returned to their heir,' he cried, 'with a thousand times their worth, a little people ye shall remain!'

"He spat upon the ground an' stamped his foot on the place, strode to his horse an' rode away, leavin' us all cryin' an' wailin' as never before, bemoanin' our condition, much reduced in stature, just as ye see us now. An' we mourned our fate, cryin' to Aperion, King of the Faere, to hear us an' to save us from this fate, an' to Beras, creator of the world, to deliver us from our calamity.

" 'Will ye not lift these curses from us, good lady?' I pleaded. 'How are we to live like this? How are we to keep ourselves from the wild animals of this wood, to feed an' clothe ourselves? How are we to find a thousand times the worth of this treasure if we cannot even leave this wood?'

" 'I do not have it in me power to lift the curses on ye,' she told us. 'An' it seems it is me fate to lay one more against ye. This curse I make: So that ye may suffer the fullness of yer punishment, the passin' of years will leave but little mark upon ye. Yet, I am touched by yer tale. This blessing I give, so that ye may have hope of overcomin' yer fate: Ye shall have no hindrance travelin' about this land, an' ye shall learn the art of movin' from place to place with quickness an' in a twinklin', though yer legs are small an' yer stride be as a child. So like a child, these fates against ye may over time be lessened, as the memory of distant pain. It is now upon ye to make yer way henceforth as do all the meek an' lowly creatures of the world. Yet, if only ye keep yer hearts alive, resolved in providence, of a time these fates may no longer seem such a burden. Fail in this faith, an' be forever the way ye are now, in form an' in favor, in spirit an' in sense. So be it!' An' then she turned away," Eldwin concluded, "an' disappeared into the mist."

Robby watched him drag the last puff from his pipe and tap it out.

"The battle of Tulith Attis was a long time ago," Robby said.

"Yes, it was. An' we have not found the means to break the curses upon us. Those first years were very hard, an' so as to clothe ourselves an' have tools we fell to thievin' an' robbery, our victims bein' any who passed this way. The lady's curse remained a mystery to us until we learned that, by snappin' our fingers, we could travel to any place within sight in only an eyeblink, as long as the place was not beyond our wood an' was a place we could otherwise walk, jump, swim, or climb to. By this means, we may quickly move about our wood, makin' our escape when needed, from animals or people. We could also steal without regard or warnin' to our victims."

"Then why the toll road? Why did you not just take what you desired from us?"

"It was in our heads to someday repay from those we robbed all that we took. An' so we chose Herbert to be our leader an' Millithorpe to make a reckonin' of all we took, that portion used for ourselves an' that that we put aside for repayment. When three years had passed, the lady returned to us an' appeared out of the mist of winter. But she was covered with cloaks an' rode alone, an' we did not recognize her when we waylaid her. When she drew back her hood an' cloak, we saw who it was."

Eldwin glanced over at Sheila, who was listening intently, just as her companions were. Robby looked her way, too, wondering at Eldwin's odd expression. But Eldwin shook his head and continued.

" 'Indeed, Lord Navis was right,' the lady said with anger in her voice. 'Thieves, justly deservin' the curse he laid upon ye.' "

"We explained that we had no other way to obtain the things we needed, or the riches required to add a thousand-fold worth to the treasure, except by takin' from passersby.

" 'Ye must start again,' she told us. 'All that ye've taken, since I was last here, must first be given away, freely an' not in trade for any other thing. When that is done, ye must find some way that is fair an' with honor. If any passerby gives ye anything, it must be by their own agreement. Otherwise, ye must render payment by yer own toil an' the work of yer own hands. That is the only way to meet the demands of yer fate. I will come again once more, when the time of repayment is nigh. Heed what I have said!' "

"Then she left us, an' we have not seen her since," Eldwin said, looking again toward Sheila.

"What is the lady's name?"

"We never asked her," Eldwin said. "We were too afraid to ask, though she is anything but frightful in appearance." Eldwin glanced at Sheila. "She never told us her name," he added.

Robby looked over his shoulder at the others, wondering whether Billy was doing something that was distracting Eldwin.

"We heeded her words, though it was hard," Eldwin went on, "especially since the winter was upon us. We made the changes, slowly, heapin' our booty upon any who chanced by, as much as they could carry away. Eventually, Herbert the Blue came up with the notion of the toll an' with a sign statin' the rules. Few people travel this way, an' fewer, still, who cheat. But our people are hard workers, an', to tell ye the truth, I think doin' things the right way, above-board, like, makes yer work lighter than it might otherwise be. So, since the lady last came, we've managed fairly well. We have a little town, we farm, an' we've found iron with which we make tools. We've traded for cloth an' beer an' various other goods. Up until about twenty years ago, a young trader named Furaman came through right regular, every spring an' fall. We don't know why he stopped comin', unless it was the Damar that took over the surroundin' parts. Still, the toll road remains our main way of obtainin' coin of silver, gold, an' copper, an' addin' to the worth of the Hoard, as we call it. But the lady has not returned, an' so must have forgotten about us. An' that's why we think of ourselves as a forgotten people."

"What do you do with the other things you collect?"

"Well, as I said, some of it we use. The rest, once counted, goes into the store with all the other things. Problem is, we don't rightly know the worth of things anymore. Why, a boot may be as valuable as a button, for all we know. Or a fine necklace as precious as a jug of beer. So as to not take chances, we collect a bit of everything we can."

"And where do you put it all?"

"In a cave. Someday, we may learn to tally the worth an' know how much more we may need. But the Hoard, the treasure, is of prodigious value, surely, so we keep on addin' our meager things, even though we haven't much hope of matchin' its value, much less addin' a thousand-fold worth to it."

"Billy!" Robby suddenly turned and startled his friend. "Who is the best person for reckoning the worth of things in all of Barley and Passdale?"

Billy appeared puzzled by the question. "Why, that'd be yer ol' man, as everbody well knows."

"And who, when it comes to reckoning trade goods, might be second best?"

"Well, that's easy, too, since it's yer own self. A reg'lar chip off the ol' block, as ever'one says."

The others looked as puzzled as Billy. Robby turned back to Eldwin.

"There you have it, and Billy is right, if I say so myself," he said to the little man. "If you give us back our things, I will, in exchange, reckon a fair and honest account of the things in your Hoard. To the very best of my ability."

"Oh? Hm. That sounds like a good trade, if ye can truly do it. It is a prodigious great number of things. Though, I regret to say, not near a thousand times the original booty carried from Tulith Attis."

"Will you take my offer to your people?"

"If that is what ye wish."

"Very well," Robby said, standing. "But, be warned: If you or any of your people play any kind of trick on us, or seek to deceive us in any way whatsoever, I will do my utmost to repay the treachery without mercy. Do you understand me?"

Robby spoke with such authority that new fear filled Eldwin's eyes. Robby's friends were amazed, too. Sheila, especially, was troubled and marveled at him, but said nothing.

"Yes."

"And will you make your people understand what I say?"

"Yes, I will."

"Then go to them now. Return with their answer with all haste. I cannot wait long for a reply."

"Very well, sir. I promise."

Robby nodded. Eldwin snapped his fingers, and in the dimming light the odd glow of his disappearance seemed to linger a long while. Robby turned to the others who were sitting or reclining nearby.

"I'll do the best I can to get back our things," Robby told them. "If they accept the offer."

"That was an interesting tale he told. If it is true," said Ullin.

"I have no doubt that it is true," commented Ashlord. "For I have heard a similar tale from another about the inhabitants of these lands, but never knew precisely where they lived. And we now know a little more about Bailorg."

"D'ye think the feller what came away from Haven Hill with Bailorg was the traitor?" asked Billy.

"Most likely. But little more do we know about him."

"Whowas, whowasthe lady?" asked Ibin.

"That is a good question, Ibin."

Ashlord drew on his pipe and said nothing else, returning Robby's expectant look with one of his own which told Robby that the mystic had likely surmised the lady's identity but would keep it to himself.

"It seems we'll be here awhile," Robby said as he sat beside Ashlord.

"It appears so. First, waiting for Eldwin's return, and longer, should they accept your offer."

"I suppose so," Robby sighed. "But we won't get far without our supplies. And, well, they have the upper hand."

"It will work out, I am sure, one way or the other."

"I hope so."

Chapter 16

The Treasure Hoard

They waited. After a while, Billy and Ibin snoozed, and the others eventually stretched out, too, until only Ashlord and Robby remained awake. Through the night they watched and waited and spoke very little. In the long hour before dawn, two pops were heard, and two forms appeared before them in a spray of soft blue, effervescent light.

"Are ye the one called Robby?" Herbert asked in a tone that, though gruff, indicated some nervousness.

"I am."

"And ye would do an accountin' of our things, fair an' honest, for the return of yer fine?"

"I will."

"Then, on yer word, an' on the condition that only ye may come into our place, we agree."

"I will come alone only if food and drink are brought to my comrades, and if they are well taken care of and protected from harm while I am away."

"I told ye he would not abandon his friends," said Eldwin to Herbert.

"Very well. Ye will come with us. We will put Eldwin in charge of ye an' yer friends. He will see to it, by me own authority, that yer friends are taken care of an' that ye make a proper accountin' for us. We hold ye both responsible," Herbert added, turning from Eldwin to Robby, who both nodded in return.

Robby slung Swyncraff about his waist and it tied itself into a neat knot, making a further impression on both of the little men. Herbert emitted an odd noise, almost a whimper, and then gruffly said, "Come along, then."

Herbert snapped his fingers and disappeared as Eldwin held out his hand. Robby took it, and at Eldwin's snap, a blur of soft light enveloped him and then faded. They now stood on the path.

"Oh!" Robby said, just as Eldwin snapped his fingers again. Again, they reappeared on the path, farther along where there was a clearing, and Eldwin craned his head, setting his eyes on the top of a little hill that jutted up about a furlong away. The next thing Robby knew, he was standing there.

"Oh. Oh, my!" He felt an odd sensation in his body, as if he had just come to rest after a stroll.

"What ye feel is natural, but takes some gettin' used to," Eldwin explained. "We call it 'poppin',' an' it only works if we can see where we intend to go. If our destination is uphill or far away, the more our bodies feel it. Almost as if we had actually walked some of the distance at a leisurely pace."

"I see." Robby felt a little dizzy, but tried to hide his discomfort.

"It took years for us to discover this power an' all that we can an' cannot do with it. It is a blessing, oh yes! One given by the fair lady. Just a few more pops to go."

Eldwin eyed a hill in the far distance and next they were there, standing on its bare top.

"Look there," Eldwin pointed downward. Below and partially hidden by nearby tree limbs, Robby could see a fair-sized town, with well laid out rows of cottages and other buildings. There was some activity in what Robby took to be the town square, and a man, he noticed, was going about snuffing out the lamps that lined the streets. Dawn was breaking, and in the morning mists beyond the town were fields in orderly terraces climbing the hillsides, along with thatch-roofed farmhouses and barns.

"What do you call this place?" Robby asked.

"We call it Nowhere."

"Oh? Well, it's an apt name, I suppose. But it looks as though your people have made a good home that would be the envy of other places I have seen."

"Perhaps. It is kind of ye to say so, anyway. An', of course, the generations born here do call it home, though we Elders do not."

"How many of you are there?"

"Of the one thousand an' seven hundred who were taken away by Bailorg, there remains of us only sixty-one. There are now many generations of offspring, though we have few children. We number altogether nearly two an' a half thousand, accordin' to Millithorpe. Shall we continue?"

"Certainly."

They landed in the town square. As Robby looked around, he was surrounded by hundreds of Nowhereans. To the south, Robby could see the hilltop where he had stood only moments before, towering steeply over the multicolored forest at its base. The shoulders of the hill stretched into those to the east and west so that on the opposite side, gentle south-facing slopes ran upwards in the neat patterned fields he had just viewed from above.

"Here is the one who will make the accounting," said Herbert to the crowd, none of whom were much taller than Robby's elbow. Turning, he saw the blue-coated one standing on a dais. "We are assured that we have nothing to fear, an' we have given promises in exchange for his. Let it be known that he is to be treated respectfully an' as a guest while he is here. Eldwin the Elder will be his guide. His companions are not to be molested an' are not to be visited by any except those who are appointed to do so. This one, called Robby Ribbon, is to give us a true an' fair reckoning of the Great Hoard, so that we may better strive for the breaking of our curses an' relieve our people of the injustices brought upon us by our fate. Do not hamper him, but give him all assistance that he or Eldwin may request. Otherwise, go about yer business an' yer chores as usual an' in peace. So be it!"

"Now," he continued, facing Robby, "Eldwin may take ye to the Hoard where Millithorpe awaits."

Robby bowed to Herbert, a gesture that seemed to impress Herbert by the look of his swelling, and then he turned to Eldwin, who led him through the crowd. They did not exactly look friendly, Robby thought, but their expressions did not reveal to him any threat or hint of deceit, either. Rather, it seemed that they watched him with some concern and, perhaps, hope. Some did smile. And others bowed as he passed. Though Robby himself was not very tall, he towered over them, and his head was well above the doorways of the houses and buildings they passed. Unlike the group that came with Herbert, most of the people were plainly dressed in working clothes, though clean, and most had some article that was gaily colored, a red cap, a yellow scarf, or blue bodice. The buildings, too, were colorful, with brightly painted doors and shutters, and Robby thought he had never seen a place so neat and trim.

"I am quite impressed with your town," Robby said. "You have worked very hard, I can see."

"Thank ye. Yes, we have. These mountains are rich in minerals an' game, plants, an' fish that we have learned to make use of. We have few cattle or poultry, but we do have some swine. Meat is precious. We have, through trade, gained seed for our crops. An' there are wild grapes we have learned to cultivate, among many other things once only found wild. By the time our trade ended with the one called Furaman, we were obtainin' through him such niceties as fabric an' some metals, such as tin an' copper. We have ample iron. Since Furaman stopped comin', we have had very little news from outside of our lands, an' have done without much trade."

"How long ago was that?"

"Around twenty years or so, I think."

"And do you often encounter the Damar?"

"Not so much any more," Eldwin stated with a slight smile. "We gained a good number of horses an' a lot of steel from them. They tend to avoid our roads, now."

While they walked southward toward the base of the cliffs, the houses thinned, and they entered a smoothly paved path rising through a wooded stretch. Soon they came to a clearing and before them yawned the wide opening of a cave.

"This is where we keep the Great Hoard."

Even before they entered the cave, Robby could see that it was well lit by oil lamps burning brightly within. The room they entered was about forty feet high, nearly as wide and about twice as deep. It fanned out into many passages at the rear that curved away and out of sight. There were shelves and racks and boxes and chests stacked up all around the sides of the room, and to the right side was an area with tables and desks. Sitting at one was Millithorpe who, seeing them enter, sprang up and hurried to them.

"Hullo to you!" he said. "I am Millithorpe, as you may recall."

"I am Robby."

"So I know! So I know! Since I heard of your coming, I have been busy putting our last accounts in order and preparing a place for you to work."

Millithorpe motioned them to the table. It had been thoughtfully propped up on four chests to suit Robby's greater height, and a hastily made stack of other chests were pushed together for a bench. There were bottles of ink, jars of quills, and a lamp giving strong light to the table. Behind the table were rows and rows of shelves filled with books and scrolls.

"These are our accounts," Eldwin said. "Kept by Millithorpe to the best of his ability these many years."

"Please, let me show you," said Millithorpe.

He showed Robby two sets of books. One set contained an inventory of each item in the Hoard in chronological order of its acquisition. The other set was divided into categories. There was one for coin and treasure, another for weapons, one for housewares, one for tools, raw materials, and so forth and so on. Robby paled a little as he realized the extent of the collection of goods, and even before opening one of the books, he realized his task would take considerable time.

"Let us begin with the sundries," said Robby. Millithorpe opened the ledger and stood aside expectantly. Robby stared for a moment at the page before him, glanced at Millithorpe and Eldwin, then slowly turned page after page, trying to grasp the scope of his undertaking. There were all sorts of lists and tick-marks and flourishes without meaning, and the margins were filled with scribbles, many blotted out or scratched over. Biting his tongue, he felt his face redden with a mixture of anger and frustration.

"Let us have a peek at the weapons ledger, now," he said, making an effort to sound confident and relaxed. It was in no better shape, nor any clearer. Neither was the housewares ledger, or, in fact, any of the rest that were handed to Robby, who examined them one by one. He quickly understood the variety of things collected for the Hoard, but after an hour of study, he was no closer to knowing the quantity or condition of any of the goods than he was when he began, due to the truly abysmal tallying. In spite of his effort not to show any emotion, Millithorpe and Eldwin sensed Robby's concern, and they were no longer smiling.

"Well?" Millithorpe asked cautiously.

Robby closed the ledger and sat back against the makeshift back rest.

"This will take longer than I imagined," he said.

"The Hoard is large," Eldwin put forward.

"I suppose it is," Robby began.

"It is not a proper accounting!" Millithorpe blurted out, crestfallen. "I know I have not done things right. I have done my best, according to my ability. Oh, my! Herbert will be furious! I told him I was a poor choice. Years and years ago, I told him."

He wrung his hands and paced around in circles.

"Now, now," Eldwin consoled him. Then to Robby, "Is it all that bad?"

Robby scrunched up his face, shrugging, and tried to find the right thing to say.

"As far as it goes," he started. Millithorpe looked up as if he was bracing for some sharp blow. "It is not how I was taught to do things," Robby finally said. "And I will have some trouble making out your methods on my own. But with your help, Millithorpe, perhaps we can do this accounting together."

"With my help? Oh! Oh, yes! Do you mean? Why, yes. Certainly. Whatever I can do. Yes, good gracious, yes!"

"And we may need the help of others, too."

"I can arrange that," said Eldwin. "How do we begin?"

"Well, first, my companions may be growing hungry."

"Of course. I'll see to them right away."

"Good. In that case, I'll need plenty of paper and ink."

"We have bales of paper!" said Millithorpe. "Some of it in bindings, too, like these, with ten-score leaves. And barrels of ink! Quills by the dozens!"

"Very good. I'll need a dozen of the bindings. I will need to examine the Hoard, too. Do you have a slate?"

"Pardon me?"

"A slate. With chalk. For writing on?"

Eldwin and Millithorpe looked at each other.

"I do not know what that is," Millithorpe said.

"Oh. Well, never mind. We'll make do. How long do you think it will take you to go to my friends with provisions? And then be back here, Eldwin?"

"Less than two hours, I imagine."

"Then please take care of them right away," Robby picked up a scrap of paper, "and please give them this."

Robby wrote a note saying that he was well and asking Sheila to give Eldwin his shoulder bag.

"Sheila, the lady in our group, will give you a bag to bring to me," he said handing the note to Eldwin. "You may read it if you wish."

Eldwin took the note, holding it with both hands, glancing at Millithorpe, and with some embarrassment said, "I cannot read."

"I was only suggesting it so that you would know I am being straight with you," Robby said.

Eldwin nodded, putting the note into his vest pocket.

"I'll be off, then."

"I'll be here."

Eldwin glanced at the cave opening and snapped his fingers. Robby watched him reappear just within sight and disappear again.

"That is an uncanny ability," he said.

"Yes, it is."

"Well, let's have a look around. Tell me about this place. Show me how you use it."

"This part we call the Foyer, where we do the first sorting and dividing of things." Millithorpe waved his hand around, then gestured for them to go to the first passageway. As they entered, Millithorpe explained that most of the passages were natural, but were carved out and trimmed and paved to ease their work. A great deal of the rock was used in the town and some ore, such as iron, was found. Robby rarely had to stoop as they went along, and Millithorpe, taking a lamp from the wall, led him into a large cavern and began to light other lamps about the room.

"This is the sundries room. Over there are dry goods, such as cloth. And you see the bale of paper. There are leather items, there, harnesses, saddles. A few pelts. Over there are cakes of soap and blocks of beeswax and crates of tools—hammers, plough blades, shears, and so forth. Axe handles, wagon parts over there, too. On that side are glasswares, dishes, cups of pewter, ceramic jars and all manner of ladles, spoons, and knives, and so forth."

Robby fingered some of the harness leather, and examined the bale of parchment and paper.

"The leather is pretty-well gone," he said. "Though the cloth is in good shape."

Millithorpe pulled out a little wheelbarrow and began stacking volumes of bound paper onto it.

"Eldwin said that some things are taken for use by your people. How does that work?"

"Yes. Well. You see, at first it was a solemn matter to take anything at all from the Hoard. Only the Elders could give permission, by unanimous agreement for anything to be taken. From the beginning, all of the original Hoard was protected, and it still is. But our early years were a struggle and so a way was made so that any person could ask for anything from the regular Hoard if only they could provide some thing to replace it of equal value. All of the Elders had to agree that the exchange was fair. It became very difficult, though, to know what may be of value as time passed. It is one thing to need some wax, for example, but how valuable to those outside our land is that wax? When Furaman came to trade, he shared some knowledge about the worth of things with us, but before that, well, naturally the Elders made laws governing the Hoard. Nowadays, if something is perishable, like, say, a side of beef, an auction is held. For other things, it is a great bother to borrow it for awhile."

"For a while? You mean the things aren't kept?"

"Oh, no! Gosh, these things do not belong to us!" Millithorpe was somewhat taken aback at Robby's question, but then understood Robby's quizzical look. "None of these things belong to us. We came here with nothing, not even clothes. The few things that we carried away from our homeland have long since been lost. Things from the Hoard are only borrowed."

"So the trade is just a fee."

"Yes, and the Elders set a time when things must be returned."

"But what about the things you make, your tools and such?"

"These are not truly our lands," Millithorpe said. "Not our mountains, not our forests, not our rivers or streams. The things we make from what we find, our food, our houses—everything belongs to this land, not to us. All must be returned to their rightful owners for our curse to be unmade. And if we ever leave here, our town and our houses will all be given back and the forest will retake the fields and the streets, and the mountains will reclaim the stones cut from them."

Robby thought about this as they headed back up the passage, with Millithorpe pushing the wheelbarrow ahead.

"How does it work, then, when someone needs something that someone else has?"

"Oh we can trade those things we take from the Hoard, or those things that we make or grow or raise or hunt. There are rules about setting values and bargaining and so forth. But because of our long struggle with the purpose of unmaking the curses upon us, a strong tradition of loaning and borrowing has come about. Gift-giving is an important way for us to celebrate special occasions. And we still retain some of the traditions of the Elders and of our original homeland, too."

Robby felt a sudden pang as he thought of his own homeland and his memories of birthday parties, festivals, and bonfires. Images of joyful faces and the sounds of laughter and lively music swept through his mind on a wave of homesickness that brought a stinging mist to his eyes.

They stacked the books on the table and then went to look at the weapons room, where Robby saw enough weaponry to equip a small army, neatly stacked and racked and packed. It reminded him somewhat of the armoury at Tallinvale, and his sense of urgency was restored. Next, they visited the cask room containing all manner of liquids: casks of wine, kegs of various strong liquors, barrels of oil, and jars of unctions.

"Some of this we traded for, and some came to us in the way of toll road fees," Millithorpe commented as Robby put his nose to a barrel of oil. "But a great portion we produce, and oil is a favorite thing to trade and to pay the Hoard tax."

"Tax?"

"Yes, that is another way we grow the Hoard. Trades are done through an Elder, and a fee is charged and the fee must be paid with something that can go into the Hoard, or with something that can be exchanged for something hoardable."

"Sounds complicated."

"Not really. Easier done than said, perhaps. Say a farmer needs a new plough, but all he has to trade is corn. And the blacksmith can make a plough, but needs no corn. They go to the Exchange and almost always the Elders work out something that satisfies all."

"I see you have things figured out pretty well, then."

"Yes. There are few disputes, and, unless there is a bad harvest, we rarely go hungry as we once did so often."

"So you trade this oil? It has an unusual odor. Earthy." Robby was rubbing his fingers before his nose, rubbing the bit of oil he had dipped.

"That is bright-oil, and it is made here in Nowhere. It comes from the nuts of a particular tree that grows here. We cook with it and use it in our lamps."

"You make it?"

"It pretty much makes itself. The hardest part is gathering all of the nuts and keeping the squirrels away until we have enough to cook. It takes a lot of nuts to make a good batch of oil. But a little goes a long way, and some years we make more than other years. We have been here a long time, you know. Some years we make oil. Some years we spend making wine or beer. Some years we labor at iron."

"I see."

"What do you make of our Hoard so far?"

"Well," said Robby as he peeked behind some liquor kegs to look at a few empty glass bottles. "I'll need to take a closer look at everything. Right now, I'm just getting the lay of things. There is certainly a large collection of goods. A variety, to be sure, and of various qualities, some good, some very good, and some perhaps not so good, or maybe even worthless."

"Hm. Yes. I suppose you are right. We know so little about what is worthwhile, valuable, or commonplace outside our boundaries."

"I notice that this cave is well-lit, yet it is not smoky and the air is always fresh."

"Oh, we have cut shafts upward to allow the stale air to escape, and it carries out the damp and the little smoke from our lamps, though the oil burns very clean. As you see, we have done other work here. One of the Elders was a stonemason before we came here, and he directed much of the work, making the passageways and floors and storerooms."

By now they had arrived back at the Foyer and Millithorpe directed Robby to the last passageway. It was wider than the others, better lit, and the ceiling had been carved smooth in an arching curve. The passage went straight, and at the far end Robby saw a massive doorway into which was set gates made of iron bars as thick as his wrists. Around the center, where the gates came together, was welded a band of steel in place of a lock. Above Robby, a shaft was cut and immediately below it was a cold forge, various tools and two heavy hammers laying crosswise on a large silent anvil. Robby observed all of these things, but his attention was riveted on the glittering display beyond the black bars of iron. On shelves of stone arranged about the room were jewel-encrusted chalices and crowns, silver chests, untarnished by age. There were ornate helmets and swords and shields, too, and a mirror of glass framed in carved rosewood. Robby saw combs and brushes, plates and cups of the most delicate workmanship, crystal brooches, fancy staffs and walking sticks, and even what he took to be a child's rattler. Incongruously, on one side of the room, were sixteen wagons and three carts, all lined up and ready to be hitched. He could see that the room stretched back into darkness where, here and there, a glint of red or green betrayed the presence of even more jewel-laden wonders.

"We do not know why dust does not gather on these things as it does elsewhere," Millithorpe said reverently, seeming as much in awe as Robby was. "These are all the things we were made to haul from Tulith Attis. The carts and wagons, too."

Robby shook his head at the wonder of it.

"How do you get in?"

"No one is allowed into the Treasure Hoard. It is sealed, as you can see, with welded bands of steel. We constructed these in the years when the Damar assaulted our lands, and we feared the treasure might be looted. It was many months in the making, and since then the gates have not been opened and the forge, here, has remained cold. The bars are even placed in such a way that even the smallest of my people cannot squeeze through, and so we cannot even pop in."

"Of course, I will have to go in there so as to make a right accounting."

"Oh? Oh, my, no! I mean, that is not for me to say, you see. I cannot undo the rules made by all the Elders."

"But aren't you an Elder?"

"Yes. Yes, I am. But I am only one amongst many. No Elder alone may make or break any rule. It requires the approval of all. Besides," Millithorpe shrugged, "you have the accounts already that we have made."

"But those are not very useful, if you pardon my saying so. They give no reckoning of the worth of things. That vase, yonder, is it of solid gold? Or is it plated? And those crowns. Are they the crowns of Heneil and his Lady? Or of some lesser lord? Only by examining them may we learn and put some value upon them."

"But the matter is beyond me," Millithorpe insisted. "And even if the

Council met and all agreed, it would take many days to cut away the band that holds the gate in place."

"Be that as it may," Robby replied, making toward the passageway. "We must have a decision, so they must meet!"

"Yes. Yes. Certainly. I do understand. The Elders must meet to decide. That is so," Millithorpe hurried after Robby. "But they must first decide to meet, and must be called together, and that will take some doing."

"Then there is not a moment to be lost. Ah, Eldwin! How did you find my friends?"

Eldwin and a small group were entering the Foyer from outside just as Robby emerged from the passage.

"They are all well, though concerned for ye, an' they send their greetings. Here is the bag ye requested. An' we have brought with us some food an' drink for ye, too."

"Thank you," Robby took his writing things from the shoulder bag and stuck a pencil from it on his ear, to the puzzlement of the others, and put a penknife and an order book into his vest pocket.

"These boys will help us," Eldwin said. "An' more may be had, if needed. This is Timbo, Jimbo, Limbo, an' Nimbo, all nephews of mine, an' this is Seltin, me grandson."

"How do you do?" Robby bowed to shake their hands. They all looked roughly the same age. But it occurred to him as they stood nervously with the plates and jugs, shifting from foot to foot, that he was less a judge of age these days than ever before.

"Shall we set a table for ye?" Eldwin asked.

"Certainly!"

He pulled down some ledgers and spread a fresh blank sheet before him. Eldwin and his helpers slid a small table over and stacked some crates to sit on around it. After inking only a couple of notes, Robby heard Eldwin clear his throat.

"All is ready, sir," Eldwin called.

Robby looked up to see a plate of food, a pitcher of beer and one of water, a cup and utensils neatly arranged on a light blue tablecloth.

"Thank you very much!" Robby sat down enthusiastically and his stomach let out an anticipatory growl. A cup of beer was poured as he picked up the fork and quickly enjoyed a morsel of sweet ham. It was not until he was reaching for the cup that he noticed the boys standing at a respectful distance, watching him intently. As he raised the cup to his lips, it occurred to him that it was the food, perhaps, that most interested them. He paused and then put the cup gently down and lifted the cover from the platter and saw it to be crammed with meat and cheese, bread, sliced apples, green beans, and berries.

"Have you already eaten?" he asked. They hesitated, and Eldwin said, "Yes, sir."

"Seltin—Seltin, is it?"

"Yes, sir?"

"When did you last eat?"

The boy looked at his grandfather and said, "Oh, I breakfasted this morning, sir."

"And what did you have for breakfast?"

"Er, well, I had a bit of porridge. Oh, and some blackberries."

"And you, Jimbo?"

"I'm Timbo, your honor. That's Jimbo. I had breakfast, too. Porridge."

Jimbo and Nimbo nodded.

"And when will you eat again?"

They looked at each other.

"Tonight?" one proposed.

"Sir," Eldwin broke in. "We need very little to sustain us."

Robby nodded, aware of their growing embarrassment.

"Then," Robby told them as he poured the beer back into the pitcher and reached for the jug of water, "I'll only take this pitcher of water to the desk. I'll eat when it is your custom to do so and, if it may be so, in your good company."

"Oh, sir!" Limbo cried.

"But you are, oh my! Our guest!" stammered Millithorpe.

"Ye need not follow our ways," put in Eldwin.

"You are all very kind," Robby said, rising. "But my mind is made up. We have work to do and may as well get started. Eldwin, the Elders need to be called to decide whether or not to permit me into the chamber where the treasure from Tulith Attis is stored. I cannot deliver a fair accounting of the things there unless they give me permission to do so."

Eldwin looked at Millithorpe, who shrugged. "He says my accounts are not sufficient. And I have no doubt he is right."

"I cannot call for a meetin' by meself, sir," Eldwin said to Robby. "It takes at least twenty Elders to do so, unless it's a regular meetin' time, which is not for another fortnight."

"It must be done. You and Millithorpe are two. You only need eighteen more. My travels are urgent, and I haven't much time. My companions and I must be on our way, with or without our things, and we cannot tarry long. And tell the Elders that I will do my part to break the curses upon your people, if they do their part."

"What do ye mean? Do ye have the power to do so?"

"Just tell them that I will do my part. But only if they give permission. Please hurry!"

"I will. Just as ye say. These boys will stay an' help however they may. All of them can read an' write the common letters, an' all can count a fair bit, too."

Eldwin took his leave and was quickly out of sight as Robby sat at the table and started making his notes. The others waited pensively and without word, but it was not long before he was delving into the ledgers and trying to translate, with Millithorpe's help, the meaning of the counts. His intention, Robby explained, was to make new ledgers. In each would be a line for every type of thing, and, off to the side in neat columns, he would write notes about the condition and quantity of the things, and an appraised worth in Realm silver. Each page was to be tallied up at the bottom, and each tally carried forward to the next page, too, as a running account of the whole value so far. He was not sure they understood, but made worksheets for his helpers to use, showing them how to make their figures, then sent them off in pairs to do counting-work while he made more worksheets for their next counting jobs. When that was done, he set to the task of organizing the ledgers and making new ones. He showed Millithorpe how to make proper lists and set him to work copying portions of the entries from the old books into the new ones.

It was easy for Robby, having plenty of practice from his earliest days. He knew the real task was not in making the books, or even in tallying up the amounts, but in working out the worth of things to be tallied. So much depended on the person that you traded with, the circumstances, and even the time of year. Nails might be commonplace things, but if they were in short supply to one who needed them, they would be quite valuable. Weapons might have no value at all, beyond the material of their making, unless there was an army to wield them. This was a task more suitable to his father, or the likes of Mr. Furaman. But even they, Robby realized, would be guessing at some things. So he made up his mind to use a variety of measures. How long did it take to make a thing? What materials were required? What was the quality of workmanship, and in what sort of condition was the thing now, after so long in storage? As he worked on the copying and mentally prepared himself for the assessments, there were moments when he felt overwhelmed by the task, but he made himself go to the next step and then the next.

"What on earth did I get myself into!" he muttered.

"Pardon me?" asked Millithorpe, raising his head from his copying.

"Oh?" Robby shook his head. "Nothing." He put down his pen and stretched his arms. "This will take a while to do. Tell me, is there much hunger among your people?"

"Hunger? There is some. But we do not face starvation. It has been a hard year, though it did not start that way. Our first crops were bountiful, but several days of bad storms washed away some of our fields and nearly flooded the lower part of the town near the stream. By the time we got our fields repaired, it was too late to get much of a second crop. We have stores put aside, though, and the woods are plentiful in nuts and berries and game, and fish are plentiful, too, so we have no doubt that we'll make it through the winter. If everyone keeps up their hard work. Which we shall."

"I see."

Robby sat back in thought. The great storm was vast, indeed, he realized, reaching over and into the mountains. His mind went back to the opening day of the festival, and the speech his father had given, expressing the community's thanks for coming through the summer in such good shape.

"I think I'll stretch my legs a bit," he said to Millithorpe, picking up one of the ledgers. "And take the air while I look over this list again."

He walked out of the cave and into the daylight, bright and clear, but instead of continuing down the path toward town, he impulsively took a right turn along a narrow, obviously seldom used trail that descended gently through the trees at the base of the cliff. After a short walk, he heard the sound of falling water and soon came to a small pool fed by the clatter of a little waterfall. It was a shady place, cool and peaceful, and though the narrow cascade of water splashed over time-smoothed rocks, there was hardly a ripple in the shallow pool below. The sound and the cool air were soothing, and he sat at the edge of the water on some rocks beside the path and put the ledger on his lap. With a sigh, he took out his smoking pouch. It was already late afternoon, and as he lit his pipe using one of his firesticks, he wondered how his friends were faring. Probably impatient, he thought, as he gave a couple of starting puffs. This sidetrack certainly hampered their progress, to say the least. Ashlord was probably beside himself with worry over Certina, who was not yet back from her errand. Ullin was restless, no doubt, and on guard, too, and wanting to scout the way ahead, Robby guessed, but was likely discouraged from leaving their camp by the cautious Ashlord. Billy and Ibin were apt to be napping as much as they could, and he worried little about them. Sheila, he felt strongly, was probably deep into her own thoughts, likely dark and full of fret, self-doubt, and regret.

He opened the ledger to look over some entries, but his thoughts wandered back to Janhaven, and his eyes nearly filled with tears thinking of his mother. He hoped by now his father had reached help across the lake, and the thought of his father's strength and determination fed his hope, somewhat. Then he remembered that his father was being pursued by Redvests, and he frowned.

"Hullo. That is a glum face yer making!"

Robby, somewhat startled, looked up from the page he had been blindly staring at and saw a young girl—at least he took her to be young—holding a baby in her arms wrapped in a light blanket.

"Do you always greet strangers so bluntly?" he asked, smiling.

"I dunno. Yer the first stranger I have ever greeted. But I saw ye in the square this morning, an' I know ye to be the one called Robby. Is it the accounting that worries ye so?"

"No. Well, yes, I am concerned over it. But in fact, my mind was elsewhere just now."

"Oh," she said as she shifted the baby. "I suppose there are troubles in the outside world that we know little about. An' besides, everyone has their own, regardless."

"Yes. I'm afraid my own little problems are hopelessly mixed up with those great ones of the world."

"I often wonder about the outside world. Besides the troubles, I mean. There are wonders, aren't there? I imagine vast cities of glass an' silver, great magic forests full of elves an' the Faerekind. An' the land ends, they say, where a great water stretches out farther than the eye can see, an' men go about in boats driven by the wind."

"I have never seen magic forests, or vast cities. Nor have I ever seen the sea, though I have seen sailboats on Lake Halgaeth, and I've been to the beautiful town of Tallinvale, with its spires."

"Still, yer free to go about to such places if ever ye choose, are ye not? But we can never leave these mountains."

"I wouldn't say never. And I travel only because I must. If ever my lot frees me to do so, perhaps I will seek out places such as those you speak of. But I'm beginning to think no one is truly free, and that all have bonds of some kind or other that may not be escaped."

"Oh! That *is* a glum way of putting it!"

"I'm sorry!" Robby laughed. "But you should be grateful for the beautiful land you live in, and the home you have, safe and peaceful in a troubled world."

"I am! Surely we strive to keep in mind each an' every day those woes that brought our people here an' left us imprisoned in these lands."

Robby nodded.

"An' if one is to have such glum thoughts, this is the place to have them, certainly."

"Why is that?"

"We call this place the Pool of Desire," she said. "Some say it is a bewitched place an' that it charms those who sit near its waters. Many of our people will not come here. They say it causes the mind to wander an' the heart to turn to impossible desires."

"I had no idea," Robby replied, looking around. He thought of the wanderings of his own mind just a few moments ago and chuckled. "Maybe it is true, though, in a way. Still, it seems a pleasant enough place to me. What is your name?"

"Eldwyna."

"And the little one?"

"He is Aldred. We came looking for Eldwin. Millithorpe said ye had gone for a walk, an' since I did not see ye on the path from town, I thought ye may have come this way. I thought perhaps Eldwin was with ye."

"Are you related?"

"He is my grandfather."

"And is this your son, or perhaps your younger brother?"

"Oh," she giggled. "No, he's me grandson."

"Goodness! Forgive me. But your people seem so young compared to most others I've met. Besides the Elifaen."

"Truly age does not touch us in the same way as it does others. So we have been told. We age, but slowly."

"A blessing."

"In some ways, perhaps. But, though we have few children, our mouths increase an' our lands do not. We are not as few in number as we once were."

"I, myself, am barely over a score of years in age," Robby stated.

"That is quite young, indeed. But ye do not act so. There is something very old about ye."

"Perhaps it is just weariness," Robby chuckled. "Tell me, you said I was the first stranger you had spoken to. I thought Eldwin and Millithorpe told me your people used to trade goods with outsiders. A man named Furaman, among others."

"Yes. But, in the first place, Mr. Furaman would not be a stranger an' would be a welcome sight if ever he came this way again. And, in the second place, all trading was done along the Toll Road, an' no one was ever before allowed into our valley or town. The Elders maintain a careful watch on our borders. Should any try to find our valley, or wander too close, the Elders turn them away. There was a time when the Damar soldiers sought us out with ill-intent. But we harried them mercilessly with all manner of pestering. They have not troubled us for many years, though we think they keep the traders away."

"I see."

"Well, anyway, I need to leave ye to yer work an' speak with me grandfather," she said, turning back toward the cave. "I suppose he's somewhere around the Hoard, or working deep within?"

"Oh, no! I'm sorry," Robby said, standing up. "Pardon me for not saying so before, but Eldwin is not here. He is in town, or thereabouts, trying to stir the Elders to have a meeting."

Eldwyna rolled her eyes in an expression of exasperation and shifted the baby to her other side.

"I'm sorry," Robby repeated.

"An' we came all this way! Do ye know if he will return soon?"

"I cannot say. You are welcome to wait."

"I wish I could, but I need to get back to chores."

"May I pass along some message, then?"

"I only wanted to know if he would be able to help us today with the new cottage we are building. If he cannot help, we will ask a cousin."

"Oh," Robby replied. "I suppose my coming has disrupted a lot of work. But I'll be needing Eldwin's help, and I don't see how he'll be able to help with the cottage. I am sorry."

"Oh, of course. I know grandfather has put himself in yer service, an' what ye do is more important than any cottage. Especially if ye find that our Hoard is of worth. Many of us have put aside their work in hopes of that. But others of us do not share such great hope, an' we continue in our work an' chores. It is hard to see how the riches taken from Tulith Attis could be matched, much less surpassed by our gleanings."

"Well," Robby shrugged, "I cannot yet say. But who knows?"

"Then I will leave ye to yer task," she said. "I have to find me cousin, an' he lives all the way on the other side of the valley, an' the day gets no longer by putting things off."

"I enjoyed talking with you. Perhaps you will pop over to see me again."

"I don't think so," she laughed. "Only the Elders have that ability. The rest of us may only be carried by our feet."

"Oh. I didn't know."

"No matter. But perhaps I'll see ye again. Good day!"

"Good day to you both!"

Robby watched her go, with the baby peering at him over her shoulder in such a way that Robby was compelled to give a little wave which was returned by the child. Smiling, he went back to the cave where Timbo was just coming from the weapons room.

"I made the list an' count, just as ye told me," he reported, holding out the list for Robby. "But there are many things that are strange to me. That is to say, I do not know what to call them. I'm afraid I didn't get very far along. But I drew little figures of them, along here, see? An' a count beside them giving their number."

"You did well. Honestly, I'm not sure I know what that is," Robby said pointing to a sketch that looked vaguely like a large spoon. "But perhaps I will know when I see it later when we look together. Next, I need you to sort things out, several stacks for each thing. Those that are in the best condition, those not so good, and those in poor condition. Be careful and ask for help with the heavy things."

Not long afterwards, Limbo appeared, and soon Robby was busy keeping up with their reports and questions, making his notes and preparing to assess all of the things. The boys came and went, and Robby often had to help them move something, or answer some question, or direct the sorting. When he returned from one such errand, he found Millithorpe had lit more lamps, and the Foyer was aglow in amber light. He was surprised when he looked to the cave opening and saw only a gaping blackness outside where night had settled on the land. The sound of Millithorpe's scratching pen was answered by the distant calls of a night bird and the subtle drone of crickets.

"I am surprised there are no bats," he said as he sat beside Millithorpe.

"They do not like the lamp oil," Millithorpe replied, not looking up from his copying. "And they have taken to other caves nearby."

Robby stifled a yawn.

"What I wouldn't do for a cup of coffee!"

"I remember coffee," Millithorpe looked up with a faraway expression. "With cream and sweet liquor!"

"Nothing quite like it, for when you need a lift."

"Aye. We have a nice tea, though. If you wish, I can pop over to my cottage and fetch a pot."

"I don't want you to go to any trouble."

"It would be no trouble and, anyway, with your leave, I'd like to look in on my missus. It being past dark and all."

"Oh. I guess I didn't realize, but of course you have a family. I suppose I am putting a great deal of people to trouble over this."

"Oh, no, sir. Not at all. That is to say, it is only my missus and myself. And what trouble we go to is nothing, oh truly, nothing whatsoever compared to what we may someday gain from it."

"Well, why don't you go see your wife? Can you come back in the morning?"

"Unless you need me before then. Where will you sleep tonight?"

"Oh. Hm. I guess it isn't practical for me to return to my friends. I'll be fine just stretched out here."

"Then I will have some blankets brought to you."

"That would be nice. Thank you."

"May I also suggest that perhaps it is time to eat? It is a little beyond our customary time. And, if you meant what you said earlier, the boys would enjoy a bite, I'm sure. I'll sup with my missus."

"Oh, yes, certainly. I'll fetch the others."

"Then I'll see you in the morning!"

Robby went to the sundries room and asked Seltin to find the other boys as he picked out some plates and cups and other things. After convincing the boys that, in the first place he would not eat unless they did, and, in the second place, it was fine to borrow the dishes and so forth, they sat together and ate from the full platter and drank the beer. The boys were polite and answered Robby's questions but said little on their own for the better part of the meal. Even with what little they did say, Robby was surprised at how well-spoken they were, and he learned that they had a very active school and even a library of books and scrolls, one of the few things that could be borrowed from the Hoard by copying.

"In the days when traders came along the Toll Road," Seltin explained, "news of the outside world was to be had. We got books that way, too, an' often we traded for stories, written down as they were told by passing travelers."

"Oh?"

"Yes. There was a family of minstrels who used to regularly come this way. Though they were poor in other ways, they were rich in songs and lore, an' in tales and stories."

"My grandmother even met a prince, once," chimed in Jimbo. "He was traveling to Tallin Valley from Vanara in the west an' gave to her all manner of genealogies of the Elifaen lines. She spent three days in his camp an' among his people an' copied fifty scrolls of tales an' lore."

"An' once," Timbo said, "me Uncle Eldwin saved from a bear a mighty hunter who came from the northlands beyond Duinnor. They became great friends, so he says. In gratitude to Uncle Eldwin, he sent to us a whole wagon of gifts, including silver and gold an' fine cloth an' tools, as well as a case of stories from Glareth-country full of sea-tales an' magic adventures."

As they went on, with growing ease in Robby's company, he realized that, for all their isolation, they seemed to be more knowledgeable and better read than himself. Although he felt their knowledge to be quaint, outdated certainly, he felt a pang that he himself could offer little better. Still, they seemed to have a genuine hunger for and delight in all sorts of lore and knowledge about all things. Which made it odd, Robby thought, that they asked very few questions about himself, his home, or his travels, even though he sensed their curiosity. Perhaps it was out of politeness, he thought. He spoke with care, not wishing to give away anything too particular about his reasons for being on the road. The boys listened intently, rarely interrupted, and, he noticed, they did not eat or drink as he spoke, though they had no inhibitions about doing so while one of their own talked.

They chatted on after the last morsel was gone and the dishes were cleaned away. Though Robby thought it was not much of a meal when divided so many ways, they looked satisfied, and Timbo, having pushed back his stool, patted his belly contentedly. They talked of the great storm and each related their own tales. Robby left out much, most, in fact, of his own tale, but he described the damage to Barley and the death of Passdale's mayor.

"No one here was killed, as in your town," said Jimbo, "for which we are most thankful. But the water pouring down the slopes brought some trees an' boulders with it, an' many of us took shelter right here and also in other caves nearby."

Robby listened to their account of the damage and the loss of crops and found himself wishing he could help them, thinking of his own people and their plight. But he did not mention their troubles, or talk about the Redvests or the invasion, or the coming war, or why he and his companions were on the road. Oddly, he had not been asked, so he concluded that some agreement must have been exacted of them to refrain from such questions. Just as he was thinking of Eldwin, the little man entered the cave at the head of a dozen or so others, most carrying bundles, some with long boards and others with tools. Eldwin had changed out of his fancy suit and now wore work clothes and waistcoat.

"Just over there, nearby those shelves, I think," he instructed those in his party who awkwardly bowed to Robby as they passed with their loads and immediately set to work on some little construction. Five of the group, who carried no bundles and who were dressed in colorful outfits, stood aside as Eldwin approached Robby.

"We have brought things to make a cot for ye," he said. "I ran into Millithorpe on the way an' brought blankets, too, an' straw for a mattress of sorts. That is, should ye decide to sleep here rather than with yer companions."

"I'll stay here. But I'd like to send another message to them."

"Certainly."

"And who are these gentlemen? Elders?"

"Just so, sir." Eldwin nodded to them, and Robby bowed and shook their hands. "This is Larris, Brolith, Arldewain, Torridge, an' Makewine. I have seen many of the Elders today, makin' yer request, an' these have come to question ye about it."

Arldewain cleared his throat and looked at the others before speaking.

"We are concerned," he said, "that the accounting done by Millithorpe is not sufficient for you to make a reckoning as to the value of the Hoard. Can you tell us why that is?"

"Millithorpe is a good keeper of the Hoard," Robby began. "He has followed the instructions given to him, and the work he has done is to be commended. But the records are not kept in a way so as to assign value to the things, or to tally up the amount of value as a whole. The Great Hoard, as you call it, those things from Tulith Attis, is to be the measure for all other things combined. Therefore, I must inspect the items in that chamber."

"You have looked into the chamber of the Great Hoard, have you not?" asked Makewine.

"Yes."

"Then you have seen how the Great Treasure does not gather dust, nor does it tarnish or decay."

"I have seen that. It is most uncanny."

"Would it not seem, then, that their condition is unchanged?"

"It would seem so, yes," Robby shrugged. "But those things were taken in a time of war, carried off through battlefields, and carted across many leagues. What condition were they in when they were taken, forcibly, from those who would not easily give them up? What damage might those things have suffered at that time or even before then? And then afterwards, on the way here? Yes, I have looked into the chamber. But a thing looked at from a distance does not always show its value, as I'm sure you may appreciate."

"Well said, I admit," replied Brolith. "I remember those days too well, as all we Elders do. The road was hard, and we cared little for our burdens except to rid ourselves of them."

"And I was one of those who went to Tulith Attis itself," said Larris, shaking his head and giving a slight shudder at the memory. "Cast into piles by the coarse Dragonkind for us to carry out. With my own shirt, Bailorg made me to wipe the blood from a headpiece of gold. I remember the horrible grin on his face as he took it from me and held it up to admire."

"So you understand why I must look at those things," said Robby. "Will you and the others give me permission to go into that room and do so?"

"Eldwin did a fair job of convincing us before we came," said Makewine. "And you have satisfied our questions, I think."

The others nodded.

"A meeting of the Elders will take place tomorrow, and we will put the question to vote. Herbert will oppose, naturally, but I think we may prevail with four-fifths of the vote needed. However, even if the Elders agree that you need to gain entry into the Hoard, they may not wish to give permission because of the labor needed."

"Our people, that is, those not already helping you," picked up Larris, "are busy making ready for winter, gleaning what food and fuel may be had, salvaging crops and salting fish."

"The gates have not been opened since the bands were forged around the bars," explained Brolith. "Our smithies tell us they will have to make cutting chisels and irons."

"That means the forge will have to be kindled and stoked with cut wood. Bellows remade and certain other tools."

"Many hands will be needed."

"We think it will take about twelve of us working several days to open the gates."

As they talked, Eldwin's workers had assembled Robby's cot in short order and were now standing with Seltin and his cousins, listening to the exchange. Robby considered for a moment what they said.

"Be that as it may," he said at last. "Let the permission for me to go into the Hoard be one thing, and let the decision to do the work of opening it for me be another thing. Please meet with the Elders and let me know how things stand. If permission cannot be granted, then I and my companions must be on our way, without our things, to make our journey as well as we can. If permission is granted, a way to open the gates will be found, somehow. But know this: The breaking of the curses upon your people depends on your wit and wisdom. If you do your part, I will most assuredly do mine."

The five Elders agreed, then quickly departed. Turning to the others, Robby politely thanked and dismissed his helpers until morning, all but Eldwin whom he asked to linger. Seating himself at the desk he began to write a note to his companions, speaking to Eldwin as he did so.

"Everyone did a fine job today," he said. "I admit I was discouraged this morning when I first saw the books. But Millithorpe and I are well on our way to sorting them out. All the helpers did fine work, too. Tomorrow, I'll begin making my notes as to the value of things. But you, especially, Eldwin, have done well, and I thank you for all your efforts."

"That is kind of ye to say, sir, an' ye should have our gratitude," Eldwin bowed. "Not all of us take great delight in our way of takin' a toll on the road or a fee as we do. I wish I could just give ye back all yer things an' let us be friends."

"Perhaps we may become friends, anyway."

"I hope so. Whether ye succeed or fail, an' whether we act wisely or not."

"Thank you for saying so."

Robby continued to write, turned the sheet over and filled that side, too, leaving just enough room to sign his name. He folded it and handed it to Eldwin.

"I'd like for you to give this to Ashlord in the morning and wait for his reply."

As Eldwin took it, Robby looked at him, noticing for the first time his muscular build, his thick strong hands, and his stocky body, and for a moment Eldwin's small size was neither here nor there in Robby's mind. Robby saw him not as a pixie, or as a servant, or even an Elder of his people, but only as a man.

"What is your trade, Eldwin?"

"I have always been a woodworker, sir, after me father before me an' his before him."

"A carpenter?"

"I have done plenty of that, yes. But all manner of things do I make an' carve. Tools an' handles, furniture, doors, beds an' posts, an' even toys. I made the simple table ye work at, those shelves behind ye an' in many of the rooms here."

"You do good work," Robby said running his hand across the smooth finish of the tabletop. "How do you cut your boards? And smooth them so? Do you have a mill?"

"A mill? Goodness no, sir. They are hand sawn, with saws made by our smithies. An' once the boards are cured, we smooth them using stones. I have an auger that I use for the peg holes, an' various tools for cuttin' mortises an' tenons. That's how we put together the cot, there."

"Quick work, too, I might say. And quite inviting," Robby said.

"Strong, but not so comfortable as what ye may be used to."

"The rocky ground is what I've been used to of late, with roots jabbing in awkward places!"

"Surely," Eldwin hesitated. "I know little of ye or the purpose of yer journey. The Elders, decidin' to allow ye here to do this, required an oath of all not to ask questions about such things. They do not wish to become involved in the outside world. Before we are ready."

Robby nodded. "I understand and surmised as much. Well, ready or not, you are involved, since I am here and of the outside world. Perhaps, before I leave, and if I'm allowed, I might tell you some of why we pass this way. But these days are a time for your people to watch your borders with vigilance and caution. The world closes in, and even my coming here may have brought danger. I do not mean to alarm you, only to put it before you. I will do what I can here, but then I must go, and go quickly. As I said, I might tell you more, but not without the consent of my companions."

With assurances from Robby that he would be fine staying by himself, Eldwin let Robby dismiss him, promising again to take the message to Ashlord at first light and then return. Robby worked for some while longer on the ledgers, and he was pleased with his progress. Closing the last blurry page, he walked the passages, having another look at the various storerooms, and putting out lamps as he went, until he arrived again in the chamber of the Great Treasure. He looked for a long while at the fabulous display of ancient articles. For the first time, he imagined Tulith Attis as it once may have been, a place of beauty and riches, surrounded by a little town of happy traders and craftsmen, secure in the watchful shadow of Lord Heneil's fortress and in the company of his many fine soldiers. The treasure he looked at was surely only a hint of the wealth and marvels that must have once been commonplace there.

At last he turned to go, but stopped a few steps away. He went back to the gates and carefully placed his right hand on the thick steel band that sealed the latch bars. He touched it only for a moment, and withdrew his hand quickly. With a satisfied expression, he left and walked back through the Foyer and on through the opening of the cave. A cool wind blew down from the cliffs above, trees bent and rattled in the little wood, and bright stars winked in and out between the branches. As his eyes adjusted to the dim light, he noticed a huddled figure, bundled in a blanket and leaning against a tree about twenty yards away down the path. Smiling, he went back inside. Realizing he would have a more comfortable night than his guards, he took full advantage of the cot.

• • •

The wind was hot and dry, and Robby tasted the endless expanse of dust and sand on his lips. Squinting, he turned, shifting his stance on the sand at the top of a high dune, and looked all around. He thought he saw a glint, but it was gone in a wink, and the faraway spot where he thought he saw it was blurred by the restless heat, shimmering like water, and blending into the distant, rimless sky. Nothing could he distinguish in any direction but sand and sky. She was nowhere to be seen. He remembered her words: *"We will not see each other again until after Tulith Morgair."*

Chapter 17

Robby Gets To Work

Day 96
149 Days Remaining

Sheila awoke from a restless sleep and sat up from her bedroll. The sky above the treetops was blue with morning, though the sun had not yet cracked over the eastern mountains. The air was cool, and she shivered, pulling her blanket around and over her shoulders. Noticing the odor of pipe tobacco, she turned and saw Ashlord sitting on a log at the other side of their camp, turning over a piece of paper and reading it silently. Ullin sat on the ground beside him, leaning comfortably against the log and smoking his long-stemmed pipe. Standing before them was the child-sized Eldwin, and behind him were stacked several small bundles. Ibin and Billy, oddly enough, were already awake and sitting on their bedrolls as Sheila now did, silently watching Eldwin and Ashlord. The Eldwin wore a blank look on his face, but from her vantage she could see his eyes wander time and again to the sword-hilt upon which Ullin's hand absently rested. Whether Eldwin was nervous or just prudent, she could not tell.

"Very well," Ashlord said, handing the note to Ullin. "We have your assurance that Robby is safe and that no harm or treachery has befallen him?"

"On me honor, I swear. When I left him last night, he was in good health, safe, an' I promise that we have played no trick upon him, nor will we."

"Then take this message to him: Say that I will do as he asks. Remind him also that time presses upon us and beg him to conclude his task as quickly as he may. Say, too, that should he need us, we will be ready to aid him in any way we can. Will you do that?"

"Yes. Just as ye say."

"Then I thank you for the food that you brought for us, hoping that you did not bring too much. I beg you now, return to do your master's bidding."

Eldwin bowed and then disappeared, and Ashlord turned to the others.

"Well!" he said, seeing their expectant faces. "We may be here for a while yet. Robby is doing the best he can, but there are problems and developments that are, well, interesting."

He went on to tell them the gist of the note and of Robby's peculiar request, that they tell stories to each other, that Ibin sing some songs, and that they be ready to depart at a moment's notice.

• • •

All through the day, Robby and his crew of helpers kept busy counting, examining, making notes, and tallying sums. He found it hard to resist doing those things himself; after all, in his family's shop he had never had anyone to order about or any reason before now to think of how best to direct one person's work in coordination with another's. He quickly learned the differences between the boys, though they were all capable and eager to do whatever was required. Seltin was the most work-conscious and always seemed to be thinking ahead to the next thing. Timbo and Jimbo seemed of a kind, both talkative and somewhat happy-go-lucky; they reminded Robby of Billy. Limbo and Nimbo were quiet, steady, and strong, rarely speaking unless prompted, and though they seemed to move slowly, they accomplished all that was asked of them. Millithorpe's nervous way was natural to him, and though the little man was too concerned with the opinion of others, Robby found him easy to work with. Eldwin was more of a mystery. Strong, quiet, like Nimbo and Limbo, but strangely world-wise and articulate, especially for one who could neither read nor write. Very businesslike, but at moments quite personable, Eldwin was definitely different from the others, and he seemed concerned with both the details and the broad lay of things. Robby thought Eldwin was sensitive, in an odd way, even more so than Millithorpe, but Eldwin's face rarely betrayed emotion. At first Robby took it for resentment, on Eldwin's part, of being forced into Robby's service. Eventually, he realized that it was not hard feelings that tempered Eldwin's behavior. No, something else preoccupied him. Perhaps the meeting of the Elders, due to convene in the evening, was on his mind. But something was bothering Eldwin, and Robby resolved to find out what it was, if ever he could.

After rushing to the sundries room to check the quality of salt kegs, and then hurrying off to help Seltin move a few oil jars, Robby had barely returned to the desk in the Foyer when Limbo showed up with a handful of small brass items from the weapons room.

"What am I to call these things?" he asked. Robby took one and turned it over in his hand, a flattened cup-like item with gold along its rim and a little ball where the stem of the "cup" should be.

"Oh, these go on the ends of leather scabbards," he said. "I don't know what they are called. Let's call them 'scabbard ends.' "

"There's a whole box of them."

"Just count them up, like everything else."

When Limbo turned to go, Jimbo stepped up.

"And what about these things?" He held up several long curved bands of heavy hammered metal, linked together with iron rings. Robby recognized them from the soldiers at Tulith Attis who did battle with the wolves.

"Those are armor pieces that go around the chest. These are all tangled. See? Like this. They overlap. Called banded armor, I think. I am no expert at such things, though there is one in my party who is. Anyway, there should be matching pieces that go underneath, down around the waist and others that go up over the shoulders."

"Yes. I think I saw some that might be those."

After he left, Seltin appeared with a question about how to measure a quantity of nails, "by the nail, or by the keg?"

"No. Sort the nails by size. Then weigh the total amount of each size. Weigh out one pound of each size and give a count of how many nails are in a pound. On your sheet of paper, draw a line showing the exact length of each size of nail and beside it put the count of a pound-weight and then the total weight of all of that size, like this."

That sort of instruction went on and on, with Robby jumping in wherever needed, making snap decisions here and there, and scratching his head over what some of the items were that they found in the many storerooms, boxes, kegs, sacks, and shelves. Eldwin, unable to use writing, kept himself busy by moving things for the others, and by sorting and stacking. Hour ran into hour, and yet they hardly noticed the passing of time, so busy they were.

They had not yet heard back from the Elders, but, except for the things in the Treasure Room, all of the rest of the inventory was nearing completion. Robby looked over the progress of the books with satisfaction. It was during a mid-afternoon lull, when Robby had time to sit at the table and catch up with some of the sums, that he looked over Millithorpe's part of the work with the ledgers.

"Fine work, Millithorpe. Very good. We should be finished with this part of our inventory by day's end, and it will be up to me to do my figuring as to the value of things."

"Thank you, sir. That means the world to me, oh yes, it does! I'm so glad that you like my work. You are very kind to say so."

"I do, indeed."

"You see, all I needed was to be shown the proper way of things, that's all. And you have been so kind, so patient."

"I take it Herbert is somewhat demanding?"

"He can be," Millithorpe nodded. "And especially for one who doesn't know numbers worth a twit. If you pardon me saying so."

Robby chuckled. "Well, he seems to have held your people together all these years."

"It might seem so. But more's to the credit of our folk and less to him. He hasn't had a good idea since he came up with the notion of the Toll Road. And even that was suggested by someone else, it is said. But he is harmless for all his bluster, I suppose. Though he knows how to make a person feel puny and low with his sharp words and harsh tone of voice. He certainly doesn't have your way with folk. But then, I suppose you have long been a great leader among your people and have seen much of the world and all manner of wiles. This work must seem so low and menial to you."

Robby's eyebrows shot up with surprise. His smile faded as a cloud crossed his brow, and he sat down beside Millithorpe and picked up a quill to ink.

"I am no leader, Millithorpe. Mayhaps someday I will be. Certainly there are those who have placed that hope in me. As for the work? If the work is honorable, it is so for peasant or king, and neither may be the worse for doing it."

For a long thoughtful moment, Millithorpe watched Robby do sums, then he resumed his own work.

Indeed, by nightfall the boys finished providing Robby with lists and counts and also other notes about the things he had asked them to do. He thanked them, and assured them that he would no longer need their services.

"I know you have been taken away from other people who need you, and I'll not delay you from them any longer," he said. "For my part, with Millithorpe and Eldwin's help, I will make the best of your efforts, and do my work as well as I can. Eldwin tells me that, if you are needed again, I may be sure to call for you."

The boys bowed and shook Robby's hand and departed, joking and laughing.

"Another day's done!" Robby said, repeating a phrase his father often used when closing shop. "I thank the both of you, again, for your help. I suppose the Elders must be gathering for the meeting."

"Yes. And Eldwin and I should go and attend," Millithorpe said to Robby, nodding at Eldwin.

"I would not for the world keep you away from it much longer, as I need your two votes."

"Ye shall have them, sir," said Eldwin. "An' by mornin', if all goes well, I may give ye the news."

"I have another request of you, before you go, Eldwin. But Millithorpe, I know you wish to depart. Thank you again, and please come again tomorrow, if you can."

"Thank you. I will."

"Eldwin, I have a couple of things I'd like to ask you about," Robby said, pouring water into a cup and offering it to Eldwin before taking another for himself.

"I will answer as best as I may."

"What do you think the chances are that my companions would be allowed to come here?"

"Here? To Nowhere? To the Hoard?"

"Yes."

"Oh, sir, I don't think that would be allowed. Herbert has made his decree that they should stay where they are an' that we should have little to do with them, except to see to their meals each day."

"I know. This is how it is: I believe we have some things you may find valuable that we would be willing to part with, in exchange for things that your folk may provide. Also, while I know a great deal about some things, I may not value some other items, such as weapons, as greatly as they should be. But there is one in our party, Ullin is his name, who is an experienced soldier."

"Yes, I know the one ye mean."

"He will know better than I the value of the weapons, beyond their material. Also, the others have knowledge of things that may be useful to your people, things that can be told to your scribes and copied for your collections. If it could be agreed that they be brought here, I would feel better for their safety, and they would surely provide what knowledge they may. Ullin, too, will be able to help me with putting a value on the weapons. Without him, I'm afraid my values will be low."

"Still, I don't think Herbert would agree."

"The decision would not be made by the Elders?"

"Herbert may be a pompous sort, but he's not without wile. Long ago, he saw to it that the Toll Road would be his charge an' all that happens upon it in the way of gatherin' tolls an' fees his responsibility. He only agreed to let ye come because it makes him look good in the eyes of others. But it was his decision as captain of the road, since it was as a result of the road that ye offered this bargain. Since yer companions remain there, it would be Herbert's say to allow them to come. He would only do so if he was made to think it was to his gain. He is elected, ye know, an' every once in a while he is reminded of that. Not that we would ever choose anyone else since he handles the Toll Road well an' that's about it; he'd be a nuisance if he did not have that."

"How would it look for him if the Hoard was valued at very little?"

"He would be mocked for makin' such a bargain with ye, an' for bringin' shame upon us by dint of our failure to grow the fortune properly as we are charged by the curse to do."

"Then let him know, if you may find a way, that the weapons may in fact be the most valuable things that you have collected, but that I, being one who has very seldom reckoned the value of such things, might deem them nearly worthless. Let Herbert know that I rely upon the advice of my companions, as they hold special knowledge of many matters, and that only with their aid may I make a reckoning that does not insult the efforts of your people. Do you think that will convince him?"

"It might, indeed."

"Good. Please tell him in the best way you know how. I know you must soon go to meet with the Elders and have your part in the voting, but there is something else I would like to ask you about. Frankly, I am a bit reluctant, though, to bring it up."

"Whatever it is, I will try to answer truthfully."

"Yes, I'm sure of that. It is perhaps a small thing, but you have seemed, well, somewhat perturbed. At first, I thought you were angry at me, and wondered what it was that I may have done. I eventually realized that it was not anger, but must be some sort of problem you are turning over in your head. You rarely smile, even when the others laugh. You do everything I ask without reluctance, and with care to do things right, but you have little enthusiasm. Is there something wrong? Would you tell me what is on your mind?"

Eldwin looked earnestly at Robby and, seeing his sincerity, sighed, put his hands into his pockets, and nodded.

"Yes," he said, "though I fear I might not have the proper words."

As Robby sat, Eldwin shrugged and gestured to the opening of the cave, trying to gather his thoughts.

"Outside," he said. "It is a big world outside." Turning back to Robby, he continued, "I worry that we are not ready. The curses laid on us have, in a way, been our protection. By bein' unable to leave, we have been forced to be good stewards of this land we occupy, an' it continues to provide for us. By bein' made small, our needs are small. We require far less than big people, like we once were, like yerself an' yer friends. By bein' able to pop quickly from place to place, we were given the power to protect ourselves without takin' up arms. True, our name an' our honor have been forever sullied, so that we are called pixies an' imps an' all manner of other names, an' we are shunned, now, by all that we would otherwise have as friends. But we never had much of a name in the wide world, anyway, truly a small people, I suppose. As for honor? What do we know of such things? We who aided murderers, we who put our hands to thievery!"

"I think you know a great deal about honor," Robby replied softly. "Others, even great kingdoms, might learn a lesson or two from your people. Though beset with misfortune and damned with curses, you took them upon yourselves as a task, a challenge. I have seen and heard enough to know a little of how you have managed. And you have done rather well, I would say."

"Those are kind words, an' might be a comfort to some. But, still, I suppose I am not so easily soothed." Eldwin shrugged. "Suppose the curses are lifted. We, of a sudden, would not fit into our houses or clothes. Our crops would not sustain our bellies. If we were no longer barred from leavin' this land, would our community be broken? Many desire to leave an' to seek out the home of the Elders. Even if we found that place again, how might it have changed? Who lives there now? Would there be a place for us? An' if we lost our power of movement, how would we protect those who wished to stay? Do ye see? Our curses have become blessings to us. They have made us into the people that we now are. These things trouble me. An' I am mindful of the words said to us by the Elfin lady, sayin' she would come again after an accountin' was made. It was she who foretold that the sting of our curses might be blunted an' the burden of our sentence turned to bounty for our children. What would she say to me worries? Would she be angry? Might she deem us ungrateful an' perhaps lay some worse hex upon us?"

"I don't know how to answer you, Eldwin." Robby shook his head, looking down and absently noticing the dust that covered his shoes. "I suppose I have not thought these things out as you have. Everyone seems eager for me to accomplish this work, yet I sense that you do not."

"No. I do not rightly know me own heart about these things. I only speak them because ye bid me do so."

"Are there others who feel as you do?"

"I keep me own counsel, for the most part. But surely among us Elders there must be some who have thought about these things. An' I've heard some words expressed that must have come from such worries as I have."

Robby drummed his fingers on the desk, wondering what to do. His eyes went first to the new ledgers and then to the passageway that led to the Great Treasure.

"I have in mind," he said slowly, uncertain whether he should say anything at all, "a way to lift the first and the second curses. The first depends on work that your people must do. The second depends on the value of the Hoard and how to return the treasure to its rightful heirs. But now, given what you have said, I'm not sure it is right to go ahead with these ideas of mine."

"Hm. What of the third curse?"

"I have no notion concerning that one. Yet, surely long life has not been such a bad thing, so far. Added to that, your way of popping about is an enviable skill."

"Perhaps. An' who would have it otherwise? Do ye think yer ideas, whatever they are, might truly work to lift the other two?"

"They might or might not. I don't want to say too much, especially if it all seems pointless or against what you and your people want. Perhaps these things are for you and the other Elders to decide. I suppose you would want to prepare yourselves, if the curses are lifted. But, as I said, if your people don't wish for the curses to be lifted, I don't see any point in trying. In fact, all of this seems pointless in that case." Robby waved his arm about.

Eldwin nodded. "Yes. Well, perhaps I should speak to others an' see how they truly feel about things. While the Elders meet."

"That might be a good idea. And you'd probably best be off to them before they begin without you."

"I shall see to yer friends in the mornin'. Is there any message for them?"

"I don't think so. Only that I hope to rejoin them soon and that I am well. Good-night, then. And good luck!"

"Thank ye, sir. Good-night!"

• • •

Robby sat in thought for a long while before at last opening the nearest ledger and resuming his work, albeit with less enthusiasm than before. It was slow going, as his mind kept wandering back to Eldwin's concerns. Naturally, his thoughts turned to home and his own people's plight, now in Janhaven, their lands overrun by invaders, and he wondered if his actions here in Nowhere might bring a similar fate on these people. It was like a story he was told as a child about a woodcutter's son who fell so much in love with the forest that he could no longer bear to fell the trees. Going to his king, he asked for a different service. The king granted the woodcutter's wish and made him executioner, since he was strong and swung the axe with precision. As fate would have it, the first victim brought to the block was the forest queen herself, who put her realm above that of the king and would not obey his commands. "If I slay her," the woodcutter thought to himself, "then surely the forest will also die." And so he turned and struck off the king's head. "Fool!" cried the woodland queen. "Do you know that every winter I must die, so that my realm may in spring be reborn? And that my blood nourishes the streams that feed my trees? Do you not know your king is my husband, who ever longs for my youthfulness when the snows melt and the sun once again brings green fire to the buds? Only by his order may this happen, and may I return. Now what is to be?" And so, aghast, the woodcutter saw her fade away and the forest did, too, and soon all his own family and all his people were gone from the earth as well, and that land was remembered only in tale.

Maybe not the most apt story, Robby thought, and he had never been sure of its meaning or moral, if it had one. But the idea rankled him that his efforts would be the undoing of these people, rather than as he intended, an aid to them. It was then that he realized that it was no longer about getting back the things taken as a fine so that he and his companions could continue their journey. It had become something more. Eldwin's words of worry hit home.

"If only I could talk with Ashlord," he said aloud. "He would know what to do. But I suppose it is for me to figure out."

After a moment, he picked up paper and quill and began writing a note to Ullin. He wrote quickly, sometimes scratching out a word, sometimes pausing for a moment to think, the nib hovering a hair's-breadth from the paper. When he reached the end of the page, he blew on it to dry the ink and flipped it over to continue. He described the situation as fully as he could, along with some estimates of value. Several sheets later, he repeated the story of the three curses laid against the

Nowhereans, somewhat shortened, and he described Eldwin's worries. He wrote about his own ideas about breaking the curses, saying that he had no clue about how to undo the last one.

"It seems to me," he then wrote, "that there may be a way to release the Nowhereans from the ill consequences of the curses without taking away too much of their safety. But only if my plan works and if you would agree to it."

He went on to put his thoughts before Ullin, and concluded by saying, " Please consider what I have said. I hope you and the rest of my companions are well and that we may see each other very soon. Please assure Sheila that I am well."

He folded the papers together and folded another sheet around them and wrote Ullin's name on the outside, and sealed it with candle wax.

"Now! I must find Eldwin."

Rising from his seat, he picked up his coat and threw it on, making for the path that led to town.

"You should probably come along," he said to the bushes just by the path. After he passed, two small figures emerged, shrugged at each other, and followed at a respectable distance, nearly at a trot to keep up with Robby's quick stride. When he emerged from the woods and headed down the slopes toward town, he could see the lamps along the lanes were already lit even though the sky was not yet fully dark. He could also see a great many lamps and torches were lit about the town square. He lost sight of it as he descended among the shops and houses, most not much higher than he, and he saw few people about, though some doors slammed shut as he approached and a few shutters were pulled in. One of the two that followed darted past and around the corner just ahead. As he made the turn, Robby saw the boy running into a throng of people, waving and crying, "He comes! The big one comes!"

Robby could see over their heads to the center of the square where there was a large circle of chairs set out, upon which sat the Elders, all sixty-one of them, Robby supposed. One currently stood in the middle of the circle and was speaking. A low murmur went up from the crowd and spread, causing the speaker to pause and look toward the crowd that was parting to allow Robby to pass through. But Robby stopped at the edge of the crowd and leaned over to speak to a lady who stood nearest to him.

"I'm sorry. I don't mean to interrupt. I only want to speak with Eldwin, if I might."

She bowed and motioned with her arm. "He is in his place, there, with the Elders."

"Please come forward, Lord Robby," called the one who had been speaking. He made a friendly gesture. "Please, sir."

Robby was nervous and a little embarrassed, and he swallowed and cleared his throat as he stepped into the way made for him through the crowd. As he passed through, the people bowed, adding to his discomfort. He awkwardly proceeded, looking for Eldwin, and saw Millithorpe seated across the circle, appearing surprised and worried. Those in the chairs nearest to him rose and faced Robby as he stopped at the edge of the Elder's circle. There was a moment when the murmuring died down expectantly, and Robby could hear the flicker of a nearby torch and a far off thrush singing its night song. Robby bowed to the speaker.

"Please pardon my intrusion," he said, trying to pick his words carefully, even though he had little to say. "I only wanted to speak for a moment to Eldwin, if I might."

By this time, all of the Elders had risen from their chairs, and he saw Eldwin step out from the right side.

"With the Council's permission," he said as he approached Robby.

"I'm very sorry, Eldwin," Robby told him in a quiet tone when he was close enough. "I only wanted to ask if you could carry this letter to Ullin when you go in the morning."

"Certainly, I will. Is there anything else that ye may need? Would ye like for me to wait for a reply?"

"No. I don't think that will be needed."

"Very well," Eldwin took the letter and put it into his pocket. "I will see to it that he receives it in the mornin'."

"Thank you. I'll leave you now. But can you tell me how it goes?"

"We only began not long ago. Each is free to speak. I went first an' put all questions before the council. Whether to give ye permission to enter the Great Treasure room, whether to grant ye the means to do so, an' whether to permit yer companion to come an' give aid with the reckonin' of things. It was decided to take the last question first."

"Well. Thank you. I'll return to the cave, then."

Robby turned to go, but the one who had been speaking called to him.

"Lord Robby, perhaps you would indulge a few questions before you depart?"

"Of course."

Eldwin motioned Robby into the circle and chairs were pushed aside to make a way for him to do so. About a quarter of the way into the circle, Eldwin gestured for Robby to stay, then Eldwin returned to his own place.

"Perhaps you may explain to us why your companion would place a different value on the weapons than you would? And why his opinion would be of more importance than your own?"

"Certainly," Robby bowed. "I will try to explain."

The rest of the Elders sat down, awaiting his answer.

"Eldwin and Millithorpe both told me," he began, "that you collect for your Hoard all things that may be of value in the world beyond your lands, but you do so without having the means to know or to estimate such value. I agreed to make a reckoning, to the best of my ability, in exchange for the return of my company's things that were taken as a fine and a punishment against my party on the Toll Road due to an unfortunate misunderstanding. I have experience at placing values on things as I was raised and trained by a master trader and store's clerk, my father. However, my experience is mostly in trade goods, dry goods, sundries, grain, fabric, house wares, and tools. I have very little experience as a soldier. I have never even seen battle, save once, a skirmish only. My companion, who is also my cousin, called Ullin Saheed Tallin, is a Kingsman of Duinnor. He has seen great battles against the Dragonkind, as did his father and his grandfather. And he is an expert in the use of weapons and a wise judge of quality. He also knows how those weapons may be ordered in the hands of soldiers on the field of battle and how each weapon, in use with others of its kind, may increase its power against an enemy. While I may judge steel and wood and somewhat of workmanship, I am ignorant of how well they may be handled or how they may withstand the hard wear of fighting. Ullin knows these things and may heft a sword and say, 'This is made well and will swing true,' or 'This is too heavy,' or 'too short.' I may place a value on so many pounds of metal, but he measures how the flesh may wield the objects of war and the blood they may draw. Such is war and the considerations of war-making and weapon-making. It is something, alas, about which I know less than I should, and my kinsman Ullin knows more than he desires to."

The Elders' expressions had gone from uncomfortable indulgence to grim, and Robby wondered if he had misspoken.

"Tell us, then," said a voice behind Robby. He turned and saw Makewine standing to address him. "As one may need firewood when it is winter and very little during the summer, does not the value of such things vary according to the need of them?"

"Yes, of course, as with all things. But a season of war is upon us. Marauding armies move in the south and send their forces northward against nearby realms. There are many small places being overrun, not for the lack of will to resist, but for the lack of arms and the training to use them. Those who do not wish to be taken must have the means to resist, and they may pay a great price to have it."

Robby realized that he may have hit a sore spot with this remark, and he quickly moved on.

"So I would say that the need is greater now than it has been in recent years, though I regret that it is so."

Again there was a thoughtful silence and after a moment Robby turned to go.

"Might I ask you of another matter?"

Robby heard a different voice and, turning back, saw an older woman, not at all frail, but leaning on a walking stick and dressed in plain working clothes.

"Yes, ma'am," Robby bowed.

"We address the question of the weapons!" Herbert said harshly to the woman as he stood from his chair. From all around, his statement was met by cries of "Sit down!" and "Let Miladora speak!"

"Very well!" he told the crowd. "Go ahead, then!" And he sat back down with an gesture of exasperation.

"Thank you!" said the woman to the crowd. Turning to Robby, she asked, "Do you have the power to break our curses?"

Robby saw that there was no expression of hope, nor any tone of doubt or skepticism in her voice. He understood it was an open and honest question, and, just as Eldwin had indicated, it was on the minds of some.

"Honestly, I do not," he stated bluntly. "But if I understand things, and have been told the story truthfully, that power does not rest with anyone but you and your people. Surely, that is what your people have believed all these years, is it not? That if you strive to fulfill the conditions of the curses, they could be lifted? If that is so, then it is a matter of will and knowledge. If you have the will, I think I have the knowledge, and I am willing to share that with you."

"What condition or price of trade will you ask in exchange?" she asked.

"Out of order! This is not the concern before us tonight!" called out an Elder nearby to Herbert, standing angrily.

"We are here to discuss the Hoard!" shouted another from across the circle. These two were seconded by a few in the crowd, but most of the villagers cried out in dismay, saying "Let Miladora ask her questions!" and "Let the stranger answer!" and "Sit down, old fools!" and a few other insults besides. Those two who objected angrily retook their seats, and when the uproar died down, and Robby could hear again the unperturbed thrush, Miladora nodded to him with a smile.

"Your friendship, only, will I ask," answered Robby. "And a regard in friendship of your people toward mine."

At first, this statement was met with silence, but then an agreeable murmur spread among the people. Arldewain, who sat near to Eldwin, then stood and, first bowing to Miladora, asked Robby, "Then will you not share with us now your knowledge?"

"With respect, sir, I will not. Your people must first decide the questions before you, since all else depends upon that. Then, should the accounting of the Hoard take place, you may then decide whether you have the will to live without the curses. Only then might my knowledge be of any use; otherwise, I will not unnecessarily delay my journey with idle notions that are bound to be fruitless."

Another Elder stood, bowing to Arldewain, and asked, "Whichever way we decide, would you and your companions share news and lore of the world with us? For reasonable compensation, of course."

"We may be inclined to do so, once these other matters are settled. But we can only stay a very short time since we are already much delayed from our journey."

After a long moment, Eldwin stood.

"Thank ye, Lord Robby. I think now we have decisions to make."

"Very well," Robby bowed and departed.

Chapter 18

The Heir of the Hoard

Day 97
148 Days Remaining

"Rise and shine, sleepyhead!"

Robby moved his arm from over his eyes and blinked in the dim light filtering into the cave from a misty dawn. Sheila's face came to hover over him, and she kissed him on the lips before he could respond.

"How did you get here?" he asked groggily, struggling to sit up. The others of his company were standing nearby, smiling at him.

"You may well ask! How, indeed!" said Ashlord. "But by the magic of these people who only an hour ago saved us from the Damar."

"The Damar? On the Toll Road?"

"Aye!" said Billy, with the look of a pent-up story in his eye. "But they got the worst of it! Or so I was told. Eldwin, here, can more rightly say what happened, since he was at both ends, so to say."

Robby had thrown himself to bed fully dressed only a few hours ago, and was quite wrinkled and disheveled as he sat up with his legs over the side of the cot, rubbing his eyes.

"Yes, sir, there was a bit of a row along the road last night. Late last night, while still at our meetin', we got word of a party of mounted Damar ridin' toward the Toll Road. By the time we got there, they had already smashed the toll gate an' were nearly on top of yer friends, here. They may well have ridden on past, but we could not take a chance on it, so we took 'em on."

"Ye should of heard the uproar!" Billy exclaimed with obvious delight and bursting to get his say in the tale. "We all heard 'em comin' an' got all up in arms. But then thar was an almighty noise of hollerin' an' poppin', an' horses neighin', an' all manner of carryin' on, just out of sight from whar we stood ready in our clearin' for far an' blood. Then come ol' Eldwin, an' four er five other of his mates an' says, 'We gotta get ye out of here!' er somethin' of the sort. An' so then a bunch of them pix—, er, them little folk started takin' us by the hands an' poppin' off with us with thar finger-snappin'. An' whoosh! Oh, man! What a way of gettin' about!"

While Billy spoke, more Nowhereans came into the cave bearing the company's things, and another, larger group was busy just outside of the cave stacking up the things they had taken from the Damar.

"Was anyone hurt?" Robby asked.

"Oh, no!" said Eldwin. "Leastwise, none of our people, though I think some of the Damar got their pride bruised, somewhat. Before they knew it, they'd lost their horses an' saddles an' weapons an' gear." Eldwin glanced at the mouth of the cave where various articles of clothing were being piled up. "And more than a few lost practically everything they had."

"Oh!"

"Oh, yes!" said Makewine, coming up and handing Ullin his shoulder bag. "Our fines for cheaters can be quite stiff!"

"Well," said Eldwin, "that is a different matter."

"It appears that we were let off very lightly by comparison," Ashlord said, chuckling at the thought of hardened soldiers running in panic back the way they had come with not a stitch between skin and night air.

"We don't much like them Damar, anyways," added Makewine, "for messing up our trade all those years ago and for being so uppity-like."

"So the council agreed to let not just Ullin, but all my companions join me here!" said Robby, clearly delighted to see his friends.

"Well, sir. Not exactly," Eldwin said.

"Some of us Elders sort of took matters into our own hands," explained Makewine. "You see, when word came to us about the Damar, we were still arguing. The meeting immediately broke up as about forty of us popped up to the Toll Road to head them off. I must say, in spite of all his bluster and stupidity, Herbert was a marvel to see in action."

"Yes," added Eldwin, "the Toll Road is his greatest pride. An' he don't take rule-breakin' very lightly. I've rarely seen him in such a fury!"

"So once Herbert and the others had the Damar in hand, the rest of us started moving your friends away. I'm afraid that started a big argument, still going on just down the path a bit, but I think we've got Herbert and his clan back on our side."

"He needs us, now," Eldwin took up, "to help justify bringin' yer friends here without council approval."

"When they hear our tale of Herbert's heroism and valor," Makewine winked, "his position will be much enhanced with the people."

"An' his head will swell to twice its normal size, I'll warrant!" chuckled Eldwin.

"Well, I don't understand the workings of your council," Robby said. "But I'm grateful and happy to see my friends."

At this point, Robby shook hands and hugged his companions, Ibin lifting him off the ground with his normal exuberance.

Herbert entered with his usual swagger.

"So! Here we are!" he pronounced. "As keeper of the Toll Road, an' sheriff of the land, I must tell ye that ye were narrowly saved from certain ill-treatment an' insult at the hands of the arrogant intruders. Yet, yer stay here—at some risk to me personally, I might add—is wholly at the whim of the Council of Elders. They will not be happy when word reaches them of yer arrival, an' I expect a mighty bout of finger-pointin' an' rule-namin' afore it's over. But let me just assure ye that little has changed an' that we still hold ye to yer word on makin' a proper reckonin' of the Hoard."

"I understand," Robby said, bowing and trying not to laugh at Herbert.

"An' now ye have more to reckon, too." Herbert motioned at the loot outside. "I have given orders to Millithorpe that it be added properly to all else within these caves as is in keepin' with our ways."

"I will begin working with Millithorpe right away," Robby said. "And I may as well make use of my friends' labor, if they are willing and if it is allowed."

"Well, why, um, I mean to say…hmm." Herbert glanced at Eldwin. "I think that would be in order, should ye need them."

"And what of the meeting of the Elders? Will it continue and decide the other questions?"

"It will resume at the noon hour," said Eldwin. "But I'm afraid I will be required before then. I should speak with some of the Elders who are with me on the question an' some others who are undecided, an' prepare for our meetin', especially since so much has happened."

"By all means. I would like some time with my friends, too, before setting to work."

They all walked out of the Foyer together.

"I'm afraid I never had the chance to deliver yer letter," Eldwin said. "Shall I do so, now?"

"No, I'll take it. Thank you. And good luck with the meeting!"

Robby and friends watched them go as Millithorpe made his way through the clearing outside the cave, now crowded with the stacks and piles of things taken from the Damar. Near the path, many horses were tethered, towering over the little people who attended them and who were still arriving with more things.

"Goodness!" Robby exclaimed just as Millithorpe came up. "How many Damar were there?"

"Why, sir, ah, oh, let's see. We reckon about seventy."

"Seventy!"

"Yes, sir. We think about five or six got away clean, with most of their things, and one or two on horseback. But all the rest went running back as fast as they could go, without even their boots. I will give you something of a count of things before I go. It won't take very long, I don't think."

"We will help. But, Ullin, I wonder if, while I help Millithorpe, you might be good enough to read this letter that I intended for you to receive this morning? Perhaps, a little later, we might discuss it privately, as it bears upon our family, somewhat."

"Yes. Certainly, if you wish. Are you sure you would not want me to help out with all these things?"

"Yes, but later. There will be plenty for you to do! Please first read, while I get these things sorted."

"RobbyRobby, Robbyguess, Robbyguess, guesswhatoneofthelittle, oneofthe, guesswhatoneofthelittleonessaid? He, hesaidhe, hesaidhewouldlikemeandSheilatosing, tosingforthem!"

"Oh? Sing for them?" Smiling, Robby glanced at Sheila who made a face and nodded.

"Yeah, yeahandthey, yeahandtheywantmetoplaymymandolin,too."

"Oh?"

"Apparently they have kept watch over us all this time, day and night," Ashlord said as he walked to where the Damar saddlebags were being stacked. "Just as you suspected."

"Last night," Ullin explained, "Ibin and Sheila gave us a few songs. To lift our spirits, somewhat. And we swapped stories, too."

"They must have overheard us," Sheila added.

"They want to trade for their singing and song-making," Ullin went on, sitting down on a nearby crate to begin reading Robby's letter.

"Yeahand, and, yeah, theymighttellusastory!" Ibin nodded, grinning as if he had just won a prize ham and was about to devour it.

As Ullin read, the rest pitched in, under Robby and Millithorpe's direction, by sorting and noting quantities and then taking the new items to the proper storage chambers within the cave. Like Robby, his companions were amazed at the work the small folk had done carving out the passageways so neatly, and they were surprised at the quantity of goods stored inside. Ullin finished re-reading Robby's letter and joined in the work. He nodded to Robby and said, "We must speak about your notions."

They made short work of sorting out the loot from the Damar, and Millithorpe departed while Robby took his friends to the Treasure Room. They were awed by the tremendous display within, standing before the massive iron gates that kept the Great Treasure secure. They stood for a long time in reverent silence. Even Ibin sensed there was something otherworldly about the gleaming and sparkling array beyond the iron gate.

"All this came from Haven Hill?" Billy asked in a whisper, as if any noise might blow away the sight as a vaporous apparition.

"Tulith Attis was not just a fortress, Master Bosk, and home to Heneil and his household," Ashlord said, "but it was also home to other lords of Men and Elifaen. There were estates in the countryside all around the citadel, and along the ridge were mansions and fine houses. Attis was a vibrant place, full of light and all the things that go with living well. A crossing point of the Saerdulin, by means of the bridge, and the northernmost place that boats could land from the faraway sea. So it was an important place on the trade routes of east-west and north-south. At the time of the great battle, the valuables of the people would have been gathered into the vaults of the fortress for protection against the invaders. I imagine that this is only a very small portion of what was looted when the summit fell."

Ashlord spoke softly, and the others felt they could almost see Tulith Attis as it once had been, and faint strains of music they heard, fading into the distant ringing of steel and the cry of battle as he ended his words. They remained for a little longer, wide-eyed in far away wonder, until Robby motioned them to go, and they lined out into the passageway with only Ullin lingering, his eyes still on the treasure.

"You understand my plan, then?" Robby asked.

"I do."

"Did I get it right? In the note that I wrote to you?"

"Yes. Yes, you did. I'm amazed by your memory."

"Do you think it will work?"

"I don't see why not," Ullin replied, his tone somewhat distant.

"Thank you."

When they emerged, Ashlord called them all together, saying, "While the Nowhereans meet and discuss things, so should we."

He was holding a sheaf of papers. "When going through the bags of the Damar, I came upon these. I thought it best to retain them and not mention them to the little folk for the time being. This document, " he said, holding it up to a lamp to read, "is a warrant for the 'arrest of Robby Ribbon of Passdale, Ullin Saheed Tallin, House of Fairoak and Tallin, Collandoth, called Ashlord in the Common Speech, as well as Billy Bosk, Sheila Pradkin, and Ibin Brinnin, of Barley County in the old Eastlands Realm. These are to be considered spies and enemies of Damar.' It goes on to say that the Damar captain—named here and presumably from whom Herbert took this bag—this captain was authorized to pay in bounty 'one hundred Damar gold coins for any one of these named to any who may deliver the spies to him alive, or ten gold coins for any who may be delivered dead.' So there!"

He let that sink in.

"Toolant must have given over our names and told the warlord of our mission to Duinnor. But that is not all," Ashlord said, turning to the next document. "This is a list of orders to be given to various Damar posts, including the one at Redwater Gorge which is just ahead of us. The Damar are to be especially vigilant, to prevent any travelers who do not bear Damar letters from crossing out of these lands, and, among various other orders, to close the bridge at the gorge to all who are westward bound except Damar soldiers or those bearing Damar letters. So forth and so on. It also directs each post to give one-fifth of their ranks over to the command of the captain bearing these orders, named in the margin, and so forth and so on."

"And these," Ashlord turned to the third parchment, "are the captain's own orders. He is commanded to destroy the toll gate, to open the toll road of the pixie-folk, to make it for Damar use only, and to then ride with all speed to Redwater Gorge to deliver orders and warrants. He is to arrest anyone he finds along the road that are without proper letters, to make whatever needed sojourns to locate and apprehend those mentioned in the warrants of arrest. He is to build his forces by gleaning mounted riders and foot soldiers from each post until he has sufficient numbers to send a force south under trustworthy command to take control of all possible crossings from the plains into Damar lands, occupying certain villages and billeting men as needed. The remaining force, under the command of this captain, is to probe and patrol all of the disputed lands within Damar along and to the north and west of the toll road, destroying all villages that do not yield to Damar control, and taking whatever prisoners that may be conveniently sent back to Damar City or otherwise employed by the captain's forces. All others are to be eliminated."

He put the documents on the table and sat on a crate.

"Yes, I fear all this is the work of Toolant," Ashlord said. "Lord Tallin's plan to have him removed has either failed or else it had not yet taken place when these orders were issued."

"The Damar seem better organized than I imagined," commented Ullin. "The tone of these orders, the ability to assemble such a force so swiftly from soldiers already in the field, the implication that the orders would be carried out without question."

"I guess those papers of passage that my grandfather gave us are now worthless," Robby added.

"They'd be our death warrant if we showed them!" exclaimed Billy.

"Maybe not," offered Sheila. "These orders have not yet reached the post at the gorge, have they? There's a chance we can get across before new orders are sent."

"Don't you think it was foolish for the Damar to send such orders only along the Toll Road?" Robby asked. "From what I've been told, the Nowhereans have always trounced them very soundly, and so the Damar have avoided the road for years. Why wouldn't they instead send important orders the safest way, along the longer road around these lands?"

"They may have done so," said Ullin. "Or may yet when those of last night make it back."

"It all means that we should conclude our business here as swiftly as possible and get away from Damar territories," Ashlord concluded, looking at Robby. Robby nodded, and they waited for him to reply, but it was Billy who cut in.

"Well, it seems to me that we're all in this thing together-like, an' I'll warrant none of us rightly understands it all," he said. "An' I'm all about gettin' our things back an' movin' on from here as much as anybody. But it seems to me like we can't just cut an' run. Them Damar's sure to come back. An' I doubt they'll come along the road like before. If I got things guessed halfway right, I'd say they're gonna set about this place like them Redvests did in Barley. I ain't for lettin' that happen to nobody else if I can help it. We need to at least tell the little folk something 'bout what's goin' on. So they have a better warnin' than we did, an' can maybe get ready."

"Billy's right," joined Sheila. "These people may have a tricky way, but they'll be no match if taken by surprise."

"We cannot protect these people," countered Ullin. "This is shaping up to be a wide war. Our only hope is to get Robby to Griferis. We have far to go and little time to get there before it is too late."

"Their only chance is for at least the first curse to be lifted," said Robby. "At least then they may move about, and leave if they must. They could still use their way of popping around to head off approaching threats."

"Yeah!" Billy agreed. "Just think what confusion an' mayhem they could set off among the Damar, if the little folk could strike outside these lands!"

"But do you know how to lift that curse?" Ashlord asked Robby.

"I think so," Robby said, glancing at Billy.

"And what about the other two?"

"Maybe. I'm not sure," Robby glanced at Ullin. "I'm working on that part."

Ashlord looked quizzically at Robby and Ullin, but he could not catch Ullin's eye, so he searched Robby's face carefully, then smiled. "I see. And if the Elders decide to permit you into the Treasure Room, how long do you think it will take to complete your work?"

"Not long."

"Well, then!" Ashlord put his hands on his knees and stood up. "Then let us hope the Elders come to a speedy decision. Meanwhile, I am willing to go and await them in the town, and leave you and Ullin to your work."

"I'm sure you will cause something of a stir," Robby replied. "I certainly did last night when I interrupted their meeting to speak to Eldwin."

"OhmetooIwanttoIwanttogo,too!" cried Ibin, standing up eagerly.

"You may as well all go."

"Bring your mandolin, Ibin," Sheila suggested. Then to Robby, "Maybe we can get this singing stuff over with!"

Ullin and Robby were left alone, and they set to work on the arms. Ullin inspected them and pronounced that much of the weaponry and armor was serviceable, some no longer in style though in good condition. The two began to work out how much they were worth in ordinary trade.

"But they would be of great comfort to the people around Janhaven," Ullin pointed out, "particularly the shields and the lances. There is also a large supply of arrows with good points, though many of the shafts are cracked and the fletching-work is crude."

This took a good bit of going back and forth as they tried to arrive at some reasonable value.

• • •

Meanwhile, the other members of Robby's company did, indeed, cause a stir. By the time the four of them reached town, Ibin was trailing far behind in a swarm of giggling, laughing, and screaming-with-delight children, squealing happily at the giant, for none were any higher than his knee. Unfortunately for the schoolmistress, Ibin passed by just as she was trying to round up her students after a period of outside play, and she now ran after them, pulling them away and off of Ibin. She had a difficult time of it, for anyone could see that she was not naturally disposed to being stern. And, in spite of her alarm at the giant, she found Ibin's charm and his own obvious happiness infectious and disarming. At last, she rounded up all of the children, and Ibin trotted up to the others.

He arrived back with his companions just as the next stir erupted from the crowd that milled around the square listening to and sometimes jeering at the Elders at their meeting. The four had not put aside their arms, and though they smiled and bowed as they made their way to the circle of Elders, they were met with more consternation than Robby had encountered the night before. The tall pair of Ashlord and Ibin—one severe in appearance and posture with his walking stick and robes, his long black hair and beard and his piercing gaze, the other obviously as gentle as a lamb with his ridiculous grin and his mandolin slung across his back—seemed a study of opposites and aroused the people's curiosity. Billy, also grinning at the little ones, who were closer to his height than any of his companions, offset some of the Nowherean's fear with his amiable nature and his mischievous eyes.

But it was Sheila who attracted most of their attention and evoked a hushed tone as she passed. Dressed in her usual buckskins and waist jacket over her bodice, with her bow and quiver over her shoulder, her shortsword on her hip, and dagger in her boot, she appeared to them wildly exotic and beautiful. They bowed especially low and murmured "Good lady," as she passed.

"Might this be her?" some whispered. "Or has she sent her sister to come in her stead?" For they all knew the story of the lady, dressed as a warrior, who put the last curse upon them and who said she would return when the accounting was made.

The Elders all stood and faced them. Herbert had been speaking, and now he addressed them.

"These are four of the five we brought from the Toll Road," he explained to his fellow council members. "The older man is the one called Collandoth, Ashlord by Men."

"Older man, indeed!" Ashlord snorted.

"The small one is called Bilaylin, of the House of Bosk. And with him, the giant, Ibin. The lady is known as Sheila, I am told."

The Elders bowed, and their bows were returned by the travelers.

"Do you wish to address us?" Herbert asked Sheila. But Ashlord answered.

"Only to express our thanks to you, Herbert, and to Eldwin," Ashlord said, "and all the rest of you who brought us into safety before the Damar came upon us. We also thank you on behalf of the other two of our company who are now busy working in your caves. Our thanks to you all!"

Ashlord bowed again and his companions did likewise.

"Yer most welcome," Herbert bowed proudly.

Another Elder stood and said, "We welcome you in peace. The Damar we waylaid would have faced our ire whether you were on the Road or not. We have decided that Herbert and Eldwin acted bravely and prudently to bring you here, and we will not gainsay their actions."

"We do not mean to disrupt your meeting," Ashlord replied, "and yet I wonder if my companions and I may observe your discussions? Afterwards, perhaps I may share with you the happenings of the world, insofar as I know and may sum them up, and particularly news of those lands nearby to your own."

The Elders looked at one another, shrugging and nodding and talking until at last one of them said, "It is agreed that you may stay. And, after we have concluded the business before us, we would very much like to hear your news."

Another Elder now stood, and she said, "We now take up the question of the Great Treasure. First, whether to open the gate barring the treasure from inspection. Second, whether to permit the visitor to examine and reckon a value of its contents. Let us first hear from Elder Sweedmiller and Elder Finniar, the blacksmiths, about what effort it would require for us to cut the bands that lock the iron gate."

For the next hour or so, they discussed all of the preparations that would be needed to stoke the furnace and forge the required tools and chisels. Many people not on the council had to be called to answer questions about which trees could be cut, which were best, who might do the cutting of the firewood and the hauling and so forth. During this time, the crowd grew larger as more people arrived to see the strangers and to hear the debate. Sheila, in particular, was the object of much staring, and a group of men, little though they were, took it upon themselves to surround her to keep back the push of the crowd. A hushed argument broke out between some of the women with some men who were apparently their husbands, until the husbands reluctantly went away on some errand. Soon they returned bearing the largest chair they could find. They placed it before Sheila and begged her to sit. Eventually, chairs were brought for the other three strangers, but they were less grand and some of the Nowhereans were justifiably concerned at the prodigious creaking that came from underneath Ibin when he sat upon the small seat given to him. Refreshments, too, were brought, some cool juice of wild berries and some bread lathered with sweet honey-butter.

It was mid-afternoon when the Council, by vote, decided to take a recess and immediately afterwards to vote on the question before them. Some of the Elders took this opportunity to introduce themselves to the strangers. And others of the town also gathered around with interest.

Sheila and Ibin were asked if they were the giant and the great lady who sang in the wood, as told to them by some who had watched over their camp. Ibin stammered his yeses while Sheila tried to explain that she was not a great lady of an ancient house, but just a country girl. Her efforts made little change in their enthusiasm or their wonder at her, and several Nowhereans who said they were musicians asked if they might trade songs.

"I see no reason why you two should stay throughout the meeting," Ashlord suggested. "And the good society of music-sharing may go far to allay any fear or mistrust of us."

"There is a grove of trees just yonder," said Eldwyna who was one of those that spoke for the musicians, "where we would not disturb the Council."

So Sheila and Ibin agreed and were shown to the grove, depleting the crowd considerably as many followed along, leaving Billy and Ashlord to stay with the Council. Just as Billy made a move toward Sheila's more comfortable chair, several of the crowd grabbed it up and hauled it, along with Ibin's, toward the departing group. Billy smiled and shrugged and sat back down. It was not long before an Elder went about the circle clapping his hands, and his fellow Elders took their chairs.

"We now decide the question before us. Shall we devote the labor and materials needed to open the iron gate of the Great Treasure? What say ye?"

Eldwin stood and called out, "I say, yes! Do any others say likewise?"

"Yes," said Makewine standing.

"Yes," said Torridge.

"Yes," said Larris.

Brolith and Arldewain, already standing and awaiting their turn, said yes.

"Yes."

"Yes."

After about twenty yes votes, there was a pause.

"Do any others say likewise?" Eldwin called out again. "Herbert, what say ye?"

After a moment, Herbert reluctantly stood, shrugging off the discouraging hand of a fellow Elder who sat next to him.

"I say, yes! Let us be brave! Yes!"

A few more of his group also stood at that time and threw in with Herbert, and others here and there weakly assented. Moments then turned into minutes and no one else stood.

• • •

Back at the caves, Robby and Ullin continued their work in an effort to finish before sundown. Having agreed to the values for the various weapons and arms, Robby set Ullin to summing up the books pertaining to them while he completed the other ledgers and worked out a summary. They spoke very little and made quick work of it so that by the time the sky began to darken outside, Robby had double-checked his sums. Since the two had nothing more to do but wait, they stepped outside, and in the dimming light they sat near the mouth of the cave and lit their pipes. Robby watched the path carefully, but Ullin seemed lost in his own thoughts. Robby noticed it, but said nothing. Ullin wandered back to the Great Treasure room and was there, still, with the same look on his face when Robby came to find him and fetch him to other tasks. Though Ullin had agreed to Robby's plan, he showed little enthusiasm for it. So Robby wondered what troubled Ullin, and at last he asked.

"Eh?" Ullin slowly turned to face Robby.

"You seem very thoughtful," Robby repeated and added, "Is there anything amiss?"

"Oh. No. Nothing, and everything, cousin. I was only thinking of Tallinvale and what the people there now face. Wondering whether our grandfather's plan will matter at all in the end."

Robby looked down at his boots, absently noticing that his feet were as big as Ullin's. He did not know how to reply.

"If Duinnor does not stir itself," Ullin's voice trailed off.

Again, words did not come to Robby, then, abruptly, Ullin spoke again.

"All those years ago, when I left my home in Tallinvale, I wanted to be like my father. Brave, a fine warrior, to know the wide world and see the great cities. To take my place as a Kingsman, as was my duty. But I wanted also vengeance, just as he sought vengeance for his brother. Or so I thought I wanted. It did not take long," he said, looking at his hands and then rubbing them as if wiping away some invisible stain. "It did not take long for me to have my fill of vengeance and of Dragonkind blood. Nor to get my fill of the ways of Duinnor and its failing decadence, its power over Vanara, the home of my kin. But I am sworn to serve and to defend the One With No Name and all the realms under his dominion, until my heir takes my place. That is why I do not marry, Robby, and have never looked for love, though I have longed for it and for the peace that a home and family may bring. I am determined to have no heir, and thus the chain of servitude will be broken when I die, and the House of Tallin will be no more. Our grandfather senses this, I believe. And, though we have never spoken of it, his eyes see the end of days. I think that is why he does what he does, knowing his name will soon be lost, regardless of what he does. Yet, I fear for all the people of that valley, and feel I am in part to blame for the wrath that will soon be visited upon them."

By now, Sir Sun was near to ending his daily walk, and his light angled low against the surrounding hilltops. Beneath them, a somber shadow lay over the land. Billy's figure appeared along the path, blinking now and then between the trees as they watched him approach. He came into the clearing before the caves and walked up to them, and he was not smiling.

"Well, they made the decision," he told them. "They give permission to look at the Treasure, but they won't help open the gates. Don't that beat all!"

Robby sighed and nodded.

"It is as I thought it might be," he said, standing. "But I am somewhat disappointed. Still, I see no reason not to fulfill my promise and to do what I think needs doing."

Ullin nodded.

"What of Ashlord and the others?" Robby asked.

"Well, Ashlord's now givin' 'em the news, though I think they oughta had it afore they made up their minds. Anyways, so he's doin' that, an' Ibin an' Sheila are makin' jolly with their songs an' whatnot."

"Will you carry a message back to the Elders? I'm sorry to turn you around so quickly, but we have to be away from here as soon as our business is done. And we need to finish up soon."

• • •

"And so, that has been the way of things this past age," Ashlord said to the Elders. He now stood, at their invitation, like a tower over them, in the center of their circle. He had been speaking to them for an hour, having sent Billy first to find Ibin and Sheila to tell them the news of the decisions, then to carry the word to Robby and Ullin.

"Vanara in the west grows weaker, losing its land and blood slowly over all this time like a wound that cannot be staunched. To the south, the realms of Altoria and Masurthia guard the southwestern passages, but Tracia in the southeast has been beset with turmoil, and its noble houses have been overthrown. Now the usurpers prepare to march their armies westward against neighboring Masurthia. And to support their conquest they have struck northward to pillage the Eastlands of crop, fodder, and provisions. Glareth, powerful but small, does not yet know of the invasions to the south, but may soon learn. Only Tallinvale remains as a thorn in the flank of Tracia. But Tracia has made an alliance with Damar and so Tallinvale is sure to be attacked from all directions. The treachery of Tracia goes even beyond that, for they have most likely formed an accord with the king of the Dragonlands. My fear is that they will drive together in the south, coming from east and from west, overrunning Altoria and Masurthia. Their forces then united, they will turn north, marching swiftly, avoiding engagement with Vanara if they can, and traveling across the plains to strike Duinnor itself and remove their most powerful opponent first. I think their plan is then to split. While the Dragonkind will catch Vanara in a pincher, bringing more forces up from the south, the Tracians will march against Glareth Realm."

"That Men should form an alliance with Dragonkind!" uttered one Elder.

"Once the thorn of Tallinvale is picked from its side," Ashlord went on, "the eastern vanguard of combined Tracian, Damar, and Dragonkind forces will no doubt sweep away the Galinots just to the north of your lands, seeking to reach the northern passes and cutting Duinnor off from Glareth. Last night was only a taste of what may come. Your lands are surrounded by those occupied by the Damar. Even with your magical way of moving, your tricks and your cunning, you cannot be everywhere at once. It is only a matter of time before the Damar come in force to take these lands. Until then, I think they will continue to assert themselves upon you, testing you and learning how you respond. They may send their hunters into your lands and set other spies upon the hills. Since you pose no armed threat, my guess is that they will wait until spring, summer at the latest, to mount their assault. That is only a guess; they may come sooner. Indeed, they may come at any moment."

Ashlord saw that they were shaken by his grim and disturbing news. They murmured to each other and shook their heads, some exchanging heated words. Billy returned during this clamor, nodded to Ashlord, but made no comment on the disturbance.

"What hope have we?" cried out one of the Elders.

"We do not have arms suitable for our size," said another. "And we have never carried them, anyway."

"Aye! What knowledge do we have of using weapons?"

"There are too few of us, anyway!"

"One matter at a time!" shouted Makewine, holding up his hands in a gesture to restore order. "One matter at a time!"

When things settled a bit, he continued. "Mr. Ashlord, your young friend Robby says he may know how to break the first curse. When may he tell us of it?"

"Yes!" broke in another Elder anxiously. "If that curse is lifted, we may escape these lands!"

"Let him answer!"

But it was Billy who answered, saying, "Robby sends me to say that if ye come up to the caves, then he'll explain it all his own self."

"Then let us go!" said an Elder who stood and snapped his fingers. Immediately there was a cacophony of popping, and all around the circle was a blur of bubbling light as the Elders disappeared. But Eldwin and Makewine and a few others remained and, approaching Billy and Ashlord, offered to take them to the caves so that they would not have to trudge back up the hill.

• • •

The clearing in front of the cave was crowded with the Elders when they arrived. Billy and Ashlord made their way through to the mouth of the cave where Robby and Ullin stood, now with Sheila and Ibin also, facing the Nowhereans. Torches were lit against the falling night, and Robby stood silent with his arms crossed in an attitude of thought. Some of the Elders tried to ask Robby about the curses, but Ullin, stepping in front of them, said firmly, "Robby will speak when you are ready to hear him."

"I tell you now how you may break the first curse laid against you, that spoken by Bailorg the Vile," Robby said loudly and abruptly to the Elders. "Find a grove of strong trees. Using all your skills at woodcutting and woodworking, build there a large platform around the trees, high amongst their topmost branches. Make it sturdy so that the wind may not shake it. Take to that place all of your swine to be raised. When the first litter is born and weaned, the curse of Bailorg may be lifted, for pigs will then grow in trees, and you may then find your borders open to your passing."

Astounded and somewhat humiliated that in all these years they themselves did not think of this solution, the Elders were dumbfounded.

"Is that all there is to it?" asked Herbert.

"It could be. You should try it," Robby replied.

"It will take some time and many laborers," said one Elder, not so much to Robby as to the others. "And winter comes and we are not yet prepared for it."

"There are many things you may not be prepared for," said Ashlord over the hubbub. "You must try, nonetheless, if you value your families and your lives. Otherwise, you will be trapped here when the enemy comes."

"We must get started right away!" Makewine declared.

"Wait!" called out Robby. "I have more to say to you. Come to the Treasure Room and hear my words concerning the value of the Hoard."

Robby turned, and they all followed him through the well-lit Foyer and passageway and into the Treasure Room. This, as Robby surmised, was an uncomfortable place for the Elders, and the shimmering jewels and precious metals beyond the bars seemed to glow and sparkle even more exquisitely in the presence of those whose hands had taken it from Tulith Attis. And, whether from the intensity of the light, or from within their own hearts, it was here that the Nowhereans felt their history most heavily. They spoke not a word, and those who wore hats removed them. Many, including Eldwin and Herbert and the other more stalwart among them, had expressions of grief on their faces.

"The curse of Bailorg against you means little to me, and I care not that it may be broken, for it was unjust and made of spite. I am glad if any work that he wrought may be unmade. Moreover, he has no more power over you. He is dead, by my own hands, and his flesh is burned in a fire of his own making. His evil craft is gone from the world, though the evil seeds he planted still spread, and, until you do as I suggest with your swine, his curse remains.

"The Curse of Navis, however, I do care about. I understand his grief and his fury, and I do not lightly undertake its undoing. Truly, as he said, you were a little people and are now despised and shunned. Yet, his sentence against you was in two parts, that the treasure be increased in value a thousand times, and that it be returned to the heirs of those from whom it was taken. It was to help you achieve the first part that I did my reckoning. Answer me now: Do you permit me to examine the treasure?"

The Elders looked at him blankly, too fearful, of a sudden, to speak.

"Answer me your decision!" Robby demanded.

"Yes," spoke Eldwin uncomfortably. "We decided, yes."

"Yet you put your own desires before the call of your duty, and you decided beforehand to make no effort to assist me by opening the gate. You give me a hollow consent," Robby accused, not without some anger in his voice. "Consent made meaningless by your lack of will to see it through. I, for my part, gave my word, and I do not need your help to fulfill it!"

Robby turned away from them and put his hand on the thick band that was welded around the gates. Instantly, a rumble was felt beneath their feet and bits of ceiling flecked down upon them. With the sound of a mighty gong, the steel band burst asunder, unbending itself like a bow relieved of its arrow, and it fell away ringing onto the floor as the two gates of iron swung inward with an earsplitting groan. In the dizzying silence that followed, Robby entered the Treasure Room and approached the first shelf where a circlet lay. It was finely wrought of gleaming gold with a single small glittering diamond on its front. He picked it up with both hands, carefully holding it before him for all to see, and with it he returned to those watching from outside the iron gates.

"I thus complete the reckoning of the Hoard," he said. "Those things added to the Hoard by you over the years on one side of the balance, and this Great Treasure on the other. It is my finding that the added things, when combined in value all together, are worth about as much as this modest circlet of gold alone, and do not measure at all against the rest of the priceless treasure."

Many of the Elders, Eldwin included, were devastated by this news and felt their cheeks redden with frustration and anger. All of their efforts, their whole way of life, all of the years of adding to the Hoard so that its value might grow seemed a pitiful waste. But they understood the honesty of Robby's pronouncement, knowing in their hearts the truth of it, and their emotions turned from anger to shame and embarrassment. Tears rolled down Millithorpe's face.

"All is not lost," Robby said firmly. "Your efforts have not been in vain, and there is wisdom to be found in your ways. You have protected this treasure with a simple and honest understanding of your duty. You have sought to bring honor to your charge by your labors and by your stewardship of the Hoard. You, Elders of your people, against whom the curse of Navis was spoken, have led your offspring wisely and have passed to them your own determination to overcome the hardships of your fate. You have, therefore, created a legacy besides that given into your keeping. As for the Great Treasure, it was taken during a time of plenty, a time when other things had greater value than gold. A time when jewels were traded among children. Since then such things have become rare and of great price, the possessions of the great and the mighty. Their value is increased also by the deep connection they make through history to that age, and surely few other objects of the world may compare to them. So, due to your protection of them and the passage of time, with the changes in the world from that age to this, their value is a thousand-fold increased, and more. Indeed, the first part of the curse that Navis laid upon you has long been fulfilled, though you never knew it. Yet, I do declare it so."

The Elders could hardly believe their ears. They shook their heads, dumfounded at the revelation.

"Now, let the second part of his curse be addressed." Robby turned to Ullin. "These things I learned only very recently. By tradition among Men, legacies are passed to the eldest male heir and to the next and to the next. By tradition among Elifaen, the blood line passes from female to female, though the males are the keepers of worldly objects. Heneil had a brother, Pellen, who by his wife, Myrium, bore a son named Dalcadian, who was but a young man living in Vanara when Tulith Attis fell. As the sole surviving male of Heneil's lineage, the lineage of Silmain who was once King of Vanara, Dalcadian would have been heir to the treasure of Tulith Attis, had it been saved. In later years, he wed Lady Finteri, a child of the Men of Glareth of the House of Tallin. In Vanara, they sired a man-child, called Metlar, who inherited the Tallin surname since there was no other of that line. Dalcadian died in the Dragonlands, and so, even though the line of the Faere was broken, the line of Men continued from mother to son, and from son to son. Metlar wed a lady of Glareth, too, and sired Danig Saheed Tallin, who in his time wed the Elifaen Lady Kahryna of the House of Fairoak in Vanara, and she bore him two sons and a daughter. Both sons were killed in battle, but not before the second son fathered a son of his own. This is he, Ullin Saheed Tallin, son of Aram, son of Danig, son of Metlar, son of Lady Finteri and Dalcadian, son of Pellen, son of Silmain. Ullin Saheed, sired of the House of Tallin, heir to that name, and the scion of Fairoak, bloodhouse of the Elifaen."

Ullin, though he knew Robby's plan, looked grim, and Robby noticed a wavering in his eyes, almost panic.

"Please bow," Robby asked him. Ullin did so, and Robby placed the circlet on his head.

"I therefore return this treasure to its rightful heir!" Robby declared and stepped away. "Do you, on behalf of those before you who once lived upon the heights of Tulith Attis, accept the return of this legacy?"

Ullin hesitated and looked over the anxious faces turned to him. He slowly reached up, removed the circlet, and said, "I do not."

Robby, astonished, looked at Ullin in disbelief. Ashlord's mouth fell open, and he glanced from Ullin to Robby, sensing some sudden conflict between them.

"I cannot, I say," Ullin spoke emphatically to Robby. "Not until these people show their worth in the world and fulfill my charge to them."

"I promised I would place no condition on releasing them from the curse," Robby stated.

"This condition is not yours. Forgive me, but it is mine."

Ullin then turned to the Elders, and said, "When you have cast off the first curse and are able to leave these lands, I bid you send parties east and go to the relief of Tallinvale. There, you must show your worth by making havoc upon the enemies of Tallinvale, joining in the defense of the city and of the people therein. Make you an alliance with the House of Tallin and show your greatness in deed. Let your stature then be measured not by the height of your brow, but by the summit of your valor. This I charge you: Be hidden no more from the world, but let it be known to the world that you protect not only your own people, but all others who are free and good, or who long to be so. As token of our pact, let all of the Hoard, all of the contents of these caves, aside from the treasure in this room, be given over to your people, to be distributed and used as needed for your welfare. And let the bands of this gate be reforged so that the Great Treasure may remain in safekeeping until the Lords of Tallinvale may reclaim this legacy. So let it be done!"

Chapter 19

Curses and Blessings

Day 98
147 Days Remaining

Ullin and Eldwin stayed low, Ullin on his belly, and Eldwin crouching on his knees, as they peered over an old moss-covered log and downward toward the gorge below. They could see the roadway running through the trees on this side of the gorge and where it joined the Toll Road about a hundred yards directly under the high ledge where they hid. Stretching from that point below and crossing over the gorge was the bridge, a long narrow affair, barely wide enough for three riders abreast. It was built by the same craftsmen who had constructed the bridge at Tulith Attis and with something of the same appearance as the stonework of its two supporting arches, one on either side of the rocky walls of the deep gorge. In between these two a full third of the bridge was supported from chains and cables, more like the bridge at Passdale. Ullin saw only four soldiers on the near side of the bridge; there were probably more of them out of sight below the treetops that blocked the downward view. He counted six on the far side and two more on the bridge itself.

Ullin's stunning refusal of the treasure, along with his charge to the little people, had created friction between Robby and himself. Robby was disappointed and upset at Ullin, and the Nowhereans were baffled. Afterwards, he and Robby had a mild argument, in the presence of their companions, but out of earshot of the Nowhereans. Clearly, Robby did not approve, but Ullin, though apologetic, stood firm. It helped that Ashlord seemed to support Ullin's decision, and Ashlord suggested that it might be a good thing to give the Nowhereans a new mission. The group talked late into the night, until the tension between them abated, and all agreed to be off and away in the morning. So they slept restlessly that night in the cave. At first light, Ullin left with Eldwin to scout the way ahead to the gorge while Robby and the others prepared for departure.

"It looks as though the far side is where their camp must be," Ullin observed. "They don't seem very cautious, since the gates are open on both ends and no one mans the guard platforms."

"Hm. Yer eyes are not blinded by the fog, then?" Eldwin asked, peering hard toward where Ullin was looking.

"Fog? It is a clear morning."

"For ye, it may be so. But I can only barely see this side of the bridge. A thick rollin' mist rises from the middle of the gorge, an' I see no break in those gray clouds from there to the sky."

"Do you not see even the mountain tops beyond?"

"No. Only, high up there," Eldwin pointed nearly straight up," some bit of blue."

"What about southward? What do you see there?" Ullin gestured to their left.

"Just a bit of road, nearby trees on hills. But behind those the fog is thick, an' I do not even see shadows in it."

"So that is the way of Bailorg's curse?"

"Yes, it is, an' has been so since it was uttered against us. Many, many times we have tried to go through the mists, only to find ourselves where we began. Nearly every year some one of us tries again, but never gets far. I, meself, tried not three years ago, on the southeast side of our lands."

"What if I guided you? My eyes can see the way."

"We have tried that. Here, take my hand."

When Ullin did so, the scene darkened into a murky cloud, boiling constantly but not moving away, blocking Ullin's view of the bridge and the gorge and the lands beyond. When he let go of Eldwin's hand, the mist evaporated, and once again Ullin could see all that he had before.

"Great stars!"

"We have tried followin' those that travel along the road, even by tyin' rope an' twine to them. But always our knots come undone, or the cord comes unraveled, an' we lose those who lead us in the fog, even though they are but an arm's reach away."

"I do not understand how such a thing can be," Ullin said, shaking his head. "Though I have encountered many mysterious things."

"We don't understand it, either, how a person's words may change the world of others before their very eyes."

Ullin turned and put his back against the trunk, sprawling his long legs out.

"I supposed that's the way of it, isn't it?" he reflected. "That so much of what we do comes from what is said. A man may take offense and lash out because of it, or fall in love at the sweetness of its sound."

Eldwin slumped down beside him.

"But how may the mist that I see come of words, an' one's size be reduced by the speakin' of them?"

"It is beyond me. How do the geese know that winter comes and fly away southward? How does a tree learn to steal fire from Sir Sun, to give it back in our hearths? And what makes shy Lady Moon to show her whole face only once a month, gaining and losing her courage little by little, over and over?"

"Such matters are too great for me own poor mind," sighed Eldwin.

"Though, if I could read, perhaps some of the answers may be found in the books an' stories we have collected in our town."

"More words!" Ullin chuckled. "But surely things may be learned from the wise ones who wrote of them. Someday, I hope to spend all of my days reading again all of the things that I read as a child, and new things, too. It is something like your way of traveling, reading is. With just a little effort, one can go far in little time. Tell me, why have you never learned?"

"Oh, sir! It is a shame upon me," Eldwin said, shrugging. "But I am too weak for the task. An', to make me shame all the greater, I am the only one among all of me family who is of age an' cannot read. I have tried, surely! An' many have tried to teach me. But I do not see letters properly. They do not stay still for me as they do for others. A word that I am taught becomes some other word when I later look upon it. Sometimes, I think I know what the word is supposed to say, but I become confused an' lose me place an' cannot find the word again."

"Yet you seem very knowledgeable, nonetheless."

"Oh, I remember things extraordinarily well. I practice what is told to me by sayin' them again an' again," Eldwin tapped his head, "up here. Me children or grandchildren read to me nearly every night, too, an' so I learn of things that way, as well. An' every seventh day, we have a gatherin' of the town, an' things are read an' stories are told to each other. On special occasions, we do the same. Such as Winter's Night when we recite our year's story an' repeat the story of our beginnings in these lands. There is much told, then, an' I listen an' listen."

Just then they heard a distant shout. Quickly peering over the fallen tree, Ullin saw the gate lowered on the near side of the bridge and some stirring on the far side. Three figures on buckmarls were being challenged as they approached the far gate, one in the lead and two side by side just behind. They drew to a halt and exchanged words with the guards and the lead rider handed down something, papers maybe, or payment more likely, to the commanding Damar in charge of the others.

"What do ye see?" Eldwin asked.

"Three riders from the westlands."

"How can ye tell?"

"They ride buckmarls. They are being made to pay a crossing fee, I think. Here they come."

Eldwin squinted hard to see into the fog and saw at last dark figures emerge halfway across the bridge, like shadows in the mist. It was odd for him to see the Damar soldiers on this side of the bridge wave a signal to the shrouded side, and then, in response to something they saw, lift the gate to permit the riders to pass.

"Now I see them. They are takin' the Toll Road," he said.

"I think we should keep an eye on them," Ullin suggested. "You know these lands. Can we get ahead of them?"

"Surely. If ye take me hand, we'll pop right through to the next bend."

• • •

As soon as they started, Ullin and Eldwin arrived far along the way at a place slightly above a bend in the road. Eldwin released Ullin's hand, and for a brief moment Ullin swayed with a slight dizzy spell from the rapid popping. After a few minutes, the riders appeared at an easy pace, and Ullin and Eldwin quickly hid behind a tree. A few yards away, the riders halted and remained still. Ullin and Eldwin heard the soft hooves stop and the nearby snort of a buckmarl, and Eldwin looked up at Ullin in alarm.

"They've smoked us," Ullin said softly. Stepping out from behind the tree, Ullin faced the travelers. The two in the rear already had arrows on their bowstrings, and one was turning to face the other way while the other urged his mount in front of their leader.

"Who goes!" Ullin called, his own hand instinctively on his hilt.

"What business is it of yours? You do not own this road or these lands," retorted the one now in front, his bow creaking and his arrow pointing at Ullin.

Ullin heard soft popping around him and understood that they were now joined all around by Eldwin's fellows, though he could see none of them, so well they were hidden. The hooded head of the rider in the middle turned, hearing the sound, too, Ullin surmised.

"I am charged with the safe keeping of these lands!" Herbert's shrill voice proclaimed. Glancing down, Ullin saw him standing just to his right. "An' I keep this road, too. The challenge stands. Who are ye? An' why do ye travel this way?"

"You are the one called Herbert," said a woman's voice from under the hood.

"I well know me own name!" Herbert shot back in his usual impatient manner. "What is yers?"

"You never asked before," she said. She dismounted and approached, her escort easing his string somewhat as she passed him. She lifted her hood. "Do you need to know it now?"

Her face was broad and round with high cheekbones and dark tan skin. Her light brown hair was loose over her back with long braids over the front of her shoulders in the fashion of Vanaran warriors. A band of red copper, burnished and studded with a single green gemstone wrapped her forehead and held her hair back. It was shaped along the sides like the narrow wings of a bird. Down from this band hung a sheer black veil to her nose, completely covering her eyes.

Ullin was struck by the powerful resemblance to Sheila but could see this woman was of ageless Elifaen blood. He bowed as the others around him knelt. He detected not only some deep respect they had for her, but also fear.

"I have come again, as I said I would," she told them. "But this is not one of your people. He has the look of Duinnor about him. Answer me, Eldwin. Come! Rise and tell me who this Kingsman is."

Eldwin nodded at Ullin, and the two of them stepped down from the bank and onto the roadway to face her. When Eldwin hesitated, she said to him, "You wonder at my veil, but fear it not. I am the same who left you here those many years ago. Those years have had their share of wear on me no less than you, and this veil I wear is the result, as a shield for my weary eyes. Please, tell me: Who is your would-be protector?"

"This is Ullin Saheed, House of Fairoak, House of Tallin."

"The Joined House of Fairoak and Tallin. I know of it. Many Fairoaks have been my friends, though it is a long time since their lands were given up. Tallin was a great lord of Men, and I recall his defiance, both in battle and, later, in the courts of Duinnor. A general who led his forces at their front. I heard that when the Fairoak lands were lost, Lord Tallin took his family back to their old lands in the east. It is a place nearby, I think."

"He is my grandfather. Tallinvale is some days ride from here."

"Hm-m," she nodded. "Then perhaps I have seen you before, too. I was told that Tallin Kingsmen are first among those sent by Duinnor to fight the Dragonkind. The honor of doing so is only given to the mighty, or to those Duinnor fears. It may be that we have fought together? Upon Tamkal Plain? Or perhaps at the Battle of Saerdulin?"

"I am not Elifaen, and those battles were before my time."

"Oh, well, there have been more recent battles. Garmitor. The Green Citadel."

"I fought at Garmitor. My father was at the second siege of the Green Citadel and died near a place called Peldown."

"Ah, the Gory Gulch," she said, and a cloud crossed her face. "I was not there. Many of our kin rest forever in that place."

During this time, the two who were still mounted put away their arrows, though they remained wary. After a long pause, the lady looked at Eldwin, then at Herbert. Addressing them all, she said, "My name is Esildre, of the House of Elmwood. We are in the northlands of Vanara."

"I have traveled through that country," Ullin nodded, "and have seen the great trees that grow there. And I have passed through the Valley of Dreams and visited the Temple of Beleron there. It is a beautiful land, and its people no less than the land."

"My father retains extensive lands there," she said, "but my relations are mostly in lower Vanara. I, myself, reside in northernmost Vanara, near the border of Duinnor."

She smiled and turned to Eldwin, reaching out her hand.

"I am pleased to see you, Eldwin. I think you have much to tell me, as you had the first and second times we saw each other."

Eldwin blushed and took her hand meekly and bowed.

"I do, Lady. Yer comin' is as ye foretold, an' those things ye divined have come to pass."

"Are they? But you do not seem happy. Tell me, is there trouble among your people?"

Eldwin shook his head, glancing at Ullin, and then nodded, struggling for words. Ullin looked on, sensing the many emotions stirring within himself and within those around him. She was beautiful, and, like Sheila, was feminine in spite of her manner of dress. But Esildre sought not to hide her qualities. And everything about her—the sensual cast of her armor, the movement of her head and arms, her poise and enigmatic smile, everything—was feminine with a natural air of confidence. Ullin felt an unexpected pang in his heart when she turned her veil his way, but, at the same time, he felt an unimaginable gulf between them. He wondered if she might be one of the First Ones who once soared lithely through the air and who later felt the wings torn from her body. One who saw the departure of Aperion and a host of her own kind, trapped ever since in a spiral of violence, steeped in melancholia alien to her fiber yet now the ruling stars of her long life. How much of the Faere was still within her? And how much of the Elifaen might she be? Ullin had seen the Elifaen in battle. Their blood ran as red as that of Men, and yet when in the pitch of the fight they fought with a viciousness and cold cunning that made one wonder if ever they had a heart. But, no. He had also seen the Elifaen in sorrow. Their tears ran as hot and their anguish as deep, perhaps deeper, than any Man. Ullin wondered how, after such losses, they found the heart to grip the hilt or pull the bowstring. Having lived among them for so long, as close relations and as comrades, Ullin was no closer to any such answer. His grandfather could perhaps tell him. Or Mirabella, who was one of them. Or Ashlord. Perhaps, as a Dragonkind once said, they lost their heart with their wings. Shaking himself, he interrupted Eldwin's stammer.

"Lady Esildre," he said, not without some wavering in his voice, incongruously wishing he could glimpse behind the veil that shrouded her eyes. One can tell so much from the eyes, he thought as he spoke. "Lady Esildre, these woods are not safe," he stated. "I beg you come away from here and join us in Eldwin's town."

She smiled and looked around at the other Nowhereans who quietly stood by. She then looked into the trees beyond them and up onto the hills around.

"I see that I am not the only source of your fear," she observed. "Take me to the treasure of Tulith Attis. First, let me look upon it. Then we shall speak."

• • •

It was in complete and eerie silence that they entered the Foyer, with Eldwin leading Esildre, and the other Nowhereans following. As Esildre passed through, she turned her head and looked across the room at Robby who was examining his maps. Raising his head at the procession, he caught her veiled gaze as she moved lightly along. Just before she disappeared into the passage leading to the Treasure Room, she turned from Robby and looked at Ashlord, giving a slight nod to his bow. When she had gone, Robby pushed back his chair and stood at his table, somewhat shaken.

"It appears as though, but for my refusal of the Treasure, all of the curses may soon be broken," Ullin said, coming over to Robby.

"Is that her? The lady of their tales?"

"Why, she's the very image of Sheila!" Billy whispered, standing close to Robby. "Only, well, *not.*"

Ullin nodded and told them her name and how they came along the Toll Road from across the bridge.

"Ashlord, do you know her?"

"I have seen her once before. Long ago. But I only know her by reputation. My associate in Duinnor knows her quite well, though, and he has told me somewhat about her. Like Lyrium, she has long been a recluse. That she is traveling in the open world..." Ashlord's voice trailed off as he scratched his chin. "First Lyrium. And now Esildre." He shook himself. "Like all her kind, she is not to be trifled with."

"Reputation?" Billy asked. "What reputation?"

"I cannot tell you now, if you do not already know. But I beg you all to speak no more than you must. Her House is closely allied with Duinnor. Her father is Lord Banis, one of the most powerful in Duinnor, second only to the King, though I understand she and her father are estranged. At any rate, do not allow yourself to be alone with her."

"Of, course! Lord Banis!" Ullin declared. "Who has not heard of him!"

"Me, for one!" snorted Billy.

"And me, for two. Will she lift her curse from the Nowhereans?" Robby asked.

Ullin shrugged. "I don't know. She seems to have chosen Eldwin to speak for his people. I am sure he will ask her about it."

At this time the Elders began emerging from the passageway and leaving the caves. They looked subdued and worried. Millithorpe broke away from them and came over to Robby.

"She dismisses all of us, save Eldwin. She wishes to speak with him alone. She tells us to assemble our people and wait for her in the town. But she asks that you and your companions remain here so that she may speak with you before she comes to us."

Millithorpe then departed with the others just as Sheila and Ibin arrived bringing the horses and all of their belongings. In addition to returning the things taken for the fine, the Nowhereans also gave them fresh provisions of hard cheese and flour, dried fruits, nuts, and a sack of fresh-picked apples. They had been especially generous since Ibin and Sheila had given them so many new songs.

"I heard there were visitors from the west," Sheila said when she entered, gesturing at Esildre's escorts at the entrance. She saw the pensive expressions of her companions, and when she was told who had arrived, she grew just as concerned as they. While they waited for Esildre's return, they talked of their preparations to leave, and Ullin told them about the bridge at the gorge while Ibin softly plucked the mandolin. Robby sat back down, but, instead of looking at the maps, he tapped his pencil to Ibin's tune and listened as Ashlord spoke about the region ahead of them.

"Beyond the gorge are two or three days of travel to the Plains of Bletharn," Ashlord said. "Between here and there, it is a thick forest, mostly uninhabited, I think. Where the mountains end, there is a road that reaches north and south along this side of the Missenflo. If I'm not too far off, we should reach our crossing on the third day out from here, where the Missenflo's waters are broad and shallow. It has been a fording place for so many years that its bottom was paved in the last age. There once was much more traffic that way, but for many years, now, most travelers have chosen a more northern route. But just north of the river crossing sits Tulith Morgair, Robby, and it overlooks the ford. And, beyond the river stretch out the plains."

Robby nodded and was about to say something, but seeing Esildre and Eldwin emerge from the passageway, he stood. The others stood, too, and bowed. Esildre turned to Eldwin and took his hand, giving him a little smile.

"Leave us, now, dear Eldwin. Await with the others. I promise I will consider what you have told me, but no other promise do I make."

"I thank ye," he bowed. And to Robby, he said, "By yer leave, sir."

"By all means. I will see you before we depart."

They watched Eldwin go, then Esildre turned to the group, looking at each in turn. She seemed as if she was about to speak to Sheila, but she suddenly turned to Ashlord.

"Collandoth, you are called among my kind."

"That is so."

"There are many stories attached to your name."

"And to yours, Esildre, Lady of Elmwood."

"It is said you are a Watcher and, as well, that you have been counsel to many of the high and the mighty, both Men and Elifaen. Is it true, that you were even an envoy to the Palace of the Sun?"

"All that was long ago."

"They say the women of the Dragonkind are as beautiful as they are fierce, and that few can resist their charms."

"Beautiful, indeed. And as fierce as any woman may be who has something to be fierce about. But the few I was privileged to know were gentle, and they were as concerned with their households and their arts as any woman elsewhere, I would say."

"It is strange to hear you speak of privilege and gentleness where it concerns the race that has brought so much pain and suffering into the world."

"Aperion is wise, Lady, as is his Creator. Surely, you need little reminding that it was not the Dragonkind who caused the Fall, nor they who first gave offense. The entire sufferings of the world cannot be blamed upon them." Ashlord sensed that he was too sharp and added, "Besides, it was a time of peace when I was there."

"Peace! A thing seldom seen. And the chill in my bones tells me that less will be seen in the days that come. Perhaps you feel it, too?"

Ashlord did not answer.

"There are rumors," she went on, looking at Robby, "spoken in the courts of Duinnor, of a new power arising in the east. Of old prophecies coming to pass, bringing change. Those who watch the heavens say Aperion stirs from his abode. Some say that the growing might of the Redvests is the power foretold. But others say elsewise. Some even whisper that a new king comes forth. Naturally, all these rumors make Duinnor wary, and the people are unsettled."

Robby remained expressionless, and none of the others spoke or took their eyes from her.

"And even though the frontiers of southern Vanara are quiet, and few Dragonkind stir," she went on. "My people grow nervous, too. It is as when the air grows still before a coming storm. Might it come from the south, I wonder? Or from the east?"

"From both, I fear," said Ashlord, "for the powers of the southeast will soon be joined to those of the southwest. The Tracian leadership, it seems, has made some pact with the Dragonlands. They gather their forces against Masurthia and Altoria as we speak. The Damar are now the servants of Tracia, and in the middle Eastlands between Glareth and Tracia, only Tallinvale stands, cut off on all sides."

"Tallinvale," she stated. To Ullin, she turned. "Your home. Knowing these things, you leave there?"

"Our hope is to arouse Duinnor," Ullin replied.

"Arouse Duinnor? Duinnor is as a person in a deep but restless sleep. It will take a great shaking, indeed, to wake Duinnor to any threat. But is that not what Vanara is for? To thwart any advance from the south? And has not Vanara always done so?"

"Yet that's our task," Billy said, somewhat defiantly.

"I see. And something more, too. Why else would such an odd company travel together? A Kingsman, a Melnari, three boys and a girl? And if it is Duinnor that you go to, why do you take this way, through the land of your enemies?"

"We take the only way open to us," said Robby. "And our business with Duinnor is just so."

"Ah," Esildre nodded. "You do not trust me. And why should you? These little people fear me, too. But look at them. They have overcome the hardships laid upon them and have turned their curses into blessings. Because they could not leave, they made an inhospitable land into a place that would be the envy of many. Because they were made small, their needs are smaller. And yet notice you their vigor? It is the match of any three times their size. Even the shunning that came about because of their early misguided ways of thieving has now given them peace from others, and their way of moving, a surprise even to me, is a gift to them. Yes, they fear me. And they fear you, too. Who are we to take these things away from them?"

"They should be given a chance in the world," Sheila said. "Whether they leave or stay should be their decision." Sheila glanced sharply at Ullin.

"Perhaps," Esildre replied, looking at Ullin, too. "Eldwin told me of the return of the Treasure to the heir. Of his refusal until certain conditions are met. Perhaps your decision was wise, Ullin Saheed, and not for the reasons you had in mind. The choice will indeed be theirs, and a serious matter to decide. Whether to leave, and, if so, where to go, east or west? If they do as you say, their effort may teach them much they have not already learned. On the other hand, if they do not go to the aid of Tallinvale, but choose instead to abandon these lands, their way of life will be unmade. Who can say what evil they may set their hearts upon?"

"Evil? Why do you speak of these people so?" Sheila asked.

"Yes, if they fall away from their ways, from this land that holds them to their ways and the fates that brought them here. For I cannot take away the gift of movement their Elders possess. They will have the ability to travel easily and quickly throughout the world. No land will be closed to them. Great things they may do, if they choose, in darkness or in light. Yes, wise, Ullin. And a great risk, too, for who can resist mighty power? And who may resist the corruption that such power brings?"

She let that sink in for a few moments.

"For my part, I will tell you why I come this way, and perhaps you will tell me how you came to be here, too?"

They looked at each other, nodding reluctantly, mindful of Ashlord's words.

"We shall let Ashlord speak for us," said Robby, "but we would indeed like to hear of your travels. There is some fine beer here in this keg, and I'm sure Ibin would be glad to hoist it to the table and twist the tap, if you'd care to have some."

"Beer, oh my, yes."

"OhI'll, I'll, I'lldothat," Ibin said, nearly throwing down his mandolin and rushing over. Perhaps he did not understand all their talk, or if he did he found it somewhat distant, but he understood good hospitality, and he especially understood good beer.

"Maybe ye'd like to sit a spell?" Billy asked, trying to be cordial and putting a blanket down on a crate for her. "An' d'ye reckon yer two fellers would like a sip?"

"Most surely they would."

"Then I'll fetch them."

"They will not join us. They will remain just outside, vigilant as they always are. And do not be offended if they do not speak," she said. "They seldom do. A nod from them is as good as a tale."

"Alrighty," Billy shrugged, taking two tankards from Ibin. "Then I'll hand 'em these an' be right back."

Esildre took off her cloak and undid her straps and light armor, and slid out of them, revealing much more of her feminine shape than any expected to see, barely hidden under a short, tight-fitting bodice, the drawstrings of which she loosened for further comfort. She wore no other clothing below her breasts and above her low, narrow breechcloth, black and crimson-edged that draped over leather leggings. But around the narrows of her waist was a thin gold chain, glittering against her tan skin as she moved in the lamplight. Whether she was conscious of her beauty's effect upon the males present or simply immodest, she gave no sign and was, regardless, very comfortable with herself.

"There! That's better, and thank you." She accepted a tankard from Ibin. She took a drink, then another deeper draught. "Mmm. Men make such rich beer! Not like the airy stuff we call beer. Well, I suppose I'll speak first."

She took another drink and sat down on the crates and pulled one leg up under her, and leaned back on one arm while she held the tankard with the other.

"Great stars!" Ullin muttered softly, closing his eyes and raising his eyebrows with a little shake of his head.

Billy struggled to close his mouth, failed, and at last did so with an audible clop. He hurried to the opening, and, while looking over his shoulder at her, he shoved the tankards into the hands of her escorts, and fairly rushed back in, stumbling into a seat, hardly taking his eyes from Esildre for even a moment.

"A very long time ago," she said, "I withdrew from the world, to live privately and in my own way. I remained somewhat ignorant of the happenings of the world, and for a long time dismissed the stirrings that I felt. But, many months ago, I received a message from an old friend, begging me to visit him in Duinnor to discuss matters that are private between us. I was reluctant, for I have no love of that place. And though it was not the first invitation I had received from him, I could refuse no longer. So I traveled there to abide for a time. I learned much and saw much. The might and power of Duinnor and the changes wrought in that realm since I was last there are profound. My father, who holds a position of authority there, is now at the center of this power, though I did not wish to see him or for him to know that I was there. We are not close, as a father and daughter should be. I will not explain why."

She took another sip, looking down into her tankard for a moment before continuing.

"I am not one of those of my kind who is gifted with Sight," she said. "Yet the west has been filled with strange omens, and the Seers go about with little to say and with worry on their faces. Though they may see meanings hidden to the rest of us, the rest of us are not without wit and can hardly ignore the things that have happened.

"A new star appeared, low over the western edge of the world, and it burned red from Midwinter last until it sank from sight on Midsummer's Eve. The astrologers called it Veritask, named for Aperion's soothsayer, and they say it foretells other omens of sky and earth and water. Three months and more ago, late on the night of my arrival in Duinnor, all of the bells of the Westlands rang of their own accord. The great bells of the towers, as well as the chimes of the temples and courts, and the service bells in all of the houses of all the people. Three times did they ring with great force and invisible agitation, causing a terrible alarm throughout the land. The people were called out to arms. Soldiers of all armies and Houses rushed to their posts. The many gates of Duinnor were pushed closed against any coming attack. Kingsmen crowded the fortifications of the Palace, and watchfires were lit throughout the countryside. A terrible calamity was feared and expected, yet no enemy came. I was in the Temple when this happened, just outside Duinnor City. A powerful urge overcame me to take up arms and fly away east against some unknown foe. It was a terrible and fearful thing to feel, and difficult to resist. After three weeks, and owing much to the influence of the Temple, I was calmer. Yet the people of Duinnor remain nervous still.

"While I abided in the Temple during those days of alarm, I heard from the monks tales of strange creatures that had been seen in the faraway seawaters off the coast of Glareth. Creatures that sang songs of enchantment and that danced upon the waves. I, who remember the First Days, before the Fall and before the world was remade, remember, too, that some of our kind arose from the sea and others of us followed their invitation to retire into the sea away from the woods and the fields. When I heard the monks' stories, a deep longing grew in me, a yearning to find those creatures and to see for myself if they may be brothers and sisters of the Elifaen who may have escaped our fate. Again, my heart urged me to go eastward. And, as it happened, there were other matters I desired to attend to in the east. Though I was advised against it, I could resist the urge no longer. So I and my two great-nephews who insisted on being my escorts set out. It was our intent to travel northeast along the Osterflo, through the mountains to the Locks of Karthia, and from there go down in boats to Glareth by the Sea.

"But on the twentieth night of our journey, a dream came to me. It was a memory-dream of when I came to Tulith Attis with my brother Navis. But in this dream, I became small, like the people here, and became lost in the fog and mist. All the while, as I fought vine and limb to find my way, a mighty bell thundered and tolled. The dream persisted in my thoughts for the next few days. At last, I understood better my urge to come east, and we turned south and rode hard to come here. We came down off the Middlemount, well east of Nasakeeria, of course, and passed through the plains. We tarried nowhere, stopped for no challenge, and rested only when our buckmarls needed rest. And here we are."

While she spoke, Ashlord remained standing, scratching his bearded chin and looking from Sheila to Esildre and back. He smiled and nodded whenever Esildre looked his way, and politely muttered, "Oh. You don't say."

Robby, who had pulled up a crate to sit before Esildre while she spoke, noted Ashlord's familiar deep-and-distant look, and wondered briefly which part of Esildre's tale he contemplated, or if the mystic was thinking at all of Esildre's words. Ullin and the others had also dragged over crates or boxes to sit on, and though Billy and Ullin appeared thoroughly enchanted by her, and Ibin enraptured, Sheila seemed stiff and wore a wooden expression.

Esildre's two escorts came in and returned the two tankards, and bowed in thanks. When they removed their helmets, it was a surprise to see that they had the look of boys not more than twelve or thirteen years of age, and were identical in every way, except one had green eyes and the other blue, with long sun-blond hair tied in ponytails, small sharp noses, and thin lips. Their skin was pale and freckled, as if they had never spent a day outside, though they had the tough, muscular bearing of two who had spent little of their life indoors. Young though they seemed, there was something in their manner indicated to Ullin, at least, that they were Elifaen, and had seen and done more, perhaps, than he ever would. The pair placed their helmets next to Esildre's gear and retreated back to the cave opening to resume their watch.

Ashlord nodded and smiled as everyone looked at him. Then he shook himself, realizing they were expecting him to speak.

"Ah. A very interesting account, Lady Esildre," he said. "I suppose it is my turn. Well. Let's see. Sixteen days ago—is that all? It seems longer—yes, sixteen days ago, we were all going about our business in County Barley when an army of Redvest soldiers from Tracia, about three or four thousand strong, invaded the lands. There was a fight or two, but most of Barley and Passdale, the chief town there, were taken by the enemy, and many of the inhabitants fled to Janhaven to the west of those parts. The Tracian Redvests seemed uninterested in advancing to Janhaven, in spite of the supplies and stores there in warehouses and factors' floors. Perhaps they did not wish to extend their forces, for the road to Janhaven has become a deathtrap for them. Anyway, the invaders took as many captives as they could. Their intent is apparently to loot the region of grain and food for transport southward where the main forces of their armies are gathering. We fear that the Redvests of Tracia have reached an accord with the Dragonkind, and that they work together toward an upcoming attack against Masurthia and Altoria. Meanwhile, my guess is that the army that took Passdale is the northernmost force of Redvests, and that the lands from there southward are under their occupation, too. Word of all this was sent to Glareth, but the messenger was pursued by enemy hunters. And Glareth is far away, so the Ruling Prince may not have word of the invasion for some time. It was decided that a small group should go to Duinnor to represent Barley and the Eastlands in an effort to bring aid. That is where we go. We first went to Tallinvale. And it was there that we learned the breadth of the war that is in the making. Tallinvale, which has held a precarious pact of peace with the Damar and with Tracia, now realizes that their valley is isolated and surrounded. Lord Tallin foresees that the Redvests will wait until the spring for their offensive upon Masurthia. But he also knows that the Redvests cannot leave Tallinvale upon its flank. And so Lord Tallin prepares for the coming attack and siege. Tallin City is a formidable fortress, and no small force may hope to take it, so Lord Tallin expects a great army will come against him. It is his aim to delay or to weaken the Redvests, making their springtime offensive less powerful. We have until then, springtime, if we are lucky, and if Tracia does not launch its westward attack beforehand. So to Duinnor we go, to rouse Duinnor to the threats that mount, and then to return with an army sufficient to relieve the city and free the Eastlands of the invaders."

Esildre appeared thoughtful, and the twins, who could hear everything, exchanged blank looks.

"If Lord Tallin remains the soldier he once was, then the Redvests will pay dearly, for he is reputed to be merciless in battle, cunning, and impassioned with the strength of ten men. And, it is said, he inspires the same in all who follow him. Yet, you haven't much time, particularly if Tracia and the Dragonlands have united. Altoria is weak and has always been well protected by the Hinderlands. If the Dragonkind can break through the passes, Altoria will certainly fall. Masurthia cannot resist an assault from east and from west by such armies as you describe. Together the invading armies would outflank Vanara, and the plains will be an easy road to Duinnor."

"Just so," said Ashlord.

"Yet, there is more to your tale than you have told. Even Eldwin did not tell me all, I suspect. He could hardly explain how the Treasure Room, barred so strongly, was opened with such ease, and much to everyone's astonishment. He showed me the bands that burst asunder, and how their welds were split."

She looked at the group, but none made an answer to her.

"And he told me," she went on, "how Ullin Saheed Tallin, here, was declared to be heir of the Treasure of Tulith Attis, and so the rightful spoils of that place have been returned, by my brother's decree. I find it curious that it was done in the manner Eldwin described, that his own cousin," she looked from Ullin to Robby, "bestowed the honor and declared the spoils returned. And that you also declared their value increased a thousand-fold from the day of their theft from Tulith Attis."

"At least that much increased," Robby said bluntly. Without being able to see her expression, he could not tell if her tone was accusative, or merely curious. "And Ullin's lineage is no secret."

"You are right on both points. I think your company is a very talented one, and more noble than you may seem, at first glance. I will not press you too hard on your secrets. The world is full of them, for good or ill."

She took a long sip of beer, and her expression, what they could see of it that was not hidden by her veil, was one of pleasure at the refreshment. She turned to Robby again.

"Eldwin tells me that the one originally responsible for his people's plight, the one who brought them to Tulith Attis as slaves, is now dead," she said. "That the one called Bailorg died at your own hands."

"That is true, Lady Esildre," Robby nodded. "Our dispute led to a fight, and it was my life or his."

"I see. And the nature of your dispute?"

"Bailorg sought to harm one of our companions, Billy, here," Ashlord intervened. "Luckily for Billy, Robby rescued him."

" 'At's right!" Billy added. "Ol' Robby, here, saved me life!"

"I see. And I sense one tale must lead into the next," she nodded. She turned her head toward the opening of the cave, still nodding as she sighed. "But why was Bailorg in your region? Do you know?"

Ashlord shrugged.

"We learned his name from Robby," he said, "who overheard one of his men address him. We also learned that one of his associates was a Dragonkind, and we suspect that another was an agent for Tracia. Bailorg's true role in things remains a mystery. Until we arrived here and heard the tale of these people, we had no idea that his ties to the Dragonkind went so far back in history. Apparently, his deeds at Tulith Attis, here in Nowhere, and elsewhere, have woven a dark weft farther and deeper than we may ever know."

"Yes, I can only believe that is true," Esildre replied, obviously unsatisfied with their answers. Turning back to Robby, she said, "Then it was fortunate for you to be where you were to save your friend. And fortunate for so many others, too."

Her tone, Robby thought, had a note of disappointment, in spite of her words.

"I deeply regret that Navis and I did not find him after we encountered these people," she finally said. "But our search was a short one. I am to blame for that tragic failure. My brother and I should have persisted. So much evil would have been averted had we found him."

Her speech drifted off with an undertone of profound distress. She took another swallow of beer, holding the tankard with both her hands to hide how they were shaking. She swallowed, and took another gulp.

"Because you will go the way that I have come," she then continued, "I will tell you that there are strange things happening in the lands west of here. We avoided the few towns along the way, but came across signs of unrest and trouble. Abandoned farms. Odd signs made with wood or standing stones placed in the fields or amongst the deserted livestock. Duinnor sends patrols, but they go no farther south than the pass between Nasakeeria and the Mossweren Heights to the west. A traveler we met along our way said that a small Kingsman army was already posted somewhere south, somewhere east of Forest Islindia. Their mission or purpose was not known to him. Later, when we forded the Missenflo and entered the mountains, we felt a strange and unsettled air within the forest. The woods there are unnaturally quiet, as if nervous and sullen. We were cautious, and did not stop but to water and rest our mounts. We encountered no one until we came to the bridge at the gorge."

A strong breeze blew into the Foyer, flickering the lamps. Esildre turned her head to the entrance as the air stirred her hair. The breeze faded away, and she looked back at Robby.

"I must go," she said, rising. Everyone else stood as her great-nephews helped her on with her armor.

"They will be glad to hear your decision," Ullin said as she strapped on her harness and shifted her sword.

"Perhaps we should all go," she replied. "After all, this now pertains to you, too."

To this they agreed, and after removing the saddles and packs from the horses ("No need to tire 'em out ahead of time," said Billy), they walked together to town. They reached the square at midday, and there were more people gathered than before. The Elders were gathered, the chairs now in a broad semicircle facing the chair that previously had been given to Sheila and was meant now for their Elifaen visitor. The Elders each stood beside his or her chair, and their families of every generation were grouped behind them. Every inhabitant was there, called away from tasks and chores wherever they were, the young as well as the old, summoned by urgent messengers sent out by the council. Now, pressing close to their Elders, the crowd grew quiet, and they bowed, opening a path for the visitors.

Esildre did not take the chair reserved for her. Robby with his company stood behind her and her escorts as she turned to the gathering.

"I will not lift my curse laid upon you," she said immediately in a loud voice for all to hear. There was a sigh of relief on many faces, for how would they protect themselves if the Elders could no longer pop around so swiftly? But others wisely waited for the caveat they felt coming.

"A curse may only be uttered in the throes of passion. The passion of love or hatred, compassion, or anger, and the Great Powers must join in sympathy to that passion, for better or for ill. When a curse is uttered, it becomes its own spirit, with its own life, one might say. In this way, a true curse is born in the same way as a true blessing and cannot easily be undone. He that utters it has never the power to revoke it, no matter how it may later be regretted. When the conditions, if any, of its being are fulfilled, and its purpose is gone from the world, so it, too, goes away. Curses and blessings are two faces of the same power, and one may sometimes become the other as it turns upon itself. I will not lift the curse because I cannot."

"You now have the power that I, in my passion and compassion, brought into the world. I made no condition upon it, and I cannot say when your long life or your power to move about may depart from you. Use them wisely I beseech you! And if you have any blessings in this life, use them to be blessings upon others whenever you may."

The Elders looked at one another solemnly. Some shook hands with arms around each other, and, after a few moments, the crowd absorbed something of the situation and the meaning of her words. Their spirits began to lift, and they began talking excitedly with each other of their prospects, speculating, as they always had, but now with a growing sense of how their plight could soon change.

Eldwin stood on his chair and, facing his people, cried, "Hear me! Hear me!" with his hands in the air.

"I put this before the Elders an' before ye all," he said once he had everyone's attention. "Let us give thanks to Lady Esildre an' to the Lords Robby an' Ullin. We have now a greater hope of saving our people an' of entering the world for our protection an' the protection of these lands. Let us resolve ourselves, now, to break the first curse as we have been instructed, so that we may freely travel from these lands as need may be. An' by the permission given by Lord Ullin, let us use the Hoard to accomplish the things before us. Let the council meet until plans are made, an' let us then carry them out with a good heart an' great hope. Let this day an' this night be one of celebration, putting aside all other business so that we might give thanks an' good fellowship to one another an' to our honored guests. What say ye?"

These suggestions were met with enthusiastic agreement, and immediately groups broke forward to join the Elders, bowing before Esildre and thanking her. They bowed to Robby and Ullin, too, and asked their permission to prepare a table so that all of their visitors could be entertained and fed. Robby, who, like Ashlord, was anxious to make their departure and to cross the gorge, was reluctant. But he could not help smiling at the pleas and excitement of the Nowhereans. Makewine and Arldewain were competing with others for Ullin's attention, asking the Kingsman about the best ways to establish watches and to make some kind of defense of their lands against the Damar.

"They may send spies or scouts to probe you," Ullin speculated. "And they may make some attempt in some force. I doubt they will come on horseback, preferring to send their soldiers through the hilly forest on foot, perhaps in the guise of hunters. But it is unlikely that a full assault will come until next year. They will be too busy elsewhere. It will be up to you Elders, who have the gift of speed, to form the main guard of your lands, since you may quickly spread word and warning of any intrusion and may assemble well before the rest of your people. Tell me, how long might it take a man such as I, without your power of movement, to walk the borders of Nowhere and to arrive back where he began?"

Makewine scratched his chin, eyeing Ullin's long legs while Arldewain shrugged.

"About half as long as it would take us?" he speculated.

• • •

Ibin, as seemed his fate, was again the center of playful attention, and he soon had two small children high up on either shoulder where they both stood shrieking with laughter as they clutched his curly hair for balance. Another three or four clung to his belt, dangling out as he spun around and around with another child in each of his hands. And another little one, who had lost his grip and slipped from Ibin's belt, was clinging onto his right thigh with arms and legs wrapped around his thick muscles like a vise.

• • •

"If ye pardon me, ye have the look of a Wise Man," a woman said to Ashlord. "This is my daughter, Eldwyna. She gathers herbs and makes use of them as medicines for our people. I have taught her all I know, and her wisdom in those things now surpasses her teacher. Still, many plants were strange to us when we first came here, and some that we used in our old country cannot be found."

"Would ye share with us, sir, any wisdom ye may have of such things?" asked Eldwyna.

"Perhaps a better instructor would be Sheila, here," Ashlord suggested. "I have taught her some along those lines, and she has learned more from a wise countrywoman of her land. Sheila is more artful in such matters than I shall ever be."

Sheila blushed at the tribute, saying, "That is doubtful, but I would be glad, in the little time we have, to share what I can."

"So in addition to singing with a beautiful voice," the woman said, "yer also a healer!"

"I wouldn't say so. I do a little bit of everything I can, I suppose. But I am a master at nothing. Except perhaps the bow and arrow."

• • •

"Sos, ye see, these cows kept goin' through thar, boggin' down an' gettin' stuck an' such," Billy regaled a group of fascinated Nowhereans.

"So what we did was build this broad bridge, sort of. A wide, high thing on piles that we drove down into the mud. Then, onto them piles we made a frame, just like buildin' a floor for a house, with joists an' such. Now, the cows go onto this thing an' they can get at them flowers an' bushes they love so much, ones what grew up along the edges an' in gaps we left in the floor. We didn't need to mind after 'em so much after then, an' our hands could do other things 'sides pullin' cows out of mud ever day er two.

"Now, ever'body knows how pigs like acorns, so I say ye just make the platform up high so they can get at the tree limbs growin' up thar, an' at them acorns what come out or fall on it. Build yer hoist first, real sturdy-like, with a heavy weight on the end like rocks in a basket or some such. Much like the gate on yer Toll Road. 'Cept higher an' stronger. Get it workin' real good, like, then use it for haulin' up yer timbers. Later, once yer all done with the buildin' of the thing, use it for haulin' up yer swine an' feed an' troughs an' such-like. An' water, too, an' such. It'd be a lotta work, but I reckon ye've done harder things. An' it ain't like buildin' fine houses, such as ye've done all through yer town. But it's gotta be strong enough for the pigs, an' dirt an' mud, too, for 'em to roll around in. An', of course, ye gotta put some fence around it to keep 'em from fallin' off. Yep, a lotta work. But, like I said, it ain't gotta be fancy. It's just gotta get the job done."

•   •   •

Robby, meanwhile, had returned to the caves with Millithorpe and Herbert to prepare for the distribution of those items from the Hoard that would be of use to the community, as well as to retrieve those things that might be wanted during the evening's celebrations, such as casks of wine and some of beer. So it was that while many of the Nowhereans prepared for an evening of feasting and celebration, the various members of Robby's company spent the afternoon separately, with Ashlord meeting with Esildre and many of the Elders. It was late afternoon, nigh upon sunset, before most of them were all assembled once more, except Robby and Millithorpe, still at the caves working. Ashlord, who pardoned himself to fetch Robby to the feast, smiled when he entered the caves and saw him bent over a ledger.

"Are you to work all evening, too?" Ashlord asked. "A fine feast is being prepared and awaits."

"Oh, no," Robby replied, smiling. "We are just finishing up."

"In that case, perhaps Millithorpe wouldn't mind letting the others know that we'll be along shortly?" Ashlord asked.

"Oh, why yes. Of, course, sir. That is, if..." Millithorpe looked from Ashlord to Robby.

"Oh, we're quite through here, I suppose," Robby said, wiping ink from a quill. "I'll just put away some of these ledgers and be right along."

"Very well, sir. Then I shall see you soon!"

Robby got up from his makeshift desk and put the stack of ledgers on the shelf behind him.

"I take it you want to have a word alone?" he asked as he pushed the book spines even with each other.

"Yes. About Esildre."

"Oh?"

"Yes," Ashlord sat on a low stool and laid his stick across his legs. "There are many rumors, legends, and tales surrounding her."

"So you implied earlier. What kind of tales?"

"Many are the kind that, now that I have met her for myself, I do not believe, calling her a sorceress and a witch. Other tales, ones that I have had on good authority to be true, are almost beyond belief. Let me sum them up by saying that she is despised and shunned in Duinnor, and her estrangement from her father is real."

"Why? I mean, why despised?"

"She was, for a time, consort to Secundur."

"No! Truly?"

"Yes. And though she managed to escape Secundur's clutches, it is said that he spited her with curses, and still has his claws in her."

"What do you mean?"

"As I just said, I do not believe everything that is told about her. How she escaped Shatuum is a mystery, but she has suffered from the experience ever since. I know more, but will wait until we are away before telling you. Meanwhile, more than any of us, you should guard your words with her. And, for goodness sakes, until we depart, do not let yourself be alone with her. You have a friendly nature, and she may delve more from you than you might intend. Mind you, I have no reason to distrust her. I only wish us to be cautious, just as we must be with everyone we meet along the way."

Ashlord stood. "Agreed?"

"I'll be careful," Robby answered.

"Good. Then let us make haste for supper!"

• • •

By the time they arrived, a long table had been made for them with Esildre at the head at one end, with Ashlord and Robby to sit on either side, and the others, except Ullin, had places along the table with an Elder in between each. It was after sunset when Ullin at last returned from a partial tour of the boundaries, and he took the place saved for him across from Sheila. He told his friends that since he had already seen the Toll Road as well as a good portion of the western border along the gorge, he felt he needed to inspect other areas of Nowhere. So he, Makewine, and a few others, had hiked with Ullin around the north and eastern sides of the lands.

"This little valley is surrounded on all sides by hills, many falling away into treacherous ravines to the north and northeast and into the gorge on the west," he reported to the table. "There are only a few places where a man, with much determination and strength, may pass. And those places are easily watched. The greater problem is to the south and east, along the Toll Road area."

The square around their table had been transformed for the festivities with lamps and a main table of food for the crowds, a sort of potluck, with everyone sharing whatever was ready at hand. And people came from their houses gaily dressed and with these food offerings in pots and trays and jugs. A number of musical groups played and sang songs, some of them newly learned from Sheila and Ibin. Many of the Elders sitting at the table with Robby's company bounced children on their knees, some still in swaddling. There was a constant coming and going of people desiring to introduce themselves or some member of their family, so that conversation was difficult to carry on at any length. Ullin, particularly, seemed amused and humbled that so many wanted to greet him. The day fell into night, the chill that normally descended with it came only mildly, and the stars twinkled bright and giddy overhead.

Later, some of the musicians strummed up a slow tune, joined by low pipes, and Eldwin said to Robby, "This song is about how we came here."

The tables grew quiet as the piper and strummers moved through the opening strains. Then a young man and girl stepped forward and sang together, tenor and soprano, and told of the trials of their people, taken from their homes and marched off as slaves. They sang of their hardships and of the battlefields they passed through, of the viciousness of the Dragon soldiers who drove them with their whips and clubs. The young man sang the words of the dying soldier that Eldwin had found, and the girl sang of the locket that hung about his neck and of the likeness within. The tenor then sang the words of Eldwin,

> *"Though I am but a slave, this locket I will take from thee,*
> *Though the drum of thy heart is still, oh soldier young and brave,*
> *This promise I will make to thee:*
> *If ever my chains are broken and freedom comes my way*
> *I will this locket take and go to Glareth Bay.*
> *And there to find your lover and say these words for you:*
> *That ever were you brave, and ever were you true."*

Though the words were simple and had little to do with the Nowhereans, there was hardly a dry eye amongst the listeners. The ballad went on, describing the terrible scene of Tulith Attis and the flight from there, laden with loot and laboring under the whips of Bailorg's drivers. When they came to the part about the curses and the tenor sang the part of Bailorg and of Navis, terrible in their wrath, the girl sang the part of Esildre with the note of hope and promise, and together they added,

"Oh Lady come again, it's been so long from now to then!
May it be soon, and the tally made,
The Hoard made equal to the redemption paid.
Oh Lady come again, it's been so long from now to then."

There was a hearty round of applause, and the singers took each other's hand and bowed together. And Esildre stood and bowed very low to the singers, which elicited even more clapping and a few hurrahs. A livelier jig followed and many began to dance, Ibin among them, having coaxed Sheila out with him, while Billy, with another tankard in hand, held forth with one of his tall tales before a crowd of enraptured little folk. Ullin moved down the table to sit nearer to Ashlord, Esildre, and Robby, and they discussed further the situation in the south and east. During a lull in the conversation, Robby turned to Esildre.

"If you pardon me asking, you are one of the First Ones, are you not?"

Esildre, who was watching Sheila dance, turned to Robby and said, "Yes."

"Yet you have a father and a mother?"

"Yes. I see your confusion. How am I a First One when there were others before me?"

"Just so."

"There was a time before the days were counted. The Time Before Time, it is now called. The world was different, then, as it may never be again. The spirit of Beras moved across the face of the earth, which he created, and his spirit brought forth the trees and the mountains, the mighty and the lowly, and made rivers to flow and the seas to rise to the shore. It was then that those things he first created gave birth to new creatures by dint of their spirit, born as their voices sang the praise of Beras and reveled in their existence under the sun and moon and stars. These were the Firstborn. Among those that came into being, some were born of the trees and forest, and some of the wind and water, some of starlight and moonlight, and some of sunlight, as Aperion himself was. These came into being with the birds and the creatures of the forest and the denizens of the sea, and all spoke to one another with the First Tongue, there being no difference among them except manifested form. These, the Faerekind, rejoiced in one another, and it is of the union of two such Faerekind that I was born in those days before days, and I remember when I had wings."

"How long was it, then, after that time of the creation until when the wings were taken from you and your kindred?"

"How long? How long is a mountain's rise and fall? How long does a falling star twinkle? Time was not heavy upon us, and not even the seasons of the year changed. All was as a golden summer. How long? A million millennia. A single heartbeat."

"Your father is in Duinnor, as you told us," Ullin said. "What of your mother?"

"My mother is with Aperion," she said bluntly. "She refused to take up against the Dragonkind and begged my father not to honor his pledge to fight them. I, my sister Atlana, and Navis, my brother, all remained in the world with my father. I because I thought I was in love with another of our kind and would not be parted from him. That was my mistake, for it was not love, as I came to learn. Atlana likewise could not be parted from her lover, and they lived happily for many years and had children who are still living. She died where your father did, at Gory Gulch. Navis remained in the world because he was ever loyal to his father and hated the Dragonkind. But he, too, is long dead."

Sadness lowered Esildre's voice, and the lamplight created deep shadows across her face. Robby glanced at Ullin, who had an expression of regret.

"I beg your pardon," Ullin said, "for arousing sad memories."

"Do not fret. But if you will excuse me," she said, rising gracefully and smiling kindly, "I wish to walk privately. I will see you off tomorrow." She nodded at Robby and turned to Ashlord. "Thank you for your news. I wish I could offer some in return, but little has changed in the west, other than what I have told you."

"Where do you and your two escorts go from here?" asked Robby.

"That is on my mind, and I will soon decide. Perhaps to Glareth, as I had planned. Or maybe to Tallinvale. Perhaps even to Janhaven. Perhaps I will know by sunrise. I do not know."

The members of the table rose and bowed as she departed along the lane northward toward the woodland groves, her great-nephews following at a respectful distance.

"If she goes to Janhaven," Robby said, "I should like to ask her to carry a note to my mother. Billy! Billy!"

Billy looked his way, and Robby motioned for him to come over.

"Pardon me, gents," he said as he bowed. Then he swaggered over to Robby.

"Billy, there's a chance that Lady Esildre may be able to take letters to Janhaven. Do you want to write to your mother?"

"Aye! That I would!"

"Then let's go back to the caves and do so."

"I should appreciate it if I could borrow paper and ink, too," Ullin said. "For if she goes to Glareth, perhaps she'll carry a missive to my own mother."

• • •

Ullin's letter was a short one, and he finished more quickly than Robby, who wrote several pages, and Billy, who struggled over every word and had hardly written half of a page. But Ullin knew that his own mother's sight was failing and that she would likely turn to her housekeeper of many years to read his letter to her, so, just as his companions were, he was cautious about what he wrote. They all agreed to say, however, that they were writing from the middle of nowhere, and Robby added to his line a parenthetical, "Ask Mr. Furaman." Indeed, none of them said a great deal to their mothers, not knowing how much to trust the couriers, but each saying how healthy and hale he was, and that they were making progress toward their goal, though at a slower pace than wished.

Ullin folded his letter, sealed it with wax, and excused himself from the others to "walk off the wine," and left them still scratching away. Outside, he let his eyes adjust to the night and then walked along the side path that led along the floor of the cliffs, passing other caves, winding its way up and down and among the boulders and trees until it brought him to the waterfall and the place where Robby and Eldwyna had met, the so-called Pool of Desire. The water danced down the sheer face of the cliff above before making a little jump over a ledge just above Ullin's height, and then it splashed into the broad shallow pool below. The night air was turning cooler, and a slight breeze shook the overhanging boughs that swung like dark boats in the air, floating at their moorings between his gaze and the bright stars above. Here the pathway ended, and he waded through the pool, little more than ankle deep, and to the other side where the brook lapped over rocks and trickled away downward and through the woods. He followed it just a yard or so down and then sat on a mossy stone and was lost to time and to his thoughts for a long while, his cloak pulled close about him, not so much for warmth as out of habit. Later, Lady Moon strolled over the hilltops, rising into the sky with half her face hidden and sending her beams floating through the trees. At some point Ullin noticed this and looked up at her, pulling in a long take of air and heaving a great sigh.

"What I would not give to have you appear before me now," he muttered softly as he fingered the locket about his neck. "Might you now be looking upon the Queen of Night as I do? Does she remind you, as she does me, of our time together under her cool evening gaze? Why must a mere thing as leagues hinder us when so much else does? Why did I ever leave?"

Ullin was not one for making speeches or unnecessary talk. He was not unfriendly in his attitude or manner; indeed, when in the society of others he was good company. He contributed to conversation, asked meaningful questions, made thoughtful observations, and related interesting stories and anecdotes as the occasion might suggest. Naturally reticent, he never showed it. But there was much he never talked about, and only the most observant company might sense when he skillfully guided conversation to other topics. Even with Ashlord, with whom he was most open among his travel companions, Ullin held back. Only when asked would Ullin speak of his years in the desert, the battles he had witnessed and fought, and the harsh living that his previous duties required. Never did he speak of the special assignments that took him deep into the Dragonlands, or what he saw and did there. Ashlord knew more than any about those experiences, and he always seemed satisfied with Ullin's abridged versions. Perhaps Ashlord had other sources, Ullin mused, and had little need to delve too much into the Kingsman's past. But those experiences taught Ullin to think for himself, to quickly size up any situation, and to take unhesitating action. Survival depended on it. It was what made him a good soldier, filling the gaps in his orders with keen judgment, taking advantage of chance when it favored. And his other skills, at weapons and tactics, at handling men, and at reading his own peculiar warning senses, made him an ideal scout, officer, and patrol leader.

When Ashlord came to him in Vanara, and offered a commission to work with him, Ullin jumped at the chance to get as far away from the desert as possible. Looking back, it was an ironic reaction because almost immediately, and ever since, he felt a deep longing to go back, to find his way, somehow, through the southern mountains of Vanara, back out into the desert, and to the Free City of Kajarahn. It was a miracle that he had survived what should have been a death trek from the desert. And though he still could not say for sure how it was that he survived and made it out, the longing to return to the place of his suffering grew stronger with every passing year. But it was not the desert itself that attracted him so, nor was it the pain that place had inflicted upon him, but the memory of the person he had left behind and had ever since longed to see again.

Robby would never understand. No one would.

Ullin fingered the locket beneath his shirt. So many things to explain! No. And now he had risked Robby's ire by refusing the Hoard and by placing unreasonable conditions on these meek Nowhereans. Could they truly be of any help? But Tallinvale, the eastern lands, needed allies, any they could get, even if they were little people, unsure, untested, naïve of the world, and, well, *small*. He rubbed his head. It was too much.

"I should have stayed in the desert," he muttered. "My bones would be better off bleaching in the sun, as do those of my kin."

"Why do you say such a thing as that?"

Ullin flinched at the voice, not realizing that he had spoken his thoughts aloud, and turned to see Esildre standing on the other side of the pool. He felt his face redden as he stood.

"I think you do not mean it," she went on, stooping to put her hand to the water. She first held her open palm near to the rippling surface, then dipped into the water and drew it up, watching the moon-sparkled beads drip away. "You have much that so many long for or would envy. Strength. Wealth. Freedom."

"Freedom?" Ullin snorted. "What freedom do I have? Bound by contrary oaths. Shackled by circumstance and jostled along paths not of my desire. What would you know of my freedom?"

"You choose, nonetheless. Your loyalties. Your way of facing that which you would rather not face. You choose. To go on, to keep moving. That is your freedom, if nothing else is. I heard how you refused the Hoard, how you made a challenge to these people. So, not only do you choose for yourself, you choose also for others. Your freedom, your choices, gives you power over others."

Ullin stepped up to the edge of the pool and looked across at her. She stood and put aside her cloak.

"I wish to bathe. If you don't mind."

"I don't mind," Ullin shrugged. "Why do you veil your eyes? The light is not strong enough to hurt them."

"It is to avoid…complications."

"Take it off and look me in the eyes with your own. Then talk to me of choice and of freedom."

"I dare not."

"Then I will help you," Ullin strode through the pool toward her, but she shrank away, drawing her sword.

"Would you strike me for such a thing?" he asked.

"To save you, I would."

"To save me? From what?" He stepped out of the pool and stood before her.

"From me," she raised the sword.

"From you! By striking me you would save me?"

Before she could react, Ullin sprang forward and gripped her sword arm, locking the weapon upright, and held her other wrist to prevent it from reaching her dagger. She squirmed, but he held her tight, his face close to hers.

"No!" she cried, though she ceased her struggle.

"Do not fight me."

"I have no wish to."

"Look me in the eye and say that."

"No." She tried to shrink away. She did not sense he had already eased his grip, or that he had stepped back from her just a bit. She was already fighting the deep swell of desire that could not be controlled, could not be pushed away. If she had any contrary thoughts or reactions, they may have been those of surprise or of disappointment. Not in Ullin, but in her own circumstance. Not since she had left her castle on the borders of Shatuum had the curse come upon her. For months, since Raynor had summoned her, she thought she was free of it. She wore the veil, as Raynor had insisted, in fear that the shadow of Secundur might return. And now it did. She shot out her freed hand and gripped Ullin's arm just as he was turning away. She shook with remorse, with futile resistance, and with animal anticipation. Ullin saw two moonlit tears fall away from her face as she dropped her sword and reached up to pull away the veil.

When her eyes met his, they burst into flame and something streaked from hers to his, setting off a fire within him. He staggered with the weight of a thousand years of sadness, crossing through into anger and remorse, and passing into shame and resignation, now released like a beast too long caged, too long humiliated and ruined by a world made small by the trap. He was unaware of the ruddy glow that surrounded them and engulfed them. Ullin was filled with desire and longing, not for Esildre—for he no longer even saw her—but for the vision he now saw, and held, of the one he longed for most in all the world. He was not capable, in his state, of questioning how it was that she could be here, how she could be touching him and pressing her lips once again to his. There was no possibility of doubt in their touch as they passionately embraced. He was happy, filled with complete joy, and they rejoiced in the pleasure of each other as only those truly in love may do when passion is at its utmost. Together they committed themselves to each other, flesh and spirit, heedless of consequence, mindless of the impossibility of their union.

Ullin and Esildre were lost. Another presence took them over, shadowy and cruel. It dogged Esildre, and she knew of it, and wore her veil because of it, to guard herself, and others, against it. It was her bane, and her weakness, her demon held so carefully in check for so many years. The shadow that she thought might be gone from her life after so many months of peace. But she was wrong, it was still with her, and it had never slept. Now, as it had done so many times before, it used her, as a hook may hold a lure. And, stabbing through each with its unrelenting barb, it made lure and prey willing puppets to its string. It delighted in tugging deeper and deeper into the couple, as vengeance for ancient rebuffs that its Master took for betrayal. And, if such long, thin shadows may do so, it laughed, revelling in their compliance.

But Ullin was strong, and the desire of his heart, she whom the shadow conjured Esildre to represent, was his true love. Still, the shadow vied with him, determined to leave its barb in him. Delivered through the hapless Esildre, it would nevertheless be a thorn that would, in its own time, continue to do its work of madness and discord. Just as it had with all of its victims before him. With Esildre as its lure, the curse upon her pulled its string, and set its poisoned barb deep into Ullin's soul.

• • •

Lady Moon hid her face behind her fan and peeked through the treetops at Ullin's body, prostrate, half in and half out of the cold pool. His heart, full and complete just moments before, now shuddered as his dreamlike swoon turned dark. He stood, warm and satisfied, as if the overhead sun glowed from within him, holding the hand of his refound love. Her smile vanished as a cloud crossed the sun, and she dropped his hand. The bright day grew black, and horror grew within his heart. Now he saw her again, standing over him in battle gear, just as she was when he first beheld her those years before, faraway and across the southern mountains. All but her eyes were covered, and they were deep tearful pools of disappointment.

"Are you so weak that you would betray me in this manner?" she demanded. "But I should not blame you. We are long parted and far away. And she is very beautiful."

Then she turned away and a shiver passed through Ullin's body. He awoke, thrashing in the pool to gain his feet, the water heavy, like the quick-blown sand of the duney desert, making him clumsy and off balance.

"Come back!" he cried out. But now he understood. His heart pounded against the crushing realization of what had happened as he turned this way and that, looking for her. And *her*. But no one was there. Esildre was gone, if she was ever actually there. And so, too, was the object of Ullin's deepest affection.

He groaned aloud at his humiliation, grabbing up his clothes and cursing as he dressed. Once he was dressed, he paced, still cursing himself, wondering how he could face his companions. Anger at Esildre swept him, then passed; she had tried to warn him. Shame, confusion, and black self-loathing racked him as the ache of his passion taunted him spitefully.

"Bones! Bones!" he cried, drawing his dagger and immediately putting it away. He took the dagger out again, looking at the dim glint of the blade. "Worthless fool! Worthless and weak!"

So easily is the worth of anything, everything, called into question! How well Doubt knows every gate and every path into the heart, never long without its companion, Pain, in the guise of whatever suffering is at hand, great or small. But Ullin knew this, familiar too much with the turnings of his own heart.

"My use is what I make it to be," he said, putting away his dagger. "A little farther I must go. For the sake of those I love and care about, though they may despise me and hold me in contempt of their favor."

Feeling a new pain in his shoulder, he reached into his shirt and flinched when he touched bleeding scratches. The growing desire to pass it all off on a strange dream was thus obliterated by this confirmation of a darker experience.

Quickly, owing to his training and to the direction of his remorse, the Kingsman slipped out of his blouse and took out his dagger and knelt over the pool, dipping the shirt into the water and washing his wound and his dagger ritually.

"Let this water wash away my transgressions," he recited as he washed. "Let not dishonor stain my name."

His hands shook as he dipped again and squeezed out the water over his head.

"Let this water wash away the hurt I give to others," his voice cracked, his eyes full of tears. "Let no enemy...let no enemy entice me to evil."

He stopped, having no heart to continue the ritual, staring at his blurry moonlit reflection in the rippling pool.

"Oh, fie upon me!" he cried, falling into the speech of the west, staring again at his dagger. "It is useless! And I am trapped! Oh, blade! Ye rightly desire my blood. And I would give it to thee, now, but I needs put thee off for a time, if I may bear it. For duty is greater than grief, and honor still requires of me some effort to my companions, unworthy though I am."

He put his blouse back on and slinked away, still trying to gather his composure, looking about as he went through the woods. He did not see Esildre hiding from him within the nearby brush.

When she could no longer hear his receding movement, she got to her feet and, dragging her clothes, went to the pool. Standing in the spray of the falls, she scooped up gravel and sand, and she viciously scrubbed, making terrible bleeding scratches all over her body. Then she fell to her hands and knees, sobbing as she let the cold water wash across her back. While she wept, the blood was rinsed away, and all her wounds rapidly healed so that no blemish remained but those that shed no blood and cannot be seen. And in that eternal moment of her Elifaen mind, all her woes and all her hopes were crossed and recrossed, questioned and confirmed. But what settled upon her at last was the wish that one man could really be with her now. A man who, if he wished to do so, might have within his heart the power to make everything good and to heal all her wounds. This thought suddenly stilled her, like something mysterious which is seen but not believed, not understood, and not even to be contemplated. Then, without a sound, her lips quivered his name, and her tears came once more.

Chapter 20

Ullin and Micerea

In the Badlands were bands of renegades that preyed on any they came upon. They seldom took prisoners, except for sport or rape, and lived so miserably in the desert that a bag of crumbs or a flask of wine was worth more than life. United only by the might of the quickest sword, or whichever one of them eliminated all who would rival his authority, these groups often split up, feuded, or combined forces, depending on the spoils at stake, or the skills and lack thereof of their bands. They were deserters from every army, Dragonkind, Elifaen, and Men, and so could never be reunited with their own kin on penalty of death. Each was once a member of a proud army, each highly trained and skilled in combat. The Dragonkind members of these bands were fewest in number and they survived the longest, but of the renegades few lived very long. Hunger, thirst, and the cruel desert took the greatest toll, while wounds received did away with the others. But their numbers were replenished, quickly or slowly, as the tides of war ebbed and flowed across the generations. Every few years, some general would determine to wipe them out and rid his flank of the aggravating stings of these marauders. More than one general made the mistake of becoming obsessed with their obliteration, to the destruction of his own army. For wherever one band of renegades was destroyed, and all its members utterly hunted down, another would soon arise from a different flank.

Ullin had encountered enough of these renegades to know that their fighting skills, added with their innate desperation, made them truly dangerous and unpredictable. He also learned from cruel experience that the Badlands was no place to be without the company of loyal swords. But here he was, alone. No horse, no companion to watch his back, and very little water left in his flask.

It was a mixed terrain, swaths of rock and rubble reaching far out from the northern mountains, formed into long thin arms of craggy broken ridges reaching southward. Once, in eons past, the terrain was covered in forest, and, no doubt, streams once ran freely through the gullies. But since before the First Age, the only green was the pale scrawny sage that somehow managed to cling beneath rocky outcrops here and there. Otherwise, very little grew between here and the southern side of the mountains, now a pleasant blue line in the far distance.

It was to the south, where the jumble of stone fanned away and flowed under the dunes, where the ground was neither too sandy nor too rocky, that a path edged along. Ullin watched, lying on his side just behind a low ridge, his light brown robe pulled over his head for shade and his shemagh over his nose and mouth against the blowing grit. He could just make out a faint trail of dust rising in the distance, wavering through the hot silver haze. He wished he had his spyglass, but it had been smashed to bits in a rockfall two days ago. Squinting, he watched the trail of dust carefully. It was coming along a route commonly used by the Dragonkind, going from their eastern provinces to the Free City, Kajarahn. Here, where the road took a turn between the sand and the rocks, was a favorite place for ambush by renegades who ever preyed upon the unwary or ill-armed. He had already seen enough signs of their activity, tracks, and rubbish from recent camps, to know they were about, but he had luckily avoided any contact. He watched intently, but he could not yet tell if the dust in the distance was from a party of renegades or whether it was the approach of travelers.

Shifting his position, slowly and slightly, hoping that his movement would not be noticed, and hoping that his robe blended well enough into the terrain, he carefully scanned the surroundings. Other than a scorpion crawling over the top of a nearby rock, he saw no other sign of unwanted company. This was little comfort. The all too familiar sensation in his gut and the prickling of the hairs on his arms and the back of his neck assured him that danger was very near. Whether it was from the approaching riders or from nearer to hand, he could not tell.

"All you need know," his commander had told him, "is that your contact will be there. He will most likely be one of their high-born and in company of armed servants. Most likely the same ones that you have met before. They will be riding under yellow pennants. As usual, your man will be wearing a red shemagh covering his face. Accept what he gives you and give him this packet in return. That is all you are to do. Identify yourself in the usual manner, with your signal glasses, and all will go well, I'm sure."

"What if it's cloudy?" Ullin quipped. The commander was not amused.

Now he could just make out the ribbon-like yellow pennants on the lances carried by the lead horsemen, and he took out his signal kit and carefully unwrapped it. Taking from it a round disc of light green glass, he put out his cupped hand and with the other held the disc in the sun until its glint was on his palm. He moved the mirror so that a flash of light was thrown at the approaching party. Three times he did this and then paused. He repeated, paused and repeated. After the fifth repeat he saw the reply: three answering green glints, like his own, pausing and repeating. Ullin put down the green disc and picked up a red one and flashed it four times, long and deliberately. He watched and waited. This red signal was to be answered by the proper colors.

After a moment the signals came, two white glares and three long blue flashes from the horsemen. Relieved, he answered with white, and put away the kit.

His sensations of danger were not alleviated. Indeed, as he gathered his things the feeling only intensified, approaching a shiver, so starkly did his armhairs rise. Nonetheless, he picked up his shoulder bag with the special packet and his water flask. He tightened his face coverings and fixed his light robe in place with a band holding his hood around his forehead and tucked the flap across his face. As cautious as ever, he began making his way forward, crouching low among the rocks, with one hand on his bag to keep it from swinging, and the other on his sword hilt. Soon the ridges were too low in the sand to offer cover, and he halted for a moment to give the landscape another close examination before exposing himself.

The party of about ten riders along with several pack animals was about a furlong away, and, still crouching, he waited before starting out so that they would come together at the same time at the path nearest to him.

This was the third time Ullin had been on such a mission, to a secret rendezvous in the south, but before he met with only one or two riders. The size of this party of Dragonkind put him more on edge. As he began his way to them, the foolishness of what he was doing, walking alone to face ten of the fiercest race, struck him cold. So much could go wrong. Besides any misunderstanding that might arise, there were other, darker possibilities. What if his contact had been captured and forced by torture to give up the signal codes? Not only would the packet he was to deliver fall into the wrong hands, but his life would surely be forfeit. Dressed as they were, with armor and robes from head to toe, with only their eyes showing, he would hardly be able to recognize his contact. His last meeting was foremost in his mind.

"Know this ring," his contact told him, holding out his fist. "Look well upon it. If any come in my place, and they do not wear this ring, know that I am taken."

They halted about twenty yards from each other. After a moment, one of the riders wearing a red shemagh wrapped around his face dismounted and came forward. As he neared Ullin, their eyes, the only portion of their bodies exposed, fixed each other. Ullin saw immediately, though, that this was a different person than he had met before, not as tall, and with a different way of walking. The figure halted a few yards away, pushed back his black robe to reveal the hilt of a sword, then removed a glove, and produced a small leather-bound packet. Ullin approached, and, before he held out his own packet, he looked closely at the ring of his counterpart. Satisfied that it was the same ring as he had seen before, he was curious as to why a different person had come this time. But he asked no questions and held out his delivery.

The Dragonkind, apparently satisfied as well, took it, and the two tucked their new burdens away as the Dragonkind looked about.

"Alone?"

"My escort was killed five days ago," Ullin replied.

"You speak our language." The Dragonkind said. It was the voice of a youngster, thought Ullin. But he could distinguish no features through the robes and armor, except, by the richness of them, that this must be a high-born of their kind. For surely only a prince would own such finery. Whoever it was, he would not have been entrusted with this assignment unless he was quite capable and trustworthy.

"Somewhat crudely, I'm afraid," Ullin answered.

"Well enough. Do you have far to go?"

"A fortnight, by foot. Perhaps farther."

"I see. Wait here."

The Dragonkind went to one of the pack animals and then returned, bringing a waterskin.

"Take this," he said. "We are but four days fast ride until we reach Kajarahn."

Ullin took the skin and slung it over his shoulder.

"Thank you. There is a party of renegades about," he said in return.

"We are well-armed."

Ullin nodded.

The Dragonkind made as if to say something, but perhaps thought better, and nodded, "Very well."

"Good journey," Ullin said, turning to go.

"And to you," the Dragonkind replied, remounting his horse. A rising breeze from the southeast fluttered the pennants. "A storm swiftly comes."

Ullin turned and looked at a wall of reddish brown clouds on the horizon.

"Yes."

He waited for them to pass westward, each of the riders eyeing Ullin warily as they went by. He watched them recede, waiting for them to be out of sight before going his own way. They were nearly a few fulongs away, heat-shimmered lines of black riders over a low trail of dust, when he turned. A brief glint in the sea of sand to the left of the Dragonkind caught his eye, and he immediately broke into a run to catch up with them just as a hot, dusty wind came at his back, as if to push him along.

The renegades rose up from their shallow sand-covered pits, and within moments their hail of arrows brought down six of the riders and four of the horses. From the sand to one side and the rocks on the other, the renegades charged the travelers, brandishing swords and lances. The four remaining Dragonkind were quickly surrounded by five times their number, but held their ground by dint of their skill. Ullin arrived just as the storm struck its first blows, and he fought his way through the renegades to join at the side of the travelers. Seeing the bowmen recovering their arrows, and realizing the fight was hopeless, Ullin grabbed the one in the red shemagh by the arm, deflecting a sword thrust from the desperate Dragonkind.

"It is I! Come away! Come with me!"

They were prevented from any further talk by arrows that took down another of the travelers, and Ullin grabbed the man again.

"To the rocks!"

By now the air was hissing with stinging sand as Ullin pulled the Dragonkind with one arm and fought with the other.

"To the rocks!" he cried again, pointing with his sword.

They ran through the sandy wind, fighting as they went, barely able to see friend from foe. But the pair slipped through the attackers, as the noise and force of the gale increased rapidly. They stumbled through the rocks while the renegades, too concerned with their spoils and too little troubled by the fate of the two escapees, did not pursue. By now the grinding howl of the gritty storm had engulfed them and was tearing at their robes and clotting their eyes.

"Here!" the Dragonkind yelled, barely audible though his face was just inches from Ullin's. "In here!"

Together they squeezed into a cleft beneath an outcrop and covered their heads with their robes. They huddled into the crevice and tried to pull their legs in as close as they could while the sand rose like an incoming windblown tide. The hiss and howl of the storm made speech impossible, battering them fiercely, and buffeting them about within their hole.

The wind suddenly intensified, and with it came a deep-rumbling roar paired with a wavering high-pitched shriek. Like ten thousand screaming banshees riding ten thousand stampeding buffalo, the horrendous noise encompassed Ullin and his companion as the powerful gale clawed and tore at them viciously. The sand that had just moments before threatened to cover them was now scoured away, and the two men twisted around to press their faces into the crevice, clutching at the rocks as their legs were pulled out from beneath them with the retreating sand. Both screamed unheard at the top of their lungs. They scratched rock and dug their nails into stone keep their hold as their robes whipped and snapped. Ullin managed to drive both his arms around a rock, and in the dim light he sensed his struggling companion sliding away, clawing and scratching at loose stones. He shot out an arm just in time to grab the Dragonkind's wrist, and he felt his own wrist clenched in return. The clutching wind shrieked and screamed, pulling them upward with invisible hands that tried to tear them out of their hiding place. Ullin felt as if he would rip apart at the shoulders, but he did not loosen his grip on the rock or the Dragonkind. Groaning, he pulled while sand and pain-induced tears clotted his eyes, until at last the Dragonkind gained some purchase with his other arm. Still they clung to one another, wrist to wrist, hand to rock, as the storm turned and pummeled them from a new direction. Once again sand poured up the little gully and down over its sides. The worst of this soon passed, the grit-laden air less forceful than before, but a mighty wind persisted for a long while, and once again it pushed sand and covered them to their shoulders.

• • •

Hours later, the storm spent itself, and it was some time in the night that Ullin regained enough of his senses to tell that the ringing in his ears was silence.

When he tried to open his eyes, sand fell into them, and he spent a long while blinking and loosening his grip on the rock he had been hugging so that he could carefully wipe the grit away until his vision cleared enough to take in his surroundings. Beside him the Dragonkind lay motionless, still clutching his wrist, his face tucked into his other arm which was still wedged around a rock. His red turban had blown away, and Ullin could see long black hair, tangled by the wind and filled with dust.

The Dragonkind moaned and released Ullin's tired wrist and pushed himself up to his knees, sand cascading down from his back and shoulders. Ullin did the same, and they slowly crawled backwards out of the sand-filled hole and into bright moonlight. In tatters, covered with dust from head to foot, they tried to brush themselves off, watching each other all the while out of the corner of their eyes.

It was the first time Ullin had ever seen a woman of the Dragonkind. Though she still had on the black armor and leggings, when she tossed out her hair, gathering it up in her hands to shake it out and toss it back over her shoulders, he was stunned by her beauty. A master at checking himself, Ullin continued emptying sand from his folds and pockets with only a cocked brow for reaction. They said nothing for a long while, each making sure they still had their documents and weapons, rebinding their leggings, and making new head-coverings from the remnants of their cloaks. Ullin still had his shoulder bag and the waterskin she had given him, and, after checking the straps to those, he took a long look around. Lady Moon, not yet at her boldest, was nearly overhead, and by her light he could see far in every direction.

The storm had greatly altered the landscape, filling the low places with sand, and heaping great banks against the ridges of the rocks. Looking back to where the ambush had taken place, he saw that a broad, high dune had poured over the spot, the nearest edge of it only a few feet away and rising steeply up far above their heads. If the storm had persisted only a little longer, they would have been entombed.

"I fear your companions did not survive," he said. She nodded at the dune.

"I do not see how they could have. But I must continue on."

"Well, perhaps the renegades suffered the worst of the storm," Ullin said. He slung the water bag from his shoulder, took out his flask, and very carefully filled it with the precious stuff. The Dragonkind woman observed his care and that he did not spill a drop. Ullin then stood and held out the water bag to her.

"I do not take back what I have given," she said. "Besides, the messages you carry must be delivered. You will need water."

"No less than you. And what you carry must also be delivered."

"You will not make it back with only your flask."

"Then I will go as far as I can, to a place I know of where my body will be found by my people. Your messages will be taken from there."

Her expression told Ullin that her people had no such contingency for her, and he even thought he saw a slight look of shame.

"I am sorry. Of course," she said. "I am afraid I am new to this sort of thing. And perhaps those I represent are not as well organized as your people. There are very few of us."

"We do the best we can with what we have," Ullin replied. "If you continue your route, the renegades will have you."

"With so little water, I must go a different way. South, at first, into the desert. Then west to the ruins of the Dead Place."

"There is water at the ruins?"

"No. But there is shade."

"How far?"

"By foot, almost two days, I think. Another ten days from there to the city. But a turn southward will take me to an oasis in four days, and from there by a roundabout way I'll have steady water a day apart for another six or so days to the city. An indirect route, but one that will have your messages safely to their destination."

Ullin gazed north, the direction back to his own people. He slung the waterbag over his shoulder and nodded at her.

"Very well. We go together to the city. Along the way, we will protect each other. From the city I will go north and cross the mountains, working my way east to rejoin my people. We may as well be off before the sun rises."

Ullin started out, striding past the woman, and was several yards ahead when she called to him.

"But, wait."

"What is it?" he stopped and looked back at her.

Now, with the silver light full upon her figure, he saw she was young, not so much by her appearance as by the slight, hesitant, girlish movement of her shrugging arms and shoulders. Such was her unexpected loveliness that he smiled.

"You are right," she said. "Let us be off."

• • •

It was difficult going for several hours, first picking their way through the sand-covered rocks, skirting the new dune, then, where they guessed the road must have been, turning west and trudging through deep, fine sand, their feet sinking several inches with each step. After a few slow miles, the sand thinned somewhat and they could discern the roadway again. Their pace quickened as their way eased, and after Lady Moon left them behind, and her gown of light helped them no more, they continued on by bright starlight, saying nothing, staying close together so that each could hear the breathing and footfalls of the other. The roadway took a southward turn and, after an hour, returned sharply westward.

"Half of our pack animals carried nothing but water," she said. "And we planned to go quickly, without rest. But if you and I follow the road, we will never make it. On foot it is at least twenty days of heat and bandits until the next outpost and oasis. So we must go south."

Ullin let the woman take the lead since she seemed to pick out the way better. For all he knew, she had been this way many times. Looking at the stars, he followed close behind. By the time the eastern sky was growing pale, his thoughts were on his faraway home, and he tried to recount the years since he had last seen Tallinvale. Later, as the sun rose, it briefly passed through the same shade of red as his aunt's hair, and he wondered how she and her family were getting along. Was it four years since he last saw them? Or was it five? He could not do the calculation, and, regardless, the Eastlands Realm was a world away. It was best to put such thoughts, such memories, out of his head.

The sun quickly changed from red to yellow, then to searing white, blasting the travelers with its heat, bringing Ullin's mind back to their predicament. Few could survive what they were attempting. But the papers she carried had to get through, and she stood a better chance with him than alone. The attempt had to be made.

The day rapidly grew hotter. He settled into a split state of mind, one part carefully making his body take each additional step, the other part struggling against the heat to stay alert. With Ullin following the Dragonkind woman, the two slowly moved deeper into the vast expanse of unbroken flatlands, their footfalls somewhat muffled by the thin layer of fine brown dust that they tread upon. After an hour and longer, the woman adjusted their course to the southwest, and Ullin, squinting at the blazing way ahead, saw a distant wavering shape that, as they drew closer, rose up as a lonely turret of stone. It was about twelve yards in diameter at the base and three times as high, at least up to where the topmost portion was crumbled away, the stones of the ancient top scattered around the northern base. They found a spot in its shadow among some of the fallen blocks, and his guide sat and leaned back against the stones. Ullin sat beside her, and surveyed the landscape before them. The hard pale floor that stretched out in every direction was by now shimmering with heat, making the distant horizon waver.

Ullin handed the flask of water to her. She nodded and took a few sips, then handed it back.

"Was this a watchtower?" he asked.

"Once. And once there was water here, so they say. In a past age. The ruins of the old city lay some six or seven leagues to the west."

Ullin rummaged through his bag and found a hard brown block. With his knife he carved off two pieces about the size of his thumb. He held out one for her, and she took it with a quizzical look. He bit into his own portion and began to chew. She watched him chew and chew, then after sniffing it, she carefully took a bite and chewed, too. They both chewed for a long while. When finally, and not without a little difficulty, each had swallowed their bite, she looked at her remaining portion.

"What is this?" she asked.

"Soldier rations. We call it jawrock."

She nodded, "Thank you," and slowly put the remaining piece into her mouth. As she chewed, her expression made Ullin chuckle while he ate the last of his portion. She smiled back at him, nodding as she tried to swallow.

"It's terrible!" she managed to say.

Ullin nodded, "I know."

"Whatever is it made of?"

Ullin shrugged as he swallowed. After a moment, he was able to say, "I don't think we want to know. Here, have another sip of water. It will help."

She took the flask and a small swallow, then handed it back as she stood. As she threw off her black hooded outer robe, she noticed that Ullin did not take another drink, but tucked the flask away. Quickly, and with the ease of experience, she lifted her spaulders and unbuckled her breastplate from the backplate, dropping her armor away. Ullin saw the outline of her form as her blouse stuck to her skin with sweat. Soon she had her leg guards off, too, and she found a place behind one of the stones to hide the equipment. With her back to him, she pulled her long black hair around her neck to reknot it behind her head.

"I will retrieve these if ever I can, "she said as she put her robe back on and refastened her head band around her hood. "Now we go west. You wear no armor?"

"Only in battle. If there is any at hand."

He stood, tucked his shemagh over his mouth and nose, pulled his hood over his head, and followed her out from the shade into the full fury of the unforgiving sun.

"You have seen many battles?" she asked without turning around.

"My share."

"Against my people."

"Yes."

"And you have killed many?"

"That has been my lot."

"I do not believe in lots, or fate of any kind."

She turned her head to look back at him as she spoke this, and Ullin caught the flash of her greenish-yellow eyes. About a mile later, she spoke again.

"These wars are unjust. Although we are sworn enemies, it is because we choose to be so, and we can choose not to be so, too."

"Hatred runs deep," Ullin replied. "Our two peoples are bound by it in oath and in blood. The bonds of the past are strong. They bind the young to the old, one generation to the next, in ways words cannot tell, and stain all hands with blood. Those who wield the sword. Those who make the sword. Those who raise the grain to feed the swordmaker. Things are not easily changed."

"Yes. But if people yearn for peace, they may hope to find it, if they try."

"Perhaps they may. If they are brave and do not fear change."

They walked on, two upright figures on a vast frying pan under a full sun that beat hammers upon the desert, causing the air, which did not move a whisper, to throb from all sides. The Dragonkind woman kept a good pace and said nothing else while Ullin followed several yards behind. Once, when he looked to his left, he saw in the distance the rim of a beautiful blue lake, bounded with tall trees. He started to say something and saw that she was gazing at it, too, but she kept to her course. He chided himself, realizing that it was a desert illusion. But such was the potency of the mirage, and so clear were the lovely trees, that it provoked a powerful temptation in Ullin. It was as if it called to him, "Come! Bathe in my cool, clean waters, and dry in my comforting shade!"

The desire to go to it did not rapidly fade. His disappointment that it could not be real nearly brought tears to his sand-stung eyes in spite of his chagrin. A few moments later, glancing again in that direction, he saw nothing but an endless expanse of shapeless dust, unbroken from horizon to horizon.

It was hopeless, he knew. In such a place as this, with no water to last their journey, they could not possibly make the distance they set out to cover. Hopeless, perhaps, but not pointless. Ullin thought the best thing was to assume you were already dead. True, fear and the desire to survive make one fierce and strong in strange ways. But in futile situations fear and desire are not enough. Like before a hopeless battle. What becomes important is not death, but how you meet it. He had seen bravery in the face of death. Once, from a distance, he had witnessed a comrade, so wounded that he could not lift his sword or parry, smash his body into a line of enemy swords in an effort to buy his brethren time to regroup. On another occasion, he watched a Dragonkind soldier race through a hail of arrows to retrieve his wounded fellow, lifting him up and jogging away, miraculously avoiding the missiles directed at them. And he had witnessed cowardice, too. Those who broke and ran. And those who did not even try to do their duty. But we, he mused, we two specks of life inching through the vast desert will try to do our duty. Right now, trying was everything, even if there was no hope of success. And that was the point. It was something that need not even be spoken, Ullin mused, and something that the unlikely pair had in common.

The effort of walking regained his attention, and he focused on his guide's shadow, his head down and his mind fairly numb from the heat. Thus he watched her moving shadow grow longer by imperceptible increments and could tell without looking up when she glanced around to take her bearings. As the sun slowly receded, and her shadow lengthened, he held his same distance from it, and slowly drew farther behind.

Their march was slow, painfully slow, trudge after trudge, step after sole-burning step. There was no sound but their breathing, their footfalls, and the occasional slosh of the water bag. Time seemed meaningless. For long spells, Ullin forgot where he was, so absorbed by his thoughts, mesmerized by the glinting sand that moved past the woman's shadow. Suddenly, her shadow was straddled by two others. Startled, he looked up to see two tall columns of stone just ahead and on either side of her. They were octagonal in shape, about twenty feet thick, each side carved in sandblasted figures and glyphs, rising upwards of sixty feet and capped by domes of gold. Beyond those lay the ruins of a once-great city.

A beautiful place it must have been in its heyday, Ullin thought, judging by the elegant curves of the cut stone, the graceful lines of the remaining walls, some still several stories high with arched windows. Much sand had blown in over the eons since its abandonment, piled into smooth dunes against walls and columns. As the two continued along what once had been a wide boulevard, Ullin wondered how much must be buried beneath their feet. They turned and went southward between protruding rubble and came to a wide round disc of sand, nearly a mile in diameter. Surrounding it to the south and east were towers and palisades of ancient palaces, now cracked and crumbled, mute signs of a once-glorious splendor.

"Surely, this was once a great city," Ullin observed as they turned westward following the curving edge of the disc.

The Dragonkind woman waved her hand toward the disc of sand.

"It is said that this was once a blue lake of cool water, made by the people who built this city, and that it flowed from here to feed rich fields and vineyards all around. But the source of the water was cut off long before the First Age. So the city withered and died as did all the lands around it."

Ullin nodded and followed on, remembering the stories of how, before the Fall, before the Elifaen lost their wings, certain of them attacked these lands and smote it with dryness to spite the Dragon People for the destruction of the forests and wild fields. From those events, nearly forgotten in the Northlands, flowed all of the sorry and glorious histories since. As they went, passing strange and beautiful carvings, and going between rows of columns, he saw that they walked along a paved avenue that curved around the lake of sand toward a large, high-walled ruin.

"I suppose the Dragon People were the first to build cities," he said. Looking at the carved letterings on a half-buried block, he added, "And the first to have writing."

"Perhaps. But, as you can see, much has been lost."

It was a struggle to speak. The sun had by now passed into late afternoon and blazed unabated. Ullin's mouth and throat were beyond parched. Already lean from the preceding weeks of travel, heat, and minimal rations, Ullin's legs throbbed dully at the edge of his awareness. Yet the wonder of the place pushed away such concerns, for the moment at least, and his thoughts were filled with the legends and tales that, since childhood, had fired his imagination, and the stories, read over and over from the old books and scrolls in his grandfather's library, that spurred his early longing for travel and adventure. He now realized that the things he had seen and experienced since leaving Tallinvale were more wondrous, and more awful, than he had ever imagined they could be.

"This way."

She led the way along many turns through rubble and ruin to a narrow stair rising steep and without a banister against a tall wall. This took them to an arched passageway, cut into the stone, and then they descended again into what must have been some sort of courtyard. She led him on through other passageways, going up and down and turning, often along narrow corridors and alleys, through relieving shade and brilliant, sunlit places. Yet, as desolate and quiet as the place was, signs of the old vibrant city were everywhere. Hardly a wall was unadorned by carvings or tilework. There were mosaic-like stones carefully cut and laid in striking patterns, lintels decorated with quartz of many colors, and stone balconies that still defied gravity and gracefully curved out here and there above them. Ullin ran his hand along one wall within a narrow alley, wiping away a thick layer of dust, revealing the gleam of a smooth surface, lush green and rich red tiles intricately laid, each piece no bigger than his fingertip.

They climbed again, and came to a roofless room, surrounded by high walls. It was long and narrow with a line of small holes at the top of the wall on the western side. Due to the height of the walls, it apparently received little direct sunlight except when the sun was high overhead. Now it was dark and cool below a clean blue sky above. Here they stopped.

"We can shelter here for the rest of the day and continue on at nightfall," the woman said.

Ullin moved to the east side and, looking out through a narrow window, put down his pack and unwrapped the coverings from his head and face. Several stories high, he could see the entire lake bed, its nearest edge very close by. Beyond the ruins that lined the far side, more ruins stretched, fanning out in patterns like spokes. It was plain that it had been a carefully planned city. And his training as surveyor and engineer suggested that the water must have once flowed out from the lake to be distributed all around along the network of avenues and lanes.

"You have been here before?" Ullin asked.

"Yes. Years ago."

"What happened to the water, and to the people who lived here?"

The woman came and stood next to Ullin to look.

"You know of the Great Stone, do you not?"

"Yes, of course," nodded Ullin.

"Kalzar made many suffer because of it. This was once a rich and fertile region with many fields fed by clean waters that sprang from here and were carried by dikes and canals to the cropland and vineyards and orchards. The city rivaled the glory of Kalzar's own city. Also, these people were renowned for their skill at building and working stone. Those two things were its undoing. Kalzar took many from here to be his slaves and to do the work of cutting the Great Stone from the mountain. But Kalzar, needing food to feed his armies and his slaves, also made the people give over so much of their grain that the people here starved. When the shipments of grain suddenly stopped, Kalzar sent men to find out why. They found only the bodies of Kalzar's slain overseers and soldiers. And a dry, abandoned city. It was as if it happened overnight. No one knew where the people went. Kalzar desperately tried to locate and restore the source of the waters, but his wise men could not delve its secret or restore the flow. Kalzar was enraged, and suspected the Faerekind had something to do with it. He ordered the name of the city stricken from all records, chiseled out of every stone marker, and all scrolls pertaining to it were burned. It was made a crime to speak its name, and all former inhabitants, who still survived as slaves, had their tongues cut out. That was when Kalzar at last gave up the moving of the Great Stone, and marched his armies north to attack the places of the Faerekind."

"Where did the people go? Those who revolted and made the waters vanish?"

"No one knows. But there are many tales told. Some say they killed themselves, somewhere out in the desert, so that Kalzar could not use them to increase his power. Others say they became spirits, and abide here still. There are even tales that say the people who lived here all journeyed north and disappeared in to the green lands beyond the mountains."

They looked for a moment longer across the lonely vista, then she turned and slumped down to sit against the wall. Ullin did the same and passed the water flask to her. She took a sip and let it dry into her mouth, closing her eyes with the relief of it for several moments before taking another sip to swallow. While she did this, Ullin brushed away with his hand the inches of sand beside him, revealing the smooth tile floor below. She handed the flask back to him and he took his turn, being as careful as she, feeling, as she had, the life-returning power of the water. When he finished, he put away the flask and turned to ask her about this place but saw that her eyes were still closed and her head tilted to one side, asleep. He studied her for a long moment, noting how different from others of her kind she was, at least different from the males of her people that he had encountered. Her hair was thick and black, her eyelashes long and lovely, her skin smooth and without blemish or scaliness, dark brown, almost walnut. Her form was full and pleasingly curved; though thin, she was voluptuously endowed, and, though she had the air of a high-born, the muscles of her legs and arms were distinctive and well-defined, and her shoulders looked strong. The men of her kind, most of whom he had only met in battle, were thin and spindly, but with intense, wiry strength, and with coarse skin, often pocked and scaly, their hair wispy thin, and their noses ill-defined. Almost like skeletons, they were. But if she was typical of the women of her people, he thought, the rumors of their beauty fell somewhat short of the mark. Suddenly he felt self-conscious, his face red with embarrassment as he looked away.

Outside, Sir Sun descended toward the edge of the desert. As Ullin looked across the room to the west wall, a shaft of light appeared through one of the small round holes just opposite of where they sat. The yellow beam shot across the room, over his head, and out through the window. The light grew brighter as the sun fully lined up with the opening, and Ullin was intrigued by it, wondering at its purpose. Overcoming his aches and fatigue, he got up and looked through the window.

Now the remains of the city cast long shadows away from him, reaching across the lake of sand. Directly opposite, among the now-shadowed ruins on the far shore, one structure stood out, bathed in an orange glow. He continued to watch, fascinated by the tranquility of the city, until the sun sank out of sight and the eastern view was lit only by the fading sky.

As he was turning away, a movement caught his eye, and he instinctively flinched to the corner of the window so that he could peer out. What he saw was just below and several ruins over. He thought he saw it again, just a small movement of brown against brown, but after watching for a long time he began to think it only a trick of the deepening shadows. His guide still slept, and he looked around the room with concern. It was not a place to be caught in, and now he chided himself for standing so boldly before such a prominent window. Any number of trackers could be following them, renegades or even Dragonkind soldiers. He looked at his guide again and wondered if he could trust her. She had nothing to gain from killing him, and she already had ample opportunity. But how can any spy, or any spy's courier, be trusted? Perhaps she was betrayed, and a party was sent to intercept her and to capture the documents that they carried. If captured, her fate would be far worse than his own, he knew. Suddenly, it occurred to him that he himself knew precious little of his own masters, or who might be party to this mission. For all he knew, his own people could be tracking them.

This, his third such mission in as many years, had gone badly from the beginning. He had started out from Vanara with five other men. After only a day's journey beyond their lines, one of the men was killed by a scorpion. The next day, a rockslide maimed two others and so Ullin sent them all back, continuing alone. He certainly regretted the death and injuries of his companions, but he was relieved to be on his own. He preferred it that way. He could travel faster and with greater stealth, and he had only himself to look after. He was forever worried about those entrusted to his command, and though he had always distinguished himself in battle, he sometimes fretted that his caution with his subordinates might be mistaken for cowardice by his superiors. It was a silly concern, as any who had served with him would readily say. But he knew that the reputation of his House was now on his shoulders, and he would not have it impugned nor improved at the cost of unnecessary blood.

This was a fairly recent change in him and a radical turn. Once, not long ago, he cared only to take revenge on the Dragonkind who slew his father and his uncle. Now, after too much gore, he was as determined to do his duty as ever, but none of the rest. Not again.

• • •

Night fell quickly as he continued to worry about the movement he had seen. And he found himself at the side door of the room, watching. The dead city was as silent as Lady Moon above who was already lending her silver light to the thankless desert. It was then that he noted that he did not have any feeling of danger that normally came to him in times of peril, the body sense that stood his arm hairs on end and gave him peculiar sensations on the back of his neck. He passed his hand around his neck. No, unless the ability had failed, there was no sense of alarm.

Calmed, he decided to have a look around. Leaving the waterskin beside the still-sleeping Dragonkind, he picked up his own small flask and left the room. He only intended to look close at hand, checking those elegant ruins that were nearby. But an hour later found him far from where he had started, carefully following a small furry creature that was a wonder to see among the stones and cast down blocks, a creature certainly not native to the desert. And, amazingly, it did not seem to mind being followed. It was the same creature whose shape he had glimpsed earlier, causing him such alarm at the window. After a little longer, Ullin realized that the rabbit was aware of his presence. It actually seemed to wait for him to catch up to it, stopping to groom its ears until Ullin was within five or six feet of it before hopping off again, checking with its about-turned ears to be sure Ullin was following. Ullin fell into an almost dream-like state of disbelief; if the creature itself was not enough of a wonder, then its behavior was certainly marvelous, for Ullin was convinced it was, indeed, leading him along, deeper and deeper into the still city. He knew that he should not have left his guide for so long, for it was possible that she would depart without him. But something made him trust that she would wait. And so, as he turned down a moonlit passage and crawled under a tumble of blocks, keeping a fair and polite distance between himself and the rabbit, his mind kept going back to her. He wondered, for the hundredth time, who she was and why she was chosen for this mission. He admired her mysterious beauty which so penetrated him that he raised his guard against the attraction. But there was something else about her that he found intensely attractive. Her manner, perhaps, or her bearing.

As he squeezed between two massive columns that held up a teetering wall, his thoughts were suddenly interrupted by the realization that he had lost sight of the rabbit. Looking carefully into the tiny alcove formed by the ruins, a sweet aroma touched his nostrils, one as out of place as the woodland rabbit. Just as he began to try to identify the smell, the little creature reappeared just a few yards away from a shadow in the wall. It hopped out into the moonlight, munching on a leafy stem. Ullin stared in disbelief as the creature finished the snack and set about washing its face with both paws, sometimes pulling down one of its ears to give it a scrub. It seemed careless of Ullin during these moments, but then it stopped, stood up tall on its hind legs, and then turned around to hop back into the shadow, shaking its head and bouncing off all fours in a delightful sideways manner before disappearing. Ullin followed, finding an opening in the shadow just big enough to slide through on his belly. The opening was several yards deep and as he reached out to pull himself through the other side, he touched something cool and moist.

• • •

Dawn was but a few hours away when he returned to the room where he had left the Dragonkind woman. Before he could greet her, she sprang to her feet angrily.

"Where have you been?"

"I was—"

"We should have left hours ago! While the night was still long and cool. Soon the sun will be up and merciless! I thought you might have taken your own way and left without me."

The anger and frustration in her voice was clear, and Ullin felt justly chastised for his absence.

"My word is my honor," he said. "I will see you to the Free City of Kajarahn. I felt you would be safe here while I scouted some movement in the shadows outside. I am sorry it took me so long, and for your anxiety."

She softened her stance a little, obviously relieved that he had returned.

"I have no hold upon you," she said. "You owe me nothing. Not even an apology. My life is yours twice over, and so it is I who am in debt to you. Please forgive me."

"There is nothing to forgive, and my apology stands," Ullin said emphatically. "I should not have left you for so long. Perhaps you will feel better when I show you this."

He held out his hand from under his cloak to show her a posy made all of the same kind of flower, but all of different colors. Her eyes widened and her mouth fell open at the sight. In disbelief, she stepped closer and carefully took them from him, glancing back and forth from the flowers to Ullin's grinning face.

"Cronosis! Some newly bloomed!" she uttered. "Surely you are a magician!"

"Hardly. This place is not as dead as you may think."

"But these only grow where there is ample moisture."

"Then come with me, and I will show you where that moisture is, along with more like these."

• • •

So it was that as the dawn began to mark the eastern horizon with its glow, Ullin took her through the silent ruins, picking his unfamiliar way carefully and giving his hand to hers to help her through and over the difficult tumbles of stone. By the time they reached the little hole in the wall, the air was filled with an alluring scent, and the night was rapidly retreating into the west. Ullin, smiling, motioned for her to go first. She hesitated, shifting her gear, then got down on her hands and knees to peer into the tunnel. She glanced back at him as he crouched, making ready to follow. Satisfied that this was no trick, she squeezed in on her stomach and crawled through. He waited for a moment to give her a little distance, then pressed in after her. It was a little more difficult for him than for her, owing to his broader frame, but he had already passed through twice and knew that he could do it again. Still, it was a struggle, and the tightness of the space was not at all to his liking. But he was too excited to mind the discomfort, and he was soon emerging beside his companion who was still on her knees, staring and gaping in awe.

It had once been a courtyard, surrounded by very high walls that were still remarkably intact. Along the base of each wall were columned porches with arches that supported tiled roofs. These left an open rectangular area about thirty yards long and twenty yards wide. And it was choked with flowers. White, blue, red, and every shade between, yet all of the same form and variety, just about knee high.

"This is impossible!" she uttered. "These cannot thrive in such a place unless… unless…listen!"

Ullin nodded. "Over there, against the far wall."

They got to their feet and carefully stepped through the flowers, wading through the profusion, trying not to crush them. As they approached the far side, they were walking through water that was about an inch deep. Ullin's companion laughed. The dripping sound became louder, coming from the space just ahead under the roof of the opposing porch. Where the arches met the high wall on the underside, water dribbled out between the joints in the stone. It ran down the underside of the lintels and dripped from there to the floor where it pooled several inches deep before running out and into the thick growth beyond. It was not so much that it could not be quickly dried by the thirsty plants and arid air of the open space, but it was steady enough to have created the pool that gently spilled over the outer curb and into the sun. Ullin was every bit as astonished as she, but only shook his head and grinned. She hardly had words, either, and was almost reverent as she looked around. She reached out to let the water fall onto her hand.

"It is cold!" she uttered softly, and then, cupping both hands, she let it gather and run down her arms as she carefully brought her hands to her lips. Her eyes widened even more as she sipped, then she wiped her hands on her cheeks and turned to Ullin.

"It is sweetwater!"

"Sweetwater?"

"Yes. Not desert water. This is like water from the north. I have tasted northern water before. This is like that."

"Well, it is clean, if that is what you mean. And it is remarkably cool."

"Cold!"

Ullin thought to himself, "Well, I don't know about cold. You probably haven't felt very cold water, before." But he did not say anything, unwilling to spoil the delight that filled her.

"So," he said instead, "shall we stay here for the day?"

"Oh, yes! Let's do!"

They filled their water containers, and themselves, then stripped off their dusty robes down to their breeches and blouses, and dipped their makeshift shemaghs into the water to wash the dust from their faces and necks. This they did on their knees, saying nothing for a long while, as the day brightened into pale blue. During this time, similar thoughts and feelings came to each of the two, for nothing seemed so delicious or as relieving than a simple wash with an old rag and cool clean water. The care with which they dipped the cloth and wiped the skin had an air of meditation as well as revelry. Once, when Ullin took his cool cloth from his face and opened his eyes, he saw her looking at him in such a way that, after they broke eyes from one another, embarrassed them both.

"Such a mystery!" she said at last.

Ullin nodded at the pool. "Yes. I wonder at the source. Somewhere behind the wall, obviously."

"Yes. A mystery." She was looking at him again, searching with her eyes, and not where he gestured. "My name is—"

"It may not be wise," Ullin interrupted, "for us to share our names."

She looked a bit startled, then said, "Oh. Of course. You have no reason to trust me."

Ullin shook his head. "I care little for my own sake. My name is Ullin Saheed Tallin, and I care not who knows it. But I know that you will guard it with your life. No, it is not you but myself that I do not trust."

Seeing the questioning look on her face, he shifted off his knees and sat with this back against one of the nearby columns.

"I was captured once. It did not go well for me. Had I known anything at all, I may have told my captors. I was very close to making up anything that might please them when I was rescued."

"Oh."

She pushed aside her things and sat as he did across from him.

"I am sorry that you were abused. Your hatred for us must be very strong."

Ullin had closed his eyes, but he shook his head.

"I do not hate anyone. Not anymore."

"Hm. Then you are different from most."

She stretched more comfortably and listened to the fall of the water as she looked at Ullin, studying his attractive features. Aside from renegades, she had only seldom seen Northmen. Once, when a group of captured slaves were being pushed and shoved through a marketplace in far-off Tyrsharat, she chanced to pass. They were Northmen, miserable creatures, dirty and depraved. And she was told by her friends that they were without culture or wit, cruel and wicked, and so despised the abundance of their green fields and forests that they made war in the desert for spite. Others she had seen, too, in the Free City of Kajarahn. But they were merchants and moneychangers, allowed by unofficial pacts to trade there so that goods could still be exchanged by the warring lands. As long as the city paid its tribute to the Dragon King, it was tolerated. And the place flourished as well as such a place could that was lawless and decadent. Caravans regularly traveled to and from the city, taking spices and gold northward and precious herbs and textiles southward. Although a Dragonkind prince ruled the city, Men gave counsel to him and oversaw the collection of tributes and taxes. There were few laws, and fewer taboos. Disputes were settled privately, often on the spot, or, just as often, by bribery, or murder. Assassins and spies were everywhere, and no one was safe without the patronage of the wealthy or powerful who provided protection and even bodyguards. Rogues were in abundance, too, and renegades sometimes worked their way into the militia of the powerful.

But this man, she mused, still looking at Ullin, did not seem like any of them. He did not seem petty, or vain, or cruel, or careless. His speech and manner were refined. He was, she concluded, as her father described the Northmen from his own experience, strong and fair, honorable, for the most part, industrious and brave. All these things she wondered about and considered. But what occupied her mind the most at the present moment, was this man's surname. She knew it well from her father's tales. Did her father know it would be him? Did he send her on this mission so that the two would meet? Should she tell the Northman her own name?

"I have guessed who sent you," Ullin said suddenly, shaking her from her thoughts. His eyes remained closed for a moment, then he looked at her earnestly.

"But, I assure you, there is only one other living man in all the world who could have made such a guess in the way I have made it, and he is my grandfather. On two previous missions such as this, I have met the owner of that ring." He gestured to the ring she wore, partially wrapped with silver wire to make a man's ring fit a girl's finger. "I knew who he was when, on my first such mission, I saw the ring. But you are the first person I have spoken to about it. My superiors know nothing of it. I can only assume that you are someone very close to him."

She looked at the ring and nodded, not only in answer to Ullin, but also to the doubts she had just been contemplating.

"General Gurasa," Ullin said the name.

"I am his daughter," she stated. "My name is Micerea."

"Micerea. I am pleased to know you. Something very serious must have caused your father to send his daughter in his stead. On a task fraught with so much danger."

"My father trained me as well as he could to face such dangers as I might encounter. But, yes, he is ill and has become too frail to make many such journeys."

"I am sorry."

"He was never the same after," she hesitated, "after a friend of his was killed. My mother died shortly thereafter, which deepened his maladies."

"I am sorry to hear that. Do you have any brothers or sisters?"

"No sisters. My older brothers died when I was very little. But, I should tell you now that my father's friend, the one who was killed, was a Northman. And my father took this ring in remembrance of him. Dalvenpar Tallin was his friend's name."

"Yes. As I guessed. I know that ring was first given to Dalvenpar by your father when the two were young men. Your father was a guest in our house. That was before I was born. There is a portrait of Dalvenpar, my father, and my aunt in my house. In it, Dalvenpar wears this ring."

"Then I am relieved, at least, that it was not your father that mine came across on the field of war."

"No, it was not." Ullin sighed, his brow furrowed as he glanced at Micerea and then away at the rabbit that had taken up near to her, sprawled flat on the cool tile, his eyes closed but his upright ears attentive. "My father died near a place we call Gory Gulch."

"Oh."

They were silent for a long while. Although they remained in the shade, the air barely moved, and the powerful heat made the place steamy as the moisture that seeped into it dried and was replenished. Micerea slept, leaning against the wall in the shade of the overhanging balcony, and Ullin watched the rabbit. Or, to be sure, he watched the rabbit's ears, for that was the only hint of the creature protruding over the tops of the flowers. Ullin saw the plants sway as the rabbit nudged through them, grazing as it went, and sometimes a stalk would topple over and disappear, apparently snipped from below.

"How on earth did you get here?" he mused to himself. And, as if to answer, the rabbit stood on its hind legs and peered over the colorful blossoms back at him, its ears erect, as if making certain that Ullin and Micerea were still nearby, or perhaps wondering why they were here.

These circumstances, Ullin continued his thoughts, the three of them in this unlikely oasis, this refuge, at the same time, each representing something the other two might scarcely imagine, must happen only rarely in the long course of the world. The rabbit's presence here was no less the result of miracle and adventure than that of Ullin and Micerea. And if Man and Dragonkind escaped the swords and arrows of renegades, the deadly windstorms, and the frying heat of this trek, then so, too, had this creature its own adventures, setbacks, and reasons for arriving here. It was a story Ullin wondered about, but would never guess. Yet it was in Ullin's character, his experience, and his history, to take no circumstance for granted and to assume neither coincidence nor fate as a cause for anything. So he knew enough, at least, to be certain that this meek little creature's story was an extraordinary one. Moreover, and this, too, was peculiar, he felt that each in his company somehow understood that much about the other two, and that made them all kindred spirits, the wee thing no less than the two humans.

As he mused, his mood changed from curiosity to marvel, as comprehension formed. Indeed, as he realized, if each could know the stories of the others, each would surely be amazed in turn.

"Providence has brought us together," he thought, silently addressing the rabbit, "and I'll not abandon you here. So, perhaps, we'll see again the woodlands of the north. It is rather a matter of finding our way, isn't it?"

By now, the rabbit had eaten its fill, and had taken a place on the cool tile. As the day progressed from heat to blaze, it stirred very little, except to drink from the pool before resuming its nap. Ullin shared more of his jawrock with Micerea, and she ate what he offered, giggling at how atrocious it tasted.

"Too bad we can't eat what he eats," Ullin commented, gesturing at the rabbit and plucking one of the flowers himself to nibble at its stem. "Oh! Bitter!"

"They will make you ill if you keep that up."

"What did you say they were called?"

"We call them 'Cronosis,' " she answered. "I am told the Northmen call them 'semiluna.' "

"Yes. I have heard of semilunas. They change color after they bloom, is that not so?"

And thus their conversation moved to lighter, happier subjects. Flowers, gardens, customs, lore, and even music. When night fell, they still talked, and they quickly agreed to stay another night and day. Jawrock was plentiful, and water, too, and neither of them seemed in any hurry to venture back into the open desert, though they both knew full well that they must eventually do so. But, for now, they talked on and on, each strangely happy in the company of the other, and surprisingly alike in their views.

The cool night did little to dampen the ardor of their talk, even when shivers forced them to don their desert cloaks. When yawns became more frequent, though, and talked lessened unto silence, Ullin offered his arm so that Micerea could nestle against his shoulder for warmth against her shivers. Her body felt good against his, and he pulled his cloak over to cover their legs. After a little while, she shifted and looked up at him. And they kissed. It was a soft, gentle kiss, followed by another, then another. And, soon, the cool air seemed not to matter at all.

● ● ●

Six months later, Micerea was only a half-day's ride from her home, and she was looking forward to seeing her father after so long and reporting to him aspects of her journey. That same day, Ullin's half-dead body was found by a party of Vanaran soldiers who were scouting the mountains along their southwest border. They transported him as quickly as they could to an outpost where his injuries could be tended. The next day, he was taken by litter to the city of Linlally and to an infirmary where he could recover from exposure and exhaustion.

Gone for nearly a year, his commanders had given him up for lost, risking no rescue to an ill-fated mission. But back he came, bringing with him the secret dispatches he had been sent to fetch. They were dismayed at his condition, injured, feverish, and so weak that he arrived upon a litter.

When his superiors met to discuss Ullin's mission, they swore they would never again send him on another such errand. One person, who happened to be attending the meeting, suggested the Kingsman might make a good candidate for the King's Post, a Special Courier, perhaps. This was agreed upon, and the man went to see Ullin at the infirmary where he was still recovering from his ordeal. He found the Kingsman sitting on his cot, his head propped on one hand while he fiddled absently with a locket in his other hand.

"Hullo!" the man said to Ullin. "Do not rise! I wonder if we might have a little chat?"

Ullin shrugged as the man pulled a stool over and sat, leaning his walking stick against the window sill.

"You are Ullin Saheed Tallin, are you not?"

Ullin nodded.

"My name is Collandoth."

Chapter 21

The Bridge at Redwater Gorge

Ullin saw the opening of the cave, a yellow blot against the hill, and hesitated. Suddenly, he turned and walked toward town, feeling the need for further solitude before facing sleep, and time to gather his composure before facing his companions. Before facing her. His shame was unabated, but he strove against it, reminding himself over and over of his duty. The town was quiet by now, and he passed through it unnoticed, his pace easy but determined, though he had no aim but to walk and walk. Every few turns and stretches, hot tears welled behind his eyes, sometimes trickling out as he thought of Micerea. It was her, not Esildre, that was most in his heart and in his thoughts. Micerea would want him to keep to this task, to honor his commitment to Robby and the others. Although she could know nothing of their quest, his memory of her spoke truly of her loving support. How could he have behaved so? It was a shame upon his love for her, upon the honor he wished to have before her, should he ever see her again.

"And, if I never do," he thought as he stumbled and nearly fell due to blurred vision, "I will at least be true to my duty, as she would expect of me."

By following the ways and paths, he circled around the far side of town, and before he knew it, he was on his way back the way he had come. By the time he returned to the cave, it had been hours since he had left the pool, and he knew dawn was not far off. He needed rest and strode on toward the opening, hoping everyone was asleep. But at the entrance were Esildre's two traveling companions, standing watch. He returned their expressionless nods as he passed, and, as he entered, he saw Esildre and Sheila sitting on blankets at the far side of the Foyer near a low-burning lamp, chatting softly with each other. He quickly determined to act as if nothing had happened, and they looked up in mid-laugh and watched him fairly slink to his bedroll. They may as well have been staring at a chipmunk for all their bemused faces told him. Sheila's eyes glittered from across the room, but Esildre wore her veil. Without speaking, Ullin unrolled his bedding and settled down near Ibin and Billy and Robby, all drowsing peacefully.

• • •

"I wonder what's gotten into him?" Sheila commented. "He looks as though he's tried unsuccessfully to wash away the wine, too. Did your bath help?"

"Yes, I believe so. And now I am warm and dry again, thank you," Esildre replied, eyeing Sheila curiously, noting again the similarity of their appearance.

"Some have made comments about the two of us," she said. "About how we resemble each other."

"I know," replied Sheila. "But they are silly."

"Do you think so?"

"Don't you?"

"We could be related," Esildre suggested.

"I don't see how."

"The bloodlines of Men and Elifaen are mixed from the time Men first came to these shores. All offspring of this mixing are not Elifaen, yet many are connected to the Faere race from times and ancestors that are forgotten. Or purposefully lost to memory. Take Ullin Saheed. He is not Elifaen, though his father was. His cousin, Robby, however, is Elifaen. Or, that is, he will be once he is Scathed, for his mother is Elifaen."

"My mother was not, though," said Sheila bluntly.

"How do you know?"

"Because I was told that my parents both died of yellow plague when I was tiny."

"Yes, only Men are susceptible to it. But you survived."

"Besides," Sheila continued, "I do not think my mother had the Elifaen sign. On her back. At least, I do not recall it."

"Still. She may not have gone through the change as those born of Men-sires must. Or, perhaps, a distant relation of ours," Esildre trailed off in thought.

"When does the change come?" Sheila glanced at Robby's sleeping form across the Foyer in the shadows beyond their nearby lamp.

"None can say of those born of Men-sires. For each it is different. For those others born of both Elifaen mother and Elifaen father, the change comes within the womb, upon conception. But not for those like Robby, whose father was not Elifaen. Often the child of such a union does not survive birth. Sometime after birth, the change comes. Usually while they are still very young, but sometimes, rarely, it comes after the body has already matured into adulthood. And, sometimes, the change does not come until old age, even until the throes of death. When the change does come, Robby will cease to age in the eyes of Men. But when might it come? I cannot say."

"What will happen to him when it does come? How long does it take, once it begins?"

"It will be like a storm. A trial for him. It will come suddenly, perhaps fired by some spark of passion or some crisis. Or, it may come during a time of peace. One that I know of had it happen while she slept. She went to her chamber of one race and emerged at sunrise of another race. It will be painful. It always seems so for males. I have known some who, after the change, were so weakened of spirit that they wasted away to nothing, though their bodies had been strong. Others, whose bodies were weak and frail beforehand became as strong as their spirit and afterwards became mighty warriors or enchantresses without equal. Ullin's father was one such, I have heard. Truly, few men were as strong or as handsome as he, it is said, nor as brave and bold in battle. Yet, so it was told, Lord Tallin was a sickly child."

Esildre looked at Sheila.

"He will need his friends about him. Even though he may see them as strangers and desire to shun all company and endure his pain in solitude. But my heart tells me he may need protection during that vulnerable time."

"Protection," Sheila repeated to herself. They sat in silence for a few moments before she spoke again.

"How long is an Elifaen child carried in the womb before birth? That is, children born of both Elifaen mother and father?"

"They grow fast. No more than four months. From the beginning of one season to the coming of the next," Esildre told her. "You have the look of something explained."

Sheila shook her head. "No. Just curious."

Again, silence fell between them. Earlier, when Sheila returned to the cave and found Esildre still drying from her bath, she hesitated to approach. It seemed to Sheila that the aspect of Esildre's manner had changed since just a short while before. As Sheila sat nearby and loosened her blouse, she watched Esildre, staring into the empty passageway, as one might stare into a fire. She absently ran her hand across her shoulders and down her arms, as if wiping away dripping water. And—was it just Sheila's imagination?—or did Esildre seemed less distant, as it were, vulnerable? Girlish, even. When Sheila got up and approached her, Esildre's demeanor instantly changed. Esildre smiled and patted the blanket beside her, and so Sheila sat. They had been chatting for a while, about nothing in particular, until Ullin's arrival. Now they felt a strange attraction for each other, a closeness and a cautiousness. While they did not fully trust each other, they felt such kinship that nearly anything could be said. Now, while Esildre remained contemplative, Sheila grew more agitated, more restless.

"There are always signs that one is Elifaen, even well before the change. Sometimes, the signs are known only to a few, and sometimes the signs are not seen for what they are."

"What kind of signs?"

"In the stars, perhaps. In nature, or in the person. And in those Elifaen of mixed unions, the power of each race is multiplied by the blending. Some special ability is not unusual, some skill, difficult to control or direct. Sometimes a sort of sight or way of knowing the world. Like the Melnari. Like Collandoth, who is neither Man nor Elifaen. Sometimes the

Elifaen has power over others, through their voice or words. Some, it is said, may even shift their shape from the likeness of one person to another, as easily as casting off one robe and putting on another. Some may even take the form of an animal or even a plant. But most, it seems, have abilities that are more subtle, less apparent."

Esildre smiled. "Now you are wondering if I possess any such power. Yes, I do. But I will not say what it may be, for he who boasts his power the gods so take it away. I think you know more of these things than you let on, and by your questions you feign ignorance greater than you have. You need not protest; that is your affair. I only warn you to be cautious. Such things are easily lost or mishandled. Like a beautiful vine, if obsessed over or ignored, it will spread throughout the garden of your spirit, choking out all else. One must pay attention to it, but pay it not too much attention!"

"You give me too much credit," said Sheila, thinking about her conversation at Tallinvale with Lyrium.

"Do I?"

"Yes. Where do you go from here? Have you decided?" Sheila changed the topic abruptly. Esildre sighed, understanding that the conversation was at an end.

"I go to Janhaven, I think," she answered, sensing Sheila's sudden distance. Rising, she said, "You should sleep, as your companions do."

"I shall do so. And you? You must be tired from your journey and all of this evening's celebrations."

"Perhaps, later. I go for another walk. To think more on today's events."

Esildre turned to go and stopped, looking at Ullin's prone form in the shadows. He was asleep, now, though he tossed about uncomfortably. She moved to the cave opening.

"Are you a witch?" Sheila blurted out. "As some say of you?"

A breeze puffed into the cave, stirring Esildre's hair. Without turning, she answered in a light voice, "No more and no less than you, Shevalia."

Sheila watched her step out into the night and disappear.

● ● ●

The following morning, Ashlord urged everyone up, and they made ready to depart. The Elders, most having made their goodbyes the night before, sent representatives to bring them breakfast and to see them off. Many of the townspeople came, too, including Eldwyna and all her family, including her grandfather, Eldwin. It was a hearty gathering, full of joyful talk, well-wishing, and more questions, too, for each of Robby's company pertaining to all the matters they had already discussed and more. They went back and forth in little groups to the Treasure Room to give the travelers a last gaze upon the splendors there. Robby, busy chatting with so many of the kind folk, was the last to make the walk through the passage to the Room, and Eldwin accompanied him. The turns of the passageway had the strange quality of quickly closing off the room from the noise of the Foyer, and as the two walked through the opened gates and thoughtfully looked over the wondrous jewel-encrusted goblets, the same mood of reverence overcame them. It was as if by touching these things they touched the past, great and magnificent, deep and mysterious. Even the helmets, black steel with threads of silver coursing over their surfaces, seemed not so much utensils of war as pieces of art.

"Ye may trust that I will do all that I can," said Eldwin to Robby, "to protect this treasure an' to see that we do as Ullin Saheed directed us."

"I know you will, Eldwin. Though I had no idea there would be any conditions placed upon you, I have every confidence that you and your people will do what is right."

"Thank ye, sir."

"In fact, you have done admirably well, these past days. I think anyone would say so. I regret the rough handling I gave you when we first met, and I now release you from any obligations to my service, to do as you, yourself, may see fit."

"Thank ye. But I would rather not give up me newfound loyalty. What I mean to say, sir, is that I will consider meself yer friend, if ye would have me as one, an', if I may ever be, yer servant. It is all that I have to give in gratitude for what ye've done for me family an' me people. Even though ye will soon part from us, I shall do as I think ye would have me do."

"That goes for me, too," spoke Millithorpe from behind them.

Surprised, Robby turned and saw the sincerity of Eldwin reflected on Millithorpe's face. His heart was gladdened by their words and their earnestness, yet he suddenly felt a strange weight of obligation, a sense of responsibility, as if these were his own family or his own people. Somewhat embarrassed, he saw Ashlord standing just beyond, emerging from the shadows of the passageway, coming to tell him they were ready to depart. From Ashlord's smile, Robby knew he had overheard the last exchange.

"You do me too much honor," Robby said. "I'm afraid that I am only starting to learn my way."

"Then we are no different," Millithorpe said. "At least when it comes to that. In a manner of speaking, that is."

Robby nodded and smiled, and they left the Treasure Room.

"Then perhaps these will help you," Robby reached into his shoulder bag and pulled out several folded packets and gave them to Eldwin. "These are maps. I doubt if I'll find much use for them from here on out. But they will show you the way eastward, toward Tallinvale. Study them. Make copies."

"Thank ye. Study them we shall."

Eldwin suddenly stopped and turned to Robby.

"Oh, sir! I almost forgot to ask. If we are able to go to the aid of Tallinvale, who shall we say sent us?"

They stopped, looking at one another, and Robby considered the question. Before he could answer, Ashlord spoke.

"Tell your people to say this, and no more: You serve the King."

"The King?"

"Yes."

"But," Eldwin looked from Ashlord to Robby and back, "shall I give the name of the King?"

"How can you?" Ashlord smiled. "For none knows his name. Let it be a mystery to all but your own people, but share not our names with any until the time is come for you to use them, among trusted people. Then it will be safe for you to do so. You will know when."

Eldwin's face went white, then reddened as he nodded in silent understanding of the authority with which Robby declared the Treasure returned to its heir, and of the danger Robby and his companions faced.

"My Lords," Eldwin bowed. "I will not ask where it is ye go. But, pray, do not forget us."

Robby took his hand and said, "We shall not forget you. And, should fortune favor our quest, we shall not neglect your people."

• • •

Instead of popping over to the Toll Road, they chose to ride through town, led by the group of Elders on foot. Robby and Esildre rode first, with Esildre's great-nephews following, then Ibin leading the packhorses and the others behind them. The people of Nowhere lined the streets and ways, cheering to them and calling out good wishes as they passed by. Never had Robby felt so honored, though he did, in fact, feel some pride—something like the day he so proudly rode out to Boskland on Anerath in his new armor and colors. Today, however, the feeling was more genuine, full of care, true, but his heart was lifted by their gestures. They took the winding way that led back up the steep hills, encountering more groups of well-wishers at switchbacks and lined along overhanging banks until at last they made the Toll Road. There, Esildre and her companions turned to go eastward.

"May you find what it is you seek, Robby Ribbon," called Esildre to him as she turned. "And may you all!"

"Fare thee well, Esildre. May we meet again, someday," he said back to her.

"Well may we! And well we may!"

Robby's party watched the three Elifaen disappear eastward around a bend, then they turned to go westward toward the bridge at Redwater Gorge. As they neared the junction where the Toll Road met the road running along the east side of the gorge, the Elders turned away, some to take their leave back to Nowhere town and others, Eldwin among them, to watch from the same place he and Ullin had viewed the bridge the day before. They popped away, one by one, Eldwin waiting the longest. At last, he waved and smiled, saying, "Good luck an' fare ye well!" His words seemed to linger and dissipate as did the glow of his departure.

Robby's group moved on, and Ullin loosened his sword and pushed his cloak away from the hilt. Robby did likewise, and put his hand on Swyncraff about his waist just as the last bend was turned. The roads joined and the gorge yawned open and the narrow bridge with its towering columns loomed before them. He had never seen such a gorge before, much less one so stark. It was wide and deep, so deep that when he looked down to the distant stream far below, he became somewhat dizzy and gripped his reins more tightly. Twisting around in his saddle, he saw the others behind him were equally impressed with the gorge and the graceful bridge ahead. They could not yet see its supporting spans, and it seemed to float across the chasm, longer and higher than the one at Passdale by four or five times, but just as narrow. Still, in spite of its size, it was a tiny work compared to the gulf it spanned.

"How deep is this place?" Robby asked.

"Oh, I'd say about three or four furlongs along here," said Ashlord over his shoulder. "This is the deepest part of the gorge. And the narrowest."

Ahead, two guards emerged from their shack and scrambled to the gate, trying to put on their helmets and pull down the gate at the same time. They were grizzled and dirty, in unkempt array, dull-looking and crude, Robby thought. As the company neared the two, Robby could see similar activity on the far side of the bridge.

" 'Ewe gaws thar!" called the grubbier of the two guards.

"Six to cross," Ullin replied.

"A Kingsmun, eh? A Duin'er mun? Whut's yer busyness?"

"We have writ of passage," answered Ashlord, handing down the document Lord Tallin had prepared for them.

"From Tallinvale?" The guard eyed the document carefully, squinting up at Ashlord and then at the others. Likely, he could not read, but recognized the Tallin-Fairoak seal. While he took his time, the other guard slowly went down their line, looking at the horses and their saddles, the packs, and each rider in turn. Robby caught a whiff of hard liquor as he passed. Ibin grinned stupidly, but the guard only glared back at him and moved on. Billy, who had slung one leg up over his saddle and sat chewing a blade of grass, nodded at the guard.

"How do?" Billy greeted. The guard only grunted in return, making a show of visually inspecting the pack animals before moving on. Billy's expression changed to wariness as the man walked slowly around Sheila at the end of the line. There, he paused, then stepped around the other side, staring at her with a look of curiosity and clear vulgarity in his face.

"What's yer name, missy?" he asked as what he hoped would pass as a grin crossed between the few black teeth he still had. Just then, Billy gently tugged on his reins and his mount backed up a step or two.

"Aye! Watch out!" the guard scolded Billy. "Keep a handle on yer animal, mind ye."

Billy shrugged and smiled, backing again.

"Did ye hear what I said?" the guard said as he was bumped.

"Sorry!" shrugged Billy.

The guard up front looked around at the second, handing up the document to Ashlord.

"Well, it looks alright to me," he said. "But it's for the Capt'n to say, ain't it? Aye! Quit yer foolishness an' get this here gate up!"

The other one glared at Billy and walked back to the gate and pushed down on the counterweight to lift it. He continued to glare at them as they went by, gawking at Sheila when her turn came. Once onto the landing, Ullin, who had been watching the other side, urged those behind to keep close.

"Don't know if I trust this bridge," Billy commented, peering down past the knee-high banister into the rocky depths below.

"It's sturdy enough," Ashlord assured him. "In spite of being ill-kept."

"I don't care for the bridge, either, Billy. But it's the keepers I worry more about," Ullin said nodding toward the far side. There, a number of soldiers were gathered and began coming onto the bridge in front of a big man, obviously their captain by the way he ordered them about with violent gestures. By now, the company was onto the wooden suspension and though the heavy beams below creaked, the bridge did not sway or sag. Midway, a strong breeze blew through the gorge, and, far below, they could see several waterfalls upstream, each at least a hundred feet high by the looks of the trees around them, looking very much like a watery staircase made for giants.

"Ooo. I feel kinda sick," Billy uttered.

"Me, too," said Ullin.

"Don't look down," Sheila scolded from behind.

"Don't get sick!" Robby ordered.

Ibin, too, was clearly nervous, and he constantly looked up and down, right and left, into the surrounding abyss, and then to his companions as if for reassurance, clutching the reins of his horse with one hand and the neck of his mandolin with the other, holding the tiny thing out delicately as if for balance.

"Keep moving," Ashlord coaxed.

The men ahead divided into ranks along each side where the suspended part met the landing. Fifteen, Ullin counted, plus their captain. The helmets that some wore were crudely riveted with flat tops, and they held short lances in one hand and round bucklers in the other. Each also had a sword on a belt. Bits of rusty-brown iron strapped onto leather slabs served as their armor, and their cloaks were drab and dirty shades of green and brown and scuffed-up black. As the travelers rode between them and toward the captain, Robby thought they looked no better than the first two they had encountered.

"Halt thar! State yer name an' business!"

"Collandoth. Traveling to Duinnor."

The captain was a barrel-chested man with a puffy face and a scruffy black beard covered with flecks of meat and crumbs under long stringy hair that was too thin even to mat. He had the look of too much drink as he swaggered up to take the paper from Ashlord.

"Well," he said after a moment of study, "looks genuine enough, though I can't say as I have much trust for Tallinvale folk. An' ye lack the looks of them folk, too. Who'd ye lift this writ off of?"

"It was given by Lord Tallin's hand," Ashlord stated.

"Oh, surely! Deserters, more likely, I'd say. An' a sorry lookin' lot, at that! Comin' off the Toll Road, too. It's a wonder them pixies didn't pick ye clean. Hold on," the Damar captain stated, looking at Ullin's Post bag. "A Post Rider, eh?"

"That's right."

"Well, ye'll be comin' along with us, then. All Post Riders are t'go report to Lord Cartu, whether comin' er goin'. So, get down from thar an' give me the bag."

"I must refuse."

"Refuse, eh? What's all the commotion?" the captain was distracted by yelling coming from the other side of the bridge. "A Redvest courier?"

All turned to see the guards at the far side pointing down the road at a rider tearing for the bridge at full gallop. In his saddle cup was a lance upright, and from it flew a set of white and red ribbons.

Ashlord and Ullin exchanged a quick look, and then Ashlord turned in his saddle and said loudly to the others, "I think we had better make way for the coming rider!" And at his kick, his horse leapt forward at the Damar captain.

"What the...! Stop 'em!" he cried, stumbling aside. A quick undercut to his chin by Ashlord's stick prevented the captain from drawing his sword. Immediately, a cramped melee broke out as the others of the company urged their mounts forward. At such close quarters, the lances of the Damar were nearly useless, and they bumped into one another, trying to grab at the reins or saddle straps. Robby whipped out Swyncraff and banged some heads, and Ullin had out his short sword, parrying the inept lances. Billy took hold of one of the lances that was thrust just past his face and pushed the wielder into his companion. As he kicked away one, another soldier took his horse's bridle while yet a third took aim with his lance. Before Ibin could spur to his aid, he heard a shrill whistle go past his ear, and Billy's attacker slumped down as the arrow passed through his chest and lodged into the shoulder of another. Robby jerked his reins and kicked with his right heel, spinning his horse around sideways on the bridge, knocking two Damar over the side and another soldier underneath the hooves of a pack animal. By now, their horses were in panic. With the tightness of space, the yelling, kicking, grabbing, and confusion of orders, the beasts sought to make off the bridge of their own will. Ibin's mount bucked, then it lurched forward into the pack animals. Turning around, he saw just behind him a soldier pulling Sheila's horse by the reins, trying to force it around so that he could jab at her with his sword. The horse reared in defiance as she fumbled to notch another arrow, nearly losing her balance. Ibin, twisting hard in his saddle, reached out with his mandolin and gave the soldier a fierce knock right in the face, sending him tumbling backwards over the banister, screaming to the bottom of the gorge.

"SheilaSheila!" Ibin cried. Looking over her shoulder as she reached to regain her reins, she saw the Redvest courier charging across the bridge, his lance now leveled at her. Quickly, she notched her arrow and pulled back the string as Ibin kicked away another attacker. She took aim, trying to find her target as her mount clopped unguided from side to side. She pulled the string taut, her bow creaking, waiting for the courier to close. But the rider crouched low in his saddle, keeping his body behind the horse's head and neck, and holding the lance steady with practiced assurance.

"Dammit!" she cried, her eyes stinging, unable to take the shot she wanted, the assailant now within twenty yards. "Dammit!" she repeated, loosing her arrow to fly deep into the horse's chest, killing the poor beast instantly. It crashed head first and flipped over onto its back, crushing the rider underneath, his lance skidding along the deck past Sheila and harmlessly coming to a stop under Ibin's horse.

"Let'sgo! Let'sgo! Let'sgo!" Ibin screamed at her, but already she was kicking her stirrups and slapping her mount's flank with her bow, muttering, "Not fair!"

By now, the remaining soldiers were scrambling to get out of the way, and giving full rein to their horses' fear, the travelers quickly reached a gallop, pounding off the bridge, up the steep road, and into the forest-covered hills. They slowed down after the second hill, but kept a fast pace for several minutes. After another half-mile or so, they drew to a halt and dismounted, to rest the horses and to tend to themselves. Sheila, Ashlord, and Ullin were unscathed. Robby had some broken skin and a nasty bruise forming on his right shin where an effort to kick had gone amiss and found the side of a Damar helmet. Billy had a minor cut on his arm, and Ibin had a short gash on his thigh where a sword thrust just missed. His horse, however, was bleeding profusely from the flank just where the blade had gone in.

"Oh, no!" Ibin cried when he saw it, putting his hands on the horse's wound in an effort to staunch the bleeding, heedless of his own blood running down his leg. All were still shaking with fighting-spirit and ire, so their injuries and pain had not yet had time to gain much of their attention. Sheila pulled Ibin away to look at his wound while Ullin examined the horse. Robby took Billy's arm to examine his cut.

"We have to assume that courier was riding ahead of a larger group," Ullin said, dowsing water on the animal's wound to cleanse it and bending for a closer look. "Easy, boy. Easy. Let me have a look."

"They will not stop at the bridge," Ashlord added, taking the wounded horse's reins and stroking its neck.

"But they would not have sent a courier if they were very close behind," Ullin replied. "My guess is they are at least a half-day's ride behind us."

"It just depends on how badly they want us, don't it, though?" Billy put in, as Robby put a bandage on his arm.

"This isn't as bad as it looks," Ullin said. "But he's no good for us. He can't be ridden, and shouldn't be made to carry a load. He shouldn't move around much."

"Ye mean to leave'm?" Billy asked.

"I'm afraid if we take him along," Ullin said, going over to the packs and rummaging, "the exertion will break the stitches. His wound might fester, and he could die."

"What stitches?"

"The ones I'm about to put in. Ibin, how are you?"

"OhI'm, I'm, I'mfine,Ullin. I'mfineandIdon'tneedanystitches."

"I'll be the judge of that," Sheila said. Ibin looked at her, wide-eyed with terror. "I'm joking, Ibin. I'm sorry. I was only joking. You don't need stitches, but this will sting. Ready?"

Ibin nodded and then Sheila smeared unction from a little tin on the wound. Ibin didn't wince and only watched blankly.

Robby removed the saddle from the wounded horse and while Ashlord held the bridle and gently whispered to it, Ullin took the tin from Sheila and smeared some of its contents into the gash. Sheila finished tying off Ibin's bandage and came over to watch over Ullin's shoulder as he sewed up the horse's wound.

"You've had practice," she said.

"Alas, yes," he said. "But not too much with horses."

"Are these Damar lands?" asked Billy, looking around.

"They claim these lands, and they once had outposts on this side of the gorge. Whether those outposts are still manned, I cannot say," Ashlord shrugged. "I would think so, particularly since they prepare for war and may not wish to leave a flank unguarded. On the other hand, perhaps they do not fear any threat from the west. Still, this part of the Thunder Mountains, this side of the gorge, has always been sparsely settled. Even before the Damar."

"It does seem awfully quiet," Robby commented, remembering what Esildre had said about the place.

"Yes. Peculiar."

"But what I mean is," continued Billy, "d'ye think they're liable to chase us this far?"

"I guess that depends," said Ullin as he continued his stitching. "Like you said, on how much they want us. On the power of Toolant's influence. On how zealous the Damar commanders are. On their resources. And the captain wanted my Post bag, so they may fear that word may reach Duinnor before their plans are sprung."

"But we cannot assume," picked up Ashlord, "that the Damar merely want to stop us from reaching Duinnor with word about their treachery. After all, they must know that Lord Tallin, with his cunning and resources, would have dispatched several fast riders along different routes. No. Toolant may serve the Damar on the face of things, but he certainly uses them, just as he used the Tracians and just as he sought to use Tallinvale. I fear he serves some darker purpose."

"Maybe Lord Tallin's spies will be able to get rid of him," said Robby hopefully.

"Even so, the Damar ruler, Cartu, must now know of us. Though he may not guess our true purpose, he may see some value in capturing us. Perhaps as hostages. Toolant or no Toolant, we will not be out of the Damar reach until we cross the Missenflo and are well onto the plains beyond."

"Then let's get goin'!" cried Billy.

"What about this fellow?" Ashlord patted the neck of the wounded horse just as Ullin finished the last suture.

"We should probably let him go," Ullin suggested. "There is ample water and forage around here, and he should take it easy. We can divide the packs among us and saddle one of the packhorses for Ibin."

"But his wound will need tending," Sheila argued.

"If we take him, and if we must fly like we just did, his wound will reopen. He could die," Ullin explained. "He has a better chance on his own. Horses have good sense. He'll follow his nose and find food and water. Perhaps even a kind farmer in these parts will take him in."

Sheila nodded, giving the animal a pat. "I suppose you are right."

"We'll just have to trust in prov'dents, as me ol' man might say," added Billy.

It was not long afterwards that they had the packs redistributed and the sturdiest of the packhorses was saddled for Ibin. Ullin walked the wounded animal into the woods several yards to a clearing where there was still green forest grass for the horse to eat. There the Kingsman gently removed the bridle and coaxed the animal to stay. Robby couldn't help thinking the beast had a forlorn look in its big brown eyes as it watched them depart. But the horse did not try to follow and turned his head to the shoots growing at his feet.

Ashlord was looking at the animal when a flutter reached his ear, and, with a look of pleasant surprise, he saw Certina shooting around their party before landing on his shoulder, puffing his hair away from his ear with her wings.

"Well, hullo Certina!" Robby laughed.

"Yes, my dear! I am very happy to see you, too!" Ashlord said. He was beaming broadly, his eyes glistening with joy as he proudly looked at his companions. "Yes, yes. Of course, of course! Just let us move a bit farther down the road. We've had our adventures, too!"

Ullin grinned back at Ashlord as he climbed into his saddle, and with a nod from Ashlord, they set off.

The road wound between the mountains and was less used than any they had yet been on. In some low places, it was so overgrown that they had to go in single file, but in other places the way was wide and ancient paving stones were visible. They splashed through many shallow streams and crossed a few stone bridges that spanned narrow banks over white-churned water dashing down from the slopes and skipping noisily below them. These little streams and waterfalls, often hidden from view by the trees, could be heard from afar, their sound bouncing up and tumbling down the slopes. But those were the only sounds of the forest they heard. After several hours, the way began to climb back and forth along the broad shoulder of a ridge. The sky had become overcast, with low, brooding clouds, as they came onto a crossroads. They took the north-leading way and traveled the ridgeline for several miles until the way turned west and plunged back into the still forest. Robby and Ashlord led, with Billy just behind, towing the remaining packhorse in front of Ibin, who plucked his mandolin and let his horse follow those ahead of its own accord and good sense. Ullin had fallen back and rode beside Sheila, where the width of the way permitted.

"You did what you had to do," he said to her.

She only glanced at him, biting off a harsh remark.

"It wasn't the horse's fault that he was being made to charge me," she said.

"No. It wasn't. But what soldier is not compelled, by force or force of honor, to do the things we do?"

"I'm no soldier."

"Maybe not. But it is the way of war that servants suffer more in battle than the ones they faithfully serve. It has nothing to do with what anyone deserves in life."

"It should."

"Perhaps. Yet, I sometimes think it might be a poor place if we all got what we deserve. However that may be, if you could have prevented your own death or the death of your friends by any other means, I know you would have."

"It's just so unfair. I have killed many animals in the hunt. Never for the sport of it. And I have always given thanks to my quarry for giving their life and their sustenance to me. This is different. I killed men, back on the road from Tulith Attis, and later, when the Redvests attacked us at Passdale and along the road to Janhaven. It was clear to me, then, what I had to do, and I did it. Just as it was clear to me that I had to kill the horse. But now I hurt, inside, thinking of the waste. And not just the horse. I wonder about those men and their families. What they may have been like with their children. Things I never knew until I met Robby. Until I stayed with Ashlord and Frizella Bosk, and, later, with Robby's family. And even those you would not think of," she said, putting her hand on her pocket where she kept the small volume of poetry from Mr. Broadweed, "they have kind hearts, too."

They rode along silently for a few minutes, Ibin's strings and the clopping of the hooves oddly soothing in the otherwise silent wood.

"We cannot always do what we desire," Ullin said.

"And I suppose we do not always desire to do what we must," Sheila responded. "How trite that sounds!"

"Yet true," he said, looking at her. She looked back at him and her expression softened, and was reflected in Ullin's own.

Meanwhile, Certina grew more annoyed with Ashlord, until at last he relented and let her perch on his hand to relate her message from Raynor. While she did so, Ashlord let his horse follow Robby's so that he could keep his eyes upon hers. Raynor's message was brief:

> *Time rushes in upon itself, my friend. Surely what we thought would not happen for another age now comes to pass. There are many signs, from you and elsewhere. Ready yourself! If you can, go to your mountain to gather your faith and grow your strength. Here, there is much confusion, and the people are restless and worried. The courtiers vie for power, and the army is in disorder and is divided among the Houses. Truly this attack in the east is timed for this season of disharmony, for I have little hope that Duinnor will send aid before spring. I will speak to those that still trust me and who I still trust. Be quick! This kingdom falters, and all with it!*
>
> *Of the other matter. Can it be true? Surely our enemies, too, suspect that it is so. Be safe! Be quick!*

That was all that Raynor said, but it was enough, Ashlord's message had gotten through, and Raynor would do what he could. Certina had more to tell, in her way, but he needed some time to consider Raynor's words. What other signs did Raynor see?

Certina was not happy, though, with Ashlord's desire to meditate on Raynor's message. Impatient, she fluttered constantly around him, begging for his attention until he gently scolded her to leave him to his thoughts for just a while. She flew off in a huff, landing on the head of Ibin's horse, then off again, only to land on Billy's head. He froze in his saddle, rolling his eyes up to try to see the bird, not daring to say a word.

After a long few moments, she flew back to Ashlord's shoulder, and Billy rubbed his head.

"Sharp-toed critter," he muttered.

She continued her agitations with a pouty air, almost as if her feelings had been hurt.

"I know, I know. It is a cruel thing to make you wait. But we have waited all our lives, have we not? And, as you have seen, much has taken place since you departed. Yes, yes," he said when she let him stroke her back, "I have been remiss. I have been anxious, too, as you, who know my heart better than any other, must surely know. Your safety was nearly all I thought of while you were gone. What would I do without you? I'd be lost. Yes, I would! I would, indeed, my dear. Now. Accept my apology, perch again on my hand, and show me that which you have so patiently waited to show me. Tell me all about the burden of your heart, my dear."

Little did he suspect what it was that she would finally show him, what made her so nervous and anxious. It made Ashlord's hairs stand on end. As he drew his horse to a halt, the rest of his companions halted, too.

"What's the trouble?" Ullin asked from the rear. Billy thumbed ahead, toward Ibin, who thumbed ahead toward Robby. Out in front, Robby gestured to Ashlord with a finger on his lips.

"He must be conversing with Certina," Sheila said, stopping her horse beside Ullin's. "I have seen him get very distracted with her."

"Me, too."

After several minutes, Certina hopped back onto Ashlord's shoulder. He sat a little longer, then, looking around as if wondering what was going on, he realized they were waiting for him.

"I apologize," he said. "I didn't mean to hold us up."

"Is everything alright?" Robby asked.

"I don't know. I mean, I suppose so. I must think about things. We may resume our travel, now."

"Very well."

It began to rain. Ibin put away his mandolin as they all pulled out their long cloaks. With the rain, the air turned much cooler, and for the first time since they left Passdale, Robby actually shivered. The steady rain filled the land with the noise of its falling, quickly swelling the streams and creating patchy mists that floated across the slopes. Some of these mists rose up to suddenly engulf the travelers only to lift away just as rapidly. They led their horses, the trail being steep and slippery, and though the rain was never heavy, it was enough to make them wet and tired long before sundown.

"We'll have a hard time making a fire tonight," Robby commented to Ashlord.

"It may be some time before we have proper shelter, Robby," he replied. "We will be able to move more quickly once out on the plain, but should most likely avoid the few towns out there."

"What is it like, out on the plain?"

"It is a vast stretch of gentle grassy hills running from Altoria northward between the western forests and these eastern mountains all the way to Nasakeeria to the north. In the winter it is a barren, snow-covered, and trackless place. In the other seasons, it is tolerable. Quite beautiful in the spring and early summer. There are towns along the trading roads that run through it, but they are notorious for their strange practices and criminal ways. Havens for rogues, bandits, and renegades fleeing from every other domain. Among them are scattered honest farmers and cattlemen, and a few towns not governed by outlaws. For the most part, it is a place that is left alone to its own fate."

"Does Duinnor not exert its will over those lands?"

"They are in no realm, properly speaking, though the territory was once recognized as belonging partly to Masurthia and partly to Altoria and partly to the Eastlands. Most settlements manage to pay small tributes to Duinnor. Enough to placate the ire of fair-minded ministers but not so little as to warrant action against them for forgetfulness. They do not molest the Post Riders or any who are well-armed or of importance in the other realms. It is the lone traveler who must be wary."

"But now that war is coming, what will these people do?"

"They will no doubt throw in with whichever side may benefit them the most and threaten them the least. One town may go with Tracia, while the next village a few leagues away may join with Duinnor, and the next with the Damar. Who can say? To the north, the Galinot warlord surely seeks to strengthen his position against the Damar. And as for the Damar, they have long looked upon Tallinvale with envy. It is likely their attention will be directed that way. The Galinots may cast their lot in with Glareth, if it comes to that, for if the Damar take Tallinvale, their lands will fall next."

"An' once we cross the plain," Billy asked, "what then?"

"We go west, then north to Minion Gap, then through the hills and back south to Vanara."

"Sounds like a long way."

"It is likely we will trudge through snow before we reach Vanara," Ashlord nodded. "It is at least three hundred leagues away, and more, depending on the way we take on the other side of the plains. So perhaps five or six weeks of swift travel."

"Why will it take us so long?" asked Robby. "Ullin, didn't you say it only took a month or so for you to come to Passdale from Duinnor?"

"Yes. But I was alone, on swift Anerath, and we took little rest. Also, I came the nearest way from Duinnor, down across the northern plains and then through the high gaps of the Carthanes. It was summertime, and there was little snow. I encountered few obstacles, and I traveled openly, unmolested by bandits or the Galinots, who still respect the King's riders. But the snows on Loringard Pass come early and deep, and that way is now closed, as I have told you before. This way that we go is much longer and through disputed and unsettled lands. And, also, there are six of us."

"And if we go to find Griferis," Ashlord pointed out, "so much the longer it may take us to reach Duinnor."

Robby wondered if having so many along was a mistake. It began for him a long and deep consideration of their mission, his own role in it, and the risk they all were taking for him.

"We are in this together," Ashlord said after several minutes, as if knowing Robby's thoughts. "Each of us has a stake in this quest. As does the whole world. Just as surely as there are those who rely upon our failure and who seek to stop us. Particularly, to stop you, Robby."

The road, not much more than a path, took them on so many turns and bends and climbs and descents that Robby had little sense of which way they were actually going. The light, subdued probably even on the brightest days by the flanks of the mountains, was even dimmer through the rainy clouds, and it was growing darker. Robby reckoned it was getting on toward evening when they came along a place where the way skirted under a long rocky overhang, at the back of which was a shallow cave.

"Ashlord!" Ullin called. "This may be as good a place as we'll have to rest tonight."

Ashlord came back and looked at the place Ullin indicated.

"It is right against the road."

"I grant you that, but it looks fairly dry. If we squeeze against the wall we may not get too wet. No room for a fire, though."

The others gathered around to look at the place, no more than a little shelf of mossy rock, not even high enough to stand under, but about seven or eight feet deep and about twelve wide, forming an almost insubstantial grotto. But it was out of the rain.

"With this rain, and nightfall, I doubt if the Damar will move very fast, anyway."

"Very well," Ashlord conceded. "But we must be off at first light."

It did not take long for the group to see to the horses and to make a cozy fit of themselves and their blankets under the outcrop. They had dried beef and hard bread to eat, with plenty of water, and as they leaned against the back wall and chewed, they said little. The daylight was soon gone altogether, and they were amazed to find that the moss that grew over their heads on the underside of the rock gave off an eerie blue-green glow. It was a very soft light, but enough for them to make out each other's shapes in the gloom. Ashlord, particularly, was interested in the stuff and said it had been many years since he had seen Peller's Carpet, as he knew it to be called. He gathered some and put it in his pouch as Certina watched.

"It is a kind of lichen," he said. "There was once a forest garden near Vanara, on the other side of the river Stayborn, where the paths were all covered with this. It was soft and silent to walk upon, and did not seem to mind the wear. Not that many people ever trod there. It was a moon garden where everything bloomed at night. You remember that place, don't you, Certina?"

Robby could see only a dark outline of Ashlord, though he was right beside him, and was fascinated not only by Ashlord's tale, but also of the gentle love in his voice when he addressed Certina. He wished he could see his expression and the bird's reaction. All he heard was a little sigh. Reaching with his left hand, he found and took Sheila's. The rain eased until only the insistent dripping of the forest was heard, and the nearby trickles of water running over the ledge in front of them was reduced to only steady drops, too. But the sound was all around in the forest, near and far in the blackness beyond their shelter. Though they all knew it was only water dripping for miles around, the drops snapped into the leaves, and tapped onto the rocks, and sometimes gurgled away down the path in an uncanny manner, often sounding like footsteps or even the sound of a distant hoof. It was, to say the least, not very restful, but neither their discomfort nor their fear ever got the best of them.

"I do believe I liked the last cave we stayed in much better than this'un," Billy said from the far end of their shelter. "Not as—*yawn!*—damp."

"Don't complain," Ullin said. "This might be the last roof over your head for a long time to come."

"Oh, I ain't complainin'. Just makin' a note, so to say."

"Ah."

Sheila moved closer to Robby, and he put his arm around her. She moved closer to his ear and whispered, "I wish we could be alone."

On the other side of her, Ullin sat, like Robby, with his back against the wall.

"How is your leg, Ibin?" he asked. Next to him, Ibin stirred, and Ullin realized that he had spoken to Ibin just as he was dropping off to sleep.

"Myleg?"

"Yes. Are you in much pain?"

"OhyoumeanwhereIgotcut?"

"Yes."

"No, no, noitdoesn'thurtverymuchanymore."

"That's good."

"Yeah, uhuh, yeahthat'sgood."

"You haven't said anything about Certina's trip, Ashlord," Robby said as the older man settled next to his right side.

"She has given me a lot to think about," he said. "And I have not had the chance to ponder it through, much less speak about it."

Robby nodded in the darkness.

"But I am relieved that she is back with us," Ashlord went on. "I'm afraid it was pretty hard on her. Wasn't it, my little lady?"

Robby thought he heard a low whistle but could not be sure with the noise of all the dripping.

"She carried my message to another of my order, one called Raynor. If you ever are in Duinnor and need help, go to him. He is trustworthy and as knowledgeable as I about how things are. Look for him at house Number Three, on Crescent Avenue, where he has his apartment. He is a bookseller and sometimes a tutor, so it would not be unusual for him to receive visitors. Remember, Raynor, bookseller, Number Three, Crescent Avenue."

"Crescent Avenue," Robby repeated. "Raynor."

"He is out of favor in Duinnor, so be discreet. And if you meet him, be patient. He may seem rather odd. Do not cross him, whatever you do."

"I won't!"

"He tells me that there is much discord in Duinnor. And the people are concerned and fearful. I will not burden you with all that Raynor told me, but suffice it to say that the government is in shambles with various men of power contending with one another for their share. I fear that Duinnor is in turmoil and is edging toward anarchy and ruin. Only some great and overwhelming change, some power to control those who plot ruin, can save the Realm. I need not tell you that, without Duinnor's aid, Tracia and the Dragonkind armies will be unchecked. I have sent news of the events in Barley and in Tallinvale to Raynor, and he will know who to tell and how to tell it. I have also sent word to him of you, Robby, and where we intend to go."

Robby suddenly became very uncomfortable as he did whenever he contemplated his fate and the expectations upon him.

"But there is more to Certina's tale than all that," Ashlord went on. "On her way back to us, she was attacked. By a black eagle."

"An eagle?"

"A black eagle. They are the minions of Shatuum, and they travel far and wide to report whatever they see."

"But she escaped. And she's alright, isn't she?"

"She is well. But she didn't exactly escape. She was set free."

"I don't understand."

"I don't either, but here is what I know. She was pursued from Duinnor over the plains. She is strong and swift, and not without wit, but no match for such beasts that stalked her. She made for Nasakeeria, and it was there, exhausted, that the black bird overcame her. Just as it was about to strike her, it was itself struck down by an arrow from Nasakeeria. Exhausted, Certina fell to the ground, unharmed but helpless for a time. At this point, her tale grows confused and difficult for even me to understand. She says, in her way, that one of her captors, a woman, spoke to her in an ancient language. But she does not remember what was said. She was fed and rested for a whole day, kept inside the cottage of the hunter who killed the black eagle. Besides the hunter and the woman she spoke with, many others she saw, and there were many comings and goings at the cottage of those wishing to see Certina. But Certina struggles to tell me, and can only show me in bits and pieces, which is not her usual way. She repeats over and over that they are desert people."

"Dragonkind? There are Dragonkind in Nasakeeria?"

"Yes. And no. She knows Dragonkind, but these people are different. Yet their manner of speech sounds like that of Dragonkind, except that it is an very old way of speaking, not like the Dragonkind that she knows of."

"What does that mean?"

"I don't know. I don't think she does, either. She does not herself understand. It agitates her greatly. It is too much for her. But whoever they were, they saved her from the black eagle, and they took care of her, permitting her food and rest. There was one in particular that she keeps mentioning, in her way, showing her to me, but it is a strange vision. A woman. This woman, who is perhaps a sorceress, was the one who spoke with Certina. She and her companion, the hunter who felled the black eagle, were very tender toward Certina. The woman sang to Certina and put her to sleep. It was a deep and restful sleep, much needed. When Certina awoke, she was released."

"Nasakeeria," Robby whispered, as if even speaking the name of the place would evoke some mortal event. "I thought none who entered there could depart alive."

"So did I," shrugged Ashlord. "I have seen the bones surrounding that land, and it is not an inviting sight. But here is a fearful thought, an anxiety that will not leave me: I'm afraid Certina may have unwittingly given up her messages. While she was asleep."

"So you think they know? About me?"

"I veiled my message enough so that I could be sure that only Raynor could understand the full import. Still, if Certina was enchanted, coaxed to reveal her true nature and the messages she carried, Nasakeeria may know something of our quest and even something about where we are."

"Do you think Certina was followed from Nasakeeria?"

"Perhaps. But they need not follow her to know she was bound for this region. And if, along with that, they picked up enough to know that we head west, they can easily surmise our track."

"What should we do? Change our course?"

"I do not think that would be wise. It will be difficult enough as it is, and we may well be forced aside by any number of obstacles that we cannot foresee. No. We should continue on as planned. But we should be ever the more cautious."

Robby shook his head.

"I have the strangest feeling, nearly all the time these days, that all of this is happening around me, not to me. That I have no control and am being swept along like some kind of leaf in the wind. Part of me is calm, but another part of me is in a kind of deep panic, not knowing what to do or how to do it."

Robby and Ashlord were so close that they were brushing shoulders, and he knew that Ashlord was listening carefully to him.

"It's like being a baby, left to mind the store all on my own. People coming and going, asking for things that I don't know about. Wanting things from the store, but I don't know where the right shelf is, or else I'm too small to reach it, or how to count the money or make the books right. I feel something akin to what Millithorpe must have felt when he was put in charge of the Hoard those years ago."

"You will know what to do when the time comes," Ashlord said soothingly.

"How do you know?"

"I have faith. Do you think your abilities are limited only to what can be seen with the eyes or felt with the hands? No, the gifts you possess go beyond the opening of trick boxes and doors and the picking of locks with ease. Those are only the crudest signs of your power. Perhaps with age and experience you will come to a fuller understanding of what I mean. Queen Serith Ellyn and her brother Thurdun understood, and that is why they made a gift of Swyncraff to you. Others understand, too, as Lyrium does, for power such as yours may take many roads. And sometimes the refusal of power is the wisest way to gain it. It is as you did when you refused the ring and the sword that Lyrium offered."

"But I gained nothing from it."

"What you gained was freedom from those things, freedom to exert your power in other ways. And you gained Lyrium's respect and friendship, too, and even her loyalty. That ring. That sword. Such things are hard to refuse when they are craved, and the evil that may come of possessing such power is profound and subtle. Once gained, it is the rare person who may willingly shed such things."

"But I have no choice in so many of these things. I cannot undo my birth, or who my parents are, or any of these things that have happened."

"No. But you do have some choice. It is who you are. Just as the rest of us, it is made into our flesh and into our breath to have choice. Since you live now, and not in the past, you have no choice but to accept the past. But bear in mind that every moment of the past was, at some prior time, the future. It is like a fabric, being ever worked upon the loom, and each of us is a thread in that fabric. Those of us alive are still being woven into it, until our coil runs out. All is connected. The choices you make not only affect your own self as well as those around you, but also the texture and the shape of the fabric itself."

"Time," Robby sighed. "Another thing I haven't enough of. I do not know how to become King. And, even if I did, I do not know how to rule.

We go to Griferis, if we find it, so that I might learn quickly. But will there be time, once there, to change the things that need changing before spring comes?"

"No doubt you will be tested, Robby. Tempted and tried. It has already begun. That is why we go to Griferis. If you survive, you will know what to do. If you do not, or if you fail in this quest, many other things will fail, too, and the warp of time will set a new pattern nonetheless. I see no other way but to try. But it is not up to me."

"No. I know. It is my choice."

Chapter 22

The Witch

As Robby and his company moved west and fought their way across the bridge at Redwater Gorge, Esildre rode very slowly eastward along the same way that the travelers from Barley had come to Nowhere. She did not urge her mount on, but let him take his own pace along the forest path. Her two companions, who rarely spoke but were always attuned to her mood, followed closely behind, sometimes exchanging glances with each other. Her silence never bothered them in the least, and they instinctively knew that hers was the silence of contemplation, of the careful consideration of possibilities, and of choices being weighed. When she had something to say, she would say it. And the two great-nephews correctly surmised that the root of her present meditation was a very simple fact, one that was only discovered the day before.

Bailorg was dead.

Vengeance for her brother's death was gone. Hope of capturing Bailorg and returning him to reveal the mastermind of his deed before the King's judges was now entirely extinguished.

"At the hand of a mere boy!" she inwardly mused. "A mortal, too, until he suffers the Change."

Her purpose was now gone. To come all this way! A needless journey, putting her servants at risk, alone in her castle without her protection. And putting her kin in harm's way as her escorts. Going all the way to Duinnor, then coming all the way here. What was the point of it all?

Raynor told her she should bide her time, preparing instead to confront he who sent Bailorg with Navis, he who rewarded Bailorg for the foul deed. Her own father! But she refused to believe Raynor. How could she believe him? She insisted on leaving, to look for Bailorg herself and bring him to justice, or to at least force a confession out of him for her own ears to hear, so that she at least would know who had planned her brother's murder. Raynor acquiesced, maintaining it was a foolish thing to attempt, convinced of her father's guilt. Folly, he said it was.

Folly, indeed, she now accepted, letting her buckmarl come to a halt. Bailorg was dead. And now what? Should she turn around and join Robby and his company westward? No. She remembered Ullin, and mistrusted herself. No, her company would only put them at greater risk.

Her two companions halted, too. They had never succumbed to the temptation to look behind her veil, taking brotherly strength from each other to resist. And they knew that she trusted them for that, as she trusted no one else. Or perhaps there was one other, one she spoke of only briefly, only once. The man who had escorted her to Duinnor. But she never said his name.

"There is only one other whom I would trust as my escort," she had told them one night when she was expressing her gratitude for their patience. It was the night she told them that she intended to go southward instead of continuing east toward Karthia on the River Osterflo. "But, with my sight restored, I would not trust myself in his company."

It was an interesting declaration, and the twins, who rarely needed to speak to each other, had even chatted about it later. But that conversation was distant from their minds as they now settled in their saddles and waited.

Esildre was reviewing again those things that Collandoth and the others had told her, and the mysterious gaps in their explanations. Why did they seem so deferential to Robby? Because he killed Bailorg? Or was there something else about him that demanded such respect? And if they went west to Duinnor, why did they not send the Kingsman ahead, to carry swift news of the invasion? What held him back from that obvious duty?

Oh, Ullin Saheed!

She should have said something to Collandoth. She should have warned them to be wary of the Kingsman. But her shame kept her silent. That the Kingsman was not immediately lost to madness was a wonder and a mystery. Truly Ullin's longing was a torment to him, long before Esildre encountered him. If it had not been for that torment, might he have resisted her? And might she, perhaps, have resisted him? No, most likely not. It was his torment that made her unable to resist, for all his loneliness. What must his love be to produce such feelings? More powerful, and more terrible, than she had ever felt from any of her previous victims. A man like that, filled with such anguish, ought to already be made mad by it. But, she wondered, why wasn't he? A man like that, carrying such weight, could be capable of anything.

She sat for a long time on her patient buckmarl, speaking not a word to her escorts, and they not a word to each other or to her. The day grew long and overcast, then it began to rain. Still Esildre pondered her questions, heedless of the downpours. Finally, when the gloom of the day could hardly be discerned from the coming night, she reined around.

"We shall abide with the little people," she said to her escorts, "and help them prepare, if we may. Then we shall decide where we should go."

• • •

The next morning came in subtle changes, gray and foggy, but a bit of sunshine tried to break through during midmorning. Robby and his companions were glad to be away from the damp, exposed place where they had uncomfortably slept. When noontime came, the clouds had gathered again and it was a wet, gloomy day of uphill and downhill. They rode where they could, but when the rains came again, they dismounted and proceeded on foot along the slippery way. There were more breaks in the clouds during the afternoon, sometimes raining while the sun shone. Both rain and sunlight were fitful and restless until, as if out of exhaustion, Sir Sun gave a last glare at the travelers and then disappeared behind a thunderstorm that came booming over the steep slopes. It was such a heavy downpour that they stopped in the middle of the way and huddled with their horses, calming them as best they could against the blinding jabs of lightning and splitting cracks of thunder. It did not last long, thankfully, and they continued with what light that was left to them. The road descended and remained fairly steady and easy, allowing them to ride again. This they did for several miles through a forest where even the trees seemed to droop from the heaviness of rain.

"Ho! Look," Billy called ahead to the others. "What have we here?"

It was perhaps a sign of their fatigue that those in the lead did not notice the little side path that Billy pointed to. Ashlord came up from the rear, and Ullin came back from the front. Dismounting and handing Robby their reins, the pair walked toward the path's opening for a closer look.

"How did I miss seeing this?" asked Ullin.

"Well, it seems to lead off to'ard some clearin' beyond," said Billy, leaning sideways out of his saddle to see under some branches. "A good place to camp, maybe?"

Ashlord craned his neck but could not see where the path led.

"We may as well have a look," he said. "It will be dark soon enough, and any Damar that passes at night will surely not see this."

"Lead on, Billy," Ullin said. "We will follow."

After passing through thirty or forty yards of a dense wood, there opened a broad flat clearing. In the center stood a wooden cottage made of hewn planks with cedar shingles. All around were gardens gone untended for many months. A dense tangle of vines had nearly taken over one side of the cottage. Otherwise, it looked as if it had once been neat and trim and well-kept. No smoke came from its chimney, and the cottage had every appearance of being empty.

"Well, if anyone is there, we've been seen, certainly," said Sheila.

"Let us put friendly faces on, and feign that we are lost if necessary," said Ullin. Ashlord nodded and then approached the cottage just as the rain resumed in a downpour.

"Hullo!" called Robby. "Is anyone home?"

No reply and no movement could be heard or seen.

"Hullo!" he cried again as Billy walked up and gave the door a loud knock. After a pause, listening, Billy shrugged.

"Shall we enter?"

"Go ahead," said Ashlord. "I don't think anyone is home."

"The door's locked on the inside," said Billy pulling and pushing on the handle. "Solid, too!"

"Robby," Ullin nodded at the door. "Why don't you have a go?"

Robby grasped the latch handle and turned it then pushed gently. The crossbar within burst from its pintles, and the door swung open with a loud protest from its hinges.

Robby stood back, peering within the gloom and sniffing. The memory of opening the house of Sheila's uncle suddenly sprang to mind, and he didn't fancy another sight like that. But he smelled nothing other than the musty odor of disuse. Billy pushed past him and confidently strode in.

"Hullo!" he called, then turned to the others. "Nobody's home, an' don't look like thar's been anybody here for some while, judgin' by the dust. It's dry though."

It was a modest, two-room place, the largest portion with a stone fireplace for heat and cooking, a table with a dried-out oil lamp and equally dried-out onions on it. There was dried corn dangling from the rafters, along with large pots, some tools, and a chair, hung upside down to be out of the way. Sheila poked at the ashes with the fire-iron and sent a crowd of swallows fluttering away up the chimney and a couple others right out and through the door, startling her. The other room had a cot and a clay washbasin and pitcher. There were clothes stacked neatly on a chest which, when opened, revealed more clothes, woolens, and the like.

Ibin and Billy looked longingly at the cot.

"It must get very cold in here in the winter," Robby said, peering over Billy's shoulder. "See all of the knotholes stuffed with bits of cloth?"

"Yeah," Ibin nodded, reaching down and pulling out a clump from a nearby wall. "Mustget, mustget, itmustgetprettycold, prettycoldwhen-it'ssnowing, Robby."

Back in the other room, Ashlord looked over the pots and pans and all the accoutrements for living, but saw no evidence of recent occupation.

When Robby came back from the bedroom, Ashlord was scratching his head, examining the door and the crossbar that Robby had dislodged.

"I don't see a very easy way to lock the door from outside," said Robby.

"Nor do I," replied Ashlord, picking up the crossbar.

"And yet there is nobody inside and the windows, such as they are, are boarded up tight, too," added Ullin.

"The only way out is through the chimney," said Sheila, "but only for a tiny person."

"Which I don't think's the case," said Billy holding up a pair of trousers that were nearly broad enough for Ibin.

"Well, let's see," said Ashlord, attempting to reassemble the pieces. By balancing them together and then closing the door very carefully, he managed it so that the crossbar fell into place as the door closed.

"There you have it," he said, unsatisfied. "Perhaps the dweller left one day, the door accidentally barred itself behind him, and he never returned."

"I guess we'll never know," said Ullin.

"Is it safe to stay the night here?" asked Sheila.

"Well, there is something odd about all this," Ashlord replied, examining the carving about the lintel. "But it is dry, at least, and the rain seems to be getting heavier. Yes. Let's stay the night and be away as early as we can. Shall we?"

Ullin and Robby nodded in agreement, and they all went out to gather in their things from the horses and to tend to them.

"Let's see 'bout gettin' some farwood, if thar's any dry enough to light," suggested Billy to Ibin.

By the time all of the saddles and bags and packs were inside, the cottage was fairly crowded. They stacked their things neatly enough to allow space on the floor for sleeping, and Sheila was already coaxing a smoky fire in the fireplace by the time more firewood arrived and the horses had been seen to.

"There's good feed for the horses," Ullin said when he entered, stamping off water. "And the well water is good. I could find no stable or barn, so I don't think this farmer had any livestock. But I found these."

He dumped some onions, radishes, and little carrots onto the table near the fireplace, saying, "Looks to me like they were laid out in the spring but let go. Deer and rabbits have had a feast, and weeds have all but choked the rest of the gardens."

It was now pouring in earnest, thunder rolled through the mountains in the peculiar way it does in such regions, and night came swiftly and dark. They shut and latched the door against the wind-driven rain, cooked and ate, and were all thankful and quite satisfied with the cozy place. Ibin took down the chair from the rafters and gave it to Ashlord to sit before the fire, and then he took away the pots and pans to clean. Certina explored the rafters and the nooks and crannies of the place, coming and going from Ashlord's shoulder. At last she found a place on the mantel to sit, and with lazy eyes she watched Ashlord smoke his pipe. A candle was found and lit and placed on a shelf on the other side of the room above where Sheila and Robby slept on the floor. Ibin remade the cot in the bedroom with their own blankets, after removing the musty covers that were tangled there. Billy commented on how the last occupant must have been a restless sleeper, judging by the state of the bed. He thanked Ibin for the favor, noting to himself that the bed was far too small for Ibin's long and heavy frame.

"The owner must've had a dog er cat er somethin'," Billy commented as he tested the mattress and pulled off his boots. "An' he must've been fond of playin' with some toy whilst his master slept. Just look at them scratches on the floor an' against the wall, over yonder near that knothole, the one what ain't got no stuffin' in it."

"Yeah,Ibet, Ibet, Ibethehadadog."

"Yep. Pro'bly follered his master to wherever he went off to."

Since there was no mattress too lumpy for Billy and no floor too hard for Ibin, the two were soon gently snoring.

In the next room, the others also made themselves comfortable.

"I think the rain will not last," said Ashlord to Ullin. "But I would prefer that you stay here the night through, rather than scouting ahead as is your custom."

"Suits me," Ullin said, trying to stifle a yawn as he stretched out nearby and leaned against his saddle. He took out his pipe and lit it. They watched the low flames together, listening to the rumble of the passing storm outside.

"It seems to work uncommon well," Ullin pointed the stem of his pipe at the fireplace.

"Yes, it will be a warm cottage, tonight."

"I do not think I have seen stonework such as that," he observed, stretching forward to tamp out his pipe into the fire. "Or the likes of these wreathed vines surrounding the fireplace. Seem something of a fire risk, so close to the hearth."

He referred to the flat stones framing the fireplace and, surrounding that, a densely woven frame made of thin knotty vines, dried and brittle. The flat stones had writing painted on them and there were runes carved into the mantel.

"I have seen them before," observed Ashlord, "and it is still a common practice among some folk. The writing and the runes on the stones are various charms, and the wreath frame is made of witchbane, all intended to keep evil spirits from entering through the chimney. You may notice, too, the few windows also have the same wreathes surrounding them as has the doorway. Similar charms are carved into the lintel there."

"Hm." Ullin looked at the door, settling back against his saddle and pulling up a blanket.

"These days, the practice is merely traditional, or even decorative in its simple way, much like the hanging of a horseshoe, or mistletoe, or wreaths of holly."

They said no more and continued to stare at the flames. Ullin's eyes closed just as the rain tapered off, and he fell asleep to the sound of a gusty breeze that shook the drops from the trees and persisted well into the night, blowing away clouds. At last, even the breeze died, and misty fogs rose up and wandered along the surrounding mountain shoulders and drifted and curled through the forest.

Robby and Sheila slept peacefully, though Sheila snored lightly. Billy and Ibin slept somewhat peacefully, too, but each snored as if in competition with the other. Ashlord continue to stare at the fire, letting it die down since it did make the cottage uncommonly warm. Ullin slept lightly, and from time to time he stirred and briefly opened his eyes before quickly drifting back into unsettled dreams.

Ibin was dreaming, too. It was a fantastic feast, with cold foamy beer in huge tankards suited to his size, ham aplenty, fruit pies and sweet cake, and juicy roasted apples dipped in sugar syrup. The best thing was that he was the only guest, and he sat at the table mysteriously located in the woods just outside the cottage with no one else around. The woodland clearing was lit by an uncanny greenish glow that also illuminated all of the wonderful victuals. As he sat on a bench to eat his fill, he noticed a tall shadow pass behind him. He thought little of it, though, for the food was the tastiest he had ever put his lips around. Yet, the more he ate, the more famished he became. No bother, since the more he ate the more food appeared, out of nowhere, on the table before him. So he ate, and he ate, and he ate, becoming hungrier all the while. So full of food that he was nearly starving, he noticed that the table seemed to be growing taller, or else his bench seemed to be sinking, and his feet could not get any purchase on the ground. As he crammed a slab of pie into his mouth and reached far up and over the table for a tankard, he had the distinct sensation that he was being pulled under the table.

He awoke with a start, relieved somehow, but saddened, too, that it was only a dream and now all that food would go to waste. Suddenly he realized he was sliding slowly across the floor. Something had him by the ankles and was tugging on him. He tried to sit up, but he could only get to his elbows. In the dim light, he perceived two long arms, the spindly hands of which grasped his ankles, and he was being dragged toward a knothole in the wall through which those arms impossibly reached. His heart jumped straight into his throat, and though he tried with all his might, he could not get any sound to come from his mouth except, "Gala-, Gala-, Gala-," choked and high-pitched. But it was loud enough.

Ullin sat up, alarmed, the hairs on his arms standing on end. Ashlord was already standing, stiff and erect, looking about, his head tilted, listening.

"Help!" came Billy's cry, loud and desperate, waking Robby and Sheila. Ashlord snatched a burning stick from the fireplace and held it up as they all burst through the bedroom door. What they saw astonished them so completely that they were momentarily frozen with fear and horror. During that moment, Billy, who was clutching Ibin under the arms while the big one was thrashing about, screamed, "He's bein' pulled out through that thar knothole!"

In fact, Ibin was already up to his waist into the wall when Ullin and Ashlord and Sheila and Robby leapt forward, and each took hold of Ibin and pulled with all their strength. Back through the knothole he came, and then there appeared those long bony arms clinging to his ankles, provoking more screams of dismay from them all. Robby let go of Ibin and flung out Swyncraff to curl around the hideous arms. Instantly the terrible hands let go, sending the others tumbling backwards into the room. A powerful metallic wail went up from outside like the grating of iron against iron inside a massive rusty hinge. Robby released Swyncraff from its grip on the arms and saw them recede quickly through the knothole. Ibin finally managed to get out a scream, adding his own wail of terror to the ferocious shriek of pain and anger from outside that struck new fear into the company.

Ashlord flew from the room, grabbing up his walking stick but leaving his sword. Flinging open the door, he ran around to the side of the cottage. Ullin and Robby, swords in hand, quickly followed, then Sheila came with her bow. When they rounded the corner, they came to a sudden stop some yards behind Ashlord.

"Begone!" Ashlord cried.

Facing him, about ten yards away, was a thin shadow, draped in black gauze, two feet taller than any of them. By the bright light of Ashlord's glowing stick, they perceived long matted hair and a pale gray face, yellow bloodshot eyes, and thick blood-red lips surrounding the bared teeth of a canine. Everything about the creature was crooked, and even though it stood on two feet, it leaned sharply sideways, defying gravity. They saw that she, for surely it was a feminine figure, floated rather than walked, and as she hissed and wailed, her mouth opened so wide, and her jaws so far apart, that all of her teeth, white and sharp from front to back, were bared at them.

"Begone!" cried Ashlord again. He repeated it in the Ancient Tongue. It was in that tongue, a version of it, and in a voice like rasping pipes of iron, that the creature replied.

"Paltera will have her dinner, Collandoth. These are my mountains, now!"

With that she swept up a rock and spat on it. The rock burst into orange flames, and she hurled it at Ashlord's head. Instantly, he held his stick upright before him and did not wince as the missile struck the stick and splintered into hundreds of sparks, trailed by sulfurous lines of smoke. One of these sparks bounced from Ullin's sword, and it instantly glowed so hot in his hand that he flung it down, hissing and steaming as it landed in the wet grass.

"Begone, I say! Or suffer the fate of your forebears!" cried Ashlord, stepping toward her as she held up another flaming missile. Sheila let fly an arrow but it only passed harmlessly through, provoking a scream from the creature as it turned to her new assailant.

Ashlord struck the ground three times with the base of his stick.
"Hold!" he cried.

He stepped again toward the witch, pointing the base of his stick at her.

"Talitempos, retempas tardas!" he uttered.

The world seemed to slow, all movements long and drawn out, and each in the company felt their own breathing become calm. The clouds racing to cover the stars seem to pause, and an eerie stillness fell upon the clearing. They heard Ashlord's voice, soft and lulling, singing in an ancient language as he slowly advanced to the creature. Her eyes grew wide, filling with a kind of mist, though she remained poised with her rock crackling with fire, ready to hurl it at Sheila. Instead, she turned her eyes to Ashlord and stared at him as he gently sang. Continuing to sing at almost a whisper, he came closer and closer until he was standing right in front of her. The song came to an end, and Ashlord thrust his stick through her body.

The spell broke, the witch screamed in terror, and the flaming stone she held fell harmlessly to the ground as she turned into smoke and floated away on the breeze.

"She is dead," Ashlord pronounced, still facing away from them and now leaning heavily on his stick, his shoulders slumped in exhaustion.

"What was that?" cried Billy, coming up from behind the others. Ashlord sighed and turned back to them, wiping his brow with his sleeve.

"A mountain witch, surely," said Ullin as he took the obviously shaken Ashlord by the elbow.

"I am not ready for this," Ashlord muttered, shaking his head. "It is not yet time for me. Yes. Yes, a mountain witch. Indeed."

"What? Like a galafronk?"

"Galafronks are just tales, Billy," Ullin said sharply, gingerly picking up his sword, which was still hot.

"I must rest," said Ashlord. "And have some water. How is Ibin?"

"I'mI'mfine," came the reply. Ibin was hiding at the corner of the cottage, peeking at the others. He cautiously stepped out as they approached. "Didyoukill, didyoukillthegalafronk?"

"It warn't no galafronk, Ibin," said Billy. "Just a dang witch."

"How are your legs?" asked Sheila.

"Theyhurt, Sheila, theyhurtwhereitgrabbedme."

"Let's go in, and I'll have a look at them."

"I guess we know what happened to the person who once lived here," Robby said as he closed he door behind the others. Then in a voice a bit softer so that Ibin would not hear, he asked "Might there be others? What would she have done with Ibin?"

"Mountain witches are flesh-eaters, Robby," Ullin said as he eased Ashlord into the chair. Ashlord appeared to be in a kind of shock or deep distraction. "But I thought they were all hunted down years ago."

Ashlord looked up at Ullin absently and then back at the fire.

"Apparently not all," he said. "And I now understand these runes better."

"And the witchbane," added Ullin.

"Yes. My stick is of the same sort of plant, though of a kind seldom found anymore. Fortunately for me."

"For us."

"Yes."

"What was that you sang?" asked Sheila from across the room. She was holding the candle over Ibin's bare legs and examining the new marks there.

"An ancient lullaby, actually," said Ashlord. Then, more to himself than to the others, he said, "It was all I could think of."

Robby handed Ashlord a flask of water. He nodded in thanks and drank it down.

"Ashlord, would you take a look?" Sheila asked.

Ashlord rose and went to where Ibin was sitting on the floor with his legs stretched out. Ashlord crouched, and Sheila held the candle so that he could see the red splotches just above Ibin's ankles in the exact form of the witch's hideous hands, fingers clearly outlined like a red shadow.

"Hm. I'd say those marks will be permanent, dear fellow. But with some salve and with time the burning pain will subside and go away. How are you otherwise? Not every person who has been pulled through a knothole has lived to tell of it!"

"I'mfine, I'mfine, ohI'mfine. ButI'mkindoftired, andmy, andmyankles-burn."

"Well, let Sheila dress your legs and you should lie down and rest," Ashlord smiled and stood.

"Should I use the same salve that would be for a burn? Or would the stuff for Slobberfang be better?"

"I would say the regular salve. It doesn't look like the skin is broken. But you should watch him for any sign of fever. He still has that other leg wound and so is already weakened. Watch for festering."

Ashlord took another drink of water and slowly paced back and forth in front of the fireplace.

"Do you think it is safe for us to remain here through the night?" asked Robby, seeing Ashlord's agitation.

"Oh, now we are indeed quite safe here. But something is not right about all this," Ashlord said. "I cannot explain, because I do not yet know. That mountain witch should not be here. In fact, all her kind should have been destroyed long ago. It is all wrong. A mountain witch, this far east, centuries after the last of them were thought to have been annihilated. I should not have been able to combat her so easily. Somehow, I knew what to do. Though it made no sense, I knew. I felt a kind of authority. You must understand that I am not of the race of Men, nor am I Elifaen. I am of another kind. I and my kind were tasked to look after things, to watch, as I have done, and to be helpers and advisors, acting only when the action was required and when the moment of action was ripe."

"I don't understand. Put here by who?"

"Not a who, Robby. The Great What. That which strives in every thing, living and nonliving, beast or fowl or lowly creature. There is a way of things that should be, and a way that should not be. There are those of us who contend for the one way. And, just as surely, there are those who contend for another way."

"Some say you are a wizard, and that is why you are so different and influential. Some liken you unto Begrimlin the Kingmaker."

"Begrimlin was not one of my kind. I am not a wizard. I don't make things other than potions and salves and such. And the age for wizards is not yet upon us, if ever it will be," Ashlord said. "It is too soon, for the power of the earth is still strong, and its spirit still abides and holds much in check. Until the Elifaen depart from the world, it is said, other powers will not arise. That such creatures as what we just saw stir once again in the world is a sign, perhaps, that a time of great change is upon us. The struggle to determine which power will hold sway over the earth has begun."

"You mean that the Elifaen might leave the world?" asked Sheila from across the room, "as did the Faerekind that went with Aperion?"

"Yes, they might, if certain conditions are met and the world is done with them. Conditions that seem impossible to fulfill."

"What conditions?" asked Robby. "What do you mean done with them?"

"That is a long tale, and sorrowful," Ashlord sighed, "and has to do with why they are a melancholy folk, and every work that they do has some shadow upon it and cannot be pure. It is also why no evil act can be purely so, and while they are in the lands, the light of goodness cannot be wholly extinguished from the earth."

"I don't understand."

Ashlord smiled and put a hand on Robby's shoulder.

"It is not in our power to understand all things," he said. "However, I think you will, in time, come to understand more than most do. Meanwhile, our hope is to get by on what we have yet learned, while we learn the rest as we go."

"I thought that the race of Men were the ones fated to go away and that the Faere would regain dominion over the earth."

"That, too, is said. It is foretold that for a time all Faerekind will be called away, abandoning the world and re-emerging only when it is the turn of Men to go away."

436

"Go away where?"

"No one knows."

"Well, what does all this have to do with that witch?"

"Much. You see, mountain witches are the creatures of darkness, a breed of hunters fashioned by one of the many demons of the First Age to serve him. After he was destroyed, they scattered until they in turn were hunted and killed by both Faere Folk and the Dragon People alike. If one persists unto this day, it must mean some other demon now walks the earth, or dwells within its bowels, for, unlike other witches, mountain witches cannot survive long lest the blood they swallow mingles in union with their liege and offspring are made. Offspring that then become servants of the demon, or servants of he who holds the leash of the demon."

"Offspring? You mean...?"

"Yes, a vile marriage, repeatedly consummated. And somewhere nearby must be her lair. She knew my name, too. That is a sign that she bears the memory of her wretched mother, and I have only encountered one other in all my days who knew my name. Indeed, I was taken by her, one called Vinkasinea, to feed her young. I managed to escape with the help of a friend who slew her. For years, I was hunted by their kind, but the hunters became the hunted by a twist of events. I, like all others, thought the threat was gone."

"This lair you spoke of, somewhere nearby you said, is that where the demon is?"

"I will not be sure until I find it. Certainly her spawn will be. And they must be destroyed."

"Collandoth," interrupted Ullin, "surely you are not considering—"

"Yes. I'm afraid I must."

"What?" asked Robby.

"This is enemy land," Ullin insisted. "What do we care if it is harried by witches or banshees?"

"Who is the greater enemy?" countered Ashlord. "If they are permitted to grow here, out of sight and out of mind, they will eventually pour out from this place, and no person would be safe from here to the sea, north to south. I must do this thing. And I must find the source of her seed, the demon by which she has continued to exist. And, by the way, do not mistake witches for banshees. They are entirely different creatures."

"You are not ready to face them! You said so yourself. It would be folly! Your sword will be useless, no metal can harm them. Did you see what it did to mine? Even now, it is still warm from her fire."

"I have my staff!" shot back Ashlord testily. "And I have my training, my knowledge, and the experience of over twenty-seven score of years. I have hunted witches before, though I have never faced a full demon. Perhaps I was put here for just such a task. I must at least find and destroy the lair. True, this is an unexpected turn, but that cannot be helped. Do you think I wish this? I do not. And yet I welcome the chance to strike a blow against such wickedness!"

His glare at Ullin eased after only a moment when he saw the worry and frustration in Ullin's eyes.

"Dear friend, how long do you think Duinnor or any realm will last when a power such as this is growing? Our little war may be but an out-of-the-way matter in the great pattern of things. This is another proof that a greater power, dark and patient for eons, is now stirring in the world, putting together its forces, one day to be drawn together from all quarters. You have heard me speak of it before. What is this war the Redvest make compared to the collision of doom that comes? What is this conflict that continues between Elifaen and Dragonkind in the face of this? They only feed the true Enemy, weakening each other and those who may oppose him. Surely it is Secundur's hand in all these workings, the disunity of Men, the oppression of the Elifaen, the rising of the Dragonkind and their aims of conquest, even the hunting down of a future king."

Here Ashlord looked at Robby.

"Do ye mean to say we'll be goin' witch huntin'?" Billy asked, standing beside Robby with his thumbs in his belt and his chest puffed out, proud and ready.

"No. Only I will hunt. The rest of you must continue on as fast as you can go. I will strive to catch up with you by and by."

They looked at one another, Billy shaking his head, Ullin and Robby silent and unhappy. Sheila said nothing, but her expression spoke her dismay. Even Ibin realized that something serious was happening.

"When will you go?" asked Sheila at last.

"When you do. After dawn. Meanwhile, let us try to rest. We will all need strength on the morrow."

They nodded in agreement, and Ashlord returned to his seat by the hearth and took out his pipe. He lit it with an ember from the fire and sat puffing while the others stood about, uncertain whether they should try to sleep or if they should abide with Ashlord. But after a while they, too, were again stretched out, this time all tightly squeezed into the single small room, the other room being still too fearful for comfortable sleep. Light snores soon came from Ibin, followed shortly after by Billy and even Ullin nodded off. Only Robby and Sheila remained awake, sitting at either side of Ashlord on the floor before the hearth.

"Ashlord," said Sheila after nearly an hour of silence. "Who knows of us? Who knows about our party and the true reason why we travel west?"

Ashlord considered the question for a moment before answering.

"Mirabella. Lord Tallin. Lyrium and her daughters. My colleague, Raynor. I suppose Bailorg's master, wherever and whoever he is, must soon learn of us. But for now, I think word has perhaps not yet reached that far. Queen Serith Ellyn no doubt knows or has guessed, perhaps Thurdun her brother, and one or two of their court. The Damar must certainly know this is an important company, but I do not think they know the true reason for our travel."

"How might we be pursued?" asked Robby. "If Bailorg's master is the Dark One, and he learns about me. What will he do to stop us?"

"I do not think Bailorg served Secundur directly, but rather some lieutenant, perhaps. Or a high-placed person of Duinnor, loyal to Shatuum. Or perhaps the traitor of Tulith Attis, wherever he is. A small distinction, but I do not think the Dark One wishes for many to know of us, either."

"Why not?"

"Because, through agents and mischief, he may hold too much sway in Duinnor under the present King. He may fear that our quest could find allies powerful enough to protect you from him. So he cannot openly put a bounty on your head, for that might in itself thwart his efforts to destroy you and actually give you more allies. Only his most trusted servants would be given the task. I fear they are his most powerful ones, too. Still, the hatreds and conflicts that have spread across the world have created many who would have no qualms in stopping you. Our stated purpose, to go to Duinnor to plea for help for the Eastlands, is enough to make enemies among the Damar and the Redvests. The Dragonkind King and his spies would surely try to stop us from that as well. But our true plan, to get you to Griferis, is likely to play into Secundur's hand, too. The closer we get to Griferis, the more apparent will be the aim of our journey. It is a risk that must be taken."

"Ashlord, do you think we will ever learn who the traitor at Tulith Attis was?" Robby asked.

"Hm. Already there are clues, if you but think carefully," Ashlord said thoughtfully. "But I think that, should you succeed in your quest for kingship, you will have the power to discover the traitor's identity. I cannot foresee how that knowledge would be of much use, though."

"Well, who might our allies be along the way?" asked Sheila.

"Those loyal to the Seven Realms. Those who long for peace, and have a hope for justice from Duinnor. Those who resent the King's treatment of them, yet love their own people and their own lands without coveting that which belongs to others. Those who have been cheated and hurt by the lords and regents of the court, and who have given their deeds and titles and sons as trade for protection or royal assistance, but remain loyal nonetheless to Duinnor and will not revolt."

"You mean the Elifaen?"

"Yes, and others, too."

"Does Duinnor have so many enemies among its subjects?"

"They are not all enemies of the Realms, nor of Duinnor, nor even of the King. Some are people who have had no redress of wrongs and are neglected. People who seek rightness and justice and who feel they have given to Duinnor and to the throne far more than is returned. They do not wish to oppose Duinnor, many even wish to serve with honor. Some may feel, in the face of Tracia's Redvests and the threat of the Dragonkind, that it is better to make pacts with the enemies of Duinnor than to remain loyal and be laid waste by invading armies. But there are others who, although they may not be friendly to the Duinnor of today, may yet be true friends of the future kingdom. Those we left in Nowhere, for example. And in Tallinvale, too. And in other places, very far away."

With this Ashlord's eyes twinkled as he glanced at Robby, and he managed a smile. "I would only counsel you to support each other. There is far to go, yet, and many things may come to pass, for good or ill."

Sheila put her head down in thought, then looked again at Ashlord.

"Is there no other way than for us to leave you behind? Surely there is something we can do to help you find the lair."

"I will have all the help I need," he replied. "And I will not expose any of you to the vulgar contents of her den if I find it. No. This I should do alone, confident that you are all far along your way. Now, I bid you let me ponder for awhile."

Robby and Sheila moved to the other side of the room and took their places in their bedrolls, spooning one another, Sheila's hand clutching Robby's arm that was around her. In spite of themselves, they fell asleep, and sometime in their slumber they separated, Sheila curled up and Robby on his back with his arm over his eyes. He awoke with a start, and he carefully sat up so as not to disturb Sheila. He could hear the snoring of Billy and Ibin, and in the dim light of the low burning fire he saw Ullin asleep in his place. Ashlord's chair was empty. Robby saw that the door was wide open. Instantly he grabbed Swyncraff and got up to peer outside. There, a few yards away with his back to the cottage stood Ashlord, his arms outstretched, his stick held high in one hand. Taking a few steps forward, Robby stopped, listening as his eyes adjusted to the dark. Ashlord was speaking so softly that Robby could not make out the words, a strange, smooth tongue. The breeze tugged at Ashlord's robes and hair and the low light coming from the open doorway of the cottage gave him a ghostly appearance. Goosebumps broke out on Robby's arms, and he shivered. Ashlord repeated a phrase three times and said more words, then the phrase three times again followed by different words. Over and again, he chanted softly until, after a few minutes, he lowered his arms, leaned on his stick and bowed his head, his shoulders slumped as if with exhaustion. He turned and saw Robby.

"Robby," he said, coming toward him.

"Were you praying? I didn't mean to intrude."

"You didn't. Yes. In a manner of speaking. I was asking for guidance. To find what I must find. And strength. To do what I must do."

Ashlord paused, standing beside Robby, looking into the darkness of the surrounding woods. He smiled.

"You will have to carry on without me. For a little while, at least."

"But, Ashlord—"

"If all goes well, we will meet again before you reach Griferis," Ashlord said, leading Robby back inside the cottage.

"How will I find that place if we do not meet up with each other in time?"

"Go to the city of Linlally, in Vanara, and to the Hall of Ministers. There is a great library there. Find the Last Book of Nimwill. Read it. The Last Book of Nimwill. Some answers may lie therein. Pardon me," Ashlord looked back to the fireplace, "I must rest before dawn. And so should you."

Chapter 23

The Barleyman

The world does not remain unchanged when our attention is upon the near at hand, any more than the stars cease their trek across the nightly heavens while we sleep. Happenings unseen take shape even when our backs are turned to them, and the workshop of time is one of ceaseless labor, one from which no product ever truly leaves. Who can say, then, how the labor of yesterday is removed from the challenges of today? Or that the thing unnoticed does not touch the matters before us?

In this way, personal events flow into the great ones of the world, and little struggles, titanic to this person or that, are swallowed by history's flood of trials and conflicts. So it was, on the morning that Robby first saw the lair of Bailorg, who had taken Billy as a captive, that the battle at Passdale was fought and lost, and the fleeing refugees tried to make good their escape. That same morning, as Robby dismounted Anerath and prepared to enter into the old troll cave, his father was standing in his stirrups, leaning low over his horse's head, racing northward toward Lake Halgaeth, desperate to reach faraway Glareth and to spread warning of the invasion. Seeing him mount and ride off, and knowing who he was, the Redvest General Vidican immediately dispatched riders after him. Whipping their horses, four Redvest soldiers crashed through those who sought to block their way. They tore out of Passdale, riding swiftly along the forested road until they reached a muddy place where cattle had recently been driven across the mere stream that was now all that remained of the Bentwide's once deep and steady flow. There were horse tracks, too, amongst the cattle tracks, leading up the far bank, and two of the riders crossed over to trace the way along Farbarley while the other two Redvests continued their own pursuit northward. Soon, these last two saw the blue waters of Halgaeth glimmering through the trees, and, knowing about the Lakemen who might at any moment appear in their boats, they cautiously slackened their pace, slowly crossing over hilltops to peer ahead before going on.

Thus they neared the place where Robby had not long ago met the Queen of Vanara, and as the two riders topped the overlooking hill, the one in the lead leaned over in his saddle to study the tracks he saw. The path forked; the left way led on and back into the woods ahead. On the right, a path sloped downward toward the lake, and the soldiers looked warily through the trees at the landing with its sculpted arm-shaped braziers jutting out over the water.

"His horse has gone lame," said the tracker, a grizzled veteran with the hard look of many campaigns stamped on his face. "The tracks are muddled. He may have headed for the landing on foot, maybe for a boat, sending his horse on to throw us off. Blast!"

The young soldier with him nodded, looking around, alert to anything that might come out of the woods at them.

"I don't like this," he said. "Might be more of them folk hiding in wait for us."

"Then you go on ahead and find out," the tracker ordered as he spurred his horse down toward the lake. "Ride back if you find the horse, otherwise keep going. I'll catch up to you once I've had a look around here."

"Aye, sir!"

As ordered, the younger soldier continued along the wooded path, winding up and away from the lake through the silent woods. He was not as experienced at tracking as his older partner, but the ground was soft enough for him to follow the hoof marks easily. Indeed, he had only gone a mile or so when he saw the tracks leave the path, and he dismounted, leading his mount through a thick bramble, going only a few yards before seeing a horse in a small clearing ahead. He silently tied his reins to a tree and pulled his sword as quietly as it would draw. Crouching, he advanced, trying to avoid any dry leaves or twigs, until he could see that the horse was riderless, its reins dangling loose. It was thrusting its head upward to get at some wild apples that hung on the edge of the clearing. Relieved that he did not see their quarry, he approached the horse and easily took the reins.

"Good boy. Here. How's your leg, old boy? Eh? Let's take a look. Easy. Easy there."

The young soldier sheathed his sword and, while patting the beast's neck, leaned over to have a look.

"Oh, that's a nasty gash there, mate. Not used to these byways and such hard riding, huh? I expect not. There. Come along, leave off them apples. I doubt if they are good for you, though tasty, I'm sure. Your leg'll be fine. Soon as we get back, I'll put a nice poultice on it, and you'll be prancing amongst the mares in no time!"

It was not until he was nearly at the hill overlooking the landing, the mayor's horse safely in tow, that the soldier realized that the mayor must still be close by.

"Unless he found a boat like Parnas said," he muttered, looking around for his partner. Craning to see through the trees, he hesitated, seeing no sign of Parnas. Sighing, he nudged his mount closer. When he cleared the trees and came onto the broad flat campground near the landing, he immediately saw his partner's horse at the water's edge, taking a drink.

But Parnas was nowhere to be seen. His heart pounded a beat as he realized something was amiss, and he dismounted, still looking, hoping to see the older soldier crouched over some track or clue. He almost cried out his partner's name but caught himself, suddenly afraid of what may have happened to the experienced soldier, who was the kind of man well able to take care of himself.

He tied off the horses on a hitching rail near the quay and went to Parnas's mount, but the horse was skittish and darted away.

"Whoa, boy, whoa!" he soothed, splashing a few steps into the water to grab the reins, but they escaped his grip and the horse trotted off toward the trees.

He had the urge to call out again for Parnas, and again he stopped himself, drawing his sword as he waded back ashore.

"This place is spooky," he muttered at the forlorn-looking arms stretching up and out from the quay. Then he swept his gaze across the cold campfire rings scattered across the flats and back up the hill. Turning, he scanned the shoreline, looked out over the water, and then back again to the quay until his eyes settled on a dark splotch on the light-colored stones near the far end. Cautiously, he walked out onto the quay toward those upstretched arms holding the cold braiziers, his chest beating with fear, though not a soul could be seen, not a boat, either, anywhere on the broad, glistening surface. Going slowly, he looked from one side of the quay to the other, hearing only the gentle lapping of water against the stone and the slight rustle of air past his ears. As he neared the end where the two arm-uplifted braziers stood as if imploring the sky for fire, he saw that the splotch was a wet spot and that it trailed over the side. He leaned over and saw a ledge, made to be just above the water, where one could more easily step into or out of a boat. There, the puddle trickled off into the lake, and as a small puff of cloud passed over the sun, the water lost some of its blinking glitter and glare. To his horror, he saw a bit of red cloth, the color of his own uniform, floating just beneath the surface, billowing like smoke in the undulating current.

"Or like blood," he almost said aloud.

He eased down to the lowest step and leaned over carefully, dreading what he would see, and he reached into the water with his sword to push the floating cloak aside. He managed to get the tip of it just underneath the hem when an arm shot out of the water, and a gloved hand latched onto his sword and pulled hard. Yelling, the young soldier instinctively pulled back, trying to get away, but the dripping hand held fast. A figure rose up from the water, gasping and coughing, and the terrified youngster let go the sword and stumbled backward against the quay, squirming to escape. In panic, he turned to crawl away but felt a cold wet hand clutching his ankle, tripping him up. He yelled and kicked furiously, getting to his feet just as a large dripping shadow tripped him again.

"Oh, no ye don't!" cried the watery figure hoarsely.

"Mercy! Mercy!" screamed the soldier, trying to get back onto his feet to make a run for it. But the flat of his own sword struck him on the shin, sending him sprawling yet again. A powerful hand gripped the back of his collar, and as he tried to get up, he was flung violently off the quay and onto the rocky shore, knocking his helmet off. His attacker spun him over onto his back, a crushing knee pushed down on his chest, and he felt the tip of his sword against his shoulder and the blade of a dagger against his throat.

"Mercy! Oh, please, mercy! I yield! I yield!" he uttered as best as he could with the knee pressing the breath out of him, the maniac's eyes glaring from behind dripping locks of hair.

"Mercy! Mercy? Like ye showed the folk in Passdale?" cried the assailant.

"I ain't killed nobody! Not my whole life!"

"Then what're ye doin' in this get up?" the man banged away the nearby helmet and deftly returned his dagger to the hapless soldier's neck.

"They made me come! They made me on account of I'm a decent tracker, and I gotta strong back."

Suddenly the knee lifted and he could breathe, but he was jerked upward onto his feet by his collar and found himself staring down into the face of a very angry man, sopping wet and shaking from cold. Or was it fury? He realized it was the very man they had been after, the mayor of Passdale.

"Whar're the others? Four came after me. Whar're the other two?" Robigor Ribbon shook the lad hard, "Whar!"

"We split up. Parnas and me came this way. The others went off across the river a ways back."

Robigor shoved him away and the fellow clutched his throat.

"I 'spect they'll be along any time, then, soon as they see no tracks."

"What happened to Parnas? My comrade?" demanded the youngster in an effort to regain his composure.

"Dead. But he forced it."

"You killed him?"

"It whar him er me!" Robigor shouted, anger returning to his face. "An' it's a good thing for ye that..." He stopped himself. "Look here. Thar ain't gonna be no more killin' unless ye force it on me. I'm goin' to tie ye up on that tree over yonder. Yer mates'll come along soon enough an' let ye go."

"Oh, no! You are under arrest. You gotta go back with me!"

"I know me duty! Now get along thar, an' do as I say!"

"You don't understand. I can't go back without you. Especially with Parnas dead. It won't be just my head. My family will be made to pay, too! You've gotta come with me!"

Robigor grabbed the boy by the collar again and pulled him along at sword-point to the horses where he took a line from his horse's saddle then pushed the boy toward a nearby sapling, where Robigor meant to tie him up.

"I've seen what they do to the families of those they call traitors!" the boy cried insistently. "If they're lucky, they'll be sold as slaves, the women, too, and used until they starve to death."

"I got no choice, sonny. I can't just let ye go an foller me an' lead them others to me."

"Then it is better that you kill me here," the boy pleaded, kicking at his captor, and swinging at him wildly with his fists. Robigor easily stepped aside and flung the boy back to the ground.

"Stop it!"

"I won't!" the boy sobbed, scrambling on all fours to attack Robigor. "Not until you kill me or come back with me!"

"Quit it!"

At any moment, the other riders would appear, and Robigor agonized over what to do as he dodged the clumsy efforts the desperate boy made.

"They'll kill my family otherwise! Better me than them!"

Robigor reached down and pulled the exhausted boy to his feet.

"Do exactly as I say an' yer life an' the lives of yer kin might be spared. Ye must give me yer word an' yer trust. Will ye do that?"

• • •

Less than an hour later, the other two Redvest horsemen came over the ridge and, seeing the riderless horses mulling around near the shore, galloped down to them. They realized something was wrong and drew their swords as they came, looking about. Seeing some objects on the quay, they dismounted and cautiously walked out to have a look. One of the objects was a Tracian helmet. The other, just at the edge of the dock, was a sword. One of them picked it up and examined the blade. The others looked at the wet tracks of footprints, muddled amid splashed water.

"A fight, for certain," he said.

"Yep," nodded the other, holding up the sword. "See these fresh notches?"

"Lakemen, probably."

"Look, look!" said his comrade, seeing Parnas just under the surface. They hastily stepped down to the lower level, crouched over the water, grabbed the cloak, and pulled together until they saw the face of the dead man. Releasing the body, they stood, looking around quickly.

Then one noticed a line tied to one of the mooring rings and pulled on it until the cut bitter end came out of the water.

"They were in a hurry, for sure," he said, holding up the cleanly cut end.

"You reckon they took the boy?"

"Naw. Probably killed him, too. Floating off around here somewhere."

They stood and looked northward across the empty water for a long moment.

"Their boats must be swift, indeed."

The other nodded. "Aye. Let's go."

"Are we going to leave him?"

"Do you want to haul him out and all the way back? Maybe you want to dive down there and get off his gear, first, eh? He'll float proper-like and be easier to haul in. Do you want to do that?"

"No."

"Then let's head back. We need to let Vidican know that the Lakemen have been warned about us."

"What'll they do, you reckon?"

"Oh, I doubt if they'll make trouble. But they'll send word on to Glareth, for sure."

"The old man won't be happy."

"Can't help it. But he'll be grateful to know rather than to wonder."

• • •

When the dam that was called Heneil's Wall gave way during the summer storm, the receding waters and torrential rains undercut a high bank of the lake some fifty yards south of the newly exposed quay with its outstretched arms. And when the bank eroded, a massive oak that was perched atop was uprooted and toppled by powerful winds. It may have been a mere acorn when Heneil built the dam to stop the lake from pouring into the Saerdulin. Or maybe it had been one of those rare older trees that, as a sapling, had overlooked the building of the ancient landing place. During its lifetime, the waters rose steadily higher until the old quay was completely covered but for the two hands that held the beacon bowls. The lake level continued to rise, eventually encroaching to within a few yards of the oak when, some few miles away, it began spilling away into the little stream that was later to be called the Bentwide River.

For nearly the entire Second Age, the old tree stood, gripping the bank and binding the hill together with its ever-tenacious roots, its trunk growing in girth and its canopy broader and higher and prouder. Then came the storm. The wind tore at it, twisting the tough sinews of its limbs, and the lake's water pounded the bank on which it stood. The torrential rain poured like rivers off the ridge above, cutting across its roots, washing away earth into sliding mud until the great tree lurched and fell, crashing over the crumbled bluff and into the lake to rest half in and half out of the waters, its roots jutting up higher than many of its limbs. And thus, having already provided countless generations of squirrels and chipmunks with its acorns, and endless flocks with the safe shelter of its branches, it now made spawning places for fish, convenient islands for basking turtles, and a hiding place for a Barleyman and his prisoner.

They squatted amid its protruding limbs, their chins just above the water, and they watched as the two soldiers looked for them. All the while, under the water, Robigor Ribbon held with vise-like grip the arm of his prisoner and, with his other hand, the tip of his dagger against the prisoner's back, just hard enough for the point to be felt. For although the boy was compliant, Robigor made it clear that he would not risk any attempt to call out or to attract the attention of the pursuers without the assurance of the weapon held ready to thrust and twist.

So they hid. With the water acting as a soundboard, they listened to every word said by the pursuers, and Robigor Ribbon was satisfied that the two soldiers came to the intended conclusions. They watched the Redvests gather the horses and ride out of sight. For several minutes longer, Robigor held his prisoner close, wary of an unexpected return. But the noise of the riders faded away, and nothing more threatening than the gentle lap of water could be heard. At last, Robigor stood, pulling up the boy, and the two made their way dripping and splashing to the bank, pulling themselves out by the upturned roots to which still clung a prodigious amount of soil.

"Well!" Robigor said, sheathing the knife. "They must've took the ruse, truly. Hook, line, an' sinker, so as to say. So, how does it feel to be a dead man?"

The boy shrugged. "Dunno. I ain't never been dead, before. Except," he shivered, "now what?"

"I took ye at yer word, son. So now ye can either try an' make yer way back home, an' risk bein' takin' by yer countrymen, or ye can come along with me, if ye'll not hold me up, an' take the risk on that way. So make up yer mind an' come along, if ye care to."

Robigor made off, squishing in his shoes as he went, and the boy followed.

"Ye know whar I go," he went on. "To warn all that I can, an' to let the Prince know that the realm has been attacked."

"Wait, please," the boy pleaded. "I know I must decide. You may not believe me, but not all Tracians do what they do willingly. But, still, Tracia is my homeland."

"What's yer age, son?"

"Twenty."

"What I figured. I have a boy just about yer age. For all I know, he's dead, at the hands of yer masters. Or maybe me boy's on the run. At any rate, he's lost his home, as have so many. But it's me hope, if me boy is able, that he's fightin' to get it back. I've helped ye as much as I can, an' be thankful it's me yer with an' not some other of me people who'd sooner cut ye down an' spit on ye as to look at ye. If ye come with me, an' ye behave, I'll not do ye any harm. But we got no horses, no food, an' it'll be a chilly night. What's more, I've got thirty leagues ahead of me, at the least, to the nearest Glareth village, Nor'wick, an' that ain't even a start to our journey. An' when we get to whar we're goin', ye'll be taken prisoner, for sure, an' no doubt questioned most severely, too, for certain. But I reckon ye'll be treated a far sight better than if ye go the other way."

Robigor nodded to emphasize his point.

"An' I might as well say a little more, to get it all out right here an' now. That's this: I'll do whatsoever it takes to get word of this outrage to Glareth. If ye try an' have second thoughts, if ye slow me down, if ye get in me way, or make any trouble, it'll not go well for ye. I'm just sayin' it plain."

The boy nodded. "Aye, sir."

Robigor turned and marched off. The boy hesitated. Behind him the lake glimmered without care, and a pale blue shape, barely discernable from the water itself, rose in graceful curves out from the surface some furlong out and swiftly sank away, leaving behind a gentle spreading wake. But the boy didn't turn to see it, and neither did he see the body of his late comrade suddenly pulled deep and away.

"I'll come with you, then," he announced, striding off after the Barleyman.

"Then ye may as well tell me yer name, son."

"Kalpis," he called ahead. "Falgo Kalpis."

"Come on along, Falgo!"

• • •

They jogged and walked, walked and jogged, up and down the northward path, not stopping to rest even once all day long. Falgo, having tossed away all his accoutrements of war except his red cloak, was amazed at the Barleyman's strength and speed, and kept up just behind though it was not easy to match the older man's sure-footed stride. When the sun set and the forest darkened around the lake, they continued onward as long as they could, slowing to a fast walk since the path was only illuminated by moonlight through the filter of the canopy. At last, Robigor halted, and they moved off the path a safe distance to rest. As soon as the boy fell upon the ground, he slept. But before any comfort could come from it, he was being nudged by Robigor's toe. Sitting up, he saw that dawn was breaking through the limbs overhead.

"Let's be on our way," the Barleyman said.

All day they marched, sometimes jogging down the hills, stopping several times to drink from streams that crossed the path, and once to pluck wild apples.

"Only eat two," Robigor ordered. "Er else ye'll be sick as a dog. Save the others for later."

And off they went again, eating as they hiked. That night was the same as the night before, and the next day the same as the day before, too. On the third day, they began to slow. Their effort, and the lack of any real sleep or food, was catching up with them, making them weak and prone to stumble. But the determined Barleyman kept on, driven by his duty, and Falgo followed obediently. During the days, sweat covered them, and at night they shivered. They ate apples and some berries and drank their fill of cold water from the many streams that poured down the slopes and crossed their path before tumbling into the nearby lake. Sometimes, in places where the path went over a bluff and the view of the lake was not obstructed by trees, Robigor halted to gaze quickly and carefully over the lake, looking, the boy figured, for boats. Seeing none, they jogged on. Once, Robigor pointed at a little stone marker at the side of the path on which was carved the number 73.

"That's the number of miles yet to Nor'wick," he told the boy.

"Are there no villages before then?"

"Not on this track. A few off west, in the hills, whar the land can be tilled. But thar no good. Thar'll be boats at Nor'wick."

They hurried on. More often than before, Robigor slowed, his legs aching and his body begging for rest. On the following day, after a particularly long and arduous climb when the sun was highest and warmest, he suddenly collapsed at the edge of the path, and sat, leaning sideways against a tree.

"Rest!" he cried.

Falgo fell on the ground across the way from him, and rolled over on his back, panting.

As it happened, Sir Wind and his children, Breeze, Puff, Gust, Draft, and Gale, along with all of the rest of his kin had been banished from Aperion's heavenly castle long ago. It had been their duty to guard the gates of Aperion's abode, the abode of all Faerekind since departing the earth. It was Aperion's command that Sir Wind and his kin were to blow from outside the gates, forcing any Faerekind tempted to return to the earth back within the castle. But they failed, it is said, and were expelled to the earth. So, now there was nothing to prevent the Faerekind from returning to the earth except their King's Edict. Even though Aperion was stern, he trusted his people's good nature, and he did not always care to enforce his will when the Edict was broken. It is said, therefore, that the Faerekind who flew away with Aperion sometimes look back from their starry abode upon the world they had left behind. And, sometimes, they send their spirits to visit, to float among the treetops, to walk with the deer and rabbits, or to look upon the doings of the peoples of the world. It is told that, from time to time, they become attached, if only briefly, to what their spirits perceive, and may even be filled with compassion, and spread their wings about the sad and lonely, or around the hurt, or over the dying in some expression of comfort, or in the desire, at least, to give solace.

So it must have been one of these invisible spirits that silently furled his wings about the drooping shoulders of Robigor as he slumped against the tree, panting and exhausted. Perhaps the kind spirit had been there all along, hovering within the tree that propped the Barleyman up, remembering how, in nearly forgotten days, spirits such as his lived as trees. And perhaps, when Robigor fell against it, this spirit felt his touch, saw his suffering, and reached out to him.

Robigor and Falgo exchanged looks, too tired to speak, each occupied by his own worries. It occurred to Robigor that the boy must be in an awful state of mind, too, and he could not help but wonder about the young Tracian's father and mother. But this put him in mind of Mirabella, and, putting his temple against the trunk of the tree, he closed his eyes and remembered the last words he had spoken to her, the last kiss they exchanged on the porch of the store, the cadence of battle drums approaching over the far hills across the river. He remembered the last time their eyes met, he in a huddle of men, looking past the blacksmith who was speaking to him, and she, some forty yards away, hurriedly putting things into a cart. He saw in his mind and felt again in his heart the smile of love she sent to him. Now, thinking upon it, his face reflected that smile, briefly, before a great lump came to his throat. His breath shortened, and his eyes watered behind their closed lids. Robigor's heart struck a note that came up out of his mouth, a painful gulp that he tried to stifle. This must have been when the spirit pulled tighter his wings and put its head on the poor man's shoulder. For suddenly Robigor felt again some comfort of his wife as all the sweet memories of their time together poured through him. The making of their modest home, the birth of their little child, and all the years of good work, watching their son grow into manhood, each precious moment of his family and home. From the quiet evenings reading by the hearth to the joy he took in Mirabella's feminine touches around the house, and the pride he had at his son's skill in the store. These were things not to be forgotten. These were things that make the fortunate rich, he thought. Even if such things pass away, their wealth remains. It may be that the invisible wings tightened more closely as he heaved a great sigh, and the Barleyman's resolve and his strength returned.

After a moment, he grunted to his feet, gesturing at his charge to come along, and they continued northward. A lake storm blew ashore, howling through the trees and soaking the two travelers with cold rain. In less than an hour it had passed, and a few miles later, the woods were as dry as before, and soon the two travelers were as hot and sweaty as ever.

• • •

That evening, they hastily made beds of leaves and ferns some many yards away from the path, and no sooner than they fell upon them were they asleep. When the earliest birds began their predawn titter and song, Robigor awoke abruptly, sensing a movement in the foggy wood. With one hand he reached out to wake his companion, putting a finger to his lips, while with the other he slipped his dagger from its sheath. Footsteps, for sure, along the path. The boy heard them, too, his eyes widening. Then they heard voices, and they strained even harder to understand what was being said. It sounded something like an argument.

"I told ye she wouldn't take the shallers with all that cordage."

"She'da been fine if ye'd reefed like I told ye to."

"I did like ye said."

"In the most lubberly way! An' right up on them rocks, smashed like I warned we'd be."

"It warn't me at the tiller, mate."

"Ain't no sense in a helm if they ain't no steerageway. Yer lucky I pulled up the leeboard when I did, else it'd a been smashed, too!"

Robigor suddenly jumped to his feet.

"Ho, thar! Lakemen! Hold up, thar, I beg ye!"

The two men, seeing the stranger stumble out of the mist, covered with leaves and ferns and waving a knife, quickly got out their own weapons.

"Who goes? Far enough, mister! Else regret the bite of me steel!"

"No, no!" Robigor sheathed his knife and raised his hands. His companion meekly came out of the woods and stood behind, looking over Robigor's shoulder.

"I'm just needin' some help, is all."

"State yer business, er move aside. We ain't got time for idle chatter!"

"I'm Ribbon, Robigor Ribbon, of Passdale in Barley. Down the Bentwide a ways, south of the lake."

"Aye, I knows the place. An' I knows the man, too. An' he's a right neat feller, not takin' to wildness 'er waylayin' passers-by. An', if I ain't mistaken, them's Redvest colors yer mate's a wharin'. Deserters, mebbe? So move on with ye."

"No, I mean, ye don't understand. He's my prisoner. I am from Passdale. I own the sundries store down thar. But, the place is invaded by Redvests. The town, the county, all 'round them parts is covered with Tracian Redvest soldiers. They mean to loot the place for certain. I'm tryin' to get on to Nor'wick, an' from thence over to the Glareth Lakemen to give warnin' an' get help for me people."

The older of the two boatmen looked askance at Robigor, but it was the younger one that spoke.

"It ain't credible," he said. "Redvests in Barley? Why that's near a hunnerd leagues up from Tracia."

"It ain't credible," said Robigor, "but it's the truth."

"It is true," put forward Falgo, still hesitant behind Robigor. "My army came all this way just to take Barley. And we're just one of many comin' into the Eastlands for grain, forage, iron, gold, and whatnot. There's a war coming, and Tracia's gonna start it."

"Now that's a tale," said the older man at last. "An' mebbe we'll just go on our way, seein' as how it's Barley we're headed to, anyhow, for a bit of lumber an' tar. It'd be by boat if me stupid mate, here, had any lake sense about him. But since we're walkin', we'll just keep walkin', if ye don't mind us passin'. We got ourselves a boat to repair, an' can't waste time fiddlin' 'round. 'Sides, we ain't Lakemen, just plain fisher-folk. So let us pass, ye hear?"

"You'll be taken," said Falgo. "My general wants prisoners to load and push wagons, and to do other work. We didn't catch enough, so you'll certainly be taken."

"If ye can't see sense, then go ahead," Robigor said. "An' we'll be on our way to see Prince Danoss, son of Rulin' Prince Carbane of Glareth. I've got tradin' friends up in Nor'wick, an' they'll sure to get us by boat over the lake. I'm sure the Prince'll be quite interested in how come two fools didn't help out when they could've."

"Now, hold up, thar. If yer bein' straight with us, then tell me this. Who's yer tradin' friends up in Nor'wick, eh?"

"Marler Janks, the fisherman, an' Tiddus Macklebee, the cooper."

"Lo," said the younger to the elder, "Ol' Tiddus is me uncle!"

"I know dang well he's ye uncle, ye lout!" To Robigor, the older man said, "Well, I guess we'll have to trust ye. Argh! It's back the way we done come, then. An' many miles it is back home, too."

The two boatmen, much put out, turned to go the other way, and Robigor smiled, following along briskly.

• • •

A week later, the four arrived in Northwick, much starved, and well exhausted. Along the way, Robigor won over his guides, and by the time they reached the village, they were all too happy to have him and his prisoner as their guests. It did not hurt that many conversations were had concerning all the new trading possibilities that might well come about between Northwick and Passdale after the current troubles were over. These conversations continued over hearty meals and welcomed tankards, along with all the important news Robigor could share with the people who hosted them. Two days later, three well-provisioned fishing boats set out from the docks of the village, carrying Robigor, Falgo, and several village elders. They hoisted their sails and set course north by northeast, lumbering for the town of Formouth over thirty leagues away, the Lakemen stronghold and residence to Prince Danoss, the son of the Ruling Prince Carbane of Glareth. From there, with swift horses, it still would be another three weeks or more to go the five hundred miles to Glareth by the Sea.

It was a long way to go, and Robigor learned to help with the sheets and rigging to take his mind from his worries, thankful that he was saved by the fisher-folk from the long trek around the lakeshore. Still, hoping for stronger winds, he incessantly scanned the lake for other sails. With luck, Robigor thought, they might run into some Lakemen, and he might be transferred to one of their swift-sailing sloops.

Meanwhile, perhaps due in great part to the rocking of their boat on the choppy lake, Robigor's prisoner became quite sick. As Robigor worked to trim the sails, under the tutelage of the two crusty fishermen whose boat it was, Falgo hung himself over the side long after he had nothing to contribute to the wake.

That night, with lanterns hung at the end of their booms, the three boats continued on while those aboard took turns sleeping. The next day the wind was light but steady, and Robigor continued to help with the chores of hoisting or trimming the foresail, spending the long in between times to chat with the fishermen. Falgo seemed no better off than he had the day before. He spent the day holding his belly, or hanging over the side, and the two fishermen aboard laughed at the boy and scratched their heads.

"Don't look green enough t'me t'be so sickly," said one to the other.

"Nar. But them southerly folk got different ways 'bout 'em, don't ye know."

"Aye. An purty useless, too, I reckon. Aye, sonny! Don't lean over too far, sonny. Ye don't want ol' Slimeback to take a snap at ye!"

He giggled and elbowed his boatmate.

Falgo fell back into the boat and looked at the two men who suddenly became very grim-faced.

"Slimeback?"

"Shor, ol' Slimeback's been takin' folk down under for as long as thar's been water in this here lake," said one.

"Ain't ye never heard of him?" asked the other. "Why I thought for certain he was known far an' wide."

"No-o," answered the boy. "I never did."

"Well, just take a care, then. Keep ye hands an' face up out of the water."

"Ye'll be fine, I reckon," continued the other fisherman. "Even if he's partial to foreigners."

"Who, er, what is Slimeback?" asked the boy, putting his hand over his mouth as he stifled a belch.

"Why a lake serpent, as long as all three of these here boats."

"Near as thick as a wagon wheel. With leathery skin, not like a fish at all."

"Teeth like a 'possum, too, but of a size to match his long snout."

Robigor eyed the two suspiciously, and he caught a wink that one of the fishermen threw his way.

"I'm so sick," said the boy, "I don't care if I do get eaten."

Then he lunged over the side, his feet dangling as he retched.

"A wonder they gots the gall t'be invadin', what with such weak bellies."

"A wonder, indeed."

"Not like them Barley folk, neither."

"A right quick learner, that one. For a lubber."

"Aye, Mr. Ribbon! D'ye care to take a spell at the tiller?"

Robigor cleated off the jibsheet, and looked aft.

"Why, I reckon that'd be a nice thing to try out," he said. "If ye don't mind me runnin' us all over the lake, I mean."

"Aw, we'll keep an eye on ye. I'll bet ye'll get the hang of it right soon enough. Let Pearly take yer place up thar, an' come on back aft."

Robigor was soon guiding the boat skillfully enough for a novice, under the careful instruction of the older fisherman. He was a quick study, and by the end of the next day he was left to guide the boat for long spells while the two fishermen imbibed from a cask, sang bawdy songs, and at last, near sunset, fell asleep on the coils of rope and canvas at the bow. One of the other boats headed up and luffed so as to drop back alongside.

"Hey thar!" called the man at its tiller.

"Howdy!" answered Robigor.

"I take it me cousins have finally given in to drink, judgin' by the snorin' I hear."

"That's right."

"Well, do ye care to have one of us aboard to lend a hand?" the helmsman called. Another fellow on the boat, one of the two men who first came across Robigor and Falgo on the path to Northwick, stood and called out, "I'd be glad to come over!"

"Well, thanks, but I don't reckon it's needed. The breeze is light an' easy."

"Alright then. Just toss a bucket of lakewater on 'em if ye need 'em."

"I'll do that!"

"An' go ahead an' get ye boy to hang out ye lantern."

"Right!"

After another hour, Robigor's boat was lagging behind again, due in part to his lack of skill and in part to the good handling of the other two boats. As long as he could see the lamps hanging from the end of their booms, he was not too discouraged. Night descended slowly over the lake, and the two drunk fishermen snored all the louder, and Falgo's retching also continued from somewhere near the mast where he still hung over the side. But Robigor, admiring how peaceful and easy things seemed, and how gracefully the boat responded to his touch at the tiller and his trimming of the sheets, thought that he might have made a decent sailor had his life taken a very different turn.

Then came the storm.

It started with a stiff breeze that sent a thrill through Robigor as the boat heeled and shot forward, the wake gurgling loudly behind where he sat. He continued to smile until, suddenly, the stars were blotted out and the breeze abruptly transformed into a violent squall with cold hard rain. Robigor yelled for the boy to rouse the fishermen, himself too busy pulling the mainsheet and letting it back out, swinging the tiller wildly to compensate for the hard, erratic gusts. At one point, the boat heeled so far over that the boom dragged in the water, extinguishing the lamp before Robigor pushed the tiller alee, swinging the bow into the eye of the wind.

"Wake 'em up!" he cried, unable to see farther than the mast. Gripped with the kind of fear that only the uncaring power of nature can arouse, Robigor fought the boat, trying to keep the wind out of the sail. Several times he released the tiller, jumping toward the mast, feeling his way in the dark to fumble with the halyard, but each time the mainsail caught air and swung the boat over. He continued to yell for the boy, for anyone, dashing back to the tiller to try to head the boat back into the wind. The stays whistled and moaned like shrill ghosts, and the hull thumped up and down so hard on the waves that Robigor feared the vessel would shatter. On his third attempt, he got the halyard loose, but it only let free the foresail that then whipped and snapped before it filled with air and spun the boat around. Diving back to the tiller, he once again straightened the boat. Taking out his dagger, he cut away the jibsheets from their nearby cleats. The boy suddenly appeared, crawling along the sole to him.

"I can't wake 'em up!" he cried over the gale. "They won't wake up!"

"Then get the sail down!"

"How?"

"Go an' loosen the line cleated thar on the mast."

Lightning cracked overhead, and Robigor briefly saw the boy standing against the mast, fumbling with the halyard.

"I can't get it loose!"

"Then come take the tiller!"

"What?"

"Take the tiller! Come on, boy!"

Falgo crawled back astern, and Robigor took his hand and put it on the tiller.

"Just keep us pointed right at the wind," he ordered.

"Aye. I mean, I'll try!"

Once again, Robigor made his way on his knees, splashing through several inches of water along the starboard side, clinging to the siderail as he went. The boat lurched over and he ducked the boom as it swung at him.

"Other way!" he screamed astern. "Put it the other way!"

The boy responded, and the boom swung back. Standing up, Robigor tried to get at the mast but another lurch of the boat threw him off balance. Trying to find something in the dark to grip, he twisted around just as another bolt split the sky. In that daylike instant, he saw oddly pinkish-red water swirling up around his ankles. Thunder cracked as another bolt shot across the lake, and this time he saw the two fishermen tumbling limply against each other at the bow, both their eyes open and lifeless. Reaching for his dagger, Robigor turned around to go back to the stern just in time for the boom to hit him across the chest, flipping him over the side and into the water.

Falgo adroitly adjusted the mainsheet and put the tiller over, heeling the boat to gain speed. Then, as if its business was done, the storm moved on to other parts of the lake, the wind calmed, and the sail went limp. The boy nervously looked around for the lights of the other boats, but they were nowhere to be seen. Once or twice, he thought he heard a yell off in the distance, and some splashing. He remained quiet, listening. After a few minutes more, the yelling stopped, and so did the rain, and he heard only the gentle creak of the boat. One or two stars peeked through the black sky, shortly joined by many others. Judging his direction by them, the boy made ready to make sail southward and back to his comrades as soon as any air stirred. Vidican would be grateful to hear that Glareth had not been warned.

A nearby splash broke his thoughts. Jerking his head in the direction of the sound, he listened all the more attentively. He heard it again, closer, and, dismayed, he picked up a boathook and stood, ready to finish off the Barleyman.

"Here!" Falgo called. "I am here! Swim this way!"

Then he saw him, some distance off the port side, moving quickly through the star-glistened waves toward the boat. He was amused at how fast and smoothly Robigor swam, with hardly a splash. The swimmer neared, and Falgo raised the boathook high to strike. The watery form approached rapidly, and Falgo saw it rise waist high out of the water, rushing straight at the boat. It was not a man. Chills shot up Falgo's spine just before dagger-toothed jaws clamped around his torso and took him right across the starboard rail before the boy could even scream, and it plunged back into the deep. The creature's long and heavy body nearly capsized the water-filled boat as it slithered across it. As its tail came over, it cracked like a whip, flinging the boom and sail against the mast with such force that both were demolished. The stays snapped, and all of the rigging—boom, mast, sail, and all—crashed over the side. The boat listed heavily, filling with water and sinking as the two dead fishermen floated out and drifted away.

• • •

Three days later, by which time they should have all been safely to Formouth with their important news, the two other boats gave up their search. After a heated discussion, with much yelling and name-calling from boat to boat and aboard each, they made their heading southwestward toward home. The two men who had come upon Robigor and Falgo, and had brought them to Northwick, each crewed on a separate boat. And each of them would grumble and curse and mutter all the way home, throwing sharp insults at their cowardly boatmates for turning back.

Chapter 24

The Request

In fact, Robby could not sleep any more that night. The experience of the witch was agitating enough, and he was surprised that the others could sleep and that he himself had actually dozed off after such an experience. Robby suspected Ashlord of some hocus-pocus to give them the little rest they found, but he did not question him about it. Though he took his place beside Sheila on the floor, he sat with his legs stretched out and his back against the wall to abide with Ashlord until morning. While the mystic sat in the chair without moving, staring into the dying embers, Robby pondered all the questions he wished he had asked Ashlord. Now it was too late to make a start. Perhaps, in a few days, if they reached Tulith Morgair, a few answers could be had. At least he would know whether or not Micerea was real or just some strange dream-creature of his imagination. He drifted from thought to thought and found himself longing for home. He thought of all the things he missed, his parents, the long walks along the hills behind Passdale, even the store. Then he realized and remembered that he had no home, that it was taken by the Redvests, and that his father was trying to get to Glareth while his mother struggled to lead the people of Passdale and Barley. As he thought through these things, he became more anxious and worried, and thinking about his parents only made him more so. He was momentarily overwhelmed by a terrible dread, the feeling that things had gone awfully wrong. The thought of his father, going alone all the way to Glareth for help, only served to increase Robby's worries. For a moment, he was certain that something dreadful had happened back east, and he could not get the image of his father's smiling face, that night at the festival, out of his mind.

Getting up, he went over and sat crosslegged close beside Ashlord's chair, and, after a moment of hesitation, he reached out to touch him on the knee. Ashlord stirred from far away thoughts and looked down at Robby.

"Oh, Robby," he smiled.

"Ashlord, I have a huge favor to ask."

"Oh? What might I do for you?"

"I know this may not be easy. And I will understand if you refuse."

"What is it, dear boy?"

"Might you send Certina to look for my dad? And, if she finds him, then to come find me and tell me of his fate? Whether he be dead, or captured, or in Glareth?"

"Oh." Ashlord turned and looked at Certina on the mantel. She had her head tucked underneath a wing, preening. "Oh," he repeated. "Hmm. I will need her help tomorrow, and perhaps longer. I know you long to have some rest from your worries about your father. But would it be a comfort to you to have her bring back bad news? Or, if he has made it to Glareth, or is still on his way, he may yet face many perils."

"I know. I'm sorry. It is a selfish thing that I ask. I know it is not easy for you two to be separated."

Ashlord looked at Robby sympathetically and shook his head, "No less nor more for you to be separated from those you care about. I will put it to her. She will pout and may even refuse; she does not always do as I ask. But I will put it to her."

"Thank you."

"You are welcome, Robby."

By now, the night was receding before a foggy dawn, and since the fire was nothing but warm ashes, the cottage was cool. Uncharacteristically, it was Billy who first stirred. He sat up and stretched, emitting a prodigious number of yawns. He slipped into his boots, pulled up his suspenders, and tiptoed past Ibin and Sheila.

"Mornin'," he said to Robby and Ashlord. He yawned again. "O-o-o! I think I need to throw some well-water in me face!"

Grinning, Billy opened the door to go out. His smile evaporated as he stood straight and rigid, blinking. He slowly closed the door. With his hand still on the latch, and still facing the door, he said, in a normal tone of voice, "It's a bar. It's a mighty big bar, too. Right outside."

He turned to Robby and Ashlord, his hand still frozen onto the door latch, and said, nodding, "A bar. As big as they come."

"Ah. That would be my guide," Ashlord said, rising. "Here to show me the way to the witch's lair."

"Oh," Billy nodded, as if it was the most natural thing in the world. He slowly backed away from the door and awkwardly came up against the table.

"Yer guide. I see. O' course. An' why not?"

End of Volume Two

144 Days Remaining

Afterword

Afterword

Thank you for reading *The Nature of a Curse*! I hope you are enjoying this tale. And I cordially invite you to share your thoughts, questions, and comments at

www.TheYearOfTheRedDoor.com

There is much more to come!

Volume 3, *A Distant Light*, continues the adventure as Robby and his friends journey westward. They must contend with growing friction between members of their company. These are exacerbated as Robby learns how to manage his peculiar and growing powers, and how to assert his will. New threats and new allies await. Killer bees the size of a fist, a monster made of vines with a penchant for human flesh, a large-scale battle, a forlorn and enchanted forest, strange and vicious beasts that inhabit the dreamworld, and a fanatical supporter of the Unknown King who is determined to stop their quest at any cost—these and more await Robby and his friends. All the while, it seems that the purpose of their quest, to make Robby into the New King, is but a dim hope, yet one that shines nonetheless, like a distant light.

Thanks again!

William Timothy Murray

The Door is Open!
www.TheYearOfTheRedDoor.com

Maps, Stories, Chronologies,
and much more.

Leave a comment or ask a question.

The Author would love to hear from you!

Sign up for the newsletter.
*Get perks and exclusives
delivered right to your inbox!*

The Year of the Red Door

Volume 1
The Bellringer

Volume 2
The Nature of a Curse

Volume 3
A Distant Light

Volume 4
The Dreamwalker

Volume 5
To Touch a Dream

www.TheYearOfTheRedDoor.com